Wonderland

NOVELS BY JOYCE CAROL OATES

Black Water
The Rise of Life on Earth
I Lock the Door Upon Myself
Because It Is Bitter,
and Because It Is My Heart
American Appetites
You Must Remember This
Marya: A Life
Solstice
Mysteries of Winterthurn
A Bloodsmoor Romance
Angel of Light
Bellefleur
Unholy Loves
Cybele
Son of the Morning
Childwold
The Assassins
Do with Me What You Will
Wonderland
them
Expensive People
A Garden of Earthly Delights
With Shuddering Fall

Wonderland

Joyce Carol Oates

Ontario Review Press / Princeton

First Ontario Review Press edition: 1992
Manufactured in the United States of America

The poem "Wonderland" first appeared
in *Poetry Northwest*, Autumn, 1970,
under the title "Iris Into Eye";
Part I, Chap. 3 appeared in a slightly
different form under the title "The Dark"
in *Southwest Review*, Autumn 1970;
Part I, Chap. 8 was originally published
under the title "Fat" in *Antaeus* 2, Winter, 1971

Library of Congress Cataloging-in-Publication Data
Oates, Joyce Carol, 1938–
Wonderland : a novel / Joyce Carol Oates
I. Title
PS3565.A8W63 1992 813'.54—dc20 91-41741
ISBN 0-86538-075-9 (pbk.)

Typesetting by Backes Graphic Productions
Printed by Princeton University Press

ONTARIO REVIEW PRESS
Distributed by George Braziller, Inc.
60 Madison Ave., New York, NY 10010

This book is for all of us who pursue
the phantasmagoria of personality—

CONTENTS

AUTHOR'S NOTE

Some of the characters in this novel are entirely fictional, a good number of the events are fictional, and all the settings—especially Lockport, New York; Ann Arbor, Michigan; and Toronto, Ontario—are fictional. Any resemblance to reality is accidental and should be resisted.

Wonderland

the spheres are whirling without sound inside
spheres
deft as ivory
tails of vertebrae interlock
hard as ivory and ice
it is a miniature sun frozen hollow

tails like the finest bodies
of fossils
are locked together
beneath the grainy surface of skin
as the surfaces circle their surfaces

a ball of air circling itself
slicing the air slowly in its circling
daylight emerges as a small hole
an eye that achieves an iris
the collapsible space begins to breathe
the vertebrae lengthen into life

this sunless ether is silent
in every dimension
the sphere turns
I make my way up through layers of old bone
the ivory fossils of old blood
clenched fists of babies softened and unborn

coils are revolving
the hot fluorescent center of the globe vibrates
the speechless muscle of the brain spins slowly
slicing the air
continents shaping like raised welts
on the skin
the space between the ribs glows iridescent
warm as the most intimate mucus
of the soul

the eye widens
the iris becomes an eye
intestines shape themselves fine as silk
I make my way up through marrow
through my own heavy blood
my eyes eager as thumbs
entering my own history like a tear
balanced on the outermost edge
of the eyelid

—T. W. Monk

We . . . have dreamt the world. We have dreamt it as firm, mysterious, visible, ubiquitous in space and durable in time; but in its architecture we have allowed tenuous and eternal crevices of unreason which tell us it is false.

—Borges, *Labyrinths*

Knowledge increases unreality.

—Yeats

Book I

Variations on an American Hymn

1

Jesse wakes, startled.

Someone has passed by his bed...? And through to the front room, footsteps going to the kitchen, to the door...?

Jesse's father, unable to sleep. All that fall and winter he has been unable to sleep much of the night. He puts on his jacket, goes outside, walks, walks.... Jesse goes to a window where he can see out back: yes, it is his father, shoving an arm through a sleeve of his jacket as he walks, in a hurry, his head slightly lowered, as if in a baffled blind rage, like a hunter....

Jesse's heart pounds with fear. He has seen his father like this in the past, but now it is nearing Christmas, now there is a light, quick tone to the air, an expectation in faces, that his father does not know about, is violating....

Jesse goes back to bed but cannot sleep himself.

It is raining there, in that country.

It is more than thirty years ago and raining, a cold, fierce, driving rain, rushing across the streets of that town—Yewville, New York—out of a thick, boiling December sky. The main street is fairly busy this morning, in spite of the weather. It is the middle of the month and the middle of the week. Cars splashed with old mud maneuver around other cars waiting to park in the narrow street; pickup trucks move by slowly; a

Greyhound bus, its exhaust billowing, comes to a stop in front of the bus station, which was once a gas station, now painted white. The white is too white on this strange day; it glares and makes the eye tremble.... Up and down the street people are walking, hurrying against the rain. As they hurry, their heads ducked, umbrellas raised, the rain begins to turn into bits of ice. A quick magical change. The dots of ice strike faces, the windshields of cars, the store windows.... On the bumpy surface of the street, which is gleaming wet, a million bits of ice strike and bounce. The sign for the Montgomery Ward's store is bombarded with hail and sounds like a drum. A Christmas streamer with its plastic bells and wreaths is struck, shudders in the wind, seems about to break in two....

Most of Yewville is on either side of this street, Main Street—shoe stores, clothing stores, sporting goods stores, the bus station, the movie house, the post office in its fortress-like building, a few taverns, a gas station, a few restaurants. Then comes an expanse of vacant land, then the library, which shares a nondescript old building with the police station, then the high school, a complicated three-story structure made of dark rough brick, its windows high and narrow, its roof covered with black, rotting shingles. The hail strikes against the broad front sidewalk of the high school, running right up to the double front doors. It strikes against the windows, as if trying to break them. The windows show no amazement, no faces behind them.

The air looks as if it is coming apart—shredding into molecules of sand or grit. It is December 14, 1939.

This is the last day of school before Christmas vacation. School will end after assembly at one o'clock. In the narrow, dingy halls of the school students are filing along, heading for the auditorium and its warped seats, its overheated boisterous cozy air. They make a crashing noise on the stairs, coming down from the second floor, the older boys clowning, almost out of control. Their legs are long, their faces bright and blurred, as if intoxicated. One of their teachers, a woman of middle age, makes an angry gesture and they turn away, laughing together. Everywhere there is a smell of wet wool. As the students pass along the corridor they strike the lockers with their fists in a kind of giddy rhythm, their excitement almost out of control.

There is a bouncy, hollow, drum-like urgency to the air. Jesse is going to remember this. Already the high school is overcrowded, though an addition was built only fifteen years ago. Boys from the country, surging and clumsy in their overalls, stomp along the hall heavy as farm animals, banging their fists against the wall. The girls walk quickly, in little clusters, as if fearful of the boys. They are all wearing bright red lipstick. Their lips move and are very red. Because it is the last day of school before Christmas recess, they are dressed up, in wool dresses and stockings and high heels. "Is it snowing? Is it snowing?" they ask, their voices lifting shrilly, as if they were testing the air itself, their necks stretching in front of the boys' eyes.

At the doors to the auditorium a few teachers are posted. The students pass close by them, bending their heads meekly, automatically, even the big farm boys, cowed for the moment. Such a quick warm crowd of them! They are excited, giddy. The air rocks with their big feet and their giddiness. The familiar odor of wet wool is mixed with the unfamiliar odor of the girls' perfume, and everywhere there is the clatter of the girls' high heels. A girl cries out in surprise—someone has run his finger sharply down her backbone, which is outlined through her pink wool dress. She turns, pretending anger. One of the teachers snaps at her: "Never mind! Keep on going!"

They file into their seats, jostling one another, laughing behind their hands; on stage, the choir is already singing to welcome them in. On the right of the stage is a large Christmas tree, donated by the Yewville Firemen, lit up with strings of light, also welcoming them in. The choir sings "Hark the Herald Angels Sing" to march them into their seats. A sprightly, energetic tempo. The girls are attentive and bright-faced. Their eyes are serious. The boys are very much together, in their own clusters; at certain places a boy must sit beside a girl, accidentally, and the two clusters come together. The choir is made up of about twenty students, mostly girls, and it is conducted by a very small, careful woman with gray curls, her back to the crowd, her arms moving in short, precise, finicky circles. The voices rise and fall, singing, marching the other students into place: "Hark the Herald Angels sing. . . ." and "sing" has two syllables, both equally accented.

The mood of the students changes gradually; it is not so rowdy now. Seated, the country boys are not so impatient. Their eyes are fixed upon the chorus and the Christmas tree. Their hands lie quiet upon their knees or are folded formally in their laps, a gesture that is automatic.

The curtain behind the choir is made of velvet, a deep magenta: the high school's color. Initials *Y.H.S.* in cream upon this magenta. Arranged in rows according to height, the chorus sings in front of this impressive curtain, and the Christmas carol is mixed with the initials, the flushed excited faces of the singers, the movements of the choir director's arms inside her frothy sleeves. . . . Something is going to happen: it is a special assembly, a special day.

No windows in the auditorium. One boy, seated on the aisle, keeps glancing back at the doors as if anxious about the weather, or about getting out. The third time he looks around, the boy sitting directly behind him thumps the back of his seat. "Hey, what're you looking for?" he says.

"No one. Nothing," the boy says.

The boy who has been looking around straightens in his seat, forces himself to stare straight ahead. He has red-blond hair. His complexion is not a redhead's complexion, though: it is darker, as if still tanned from the summer. The boy's face is broad and intelligent, but creased with thought or worry; he has become very nervous. For the fourth time he looks around—now they are closing the doors to the auditorium! He will not be able to get out. The boy stares up the narrow aisle to those closing doors, ignoring the taunts of the boy behind him, ignoring his teacher's concern. She is a woman in her forties, heavyset and hearty and wise, with a liking for Jesse, but today Jesse has no mind for her or for anyone else. The chorus is beginning another carol. The words are soft and cajoling, like snow; they are meant to entice and make quiet—"O Little Town of Bethlehem"—but Jesse can't pay attention to them. He must get out of this seat, out of this packed hot auditorium, he must get back home. . . .

His father had gone out that morning before dawn. Stomping out the back path to the woods, his head lowered. . . .

Jesse suddenly stands, confused.

He feels himself blushing, even his neck is blushing. He hurries up the aisle, which tilts slightly, so that he has the impression of forcing himself up an invisible hill, a small stubborn obstacle meant to tease him. Someone whistles and calls out, "Hey, Jesse!" It is his cousin Fritz, grinning. He does not make any sign to Fritz. At the very rear of the auditorium his sister Jean is sitting, and his eye flies immediately, miserably, to her, to her stern face. She is two years older than he, sixteen, with a full, spry little body and an attractive red mouth. But now she looks angry, because Jesse has embarrassed her. There is a fierce, fine little frown on her forehead.

Tonight at supper she will say, "Jesse couldn't go to the bathroom *before* assembly, oh no, he had to wait until it began and *then* he excused himself. . . ." And Jesse will sit at the table in a fury of shame and hatred, unable to defend himself, wishing his sister dead.

The high school principal, Mr. Fuller, is standing at the doors. Jesse whispers that he doesn't feel well, may he be excused? But Mr. Fuller can't hear him and so he has to say aloud, in his raspy, hoarse, frightened voice, "I feel sick . . . may I be excused . . . ?"

Mr. Fuller nods gravely, suspiciously. But he does not allow Jesse to open the door himself; he goes to it and opens it wide, so that Jesse must pass through close to him, half stooping beneath his arm.

Jesse hurries down the corridor. His heart is still pounding, his face flushed. The skin of his face is almost painful, it is so flushed. Behind him the choir is singing now of a little town that is filling up softly with snow, its music misty and unreal, fading now behind the closed doors; outside there is hail, real snow, violent and wild. Jesse stares out a window. The sidewalk is trod upon by a thousand angry feet—invisible feet; there is a raucous ringing to the air that drowns out the choir's song for Jesse. *Bethlehem. Christmas.* His mind jumps from high school and Yewville to the highway, to his home, his father's gas station and the house a hundred yards behind it, off the highway, meager and dull in the storm. The gas station is now closed. Closed permanently. Jesse's father had closed it, boarded it up, just the day before.

Closed: a sign Jesse's father had painted himself with old black paint.

Jesse helped him nail up the boards without being asked. He wanted to say to his father's angry, silent back: "Why are you hammering so hard? Why are you making so much noise?" Nails struck deep into the wood, nails struck sideways and bent, twisted helplessly . . . nails dropped and lost in the tall grass. . . . But Jesse said nothing. He helped his father board up the little gas station, with lumber from an old pile behind the house, and his father hammered the boards in place, in a row, then crisscrossing on top, as if there were thieves who might want to break into this old place, cunning thieves who might be watching them right at this moment, plotting. Jesse wanted to say to his father gently: "But nobody will break in *here*. . . ." He wanted to ask, while his father hammered so loudly: "Why are you so . . . why are you so strange today?"

Why are you so strange? he thinks now.

The high school is seven miles from home. Out there, at the intersection of the highway and the Moran Creek Road, the gas station is boarded up, *closed permanently,* and behind it is the old jumble of wrecked cars and motorcycles and lumber and tires, and behind that the small frame house is gleaming with a sudden freakish burst of sunlight, hail bouncing on its roof. . . .

He must leave school and go home. Closing his eyes, he imagines the house: the gleaming roof, the hailstones, the rotting lumber pile. His father had bought the gas station, but he had built the house himself over the years. Hard work. There were a few sheds, and a garden ragged from late fall, a few trees. Wild bushes. Then the fence of rusted wire and the beginning of Mike Brennan's farmland . . . but it was not Brennan's any longer, it had been sold to someone else, a stranger, who did not live in the area or even in Yewville. A stranger. Everyone talked about this stranger for a while, wondering when he would show up. Jesse's mother said, "It's somebody with money to throw away, that's for sure. What would he want with that old dead farm!" She always spoke of other people's farms and businesses with a certain haughty, mocking look.

Jesse can hear her voice plainly.

She is seven miles away.

School will be dismissed in another hour, but Jesse won't be able to go home then. He has to work at Harder's, then get a ride home with a neighbor at five o'clock. That is four hours away. His heart pounds, seems to lunge in his chest.... He thinks of his mother: her light, red-blond hair, her eyes almond-shaped and clever and frank. He takes after her, people say, more than after his father. But he is thinner than either of them. He is very thin, his feet long and narrow. He is quite tall for his age—five foot seven—taller than his mother now. *Did she hear Jesse's father go out this morning so early?— out the back door and into the woods, alone?* If anyone talks about Jesse's father she smiles and looks away, something passes over her face, quickly, cleverly, and she is silent. She hums under her breath. She sings out loud, meaningless snatches of words. Her hair is curly and tumbles untidily down to her shoulders. Sometimes she is pretty, and Jesse and his sisters are proud of her. At other times, strolling through Yewville, she is sloppy and critical of things in store windows, she talks too loudly, and Jesse and his sisters are ashamed of her, wishing she would stay at home.

That September, not long after school started, Jesse's sister Jean told him a secret. "What do you *think*? She's going to have a baby!"

"Who?"

"Oh, you dope! Ma, of course! *Ma* is going to have a baby!"

Jesse stared. He could think of nothing to say.

Jean clapped her hands. "It's a secret right now but she told me... I'm not supposed to tell anyone else...."

"... going to have a baby?"

Jesse felt panic. A baby? Another baby?

Bob, the five-year-old, ran over to them and Jesse was startled, thinking for a moment that this was the new baby. Jean picked Bob up and swung him. The flesh of her upper arms was solid and warm. "There's a surprise coming, a surprise coming," she crooned. She winked at Jesse over the boy's squirming shoulder. "Remember, it's a secret," she said.

Her happiness stung him. *His mother was going to have another baby. In this little house, all of them crowded together....*

"How do you know?" he said angrily. "You think you know everything!"

"I know because Ma told me," Jean said.

"Why did she tell *you*?"

"Because she trusts me. Because I'm a girl."

"I suppose she told Shirley too?"

"No, not Shirley. Shirley would blab it everywhere." Jean let Bob down and Jesse saw that her face was hectic with this news, as if the baby were her own. He felt a pang of jealousy at the look of her face, that bemused female secrecy; as if conscious of his feelings, Jean lifted her chin so that she seemed to be eyeing Jesse over the full curve of her cheeks, through her thick brown lashes. "Listen, kid, don't say anything about it right now. Pa doesn't know that Ma told me. He's mad."

"Why?"

"Because he doesn't want a baby."

Jesse stared. He wanted to turn away in panic and disgust—as if Jean had exposed him to something ugly, opening a door and exposing herself, exposing a secret of womanhood he did not want to know.

"There's trouble over money. Again," Jean whispered.

"What trouble?"

"Oh, to pay the doctor, you know, the hospital . . . buying food and all that. . . ." Jean said vaguely. "You know how Pa gets. . . ."

You know how Pa gets.

Jesse put his hands to his head. Confused. Frightened. He felt the hard substance of his skull beneath his wavy hair. He could remember the soft, delicate skull of his little brother, when Bob had been just a baby . . . so precarious, so dangerous. . . . And now another baby. Why another baby? Why was she having another baby? Jesse knew what to expect; he could remember everything from last time: his mother would waddle around the house, enormous and self-pitying and tender, her eyes filming over with pain and love, her hands dropping onto her belly, caressing herself. That baby had turned out to be Bob. *Robert Harte.* He himself was *Jesse Harte.* He had two sisters, Jean and Shirley, and soon he would have another sister or brother, all of them crowded into this house, this shanty, with its two back rooms and its "front room" and its kitchen. Jesse wanted to yell into his sister's rosy, pleased face that they were all crazy—

Instead, he tried to smile.

"Yeah, isn't it great?" Jean said at once. "I kind of like babies. I told Ma I'd help her with it, you know—get in practice. . . ."

She giggled and Jesse laughed with her breathlessly.

"It's going to be next March," Jean whispered. "I want to take the whole week off from school. I'll take care of the house and make all the meals."

"Next March. . . ."

"Don't look so strange," Jean said, poking him.

Jesse smiled shakily. There was still something about Jean's face, her expression, that alarmed him. The tip of her tongue appeared between her lips, moist and pink. Secrets. Whisperings. Sometimes Jean and their mother whispered together, and if Jesse came near they would go silent. Whisperings, secrets, then silence. Were all the secrets about this new baby, or about other things . . . ? He wanted now to ask Jean about the baby. He wanted to know more. And why was their father unhappy, what was the trouble about money? Always there was talk of money, of not having enough. The gas station was not making enough money, there was a mortgage on it, and before that there had been other ventures—a partnership in a lumberyard, a partnership in a diner on the Five Bridges Road. Jesse had heard the word "mortgage" often. *Interest payments. Partnerships.* If his father and mother whispered together, it was often about these things, kept secret from Jesse.

And now, on this Wednesday, on the day before Christmas recess, Jesse stands in the corridor of the high school, miles from home, and hears this conversation again. It is so clear to him, so strangely clear. Will he never forget it? Jean's terse whispered words: *Because he doesn't want a baby.*

He will never forget it. He will never forget this Wednesday.

He walks quickly down the hall. Strange, to be the only person in it. On either wall there are lockers, dented and rusty, and everywhere the smell of wet wool, wet rubber. Galoshes are lined up on the floor. Someone has kicked a pile of them around. The floor is slightly warped, but it has a smooth, pleasant, dreamy look to it, as if it were hundreds of years old. High above, the ceiling is cracked in many places. Spider webs of cracks. They are dreamy, too, the kind of frail formal pattern that dreams suggest. An editorial in the *Yewville Journal* complained about the high school being a firetrap. Jesse thought that was an interesting expression: *firetrap.* Every week, at odd times, the fire bells rang and all the students filed out into the halls, down the stairs, and outside onto the walk, preparing themselves for a real fire. It was exciting, a rowdy half hour. But no real fires ever came.

Many of the girls had decorated their lockers for Christmas. Cutouts from magazines of Santa Claus, cutouts of Christmas trees and angels.... Jean's locker, at one corner of the hall, was decorated in green and red ribbons, pasted onto the locker in the form of a Christmas tree. When Jesse saw his sister around school he was startled—her adultness, the authority of her firm little legs and her frizzy red hair, her lips, her eyes, her manner of being in a hurry, always amused, always with other girls. If she dawdled after school with a boy, other boys teased them, hung around them, but Jean paid no attention. Jesse heard boys whistle at his sister on the street, but Jean paid no attention. She would turn away gravely and stare at something distant, sighting it along the curve of her cheek.

In the distance the chorus is still singing. A song Jesse can't recognize because the words are blurred this far away, and only the hypnotic, light sound of the music itself comes to him.

He hurries to the boys' lavatory. The smell of this place makes him gag; suddenly he knows he is going to be sick.

Yes, he is sick.

He gags and chokes, his eyes closed. Tears stream out of the corners of his eyes. Hot, everything is hot, stinking.... He spits into the toilet bowl, trying to clean his mouth. The bowl is not very clean. Oh, everything stinks, everything is dingy and pressing upon him, stretching his skull out of shape.... That morning his mother was sick. Vomiting into a basin. The sharp acrid smell of it: now he is vomiting himself. He spits again and again, running his tongue around his mouth over the hard ridges of his teeth. Tiny particles of vomit, like particles of food. Slimy, clinging, a film inside his mouth.... When he is finished, trembling, he reaches up to pull the chain and the water begins to flow noisily, lazily. He has a moment of panic, thinking the vomit won't flush away.

Jesse has not been sick for years, so this is a surprise to him. Nausea: the internal trembling, the weakness, the panic. A panic located in the stomach. He does not remember having felt so sick before, ever in his life, so helpless and frightened. Shirley is often sick to her stomach, and their mother takes care of her in the kitchen, with the basin. It is too cold to go to the outhouse to be sick. Too nasty there.

That morning, by accident, Jesse came upon his mother when she was being sick. She was hunched over and, turning to him surprised, her face was pale, her thin, arched eyebrows too severe in her delicate face; she seemed a stranger, with a forlorn, witch-like beauty that struck him. Her beauty. Her face. The odor of vomit, a streak of vomit on her bathrobe. Both she and Jesse were embarrassed. She said quickly, "There's more privacy in the barn with the cows!"

It was an expression of hers from her girlhood. Barns and cows. Her father owned a farm.

"I'm sorry," Jesse said, backing away.

That had been about seven-thirty in the morning. His father was still out walking. *Don't you know, don't you want to know, where he has gone? Why he can't sleep anymore?* But he said nothing, standing aside for her to pass, and followed her out into the kitchen. More bickering there—Jean and Shirley. Jesse sat at the table. Bob was snuffling, his eyes watering. Talk around the table was edgy, musical, teasing. Jean was always teasing someone. There was a kind of rhythm to her teasing—a cruelty, then a tenderness. She had a quick, high yelp of a laugh, which was a surprise in her because it was boyish and abrupt. But her smile was slow, teasing. Bob was asking when the Christmas tree would be put up, and Jean was saying there might not be any tree this year. "If you're bad, there won't be any tree," Jean said. "Just because of him?" said Shirley. "Why him? He's not the only one that counts!" "Be quiet, baby," Jean said. Jesse thought with pleasure of the Christmas tree. His father would bring it home, tied to the front fender of the car. It would be put up in the front room, inside a small metal tripod with a basin of water beneath, and they would decorate it with things from the two big cardboard boxes kept in the attic—very light glass globes, spirals that looked like icicles, strings of frizzy silver material, colored bows and papers, and figures in Biblical dress. Two or three birds, with feathers that seemed real. An angel. A star of tarnished gold. Candles drawn on cardboard and colored in crayon, which Jesse himself had made years ago. Beneath the tree they would put their presents for one another.

Their mother made breakfast for them. She still looked pale, shaky. Jesse wondered if the girls noticed. Her bathrobe was damp from where she had wiped off the vomit—a large damp stain in the blue material. But no one else would notice. She put plates on the table, gave them hot oatmeal in spoonfuls. She avoided Jesse's eye. He hated himself for seeing so much, always seeing so much. He couldn't help it. They lived so close together, he could not help noticing the straps that sometimes slid down Jean's shoulder, the flushed, mottled flesh of his mother's chest if her bathrobe swung open. Sometimes he found himself staring at his father—that strong, large face, the strong jaws, the grinding, relentless motion of his teeth as he ate. He wanted to see, and yet he did not want to see. He wanted to see the underclothes Jean kept in her bureau drawer, the top left-hand drawer, and yet he did not want to see.... He couldn't help noticing his sister's breasts. Her firm legs, the hint of her thighs. At school, he saw other boys watching Jean. The boys even watched his mother when she came to town in the summer, wearing slacks, sometimes with her hair done up in a bandana, looking like a gypsy. Hotly, warily, his eyes took in these sights. The moist outsides of his eyes became seared with such sights. *His father going out to tramp in the woods, hours before dawn....* Once, in the Brennans' woods, he had come upon a heap of cigarette butts and ashes, and he knew this was where his father had sat, unable to stay in the house or in bed. Unable to sleep. He had kicked at the pile with his foot, as if this were a secret that embarrassed him.

His mother pulled a chair out and sat down. Wiped Bob's nose. Now Shirley wanted something; her whining. Jean went to the cupboard and stumbled over Jesse's feet. "Biggest feet in the world," she muttered. Jesse drew his feet under his chair angrily. "Watch out for yourself," he said. "You two," said their mother, sighing. The table was crowded with things. Now his mother must sit down, with a bowl for herself, a spoon, a glass, a cup filled with hot coffee. Everything was crowded. Jesse wanted to knock things off, clear a path— He wanted to shout to Jean to let him alone. Who did she think she was? But he ate in silence, sullenly, quickly. Too much sugar on his oatmeal; he'd spilled a teaspoonful on in one place. Sickening sweet on his tongue. He glanced up to see Bob wiping his nose with the back of his hand. If his father were to come in now, they would have to make room for him. Another chair. Another place at the table. No hiding here. His father's coarse, discolored teeth, the grinding, rhythmic motion of his chewing, his swallowing. Hypnotizing Jesse. Jesse's stare, his habit of staring, would get him into trouble. Must not stare. Must not notice. *His mother's bathrobe, loosely tied at the waist.* He could hear his mother and Jean and Shirley talking, talking about Christmas. The Christmas tree. Presents for Grandpa Vogel. The three voices blended together, mingling and clashing, drawing apart, easing together. Disagreeing. Agreeing. Switching sides. It was like music. The radio was turned on to the morning news, but the station must have shifted, most of the sound was static. Why didn't Jesse's mother notice that and fix it? Jesse ate fast, gulping his food. Since he had seen his mother being sick, he felt a little sick himself. And what was behind that static, what was behind the noise of the radio and his mother and sisters? Was there something he should be listening to?

He said abruptly, "Where's Pa?"

His mother did not look at him.

"He's gone out already," Jean said.

"Why?" said Jesse.

"How do I know why?" Jean said.

"Where did he go?" Jesse asked his mother.

She was picking at something on the edge of the table. Picking it off the faded oilcloth.

"He couldn't sleep, so he went for a walk," she said finally.

"It's cold out to take a walk," he said strangely, staring at his mother.

"He couldn't sleep," his mother said.

They were silent. Shirley sucked at her milk, oblivious to their silence, not understanding. Jesse and Jean and their mother sat so close together that their faces were like balloons hovering close, about to knock together lightly. The windows were frosted with ice on the inside—a very thin, flaky, delicate coating in odd designs. Jesse stared at the window behind the stove. What if his father appeared there suddenly, staring in at them? He must be hungry, out walking in the woods for so long. His breath coming in puffs of steam. His breath smoking about his mouth. Walking with his head down, bowed, his dark hair spiky and wild, uncombed, his eyes straining in their sockets to see, to make sure nothing was being kept from him, hidden from him—that was Willard Harte. Everyone knew Willard Harte. He was from Yewville and everyone in Yewville knew him.

Jesse felt his father's presence, as if that face was really in the window, spying on them. So he said daringly, hoarsely, "What is he going to do now? Are we going to move?"

"Go ask him yourself," Jean said quickly.

Their mother did not reply. She was wiping Bob's mouth.

"Ma," Jesse said deliberately, "are we going to move again?"

"Are we going to move?" Shirley asked, surprised. "How come? When?"

"Shut up," Jean said. "You keep out of this."

"Where are we going?" Shirley asked. She had a full, moonish face dotted with freckles. She gaped at Jean. In this family, Jean often knew secrets; what passed between their mother and father, unvoiced, might be put into words by Jean.

"He's going to ask some people . . . maybe ask around. . . ." their mother said evasively.

"Ask around what?" said Jesse.

"To see if he can sell it," their mother said.

"All it says is *Closed.* Nothing about being for sale," Jesse said.

His mother glanced up at him. Pale, transparent, fed by tiny glowing veins, her face seemed to be confronting his boldly. Her eyes were a faint gray, a faint green, slightly slanted, almond-shaped, their playfulness now gone stern.

"Jesse, if you want to know so much, go ask him yourself," Jean said angrily. "Go on out, you're so smart—big goddamn loudmouth!"

"Jean," their Mother said.

"Don't 'Jean' me, Ma. Listen, Ma, don't 'Jean' me," Jean said quickly. "I'm not a goddamn little baby like these two. Don't look at me sideways like that. Today is Christmas assembly and he tries to start a fight right away, and *he* is acting crazy like always—outside tramping around, what if somebody sees him! I heard him drinking last night. Stumbling around in the dark. Why's he always going out like that, out late and up early, roaming around like a bum—the kids ask me about him, they say they see him as far away as town, on foot— Now he put that goddamn sign up and boarded everything up, and the kids are going to ask me about it—just in time for Christmas assembly—"

"Don't talk to me like that," their mother said.

"I wish I was dead!" Jean said.

She began to cry. The dog ran in from the other room, barking. Bob stared at Jean, amazed, and struggled to get down from his mother's lap.

"You hate me! I wish I was dead!" Jean cried, jumping up.

"Sit down and be quiet. Who hates you? Who the hell hates you?" their mother said in a light, hot, sullen voice. She was brushing at the front of her bathrobe. Short fluttery motions of her hands, as if brushing off crumbs. She eyed Jean sideways, turning her head sternly, severely aside. Jesse saw how her eyes pinched at the corners.

"Cut out that sniveling. It's only more trouble," their mother said.

Jean's face, streaked with tears, was not so pretty now.

"Do you want more trouble?" their mother said.

"Jesse started it," Jean said.

"I only asked if we were going to move. If he was going to sell the gas station," Jesse said. He felt shaky, uncertain. The tension in this room was between his mother and Jean; it seemed to exclude him. By raising his voice, by avoiding their eyes, he was able to blunder into it, to capture some of it for himself. He said recklessly, "Sure, this morning the kids on the bus will see the sign—why'd he have to put a sign up anyway? And they'll kid us about it, they'll want to know what happened—"

"So tell them to go to hell," their mother said.

"But what is he going to do?"

"I don't know. Ask him when he comes in. Ask him yourself."

This confession of his mother's—that she knew no more than Jesse himself—stunned him. He stared at her. He felt perplexed, resentful, cheated. The food he had been eating was cold. What he'd eaten was a cold hard little ball in his stomach. The hell with food. The hell with breakfast, this breakfast table, these people sitting and staring at one another, their faces flushed and frightened.

"All right," Jesse said, "I will."

"You damn little loudmouth!" Jean said savagely.

"Watch your mouth yourself," their mother said. Her face was weary and yet bright, as radiant as Jean's. It was as if she were dancing closer and closer to a central, furious heat, a core of brilliance she did not dare touch. Once or twice she glanced over her shoulder, to the window Jesse had been staring at. Did she expect to see *his* face there . . . ? Yet when she looked back at them it was Jean she looked at. Always Jean. Jean, two years older than Jesse, with the figure of a small, mature woman, her lipstick too brightly red, her breasts pushing too aggressively against the front of her dress. Jesse felt how they excluded him, his mother and his sister. He hated Jean. He hated his mother too when she was like this—united in that fierce, sullen, silent understanding with Jean, the two of them selfishly shut off from everyone else.

"If you're going out, go on and go," Jean taunted Jesse.

Jesse got to his feet.

"I hope he lays your fat mouth open," Jean muttered.

"Jesse," said their mother.

"What?"

"Sit down."

He remained standing, his legs apart. He stared at his mother.

"Sit down and finish your breakfast."

"Why?"

"I said sit down."

"I finished it, I'm through."

"Don't you go bothering your father, not this morning. Get it out of your head. He wants to be alone."

"I'll ask him."

"I said not to bother him."

Jesse was so angry, so agitated, that a flame seemed to pass over his brain. He seemed to see his father's face, right here at the table, an ordinary suppertime and his father's reddened, muscular face, his cheeks bunched with food, his jaws moving with the effort of grinding up food—chewing, chewing, eating hungrily, eating fast, never getting enough—his neck not clean, lined with grease from work in the garage, the cords of his neck standing out strong and hungry.

"Why?"

Around the table in this kitchen, all of them frightened. Outside there was air so cold it might hurt. Inside, their breaths mixing hotly together, and Jesse standing above them, staring at them, around at the faces, looking from face to face, his own eyes powerful, as if protruding slightly from their sockets, pushed forward by an enormous angry hurt.... They were all quiet. Even Bob. Even the dog. Jesse wanted to shut his eyes and turn away from them. *The hell with this, all of this.* But something tickled in his throat, the beginning of a sob. He could not speak. He loved them and he could not speak. He did not want to see, so clearly, his mother's tired, frightened face, the way her head lifted from her neck, birdlike and wary and sharp, as if listening all the while to that sound that was behind the static on the radio, the sound of someone's boots outside on the crusty ground.... He did not want to see his little brother's face, his silky hair, he did not want to trade looks with Jean, who always knew more than he did, and whose scared, bold, make-up face might tell him more than he wanted to know. He did not even want to look at Shirley—her dumb freckled face, her brown hair in snarls, her amazement at the way this breakfast had turned out.

"All right, I'll go live with Grandpa!" Jesse shouted.

He had not known he would say this. He had never even thought about it before.

But his mother accepted his words, his ugly shout, and with an ugly shout of her own brought the flat of her hand down hard on the table.

"Go to hell, then, if that's how you feel, go right to hell and get out of here!" she cried.

Jesse ran out of the room.

He went to the woodshed and yanked on his boots. His heart pounded violently. The tickling in his throat became painful. He began to cry soundlessly. Back in the kitchen his mother was saying something—her voice mixing with Jean's in exasperation and anger. What had he said? But he would not go back to say he was sorry. Would not go back. No. He would go to school and get out of here. The stink of that gas stove! The stink of this woodshed, piled with junk, boxes and crates of junk, probably hiding the corpses of little animals that had crawled in here for warmth and died! And his mother's anger, his mother's fear.... He could not stand it.

He ran out to wait for the school bus.

Shivering. A light rain fell. In a few minutes Jean and Shirley trudged out to join him. Jean handed him his lunch bag.

"Little bastard," she whispered.

Shivering, he could not stop shivering. He wiped his nose with the back of his hand. He would not let them see he'd been crying; the hell with them. The cat wandered over. Jesse took no notice. Shirley stooped to pick it up, crooning to it. Jesse looked back at the gas station—there, the windows boarded up, the sign that said *Closed*—a small stucco building at the corner of Yewville Road and the Moran Creek Road, with two gas pumps. Behind it a patch of land, gone over to dump heaps of motorcycles and cars, partly dismantled, a few jalopies on blocks, a pile of rubber and metal and lengths of wire. And, behind that, across a small ditch that had frozen over, the house itself—the house. Attached to the house a woodshed. Behind the house an old coop. In the driveway their father's car, a 1930 Ford. Behind this was a clump of trees that divided their land from the Brennan land, at this end mostly trees and bushes.

Was his father hiding in the Brennans' woods? Sitting on a log, smoking, tossing down the cigarette butts and grinding them out with his heel?

Jean said nothing to Jesse. He felt the stern, angry glare of her hatred tingling the side of his face and he did not look at her. The air was very cold. It seemed to pierce their lungs, to numb them. Hazy pale light radiated from the sun and could not penetrate the clouds. Jesse kept narrowing his eyes, sensing that Jean watched him. His eyes pinched at the corners as if ready to shield him from something he should not see. At the horizon, down the road where the school bus would first appear, a clump of thick dark clouds had formed. Jesse guessed it would snow that day.

"Little loudmouth bastard," Jean whispered.

The school bus has appeared, has stopped, has taken them to Yewville; and now he is in school, safe in the warm stinking lavatory, safe and weak. He thinks still of that morning and the smell of oatmeal and milk. He thinks of his mother's face. Why had he said that? Why those particular words? *I'll go live with Grandpa.* He doesn't like his Grandfather Vogel, hardly knows him, because there is bad feeling between his grandfather and his father. A fight over borrowed money, and over a motorcycle race that Jesse's father had had once on the old man's farm. He chooses his father over his grandfather, of course. His grandfather is a stranger to him. His father is so near that his face can explode in Jesse's head, startling him with its intimacy, its power. He sees that face. The blood rushing into it, animating it. Sometimes, sitting around in the garage with his friends, his father tells jokes, they hang around out back, perched on motorcycles, their legs spread lazily apart as though they are content to sit for hours, talking, laughing with their short, hacking laughs. Jesse loves to hear his father talk to other men. Telling jokes. Kidding. Telling stories. His father's voice rises with the men's voices, wrestling with them, bringing them down. They are all mocking. They laugh a lot, mockingly. Jesse hovers nearby, not quite with them and not quite excluded. His father glances at him out of the corner of his eye, to see if he is listening. His father's stories move fast: *And then I... and then I....* Stories of fist fights at country picnics, fairs, firemen's outings; at Lake Ontario; at taverns on the highway. Stories of races, stockcar and motorcycle races... and Jesse can sense in his father and his friends, these unshaven, big-thighed, muscular men, with their stomachs a little flabby, their hair thinning, an excitement that has nothing to do with this back yard of junk, the odor of smoldering rubber from a fire that is perpetually burning invisibly, an excitement that shows itself most starkly in Jesse's father's face, which they all watch. Though he is sitting on the soiled, scuffed saddle of a motorcycle, his booted heels hard in the ground, his face is turned to the sun, the searing wind of a race, his eyes are narrowed as if sizing up his chances for coming out of a turn, beating out someone else. This face is not flat or soft, like the faces of other men. It is massive, somehow—the long nose rising eagerly out of its bluish depths, the shrewd, squinting eyes fixed deep in sockets and very quick, turning from side to side, having to see everything. A strange hard whiteness to the whites of his eyes. The dark part fierce, dazzling. He is urgent in his retelling of a fight or a race, talking fast, a little too loud. They lean toward him to listen. He draws them forward—their eyes, their nerves—his voice moving on imploring and hot and hard, while his wavy hair lifts above his forehead like a rooster's comb, stiff with excitement. His arms are bare to the shoulders, where his sleeves have been cut off. Big arms, biceps, big shoulders. His shirt, opened at the top, shows tufts of dark curly hair. He is always checking a watch he wears on a black leather band, as if time is important to him, even shaking the watch to make sure it is running, as if he has other things he must do, other places to be right now, and his days were not these long sluggish afternoons of talk and beer. . . .

His father's nearness unsettles him. That face caught in his brain, a face brought up close to Jesse's own face. He can almost smell his father's tobaccoey breath. Almost hear his hawkish laugh. He shakes his head to clear it. He examines the walls of this lavatory: words that have been scribbled everywhere, some of them fresh, some crossed out, rubbed out, scrubbed away. A drawing catches his eye, intricate and detailed and puzzling—a woman's body seen from the bottom up, the legs muscular and very long, spread apart, the head at the far end of the body small as a pea, with eyes and eyelashes nevertheless drawn in very carefully so that they look real. Someone has added to the drawing with another, blunter pencil, making the body boxlike, the space between the legs shaded in to a hard black rectangle like a door. The arms have also been changed to walls and even the suggestion of brick added to them. . . . It is a mysterious drawing, two mysterious drawings, one on top of the other like a dream that fades into another dream, a nightmare conquered by another! Jesse stares at it. He has probably seen it before but he hasn't bothered to examine it. It is freakish, it is somehow unsettling. Better not to look at it. . . . But why did the second boy make the body a house, with walls and entrances? A house or a barn or a warehouse. It is something you could walk into and lose yourself in, all that empty blackness. . . . And at the top of it that head, far away, that small round head, watching you patiently.

Jesse thinks suddenly of his mother, of her anger. Why did he say that to her? He is a stupid fool, a bastard. A loudmouthed bastard, yes. *I'll go live with Grandpa.* And she had shouted for him to get out, to get out— Sometimes, late at night, she shouted at his father. His father stayed out and when he came home there might be a fight. And Jesse would lie in bed, straight as a statue, listening. He knew that Jean and Shirley were both awake and listening, and Bob, in his parents' room, was awake, whimpering, cringing in his bed. Jesse did not try to make sense of the fights. They stormed one way, then turned abruptly and stormed back. It was really like a storm in the house, gusts of wind that whirled and turned frantically. Once Jesse had seen his mother slap his father, a hard clapping blow to the face. She had been shaking a shirt of his at him, shaking it like a maniac, screaming . . . and his father had backed up, grinning stupidly, trying to make a joke of it. But that blow to the face, turning his father's handsome high-colored face aside, making the eyes jerk to slits, the forehead furrowed, the thick dark hair rising like a crest!—that had not been a joke, no. No joke.

So on those nights he lay straight as a statue. He thought of himself as a statue on the prow of a ship—thinking of pictures in the history textbooks of ships with figures on their prows, the figures of women, smoothed as if by the caressing of centuries of freezing water, the faces blank and calm and neutral, turned out into the storm of the sea. Unchanging. Jesse would lie in bed, his hands folded across his chest, his knees straight. He heard everything. He heard nothing.

Listening.

Not listening.

This day is filling with bits of ice, he sees. He stands at the window, which won't open any higher. The lavatory smells bad, it is overheated with a dry, stuffy heat. The radiators are always knocking. Jesse grunts, trying to push the window up higher. The frame is warped. At the bottom sill there is a thin crust of ice, a tiny drift of ice. Cold air blows in against Jesse's cheeks. A relief, this cold air . . . air to turn the lungs into ice. . . . He should return to the auditorium, he thinks. His seat is vacant. Everyone will see that he is still gone. If someone is sick and stays away too long, they send someone else after him. A male teacher. Or Mr. Fuller himself. He should go back to the auditorium, but he is too weak. He should go home. *He should go home.*

Before it is too late.

He stands breathing in the cold air. It is clean, it refreshes him. He spits into the sink. He runs water from the rusty tap and tries to rinse out his mouth. The taste of vomit. This sink becomes the basin at home, with its scuffed, scoured bottom. Rusty brown streaks showing through the white. At the back of his mind is music, the sound of children's voices, angelic voices, singing. Singing words he can't hear. There is a slight rhythmical feel to the day. His eyes partly close, as if he were trying to hear those words, trying to hear the mystery in the notes, the relationship of notes, the percussive sounding of the rhythm. But he does not know anything about music, he doesn't know what music is, he senses only its calming, caressing secrecy, its hypnotic power, the way it works to turn off the mind.

The door of the lavatory opens suddenly.

It is Mr. Fuller.

"Jesse—?"

Jesse whirls around, startled. Guilty. He feels as if someone has been spying on him all this time.

"I was . . . I had to . . . I had to throw up," he says.

Mr. Fuller nods in embarrassment.

"I'm all right now," Jesse says.

Mr. Fuller looks at him doubtfully. "Do you think you have the flu?"

"No, I'm all right now."

"Does anyone in your family have the flu?"

This man, Mr. Fuller, is edgy and embarrassed. He does not like to meet Jesse's gaze directly.

"No. Everything is all right. Nobody's sick," Jesse says at once.

"You look a little . . . a little sick. . . . You look feverish."

Jesse feels his face. Yes, it is very warm.

"I'm sorry," he mumbles, not knowing what he is saying.

"Maybe you'd better go home," Mr. Fuller says.

"I have to work after school," Jesse says.

He wonders if these words have been too abrupt, if Mr. Fuller will think he is arguing with him. Jesse tries to smile. He thinks of how much taller, stronger, how much better his father is than Mr. Fuller. His own father a better man than this man, though everything he tries goes wrong. The gas station. Before that, a lumberyard. Before that, a diner on the highway. When Jesse was very small, his father had tried to raise chickens and pigs on a brokendown farm his parents had owned. In those days they had lived in the deep country, the real country, back on a dirt road, no electricity, no neighbors, "no nothing," as his mother would say, speaking sourly of those years. Mr. Fuller lived in Yewville, somewhere near school. Nobody talked about him except to make jokes. They mocked him behind his back. But to his face they were afraid of him, even the older boys were afraid. He had a stern, pale, pasty anger in him, a weak man's anger, quick to be released. His voice, when raised, sounded shrill and alarming. He was all right in Yewville, because he had a job and everyone knew him. Everyone knew Willard Harte too, and didn't dare to make jokes about him, but he wasn't all right. There was something wrong with him. Something wrong. You couldn't figure out why, what made the difference between these two men. There had to be a difference. If Willard Harte were to rush into this room, his hair wavy and stiff, his footsteps making the floor shudder, Mr. Fuller would have to step back; there wouldn't be room for both of them. If Willard Harte were to tell one of his jokes, laughing and moving his big hands around, drawing shapes out of the air, Mr. Fuller would have to retreat, to cringe . . . that nervous smile of his would be no match for Willard Harte's grin. Willard Harte was tall—about six feet four inches—and his shoulders were broad with a restless, urgent look to them, even under his clothes, and the cords and arteries in his neck looked urgent too, impatient with silence or with standing too long in one place. You had to keep on the move! Had to keep going! Out hunting, Willard Harte always took the lead. His friends' dogs sidled up to him, bending their heads to him, panting to be petted by *him*, grateful when he rubbed their heads with the stock of his shotgun. Mr. Fuller, who had lived all his life in Yewville, who did not hunt and would have been frightened of a gun, would have to retreat in shame before Willard Harte. Shouldn't Jesse feel pride in that?

But no pride. Nothing. He feels shabby and meager in this man's eyes—just a boy from the country in overalls, Willard Harte's son.

"There's no need to return to assembly," Mr. Fuller says.

"Thank you," Jesse says.

Left alone, he feels relief; then he feels a peculiar looseness, a lightening, as if he has been abandoned. His face is very warm, maybe feverish. Maybe he is sick? It will be a relief to be sick, he thinks, to lie in bed and have his mother worry over him. He thinks of what he had to eat for breakfast that morning—but it is gone, vomited away, not enough left to make him sick again. He has a fear of being sick to his stomach in front of other people, but his stomach seems empty now, so he steps out into the hall. Strange, to be alone here. The corridor is deserted and he can do anything he wants. No one is watching. Up and down the narrow hall there are decorations for Christmas the girls put up—bells that open up, made of red crepe paper, slick paper cutouts of Santa Claus, angels made of tinfoil—and they wobble in his eye. He would like to tear them all down. He walks quickly to his locker, which is in the ninth-grade corner. Nearby, a picture of Abraham Lincoln, high on the wall, has been decorated with green and red crepe paper. Down the hall George Washington's heavy ornate frame has been decorated the same way. Jesse puts on his frayed, quilted blue jacket, feeling that he was mistaken in thinking no one was watching him: the men in these old portraits are watching him. Kindly, abstract, surrounded by fuzz or clouds, these dead men contemplate Jesse with their pitying eyes and seem reluctant to let go of him. He yanks on his boots, noticing that they are beginning to wear out above the heel, where he has kicked them against the porch steps to get them off. Too bad. The hell with it. He puts on his mittens, which his mother had knitted last year, runs feverishly to the door, his boots flopping about him. No time to fasten them. He doesn't care, he only wants to get out of that school, as if he senses he is finished with it.

Cold driving snow, no longer hail; it strikes against his warm face like a blow. A command. Leaving the high school, he senses himself floating, free, abandoned, strangely adult. He runs the several blocks to Harder's store, where a truck is already parked and Jimmy, a boy of sixteen who has quit school, is helping unload. Jesse runs up to him. "I got out of school early," he says breathlessly. "You want me to help?"

Jimmy works with a cigarette in the corner of his mouth. He stares at Jesse as if there is something odd about Jesse's face.

"Sure. Go tell him you're here."

So he begins work early, not certain of the exact time. Work. He will work hard. He has been working at Harder's three days a week after school since September, and he is proud of being able to work as hard and as long as Jimmy. They are unloading cases of tinned goods. Case after case . . . his arms ache in their sockets, his shoulders ache with a sharp, sweet sensation . . . as long as he works he does not have to think, his mind is too pressed upon by the heavy cases, too burdened. Snow flies against his face and numbs it. Good. The sensation is good. He needs the empty white cold of the snow to heal his face.

Inside, they work a little more slowly, stacking the shelves. Perhaps they work slower because their hands feel swollen with the relative heat—the fingers bulky and clumsy. Jesse has the idea that someone is watching him. But when he looks around he sees no one special, just a woman shopper at the end of the aisle. Where is Mr. Harder? Up front at the cash register. Jesse drops a can on the floor and it rolls down against Jimmy's feet. Jimmy kicks it back toward him.

"Hey, you sick or something? You look sick," Jimmy says.

He is a short, squat, muscular boy with a ruddy face.

"I'm all right," Jesse says.

"Yeah, you look like hell."

Jesse finds himself staring at a can; its label has peeled off. Just a blank—all surface—a mystery. It has come out of a case of canned corn, so probably it's corn, but still he stares at it, turning it slowly. Jimmy reaches over and grabs it away from him and puts it on the shelf.

At three o'clock Jesse is finished with this chore; now he is sweeping the floor at the back. The broom is very big, a man's broom, not like the small frayed broom his mother uses at home. With this he can stride across the floor and push dirt and papers ahead of him in massive strokes. He is working fast, nervously. From time to time a prickling at the back of his head makes him think someone is watching him, but he does not turn around. Women are shopping in the store, their children are running around, but no one is watching him. He keeps seeing more dirt, loose dirt. It has collected in corners, in the aisles beneath the counters, in places that are difficult to get at. A cousin of his mother's comes in—a heavy, beet-faced woman who nods briefly at him. Unfriendly, that side of the family. There was the argument over money, the choosing of sides between Jesse's father and Grandpa Vogel when the motorcycle race turned into a fistfight, and other things, other squabbles. Anyway, his mother is not friendly with her relatives. Too many of them, she says; it's like seeing yourself come around every corner.

He turns suddenly and there is his father, watching him.

They both start, as if unprepared for this. His father is standing in the aisle, between shelves of cans, his fists stuck in the pockets of his navy jacket. He stares at Jesse. He has not shaved for two or three days. His eyes seem very white above the dark, shadowy beard; a limp strand of hair has fallen onto his forehead.

He takes the broom from Jesse, finishes the stroke Jesse has begun, and sets the broom aside.

2

"Get your jacket," his father says.

"But—"

"Come on, get your jacket. We're going home."

"But why did you . . . why did you drive in?"

"Just tell Harder you're leaving. Come on."

"But Pa . . ."

His father stuffs his hands back in the pockets of the old jacket, so that his arms stick out jauntily on either side. His face is pale, his teeth almost chattering with cold. The whites of his eyes are almost luminous. Jesse looks at him and begins to protest, but his facial muscles go slack. He wants to tell his father how wrong this is—why should he leave his job early? Why? He is confused and embarrassed, his heart is pounding tightly with embarrassment because Mr. Harder is watching them and his father is standing there, just standing there, in his soiled old jacket, his trousers worn and shiny and stained, probably with grease, his boots stained with something dark and moist, probably oil that has soaked into the leather. The lower part of his face is shaded, shadowy. His jaw moves sideways, the teeth grinding together silently. Jesse can still taste the vomit in the very back of his mouth, as if there is a permanent stain there.

"But Pa, Walter Hill will come to pick me up at five. . . ."

"I'll see to that."

"But why did you drive in to get me? What's wrong?"

"Nothing."

His father's jaw moves again, almost imperceptibly. Jesse sometimes hears his father grind his teeth at night—that eerie, light sound, as of charms being rolled about gently in the palm of a hand, charms from a gum-ball machine. How strange, how intimate, to hear that sound at night and to picture his father finally asleep, his father's big arm flung across his face as if he is ashamed, even in sleep, of being so open, so innocent! There is always a shame beginning deep in his father's face, a dark blood-red glow that creeps up from his throat.

"Do I have to leave right now?" Jesse persists.

"I told you."

His father doesn't wait for him but leaves the store. Jesse goes to get his jacket, goes to explain to Mr. Harder that he must leave early.

"Is something wrong at home?" Mr. Harder says.

"No," says Jesse.

He hurries to catch up with his father. His father is walking ahead, to the car. He walks quickly, striding along, and there is something jerky and mechanical about his walk. Is he drunk? Jesse can't tell. The battered old car is parked in front of the Five Bridges Tavern, but maybe this is just a coincidence. Somehow there is an air of formality about Jesse's father this afternoon, not that smiling, boyish, arrogant tilt to his shoulders that comes from drinking. When a little drunk he sways to one side, as if to emphasize his playfulness; when he is very drunk he is mean, short-tempered, it's better to avoid him; when sober, he is himself, clear-eyed and impatient, eager to make jokes, restlessly slapping the palms of his hands together or against his thighs, humming under his breath, singing snatches of nonsense syllables under his breath. But now, today, he is different, he seems altogether different. Jesse runs after him and gets in the car. There is no figuring this out, he thinks.

"Is Ma sick?" he asks.

His father jabs the key toward the ignition, missing the first time, leaning over the steering wheel and breathing heavily. A fine cloud of steam forms at his mouth. His nostrils expand darkly with the effort of putting the key in the ignition.

"Ma's sick?" Jesse says, frightened.

He stares at his father. Nothing. That blunt, hawkish profile, that bush of hair, the eyes rather heavy-lidded as if with concentration, weighed down with concentration on the task before him.... Jesse remembers the night his mother had Bob, how his father drove her to the Yewville Hospital and was away all night, and Jesse and Jean and Shirley stayed up, together, sitting around the radio, listening to distant stations and giggling crazily, ready to jump up and turn off the radio and the lights if their father's car turned in the driveway. They had stayed up all night, unsupervised, night was turned into day, everything upside down, and in the morning Shirley had begun to cry, a baby herself. Jesse thinks of his mother's stomach, that swollen stomach, the baby coiled up wetly inside.... He has never allowed himself to have this thought before, but now it flashes to him clearly, coldly.

"Is Ma sick from the baby?" he asks.

"She's all right."

"Where is she?"

"I said she's all right."

"Is she at home?"

"Yes. Home."

Jesse's father has started the car but waits for a few seconds, his eyes roaming the street and the sidewalk as if freed from the tension inside this car. Jesse tries to see what interests him so much. Nothing? Is nothing out there? There is a strange abruptness about his father, a mechanical urgency and then a slackness, an alternating of tension and relaxation, that Jesse cannot recognize and that frightens him. No, his father has not been drinking. He can't smell that comfortable, pleasant odor of beer or whiskey on his father's breath, so it isn't that. There is another odor. It is indefinable, it puts Jesse in mind of that lavatory at the high school, an acrid, impersonal, gray odor, an odor of fear. . . .

Jesse's father frowns. His entire face seems to contract. A man is passing on the sidewalk—McPherson—who once lent his father money, so Jesse has been told, and now, in overalls, he is walking toward the car with one of his grown sons. The two of them seem to be arguing about something. They don't notice the Harte car, both of them are staring stonily at the sidewalk, arguing, and so they pass by without even glancing up.

"Somebody's getting bawled out," Jesse says, trying to laugh.

His father doesn't reply. He has dismissed the McPhersons and shifts the car into first now, forcing the shift into place. Jesse folds his arms, sits back. The car is very cold. The windshield wipers work slowly to clear the windshield of a coating of very white flaky snow. They move like old men. On the Main Street other cars pass slowly, their windshield wipers moving without grace, back and forth stupidly inside a fanlike shape; the faces inside the cars are all familiar, nameless faces Jesse has been seeing for years in Yewville. They glance at him unseeingly.

Jesse's father is impatient to get started, but when a farmer's pickup truck blocks his way he sits back, oddly patient, his bare hands firmly on the steering wheel, gripping the soiled red covering. He checks his wristwatch. Out on the street are boys from school. They are tossing snowballs at one another. Jesse hopes they won't look his way, then he hopes they will; he is proud of being seen with his father. His father owns motorcycles, sells and trades and repairs them; his father drives a motorcycle and has won races. But the other boys don't notice him. Traffic begins to move again and Jesse feels giddy, intoxicated by the whirling snow and the lights and the bells, the figures of Santa Claus that bob everywhere in the wind, the fat red body, the white trim of the suit, the white beard, the plump cherry-cheeked face. What does that mean, that figure? Jesse stares at it, waiting to be coaxed into smiling, into trust. The figure of Santa Claus seems to be flying through the closed-in air of the store windows, with his reindeer and sleigh, bundled with presents, one hand lifted in a merry salute. Everywhere there is real snow, and everywhere powdery fake snow, glistening and perfect. It is urgent to get to Christmas morning, Jesse thinks. Everyone is hurrying in the bitter wind this afternoon in preparation for that morning; it is sacred; it is like a darkness you must push yourself through to get to; grimly, with vomit at the back of his mouth, Jesse thinks of that morning and how it must be reached, it must be reached.... Now his father is doing something strange: he is parking in front of Montgomery Ward.

"Are we going in here? To get some presents?" Jesse says, brightening.

"You stay in the car."

"Why?"

"Stay here."

Jesse waits until his father is inside the store, then he gets out. He goes to look in the crowded display window. A galaxy of gifts, with ribbons around them, radios, bicycles, sets of china, hair-brushes, lamps, rifles, shotguns, boxes of ribbon candy opened to show the sharp red and green twists of candy, small plastic Santa Clauses and reindeer on a field of tinselly white. There is a village you can buy, tiny cardboard houses on a white board, with a church at its center. Jesse's mother wanted one of these but they were too expensive. Everything is too expensive this year. Last year. The year before that: everything too expensive. They have no money.... Jesse's eye fastens upon the hunting equipment at the rear of the display. He wants a shotgun but there is no chance of getting it. No, no chance. There is no money. His brain boggles at the display of things—shotguns, rifles, a red hunting cap, a fishing rod, a tackle box open like the candy box to show the bright-feathered lures inside. Who can afford such things? Where are the people who can afford such things?

Jesse's father comes out in a few minutes; Jesse is already safe in the car, waiting. His father is carrying a single paper bag. Jesse wonders eagerly what is in the bag...? But his father says only, "Now for Walter Hill." He checks his wristwatch again. He sounds buoyant, eager. Something sly and flushed about his face, as if he has a surprise for Jesse. Is it in the bag? Now he is talking rapidly: "I'll stop and you run in and tell Walter you're going home with me. Tell him you're taking Christmas vacation early. What the hell, he should walk out himself. He's crazy to work there. Tell him I said so. Working in the machine shop! He can have it, he's crazy.... Tell him you don't need a ride home with him tonight or any other night. Tell him you're quitting. Tell him he should quit himself, I said so, *I* said so, only a stupid son of a bitch would keep working in that place. . . ."

Jesse isn't allowed in the factory, so he leaves word with the plant guard to give Walter Hill the message.

And now the ride home.

Always he is riding home, beside his father, in that car. A 1930 Ford. Mud-splattered, rusty, rattling. A good old car. Sometimes it is real, sometimes it is a phantom car, a car of lurches and squeaks and the pocket of very damp, freezing air that is carried inside it, unwarmed, in which he and his father seem to sit permanently, forever. They are a few feet apart, permanently. Riding home. Gliding home. Jesse sees himself outside in the snowy fields, gliding, his feet skimming the grass, going home, running desperately home, gasping for breath, his face pale and slack and stupid with the need to get home, to get home. . . . They are driving into dusk, passing apple and cherry and pear orchards, the many acres of fruit trees, passing farms, ruined old barns and newer barns, with that Mail Pouch sign in black and yellow everywhere, and silos thick and fuzzy in the gathering mist, and fields filling up with snow and time. There are animals in the fields, stray horses that lift their heads at the sound of the car, but stupidly, massively, without sight. They pass the canning factory where Jesse's mother once worked years ago. It is closed now for winter. They pass more orchards, fruit orchards, farms. On this highway a few cars pass them; it is dark enough now for headlights because of the storm that is on its way, and lights from oncoming traffic shine into Jesse's father's face, making him squint.

They turn onto the Moran Creek Road and now they are nearly home. Things move toward them quickly and silently. A wilderness of trees, unrestrained shapes, and then a sudden opening, a break in the thicket, and there is pastureland around a sharply meandering creek, where in better weather cows graze, stupid as the horses. The creek has meandered so that it resembles a series of S's, one fixed onto another, a child's scrawling. Logs protrude through its ice. Jesse has fished and waded in this creek for the past several years, but today it seems distant, snaking away into the dusk while he is being carried home in the opposite direction.

His father sniffs suddenly. A snorting, angry noise as he tries to clear his head.

And now they are nearly home. Over one of the bridges . . . the clapping of the boards beneath the car . . . the Snyder farm, with its gaunt, ugly, exposed house on a hill . . . and now the gas station is suddenly in sight, and it is really boarded up. Closed. And the field of junked cars and motorcycles is really behind it, as always. Jesse is being brought home. What is the secret of this scene? The look of the gas pumps and their hoses thick as arms, thickly looped? Behind everything is the gauzy late afternoon sky, wintry and evil, and there is nothing in that sky to give a form to the day, nothing permanent, nothing to be outlined with the eye. It is all a blur, shapeless, a dimension of fog and space, like the future itself. Jesse stares at it and as he stares he is being driven into it relentlessly.

Dear God, Jesse thinks. . . .

His father turns up the driveway joltingly. He shuts off the ignition.

"Go in the house," he says.

Jesse thinks this is strange—of course he will go in the house. Why not?

"Aren't you coming in?" he says.

"In a minute."

Jesse gets out, goes to the porch. He hears his father get out of the car behind him. But his father goes to the trunk of the car. Jesse half-sees that he has opened the trunk . . . maybe there is something inside, a small Christmas tree, a present, a secret . . . ? And he turns away before his father sees him watching.

When he opens the door, he is grateful for the warm air. His face burns with it. And a smell of something sweet: some kind of food. The house is quiet except for a noise like arguing, almost inaudible. Jesse stands in the kitchen and his fingers instinctively grope for the zipper of his jacket. Then he sees a smear of blood on the floor.

A faint smear. It seems to lead into the front room.

Jesse's face comes open with the warmth of the house. His mouth opens into a question. He comes forward on legs that are suddenly elastic and springy.

Someone is lying there—in the doorway to the front room. It is a joke, Jesse thinks. His brother is hiding from him. It is Bobby lying there on his stomach. His face is turned to one side, far to one side, the eyes open, a pool of blood beneath him. Jesse stares down at him. "Bobby," he says. The boy's eyes are open. It is strange to see that they are open, that he is lying right in the doorway, not hidden at all.

"Bobby . . . ?"

Jesse looks up, his head springing up, and now he sees them all: he has been seeing them without knowing it. There is a jumble of bodies, arms and blood, drifts of hair like field grass, stiff with blood. His sister Jean lies with something shattered beside her—a lamp, maybe—and there is white glass mixed with the blood. A lampshade is splattered with blood. Jean's face is turned away; no, it had bled away, half of it is soaked in the rug, half of it is gone . . . and at the very tips of her fingers, as if straining to get away from her touch, is Shirley, doubled over, lying doubled over with her arms shielding her stomach. Jesse steps forward into the blood. He has begun to hear a whimpering sound. It is the dog, Duke, locked up somewhere . . . ? Jesse sees blood on the rug. It is glistening, it is still wet—where will he be able to walk? What if he steps on it? His mother is sitting in the armchair by the radio, her head back, her throat and chin and the upper part of her chest blasted red, raw, the bone somehow showing through the mess of bleeding flesh. All down the front of her body there is blood, a cascade of blood, on her great round stomach and in her lap, on her parted legs, on the chair, the floor. . . . The radio is still on, its dial glowing, but the station is too faint to hear and there is only an irritable, arguing noise.

Jesse stands there.

The blood smells so sweet, it is like summer; it rises to him in a cloud, blotching his sight. The whimpering from another room is sweet because it is so muffled. *Why did he lock the dog up?* Jesse asks lightly. The words whirl in his head, lightly, like snow.

His father's footsteps on the driveway outside, the quick crunching steps.

Jesse stands there, not thinking. His face is hot with the welcome air of the house. His brain has dissolved in this warmth, this sweetness, and he looks around at these dead people as if to figure them out—is it a joke, are they playing a game? He looks carefully at Jean, who might jump up to tease him. But everyone is so quiet!

His father opens the kitchen door.

Jesse steps forward suddenly into the blood. Through the blood. His feet carry him through it and something is knocked over—a splintering crash—and Jesse is at the bedroom door now and fumbling with the doorknob, getting it open. Jesse pays no attention to the yipping dog crouched in a corner of the room, but throws himself against the window. Everything bursts—it gives way—comes apart as if in a dream. Jesse falls through the window, covering his face with his hands, and then he is outside and running.

The shotgun blasts behind him.

He knows that sound and he runs with his hands up to his face, his shoulders hunched. Running, he seems to charge the air, still falling out of that window but already on the run, while the blast from the gun shudders in the air around him. Something strikes his shoulder, high. A clot of mud? A rock? It is solid and hot and heavy, dragging his shoulder down, but he keeps running. He heads for the thicket. Another blast from the shotgun—now he is in the thicket, gasping, his hands quick to make a way clear for his body—

He runs. His lungs and stomach define themselves terribly inside this body, expanding as if they would burst, and his eyes are like bubbles in his skull, bulging. Everything wants to burst! He hears his own voice, which springs out of his throat like Duke's whimpering, leaking out of him. He runs through the thicket and out the other side and throws himself over the barbed-wire fence, noticing with part of his mind how the fence catches at him, stinging his hands, but still he is running, running, against the wall of snow—

He runs into the dark.

3

Is that the one over there? The first bed?
Be quiet, he can hear you—
He detached himself quickly, guiltily, from his hearing.
He slept.

Has he been sleeping all morning? I better wake him up—
He's a good-looking kid. Christ, it's a pity—
Pretending to sleep so the nurse could wake him. Politely, fuzzily waking. He rubbed his eyes and felt the innocent sandy grit in his lashes. *Good morning!* said the smiling nurse. His mouth smiled and replied, a formal, distant set of words. In this hospital bed he held himself stiff, rigid, out of a fear of making some mistake, showing that he didn't know how to behave. It was always a shock to lie in bed like this and to see a woman, a stranger, standing beside him.

His eyelids were heavy with shame.

Behind him, inside him, was the place where he had been lying just now, partly unconscious, suspended between this hospital ward and the darkness that had no exact shape to it. The hospital ward was one big long, wide room, two rows of beds with many yards of floor space between them where nurses and attendants and doctors walked, usually in a hurry. Things were wheeled by on carts with creaking joints; dishes from meals clattered. Out there everything was public and open and noisy; the darkness was Jesse's own private place, a place deep inside him like a well.

How do you feel? the faces all asked him hopefully; hoping he would give the correct answer, which they already knew. He was sitting up now, smiling, drinking orange juice and milk. A healthy boy. A healthy boy, damaged but still healthy and eager to be a boy again, to be released into boyhood again—which was not found in the hospital but only outside.

There was a bright, glittering pinpoint to their stares, the focus on his face, only his. He had to sit still in bed and accept those stares. No escape. No pretending to sleep in the middle of the day. So he looked right into the stares, right into the piercing blinding point of their attention, and felt with a kind of surprise how readily he could accommodate himself to them. He had become a polite boy.

And what do you remember next? the policeman asked him. He was not dressed in a policeman's uniform; he wore a suit and tie. A young man was with him, taking notes. *And then . . . ? And then . . . ?*

How old are you, about fifteen? asked a chatty nurse on night duty.

It was night now; Jesse woke to discover that time had passed; his mouth and throat were very dry from the sleeping pills he had been given.

Fourteen, he said.

I have a brother your age. Real pest. Well, how do you feel?

Ready to go home, he said, because he supposed that was what everyone wanted to hear. But he felt the startled jab of the woman's stare and knew that he had made a mistake. He amended his answer slightly: *Ready to leave the hospital.*

She smiled. He must have given the right answer.

On one side of Jesse was the wall, several yards away. A white plastered wall with many fine cracks in it. On the other side was a young man in his twenties who had had an operation. Gall bladder. Jesse did not know what that meant. A small tube had been placed in the man's skin on the back of his wrist, and from a contraption that hung over the side of his bed fluids were moving into him. Jesse tried not to look at him, knowing how shameful sickness was, how you wanted only to hide, to hide yourself from the curious faces of the healthy.

His grandfather came to visit him. Grandpa Vogel himself. An old man with a blunt bald head and a bald face, smooth and hairless, the skin very smooth, almost shining, crisscrossed with hundreds of small, nearly invisible wrinkles. His skin had been burned and baked by the sun for years. Years of suns. He carried the air of the deep country with him, a shiftiness of the eye, a pursed, cautious mouth inside pouches of fine wrinkles. When he stirred, Jesse could smell must about him; he carried it like a cloud, a vapor—the mustiness of old closets, old clothes. The suit he wore for these visiting days was dark, probably thirty years old, too large for his slightly shrunken body. The white shirt had turned a faint gray. No necktie. His hands, on his sharp knees, were very large, distorted, even freakish, the knuckles hardly more than bunches of bones that looked swollen, but the skin over them was very smooth, as if drawn tight, painfully tight, and fastened that way, while the old man gripped his knees and talked about Jesse coming to live with him.

Your dog is right at home, he said slowly, with the shifty, cautious look of a liar.

While his grandfather was there the doctor came by on his rounds. He had Jesse lean forward so that he could check the bandages. He was springy and young, with glasses that were wire-rimmed and severe. He listened to Jesse's heart and Jesse stared anxiously into his bright, young, closed face, not flinching at the cold metal of the instrument. *Well, Jesse,* said the doctor, *how are you feeling today?*

Okay. Ready to go home, he said. Then he said quickly, *I mean, ready to leave the hospital....* But the doctor gave no sign of hearing these particular words. He nodded. He smiled down upon Jesse as if from an enormous height.

You are healing well, he said kindly.

Jesse began to cry.

Why are you crying? Living begins when crying leaves off....

After a while he went away and Jesse heard him ask, a few beds down, *How do you feel, Ed?*

The wound ached. It was high on Jesse's back, his right shoulder. It would heal, but what if, somewhere deep inside it, some of the shot remained? A piece of poison, a tiny invisible piece of metal? What then? Jesse did not want to ask the doctor about this. It might make him angry. No use to ask for more pity, more pitying stares.... Jesus, but he was tired of them! He admired the doctor because he was so busy, because he was impersonal and wise. His name was Alvin Farley and he was the son of a Yewville doctor; the nurses talked about him and Jesse could overhear. Young Dr. Farley and old Dr. Farley. Jesse gathered that they were both important men. He tried to imagine Dr. Farley with a father. A man like him, but larger, the two of them wearing glasses, with that clipped, fleshy, confident nose, that intelligent smile, that short, chunky body....

Tears rushed into Jesse's eyes.

His grandfather might have seen him cry, but he said nothing.

That evening Mrs. Brennan stopped by to visit him. She was in town for Friday-evening shopping and she wore a dressy coat, black with a maroon suede collar, with large rhinestone buttons. Her face was coarse and reddened, as if with permanent embarrassment. She held her large patent-leather pocketbook on her lap. Inside her thick brown stockings her legs were beefy, strong; she sat with her coat pulled tight across her lap, primly, her eyes darting shyly about the ward as if she had no business looking at anyone except Jesse.

It's funny how all these beds are together, people sleeping in a row like this, she said. *I never been in a hospital myself. Had all the kids at home, there wasn't any trouble.... Oh, Matt said to ask you are they feeding you right?*

Jesse hoped none of the nurses could hear. *Yes,* he said.

You get enough milk? Eggs every day? Is the butter fresh?

Yes.

Jesse's smile was wobbly.

Well...

Her face went slack with a bleak, dumb worry. What to say to him? A neighbor boy. Just a boy who lived next door to her and her own family, no kin of hers, not even a boy she knew very well. She didn't know any of the Hartes well. If he wouldn't talk about food, what was there to talk about? Jesse could understand her uneasiness. But he could not think of anything to say to her. If only she would go away.... But when she shifted the pocketbook on her knees he was startled, thinking she was about to leave him.

Jesse, you know if you ever need... if... Her gaze dropped in sorrow. She was a large, clumsy woman, built in the shoulders like a man, her graying, frizzy hair short and shapeless about her face. Her skin was prematurely creased from the sun and tiny veins had worked their way to the surface of her nose and cheeks, giving her a flushed look. *If you ever need anybody to take you in...*

Jesse remembered her screams that night: *It's the Harte boy, somebody shot him!*

Her voice now was not a scream but an ordinary voice, floating on a shapeless, dark space within him, a fluid space that shimmered and tilted when he moved. He adjusted his perspiring body in the bed. His body was private and warm and agitated, but the bed was public. It belonged to no one. With part of his mind he could hear her voice—she fumbled on, talking now of their sick cows, of how lucky Matt was to sell the farm the way he did, how everything needed fixing, how they were going to move in a few weeks; and here he sensed her hesitating, her wondering if she should say how lucky Jesse was that they hadn't moved yet— And with another part of his mind he could hear that other voice, that terrible muscular yell of hers: *Get the car started! Get it going fast!*

They saved his life.

We heard about your grandpa going to take care of you, she said, *that's real nice.... A man his age shouldn't live alone anyway. But if you ever need help or a place to live...*

Jesse could not look at her. The Brennans had nothing of their own; Matt Brennan had had to sell his farm, and yet she was offering him...offering him what? A home? A chance to be a son again? The Brennans had five children of their own. They were very poor. And yet she was offering to take him in.

He was relieved when she stood to leave. She had waited until visiting hours were over, as if leaving before the very end would have hurt Jesse's feelings. *Here are some things, just some... I don't know if you want any...just some brownies and...* She spoke apologetically, her face reddening. She handed him a box and Jesse thanked her.

Well! One thing I'll tell them is that they feed you all right in here. Matt was real curious about that!

Jesse smiled good-by. Good-by. When she left, his warm face turned pale.

He hoped he would never see her again.

He was discharged from the hospital the following week. His grandfather came to get him in a pickup truck, which rattled and bounced because it was empty in back except for some straw. From time to time the old man made a sharp noise with his throat and nose, a *tsk*ing noise that made Jesse glance at him. But he was not conscious of what he was doing. He leaned up close against the steering wheel, squinting peevishly; finally he said, "What's that say? Why's that so big over there?"

It was a large white sign advertising automobiles.

"Just to sell cars," Jesse said.

"What?"

"A sign to sell cars."

Jesse's grandfather shook his head angrily. He did not understand what the billboard meant, why it was there. He seemed irritated by it and by the other signs along the highway. They were just leaving Yewville and there were many things to see, a confusion of signs and houses and traffic. It was a Saturday afternoon; farmers and their families were driving in to town. Jesse stared at the cars that passed by, dreading a familiar face—someone he might know from school—he dreaded faces turning in surprise at the sight of him, fingers pointing toward him. He held himself still, his arms folded and pressed against his ribs as if he were conscious of the gift of himself, the gift of being here, living. He would never forget. He listened for the beating of his heart, remembering Dr. Farley's swift professional concern for that heart: it was saying gently *Here I am, I am here, I am beating*. So he would not be frightened at the thought of seeing someone he knew. That would happen, eventually. Fingers would be pointed at him. Eventually.

Mrs. Brennan had held him in her arms on the drive in . . . the bouncing drive in, through a snowstorm . . . held him in her arms as he bled onto her. . . .

He narrowed his eyes sharply to stop this thinking. He would not think about it. His grandfather was muttering something about Yewville, about all these people making fools of themselves buying things and hanging around on the streets, the kids running loose, the women dressed up as if for parties, the men piling up debts at Montgomery Ward's for things they didn't need, and when Jesse opened his eyes again they were out in the country. Safe. The air here was cold and sunny. Fields were stubbled with snow; everything was raw and frozen hard, the ditches jagged with ice. Jesse belonged in the country, like his grandfather. The hardness of the sky, the hardness of the flat earth matched something in himself.

Getting to his grandfather's farm was like sleepwalking: you drove in one direction and then turned and drove in another, as if by instinct, groping in a dream, turning from one narrow dirt road to another road more narrow, until the last road was hardly more than a cow lane leading back into the wilderness. Tall cattails stuck up out of the ice in the ditches in stiff, frigid clusters. Everything was silent here—no other cars or trucks, only a few homes far back from the road, looking vacant. No telephone poles this far into the country, no electricity at all. Distance. Silence. Something began to throb in Jesse, deeply and heavily, this thought of their being so far away from the town and from his old home, from what he could remember of himself ... out here everything would become flattened by the brutal sweep of the land, the wind, neutralized by distance.

He would forget.

The drive had made his shoulder ache, but he held himself tight, carefully. His grandfather had fallen into a sullen silence, as if he were alone, and Jesse was grateful for his silence, watching the fields blotted out by woods and the woods falling back to open fields again, a rhythm of fields and woods and fields that was peaceful, hypnotic. Yes, he would forget; he would be lost in all this distance, this wilderness, the electric nervousness of his own soul neutralized by the silence of this old man and the land he lived on.

He had bled all over Mrs. Brennan....

The fields opened and closed; the woods opened and closed. It was silent out there as if uncreated, unimagined. Except for the road itself, you would not suppose that anyone had been this way before. The winter fields looked crushed and obliterated, a jumble of ancient cornstalks, the irrigation ruts hard as iron, lined with jagged hunks of ice that gleamed hotly in the sun. An inhuman landscape. A healing landscape. *Wheeled in the emergency ward ... skimming along the floor on a creaking cart ... the smell of rubber and metal and gas ... the pumping of his heart, pumping blood out of him in gulping surges....* Now his grandfather drove the old truck slowly, but still it lurched in the road's potholes and ruts, making Jesse's wound ache. He said nothing. Once the old man glanced at him, as if just remembering him. "Your shoulder acting up?" he said.

Jesse shook his head *no.*

Almost there. He remembered the turn in the road. And now he saw the old farmhouse that would be his home—half a mile back from the road, at the end of a lane that led through two cow fields. No mailbox out front. Great oak trees lining the lane. The farmhouse itself was a surprise to Jesse, who had remembered it as being much larger. It was unpainted and its wood looked very dark, very damp, as if sour. He had the idea it would smell sour. It had originally been a small cabin, but other rooms had been added onto it over the years, so that now it had an uneven, unbalanced, lopsided appearance, as if its various parts had been jammed together by hand. Down a slight incline from the house was the outhouse, made of the same dark, unpainted wood. The door was ajar. The lightning rod on the peak of the house roof looked thin as a straw, a needle. *I don't want to live here,* Jesse thought in a panic. It was very cold. Bitter cold. His heart pounded wildly, as if to warm his blood against this cold.

His grandfather seemed about to say something, then thought better of it. Jesse said feebly, "Here we are. . . ." and was startled at the childlike sound of his voice. He stared at the house and the barns. Why did everything look so uncreated, so mean? Though the air was sunny, this place had the appearance of being in shadow, as it it were the underworld somehow, the bottom part of the real world, reflected in a substance like water. *Would he have to live here?* When his mother had brought them out to visit, long ago, the farm had looked larger, it had looked different. . . . Maybe it looked bad now because of the time of year. Their mother had brought them out in the summer; the air had been fresh and welcoming. The big hay barn had not looked so ugly and rotted. Jesse stared at the smaller barns, the dilapidated corn crib, the chicken coop, the pump on its concrete base, with its handle still up in the air, as if the old man, hearing the news, had flung the handle up and run. . . .

A sudden barking. A dog's yipping. Duke came running out of the woodshed, crouched low to the ground. His body shook as if with a convulsive terror. His ears were laid back close to his bony head.

"Duke!" Jesse cried. "Hey, you Duke! Hey!"

His dog froze, as if not recognizing him at first. Then he ran to Jesse, barking loudly. His body swayed with the violent motions of his tail.

"Hey, you crazy dog, don't you know me?" Jesse squatted and embraced Duke. He pressed his face against the dog's cold fur. "It's all right, it's okay, I'm back now . . . it's okay. . . ." Squatting, Jesse watched his grandfather approach him and tried to interpret the old man's sorrowing, closed-up look. Grandfather Vogel wore black, an old black suit. Behind him the farm buildings he had put up shared that black; the snow was a painful glaring white, but beneath it was black, a black substance. Trees and bushes were black but ornately covered with white, their skeletons decorated with a fine hard white. It was a sight that transfixed Jesse. The dog's wriggling in his arms brought him back to life.

Stooping slowly, with little enthusiasm, Jesse's grandfather patted Duke's head. "He's gun-shy now," he said.

Jesse nodded.

Jesse got his suitcase from the truck and followed his grandfather to the house. He had to push the dog gently down from him; Duke was on his hind legs, pawing Jesse's chest. He yipped hysterically. *What if the bleeding starts again?* Jesse thought weakly. It was such a struggle even to hold the dog. But he carried his own suitcase to the house. The kitchen was cold, unheated. His grandfather had evidently gone off that morning without heating it, to save fuel. Now he lit a fire in the big iron stove, grunting as he bent. Jesse looked around at the walls, which were just boards, and the wooden table in the middle of the room, and the tin sink with its short-handled pump. He was careful to show no disappointment. When the fire was started, Jesse's grandfather went into the next room and shut the door. Probably going to change his clothes, Jesse thought. *But what do I do now? What now?* The few times his mother had brought him and Jean and Shirley and Bob to the farm, the old man had kept at a distance from them; it was their grandmother who liked them, loved them, fussed over them. But she had died three years ago. The old man had always been out in the fields, working. Only happy when working, they said of him. He worked the whole section without hired help, except at harvesttime, using two teams of horses—one for the morning, one for the afternoon. Jesse and the girls had run out to spy on their crabby old grandfather, giggling, and there he would be, half a mile away, behind his team of horses, plowing, endlessly plowing, absolutely alone, a bony-faced old man with a filthy straw hat drooping about his face, his shoulders rounded inside his overalls. They had stopped giggling when they saw him. He moved in absolute silence, alone, a kind of nullity in the midst of the green corn, moving as if in a trance or a dream, making their eyes film over with the starkness of his isolation and his indifference . . . how unlike their own father he was, to be so lonely, to move so slowly behind a team of plodding horses! Their own father needed talk, laughter, beer, speed, noise, other men, other people to complete himself. . . .

I'll work like hell for you, Jesse thought. *I'll show you.*

Every morning he woke before dawn. Sometimes he woke as if jerked out of sleep by a hand, his mother's hand. Then he would sit up and not know where he was. Sometimes he woke because of his grandfather's noises in the other room. The old man snored raspily and moaned in his sleep. Jesse would lie in the warmth of his bed for a while, dreading the freezing air of the room, hearing the birds, the wind, a constant flow of sound that was inhuman and soothing. Then he got dressed, stepped into his overalls, into his boots, and went out to the kitchen. The floor creaked. Gusts of cold air rose from it. Duke, sleeping behind the stove, shook himself awake and whimpered around Jesse's legs as if questioning him—why were they here? What was this place?

Outside, the birds sang in a maniac chattering as the sun rose. Faster and noisier. A frenzy of callings. Jesse listened to them, as if transfixed by their bright, staccato notes. The birds were almost screaming a human language; if he listened closely, very closely, he could almost hear words. He worked the hand pump and splashed water onto his face, sucking in his breath with the cold. He made himself coffee. In a while he would hear his grandfather getting up—the creaking of the old bedsprings, the creaking of the floor. In the country people moved, silently, unspeaking, against a background of noises—the chattering of small birds, the cries of crows, of owls, the sound of the wind, a dog's distant barking. A car, passing along the road, was a surprise.

One day a car had turned up the lane and a man and a woman came to see Jesse. They were from the Niagara County Welfare

Board, the Department of Child Welfare. They asked Jesse questions about his life here; they looked around, prudently, with smiles. They asked Jesse about school. Why wasn't he going to school? Was he still in pain? He was alone in the kitchen because his grandfather had walked out when the man and woman came in, not excusing himself, just walking out to show his disapproval of visitors. Jesse had been very nervous, left on his own. He had never spoken to adults like this, people who wanted him, who had something to say to *him*, plans for *him*. He said that his shoulder still hurt and that he wanted to stay home for a while. He would go to school in the fall, he promised. In the fall. Wasn't that soon enough?

They left and his grandfather came back in the house. He never asked Jesse what they had wanted.

Most of the time they did not speak.

But Jesse felt that they were together in their silence, flowing the same way with the passage of each day, time itself a tangible element that carried them forward, always forward, away from the past. He helped the old man with everything. His arms and shoulders and chest ached from the heavy farmwork, but he thought that this kind of pain was good for him; it made him sleep, it pitched him at once into a deep, dreamless sleep, which was healing. Time itself was healing. He woke every morning at four-thirty or five, and then the day would begin for him and there was no staying in bed, no going back to sleep. It began by jerking him awake so that his heart hammered as if sensing danger—had someone awakened him? taken hold of his shoulder to shake it? But it was good to sleep so heavily and good to wake up, good to work so hard.

There were two things on the farm that Jesse hated, though: the chicken coop and one of the barns. The chicken coop was a long, low structure, kept in fairly good condition, but Jesse hated the chickens and their clucking and their stink, the awful crusts of their droppings everywhere—on the ground, thick on their roosts and the dirt floor of their coop, everywhere. They were nervous, filthy things. They moved like women, tiny, feathered, dumpy women. He hated their bleary red eyes, which were sometimes diseased or surrounded by tiny grublike worms, he hated their quick, stealthy walk, their dirty feathers, their perpetual hunger. When he went out to feed them they rushed upon him, wings fluttering, their eyes darting, darting, their scrawny little feet rushing them inward, to him, as if he were the center of the world for them, existing only to toss out feed. Brown hens. White hens. Jesse stared at them in disgust. When he walked out anywhere, on any task, the chickens converged upon him, clucking and excited. A few of the bolder ones would peck at his boots. It didn't matter that he had fed them only half an hour before, or that their feeding time was hours away. "Get out! Scat! You dirty things!" Jesse would whisper. He had begun to talk to himself, usually in whispers. "Dirty. Dirty. Dirty things," he said, hating them. He especially hated to collect their eggs. Still warm from the hens' bodies, some of them damp, with feathers or excrement on them . . . he so hated collecting these eggs that he had no appetite to eat them, he felt like gagging over a plateful of eggs, though he had liked them well enough in the past. His mother had made them scrambled eggs on Sunday. Chickens . . . fluidy droppings freezing to stones . . . their eggs half-hidden in straw . . . their perky heads, their little beaks, their scaly legs and feet— His scalp crawled when he had to feed them.

The animals he liked best were the horses, his grandfather's two aged horses that had no interest in him, big, gentle, stupid animals with great eyes, eyes nearly as big as Jesse's fist, black and bulging. These eyes fascinated Jesse: they were so huge, and yet they were used to see very little. As if there were little to see. As if the world contained nothing more than hay, feed, a water trough. Jesse liked to feed the horses, and he lingered in the horse barn, sometimes pressing himself against the horses' sides, his warm face against their cool sleek sides, his eyes starkly open and unthinking, unseeing. The horses were so still you did not have to think of anything. They munched hay, their heads were lowered almost permanently, they were still, silent, occasionally shifting their weight on their eroded hoofs, but there was nothing to think about or to remember, nothing. So heavy, the horses were like life that had run down into pure flesh, enormous muscular mounds of flesh, perfectly obedient and indifferent. Unlike the chickens, they were still, as if sleeping on their feet. There was no change in them.

Yet he felt their separation from him, their isolation. He could not cross over into it. What was massive in them, the powerful neutrality of their legs and shoulders and backs, was separate from him and baffled him.... It did no good for him to embrace their necks, to rub his face against their rippling necks, their dry, fine, stinging manes, even to talk to them, because they did not notice him, not really. There was nothing in *him*, nothing in Jesse himself, that could touch them.

He would walk quickly through the yard, his face turned away from the scurrying chickens. He spent less time with Duke now—the dog was a nuisance. He seemed to be always dragging Jesse back to Jesse's own childhood, a time in his life when he had been wriggling and stupid with energy, like the dog—a scrawny black Labrador retriever who had never been much good at hunting. Jesse's father had kicked the dog once in disgust....

Since the day he discovered what was kept inside it, Jesse walked by one of the small barns quickly. The door was padlocked. Furniture from his parents' house was in the barn, piled up. Jesse had peered through the cracks to see the old sofa, the chairs, the floor-model radio, the kitchen table, some beds. On the floor, wrapped carelessly in newspaper, were plates and silverware and what looked like Christmas tree ornaments, though Jesse couldn't be sure. He had felt nothing, seeing these things for the first time. He had simply walked away. But after that, crossing the yard, he had been unable to even look at the barn. His mouth twisted upward into a grin just to think of it, of himself peering through the cracks and seeing what he had seen.

On Sundays he and his grandfather went to services at the Benton Center Methodist Church, about ten miles away. Jesse sat in the drafty old church and did not look at the people around him, who might have been curious about him, *Jesse Harte... you know what happened to him....* He could almost hear their crackling thoughts, their curious poking questions. He kept a hymn book opened on his lap, though he never took part in the singing; his face went slack and dead in church. He tried to think of God, but his mind had no skill—it wobbled and shivered, confronted with such an idea. God. *God.* He needed something he could touch, turn over in his hands, get hold of. He needed to use his hands. He could believe only in things that had weight and toughness, that resisted him. When he tried to think of Christ, who had been a real man for a while, his mind leaped immediately to Christmas, to the tinsel and candy, the Santa Claus cutouts, the manger scenes with the Infant Jesus, the crepe-paper bells and candles; and then he thought of nothing at all, his mind going blank like a light that has been turned off.

In the midst of the church's small congregation, the country men and women and their children, some of them grown-up children, Jesse felt his strangeness. He and his grandfather were both strange. People glanced at them wondering. Curious. *That there is the boy whose father... But old man Vogel was always pretty strange himself. Must run in the family.* Jesse was grateful that his grandfather never lingered to talk with anyone except the minister, that he had no friends and had broken off ties with most of his own kin over the years, one squabble after another, the old man certain that he was right and everyone else wrong, out to cheat him. So there was a space about them, a dry, holy space that no one else entered. Jesse had little to say to the minister, Reverend Wilkinson, who always asked him and his grandfather how they were. Wilkinson was a man born for pitying, with mousy eyes that ran pink at the very sight of Jesse, a victim, someone who might be like Christ— "Christ, too, was a victim," Wilkinson had said once to Jesse, out of nowhere, as if he had planned saying it for a long time. Jesse had not replied. He held himself apart, quiet, content. Everyone else sang—the old women off-key but loud—and the organ, pumped by foot, was played by a girl Jesse's own age who labored with the hymns slowly and shrilly, her shoulders bent over the cold keyboard the way Jesse's grandfather bent over his plate at meals. Thumping—the organ's shrieking high notes—the slow rising voices of the people around him—the dusty maroon hymn books with their faded gold letters: Jesse took these things in but did not allow himself to be touched by them. He felt nothing, not the presence of God or of other people; he sensed nothing, no closeness, no intimacy. Confessing for Christ, some members of the congregation burst into tears and came forward to kneel before the Reverend Wilkinson, but Jesse only stared at them through half-closed eyes, fearful of their ecstasy, their coming loose. He was terrified of people, strangers, coming loose in front of him. Better the horses. Yes, the horses and their heavy, massive indifference, their brainless slumber.

But the rest of Sunday belonged to him. He and his grandfather did not work on that day and so Jesse was free to go out, tramping the fields in the misty suspension of Sunday, taking in the silence of the land. In late March the thaw began. Jesse walked for miles, his dog running with him, looking eagerly, alertly about into the fields where rivulets were draining into ditches, feeling a sense of excitement, almost dismay, in the bright sunlight. Everything was coming back to life! If he listened, he could hear the breathing of the damp earth, a soft oozing sound like a human sigh, a sucking. Jesse's eyes began to water because he could not look closely enough at everything. He had to look closely, severely. It was important. The odor of late winter was hypnotic to him: the smell of timber, of the earth, of sunlight. He came upon the thawing carcasses of small animals that had died in the winter. Their shabby, inert bodies were like cast-off articles of clothing. They were so final, so still; he found himself staring at them while the dog sniffed eagerly. *Closer to those dead animals than to the living dog.* Irritated, he chased Duke away. "Leave them alone!" he said.

He would come to a stop suddenly, not breathing. What was all that noise? The constant chatter of birds, the belligerent cries of crows. The wind. Branches came wildly to life in a sudden gust of wind, crushing against one another, tapping together. Was it a warning? What did it mean?

His body was tired from the heavy farmwork. Yet he was pleased with it—the persistent, inhuman work. He was not the same boy he had been a few months before. He had become transformed entirely. When he went to bed not long after dark he fell asleep at once, exhausted, urgent, his body tightened until the moment at which he actually slept and was lost to himself. And so, he thought, the rest of his life would pass. Sleep, waking, work; sleep, waking, work. Jesse sleeping. Jesse waking. Jesse at work, hard at work. He would not have to think about his life because it would pass like this, one day after another, carrying him forward. When he walked he could feel the muscles hardening in his legs and thighs; it excited him to think of the inhuman growth of the muscles in him, the strange, neutral strengthening of his body, which would push him forward into his own future.

The soft, sucking noises of the earth—what did they have to tell him except that he could walk quietly through the mud, in his boots, and be free of it and of anything that tried to hold him down?

One Sunday in early April he went with the dog along the bank of the creek—the "crick"—that ran about a mile behind his grandfather's house. The underbrush was thick on the banks and he had to force his way through. Birds flew up about him, as if to startle him. Partridges, pheasants, trying to terrify him with the noise of their flight. Across the creek he saw some boys, five or six boys. Were they his own age? He could not see how old they were. He hid, not wanting them to see him. They were hunting, probably for rabbits. Jesse hid and watched them. The day was filmy and glaring; he had to shade his eyes in order to see them. It crossed his mind that they might fire idly into the bushes and hit him.... Their voices came, indistinct and light as girls' voices, across the distance. He wondered what they were talking about. Two dogs ran along with them. Jesse had to comfort Duke, who had begun to whimper. "Quiet. It's all right. Nobody is going to hurt you," Jesse murmured. He watched as the boys climbed the long high hill of the creek bank and he could almost feel the strain of their climb, the tug of their leg muscles. They were about to disappear. Jesse had an impulse to call out to them— But he said nothing. Displeased with himself, he grinned angrily, mockingly, and stood with the heels of his boots firmly in the sucking mud. He did not move.

When the boys were out of sight he hacked his way to the creek bank. Slid down a few yards of earth, sliding in the mud, almost falling. His arm shot out mechanically to steady himself and the pain in his back began. *God damn it.* He shaded his eyes to look across the creek, but the boys were gone. Now, standing alone on the bank, he began to realize that this place was familiar. His grandfather had evidently built a dam across the creek at this point, to force water back into a stream for his cows. Yes, he remembered that old dam. It was nearly gone now, only a few of the heaviest rocks remained in place. Water splashed across them, thick with mud, propelling debris, and in between the rocks water rushed freely and smoothly.... Jesse fingered his shoulder. The wound pounded strangely. What was this place, why was it so familiar to him? He stood on the bank and wondered if he could walk across on what remained of the old dam. The water was quite shallow. He stepped onto the first rock, which was larger than a man's head. It was shaky. He put his foot on the next rock but it was precarious, it would probably turn if he shifted his weight onto it. He paused. Duke had splashed after him. He shaded his eyes and looked up the creek again—he knew that this was a familiar place but he could not remember why. Was someone watching him?

Then he remembered: Six or seven years ago his father had gathered a group of motorcyclists out here, men from Yewville and Lockport and Ontario, and they had raced across the creek and up the bank and a mile out to the road and back again, around a big, crazy looping circle.... Jesse and some other boys had watched them. A few women had watched them. It had been a hot sunny day in midsummer and the men had been drinking beer, and at some point there had been a fistfight: Jesse's father bellowing at someone, the sudden exchange of blows, Jesse's father lifting his knee into the pit of another man's stomach, cries of alarm and rage, some of the women screaming. It was all mixed up in Jesse's head with the roar of the motorcycles and the speed of their racing. Flattened grass, grass torn out by wheels, caught up in spokes and torn out like hair from a head— Yes, they had raced here. Down that long creek bank, into the creek and up the other side, and back around again, turning sharply, back into the creek and up the hill, some of the motorcycles falling sideways, the men leaping clear, the laughter, the swearing.... Jesse's father had gone home with a tooth missing. Blood all over his shirt front. Grinning at Jesse's mother and her angry surprise. *What, what did you do to yourself!* He had shown her the empty socket, as if proud of it. Jesse had stared into his father's mouth, feeling his warm breath, the scent of blood, the warm dark damp scent of blood.

The sun seemed to break above him and to be reflected suddenly in the churning water. Fragments of light darting like bugs, like fragments of thought he could not bring together. He stood paralyzed. He could not move. Around him the water surged, high because it was April, with the light inside it. He felt that he would become lost in the light, in the broken water. What if he could not make his way home again? Where was his home? He might slip and fall, the wound might open again and bleed, pouring out of him the way this water poured downstream. He tightened his fingers on his shoulder. There it was, the pounding of his blood, that thrilling beat that pronounced his name for him, the triumph of his blood, changing inside him, making him silent and separate and safe from himself as his grandfather's horses. He wondered if the wound was clean. There might be germs.

Living begins when crying leaves off.

The day multiplied around him. The water seemed to thicken as it rushed around his feet. It sparkled, caught fire, shaping and breaking and shaping itself again, like darting insects or stars or thoughts not quite thought. He would spend the rest of his life like this, in the country, safe in the country, where the water and the light and the expanse of empty land could hide him. . . .

That evening, after supper, he said to his grandfather, "Can I look at those things in the barn? My parents' things?"

The kerosene lamp threw up long faint shadows across the old man's face. He was impassive, as if he had heard nothing.

"Please," Jesse said, raising his voice. "Can I look at them?"

His grandfather looked away. "You better leave all that alone."

"Please—"

"Why do you want to mess around?"

"I just want to look."

"That won't do you any good."

The old man pushed his chair away from the table and stood. Jesse stiffened. He could hear his grandfather's disturbed, raspy breathing, and he knew that he had made a mistake. But he did not care. He said recklessly, "Grandpa, please, it won't hurt anybody. . . ."

"No."

"I only want to look. I know I can't use the radio or anything. I know that. I only want to look."

"I said *no*."

"Why not?"

His grandfather's hairless, stern face was eager now, eager to say no. *No.* And Jesse, standing to face him, was eager to oppose him. "I only want to look in there. Why is it locked?"

"Because I want it locked."

"But why?"

"That junk is no good to nobody, it's staying where it is. It's piled up neat out there and it can rot, just junk, nobody would buy it, the barn is locked and it's staying locked."

"My bed is in there. I could use my bed," Jesse said.

"You have a bed."

"I want my own bed."

"The barn is staying locked." Jesse could feel a swaying motion between them, a movement of the air. He and the old man were staring at each other. Jesse felt how immune he was, at this moment, as if he were still on that rock in the creek, buoyed up by the energy of the water. And his grandfather, with that coarse, flushed face, the mean little eyes, was as immune as Jesse himself; stern and aged and nullified, he faced Jesse across the kitchen table.

"You're like *her*," the old man said suddenly, sneering.

"Like who?"

"You know who."

"Why? What do you mean?"

"Like *her*, just like *her*! You don't let trouble alone, you hunt it out! All right, go after it, marry it, lay down with it, but when you get up again all filthy don't come to me—you get what you deserve. Don't come to me for help, any of you!"

Something flew up inside Jesse, a sensation of terror. It was almost giddy, it was like the fragmented sparkling water with the darkness beneath it, inside it. He stared at his grandfather's angry working jaws. He could not believe that his grandfather had said those words—so many months of silence, a dry, holy silence, and now those ugly words. He thought: *Don't say anything more! Not one word more!*

"The two of you are alike, you and her," his grandfather said. "You ask for trouble. You want it. I told the doctor and the others, I told them I was an old man and sick to death of all this, that family, all my family—why don't they let me alone? People should let one another alone! But I drove to Yewville and there you were, in bed, and your father was dead by then, and you were in the hospital and they said you would be alone, so I gave in and said all right. All right. I would take you back with me. All right. But I'm an old man," he said hotly, "and I'm tired, I want to come to the end of things, I don't want starting all over again with a kid and a goddamn noisy nervous dog and trouble—I knew what *he* was, your father, the first time I saw him. I knew. And that day he came out here and tore up the land and I called the police on him, I knew what he was, everybody knew—"

"Don't—" Jesse said.

He put out his hand as if to caution his grandfather—how could he be saying these things, how could he be putting them into words at all? For months there had been a silence in which certain events still existed, stark and invisible, and now that silence had been dirtied by words, by an old man's whining voice.

"Fifty years I worked this place, you know that? You know what fifty years is? No. You don't. You don't know."

"I only want to see those things. They're mine," Jesse said.

"Yours! What's yours! You don't own anything on this earth, not a thing! *Yours!* I should sell that junk to the junkman! Should ask him for five dollars and he could haul it all away!" the old man said angrily. "What do you think that hospital cost? Who do you think has to pay for it—all that blood and medicine and the doctor and the bed? Huh? Do you think the hospital is free? Your goddamn bastard of a father lived for two days, did you know that?—two days with part of his head blown off because the stupid goddamn bastard couldn't aim right when it was between his own eyes he needed to shoot—he lived and sucked up blood and money, and who do you think has to pay for that? Bastard —bloodsucker—cost me money while he was dying—and the funerals—the goddamn son of a bitch, that undertaker—"

He screwed up his face and spat. He spat onto the floor but some of the spittle clung to his chin. Jesse stood with his hand outstretched toward his grandfather.

How could such words be said out loud?

Jesse ran to the back room, to his bed.

He lay awake most of the night. He could not believe what he had heard. It was not that his grandfather had said anything wrong, but that he had said anything at all. It couldn't have happened. They had had a partnership of silence; Jesse had thought he understood that silence, but his grandfather had violated it... and he had spat onto the floor of his own kitchen, his eyes narrowed with hatred.... Branches rubbed against the roof and the side of the house, as if signaling Jesse. The windows were very dark. Black. It was all an inhuman place outside, no words, no betrayal. No words. He watched the windows turn slowly from black to gray, a fuzzy bright gray, and his head ached with the certainty of the morning and his return to himself, to Jesse, the inescapable beat of his heart: *Jesse, Jesse, here is Jesse, this is Jesse.* That heartbeat got him out of bed, it was so strong, so demanding. He could not lie in that bed any longer. He was finished with it.

He walked for several miles before he caught a ride with a farmer. It was a Monday morning and there wasn't much traffic. The farmer drove a rickety old car and hadn't much to say to Jesse, didn't recognize him, didn't ask him any questions. He let him off on the highway. Jesse began to walk toward Yewville, between empty fields. A man driving a truck piled high with fresh new lumber picked him up. "Where you headed, kid? Yewville?" Jesse said yes. He wondered if this man recognized him. But no, probably not, he chattered about the long drive and about a boxing match he had seen in Buffalo. "Do you like boxing?" he asked Jesse. Jesse seemed to think for a moment, then said no. The driver glanced at him, peeved.

He stopped at a bar near Yewville, one Jesse remembered his father going to, and Jesse walked the rest of the way. The air was very damp. He walked along the edge of the road quickly, his hands in the pockets of his jacket. This close to home, he did not want anyone to recognize him. He walked fast, faster. As he neared his old home he felt strangely lightheaded, as he had felt as a child on important days—his birthday or Christmas—when the day loomed up gigantic and unpredictable, an uncharted day that might be too much for him to live through. His skin felt bright. He found himself smiling brightly.

There it was: the gas station, the small house, the junkyard. There. But something new was out front, a FOR SALE sign, black letters on a yellow background. FOR SALE. Why did the sign look old? It was dented and chipped and weatherworn. There were small pits in it, as if kids had thrown stones at it or shot it with BB guns. Jesse's face was numb, but inside his face, where the nerves and blood vessels worked like tiny electric wires, everything was subtle and alive.

What would happen? He was coming home. At any minute Duke might come running down the drive to him, barking. He might see a movement at the door of the house—his mother waiting for him, wondering why he was home from school so early. *I just walked out. I wanted to come home.* He thought of the Christmas assembly and of how he had hidden in the lavatory, afraid to go home, where he was needed. He could have changed everything if he had gone home.... He touched the realtor's sign, running his fingers along its edges. He had never heard of Martin Realtors before. What business did they have selling this house?... He walked up the drive, which was in bad shape from the long winter, its gravel sparse and eroded. Mostly mud. He seemed to be floating to the door. It was splashed with mud from the dog's paws. Jesse tried the handle. Locked. He looked around to see if anyone was watching. The back of his head tingled. But he was alone, the highway was empty, everything was still except the birds. A flock of crows. Calling at him, taunting him from the Brennans' side of the fence. His heart pounded slowly, stubbornly, *I'm here, I'm here, I'm here. Jesse Harte is here, a survivor.*

A lone car passed out on the road, not slowing.

Miles away, his grandfather would be alone—maybe glancing up at the sky, a habit the old man had, just as his father had had the habit of glancing at his watch. Checking the weather. The time of day. He would do the farm chores and he would think, now and then, of Jesse. He would keep on living—an old man, sour and tired, a failure, but living—and Jesse would keep on living, the two of them now separate, in separate dimensions. The old man had been his grandfather for a while. A partner for a while. They had worked together, lived in the same house together, they had shared months of silence together . . . and then it had all ended, his grandfather had broken the silence, had spat. It was ended. Jesse felt his eyes well with bitterness at the thought of that old man's betrayal. He had loved his grandfather and his grandfather had betrayed him.

He smashed the door window. He reached inside and unlocked the door, cutting himself on a piece of glass. He wiped the blood absentmindedly on his jacket and went inside.

Unheated. The kitchen was nearly empty—only the old stove and the icebox remaining, very dirty. He looked from corner to corner. Was this the right house? So empty, so cold.... His heart slowed as if coming to rest. Yes, this was the right place. It was restful here. He was stepping into his true home, out of the strife of crows and the moist, sinking sound of the earth.

Walking through the rooms. Floating. The living room—the empty, stained walls—the floor with its worn-out carpet—the cardboard boxes in a corner, the puffs of dust, the window shades yanked halfway down. For a moment the roof of his mouth ached. In the back room one of the windows had been boarded up. Boards nailed in place. Jesse recognized this room. Who had nailed those boards up? His grandfather? The police?

There was a box, an old crate, in the corner. Jesse went to sit on it.

On the wall before him were patches of sunlight that flickered and faded and grew bright again. He could see out into the other room and there the sunlight looked stronger. A movement of cloud: patterns of shadow upon darker shadow. The wallpaper was ragged. Yet there was something compelling about it. Ripped, smeared. A certain design. His heart announced to the place, *I'm here, here I am....* Jesse narrowed his eyes to hear more closely the sounds of his family—his brother, his sisters, his parents—and he felt them watching him from the doorway, wondering at his being so alone, sitting on this crate. He would be teased for walking out of school so early. *I wanted to come home. I just walked out.* He remained sitting, his nerves tightened, his face brightened as if with fever. He would not go back to school. He would not go back to his grandfather's farm. That was over. He would not go back to the hospital because he was well. He was healed. A face seemed to be shaping itself out of the torn wallpaper, nicks and scratches and a deep tear that was like a mouth, a gouge of a mouth, his father's mouth, his father's staring face....

They had left him and were buried in a cemetery outside town. But they were spying on him, about to giggle at his loneliness, his sitting in this back room—why wasn't he in school? why had he left school at noon? But he did not move. He felt his father watching him, but he did not move. Let his sister Jean run in and tease him, laughing at him the way she always did—he didn't mind—she would say *Jesse couldn't go to the lavatory before assembly, oh no, he had to wait until it began and then he excused himself*. . . . Let her tease, he didn't mind.

The house slowly darkened. He felt how cleverly he was camouflaged in it, like an animal in the woods, like one of those carcasses he and the dog had discovered at the end of winter. From time to time he saw the flash of headlights and, for an instant, he understood that it was his family coming back—they had gone out shopping late and were just coming home. But the car never turned up the drive. He sat on the crate, feeling how the room was so much smaller without things in it—how the floor seemed to slope—it seemed to slope toward the rear of the house, toward the woods out back, and he had to brace himself firmly against that tugging, his feet out in front of him in his muddy winter boots.

4

Jesse lived for a while with his aunt and uncle in Yewville. They had one son, Fritz, who was a year older than Jesse and who had always seemed to like Jesse well enough. But now, thrown together, the two boys were unwieldy and self-conscious; Jesse was aware of Fritz's trying, trying hard, to act as if nothing had gone wrong. Everyone talked to him, as if fearful of silence. Fritz came home from school and talked to Jesse about what was going on—rapid, nervous chatter about people who had become hardly more than names to Jesse now—and Jesse began to nod quickly, without hearing, his face slack and peaceful, as if on the verge of perpetual sleep. He had the habit now of sitting without moving for long periods of time. His brain operated slowly, without agitation. He liked to sit in the kitchen while his aunt prepared food, and not even her chatter and the radio above the sink with its music and news broadcasts could keep him from a dark, pleasant drowsiness. He could feel the darkness rise at the back of his head, coming up from the mysterious thick vessels in his throat; sometimes, while his aunt talked toward him, he put his head down on his arms and fell asleep. His uncle came in late from work—he worked at a planing mill—kicked off his shoes, opened a bottle of ale, talked loudly and heartily to Jesse, with the boisterousness of a man not accustomed to talking to children, and then, as if puzzled by Jesse's silence, he would suck in air and blow it out again, slowly, thoughtfully, so that his cheeks belled and his eyes moved cautiously about his own kitchen, not quite recognizing it. Jesse slept in Fritz's room, a small attic room with a sloped ceiling, and even at night Fritz would try to talk to him in the dark, a questioning, brotherly, gentle murmur punctuating the chilly dark of the room: "Hey, Jesse, what do you think of Barbara Stanley, huh? What do you think of *Agnes* Stanley?"

But when he was not with them he could hear them talking softly together, sometimes whispering. So careful. So cautious. He hesitated to enter a room because it would break them up—his aunt and uncle drawing apart, smiling nervously over at him, even Fritz, who resembled Jesse a little, with the same red-blond wavy hair and the same tall, thin frame, drawing away from his mother as if to show that they had not been talking about anything at all. Jesse sensed how he altered their lives, stirring the air of any room he entered. He sensed their kindness, the pity in his aunt's eyes that might have been pity for any freak—Jesse a boy of fourteen with no family, a boy who was not going to school, who moved about in a kind of daze.... One evening in the kitchen Fritz slammed the icebox door and the noise startled Jesse, who was easily startled by noises now, and his aunt said angrily: "Fritz, were you born in a barn? Don't you have any manners?" Fritz looked at her, baffled. It occurred to Jesse that she was saying words she had never said before, before Jesse's coming to live here. She was speaking in a voice, staring at her son in a way that Jesse himself had caused. *Don't you have any manners?* It was not something she would ordinarily have said, just as her dead sister, Jesse's mother, would not have said it to Jesse....

In May his uncle drove him to the Niagara County Home for

Boys, outside Lockport. It was a large building of dark red brick, set back from the road and surrounded by a wire fence. The front yard was bumpy—grass and lumps of weeds and bare, rutted earth, as if trucks and tractors had been driven back and forth over it. A circular drive was made of cinders. The front of the building was weathered, the bricks beginning to chip, like the bricks of the old high school back in Yewville. Jesse's uncle talked with the supervisor and the welfare worker, who had a manila folder open on her lap, papers that referred to Jesse, to *Jesse Harte*. She consulted these papers now and then. Jesse did not bother to listen to most of what they said, these three adults who conferred together, deciding his fate. He sat politely in his new suit, which was a rather bright blue, bought at Montgomery Ward's a few days ago. His aunt, who had been nervous for a week, took him shopping and bought him the suit as a "going away" present. She had wept that morning while making them breakfast. Her face had a stricken, thin, witch-like look about it that frightened Jesse. She stood at the stove, her shoulders slumped, and the smell of the frying bacon and eggs and the way his aunt stood there, weeping, made Jesse think of his own mother. He was grateful to be leaving. He had to leave. His aunt had wept, but she had not come along with Jesse and his uncle to Lockport.

Everyone stood. The discussion must have come to an end. The welfare worker, a woman whose name Jesse had forgotten, shook hands with him and said good-by. The supervisor, Mr. Foley, led Jesse and his uncle up to the dormitory where Jesse would sleep. It was a long room with a high ceiling. Two rows of beds. Everything empty, too quiet. "We have school-age boys here only," Mr. Foley was saying. "The others, you know, the younger ones, are sent to the Clinton Street Home." Jesse was unpacking his suitcase and he moved self-consciously, taking out underwear and socks. The suitcase was not his; his uncle would be taking it back to Yewville with him. He felt that the two men were watching him closely but absentmindedly, as if they had nothing else to look at.

"...and in addition to Sunday School there are weekday instructions, Wednesday afternoons. The public schools in Lockport dismiss classes early so that children can go to these instructions. Jesse will be going to the Methodist Church...? And we have a busy schedule for this spring. There is a softball team, and the Episcopalian Women's Association is going to take the boys to the Buffalo zoo...."

Jesse's uncle kept nodding and saying, "Yes. Yes, is that so? Yes. I didn't know that."

He was awkward here, in his working clothes, unaccustomed to the kind of intense talk Mr. Foley was giving him. He seemed to be perspiring. Jesse wanted to tell his uncle that it was all right. It was all right, he knew he had to leave, he couldn't live with them. He would not hold it against them. Anyway, when he was eighteen he could leave this place and this part of the country.

But when his uncle was about to leave, Jesse tasted panic.

"I better be starting back, Jesse," his uncle said clumsily. "It's a long drive."

He shook hands with Jesse, something he would never have done ordinarily, and Jesse felt again the contamination of his own presence, how he ruined things, made people jumpy and awkward.

"Well... I better start back. We'll come up to see you on Sunday, Jesse. And sometimes you can come back with us, if it's all right with Mr. Foley, you can stay overnight with Fritz... he'll like that a whole lot...."

His uncle was leaving him here?

They went back downstairs. Mr. Foley showed Jesse and his uncle one more room, a large dining room. There seemed to be nothing to say about it. Jesse's uncle tried to say something, to make a comment, but there was nothing to say. Several rows of ordinary tables, chipped a little; ordinary chairs; windows that looked out upon the cinder drive. A smell of dishwater. It was in this room that Jesse's uncle shook hands with him a second time, gravely and miserably. "It's a long drive back. I better get started," he said.

At about quarter to four the Home's bus brought the other boys back from school. Jesse felt panic at the sight of them—boys piling off a battered orange-yellow school bus, a noisy group, not the kind of boys Jesse had imagined. He had thought of orphans as being weak, slight, sickly. But these were ordinary boys. Ordinary shouts, scuffles. He was not going to be equal to them.

What had he to do with these people?

It was too late in the year for Jesse to start school, so he stayed at the Home every weekday while most of the other boys left. Two other boys also stayed behind—they were twins, large, stooping boys with bumpy faces, older than Jesse but evidently retarded, and the three of them worked around the Home with the handyman, or cleared away dead grass in the fields and orchard, or helped unload supplies of food from delivery trucks. Jesse liked the work, which was tiring and kept his mind occupied. When his mind was not occupied it kept thinking, plotting the route back to Yewville, skimming along the highways and roads to Yewville and to that intersection, the gas station, the house, the FOR SALE sign. Jesse slid in and out of dreaming, awakened by someone jabbing him in the ribs.

"How come you never talk? How come you just stand there?" one of the twins would ask Jesse curiously.

On Sundays they all went to church in Lockport. Jesse disliked church because it gave him too much time to think, but he looked forward to the bus ride. He was fascinated by the bridges and the canal in Lockport. He had never seen anything like the canal. He asked the bus driver questions about the canal—the Erie Barge Canal—and he yearned to stand on the widest of all the bridges and wait until a boat came through the locks. But there was never any opportunity. He had to stay with the other boys. In church he sat without fidgeting, wearily sensing himself an adult already, too old to bother with the whispered jokes and scuffling of the other boys; and he had no interest in, could not bother with the church ceremony itself. His brain retreated to an area about the size of a walnut.

One day Mr. Foley brought Jesse to his office after breakfast.

"Jesse, there is a gentleman from the city, Dr. Pedersen, who would like to have a talk with you," Mr. Foley said.

Jesse had already been examined by a County doctor and for a moment he thought this must be the same man.

"Dr. Pedersen has expressed an interest in your case. He and his wife have been considering the adoption of a child for some time . . . he has been in contact with me before but . . ."

Jesse leaned forward as if someone had struck him between the shoulder blades.

Adoption?

"I have set up a tentative meeting for Sunday afternoon," Mr. Foley said. He showed Jesse a pleased, rabbity smile. "Dr. Pedersen is a very busy man and Sundays are his only free day. You have probably never heard of Karl Pedersen, but he is very well known in the city. He and his father and two of his brothers, and even his wife's father, I think, are physicians who have made quite a name for themselves here. They're wonderful, wonderful people. Of course, as you know, it's a little unusual for a boy of your age to be adopted; in fact, very few of the boys here are ever considered for adoption . . . but . . . Dr. Pedersen spoke to me several times over the telephone, in person, and he has assured me that this is what he would like. . . ."

Jesse sat, numb.

"Jesse, you haven't said anything. I know how strange this is, in fact, I . . . I find it very strange myself, and I wonder . . . but . . . Dr. Pedersen assured me . . . What do you think, Jesse? Would you like to meet him?"

Jesse nodded yes.

Yes.

He met Dr. Pedersen in Mr. Foley's office. Mr. Foley introduced them nervously. Dr. Pedersen was a tall, fat man who stared frankly into Jesse's face, as if trying to place him. "Yes. Jesse Harte. How do you do," he said. His face was large and pale and moony. It seemed to give off a subdued, clammy light. "Well, my boy. We must talk alone now. Sit down. Please sit down. Mr. Foley, you won't mind if this young man and I talk alone together?"

Jesse looked to Mr. Foley in a panic, *Don't leave.*

But once they were alone Dr. Pedersen smiled at him and settled back in his chair. A wait of several seconds. Then he said, in a very kindly voice, "My boy, you are fourteen years old?"

"Yes," said Jesse.

"When is your birthday?"

"October third."

"You did not attend school this spring, I was told. Why was this?"

"I'll be going back. I was sick for a while."

"Oh. Yes. You were sick for a while," Dr. Pedersen said. He

smiled slightly, as if to encourage Jesse to speak. Relax, Jesse. Smile. Jesse was conscious of sitting very straight.

"You are interested in school, aren't you? You enjoy it?"

"Yes," Jesse said.

A lie. But maybe it would become true.

"Which subjects do you prefer?"

"I don't know. . . ."

"You don't know," Dr. Pedersen said flatly. "You don't know?"

"Well . . . science. . . ."

"Science," Dr. Pedersen said. "Which branch of science?"

Jesse had no idea. He stared at the floor.

"Are you primarily interested in living things or in dead things?"

"Living things."

"Ah, then—biology! You are interested in biology."

Jesse could not bring himself to say yes. He nodded vaguely.

A big man, this Dr. Pedersen—an immense torso, an immense stomach that bulged out against the front of his suit coat, straining the material. Enormous thighs. Knees that strained the material of his trousers so tightly it looked as if it might rip. Jesse could not help but stare at the man's large ankles, the size of an ordinary man's knees, swelling out against his black socks. His feet, though, were rather short. His hands were pudgy but rather short.

"You intend to go to college, of course," Dr. Pedersen said.

Jesse raised his eyes miserably to the man's face.

"College. . . ?"

"You intend to continue your education beyond high school, don't you?"

"I don't know . . ."

"Why are you in doubt?"

"I don't know anything about college . . . nobody ever went that I . . . I knew. . . ."

"But you have a willingness to learn?"

"I guess so. . . ."

"To go as far as you can, as far as your abilities will take you?"

"I guess so," Jesse said faintly.

Silence. Dr. Pedersen's voice was subdued and lethargic, his face pale, moony, damp. Yet there was a peculiar excitement in him. It had something to do with his clothes, his expensive stylish clothes, and the way his body strained at them so fiercely. He seemed very pleased with Jesse's last reply. Jesse stirred himself to add to it, to continue. "I . . . I want to go as far as I can. . . ." he said.

"Yes."

Dr. Pedersen smiled at him, watching him as if from a distance. He needs a telescope to examine me, Jesse thought dizzily. His face was strained from the small frightened smile he had brought with him to the interview, but he could not relax, there was nothing to take the place of that smile. He felt as if Dr. Pedersen were staring into the hollow spaces of his skull, seeing everything, assessing everything. The doctor nodded from time to time, as if their conversation were continuing in silence, while Jesse sat in an unnaturally straight position, conscious of being very skinny. He had lost about fifteen pounds since winter.

"Do you believe, Jesse, that there are human destinies just as there are national destinies? That a human being must realize himself, redeem himself, by becoming what he was meant to be?" Dr. Pedersen asked. Jesse stared at him without comprehension. He went on, more gently, as if speaking to a child. "You are perhaps too young to understand the currents that pass between people, the relationships that are too subtle to be talked about, that elude analysis. Yes, you are very young. These things must be explained to you. There are certain tugs of feeling between people—an almost literal tugging, a pulling—that cannot be predicted or understood, and yet they exist as surely as our material universe exists. Though I am a doctor and a man of science, and as such committed absolutely to the world of the material, the world of measurement, yet I believe also in the world of the spirit as well . . . I believe that the spirit is very strong, stronger than the body . . . and that it is our spirits that commune with one another, in silence."

Jesse nodded slowly.

"Well, I will say good-by to you for this afternoon," Dr. Pedersen said in a more formal voice. He stood and shook hands with Jesse, taking Jesse's thin hand in both of his and squeezing it.

All that week Jesse asked Mr. Foley if he had heard anything. Had Dr. Pedersen said anything to him? What would happen?

Jesse kept going back over the conversation, angry with himself for not having said more, for having sat so passively, so stupidly.... He had been a child of action, always doing things, running around, getting into trouble; he could remember that part of his life clearly. And yet it seemed to belong to another boy, another Jesse, and he didn't know how to get back to being that person, that self. Sometimes he felt a flurry of panic, to think that he was nothing at all, that he did not exist. What did that mean—*to exist*? He tried to remember the strange things Dr. Pedersen had said to him, as if he, Jesse Harte, could understand them. No one in his life had ever talked like that to him. He did not understand. It made no sense. *A human being... must become what he was meant to be....* But though the words made no sense, though back in Yewville people would just have laughed at them, Jesse had the idea that they were attached to something real, something invisible and terrifying in its reality.

He went around arguing with himself. Angry and yearning. Here he was: in an orphanage. The Niagara County Home for Boys. His heart hammered when he thought of Dr. Pedersen, the bulk of the man, the enormous swelling energy of the man.... He had never met anyone like Dr. Pedersen. He had never heard anyone talk like that. As the week passed he kept hearing Dr. Pedersen's voice in his ears, as if he were still close by, talking gently and relentlessly at Jesse. He was baffled, angry. He did not want to remain in this place, and yet there was no way for him to leave except by being adopted, or taken into a foster home. Since he'd come here to live, one boy had already gone out into a foster home and come back again. The boys were scrawny and rat-faced and stupid, most of them. There was a look of quick, evasive cunning to them, as if they were happiest in small packs, mumbling jokes behind their hands... and Jesse was among them, scrawny himself, his face so thin that it, too, had that ratty, sharp, deprived look, and also an expression of vagueness. The boys' faces were sharp, but they were also vague and anonymous. One of them might turn out to be another one; Jesse often mistook one boy for another, mixing up their names but also mixing up their faces, mixing them up. He lived in the Niagara County Home for Boys. He hated the Jesse Harte who lived here, who was in the files, here, in someone's manila folder.

He kept hanging around Mr. Foley. He asked about Dr. Pedersen—did he operate on people? Did he save people's lives? Jesse half shut his eyes and saw again the big puffy knees straining the material of the trousers. Did Dr. Pedersen have any children? How many children? Where did he live? On the brink of tears, feeling himself skinny and defeated, he followed Mr. Foley around for a week. Dr. Pedersen was a strange man, he kept saying. But Mr. Foley never agreed to this, not really. Dr. Pedersen was so fat, Jesse said, *fat*. But maybe he was too thin himself. His ribs showed. His wrists were bony. His upper arms were too thin for a boy, weren't they? He tried to recall Dr. Pedersen's words for Mr. Foley, but he could not quite remember them. *To go as far . . . as your abilities will take you. . . .* "Do you think he'll come back?" Jesse asked Mr. Foley.

On Friday afternoon he went to Lockport by himself, hitching a ride in. This was not allowed but he hardly thought of it, every cell in his body strained forward, eager, perspiring, alert, anxious to get him into the city, the city where Dr. Pedersen lived! He had been hacking away at some dead weeds and near the edge of the field he had simply put down his small scythe and walked away. One of the boys called after him, "Hey! Hey you! Jesse!" Jesse had not bothered to reply. It did not matter what he was called in that place, which name they called him. His name, "Jesse," was not a word he acknowledged there. They might call him anything and he would not acknowledge it.

He wandered around Main Street, walking slowly. He had the idea that Dr. Pedersen might come along at any moment. He felt confused, a little frightened. What was going to happen to him? Traffic passed continually and he was impressed with how busy this city was, much busier than Yewville, many more people . . . small crowds of shoppers on Friday afternoon . . . many boys his own age, in little groups, glancing at him but not bothering with him. . . . In a drugstore he looked through the telephone directory and came across Dr. Pedersen's name. There were two addresses after the name, one for his home on Locust Street and one for his clinic on Plank Road. Jesse was very excited. He memorized the addresses. Then he looked through the Yellow Pages and came across Dr. Pedersen's name under the heading *Physicians*; eagerly he underscored the name with his finger: *Dr.*

Karl Pedersen, General Medicine. The same addresses! Jesse wandered out onto the street again and looked at the street sign. He would find Dr. Pedersen's home. He walked for a while in one direction, but could not find Locust Street. He was not really lost, he believed, yet it would have been difficult for him to find his way back to the Home. After a while he asked someone where Locust Street was; the girl, who was his own age, seemed to look at him strangely. How shameful it was to be so weak, so skinny! He wondered if Dr. Pedersen had forgotten him, if he had decided against him and was making plans now to adopt another boy. Why, why was he so thin, so scrawny? He climbed to Locust Street—Lockport seemed to be built on a number of hills—and was alarmed at how weak he felt when he got there. His brain raced. He argued with himself, snatches of words that made no sense, he even put his fingers around his wrist, nervously measuring it. . . .

There, there was the Pedersen home!

A vast three-story house made of a very dark gray stone. Many windows, framed in white. Yes, many windows; it dazzled Jesse to see so many of them. In front, there were two high pillars and a large front door made of heavy wood, and, just before the steps, two stone animals—maybe lions—that seemed to be guarding the house in their sleep. The lawn was a very bright, neat green, and had evidently been seeded only recently. The grass looked fragile; Jesse could see faint rake marks in the earth through the blades of grass. The house and its large lawn were surrounded by a waist-high iron fence with leafy patterns in it. Jesse stood nervously on the public sidewalk, staring at the house. He was afraid that someone would notice him out here, that someone in the house might glance out the window and see him. What if Dr. Pedersen himself looked out? . . . Jesse walked by the house several times, staring. He ran his fingers along the iron fence. They came away a little dusty. He was aware of danger, yet he could not leave . . . he walked by the house again . . . he wondered what would happen if he went inside the gate, up the steps past those stone lions, what would happen if he rang the doorbell?

But he hadn't the nerve for this. So he hesitated on the sidewalk, looking around. And he saw a very fat woman approaching him from the corner. She walked with her shoulders slumped forward and her head bowed, so that her thick, babyish chin was squeezed against her throat. She wore a white blouse out of which her thick upper arms pushed, like pale sausages, and a dark cotton gathered skirt that billowed out about her wide hips. Jesse backed away, seeing her. She looked familiar. But she did not seem to notice him, she hardly glanced up as she approached, and when she came to the Pedersen house she turned up the walk, moving slowly, wearily, as if she were very old. But Jesse had been mistaken about her age—she was not even a woman, but only a girl about his own age, or younger, with a very fair, luminous skin, eyes that were heavily lashed and almost shadowed, but a small prim pink mouth that resembled Dr. Pedersen's.

He stared at her as she walked so slowly and laboriously right up to the Pedersen house, entering it as if it belonged to her, so naturally and easily entering it, coming home. His heart beat with a terrible yearning. He wanted to call out after her. But he only stared, and after a few minutes he backed away, across the street to the other side, backing away from the big stone house, amazed at its size, at the spread of elms and oaks and bushes around it. He kept measuring his wrist nervously, absentmindedly.

That evening Dr. Pedersen and his wife came to see him.

He escaped being punished because of their visit. Good luck, what good luck, he thought greedily, dizzily, as Mr. Foley led him to the office. Dr. Pedersen shook hands with him as if they were old acquaintances and introduced him to his wife. She was a short woman with an immense body, though not as large as her husband's, but squat and soft and strangely lifeless, as if the weight of her flesh were a burden she was not accustomed to. Her face was high-colored and strained, the cheeks flushed, the eyes very bright. Out of the soft, inert ripeness of her flesh her features stared with a bright, hectic alertness. Yet beneath the face, beneath the plump chin, her body seemed to ooze without shape, inertly. She smiled at Jesse and was too shy to extend her hand when Dr. Pedersen introduced them.

"Well. It is a warm evening," Dr. Pedersen announced.

Mrs. Pedersen nodded at once, smiling at Jesse. Jesse imitated her and nodded. His heart was pounding very hard and he wondered if Dr. Pedersen could sense his nervousness.

"Well. Jesse Harte. We must sit down together, commune together." They sat. Dr. Pedersen seemed larger than Jesse had remembered. He wore a gray suit of fine, expensive material, and a silvery-gray vest, and a dark tie. He crossed his legs with care, raising one leg and easing it over the other, then drawing it back slightly so that his ankle rested on the knee of the other leg, and the large sole of his shoe faced outward, facing Jesse, a blank smooth gray sole. Jesse could see his flesh above the top of the black socks. Dr. Pedersen looked at him gravely. His face was prim, pursed. He drew in his breath slowly, not opening his mouth but widening his nostrils. It was a luxury, the way he breathed—he seemed to be tasting, assessing the very air.

"Yes. Jesse Harte is our subject," Dr. Pedersen said, as if he were addressing Mrs. Pedersen. But he seemed unaware of her existence; he was staring only at Jesse. "It is a matter of fate that we are together, in this room this evening. It was ordained to take place. We are going to establish precisely the nature of our several relationships, we are going to attempt to organize the future so far as it is possible. We imagine that we exercise freedom of will, but beneath all gestures, beneath all desperate assertions of the self, there is the stratum of fate, hard as the hardest rock.... Well, Jesse, what is your opinion?"

Jesse stared.

"I—"

Dr. Pedersen waited politely. But when Jesse did not go on, he said in his prim, courtly way, "Is the world a mystery to you, Jesse?"

"I... I think so...."

"Yet you were brought up in a conventionally religious household?"

"Yes, I think so...."

"You attend church now, with the other boys?"

"Yes."

"Do you pray very often?"

"I don't know... maybe.... Maybe I do...."

"What do you pray about?"

Jesse could not answer. Dr. Pedersen watched him. He breathed slowly, deliberately.

"Do you give thanks to God that you are alive, a living thing? That you still possess your God-given soul, your unique spirit?"

"Yes. . . ."

"Ah, good. And you believe then in the Incarnation and the Redemption of sinners," Dr. Pedersen said flatly, "and you believe in the prophecy set down in the Apocalypse, that the cities of the earth will be leveled and the sinful destroyed?"

"Yes."

"But it is all a mystery. And how do you propose to confront that mystery?"

Jesse did not understand.

"How do you, Jesse Harte, intend to confront the riddle of existence? How do you intend to organize your own life?"

Jesse's brain raced. "By . . . by going as far as I can go, as far as . . . my abilities will take me. . . ."

"Ah, good. An extraordinary answer. Yes. Good," Dr. Pedersen said, a little surprised. He smiled and a half-dozen dimples suddenly blossomed around his mouth. "Fourteen years old, Mary," he said, though not turning to Mrs. Pedersen, "and he gives an answer like that. . . . It is fate, obviously."

Mrs. Pedersen nodded.

"Now, Mary, if you will please leave us, I must talk more frankly with this young man," Dr. Pedersen said. He got to his feet, and, with a grave formality, opened the door for his wife. She paused at the door and smiled again toward Jesse, though without really looking at him; she seemed girlish. Dr. Pedersen returned and sat down, his arms folded. He rested. His breathing was contemplative, slow, regular. Jesse found himself keeping pace with it. He was sitting very straight, his eyes burning in their sockets, staring at Dr. Pedersen and waiting for something to be said. It seemed that he had been sitting there, in that position, for most of his life.

After a wait of a minute or two, Dr. Pedersen took two things out of his inside coat pocket—a leather case with a pair of glasses inside, and a piece of paper. He put on the glasses and his eyes became womanish and even more kindly. "Jesse," he said, "I have not told you very much about myself or about my interest in you. Perhaps you are curious. I will not trouble you with details that concern the past. I am a scientist, and I believe in the present and in the future. I am first of all a scientist, and then a physician, and then a father, and then a member of the American community. I owe no allegiance to any foreign power nor am I interested in politics of any kind. The delusions of Europe do not concern me at all. I do not think of them. I am a citizen of the world and of the twentieth century. Mr. Foley has perhaps told you that I am considered a dependable physician. Patients are sent to me from all over the country, but my interest is not in establishing a reputation, or in making money, but simply in doing my work. I am a diagnostician by instinct. I cannot explain my talent except in terms of its being a unique gift that has never failed me. Never. My talent is God-given and I do not explain it or exploit it. I am a humble man. I want only to help mankind. I believe that God has given me a gift and that I am responsible for it, and He has given my daughter and my son gifts also, gifts peculiar to them, and I am responsible for them also, for guarding them. I have a daughter who is thirteen years old and a son who is seventeen. No other children. I am responsible for them and I believe that I am responsible for you . . . I believe that there is something in you, a certain destiny, a certain fate. . . ."

He brought one hand to his face, shading his eyes as if Jesse were too brilliant to look at, and once again he was silent. His pale, protruding forehead seemed to brood over the mystery of the boy before him.

"You must be saved. You must be fed, clothed, sheltered, guarded. Loved. You must be loved. Your destiny is . . . it is almost clear to me . . . almost visible to me. . . . It is in you, in the structure of your bones, and it must be cultivated or it will die with you. Do not be alarmed, but I see this in you: that you will die shortly, in a year or two, unless you are loved."

Jesse tried to smile.

But Dr. Pedersen did not seem to notice. He passed his hand over his forehead again, then over his head. His hair was thin and gray.

"I am a scientist, yes, but I rely upon intuition. I was born with a gift of prophecy, whatever you like to call it. Men have tried to analyze me, assess me, but they have come away puzzled.

I am a puzzle to myself.... To speak quite frankly, Jesse, my private life is incomplete. My family is incomplete. My daughter, Hilda, is a remarkable child but, so far as I can foresee, an incomplete child who will grow into an incomplete woman. My son, Frederich, is also something of a disappointment to me. My wife, Mary, is a most generous woman, religious and good, an excellent wife and mother, though rather spoiled by her father ...but she has failed to give me the child I had foreseen for myself, it has not worked out quite the way I imagined it would twenty years ago.... Not that my marriage is an unhappy one," Dr. Pedersen said slowly, "but that it is somehow incomplete. I want more. I need more to nourish me. I need another son. Jesse, I will show you something."

Jesse waited, staring.

"I will show you a certain clipping from a certain newspaper. It is the basis of my interest in you. It dates back several months. I will not go into the sequence of ideas that this clipping began in me, in my imagination, I will only show you the clipping. And then, when you have read it, you will tell me your feelings quite honestly and frankly."

"Yes...?"

"You are prepared?"

Jesse nodded. The roof of his mouth tasted of panic—dark, dank, acrid.

Dr. Pedersen smoothed out the clipping and Jesse read:

BOY ELUDES GUN-TOTING FATHER

> *Yewville, New York (UPI)*—Fourteen-year-old Jesse Harte, who ran from home when his father opened fire on him with a 12-gauge shotgun, was the only survivor Friday from his family of six.
>
> His parents, two sisters and brother were dead in what police have called a quadruple murder-suicide. State Police said that Willard Harte, 35, shot his wife, Nancy, 31, and three children, Jean, 16, Shirley, 11, and Robert, 5, then turned the shotgun on himself in their home outside Yewville. Harte died in the hospital.

> The murders were apparently committed in the morning or the early afternoon, because Harte was seen in Yewville with his son, Jesse, late Wednesday afternoon. He picked his son up at a store where he worked after school. Jesse ran from the house after his father brought him home. He fled to a neighboring farm, wounded, and was driven to the Yewville Memorial Hospital, where he is in critical condition.
>
> The mother and children were found dead in the living room of the small house, which is adjacent to a service station run by Harte.
>
> Harte was found in critical condition just outside the house, the gun beside him.
>
> Niagara County Prosecuting Attorney Virgil Block ordered an inquest as police completed their investigation.

Jesse read the article through once. Then again. He felt his spirit skimming back across the miles of road to that house, that intersection of roads, that clump of trees, that junkyard . . . and at the same time he felt how solidly he sat where he was, how awakened he was now, how real, how vivid to the man who sat watching him through those round, gleaming glasses. How real this moment was!

It was the only fact.

Jesse handed the clipping back to Dr. Pedersen. He said nothing.

"Ah, yes. My boy. Yes," Dr. Pedersen said, nodding. His head bobbed with sympathy. He took off his glasses and, like a girl, began to weep. Jesse looked up at him fearfully, himself girlish and suspended and astonished. Dr. Pedersen took Jesse's hand in his and shook it. "Yes, you have said nothing. You simply hand it back to me. Yes. You have dignity. You will grow beyond that, that terror. Already you are pushing into the person you will be, the future that belongs to both of us. Yes, already, already the future has begun."

His tears fell onto Jesse's hand.

5

In this way he became Jesse Pedersen, the third child, the second son, of Karl and Mary Pedersen of Lockport, New York.

6

One morning in August, 1940, Jesse was standing at the railing of the largest bridge in Lockport, high above the Erie Canal. He was gazing down at the locks. He held a library book tightly, as if fearful it might somehow fall; he was fascinated by the depth of the bridge, the steep damp sides of the canal, the different levels of water. So he was here at last, standing here alone.... Everything in sight was illuminated with a hazy, pearl-like glow because of the humidity and the brilliant, glazed sunlight, and Jesse saw how his arms glistened with minute particles of dampness, the pores of his skin like tiny eyes, the red-blond hairs rising delicate and yet powerful from his flesh. *He had survived. He was here.* His hands were no longer so bony; his knuckles were not so prominent.

Beneath him, a long dizzying drop to a pit of water that was dark and fairly still. In front of him the other locks, the other levels of water, vibrated with energy—the noise of water splashing angrily from one level to the next. A continual racket. Jesse felt how the brain might grow dizzy exposed to such frenzy, the spectacle of water churning and splashing and passing away, endlessly, within the human contrivance of falls and locks.... A few other people, men of a certain aimless, apologetic age, stood on the bridge, leaning on the railing as he did, staring down. Nothing else to do. They were men who for some reason were alone, and Jesse glanced away from them, as if in shame, in fear of their loneliness. He thought of his Grandfather Vogel. He erased the thought. Behind him traffic moved as usual, not very much of it on a weekday morning in Lockport. Women strolled downtown to shop, in no hurry. In the distance there was a church steeple, hazy in the sunlight. What was so fascinating about this, Jesse thought, was its ordinary nature—the canal, the locks, the noisy water; the town itself ordinary and quiet, as if it had existed for centuries, with a profound certainty of its right to exist, no awareness of the fact that it had no reason for existing, no guarantee of its right to exist. It was here; it moved in a slow, timed orbit. Already he could define himself against it: *Jesse Pedersen on the big bridge, waiting for a barge to come through the locks.* But he saw none in sight. He would not be able to wait for hours, like the solitary men who hung around the locks having nothing else to do. He had to be home by noon.

. . . That terrible rush of water out of a pipe, a large rusty pipe . . . the explosive fall of water from one level to the next, down a series of small cliffs of water, the water boiling and frenzied and yet, in places, oddly tranquil, as if its surface were somehow firm, hard enough to walk on. . . . He stared, fascinated. Hypnotized. A dank, fetid odor rose from the deepest pit of water, directly below him. Jesse leaned over the railing. It was important for him to see everything, as much as he could see. Along the canal's banks buildings had been built, decades ago, that seemed to descend into the foundation of gray, dreamlike rock itself, their peaks and arches and chimneys rising to the sky, their lower parts descending into the smudged, rain-washed gray rock, as if going back to a time when there was no distinction between human life and the life of rocks. Had they slept for thousands of years before being wrenched out of the earth, dug up to make way for the canal . . . ? Jesse frowned and thought of the calm, wide, muddy canal that existed away from the sequence of locks, winding into the distance. No one would suspect, approaching the locks, that the water could turn so violent and dangerous. . . . Below, workmen were talking about something. Maybe arguing. An official with a white shirt and tie approached them. Jesse would have liked to hear their conversation, for they seemed to him privileged, walking so casually in an area forbidden to everyone else, blocked off by high fences and "No Trespassing" signs. They moved their arms, gesturing, but Jesse could not hear anything they said. He could not even make out the expressions on their faces.

He looked away from them, disturbed by their remoteness and by the fact of their activity, their work, their arguing. He was reminded of the Pedersens. Very soon now, at luncheon, he would be quizzed about how he spent the morning. In the evening, at dinner, he would be quizzed about how he spent the afternoon. Dr. Pedersen asked each of the children in turn what he had done, what "progress" he had made... what "observations" he had made.... At first Jesse had been allowed to sit in silence, amazed at the things Hilda and Frederich reported, too amazed to realize that he would have to take part in this himself. But his newness wore off after the first week. Dr. Pedersen had turned to him and asked, in his grave, kindly, rather maidenish voice, "And what use did you make of today, Jesse? Please tell us."

He had stammered something. His voice had faltered, faded. Hilda and Frederich had stared down at their plates, as if in sympathy for him, and Mrs. Pedersen smiled nervously at him, encouraging him, not quick enough to realize that he was hopeless. Dr. Pedersen had kept after him, though. Several minutes of questions, questioning. He was very patient. He said nothing that was critical to Jesse, but Jesse understood that he had failed....

"I'm sorry," he had said miserably.

Dr. Pedersen had nodded, as if accepting this, his lips pursed and mute. After that, Jesse was prepared for the quizzing, he made sure that he had something to say: he had read another chapter in the chemistry textbook he would be studying in the fall at the Lockport high school, or he had read a biography from Dr. Pedersen's library—on Czar Nicholas, on John Paul Jones, on Rembrandt; or he had played with the microscope and slides Dr. Pedersen had given him—not played, *worked*—for the word "played" was not used in the Pedersen home; or he had written a thank-you note to his "Grandfather Shirer," Mrs. Pedersen's aged father, thanking him for the set of the *Boys' Wonder Books* he had given Jesse; or he had written a letter to his grandfather, his old, other, real Grandfather Vogel, who never answered these letters. Dr. Pedersen insisted that Jesse write every week. That was one of his duties, Dr. Pedersen said.... Today he would say he had been reading this book, a history of the Erie Canal.

He had taken it out of the Young People's room of the library, a bright yellow-bound book called *Clinton's Ditch: A History of the Erie Barge Canal.* Jesse had never read very much in the past, he hadn't had the use of books, but now he understood that it was through books he would make his way into the Pedersens, more deeply into them. Anxiety often lifted the short hairs at the back of his head: he had wasted too many days of his life already, he would never be able to catch up. "You will not hurry," Dr. Pedersen had said to him, "but you will catch up with Jesse Pedersen. Do you understand?" Yes, he understood. He had slept away his life, it seemed to him now, even after the adoption process had begun and he had made his way carefully through the crowd of boys at the Boys' Home, marked off from them as if by a physical distinction. They had disliked him, they had envied him—he was a surprise to them, a disturbance. *You're really lucky,* they said. And he felt the truth of that remark, the truth of his luck, his good luck, in being picked by Dr. Pedersen.

Below, the waterfall hammered away at the sides of the canal. Jesse felt its urgency as his own: to become Jesse Pedersen, to catch up with Jesse Pedersen. The Pedersens sat at a dining room table, in Jesse's imagination perpetually sitting, monumental and immense, towering in his dreams at a perpetual meal, at the center of which Dr. Pedersen sat weighty with judgment and patience. Even their shadows were enormous.

Now he was never alone. Never by himself. He was not Jesse, but *Jesse Pedersen.* Even when he went to bed at night in his own room he was not really alone. Out here, on the bridge, he was not really alone. They were present, watching him. Grave and patient and kindly. Jesse could not remember clearly now what his life had been in the past. He had been alone, often. That other Jesse: pale, scrawny, much younger than this Jesse. That boy had died, perhaps. He had passed out of existence. Or, if he existed anywhere, it was on Grandpa Vogel's farm, out in the deep, vast, silent country, the country where language itself had yet to be created, a world of grunts and nudgings and sorrow, too much sorrow. That Jesse had worked until his body ached, until the wound in his back pounded with a sullen, demonic rage.... And Grandfather Vogel: he still existed, out there, in the same world. But his power had been taken from him. He did not count. He was remote and silent and forgotten.

At the Pedersens', each day began at seven o'clock. They sat down together at breakfast at seven-thirty, the five of them, and Dr. Pedersen began by asking them what they had done the evening before. He was usually brisk and jocular at this meal. Then he talked about the "Map of the Day," the general structure the day would take for each of them—what plans did they have? what did they think they would accomplish? At dinner this "Map" would be measured against their actual achievements. Dr. Pedersen was always very demanding of himself, listing his intentions and then, hours later, stating how far he had fallen short. "The world begins every morning," he was fond of saying, "and it ends every night."

His voice buzzed in Jesse's brain, louder than the noise of the waterfall. Jesse started home, leafing through the book as he walked. He was beginning to feel a little anxious. The book struck him as a child's book, much too young for a fourteen-year-old. He skimmed the paragraphs as he walked. Quick. Hurry. Maybe he should write a short report on the book and not try to remember any of it . . . his memory was not very good. . . . Both Hilda and Frederich could remember pages and pages of detail. They were strange children; they had been written up in newspapers and magazines, Jesse had discovered. They were extraordinary, and Jesse was ordinary, only ordinary. . . . He tried to make up for this by being more obedient than they, more docile, more eager to please Dr. Pedersen and his wife. He had trained his face to show no expression except one of intense, contemplative respect.

It always excited Jesse to climb the long, low hill to High Street and over to Locust Street. *Coming home. Here was home.* Houses gradually became larger, more impressive. Great elms, high rippling leaves that blocked off the hot sun; houses that were mansions, fearful in their size. He remembered how exhausted he had been from climbing the hill the first time he had walked out here. That Jesse had had no idea, hadn't guessed what would happen. . . . He could never have guessed at the size of the Pedersen house. A shout might echo forever in its vast foyer and its hallways and rooms. The foyer was cavernous. "At Christmastime we put up a tree here," Mrs. Pedersen had told him. The staircase curved around this foyer and opened to the second floor, which was lined by a balcony. From the center of the ceiling a great mass of crystal hung—this was called a "chandelier"—and the staircase was carpeted entirely in dull, dark gold. Jesse had never seen such things. There were no words for him to match to them. Behind the house there was another house, a "carriage house," where the Pedersens' Negro servants lived, a couple named Henry and Dora; Jesse did not know their last name. His own room was on the second floor, at the back of the house. It was a room in which he slept alone, he might close the door and sleep, alone, for the first time in his life. In this room, which was so quiet that it frightened him, he pressed his hands against his face as if to obliterate it and prayed, *Let me be like them, let them love me, let everybody know that I am one of them.*

Jesse hurried up the long flagstone walk and let himself in the front door. He smelled food cooking. Rich, heavy odors of food. It was nearly time for Dr. Pedersen to come home for lunch; he came home every day to change his shirt and to have lunch with his family. It was strange, how this family had lunch together; Jesse had not known families did this. It was important that everyone sit down at the table together, eat together, sit together for a certain amount of time. Jesse was nervous and hungry, thinking of the meal ahead. He hurried through the foyer, feeling once again a sensation of disbelief, as if he were in the wrong house. Since the adoption had been completed, he had no reason to feel this way, this sense of unreality, of suspension; he knew now precisely who he was. . . . From the rear of the house, from the "music room," came the short, choppy, blunt notes of a piano, Frederich's playing. Every day Frederich sat at the handsome grand piano, picking out notes, shading in small intricate spots on a piece of paper, "writing music," as Jesse had been told. A page of Frederich's music was incredibly elaborate, and also messy—there were hundreds of notes, some shaded in carefully, very deeply with a dark lead pencil, others hardly more than scrawls, with many erasures and areas that had been crossed out so roughly that the paper had torn. The music room was a large oval room at the rear of the house, its outside wall made entirely of glass. In this room were the grand piano—which smelled of fine, rich, polished wood and wood oil—and several tables piled with books and sheet music, either Frederich's own compositions or those by established composers, and a filing cabinet in which Frederich kept cards on everything. Jesse had not known what to make of Frederich at first. But now he understood that Frederich had a "gift," a "talent," and that this set him apart from other boys.

Jesse went back to the kitchen, where he knew he would be welcome. There Mrs. Pedersen and the Negro woman, Dora, were preparing lunch. "Jesse, hello! How are you, dear?" Mrs. Pedersen said. "Did you go out to the library and get back again so fast?" She was always surprised at anything Jesse did, no matter how simple, as if she did not believe him capable of doing much; and she was always pinching the flesh of his upper arms and frowning at his thinness. "What are you reading today?" she asked. She frowned and held the book up to her shortsighted eyes. Leafing through it, she frowned more intently and Jesse understood that she thought the book a mistake but she was too polite to say anything. "We're all very pleased that you have such an interest in this area," she said. "I think everyone should know the history of the city he lives in. Don't you, Dora?" Dora agreed, but without much enthusiasm. She was a short, squat woman, not nearly so heavy as Mrs. Pedersen and not so soft; she was muscular, quick on her feet, always busy. Her skin was a dark, troubled purplish-brown; she did no more than glance at Jesse. She was busy with the meal, stooping to pull something out of the oven, while Mrs. Pedersen glanced through Jesse's book. "Yes, it seems interesting. Informative," she said, and handed it back. "You certainly do walk all over, Jesse. Have you ever seen anyone like this boy, Dora, to walk all over the city? You must be very tired!"

Jesse was the only Pedersen who walked any distance.

"You're not too tired to have lunch, are you?" Mrs. Pedersen said. She touched Jesse's forehead and with a slow bemused movement of her thumb stretched the skin there, so that she could peer into Jesse's eye. But this must have been a joke, her pretending to be a doctor, because she laughed girlishly and released him. She sat at the large worktable in the center of the kitchen, a table made of plain, untreated wood, and began chopping onions. She sighed. Seated like this, her weight eased down in a chair, she was most at home, most herself. Jesse liked to watch her work like this, she was so intent and uncritical. Her thick legs were outspread slightly beneath the table; she wore neat white shoes that were like nurses' shoes, with white laces tightly tied. Her apron was white also, but a little soiled from the morning's work. As she chopped the onions Jesse saw large, delicate beads of perspiration forming on her face and dropping occasionally down onto the broad expanse of her breasts. She was a big, wide woman. She wore white most of the time beneath her work-aprons, and when she moved Jesse could sometimes see faint stains beneath her arms; but there was usually a smell of perfume about her, not a smell of perspiration, a rich, sharp, concentrated fruity odor, and Jesse could sometimes see where her talcum powder, patted heavily on her skin, showed above the collar of her dress and turned her soft, pale flesh to a flourlike coarseness.

She glanced up and Jesse's attention must have pleased her. "Jesse, why don't you sit down and keep us company out here? Dora and I need a man's presence, we need a man's judgment. Give him a taste of that sauce, Dora. What do you think of it?" Dora spooned him some white creamy sauce and Jesse, a little embarrassed at her closeness, her lifting the spoon to his mouth, tasted it. He nodded. "It isn't too strong?" Mrs. Pedersen asked. "Well, good. That's a relief. Jesse, sit down and rest after your long walk. You can read your book if you want."

He sat at one end of the table, clearing a small area for himself. While Mrs. Pedersen and Dora worked, he began reading *Clinton's Ditch.* He forced himself to read quickly, skimming paragraphs. At the end of the first chapter he realized that he did not remember much of what he had read, so he forced himself to go back. Mrs. Pedersen was humming. She glanced down at him and said, "Jesse, am I disturbing you?" He shook his head no, and for emphasis closed his book. "I'm afraid I am always disturbing my children. They have so much work to do, they're so serious, and I come along and disrupt them. This morning I had to bother Hilda about the clothes she's going to take to Chicago—don't you wish we could all go along tomorrow? In the beginning I went along to Hilda's examinations—of course she was a small child then, and she needed her mother.... But Dr. Pedersen says this trip is special and that there wouldn't be enough for the rest of us to do. And, of course, Frederich would be home alone. I don't like to leave him alone.... But isn't Hilda brave, to face those doctors and professors? I don't think I could do it, do you Jesse? Would you be frightened? But maybe you wouldn't—you're a brave boy yourself...."

"I don't know," Jesse said.

When she stared at him as she did now, her eyes bright as if with tears, thick-lashed and glittering in the lardy expanse of her face, Jesse sensed that she was thinking of what had happened to him. His past. His father. *His other family.* He wanted to change the subject, to make her think of something else.

"Or am I embarrassing you, Jesse? I'm always embarrassing my children!" She got to her feet, pushing herself up with her elbows, and came over to Jesse. With the edge of her apron she blotted the moisture off his forehead. He submitted to this, feeling very young. He was never certain of how to act around Mrs. Pedersen—should he give in to her mothering or should he draw away like Hilda and Frederich, so she would know he was too old for this? "Jesse, I need your opinion on this, this little muffin," she said, buttering a muffin for Jesse, as if she thought he might not be able to butter it for himself. "I'm trying a new recipe."

Jesse's mouth watered. He realized he was very hungry.

"Thank you," he said.

She smiled happily and returned to her end of the table.

When Jesse was out of this house, walking the streets of Lockport, becoming familiar with this city—in which he would spend the rest of his life—he felt at times, undetermined, undefined, as he had felt in that awkward period during which the adoption was taking place. For weeks it was "taking place," his fate being handed from one official to another, one welfare worker to another, adults who had no real interest in him, who did not know him. For a few minutes on the bridge this morning, his head ringing with the noise of the crashing waterfall, he had felt the same way. But when he was here, at home, especially when he was in the kitchen with Mrs. Pedersen, his very blood seemed to warm, to murmur his name to him. *Jesse Pedersen.* He ate the muffin hungrily, as if it were somehow mixed up with this feeling.... He must remember this. This moment in the kitchen, here, Mrs. Pedersen bent over the table, scraping a pile of onion skins into a container used for garbage, her nose round at its tip, a pudgy, girlish nose, her eyes slightly watering from the onions, her forehead warm and moist from the heat of the stove. He felt a fierce, powerful love for her, a certainty of love. He must remember this feeling. Sometimes when he strolled around Lockport alone, circling the high school he would attend in another month, he felt a strange despair, a sense of hollowness, emptiness, that was located in the center of his body, beneath his heart. It was a hunger that alarmed him. And when he turned toward home, headed home, his hunger increased as he walked, until by the time he entered the Pedersen home he was ravenous with hunger. This seemed to happen all the time.

"Jesse, dear, have another little muffin. It won't spoil your appetite," Mrs. Pedersen said. She buttered him another muffin and then buttered one for herself, her plump fingers moving quickly and deftly with the knife. On her fingers she wore several rings. One was a wedding band studded with small diamonds; the ring with it had a single large square-cut diamond. Flashes of light from these diamonds seemed to transfix Jesse. Diamonds! Mrs. Pedersen was a beautiful woman in spite of her size. Sometimes she smiled at him while Dr. Pedersen was speaking during one of their meals, and Jesse felt surprise, almost alarm, at the beauty of the woman's face, squeezed and condensed by the bulk of her flesh, as if she reminded him of someone else, and the face she presented to him was not her true one.

"This is a delicious muffin, if I have to say so myself," she said. She licked her fingers. She buttered another muffin for Jesse and another for herself, smiling happily. "Jesse, will you help me in the rose garden this afternoon? I hate to bother Henry. He has so many other things to do, he's such a help to Dr. Pedersen and me, I hate to bother him with the roses. . . ."

"I'll help you," Jesse said.

"Oh, thank you. I would really appreciate it. Hilda hates the sun, she hates the outdoors and she's contemptuous of my flowers—and Frederich, well, you know how Frederich is, he's so wrapped up in his music—" She paused, her head inclined to one side. From another part of the house, as if from a distance of miles, came the single, spaced, choppy piano notes. For some reason Frederich played only one key at a time, with his forefinger. "Oh, dear," Mrs. Pedersen said, looking at a tiny diamond-studded watch on her wrist, "dear, it's almost time for Dr. Pedersen to come home! Please go and wash your hands and face, Jesse. Be sure you wash very carefully. You know how particular Dr. Pedersen is. . . .

Jesse finished the muffin, brushing crumbs off his face, and went to wash up. Washing was a ritual, careful and solemn. All the Pedersens washed carefully, with a special medicinal soap; Jesse had been surprised at first, but after Dr. Pedersen explained to him the reasons for washing, for "scrubbing," he understood, and remembered with disapproval the years of his life he had been dirty, his hands crawling with germs. Now he understood how the invisible world of germs ruled the visible world, how there were friendly bacteria and unfriendly bacteria, and how it was necessary to control them as much as possible. So he scrubbed his hands up to the elbows and washed his face.

When he went out to the dining room, Dr. Pedersen was just coming in. "Good afternoon, Jesse," Dr. Pedersen said. The dining room was a large, sunny room with glass doors that opened onto the deep back yard, where roses and other flowers bloomed. Jesse's heartbeat quickened at the sight of the table. In the center, a bouquet of yellow and pink roses in a silver container; a set of silver candlesticks; the tablecloth itself made of white lace, gleaming white, like an altar cloth. The five chairs around the table were cushioned in deep red velvet, four of them without arms and the fifth, at the head of the table, Dr. Pedersen's chair, with elegant curved arms that were also cushioned.

Dr. Pedersen went up to wash and change his shirt, and when he reappeared, Mrs. Pedersen and Frederich had come to the table. Dr. Pedersen's face was rosy. He clapped his hands together. "Ah, Mary, something smells delicious! You and Dora have been working hard all morning, I can tell." He sat, beaming at them. Mrs. Pedersen made an impatient sound and got to her feet to fix a rose that was dangling over the side of the container, and Dr. Pedersen said, "Now, Mary, please relax! That rose is perfectly all right the way it is."

"I'm sorry," she said at once, sitting again.

She sat at the far end of the table, across from Dr. Pedersen. Jesse sat on Dr. Pedersen's left, and Frederich would sit on his right. Hilda, who was not yet downstairs, would sit between Jesse and her mother.

"It has been a most exciting day at the Clinic so far," Dr. Pedersen said. "You recall that puzzling case from Tonawanda, Dr. Harvey's patient? The mysterious blood count? Oh, the lovely pink cytoplasm, the dark blue nuclei, what a puzzle to everyone! Well, it is finally solved; I hit upon the answer this morning. I had told Dr. Harvey again and again that only if I could see his patient, only if I could take hold of his patient's hands and examine him, could I give him any kind of diagnosis.... Frederich, how are you on this excellent day?"

"Very well, Father," Frederich said politely.

"Did you have a profitable morning?"

"Yes, I think so."

Frederich's manner was cool, courteous, even a little distracted.

"I'm glad to hear that," Dr. Pedersen said enthusiastically. His face was slick and luminous when he was surrounded by his family. At such times his skin took on a damp, eager, healthy tone, as if the flesh were somehow in motion, warmed by motion. He was a wonderful man.... Jesse found himself staring at Dr. Pedersen as if memorizing his face. No matter how much he tried to remember, he was always surprised by the actual man, the actual face. Dr. Pedersen, so many years older than Frederich, really looked as young as his son. It was uncanny. Frederich was seventeen years old, but he looked middle-aged at times. He was very happy, very fat. He weighed more than two hundred fifty pounds, perhaps three hundred pounds.... He was not tall, not even as tall as Jesse, so that this weight was squeezed into a series of ridges and rolls and protuberances. He carried himself slowly, ponderously, with a habitual drag to his left foot. He spent most of his time in the house, up in his room on the second floor or back in the music room, where he sat in a special leather armchair at the piano, studying his music, picking experimentally at notes, scribbling onto a large piece of paper. The air of the house vibrated with his music—single notes, clear and stubborn little notes that were never hurried, like Frederich himself. Frederich's face was small for the rest of his body, prematurely lined, with a mouth like his father, small and monkish. His forehead was pale and rather bony, unlike the lower part of his face. Perhaps because his brown hair had already begun to thin out, his forehead looked prominent. He sat quietly at the dinner table, unfolding his white napkin in two even, measured movements, and placing it on his lap. Jesse could see how his forefinger, at rest on the edge of the table, moved nervously, almost imperceptibly, as if it were still picking out notes on the piano.

"That Hildie," Dr. Pedersen said, shaking his head. "Why is she always tardy?"

"I'm sure she'll be right down," Mrs. Pedersen said.

Dr. Pedersen frowned. Jesse watched his face intently, hoping that he would glance over at him and see that he was right on time, nicely washed and scrubbed and ready for lunch. Dr. Pedersen had instructed Jesse on the proper behavior for mealtimes, at home or away: "There is a small statue of yourself in your body, and it is that statue you must observe. Stability. Certainty. You will have the patience and the faith of concrete."

Jesse tried to imagine a small statue of himself inside himself.

"And you, Jesse, how have you passed your morning? Have you been helping your mother with her rose bushes?"

"He's going to help me this afternoon," Mrs. Pedersen said.

"What have you been doing then, Jesse?"

"Reading a book."

Dr. Pedersen sighed and smiled. "No. Not reading a book, Jesse. You do not reply to questions in that guttural, abbreviated way." He reached out to pat Jesse's arm. "You reply in quite another manner, don't you?"

"I was reading a book," Jesse said, embarrassed.

"Yes. And what is this book, Jesse?"

"A book on the canal—"

Dr. Pedersen shook his head, annoyed. Frederich, who had been staring down at his plate distractedly, now glanced up at Jesse in surprise.

"I mean—I meant *it is a book on the canal,* a book about DeWitt Clinton and the political background of the Erie Barge Canal, the building of the canal—" And Jesse talked on quickly, while Dr. Pedersen nodded. He gave the appearance of being very interested in what Jesse said. He blinked in such a manner, so studious himself, that Jesse had the idea he might be checking off Jesse's account against his own account of the book.

"Yes, that sounds fine. I very much approve of your interest in local history," Dr. Pedersen said when Jesse came to a halt. "You need to go more deeply into the subject, though. The account you have given of the political times is sadly superficial. Is the book you're reading a child's book, by any chance?"

"Yes," said Jesse.

"Yes, what?"

"It is a child's book. It is from the Young People's room of the library."

"But, Karl, it seems like a fairly good book," Mrs. Pedersen said quickly.

"Mary, please don't interrupt us. Now, where is Hildie?"

They waited. Just then they heard Hilda on the stairs—a heavy, fast thumping. She hurried into the room and came to sit beside Jesse, breathing hard.

"You are a little late. Have you been busy?" Dr. Pedersen said.

"Oh, yes, Father, very busy, I've been—" She bit her lip and stared across at Dr. Pedersen. "I've been so nervous about tomorrow—I'm—"

"Nervous, why?"

"I've been doing what you said, I've been trying to get hold of myself, doing those breathing exercises—but I'm so nervous—"

"Hildie, you must not talk in a rush like that. Speak slowly. When you address the professors tomorrow, you must speak clearly, you know that."

"Yes, Father. I'm sorry."

She patted her cheeks and tried to calm her breathing.

"Repeat to us what you have said, please."

"Yes. I have been very busy. I have been trying to rest my mind, to empty it of distractions. I have been doing the breathing exercises. You have instructed me not to worry, and I am concentrating on that. I am concentrating on not worrying."

"Good. That is fine, very wise," Dr. Pedersen said.

At last he bowed his head and pronounced a blessing on the meal.

Dora came out to serve lunch.

A first course of chicken noodle soup: in large gleaming white bowls, with mushroom caps and rough, coarse buttered toast. Jesse ate slowly in spite of his hunger. He felt a little shaky, he was so hungry. Across from him, Frederich raised his large soup spoon to his mouth in a monotonous, mechanical way. Hilda ate quickly, blowing on the soup to cool it, but leaning back behind Jesse so that Dr. Pedersen would not notice her. Jesse hoped she wouldn't be scolded.

"Mary, this soup is excellent. It's perfect," Dr. Pedersen said.

"I'm so glad you like it," Mrs. Pedersen said shyly.

Everyone brightened and smiled back and forth across the table, even Frederich.

The blueberry muffins were served hot, in a silver bowl, with a white napkin covering them. They were passed around and Dr. Pedersen began to talk of his morning at the Clinic. In addition to his solving of the case of the man from Tonawanda, he had taken on another case, a baffling one: "Herbert Kramer referred the man to me. I met him, shook hands, said nothing at all, observed his behavior, the size of his pupils. All very placid. Then I withdrew in silence. Stella pulled the dark blinds in my office and left me in perfect peace, with instructions not to interrupt me for any reason. No telephone calls. Not even emergency calls from the hospital. I sat in perfect stillness, with the ice pack on my head, and reviewed this problem. I believe I was able to communicate with the man after about ten minutes. It was an ordeal, an exhausting ordeal, and I will be returning to it this afternoon... I feel I'm very near victory.... You remember, Mary, Dr. Kramer from medical school? He telephoned only this morning and was very upset. The patient does not respond to any kind of medication. He is very anxious, very argumentative and frightened. He will not go to a hospital. His problem is a ringing in his ears, fainting spells, strange jumps and twists—he calls them *twists*—of the heart. But he has an ordinary cardiac shadow, a normal EKG, the blood tests have shown nothing, the urinalysis nothing. X rays, nothing. He will not submit to a spinal tap or a bone marrow test. He describes the fainting as a whirling of the head rather than the walls of the room. After about ten minutes I was able to make contact with him, my spirit and his spirit—it was an exhausting hour I spent and I had to come away without accomplishing much—"

Dora took the soup bowls away. She returned with a large platter, which she brought to Dr. Pedersen. He said, "Mary, what is this? Not braised duck?"

"Yes, dear, with that cream sauce you're so fond of. Is it all right?"

Dr. Pedersen tasted it. "It's delicious," he said.

Everyone smiled again. Dora went to Frederich and served him; he thanked her with a curt nod of his head. Dora then came to serve Jesse. She always served Mrs. Pedersen and Hilda last.

"Yes, Mother, this is certainly very good," Frederich said.

"I hope you all aren't just being polite!" Mrs. Pedersen laughed.

Jesse began eating hungrily. The duck was delicious. His mouth nearly ached with hunger now. Tiny pinpricks, tiny sparks, seemed to be rushing from every part of his body toward his mouth, concentrated most fiercely in the moist flesh on the inside of his mouth.

"Your mother is the only consistent genius in this family," Dr. Pedersen said.

Everyone laughed.

"Father," Hilda said, "don't you think that Mother could come to Chicago with us? I wish she could."

"Perhaps your mother will accompany you the next time, Hilda. You know how much trouble these trips are," Dr. Pedersen said.

"I'd be happy to go—" Mrs. Pedersen said.

"But no, Mary, not this time. Some other time."

Hilda sighed as she ate. Her elbow sometimes brushed against Jesse's, as if she were not conscious of him.

"I hate to be bothering you, Karl," Mrs. Pedersen said, "but it's really all right if I stay home. I don't like to leave Frederich anyway. I was going to ask you if you'd thought any more about my driving lessons. . . ."

"I haven't given it much thought, really. I've been very busy at the Clinic."

"I know. I understand."

"Mother wants to get a driver's license, at her age!" Hilda laughed. She was addressing Frederich, but he did not return her glance.

"I know I'm very excitable, I probably shouldn't be allowed on the road," Mrs. Pedersen said.

Dr. Pedersen smiled toward her courteously, but when he spoke it was only to request more butter from Dora.

"Oh, yes, and more muffins, please," Mrs. Pedersen said.

There was a surge of emotion around the table, as if the family were about to exclaim out loud their joy with one another. Jesse felt their unity, their happiness. He smiled at Hilda and she smiled back shyly. Most of the time she tried to ignore him. He wanted very much to be friends with her, to be a real brother to her, but he did not know how to begin. Most of the time she would not quite meet his gaze—her small, sad, darting eyes eluded his—and she rarely spoke to him except at mealtimes. Like Frederich, she spent most of her time with her "work." She was a mathematical genius, Jesse had been told. Mrs. Pedersen had tried to explain to him the kind of work Hilda did, but Mrs. Pedersen herself did not really understand. "Some things she works out on paper, but most of it she does in her head. I don't begin to understand it," Mrs. Pedersen had said. Jesse would have been frightened of Hilda, but she was shy, childlike, modest. Neither Hilda nor Frederich attended school. Frederich, years ago, had received a high school diploma, having received perfect scores on specially administered New York State Regents examinations without taking courses, but he had no interest in leaving home in order to attend college. Anyway, Mrs. Pedersen said that no one could teach Frederich anything. If he wanted to learn something he simply learned it on his own. And his musical compositions were his own, uniquely his own; no professor of music could help him. Hilda, though four years younger, had received perfect scores on the mathematical sections of the same exams, but she had failed the other sections and had shown no interest in improving her grades. For health reasons she did not attend school. Professors at nearby universities had invited her to study with them, but she had always declined.

She said sweetly to Mrs. Pedersen, "Oh, the mashed potatoes

are just the way I like them! They won't make mashed potatoes like this in Chicago."

The potatoes were passed around a second time and Jesse took another helping. Rich, creamy mashed potatoes, with cheese and onion. His mouth watered violently. All the dishes came to rest finally in a little semicircle around Dr. Pedersen, who continued talking about his work at the Clinic. ". . . oh, and I dashed over to make morning rounds, and Dr. Thorne had to humble himself and ask my advice. Why, everything that man did was routine and unimaginative . . . I was embarrassed . . . monitor urinary output, an examination of the intercostal vessels and the internal mammary vessels. . . ."

On and on he talked! His pleasant, well-modulated voice filled the room. Jesse ate hungrily and listened hungrily. The tablecloth gleamed with a snowlike intensity, a vista that excited Jesse and made him a little dizzy. He might have been standing on the edge of something, perhaps a cliff. At night he lay on the edge of sleep as if on the edge of this glowing white rectangle, this lovely lace rectangle, and felt how its whiteness filled his brain, his skull. The table fairly rocked now as Dr. Pedersen confided in them: ". . . the complexities of the case are certainly challenging, beyond any I've had for the past month. And I hate to show up a doctor in front of his colleagues, but . . . but it looks as if his diagnosis is wrong and his treatment may have been tragically mistaken. . . ."

They all listened closely. Even Frederich nodded as he ate. Now a large plate of vegetables was being passed around—creamed cucumbers, green scallions on toast points, glazed carrots. And more mashed potatoes. Dora brought out another platter: a small roast surrounded by boiled potatoes and onions. The smell of the roast made Jesse's heart jump.

". . . it is a joy, how the multiple parts come together, strain together, as if urging me to a premature solution!" Dr. Pedersen said. "But I am purposefully going slowly. It is a test of one's commitment to medicine, the slowness with which one is able to go when all temptations urge him to rush. I review the symptoms endlessly: loud P2, the second sound of the pulmonary louder than the aortic. Yes. Yes. A back-up in pressure that puts enormous strain on the heart. Yes. Perhaps. Blood pressure one ten over seventy. Breathing at thirty to forty a minute. In heart failure, but we pulled her out; no danger there. Now, now is the time that will test me, my imagination. She lies there waiting for me to pronounce her fate: will she be saved, will her body be corrected and sent back out to live, or will Dr. Thorne summon her husband to the hospital, will he admit defeat . . . ? What a drama life is, every minute of it—sheer drama!"

Jesse stared at Dr. Pedersen, nodding.

"Jesse, my boy, you look very serious today. You're thinking of my work, eh? You're thinking of how you would approach it?"

"No. . . ."

"No, not really?" Dr. Pedersen said, teasing. "But you are fascinated by my cases, I can see that. I was like that when my own father talked about his work. Yes, I see that in you. I see that in you," he said slowly. "You alone, perhaps, of my children, will attend school in such a manner as to be licensed by the moronic—but highly necessary—officials of the structure of society, you will conform intelligently though not brilliantly to their demands, you will allow yourself to be educated according to their system, and you will perhaps one day join me in the Pedersen Clinic. I see that."

Jesse's heart pounded. Everyone was watching him.

"I have been calculating for some time, I have been planning, imagining how you will grow up into my place, into my very being. It is a challenge to me, this shaping of you, Jesse, because you do not have my genes, my flesh has not contributed to your flesh. You are a total mystery to my flesh. And yet I believe I will succeed with you. . . . Correcting defects of nature, modifying certain freakish twists of fate, has always been my specialty."

Jesse could not follow all this. He nodded as slowly and as gravely as Dr. Pedersen himself.

There was a pause in the meal, as if everyone held his breath: then the meal continued.

The platter of beef was passed around again. Jesse helped himself to another slice. He poured gravy onto his mashed potatoes, he helped himself to another serving of onions and carrots and cucumbers. Mrs. Pedersen smiled happily down the table to him. More muffins were brought out by Dora, uncovered, and passed from place to place. "Mary, these muffins are superb. Were they made from a new recipe?" Dr. Pedersen asked.

"Yes. They're made with sour cream. Are they really all right?"

"Excellent," Dr. Pedersen said. "By the way, Mr. Brewster was in to see me this morning, and he has drawn up the contract for the apartment building. I will check it through and sign it this afternoon. On Friday I'll have to have luncheon with that Mr. Young, who's flying in from Detroit. So I won't be home. You remember my mentioning Mr. Young from General Laboratories? He's going to discuss my patent of that vagotomic instrument—you remember—"

Mrs. Pedersen had just discovered a spot on her white linen dress and she was rubbing at it. She looked up attentively.

"I'll repeat what I said, since you were distracted. Mr. Young, from Detroit, is coming on Friday to discuss the invention I've been working on. But there's no need for me to go into details if you're not interested."

"Oh, of course I'm interested. . . ."

"I suspect you don't really recall my work on this little device. It's been in the back of my mind for years, and last week I finally took time to draw up plans."

"Yes, I think so," Mrs. Pedersen said nervously.

Dr. Pedersen held her gaze sternly, then with a brief explosive laugh turned to Frederich. "Women cannot concentrate. Even gifted women, even women singled out for exceptional histories, cannot concentrate. Is this why they are so charming?"

"Father, *I* concentrate all the time!" Hilda cried.

"Even you, Hildie, with your enormous talents, even you must be carefully disciplined. The discipline must come from other people," Dr. Pedersen said with a wink.

And now dessert was served: peaches and cream, and chocolate cake with a stiff, white frosting that had been shaped into tiny points, like the surface of a stormy sea. Jesse was surprised to find that he was still hungry. He accepted both kinds of dessert; he recalled vaguely the night he had spent in the empty house outside Yewville—that empty house his parents had once owned—sleepless and weak with hunger. Now his stomach strained against his belt—since coming to live with the Pedersens he had grown through three sizes of clothing—but still he was hungry and thought it a good idea to eat.

Luncheon finally came to an end. It was one-thirty. With reluctance, Dr. Pedersen got to his feet. "Well, Mary, in spite of the many distractions of your life, this was an excellent meal. What have you planned for dinner tonight?"

"I thought I'd keep it a surprise. . . ." Mrs. Pedersen said.

"Fine, good. A good idea," Dr. Pedersen said cheerfully. "And Frederich, this afternoon you are devoting yourself to . . . ?"

"The same composition," Frederich said. He spoke slowly and distantly, as if he had answered this question many times. Jesse had the idea that he found it difficult to hide his contempt. "I am in the fourth movement now, the presto. It seems to be evolving into a kind of double fugue. I had not intended this, in fact, I have tried to resist it, and to resist as well variations on my theme that seem to me obvious and melodramatic. But the variations are relatively restrained. There are two strongly contrasted sections, one fast and one more rhapsodic, but I find them bearable. . . ."

"Ah, I see you're working very hard, as usual," Dr. Pedersen said.

"I have no choice about it," Frederich said coolly. It was astonishing how much he resembled his father at times—a triangle of features inside a bulky expanse of face. But he seemed to possess none of his father's youthfulness.

Dr. Pedersen returned to the Clinic. Hilda and Frederich returned to their work. Jesse went out with Mrs. Pedersen to help in the garden. He had begun to worry about his book on the Erie Canal—it wasn't suitable for a report and he had little time to substitute another book. Mrs. Pedersen slowly drew on work gloves, straining to get them on her pudgy hands. She was strangely silent. On top of her head, perched there, was a new, greenish straw hat that looked as if it might fall off at any moment. She moved slowly, sadly. She went to look out over the rose garden and stood with her back to Jesse, in silence.

Jesse was dazzled by the roses. So many of them! Their lovely petals moved gently in the breeze, he had never seen such beauty; for some reason he felt a little hungry.

Mrs. Pedersen had begun shaking her head.

Jesse did not know what to do—should he say anything? He waited. When she turned to him her face was damp with tears. "I can't do this. All this," she said faintly.

"What— What's wrong?" Jesse said.

"I can't go on," she whispered.

She had put on another work-apron over her white dress and she looked enormous, sad and enormous in the sunlight.

"I feel dizzy. I have to lie down," she said.

Jesse helped her back into the house. She pulled off one of the gloves and dropped it on the flagstone terrace; the other she pulled off and threw a few feet away, as if it had angered her. The straw hat fell off her head as Jesse helped her up the back stairs. She was weeping quietly now. From the kitchen came the smell of something frying—hot fresh fat—and from the music room in back came the sound of Frederich's piano playing, several clear sharp notes in sequence, one-two-three, one-two-three, the same notes played again and again. "Help me upstairs. I must lie down," Mrs. Pedersen said. Jesse was alarmed at her quick, shallow breathing. He wondered if she could be having a heart attack. She leaned heavily against him. Near the top of the stairs she swayed, and he was afraid she would fall back on top of him—and both of them would fall downstairs—"Jesse," she said, "help me, please help me— Will you take a message to my father? Will you?"

He helped her to her room. He had never been in it before—a large pink room with several mirrors. She sat at a writing desk and wrote a note quickly. Droplets of perspiration fell onto the paper.

"And don't say anything about this to anyone," she whispered.

Jesse hurried with the envelope to his Grandfather Shirer, who lived in a large home about a mile away on Willow Street. He was a tall, heavyset man, a retired surgeon, who sat at one end of a sun porch; a nurse, reading a paperback novel, sat at the other end. Jesse gave him the note and he opened it and read it at once. His head was totally bald, a clean, pinkened, gleaming area of scalp; his face, like his scalp, was clean and fresh and shrewd. He sat with his daughter's note in his fingers. For a while he said nothing. Then, lowering his voice so that the nurse wouldn't hear, he said, "Thank you for bringing this, Jesse. And you understand you must not talk to anyone about it?"

"I think so," Jesse said.

"Not to anyone. Not to your father, or to Hilda or Frederich."

Jesse looked down.

"Not that there's anything in this note that your family should not know—of course not—but... but... it is advisable that my daughter and I have a correspondence that is confidential, do you understand? Your mother's privacy is an important issue, though what she does with it is perhaps not important. Do you understand?"

"I think so," Jesse said.

"You know that your mother loves you very much," Grandfather Shirer said, focusing his gaze upon Jesse now as if he had only discovered that this particular boy filled a blank slot in the air before him. "You know that...?"

"Yes," Jesse said.

He went back home. He felt obscurely weary, soiled. A secret from Dr. Pedersen was bad, perhaps a mistake... he might regret it.... But he could not refuse. He had no choice.

Only four more hours to read and prepare his report on the Erie Canal.

7

That voice.

It was with him everywhere.

At the edge of sleep, fearful of surrendering himself to its emptiness, he heard Dr. Pedersen's voice pronouncing his name. *Jesse. Jesse.* The voice seemed to call him back from a deep, dangerous emptiness where anything might be dreamed, anything might be remembered. It was loving, stern, watchful. Walking to school, pausing at the edge of a curb, he seemed to hear the voice, pronouncing his name clearly, cautioning him as if the curb were the edge of a cliff and he was in danger of falling to his death. Sometimes when he studied in the evening upstairs in his room, he heard the words of his books pronounced in his head in Dr. Pedersen's voice, so that he would not forget anything he read. It became permanent once it was heard in Dr. Pedersen's voice. It became sacred.

He had never really heard his name pronounced until Dr. Pedersen pronounced it.

He had begun school and discovered that it was not difficult for him. He was anxious to do well, he studied all the time, he was always far ahead of his assignments. In a way, he felt that he had never attended school before; he had never taken it seriously before. Why that was he did not know. But now he took it seriously, he took everything seriously.... He felt himself an adult among large, chattering children in the school. He had nothing to say to them. They had nothing to say to him. The high school building—with its VNION SCHOOL sign above its front door, the "U" shaped quaintly, like a "V"—was antiquated and ugly, dating from the late eighteen-eighties, and it smelled sharply of disinfectant and polished wood and chalk dust, and the perfume and hairdressing of girls, so many chattering girls. Their voices were hectic and insubstantial and wordless, sounds rather than words, like music too trivial for Jesse to bother with. He moved among them shyly, detached from their perpetual excitement. If they brushed close to him, he felt a sensation like small sparks jumping through his body, sparks of panic. He did not allow himself to stare at them. He did not want to see them, did not want to remember them... there was something about the chunky, hotblooded fleshiness of girls that he did not want to remember.... Their skirts were long, well beneath the calves of their energetic legs, but their sweaters were tight across their breasts and shoulders; their hair, worn long, fell in bangs onto their foreheads or in languid strands into their eyes, to be brushed back impatiently, perpetually. The boys seemed much younger than the girls. They milled around together as if for strength, laughing harshly in the lavatories and on the stairs, smoking, calling out to one another in a language that seemed to Jesse partly code, made up of words he did not really understand. They were children, tall, scrawny children, and he was an adult. Something in him yearned for their childishness... but then he remembered who he was, who he must become, and he looked upon them as if from a height, Jesse already grown into the man he must become, grown safely free of their spurts of friendship and their spiteful little feuds.

They are not very real, Jesse thought. He was echoing Dr.

Pedersen's remarks about the war in Europe: *This war is not very real to us yet.*

No, other people were not very real; there was not time to think of them, to invest them with reality. Dr. Pedersen's voice was real. It was close, intimate, like the murmuring of his own blood. It was somehow contained inside his skull. Other adult voices were important to Jesse—Mrs. Pedersen's voice, the voices of his high school teachers—but only Dr. Pedersen's followed him everywhere. It prodded him on, it gave him courage, it chided him when he was lazy. It was always quizzing him, bringing him up short by saying, *What have you just read?* Jesse read his textbooks and other books on chemistry, biology, physics, and mathematics; at the back of his mind he could hear Dr. Pedersen saying, *Yes, good, but why are you so slow? You have so much more work to do!* Hesitant, as if listening for a distant summons, Jesse would pause on the narrow school stairs. His classmates surged impatiently around him, noisy and shrill and prematurely knowledgeable, their legs straining as if ready to leap into a dance where he could not follow them, their voices hard and musical and hectic, yearning for the future. At the end of the school day they burst out of the old building and gathered together on the sidewalk in front of the Palace Theater or in front of the YMCA building, or they went to join friends who had quit school at Harrison's Radiator Company, a factory right behind the high school. Or they dawdled on the bridges of Lockport, staring down at the tugboats and the dirty barges, pushing pebbles absentmindedly down into the water with the edge of their feet. Restless. Aimless. They strolled up and down Main Street, eager to be transformed into adults so that they could escape forever the small, maddening confinement of their childhoods. The boys wanted cars, dreamed of cars or of joining the Navy, echoed their parents' excited fears about the future: What was going to happen in Europe? What was Germany going to do next? The girls chattered about friends who were getting married, or about older sisters who were already married, having babies, always having babies. If Jesse happened to overhear them he felt at times that he had blundered into a crowd, an entire little nation, of strangers.

He thought of himself as large and vulnerable among them,

a tall boy, too serious, soft in the body, with a countrified apologetic look that drew out their puzzled scorn—but they respected him, too; they did not quite know what to make of him, because he was the new adopted son of Dr. Pedersen, Dr. Karl Pedersen, whom everyone in Lockport knew. He seemed to take on for them the gravity of his father's importance. Glancing at him, they saw Dr. Pedersen instead. He was so serious, with his books and his quiet, stern frown, his manner of walking slowly as if figuring something out in his head, always a problem in his head, always something. He passed among them in silence, grateful for their lack of interest in him. Except for a few remarks he overheard—made up of jargon he did not quite understand, except to know that it marked him as strange—they ignored him, forgot him almost as soon as they discovered him. He was grateful. He wanted only to be left alone by these noisy children, especially by the girls. But one day on the street a group of boys parted and one of them called after him in a voice that sounded familiar, "Jesse! Hey, Jesse!" He pretended at first not to hear, this alarmed him so. Why should anyone be calling after him? When he finally turned he saw his cousin Fritz running to catch up with him.

"Hey, I thought that was you! What the hell!" Fritz said.

He was wearing a Navy uniform.

"Hey, Jesse, look at me—you didn't know I was going in so soon, did you? I've just finished basic. How do you like that?"

Jesse was very agitated, seeing Fritz like this. For a moment he could not speak. His mind had gone blank. Then he said, stammering, "How do your—your mother and father feel about it? Is it all right with them?"

"Oh, hell, you know my mother—hell— It's okay with them, I guess. They worry a lot. They think we're going to get in the war and everything and I'll be on some boat that will sink, Jesus, you know how they are, Ma especially—she's been bawling a lot since I signed up—Bob Door and Walter Cleary and I all signed up together. The base I'll be stationed at is in Florida, how do you like that? Nice summer weather, it's supposed to be! The hell with how cold it gets up here! . . . Well, I thought that was you there. You're looking good, Jesse, Jesus, you're a lot bigger than you were— Is everything okay?"

Fritz shaded his eyes and grinned at Jesse. When Jesse nodded he went on, his shoulders moving restlessly beneath the dark material of his uniform, "We heard you got placed with a family in Lockport. Heard all about it. Is it okay there? Is everything okay?"

"Yes."

"Jesus, I felt bad about what they did. Pa felt bad too. But—"

"It's all right," Jesse said.

"Well, no, Jesus.... How come you don't come back to visit sometimes? Is that against the rules or something? You like living in town, huh?"

"Yes, I like it a lot."

"Well, you seem sort of different. Bigger."

"I feel better than I did before...."

Fritz smiled in embarrassment. His hair had been trimmed very close to his skull. He looked as thin as Jesse had been, his shoulder bones restless and awkward. Jesse could see a blotch of red moving up his neck.

"Well, that's good. Well...."

"How is everything at home?"

"Real good. It's the same. You know how it is.... You know, it was hard for them to do what they did. Turn you over to the Home and all that. I don't know. It was strange... it was hard for them... I heard them talking about it a lot and Ma would cry.... You sure it's okay where you are? What are they like, the family you're with?"

"They're very nice people," Jesse said.

"And you live with them full-time? I mean—just like a regular family? Are you adopted or what?"

"Yes, adopted."

"Is your name different?"

"It's Jesse Pedersen now."

Fritz stared at him. "No kidding? Hell. That's something to think about.... What is it?"

"Pedersen."

"Pedersen...."

Fritz nodded and could not think of anything else to say. They were separated by a yard or so of sidewalk. Fritz was still shading his eyes from the sun and his grin had become strained.

After a few minutes they parted. Jesse felt confused with an emotion he could not understand—shame, fear? His heart pounded hotly and he seemed to hear Dr. Pedersen's voice in his head. *Let him go, abandon your cousin, don't allow him to recognize you on the street after this. If he dies in the Navy . . . If he dies in the Navy . . .*

But Jesse could not hear the rest of this.

"If he dies in the Navy there will be one less person to know me the way I used to be," Jesse thought.

Each day he was away from home, consciously "away" from his home, and yearning to return. He felt himself gravitating toward that house, drawn to it as if by an actual, tangible force. As he climbed the hill, he experienced a slight confusion of times, as if he were the old, skinny Jesse coming up here to stare at the Pedersen house, and to watch in silence as Hilda Pedersen passed by him, not recognizing him. Then he remembered that he lived there, that he was "Jesse Pedersen" and would take his place at the dinner table, recognized by everyone. . . . He prepared himself all day long, reading and memorizing pages in his schoolbooks, his mind working, analyzing, discarding, retrieving, getting ready for that moment in the evening sometime during dinner, when Dr. Pedersen would ask him what he had learned that day.

He would recite what he had learned. In his quick, respectful voice, making no mistakes, he would recite as much of it as Dr. Pedersen required. Now both Frederich and Hilda listened to him as well, though Frederich would not look at him. Hilda ran her finger round and round the edge of her messy plate. Dr. Pedersen nodded his head sharply as if checking Jesse's words against his own memory. Once he interrupted Jesse to ask, "Explain the term *homeostasis*, don't define it. Explain it to us, please." And Jesse said, "Hippocrates believed that disease could be cured by natural powers within the living organism. He believed that there is an active opposition to abnormality as soon as the condition begins. In 1877, the German physiologist, Pfluger, said that the cause of every need of a living being is also the cause of the satisfaction of the need. The Belgian physiologist, Fredericq, said in 1885 that the living being is an agency of such sort that each disturbing influence induces by itself the calling forth of compensatory activity to neutralize or repair the disturbance.

The higher in the scale of living beings, the more perfect and the more complicated the regulatory agencies become. They tend to free the organism completely from the unfavorable influences and changes occurring in the environment. In *The Wisdom of the Body,* the American physiologist Walter Cannon quotes the French physiologist Charles Richet: *The living being is stable. It must be so in order not to be destroyed, dissolved, or disintegrated by the colossal forces, often adverse, which surround it. By an apparent contradiction it maintains its stability only if it is excitable and capable of modifying itself according to external stimuli and adjusting its response to the stimulation. It is stable because it is modifiable—the slight instability is the necessary condition for the true stability of the organism."*

Silence.

Jesse had a dizzying vision of Dr. Pedersen's stern face. He waited. At the other end of the table Mrs. Pedersen made a sudden gesture, as if straightening her plate, adjusting her plate on the tablecloth.

"Yes, fine," Dr. Pedersen said slowly. "Fine. But you must read Claude Bernard. He has the idea of "homeostasis" even if he doesn't use the term itself.... You must read the *Introduction to the Study of Experimental Medicine*, it's a marvelous, exhilarating, inspiring work.... Bernard is one of the giants of medicine, working at a time when science was young, fresh, mysterious, open, anything was possible then . . . anything. . . ." He broke off, staring at Jesse. His face brightened slowly. "Well, Jesse," he said, "it seems you are becoming yourself."

And Jesse understood then that he had done well.

He began taking Jesse to the Clinic on Sunday afternoons. They drove out in Dr. Pedersen's black Rolls-Royce, a stately, archaic vehicle that caught the eyes of other motorists. Jesse felt as if he were in an unearthly vessel with Dr. Pedersen, propelled silently and rather swiftly along the ordinary Lockport streets, while Dr. Pedersen talked energetically to him about his patients and his inventions and his plans for the future. The Pedersen Clinic was not very large, but it was a handsome, modern building just on the outskirts of the city. "For a while Hilda would come out with me on these special little visits to my Clinic, but then she lost interest," Dr. Pedersen said. He and Jesse would be the only ones in the building and his voice would echo importantly.

"Frederich, of course, does not like to leave the house. His asthma bothers him, he has shortness of breath... and of course he is totally devoted to his music.... But here, Jesse, look here," he would say, pulling out a giant blueprint, "here are plans for my addition; you can see the operating theaters here, these large areas, and along this side private rooms for special patients.... It is a marvelous adventure, the future. You and I believe in it, don't we?" He put on his glasses to peer down at the intricate blueprint, as if looking directly into the future and finding it good. "Jesse, there will be people in your life who claim that the future of the world is bleak. Listen to these people, be respectful to them, but never believe them. They are already dead. It is death speaking in those words. At this moment Europe is at war, it is even claimed to be a threat to us—but don't take it too seriously. A very wise man said that war is not adventure; it is a substitute for adventure. And that is very true, because adventure is here, here," he said, tapping the unwieldy, smudged blueprint, "it is what we create, not what we are thrust into. You and I are not at war. We are not being shot at. Our world is thriving, Jesse. It is expanding every day, every minute. I own a great deal and it is expanding minute by minute, and because you are my son you share in it too, this extraordinary growth.... You must understand, Jesse. All life is a movement into the infinite... or it is a shrinking back. Make up your mind. They come to take their turns, step by step, the people of the earth—well, make up your mind, I say to them!—will you thrust yourself into the infinite, or will you shrink back? If you shrink back I have no time for you. If you make claims about history and death and sickness and chaos I have no time for you. What can history tell us? It is all a joke! Manure! We are not to be dragged down by the stupidities of the past. Hegel says, quite correctly: 'People and governments have never learned anything from history, or acted on principles deduced from it.' And so, what have we left...? We have the health of the living organism, the living body, which maps itself outward and defines limitations for itself, for *itself*—it does not allow others to do this for it! Never! It is the living organism that strives to become God. I am striving, straining—" And here he would press both hands against his chest, as if he had to keep back the straining of his big heart. "I am straining to be God, to move into that place which is God's place, to take from Him all that He will allow me to take. I am a perfect protoplasm. That is because every cell in me is growing, straining outward into infinity, and because I am able to make a map of the life that will be mine, while other people bump into one another in stupid crowds and herds, like animals. When this war is over, Jesse, there will be a marvelous growth. Everything will grow, expand, come alive again. And after that there will be another war, because the economy demands it; there will always be a war, and we will watch it from these shores, and some of us will direct it, because it is a fact of life that certain people must direct wars and other people must die in them. It is Fate. Do you understand? What is war, Jesse? What is war? Is it death? Never! It is the very heartbeat of life—the last resources of life's energies! Do you understand?"

He spoke excitedly. He took off his glasses so that Jesse could stare into the perfect gray-green irises of his eyes, the peaceful, wheel-like circles of his eyes, and see Fate itself.

Jesse answered as if hypnotized. "Yes, I understand."

"It is easy to die, Jesse. I see it every day—the bodies that surrender, die. The most expensive bodies surrender and die. They claim that they want to live, but really they want to die, because the mystery of their bodies is too exhausting for them. They die, they surrender. It is easy to die. But not to live: that is not easy, that is the challenge, the strain. To displace God is not easy. To be higher, a higher man, that is not an easy fate. And I believe you will share this fate with me, Jesse. I am certain of it. Once you become the man you are, Jesse, you cannot ever rest, but must prove yourself continually. Again and again. It is the fate of the higher man."

Ruddy with the joy of such good news, he rolled up the blueprint and put a rubber band around it.

He took Jesse into his inner office, his private office. "My special office where I commune with myself," he said. Every time he showed Jesse this small, dark room it was a surprise: a single black leather chair, built especially for Dr. Pedersen's large, heavy frame; a single lamp; no books; not even a carpet on the floor; windows with dark green shades that were partway drawn; a sacred silence.

"Like this," he said. He went to sit in the chair, easing his bulk down slowly, with a peculiar grace for so heavy a man. "I sit alone. I am alone." He closed his eyes. "No one is near me. Here is where I solve mysteries that are not understood, even by me. They go against laboratory tests. All right, yes, laboratory tests are not always accurate. The organism changes, suffers, grows, shivers, its secretions change, its heartbeat goes wild, its lungs fill up—all right—but still it is a mystery to me, how I can outguess these tests, and I am humble in the face of my own gift. I am passive, sitting here. At such times I am close to God, very close. My thoughts arrange themselves—the symptoms, the clues that bodies of sick strangers are giving to me, the data other physicians cannot interpret, and the whispering souls of the sick themselves—yes, sometimes I feel their souls in this room with me, brushing against me like bats in the dark! And then, as if God had sent an angel to whisper in my ear, somehow the truth comes to me. It comes into my waking mind and I understand. Yesterday I knew, I understood, that a woman was dying of a simple deficiency disease, though no one could figure out what was wrong with her; I *knew*, I saved her. . . . But I take no claim for my gift. I am only to sink into my deepest self until the truth comes to me; it is Fate operating in me and not myself."

On Monday mornings Jesse was sometimes allowed to miss school and to attend Dr. Pedersen's rounds at the local hospital. Dr. Pedersen was merry and sociable in his hospital whites, an enormous billowing outfit that made him look larger than ever, and very chaste and earnest. Jesse was proud of accompanying him; his father (though he could never quite bring himself to think of him as "father") was extremely popular, known by everyone on the staff, by the nurses, by stray patients in the corridors and those sitting up in bed, waiting for him. "Dr. Pedersen!" they would cry, waving, and he would go to shake hands, knowing everyone by name. Jesse stood proudly at his elbow.

"And this is my son Jesse, who is very interested in medicine."

As Dr. Pedersen went on his rounds he was joined by one person after another—a young physician on the staff, a nurse who was an old friend, even the Chief of Surgery himself, a Dr. Gallimard who was very courteous and very friendly, though Jesse thought him a little odd. He was so *curious* about Dr. Pedersen and his patients! Dr. Pedersen would chat with patient after patient, never hurrying, hardly needing to glance at the patient's chart, knowing present ailments and past ailments and the names of the patient's family, the patient's work, where he lived, where he was from, everything. He smiled heartily, told jokes. Occasionally his face shifted and Jesse saw in it that expression of sternness, as if he were remembering precise material, scanning paragraphs in his head. He never forgot anything. His sickest patients grew ruddy in his presence, as if rich fluids were pumped into their veins.

One day a nurse was having difficulty with an old woman, not one of Dr. Pedersen's patients, and she asked him for help. The woman was wiry and gray, her face sexless, tense with maniacal energy; she had thrown herself around in bed and dislodged a tube that was feeding blood into her arm. When Dr. Pedersen came into her room she was yelling. Jesse, out in the hall, could make no sense of her screams; he felt shaky himself, almost nauseated. Dr. Pedersen went right to the woman, bent over her, began speaking in a slow, gentle, courteous voice. "Mrs. Lowe, may I introduce myself, I am Dr. Pedersen. . . ." The woman screamed and threw herself from side to side. "I am Dr. Pedersen and I must find a way of helping you, my dear, you are going to do yourself some injury . . . you should lie still, my dear, lie still. . . ." He took a needle and seemed to be showing it to her. She stared at him. Jesse thought he could see, in her widened eyes, a look of absolute terror. But she lay still, she seemed to be listening to Dr. Pedersen. "Let me examine this arm," Dr. Pedersen said, and he scanned the woman's thin arm, looking for a vein. "This will only take a minute and it must be done, my dear, you know that. . . . You must allow us to help you. It will hurt a little, yes, but the needle is very small . . . it's very clean. . . . We must feed you, my dear, nourish you. . . ." He examined the other arm, testing her veins with his thumb; he tried an experimental prick with the needle and the woman drew back only slightly. He gave up on her arms and began on her legs. Something drew Jesse to the doorway; he must look; his instincts were to turn away from the sight of the old woman's white, blue-veined, splotched legs, her agitated face, her odor of sickness, and yet something else drew him, forced him forward, inward, to watch Dr. Pedersen, as if this were a scene he must memorize.

In went the needle. Testing, probing. "You are very patient with me," Dr. Pedersen said. His large white back was to Jesse. It was enormous, broad with the strain of concentration. If there were other people around—nurses, a young doctor—Jesse did not really notice them. He watched Dr. Pedersen. He listened to that voice. "The next one should do it, I am suddenly certain," Dr. Pedersen said lightly, and indeed he did find a vein, in the woman's cadaverous ankle. "Ah, here. Thank you, my dear. Thank you for your enormous patience. Now we are all set, now we will take care of you as we should.... I hope that didn't hurt...?"

The woman lay back on her pillow, her eyes heavy, lined, exhausted. She shook her head slowly. Dr. Pedersen remained to chat with her and she managed to speak to him, to say something that sounded like a name, her own name. Jesse felt a little faint. He went to get a drink of water at a fountain in the hall. He felt faint, yet very excited. Yes, yes! He had witnessed something wonderful!

Dr. Pedersen always ended up in the staff lounge, sipping coffee, with a small crowd of people around him. He talked about strange new cases: "The patient was originally admitted to a hospital in Potsdam with a headache, a fever of a hundred and four, complaints of pains in the neck, pain in cheeks, cheekbones, eyes, ears. She could hardly move her head by the time I saw her. She was twenty-nine years old, no previous illnesses except measles and mumps, no previous hospitalizations. The LP was clear, absolutely clear!—and yet it looked as if she was going downhill fast; she was tense, nervous, half out of her mind—her lungs began filling up with fluid, she was in heart failure, and spasms began up and down her body—tiny pinpoint hemorrhages on her arms and legs and in her eyes—she was dying right in front of everyone—and—"

But a paging over the loudspeaker interrupted this: "Dr. Pedersen, Dr. Pedersen—" and off he went to the telephone, with his listeners gaping after him.

But he was at his best when giving guest sermons at the Lutheran Church, handsome and fresh-faced in a new gray suit with a vest, his hair perfectly combed across his large head, his glasses glinting angelically, his forefinger raised to the congregation as he pointed out certain truths: "The scientist is not at war with the man of God. No. It is an idle mind that suggests such nonsense. I present myself as a man of science and also a man of God. Truth is to be honored wherever it is found, absolute truth; it is only truth that matters. The destiny of man is to claim new territory, to pursue the infinite, to create maps and boundaries and lines of latitude and longitude with which to explain reality—the terrible darknesses and odors of reality, the terrible silence of the universe that does not know our human language. America is blessed by God. America is all men, all humanity, blessed by God and pushing outward, always outward, as we yearn for another world, we yearn to be assimilated into God as into a higher protoplasmic essence.... Though many of us here today are frightened of the future, I think we should know that the United States is a unique, blessed, powerful nation, and that it cannot be conquered, not in our lifetimes or in our children's lifetimes.... There is something magical about the United States. This is a time of magic...."

Jesse sat in the midst of the congregation, staring at Dr. Pedersen. Beside him Mrs. Pedersen fussed nervously with a handkerchief. He could not tell if she was self-conscious or restless; Hilda on the other side of him, sat with her gloved hands folded and stared up at her father just as Jesse did, listening intently. The church was well attended at this eleven o'clock service. It's off-white interior, dingy with a look of disuse, seemed to fall back before the passion of Dr. Pedersen's voice. Everything took heart, took on color—the faded grape padding of the pews, the dull wood, the stained-glass windows that looked out upon an overcast November day, invisible from here. Dr. Pedersen's magic hung in the air, almost scented. The man himself, poised over the pulpit with the occult grace of the very fat, smiled out upon the Sunday faces with a look of vast, benevolent wisdom.

This is a time of magic....

Then the Reverend Wieden led everyone in prayer, and Jesse's mind skidded from idea to idea, from image to image, excited by what he had heard. It was as if Dr. Pedersen had ascended to the pulpit to speak to him, only to him.... He carried his father's words inside him, sacred words hoarded in a part of his mind, and not even the commotion of the organ and the singing could dislodge them. On the way home he sat in the back seat of the car with Hilda, and Dr. Pedersen and his wife sat in front —Frederich, who would be upset too much by the church's attempt at music and by its musty congested air, never went to church—and still his father's words echoed in his head, though Dr. Pedersen might now be chatting about other, ordinary things. Jesse stared out the window at the sidewalks of Lockport and saw how they were transformed, transfigured, by the magical air of Sunday. In the corner of his eye he caught sight of children on the street, stray anonymous children, skinny boys in canvas jackets with nothing to do, their hands stuffed in their pockets, staring at Dr. Pedersen's immense black car as it sped up Washburn Street. . . .

Jesse's first Christmas in the Pedersen home was a confusion of delights—the great evergreen tree that filled the foyer, decorated with hundreds of gleaming ornaments, some of them fragile as eggshells, puffs of silken angels' hair, with a plump feathery female angel at its highest point, piles of brightly wrapped presents, baskets of food and flowers, wreaths of evergreen that smelled of vast snowy fields and bunches of ivy and holly and tiny red berries, poinsettia plants in heavy pots wrapped with green tinfoil and red satin ribbons. Lights that made Jesse's eyes water glimmered everywhere. He seemed to float with the light, with the music of Christmas; his feet seemed springy on the floor. He had never understood Christmas before. The house was filled with the smells of Christmas food—roasting turkeys, roasting ham, baking pies, Christmas cookies, Christmas candy. Christmas dinner itself lasted for many hours. Dr. Pedersen began it with a long, happy, conversational prayer of thanks. The dining room table had been opened as far as it would go, extra leaves put in, so that all the Pedersen relatives could be with them; Jesse sat between his sister Hilda and his grandfather, Grandpa Shirer. There was so much for everyone to talk about! Everyone was excited, buoyant as weights bobbing in restless water, with no fear of ever sinking. What force could sink the Pedersens?

Many friends of the Pedersens came over during the day. Jesse stayed near Mrs. Pedersen, shy of so many strangers, and she kept pushing him forward, introducing him, pouring champagne for him so that he could join in the numerous toasts.... He felt giddy, intoxicated. He had never understood Christmas before. "A toast to Dr. Pedersen, the Citizen of the Year!" cried someone—and it turned out, Mrs. Pedersen told him, to be the Mayor of Lockport himself, an old friend of Dr. Pedersen's. In the early evening Dr. Pedersen had a large pen-and-ink drawing put up on an easel, and he and Mr. Erikson, the architect who had drawn it, explained to the group how the Pedersen Clinic would expand and how, one day, an entire medical village would surround it. "And, my friends," Dr. Pedersen said with a rowdy wag of his finger, "the city of Lockport will expand with it, believe me! The value of your property will rise! I dislike prophets, because they are usually shabby melodramatists, but I would like to prophesy that by the year 1975 our city will be famous, world-famous, as a center for the diagnosis and cure of hundreds of diseases by long distance, by computer—by a system of memory-core devices that, upon being fed the symptoms of a patient as far away as Brazil, will diagnose both disorder and method of treatment in a matter of seconds. What, you look incredulous! Even my dear wife looks disbelieving! But we'll see—yes, we'll see who is right, who knows how to read the future! How can you be so certain that what I say is outlandish? Yes, I may be a little giddy tonight, I may have drunk more champagne than I should, but how do you know that I don't stand at the very center of the known world, I, Karl Pedersen himself? Eh? Are you all so very certain of the identity of the ground you stand upon?"

Though he spoke of himself as giddy, Dr. Pedersen talked as always with a rapid, wonderful clarity. And yet—there was something about his voice and his face that confused Jesse and made his saliva run with panic, as if, at the very center of his being, there was a light too powerfully bright to be borne.

Jesse ate so much that day that his new olive-brown suit strained at the waist and caused him discomfort. He stumbled and would have fallen into the Christmas tree itself if Mrs. Pedersen hadn't laughingly caught hold of him. "What, are you drunk? Is my Jesse drunk?" she cried. Her own face was bright, her eyes glittering. For this special day she had done her hair up in rows of curls, layers of curls, that looked artificial and not nearly so pretty as her everyday hair, but she wore a magnificent scarlet dress with an ermine collar, and a large diamond bracelet—Dr. Pedersen's main present to her—and Jesse thought she looked beautiful. He kept wanting to cry, she looked so beautiful, and Dr. Pedersen, always the center of a group of intense, laughing people, was so wonderful a man, so wonderful a father.... In the late evening the guests began to leave, slowly and reluctantly, and by midnight everyone had gone: at last they were alone, just the Pedersens! Dr. Pedersen went right upstairs to change into the elegant blue wool bathrobe Hilda had bought for him, and the leather slippers Jesse—with Mrs. Pedersen's help—had bought for him, and he came down again eagerly, rubbing his hands together as if, for him, the party was only beginning. Mrs. Pedersen kicked off her shoes, giggling. Hilda, who had had too much champagne, pressed her flaming cheeks with a damp cloth. Frederich, who had left the party off and on, perhaps annoyed by the noise, came down from his room now, fully dressed as he had been at dinner; his face looked unusually rosy and expectant. Jesse had been ready for bed a few minutes before, but now he felt eager, his heart almost pounding with excitement. He had never understood Christmas before, he thought dizzily. All the Pedersens went out to the kitchen, where Mrs. Pedersen opened the refrigerator and took out food, bowls of food, food wrapped carefully in waxed paper, and made them a supper. Hilda helped her, giggling and pretending to be drunk. They had warmed-up turkey and gravy and dressing; warmed-up ham; several loaves of good rye bread; whipped potatoes; and omelettes stuffed with mushrooms and chunks of ham, made just for fun by Mrs. Pedersen and Hilda who was supposed to learn how to cook someday soon, taught by her mother.... And slabs of leftover apple pie and minced meat pie that Mrs. Pedersen said would not keep, and an entire orange chiffon cake that Mrs. Pedersen had kept hidden just for midnight supper. Jesse and Hilda had several tumblers of milk, and the others had coffee with whipped cream spooned into it.

"Now we will read a little, just a little," Dr. Pedersen exclaimed, and they went back into the big living room, where Dr. Pedersen built up the fire again, and they sat together on the sofa. Dr. Pedersen brought in a heavy book from the library, the family scrapbook, which had hinged wooden covers and which was usually kept on a little podium in the library. The covers had been decorated many years before by Hilda with a wood-burning set. The letters of the title were large and deep: THE BOOK OF FATES.

"Now, now, we will read about ourselves just a little. On this Christmas Day of 1940, we will give thanks for all that we have, we will assess it," Dr. Pedersen said happily. Mrs. Pedersen passed around a plate of fudge. They gathered around Dr. Pedersen, who sat with the heavy book on his lap, turning the pages slowly. Jesse sat beside him, pressed up close. He wanted to see everything. His eyesight blurred and wavered, he was so determined to see everything. He felt that he had never understood Christmas before and now it was going to be revealed to him, explained to him.... Mrs. Pedersen sat on Dr. Pedersen's other side, and Hilda hung over his shoulder, girlish and silly. Only Frederich sat a little apart, pretending interest. He was much more alert than usual, however; usually he sat with his fat legs before him, his face sallow and bored and detached. "Now we begin at the beginning, as if this were a novel," Dr. Pedersen said, and the first page was a series of photographs of himself as a child, a plump, handsome child. Hilda screamed with laughter at something—an old joke, evidently. "Hilda, please!" Mrs. Pedersen laughed. Dr. Pedersen turned the large page and there was a photograph of himself in a graduation cap and gown, evidently taken on the day of his graduation from college. "Isn't your father handsome!" Mrs. Pedersen cried, reaching across to poke Jesse. Jesse, who was chewing fudge, a mouthful of delicious nut-studded fudge, did not even know at first what she had said. Then he smiled; he grinned happily. *Yes. Yes.* His father was a handsome man, *yes.* He glanced up to see that Frederich was just now taking out a handkerchief from his pocket, and along with the handkerchief something flew out and hit the carpet—it looked like a black, lint-covered piece of something, maybe a jellybean—and, stooping sluggishly, Frederich picked it up and popped it into his mouth mechanically, as if he hadn't known exactly what he was doing. Jesse blinked, wondering if he had seen right. Had Frederich really popped a dirty jellybean into his mouth? Frederich gazed at him through half-closed eyes, contented; he did not seem to be really looking at Jesse.

"Ah, here, look here!" Dr. Pedersen cried. The large glossy photograph before him was of the Pedersens on their wedding day. "My modest bride—isn't she charming?" Jesse was surprised to see that Mrs. Pedersen had been so slender. The photograph showed a woman in her twenties, only a little thick about the hips and thighs, her face eager, glowing, lovely, the eyes spaced wide apart. The photograph had been touched up a little and her lips were too clearly outlined in red; but she had been a beautiful young bride, in yards of fine white lace. Dr. Pedersen, a stoutish young man with metal-rimmed glasses and a stern, handsome face, stared directly into the camera. His cheeks had been retouched too, rouged, so that he looked unnaturally festive.

"Oh, don't look at this—turn the page—" Mrs. Pedersen said quickly.

The next photograph was of Mrs. Pedersen as a girl, standing in front of a rose bush in someone's garden. The garden was immense. Mrs. Pedersen, squinting a little, smiled a sweet maidenly smile into the sun. Her skirt drooped down on her legs and her arms were crossed self-consciously across her bosom. Jesse guessed she was about twenty years old in the picture.

"Pretty. Such a pretty woman," Dr. Pedersen said, as if making a diagnosis.

"That was so long ago, please don't look," Mrs. Pedersen said sharply.

She turned several pages in succession.

"Mama, don't turn them so fast, you'll rip them," Hilda said. "Show Jesse this one. Look, Jesse, it's Mother—would you recognize her?" A large newspaper clipping from the Women's Page of the newspaper had been pasted into the scrapbook. It showed "Mary Shirer of Willow Street" receiving five blue ribbons at the Niagara County Fair of 1920 for her baked goods. The clipping had been sealed inside a piece of plastic. "Oh, please don't look at that, that was so long ago," Mrs. Pedersen said in distress.

She turned the pages quickly, and Dr. Pedersen, with an amused sigh of resignation, did not try to stop her. Jesse saw how this Mary Shirer was transformed gradually into Mrs. Pedersen —heavier hips, arms, a face that grew rounder, that grew almost round, a bosom that suddenly billowed out, the breasts like sacks of something soft and protruding, the upper arms fleshing out like sausages, the whole body thickening, growing outward like the trunk of a giant tree, corseted tight and rigid. One recent photograph was of Mrs. Pedersen standing—perhaps half hiding—behind a large table piled with baked goods for a bazaar at the church, pies and cakes and tarts and brownies and cookies, baked goods piled everywhere on the table in front of "Mrs. Karl Pedersen, Chairwoman of the Autumn Baked Goods Sale" at the Lutheran Church. One pie was so cut—the fork marks so placed—that Jesse for an instant saw a face there, a child's sweet, happy face smiling toward the camera.

Then the photographs and clippings of Dr. Pedersen began.

Pages and pages of them—Dr. Pedersen being awarded a trophy at a Fourth of July ceremony at Atwater Park, 1931, a bald man shaking his hand, flags in the background; Dr. Pedersen standing at a banquet table, flanked by flowers, a large copper medallion on the wall behind him with the face of Abraham Lincoln on it, and writing Jesse couldn't read; Dr. Pedersen on the cover of a Sunday supplement magazine, in full color, standing in front of the Pedersen Clinic, which had evidently just opened, in 1933; Dr. Pedersen in the children's ward of a hospital; Dr. Pedersen photographed for a Buffalo newspaper with a child in a wheelchair, a small girl, the two of them posed smiling awkwardly at each other—the caption for this read, "Gloria Spanner shows her gratitude for the efforts of Dr. Karl Pedersen, of Lockport, who is credited with saving her life by making a diagnosis of her condition, a rare bone-marrow disease." There were large glossy photographs of Dr. Pedersen boarding a train, boarding an airplane, receiving strange objects of honor from groups—a large candy cane, a key as big as his arm, a huge bouquet, a giant stuffed rag doll, many trophies, a medallion, even a baby lamb, a real baby lamb; and of Dr. Pedersen with some friends at the golf course of the Lockport Country Club, and at more banquet tables, and at ground-breaking ceremonies for buildings; and at an Elks' Club Halloween Party for Crippled Children, Dr. Pedersen enormous in a harlequin outfit, all rags and diamond designs of red and black and yellow, wearing a fool's cap and bells, holding a kind of scepter; and of Dr. Pedersen on stage somewhere with a small, elderly man, the two of them facing each other in front of a large chart that showed great progress in something—the Community Chest Drive for 1939. There were several pages of a magazine story on Dr. Pedersen—Jesse caught sight of a headline that declared, "In his patients' eyes this man can do no wrong"—and another front page of the same Sunday supplement, this time showing Dr. Pedersen in his hospital whites, sitting at a desk; the story promised on the inside pages was called "Scientist or Mystic?—Dr. Karl Pedersen of Lockport." As the years passed, Dr. Pedersen's face grew wider and merrier, like a balloon being blown up. Jesse would have liked to study these pictures and stories. He felt dazzled, there was no time to make sense of this . . . and now Mrs. Pedersen was passing a bowl of salted nuts to him and Frederich. . . .

"Oh no, not these ugly things," Hilda said. She turned away as the photographs of herself began: a child of about six, already heavy, a child of nine, of eleven, of twelve, some of the pictures just snapshots, others professional photographs, others clipped out of newspapers and magazines—the biggest story had been in *Life*, called "Math Prodigy from Upstate New York Baffles Professors." As a small child Hilda had been pretty and cheerful, but as the photographs progressed her smile faded, her face soured, until the picture in *Life* showed a beetle-browed girl with a woman's body shapeless as a tub.

"They're not ugly, Hilda," Dr. Pedersen said.

"At least you let me throw out that one that called me a freak," Hilda said.

"Oh, Hilda, that wasn't serious, that was just a journalistic method," Dr. Pedersen said. "The word 'freak' had quotation marks around it, after all. . . ."

"A freak is a freak," Frederich said.

It was the first time he had spoken for quite a while.

Dr. Pedersen ignored him. He was turning the big pages of the scrapbook slowly and reverently. Jesse, pressed up close to him, his own body close to Dr. Pedersen's, stared at what was being shown to him—he could not look hard enough. He must see everything, remember everything. *The Book of Fates*, kept in Dr. Pedersen's library, was not to be touched by anyone except Dr. Pedersen himself. There were a few more pictures of Hilda, only one glossy photograph of Frederich at about the age of eleven; then pictures of the family, of relatives and friends, perhaps twenty or thirty pages of these domestic snapshots, page after page until Jesse's eyes began to ache. Then, at the back of the book, there was a section entitled "Impersonal Fates." Dr. Pedersen showed Jesse a few of these pages, but it was clear that he too was tiring and his interest was ebbing. Most of these entries were clippings from newspapers and magazines. They were about strangers, and the destinies of strangers; Jesse gathered that they had for some reason attracted Dr. Pedersen's attention. A barber in San Francisco had been struck by a nineteen-year-old boy in a Cadillac convertible, thrown into the air, lodged in the back seat of the car, and, dying, dead, had been driven around for three hours by the panicked driver, who had gone mute from shock.... An eighty-seven-year-old Cincinnati grocer had been held up by robbers three days in a row, once in his store, once in a parking lot, once entering the side door of his own house, and on his way downtown to report the third robbery he was struck by a delivery boy on a bicycle and killed.... A family in Portland, Maine, had been awakened by an elderly female neighbor who told them she had dreamed of an angel sent to flatten their house, and within ten minutes of her telephone call their house had collapsed, injuring the mother and two of her children, but not seriously.... In New York City, twin brothers of fifty-five years of age were reunited after many decades' separation, only to discover that they had been wounded in identical organs in World War I.... In Montreal, a thirty-year-old woman woke each night hearing a baby's wail coming from the wall of her furnished room and, after calling police and notifying them for several days in a row, she gave birth herself to a dead infant, though she claimed she was not pregnant and "did not know" how the baby had got inside her.... In Galveston, Texas, a taxi driver reported that his cab had been flung in the air by a waterspout that preceded a small local hurricane, and that his fare, a white woman of about sixty, had been sucked out, never to be seen again, though no one was reported missing to the police.... Jesse's heart hammered as he read these items, his eyes snatching at them. Dr. Pedersen began turning the pages faster and faster. For some reason he did not want to close the book, perhaps it was a ritual with him to go through the entire book, yet he was obviously eager to get to the end. Jesse wanted to slow his hand, to protest. Only a few more pages to go . . . Dr. Pedersen turned them rapidly . . . and, at the very end, Jesse caught sight of a familiar clipping, he had only time to glance at the headline before Dr. Pedersen closed the book, a headline that had nothing to do with him and that he rejected at once: BOY ELUDES GUN-TOTING FATHER.

No, that headline had nothing to do with him.

8

April, 1941.

She seemed to be deep inside a body.

The body was being addressed at its uppermost part, the head.

"Hilda, are you listening?"

The head responded by nodding. Yes. *Yes.* Her father was talking to her in his stern, clear voice, the one he used when he was trying not to scold her. Hilda shook herself, made an effort to get everything into focus. She had to get her brain clear so that she could obey her father properly. Her brain filled with numbers, a blizzard of numbers. They added themselves up into a pyramid, a mountain, then became a single number branched out into other numbers, a sudden crowd of them. She had to get her brain clear of all this so that she could listen to what her father was saying.

"So your mother will wake you early, around six. That should give you enough time to take a nice bath so that we'll all be ready to leave around seven-thirty. The plane is scheduled to leave the airport at eight-thirty and we want to have enough time to get there. Is that understood?"

Shame, that Father should say the word *bath* in front of Jesse, who was looking down at his plate. Was he embarrassed? It would have been natural for him to be embarrassed, to be forced to think of her, his fat sister, his ugly adopted sister, lowering herself into a tub of hot water.

"Is it understood, Hilda?"

"Yes, Father."

She noticed how meekly the head nodded at the top of its squat stem and the torso of the body leaned forward, eager and obedient, as if prepared right now to get into that hot water.

"What are you going to wear, Hilda?" her father asked.

"Oh, I don't know."

"Did you buy her anything new for the trip, Mary?"

"She wouldn't let me. She wouldn't go shopping," Hilda's mother said.

"Hildie—what is this? Do you want to look bad in New York? Don't you want to look pretty? Why are you trying to disappoint your father?"

More talk about her! She blushed and looked down at her own plate. It was clean—cleaned of food—and she automatically reached for more. There was a platter of roast beet just in front of her. "Oh, I don't know," she said in a childish little whine. She could not look at her father.

"She didn't want me to take her shopping. She refused," Hilda's mother said apologetically.

"Then I will take her myself," her father said.

Hilda chewed her meat in silent, burning agitation. Her father would take her shopping himself! Dr. Pedersen shopping with his daughter! She was aware of Jesse sitting beside her, listening to all this, and she wondered what he thought of her. Did he think anything of her? Was he ashamed of her? When they met in the upstairs hall, just the two of them, on their way to their rooms or to the bathroom, meeting accidentally, they glanced at each other with a kind of quick, furtive surprise, smiled shyly, looked away.... What did Jesse think of her?

"Since you seem to be unable to guide your daughter," Hilda's father was saying severely, "I will take her shopping myself. This might at least prevent her from making a bad impression in New York."

"But I—"

Hilda's father interrupted her mother. "Please don't annoy me. This discussion has gone on long enough."

Food. Bowls being passed. Hand to hand, around the table, bowls passed carefully, as if their contents were living, precious forms of life. Hilda sensed her mother's distress but she did not look at her. Not that round bell-cheeked reddening face—the face she would inherit—no, she wouldn't look at it. No. She wouldn't look up at Frederich, across the table from her. He was no more to her than the boys she sometimes saw out her bedroom window, far out on the street, passing the Pedersens' iron fence without even glancing at the house. She hated his music, his finicky compositions, big sheets of paper covered with fine, spidery notes and scrawls and lines and signs that looked like code, a crazy code. She hated his wheezing on the stairs, she hated his pale oversized face, the slushy chewing of his jaws. She sensed his pleasure at her being scolded and she hated him. And, right next to her, Jesse sat in embarrassed silence, feeling sorry for her and for her mother both, lumping them together and feeling sorry for them both. . . .

Hilda closed her eyes and prayed: *Let Father not say anything more.* A string of numbers appeared and swung around in her head, like a line of bees. Buzzing. She opened her eyes and continued eating. Jesse now was eating again, wiping gravy off his plate with a piece of rye bread. She saw how neat he was. But he stiffened as her father went on: "During the past year Hilda has not been very cooperative. She is becoming too spoiled, Mary. She makes very little effort to please me."

"But I don't think—"

"Please don't pretend to be ignorant of what is going on in your own family," Hilda's father said. "She is becoming willful and silly. She embarrassed me greatly by pretending to be sick so that the interview at the University of Pennsylvania had to be canceled—"

"But she really was sick, I'm sure of it."

"Sick! Of course she wasn't sick."

"But—"

"Of all people, I should know who is sick and who isn't. And Hilda was not sick. She was pretending."

Hilda looked slowly, sorrowfully up to her father at the head of the table. It was true, yes, that she had pretended to be sick, but she had been so nervous. *Leave me alone*, she prayed, *or I'll wish you dead.* But then she stiffened. Ashamed of herself. Guilty. Her father, who knew nothing of these thoughts, was speaking sternly at her mother, ignoring her. He shook a forefinger. They were discussing her, fat ugly Hilda, arguing about her in front of everyone. Now she was being asked a question—her head nodded—yes—her head nodded at the end of its clumsy stem. A head of ordinary size, with a thatch of straw-colored, listless hair, still frizzy from a permanent wave given to her the month before. It was strange that her head was of ordinary size. The skull was ordinary but the flesh packed on it was not ordinary. Everything ballooning. Swelling. Bloated. Upstairs, in her room, Hilda would smirk at herself in the mirror, bunch her fat cheeks up so that, when she released her smile, sharp angry creases showed in her skin.

"Why else does she appear at luncheon in a dress like that? It isn't even a dress! A sack—not even very clean—"

"Hilda dresses nicely for church, Papa. She—"

"Mary, you must not contradict me. I am speaking of Hilda's appearance right now. Why does she come to the table in a dress like that? It looks as if she made it herself."

Yes, she had made the dress herself, out of several large pieces of cotton. It had started out as a joke, a mockery of a dress, a shapeless bag. Trying it on, she had discovered that it was so ugly that it detracted from her ugliness—really, it was a wonderful dress for her! She had insisted upon wearing it, in spite of her mother's doubts.

"Hilda has trouble.... We have trouble finding nice clothes for her...."

Her mother faltered.

"Then I will take her myself, right after lunch. Yes. I want my little girl to look as pretty as possible. Obviously, I will have to take care of this dimension of our domestic life myself."

Yes, Father. Hilda and her mother both nodded obediently.

"I assume that Jesse is equipped for this trip . . . ?"

Jesse was going along with them. It was the first time in years that anyone had accompanied Hilda and her father on one of her "examinations."

Yes, Father. Mrs. Pedersen was demure and eager to agree.

"And we will all look as nice as possible, won't we?"

Yes, yes.

There

beneath her heart

there

in that small sac of a space where a baby might grow, where the medical books in her father's library showed that a baby might grow, she lived in secret from them. From all of them.

She did not need to watch them, to study them. Did not need to spy on her adopted brother Jesse. They were *there*, memorized there, in her, in that secret space. Her father was there, populating the space with his busy face and voice; her mother was there, always, silently and helplessly smiling; Frederich was there, puff-faced, his teeth rotting because he was too lazy to brush them; and Jesse....

Jesse: a boy of sixteen. His eyes green and silver, always moving, restless and precise inside his strong facial bones. Freckles on his forehead, a look of childlike innocence, awareness. Yet there was something uneasy about him—a hunted look. Inside that growing face with its clear-cut eyes and its strong nose and mouth there was a child's face, the precariousness of a child's face inside the tough enlargement of his flesh. His complexion was good, healthy, tanned. He was the only one of the family who spent much time outside. Sometimes Hilda watched him from the window of her room, safe behind the curtains, as he worked outside with the hired man, digging in her mother's big flower gardens. He had grown big himself. She paced nervously in her room from about three-fifteen until he came home from school, when she would hurry to the window to frown down upon him, this stranger, this adopted "brother," who walked along the street with an armful of books, a boy with red-blond hair in which light seemed to streak as if with the agitation of his brain.... She held her breath, wondering if that boy was really going to turn into the gate. Did he live here really? Was his room only across the corridor from her own?

Sometimes she stared secretly at him and saw that he seemed to be thinking rapidly, his mind racing. It showed on the surface of his skin, which was like the surface of water, rippling and shivering in tiny pinpricks. Yet when he answered her father's questions he was not nervous at all. He spoke like her father himself, echoing his rhythmic pauses, emphasizing certain words.... It was uncanny, how he drew himself up into a boy who was so precise and articulate, who spoke almost in the voice of an older man. The other day Dr. Pedersen had pursued him for thirty minutes, thirty minutes straight, asking about anatomy, even for verbal diagrams of human anatomy. Evidently Jesse had memorized a book on this subject. They had all sat at attention, letting their food grow cold, while Jesse answered these questions with only the briefest pauses. Hilda had felt her face get cold and hard, hearing all this. Jesse! The surprise of an adopted brother! The soft puffy surface of her skin broke into a dozen frown lines. *Why are you making faces?* her father had asked sharply.

She subsided into herself. Eating. All of them eating around her, at peace. She subsided into that secret part of her, as if she were the baby growing inside this immense body, herself the body, nourishing herself. At the outermost level of her flesh there was activity—she was eating. The jaws moved, the teeth ground and ground, there was a coarse, sinewy, dance-like motion to them. It was fascinating, that activity. The lips parted, the mouth opened, something was inserted into the opening, then the jaws began their centuries of instinct, raw instinct, and the food was moistened, ground into pulp, swallowed. It was magic. Around the table, drawn together by this magic, the family sat eating, all of them eating, glowing with the pleasure of eating together, in a kind of communion, their heads bowed as they ate. Hilda watched her father covertly and saw how his nostrils flared with the exertion of eating, his face slowly reddened, a handsome face, sharply handsome inside that pouched, bloated encasement of skin, his eyes sharp and glistening as the eyes of skinny, devilish birds.

Luncheon was over. They pushed back their chairs, rose from the table, Hilda among them. The bulky flesh called Hilda among them. Up. Chairs back. Walking, going away reluctantly. Dr. Pedersen came to her side and sighed wistfully, comically, sliding one arm through Hilda's. "You are a temperamental young lady, eh? A sensitive young lady? We must outfit you to your best advantage."

Yes, Father.

The big closet near the front door, where the coats were kept. A smell of redwood. Hilda's lightest winter coat, held up for her to slide her arms into—but Dr. Pedersen held it a little high, she had to struggle awkwardly to get it on. Hilda wished she could sit back at the table, all day long at the table, blind and deaf, alone, feeling the food quiet inside her as it was being digested and turned into blood and flesh. But no. She must get up from the table, must get dressed for the outside, must face the curious eyes of strangers.

Her father opened the wide front door and sucked in the chilly air.

"Ah, excellent! An invigorating day. This is a marvelous inch of history in which we are living, Hildie," he declared.

"Yes, Father."

"Never mind the pessimistic news broadcasts. Believe only what I tell you. I know how to interpret reality for you," he said.

They went out to the big black car.

"You must allow me to interpret everything for you, as Jesse does. Jesse is a child the way I was a child—watching, learning, grateful for all that is being given him. He understands what it would be like if I were to cast him back into that orphanage—he understands—he appreciates everything. And he is a child the way I was a child, absorbing everything, focusing his mind, his entire being, upon what has been pressed upon him. He will become the complete form of the self I have imagined for him. It's as if his future spirit and my spirit were in communion, right now. You and Frederich are geniuses, of course. Jesse is not a genius. You and Frederich are supernaturally gifted but you lack courage, you lack direction, you must be more obedient... you especially must be more obedient.... Is this understood?"

"Yes, Father."

"Yes, you are a genius and that is an awesome responsibility. But you are also a very pretty young lady. Is that understood?"

"Yes, Father."

They were driving down Locust Street now. Hilda wondered: Did her father speak of her as a genius because it was true (newspaper articles on her had always used that word), or because he wanted to wake her up, to reach into that deep private space beneath her heart? Did he know about her secret self, which was not his daughter at all or even a female? Did he know about the self that held back from him, that plotted against him?—she had even smashed a water glass once, wrapped in a towel, with the idea of grinding the glass down fine to put into his food, to kill him!

Maybe he knew everything.

Maybe he had made her up, given birth to her himself. Maybe he had sat in that dark inner office of his, in all that silence, and imagined her into being. A genius of a daughter. And a genius of a son. And now an adopted son, whom he obviously loved more than he loved his real children....

In the dress store.

The saleslady's smile wobbled like Jell-O. "Good afternoon, Dr. Pedersen," she said. Hilda's father greeted her cheerfully. He then sat with care in a gold-cushioned chair with curving arms that was a little too small for him. Crossed his legs and rubbed his hands together enthusiastically, as if this little outing into a women's dress shop was quite an adventure for him. The saleslady brought out three dresses. Very large sizes. Hilda shut her eyes for a moment. At the front of the store two women shoppers were watching.

"The green dress," Dr. Pedersen said.

The saleslady led Hilda back to the dressing room. "Would you like help?"

"No."

"Let me unhook your dress for you...."

"No. I can do it myself."

Hilda turned away.

She tried to close the curtain to the dressing room, but it was not wide enough. For a moment she froze. The space inside her cringed... she had all she could do to keep from counting, multiplying, dividing, imagining a mountain of numbers.... She could imagine a pyramid of numbers that was fourteen feet at its base and eleven feet high....

The saleslady was trying to help close the curtain.

"Nobody will come back here," she said.

"Somebody will see me...."

"No, dear, really... nobody will come back here...."

"Don't let anybody come back," Hilda said.

The saleslady smiled and left. Hilda tugged at the curtain again. But if it closed on one side it was about two inches too short on the other. "Oh, damn it, damn it," Hilda whispered. She gave up on the curtain and decided to try on the dress. The fitting room was very small, like a cage. She didn't understand how anyone could dress back here. Mirrors on three sides—she tried not to look into them. It was hard for her to unhook the dress. She had sewn the little hook in herself and now she had trouble getting it undone. Then the zipper. What if the zipper broke? Her elbow bumped against the wall and shocks ran up her arm. "Please, God, let me do this all right. Don't let Father be angry with me," she muttered. She had gotten the zipper down and now the dress was around her hips. It was strange that this dress was so tight, when she had made it herself as a joke, just a sack—but, yes, already it was getting tight. She pulled it down over her hips. She held her breath, hoping it would not rip. Then it was safely past her hips and down around her ankles.

Sweat.

Now the other dress! She hurried to get it on before someone came back and happened to see her. What if a delivery boy were to come back here? What if Father himself came back? Sometimes the back of her head tingled, she was so certain someone was watching her, and it never did any good to turn quickly and see —knowing that no one was there did not erase the guilty tingling sensation. She got the dress off the hanger and saw with dismay that it looked too small. Too small! She held it up against her body, staring down at it. A green dress with a white velvet bow at the neck, a party dress, it would make her look enormous . . . a huge cow. . . . Her armpits itched as if beetles were stinging her.

"Hildie. Hildie."

Her father was calling in a perfectly flat, uninflected voice.

"Yes, Father," she cried.

Ah, to get this new dress on!—she decided against bringing it down over her head and stepped inside it instead. She tugged at it. It was too small at the hips. But she had to get it on, she had to get it on. . . . Her father was calling. "Hildie. Will you hurry." She didn't know if he was really impatient or if he was just teasing. Her cheeks belled out in despair. She wanted only to shut her eyes, go blind and deaf, let her arms and legs float out anywhere, and imagine numbers: a cascade of numbers that multiplied themselves cleanly, without bodies, without substance, needing nothing that was flesh. Numbers. . . . But she shook herself awake. She was in a fitting room at the rear of Modern Fashions, her father was waiting for her, she had to get this dress up on her body. . . . She lost her balance and almost fell, she stepped forward abruptly and the dress caught her legs short at the knee. . . .

But it hadn't ripped!

Slowly, ah, slowly, she drew the dress up. She avoided looking in the mirror. Over her hips, slowly, slowly, but what a bright green it was—too tight—a droplet of sweat fell from her face onto the front of the dress—

"Hilda."

"Yes, Father. Yes."

Suddenly the saleslady was back, on the other side of the curtain. "Do you need any help with the dress, Miss Pedersen?" she asked timidly. "I'd be glad to—"

"No! go away!"

It was a terrible strain, getting the zipper up. She had to reach up behind herself, her arm twisted, her shoulder contorted . . . then, suddenly, she felt the dress rip under one arm. . . . She hesitated. Then she regained her courage and this time she got the zipper all the way up.

The dress was on!

She seemed now to be deep inside a body wearing a very tight green dress with a white bow in front.

Could she breathe? No time for that. The dress was too small, but there was no time, no time—her father's time was expensive and in the morning they were to fly to the MacLeod Institute— She hurried out to her father, whose suit coat was buttoned tight across his stomach, straining with impatience.

"Oh, no. No," he said.

He shut his eyes.

Back in the fitting room. Straining, struggling. In a few minutes she was stuffed inside another dress, two sizes larger than the green. Good. This was a brown dress with a small girlish collar. Fiercely she returned for her father's approval, hunted and panting in a body that had been measured, according to the clothing merchants of the world, as demanding a size 23 dress. Numbers whirled in front of her eyes, on the back of her eyelids, but she did not give in to them. Not yet.

Her father smiled this time. "Ah, yes, that is much better," he declared.

And so the dress was bought. It was only $29.98, in spite of its size.

Because she had been such a good girl, Dr. Pedersen took her to the Royal for a sundae. She did not mind people staring at them as they walked on the street. Alone, she would have been ashamed—she almost never went out by herself. But she was proud to be with her father, whom everyone knew. She considered slyly how striking they were, father and daughter, how terrible it must be for ordinary people to see them—Dr. Pedersen and his daughter, on the drab ordinary streets of Lockport, New York. The city was not large enough for them. It was not imaginative enough. Hilda felt as if her deepest self would explode, bursting open like a star, like a tiny seed in a speeded-up botany film. She was very happy.

They each had a sundae. Then Hilda had a banana split, because tomorrow was a special day. She was served the Banana Royal, which cost fifty cents: an enormous dish of puffs of cream, walnuts, dyed cherries, strawberry ice cream, chocolate ice cream, peppermint ice cream, and large bruised slices of banana. It had to be eaten quickly or it would melt. Hilda's mouth watered with hunger. There was no use now in thinking of numbers, the bodiless purity of numbers, adding up a column fifty digits high, reducing the galaxy of numbers to one—there was no use thinking of anything except the Banana Royal, which had to be eaten quickly before it melted.

She discovered that she was ravenously hungry.

As she ate, her father spoke gently: "If anything should happen to me, Hilda, you must remember the strength I have tried to give you. Always remember me like this, Hilda. That way you will always be strong. You will have me inside you, in a way, even after I am gone—inside you, carried around inside you. Do you understand?"

She stared.

"Do you understand, Hildie?"

She nodded. She understood, yes.

He talked and Hilda nodded as she ate. The ice cream seemed to be making her hungrier. Why was that? Of course she understood what her father was telling her. He knew about the tiny sac inside her, that elastic, magical emptiness that could never be filled no matter how much she ate. It was the size of a universe.

"It will go well tomorrow, my dear, don't worry. You are my good, good girl."

Her mouth watered like tears.

The doctors, the professors, greet me with those faces I have come to expect. I stare past them coldly, I don't talk, I let Father do the talking. There, there is my opponent . . . I find myself staring at him, my face going bright and tense while the doctors chatter their instructions. It is "Dr. Pedersen" this, "Dr. Pedersen" that. They are anxious to please him. They talk about me, around me, as if I can't hear.

Certain facts are stated and restated: This body I inhabit is fourteen years old.

The man at the other end of the table from me is thirty-four years old.

My name is Hilda Pedersen.

His name is Oscar DeMott.

Father is beside me, always beside me. I glance out at the audience in the little amphitheater—they are doctors, medical students, professors with curious faces. Jesse is sitting in the first row, large as an adult. One of the doctors is introducing us to the group. He is saying something about mimeographed material that has been passed around. Down at the other end of the table sits my opponent—that isn't a nice word, but it is true—and he looks younger than thirty-four. He stares at me and maybe he thinks I am older than fourteen. Well, we have not chosen our ages. We have not chosen our bodies. Oscar sits humped over in a wheelchair; his mother is sitting beside him, but unnaturally close to him, and she stares down at Father and me. The doctor is talking about Oscar now, who has come all the way up from Gainesville. I pay no attention to this but suck on a piece of hard candy. My mind teases me, anxious to escape. I run up numbers in the shape of a pyramid, as if flexing a muscle, set the pyramid upside-down, then on its right side.

"—Hilda?" the doctor is saying. He must have asked me a question. I didn't know that the examination had begun and I can only stare at him. I see in his face that look—that certain look—that everyone shows to me.

Father answers the question for me.

A long gleaming table. Ashtrays in front of all of us, even me. The brown dress feels too tight for me already, especially under the arms. Oscar is wearing a new bright blue suit and a striped tie. His mother, a gray-faced stringbean of a woman, is wearing a new yellow dress, obviously bought for this trip. Oscar DeMott: parchment skin, his teeth turned slightly inward and tainted, his nose long and skinny and nervous. I can see tiny hairs in the nostrils. His eyes are shadowed, like bruises. Perhaps he rubs his fists into his eyes. There is a tic in his cheek, hardly visible; I wish I couldn't see it. I see lots of things. My face tries to make itself smile across the table at Oscar's face.

Why isn't he Jesse, so that we could fight face to face?

Wired up. We are being wired up, Oscar and me. Lucky that the sleeves of my dress are so short. A strange device is put around my forehead. I ignore it. I ignore the young man who is wiring me up. I am back of my forehead, hiding. Oscar is too close to the surface of his skin, even if he is thirty-four years old and should know better—the tic jumps in his cheek, he seems frightened of the apparatus. They tell him it won't hurt. "It won't hurt, Oscar," his mother whines. She glances out at the audience, embarrassed. The lights glow. I pay no attention to them or to the men in the audience, not even to Jesse; I am dark and safe inside myself, multiplying numbers, crossing them out and multiplying them again.

". . . a casual session, chiefly conversation. . . . I hope you will look up and speak clearly. . . ."

Here we go.

The doctor is preparing to hold up a large white card with numbers on it. He stoops to get something else and in that instant I notice that there are forty-seven numbers on the card. I add them up at once and say the answer: "Five thousand, nine hundred, and—"

"Five thousand, nine hundred, and sixty-three," Oscar interrupts.

The doctor looks around at us, startled.

I shut my eyes and say loudly: "Multiplied in a series: four hundred and seventy-three million, seven hundred thousand—"

"Four hundred and seventy-three million, seven hundred thousand, two hundred—" Oscar cries shrilly.

—"and ninety-one!" I cry.

The audience stirs.

The doctor smiles nervously at us. "I hadn't intended the examination as such to begin yet," he says. "First, I thought we might begin with a simple demonstration of your ability to memorize numbers. . . . However . . ." He consults something in front of him, a batch of papers. He is uncertain. He must be looking up the answers; but we have already given him the answers. A few seconds pass awkwardly. I unwrap a candy bar and eat it in three swift bites. "Yes . . . I believe your answers are correct. . . ." the doctor is saying. "Now, Hilda, can you tell us how you came to your conclusion? Your first conclusion, the addition of those numbers?"

I crumple up the candy wrapper.

Silence.

"Well, Oscar, can you tell us? What were the thought processes you experienced?"

Oscar wipes his nose with one bony hand and says nothing.

"Is either of you aware of any process at all?" the doctor asks.

Oscar and I wait impatiently for the next card.

"Do you know the answer at once? Does no time at all elapse?"

Silence.

Out in the audience someone coughs. I stop looking out there, I turn my mind off. I run the numbers on that white card back and forth in my head, for something to do. Beside me Father sits proudly. He is at the end of the table. On my other side is another doctor, then Oscar and his mother, and at the far end of the table is the doctor who is talking. He is explaining that he would like to begin with a simple test of memorization. He flashes a card—what a joke! I shut my eyes after the first second and begin chanting the numbers. There are seventy-two of them. Oscar joins me, the two of us chanting as fast as we can. I think I finish a little ahead of Oscar.

The doctor beside me is taking notes.

"Would you please add up the numbers you have just seen . . . ?"

Oscar and I give the answer in unison.

"Correct . . . yes, that is correct. . . ." the doctor says. "Now, Hilda, could you comment at all on your performance? Do you know the answer instantly?"

I shut my eyes and see nothing.

"Hilda, you are being asked a question," Father says.

No. I shake my head.

"Oscar . . . ?"

Oscar says nothing. I can sense his impatience.

"Would you say that this process is at all visual? Do you actually see,

in your mind's eye, the numbers themselves? Or do you simply see the answer? Do you 'see' anything at all—or do you simply know the answer?"

Why does he ask such stupid questions!

After a few minutes he gives up. He holds up another card for us to memorize and multiply. At once Oscar and I look away from the card, shutting our eyes, and begin giving the answer at the same time.

"Correct . . . yes . . . that is correct. . . ."

The audience is stirring. Someone laughs incredulously. I am unwrapping another chocolate bar and my mouth aches to see that it is an almond cluster bar, my very favorite. I can sense people around me, uneasy people. Even Father is uneasy. Out in the little amphitheater some men are smoking. Smoke rises. I am careful not to look at Jesse there in the first row. Am I doing well? Are these people pleased? Father whispers, "Excellent, my dear," and pats my hand; his hand is like a paddle.

". . . a more difficult type of problem . . . involving several separate processes. . . ." the doctor is saying. Oscar and I have only to wait for him to finish all this, to come to the important part: the numbers. All the answers are in us, waiting. We know the answers to all questions. Why does it take these men so long to ask us the questions?

At last!

". . . the number whose cube minus fourteen, multiplied by seventy-nine is six hundred seventy-one thousand, five hundred and twenty. . . ."

Oscar and I give the answer instantly.

Now we look shyly at each other. He doesn't look much older than Frederich. He is sallow and sick and skinny; just looking at him makes me hungry for another almond cluster. I make too much fuss unwrapping it and Father has to say, "Don't be so eager, Hildie," and I see the eyes everywhere, watching me. I try to hide the candy bar in my lap.

The wires are uncomfortable on my head.

". . . you will raise to the sixteenth power," the doctor is saying slowly, reading out from a card, "the sum of the numbers I am going to show you . . ." and he holds a card up to us containing eleven numbers. I feel giddy. Oscar and I begin giving the number at once, rattling it off.

"Yes, that is correct. . . ."

A moment of silence. The doctor seems to have lost his place.

". . . these unusual gifts of the mind are often evident at an early age . . . in both Hilda Pedersen and Oscar DeMott this has been true. . . ." The doctor talks about us for a while, uncertainly. Someone in the audience puts up his hand; he asks a question; the doctor who sits beside

me answers it. I sift through their words and find no numbers, nothing to work with. I stop listening to them. At one point Father answers a question. He speaks for several minutes. Though I am not paying attention, I can sense how interested they are in him, in his answer. I take the candy bar out of my lap and bite into it.

Now a question begins: "... in an area of 143,658,992 cubic miles, how many units of 14,322 yards long by 443,225 yards wide by 36,115 yards thick...."

It takes me one, two, three seconds to think about this; Oscar hesitates too. Then we begin giving the answer, almost at the same time. We are both shouting.

Someone exclaims in surprise but I don't bother to look up. My heart is pounding. I want to snatch the wires away from my head and get free —I want to run around the table—and Oscar squirms nervously, one shoulder twitching. Another man is being introduced: "Dr. Miles Gordon of the MacLeod Institute will now conduct this examination...." Who are these people? I am a little confused. Father hands me a chocolate-covered marshmallow ball wrapped in tinfoil. I am starved. Saliva runs in a quick stream down the side of my chin and I have to wipe it away with my hand.

"The next series of questions will involve..."

I stop listening and begin again when the question is asked. Now I am so agitated that I have to take off the wires, I can't stand them holding me down.... So I snatch them off and push my chair back and stand up. I yell out the answer a split-second ahead of Oscar, I think. Father tries to get me to sit down, but I am too excited.

Great panting breaths. Gulps of this light-hot air.

Is Jesse watching? Is he proud of me?

The examiner asks another question and this time I can't stay still. I run to the end of the table and back again, giving the answer as I run. Oscar thumps his elbows on the table as he gives the answer, racing me. His wheelchair trembles.

"Yes, yes, that is correct... yes...."

The examiner smiles vaguely at Oscar and me. That look in his face: Oscar and I both recognize it.

"The next question will involve a slightly more complicated process of thought," the examiner is saying. What is this man's name? I know he is a doctor, I heard his name only a minute ago, but I can't remember.

"What are the days of the week?"

I answer at once: "MondayTuesdayWednesdayThursdayFridaySaturdaySunday!"

But Oscar says nothing.

He throws himself forward against the table. He begins to stammer and then cannot speak.

After a pause the examiner says: ". . . the months of the year? . . ."

Oscar cannot answer. I see this at once and I look away from him as I answer: "JanuaryFebruaryMarchAprilMayJuneJulyAugustSeptember OctoberNovemberDecember!"

Everyone is silent.

"And here is a quite different question. . . . What is the date of the second Sunday of August, 1941?"

I—

Oscar says at once: "August 12."

"Correct."

My mind is blank.

"And the third Wednesday of June, 1444?"

"June 20 on our calendar," Oscar says quietly.

"Correct."

Ashamed, I cram my mouth with something—some chocolate—I am ravenously hungry and dare not look at anyone.

"Oscar, would you explain to us your ability to answer these specific questions?"

Oscar says nothing.

Now they are hooking up the wires on me again, on my forehead, on a mountainous arm, around my mountainous chest, deft and furtive, as if they are anxious to get away from me. I ignore them. A young doctor and a nurse, I think it is a nurse, I ignore them. I hardly bother to chew the chocolate in my mouth; it is my jaws, my perfect teeth, that do the work.

". . . Hilda and Oscar, will you tell us exactly where you are?"

I look down at my hands sullenly. This is a joke. Oscar does not answer at all.

"Can you tell us the name of the place you are now in?"

"The MacLeod Institute," I say. This seems to be the right answer, so I go on. "235 West Bryant Drive, Queens, New York."

"Yes. And what is the date today?"

"April 23, 1941," I say.

But Oscar cannot answer.

The audience buzzes. Am I happy?—why am I fighting to get up again, pushing myself away from the table? I bump against someone's chair—the doctor next to me—and start to run to the end of the table, again, panting. I bend down to pull up my socks. Father calls out, "Hilda. Hilda, you are disturbing the examination—"

"It will be over in just a few minutes," the examining doctor says nervously, "just three or four minutes—"

"Ah, it is the eccentricity of the gift," Father says.

I yank up my socks. Is Jesse watching? Is he proud of me? My socks are a little dirty from the chocolate on my fingers. I run back to Father and I know that everyone is staring at me. Oscar's face working violently, as if he would like to get up too and run around the table. The wires on his forehead have slipped because his face is so damp.

Father catches me playfully and makes me sit down.

"The next several questions... the next several questions deal with feats of both memory and calculation," the examiner says. He speaks slowly and apprehensively. "Would you, Hilda and Oscar, would you multiply the fourth number on the first card that was held up to you by the seventh number on the second card—"

It takes me a few seconds to answer this question, but even so I am a little ahead of Oscar. But he too answers it, shouting. His eyes are darker now, as if the bruises have spread. His lips are trembling.

"Would you divide the sum of the numbers on the third card by the cube of the forty-third number on the eighth card...."

Five, six seconds pass. Where is the answer? And then the answer comes to me: I give it, fast. Oscar is answering at the same time. Before the doctor can ask us another question, I take a piece of candy out of Father's pocket and tear off the wrapper. Oscar's eyes are bulging. He is skinny as a crow, Oscar, with a caved-in chest. Poor Oscar!

"Oscar, are you all right? Should we terminate this session?"

He moans, shaking his head from side to side.

"Perhaps we should terminate... ?"

Everyone looks at Oscar. But why should I believe in those faces? In my own face? Behind Oscar's face someone is hiding and I see him, in the shadowed eyes, in the tic in his cheek, struggling.

"No you don't!" Mrs. DeMott cries.

Oscar says nothing.

"But is your son... How is your son?" the doctor asks.

"You just ask him the next question. He's fine."

Oscar takes the handkerchief from her and wipes his own face. He seems better now.

". . . this final question . . . involves a number of distinct assumptions and processes. Would you please, Hilda and Oscar, add to the date of the third Wednesday of April, 1265 by our calendar the total of your two ages multiplied together. . . ."

Choking.

The chocolate is choking me.

Oscar begins to whimper.

I am choking, suffocating. My eyes bulge like Oscar's; but he is moaning, shaking from side to side—

"Oscar!" his mother cries.

She falls across him. Someone shouts. There is confusion, people are moving around, the big stage lights go out. Like the blinking of an eye! We are suddenly in shadow, in an eclipse. Good. Now they will not stare at me. I manage to eat the last chocolate while everybody is standing, moving. Father himself springs to his feet. Oscar has fallen over sideways, blood is streaming from his nose, one of the doctors is bending over him. I can't see. I don't want to see. I shut my eyes hard and my mouth chews away on something soft, a sweet gushing circle of chocolate. Is it Mother weeping over me? That sound of a woman weeping?

They are bringing in a stretcher for Oscar. Mrs. DeMott is yelling, "Oh, this always happens! He's a freak, a curse! You keep him, you people take care of him! Wets his bed, can't feed himself. Call him a genius! Well, he is a freak no matter what the newspapers say and you bastards can have him for good! Put him in a cage with that other one!"

I run over to the other side of the stage.

Father comes after me, saying my name. But I turn away from him. A fountain of numbers shoots up in the air. . . .

I am saying No. No. Father takes hold of my arm. I jerk away from him. No. The numbers spin into a tower, fatter and fatter at the top, not like an ordinary tower. "Get away! Leave me alone! I have to figure it out!" I scream. Father's face is white, white as uncooked dough. "Add to the date of the third Wednesday of April, 1265 by our calendar the total of your two ages multiplied together—" I shove something in my mouth, I press it into my mouth with both hands—

Someone is screaming. It is a girl's voice. She is screaming up into the white shocked face of Dr. Pedersen. "The tower will give me the answer! It will figure itself out if I wait! Don't touch me, don't come near me—nobody come near me—" And still the tower floods upward, a galaxy of numbers. How can I make them into a single number? How can I still the bursting of these numbers? She clutches her own head, her own face, squeezing it hard. Must stop that screaming. Must make the numbers slow, slow, come to a stop, turn into a single number....

"Hilda, you are going to be sick—"

"Don't touch me!"

Screaming. Stumbling backwards. The faces in the audience are scattered now. Hilda is baffled. Hilda clutches her own head. Her father tries to quiet her, but she jerks away from him. "You want to stuff me inside your mouth, I know you! I know you!" she cries. "You want to press me into a ball and pop me into your mouth, back where I came from! You want to eat us all up!"

"Hilda—"

And now another face appears—a boy has run up on stage—

"Don't touch me, any of you!" I cry.

"Please, Hildie—" says this boy.

Jesse.

"No—"

"It's all right, Hildie, it's all right—"

Add to the date of the third Wednesday of April, 1265....

Father is going to take me home now, Jesse says.

"No, don't touch me! I don't want—"

I am crying.

Jesse takes hold of my hands.

"You hurt Father's feelings," he whispers.

Father is standing a few feet away—staring at us. Father is staring.

"Father wants to kill me. Eat me," I whisper.

"No," says Jesse.

I am very cold. Someone is shivering on the surface of my skin.

"I don't want anyone to touch me...."

And now I am weeping.

Like a girl. Fourteen years old. My new dress is soiled, wrinkled, I am ashamed. I have been saying crazy things. Now the tower of numbers has faded... the last number has left my head... I am standing here with my brother, who is trying to talk to me, to explain something....

"... over to Father now? You don't want to hurt his feelings," Jesse says.

"Yes."

Jesse gives me a handkerchief. But I am too clumsy to use it. So he pats my forehead with it himself. Forehead, cheeks, chin. A thread of saliva hangs down from my mouth and Jesse wipes it away. He is very nervous—a tall, stout boy, the freckles on his face glowing from perspiration—but still he cleans me up as I stand here in my heavy hot body, weeping.

"Now you're all right, Hildie. Everything is all right," he says.

He takes me to Father.

I stumble, almost lose my balance. I have to stop my mind from scattering and flying back to—to what?—to a question that doctor asked me? But now Father is speaking gently to me. There are tears in his eyes. He takes the handkerchief from Jesse and wipes my nose with it. I go into myself, coiling inward. Inward. Back to that small hollow space beneath my heart, where I will be safe.

"My poor girl.... You don't know what you said to your father ... the awful things you said to your own father...."

I am walking between Father and Jesse. Faces in the hallway peer at me but I don't care. I am already deep inside myself. I am a good girl. I will not scream at Father ever again in my life.

A drinking fountain. Oh, I am so thirsty! So thirsty! "Everybody loves you. You are a good, good girl," Father is saying. "You are a genius and a very pretty young lady." The water bubbles up onto my face, into my nose. I begin to cough.

Now we are riding somewhere. Pavement, traffic. At the airport I sit without seeing anyone. I run the numbers back and forth in my mind, all the numbers on all the cards, rearranging them, multiplying them, dividing them by one another. Father reads to Jesse and me from a newspaper—an article about a woman in El Paso, Texas, who had five babies and named them One, Two, Three, Four, and Five. Father laughs at this. Must clip it out for the Book of Fates, *he says. Hilda laughs like any fourteen-year-old girl, but I sit puzzled and silent and frightened. Where did those babies come from? What is a baby, exactly?*

The seat belts do not fasten across our laps. Father and I are sitting together in the plane; Jesse sits across the aisle from us. The plane rises into the air. Hilda looks out the window, interested and perky, but I sit very still, in a panic. Panic. Hilda is a good, good girl, but I am not a girl at all, not even a woman. I don't know what I am. Is there a part of the soul that is not male or female? Hilda loves Jesse, her own brother, but I am not Hilda and I do not love Jesse or even know who he is. I don't understand him. "Look, Hilda," Father says, to cheer me up, and he points out the window at what I am already looking at—a city down below of buildings, so many buildings—enormous buildings—a city of walls and streets and strangers—and they multiply out to the horizon, they cannot be held back, they have been created by Father, or men like Father, all over America—

"Beautiful! Isn't it beautiful?" Father says happily.

I am eating peppermints, light, wafer-thin peppermints, because I am not really hungry. Hilda eats, knowing that she will get an appetite as she eats; I am not hungry at all. I am dead. Down below there is a stretch of land that is made up only of buildings and houses, crisscrossed by roads, streets, avenues, highways, everything multiplying itself as we rise higher—

We are at the center of the universe.

"Jesse has promised not to say anything to your mother or to Frederich about what happened today," Father says. "They wouldn't understand. Hilda, don't you want these? Aren't you hungry?"

He hands the peppermints to me.

No.

"Yes, thank you, Father."

I eat. I am curled up in a sac, in a body. A mountain of flesh on a cushioned seat. Stumps of legs ending in ankles and feet and shoes. Oh, I am resting here with my father; I am very tried.

"We won't take you on another trip like this for a while," Father says. "Until you're ready."

"Yes, Father."

"Until you are more mature, perhaps. Perfection is difficult, Hildie, but ultimately it is not as difficult as imperfection. The demands we make upon ourselves constitute our salvation. It is necessary to be perfect. It is not necessary to live."

"Yes, Father."

"How do you feel now, Hildie? Are you better?"

"Yes, Father."

"You are a little tired?"

"Yes, Father."

"Well, then. Sleep. Sleep, my dear."

Hilda lays her head on Father's shoulder and sleeps. I do not sleep. I do not think.

I am dead.

9

He was aware of her in the house with him, treading on the stairs heavily, sighing. When he worked at his mathematical problems—he was studying calculus on his own, with the help of one of the teachers at his school—he thought of her, in her room or downstairs where she often worked, and he thought of her mother, the two of them mixed up in his mind, pressing against him with their soft, gelatinous bodies.

Hilda.

Mrs. Pedersen.

Sometimes his mind went blank. He did not like calculus; it seemed to him like a dream; there was nothing behind it, its formulations. Other textbooks did not trouble him like this—he could memorize anything that had a reality behind it. He did not have to touch this reality, to move his fingers across it, he had only to know that it existed somewhere and might be measured, might be cut out and held up triumphantly to the light.... But mathematics disturbed him. A stunning whirl of numbers, insubstantial numbers, signs with nothing behind them that somehow corresponded to ideas in the brain.... No, he could not understand. He sat in his room at the large, glass-topped desk Dr. Pedersen had bought for him, his hands kneading his face, until he gave up and went to ask Hilda for help.

What was a freak?

No, he did not ask her that. He asked her about his calculus problems, shyly, knowing that she was contemptuous of him. Each afternoon Hilda worked downstairs on the sun porch at the rear of the house, and Frederich worked in the music room, off and on, out of sight. When Jesse knocked on the opened door politely, he saw how severely his sister looked at him—her face strained, her small, close-set eyes leaping upon him. Jesse thought of the mother of that other prodigy, Oscar, who had called both her son and Hilda freaks. But what was a freak, exactly? Jesse was uneasy in his sister's presence, unnerved by her solid, silent, ponderous face, her pudgy ink-stained fingers, her ironic smile, which was an exaggeration of her mother's generous smile. She had a face drained of blood, of energy, and yet it was intensely alive, alert, suspicious, as if she could read his mind or was aware of him listening for her heavy footsteps on the stairs—Jesse listening for her sighing, her wistful, lonely sighing—Jesse conscious of her contempt. When she lowered her eyes, he gazed at her bluish lids, which were shaped like half-moons or thumbs, like her mother's, quite thick and prominent against the bone above her eye. He stared at these eyelids, sensing the rapid movement of this girl's mind, the incredible flash of illumination that always gave her the correct answers to any mathematical questions.

Always the correct answers. . . .

She was never wrong. But it gave her no joy, he saw. She was like an instrument to provide answers to questions; always polite to him, coolly polite now in the months since that examination in New York, always patient with him while he sat and tried to work out the problem in orderly, logical steps, using a normal method. He sat across from her at the table on the porch, his ankles linked around the bottom rung of his chair, his face turned down to the paper before him. He was slow and firm, pressing down hard with the point of his pencil, staring at the blank white paper and the numbers that slowly filled the page, always ending with the number Hilda had given him minutes before.

And he would sit back, dazed, exhausted.

What was a freak?

She was like a princess in this part of the house, "her" part of the house. She liked the sun porch and worked down there every afternoon, sitting with a piece of long yellow scrap paper before her, doodling with a fountain pen, thinking. Occasionally she wrote down a number. But most of the time she drew lines and circles and meaningless figures. It was impossible to know what she was doing. She could not explain. She had no interest in explaining. Dr. Pedersen had encouraged her to begin a correspondence with someone in England, and she had answered a few of this unknown man's letters, but then she gave up, bored. She was always alone like this, always thinking. Fallen deep in thought. Jesse came to the doorway with the tentative note of

Frederich's piano behind him, and he saw how sharply Hilda's eyes swung up to him, as if out of a dark, somber spell; her face became more guarded and strained.

"Oh, you want help again today . . . ?" she said ironically.

The sun porch was a large airy room at the rear of the house. Two walls were made entirely of glass. Everywhere were Mrs. Pedersen's plants—some in large earthernware pots, some hanging in delicate china bowls, pots of small-leafed ivy, pots of flowers, even an orange tree in a dumpy ceramic pot, all the plants erect and bright and mysterious to Jesse. They had about them the shiny, hopeful manner of Mrs. Pedersen herself, only wanting to please.

Since the trip to New York, Hilda had grown more silent in Jesse's presence. She had gained weight. Beneath her chin flesh was squeezed cruelly, as if held back. She helped him with his work in silence, scrawling answers for him. In the background Frederich was working at his music—always the slow notes, the single notes, falling with the precision of icicles, relentless and maddening. For many months Jesse had often shut his eyes hard, grimacing, in order to bear his brother's music, but nothing changed, the notes did not stop or speed up, they did not blossom into anything, and after a while Jesse really stopped hearing them. *What is a freak? Was he turning into a freak himself?*

When Jesse and Hilda worked together, Mrs. Pedersen sometimes hovered in the doorway, come to water her plants or to pinch off buds or to join them in a snack, tempting them with food. Hilda would often turn irritably away from her mother. "I can't concentrate with you here, Mother. Your breathing annoys me. You make the floor creak."

Jesse was shocked at her rudeness.

"Mother makes the floor sag," Hilda said. "The whole house will collapse around her one of these days."

"She's just teasing," Jesse told Mrs. Pedersen.

"She's always teasing me, she's always picking on me," Mrs. Pedersen said hesitantly, but with a little smile, while her daughter sat looking away from her, drumming her fingers. "That's because she spends too much time alone . . . she should get outside with other girls . . . she's always teasing me because we're home here together all day long, every day. . . ." She would laugh breathlessly, as if her daughter's odd behavior were just a joke. But, once allowed on the porch, she became animated and jovial; she peered at Jesse's calculus textbook and at the pages of numbers and symbols he had been working with, and shook her head. "At first it was just Hilda who could manage things like that, and now you too.... When you came to live with us, Jesse, I was grateful for you because you were just like me. I said to Dr. Pedersen, thank heavens he's like me! He isn't like those other two! But *now*—now you're getting like Hilda herself—"

"No, not like Hilda," Jesse said quickly.

Hilda snickered.

"There's a big difference between us," Jesse said.

"But at least you're going to college. I'm so proud of you, skipping a year of high school and being accepted at college already, so fast.... Dr. Pedersen is very proud of you too. He might not say so, but he is. Our little friend here, Hilda, has refused to continue her education at all. It seems to everyone in the family that a genius might want to develop herself as far as possible, but not our Hilda."

Jesse had been accepted at the University of Michigan for the fall semester; he had written for syllabi for some of his courses and was preparing for them. But he was embarrassed to talk about this in front of Hilda.

"Well, what do you say?" Mrs. Pedersen asked her daughter.

"Suppose I left home," Hilda said angrily. "You'd only try to get me back again!"

"Would I?"

"Yes, you would!"

"Oh, would I miss you?" Mrs. Pedersen laughed. "All you do is sit out here and mumble to yourself... grumble... don't even help me with my plants or with the cooking... always finding fault with me... can't even put your clothes in the laundry before they're filthy—"

"Mother, leave me alone! Go away!"

"Isn't she saucy? She always was saucy," Mrs. Pedersen said heartily. Jesse was embarrassed. He looked at the two of them, mother and daughter, two women with soft, rather pretty features that were similar, the same fair frizzy hair, the same tublike shapes. But Mrs. Pedersen's skin was of a lively, tender color, while Hilda's was sallow, even a little discolored, as if from ill health; Mrs. Pedersen's manner was girlish and bouncy, Hilda's was sluggish; Mrs. Pedersen was like a young girl at a party, crudely curious, looking around to see what she might be missing, ready to march up and intrude upon any group, while Hilda always hung back, cautious even when she sat in her usual chair here on the porch or at the dining room table. Her eyes swung around morosely to meet her mother's smile.

"You bring chaos in here. More than anyone else," Hilda whispered.

"What?"

"Chaos will absorb me," Hilda said, pressing her hands against her eyes as if to blot out her mother.

Jesse was not sure if he had heard her correctly. "What are you mumbling about now?" Mrs. Pedersen said with an exasperated sigh.

Hilda sat lumpish and still.

Mrs. Pedersen went on brightly, "I'll make her come around and be nice to us, Jesse, just watch! I spent all morning making peach ice cream, Hilda's favorite kind. Just you watch her come around!"

Hilda smiled.

"Oh yes," she said.

"Would you like some ice cream, Hilda? Homemade peach ice cream?"

"You know that my nature is coarse and greasy and bottomless. You know there is no end to me. You know I am always hungry," Hilda said.

And Mrs. Pedersen hurried out to the kitchen.

"What did you mean—chaos?" Jesse asked.

Hilda screwed the cap on her fountain pen angrily. She said nothing. She would not look at him.

Sometimes Mrs. Pedersen brought them ice cream, sometimes fudge or cake, puddings, candies, slabs of pie with whipped cream; tall icy milkshakes in hot weather, or fruit drinks with scoops of sherbet in them. She brought these things in on a large silver tray, as if she were serving important guests. She always seemed pleased to sit with them. Sometimes Hilda remained at the table, but sometimes her mother's lively chatter got on her nerves and she excused herself with an excessively polite smirk, and went up to her room as soon as she finished eating.

Mrs. Pedersen wore bright colors, like her flowers. Big splotches of color—plaids and checks—straining enormously across her broad back, her hair pulled back cheerfully, tiny diamond earrings in her ears. She was always panting with merriment, eager to joke with Jesse and her daughter, ignoring Hilda's odd pronouncements. If Hilda said flatly, "Mother, none of us washes often enough, not even you," she pretended to have heard nothing or to have heard a joke instead; the flash of a smile she sent Jesse was pitiful. Once Hilda said, "Jesse will want to leave us, he'll want to run away before it's too late." Mrs. Pedersen shook her head and caught Jesse's eye, exasperated. "Yes, he will, Mother. He'll run away. He'll escape. He knows more than Frederich and I do," Hilda said mockingly.

When Mrs. Pedersen left them, Jesse said to her, "Why do you insult your mother? You know she loves you."

Hilda stared at him.

"She loves you. You know it. They all love you. We all love you," Jesse said.

Hilda's gaze moved slowly down, away from his face. Her face closed into an expression of inestimable sadness.

"We all love you," Jesse said, his heart pounding.

As soon as Dr. Pedersen came home in the late afternoon, however, the mood of the house was changed. Everything changed. The dining table was being prepared for dinner. Dr. Pedersen sometimes went upstairs to change his shirt again, and reappeared with a freshened, robust complexion; he clapped his hands together, teased his wife, asked Jesse how the day had been. Dinner began promptly at six-thirty. The meal was like a race—everyone ate fast, skillfully, as if there might not be enough food—but it was also like a race because they were being questioned closely, eyed closely, by Dr. Pedersen. He would begin casually with his wife. *What did you accomplish today, dear?* And Mrs. Pedersen would haltingly list the things she had done around the house: food prepared, closets cleaned, a telephone call to check on her father, letters written, some checks sent out, a call to the Reverend Wieden about some matter. . . . And then Hilda was examined briefly. Hilda's replies were laconic. Jesse did not understand them and he began to see, as time passed, that Dr. Pedersen did not understand them either. When Frederich was questioned he replied at once, but his replies often did not make sense. *Transcribing a Brahms string quartet into a parodic suite in the style of Ives . . . ?* Jesse did not know what this meant. It was a composition Frederich had been working on for the last several months. Jesse glanced at his brother and thought he could see, in Frederich's courteous expression, a certain lidded, mocking, heretical look. Did Dr. Pedersen notice? Frederich was perhaps no longer the favorite son. . . . He had had several teeth extracted in June, and in July his gall bladder had become infected; he had not lost weight, but he looked smaller, like a partly-deflated balloon, the skin hanging sullenly and evilly about the sides of his face, down toward his neck, giving him the appearance of an intelligent frog. His voice was lazy and rather womanish. When he had been admitted to the hospital for the gall-bladder operation, it had taken five attendants, so Jesse had heard, to load him onto his bed, and his doctor, a colleague of Dr. Pedersen's named Wascom, had complained of his behavior there—he hadn't cooperated, he had been childish and demanding, he had insulted the nurses. Dr. Pedersen had defended Dr. Wascom, a member of his profession, against Frederich himself, who had wanted another doctor: "Why are you such an infant, at your age, with your powers! Do you want to degenerate, do you want your brain to turn into baby food? A son of mine!" Red-faced, very angry, Dr. Pedersen had been ashamed of Frederich's behavior at the hospital, and in the several weeks since that time there had been a tension between them, so that Dr. Pedersen's questions at the dinner table were put to Frederich in a detached, cool way, as if he did not really expect any sane reply.

"Would you explain that further, please, Frederich?"

"I am extending the atonal scale; I am seeking to dramatize, by means of tripartite harmony, the essential suicidal nature of the traditional quartet. The quartet is notoriously difficult to write, you know."

And then it was Jesse's turn.

If Dr. Pedersen could not make much sense of his other children, he could always make sense of Jesse. Jesse had a great deal to report: halfway through the calculus textbook, then all the way through it, all the way through the syllabus for one of his Michigan courses, chapter after chapter of a book on organic chemistry, the memorization of innumerable charts in the physiology book Dr. Pedersen had given him, charts showing blood pressure, the size and admixture of tissues in the walls of the different blood vessels, everything about the heart and its properties.... He could recite for minutes at a time, while the family sat and listened: "The primordia of the heart are contained in the mesoderm on either side of the foregut invagination of the mammalian embryo. The embryonic cardiac tube is formed..." He saw the glaze in Frederich's eyes—now it was Frederich who did not know what he was talking about!—he felt Hilda's restlessness, Mrs. Pedersen's awe. He could talk about the endocrine system, answer Dr. Pedersen's most minute questions on it, he could recite the gross anatomy of the various glands. Sometimes dinner was halted temporarily while Dr. Pedersen, growing taller at the head of the table, pursued Jesse with enthusiastic questions. He was always asking, "Well, then, how can life be maintained *if*..." and Jesse always had a reply, slow and firm as the steps he took in his mathematical problems, his brain working without much imagination. He groped his way, he crossed a dangerous stream stepping on big round firm stones, he rarely made a mistake; if, finally, he did not know the answer to Dr. Pedersen's question, he admitted he did not know.

"Ah, that is the beginning of wisdom," Dr. Pedersen would say.

On Sundays, Grandpa Shirer often came for dinner if he was well enough; and the Pedersens often invited some of Jesse's teachers from the high school. Once Dr. Pedersen had Jesse recite an entire chapter from a text on physiology. Jesse spoke easily, slowly; he obeyed his father in everything. But he believed he could sense uneasiness around the table—were they bored by his knowledge or disturbed by it? Was he beginning to frighten people the way Hilda frightened them?... When he finished, everyone congratulated him. Frederich smiled a kind of smile, curt and frosty; Hilda with her heavy-lidded mocking smile, whispered, "You sound just like Father!" Dr. Pedersen was so pleased with Jesse's performance that the next day he drove downtown to an automobile agency and bought him his own car.

Now that he had been admitted to the University of Michigan

he already thought of himself as a college student and therefore a very serious person; so, in midsummer, he began driving the twenty or so miles to the University of Buffalo library, conscious of the beginning of a new segment of his life. And yet it was a seamless break, a gentle transition from the Pedersen household to this car—a black Dodge, modest in its trim and equipment—and to the university library in Buffalo. Driving the car his father had given him was a precious responsibility. He was conscious of Dr. Pedersen with him, in the car with him, guiding him, warning him of oncoming speeders and tricky intersections; he carried the presence and the power of Dr. Pedersen with him all the way to Buffalo, Dr. Pedersen's being extended in Jesse's no matter how far he might drive. He went to Buffalo two or three times a week.

On other days Mrs. Pedersen begged him to take her out for little drives below Lockport, down toward Lake Ontario and Olcott Beach. She could not drive; she had never learned, and Dr. Pedersen believed now that it was too late for her to learn; anyway, she told Jesse apologetically, she was a nervous person so perhaps it was better that she had never gotten a driver's license. Didn't he agree? He avoided answering this question, and to offset it he agreed to take her out for drives. It took so little to please her—she loved the look of warm summer fields, the orchards of apple trees, pear trees, cherry trees, peach trees, the farmers' roadside stands where she could buy baskets of fruit, eating them right in the car as Jesse drove along the dusty country roads, his mind half attending his mother's happy chatter and half attending its own concerns, his work, his studies, which had nothing to do with the heat-riddled landscapes of Niagara County. Sometimes on the warmest of days when the sun porch was stuffy and Hilda's round, pale face was blotched with heat rash and even the numbers in her head were not enough to absorb her interest, Mrs. Pedersen talked Hilda into joining them.

"Hilda is hungry, I know," Mrs. Pedersen would tease. "Let's stop right away for some ice cream!"

And they would stop—at ice cream stands, fruit stands, at roadside diners, anywhere. Food bought on the road, the surprise of food bought from strangers: what a joyous summer! Jesse was pleased that he could make his mother happy so easily.

He wanted to think about his work, he yearned to get back to the university library, and yet he found himself with Mrs. Pedersen constantly.... Her own children had grown morose and strange, and so Mrs. Pedersen had herself become childlike. Even her puffy legs in their silk stockings—tight to bursting—had a childish, innocent appearance, sticking out like gay light-tinted sausages beneath the hem of her flowery dresses. If Hilda accompanied them, she directed her remarks to Hilda so that Jesse might overhear: "Why can't you and Frederich be more like Jesse? He has such good manners. *He* doesn't go around with a long face, moping all day like a certain young lady I know. Grandpa Shirer always says, *If you make a face, it'll freeze that way.*" And Hilda might reply at once: "My grandfather never said such rubbish in his entire life." If they were alone, Mrs. Pedersen talked to Jesse endlessly and wistfully as she ate cherries and spat the pits out carefully into her stained palm and then put the pits in a paper bag; she talked of Dr. Pedersen's many projects—it seemed they were always passing land he had just bought or was trying to buy, or a roadside poster put her in mind of a new invention of his he was having patented—or she talked of her girlhood, which had evidently been spent exclusively in Lockport, or she talked of her children and how she suddenly felt so lonely now, in her forties, of how the big house frightened her even though Hilda and Frederich were always at home, of how she feared that Dr. Pedersen might overwork himself and have a heart attack, she feared that Frederich would become seriously ill, that Hilda would become more silent, more abrasive, until, like one of Dr. Pedersen's brilliant younger brothers, she would have to be "put away"—this terrified Mrs. Pedersen and she did not even dare to talk about it with her husband.

"I don't have anyone to talk to, Jesse," she said softly.

Sometimes she came across a tiny white worm in one of the cherries she was eating and, with a stifled scream, she threw the cherry out the car window.

Jesse brought along books to read, and on a deserted stretch of beach on Lake Ontario Mrs. Pedersen would wade in the cold water, avoiding the small dead fish, shrieking with pleasure as if to call Jesse's attention to her; but Jesse turned off his mind politely. He had work to do. He felt, uneasily, that time was running out for him. Mrs. Pedersen would stroll up the beach a quarter of a mile, gathering bits of driftwood and odd-shaped stones, walking barefoot so that her feet made deep prints in the sand that filled slowly with water, while Jesse read or tried to read, conscious of something strange in the crashing of the waves, something inexplicable and dangerous in the loneliness of the beach.

When they drove back home, Mrs. Pedersen was always reluctant to return to the house on Locust Street, and so Jesse would find himself driving slowly up and down the hills of Lockport, along Clinton Street and Gooding Street, Water Street, Plank Road, down by the sewerage disposal units, out by the city dump, out by Atwater Park and the gorge; he sometimes parked at the "world's largest single-span bridge" while Mrs. Pedersen stood at the railing, watching for barges to come through the locks. If a barge was actually partway through the locks, Mrs. Pedersen exclaimed as though she were a tourist and had never seen such a sight, and had to wait until the boat got all the way through. Her posture was arch and expectant, as if she believed that at any moment something extraordinary was going to happen. The barges and the occasional tugboats were drab and ugly, loaded with coal or steel or scrap metal, or not loaded at all, riding high upon the canal waters. They made their passage through the series of locks very slowly, like ancient vessels. Jesse got out to stand beside Mrs. Pedersen at the railing, recalling how he had stood there many months before, when he had been a stranger to Lockport and to his new family.... How long ago that was! And how different he was now, how totally changed he was—for his face had matured, and certainly he looked different, having gained over eighty pounds.

People who passed Mrs. Pedersen and Jesse on the bridge glanced at them oddly. What did they see?

It distressed Jesse that he must always exist in the eyes of others, their power extended in him though he did not choose them, did not choose them deliberately at all. They were a pressure on him, in his head, a pressure he loathed. He turned his mind away. Yes, he still liked to stare down at the locks. Water levels rising, falling—furious little man-made waterfalls—men far below the bridge, going about their work. Everything was ordinary. Everything was perfect, in miniature. Long, thin rays of sunlight stretched everywhere, onto the rock at the side of the canal, onto the cement and iron railings and warning signs and the glinting windows of the officials' building far below, scanning the surface of the dark water. There was a cool, bluish tone to the shadow that fell from the bridge onto the water. Jesse felt a little dizzy. He could not distinguish between the crashing drone of the water and Mrs. Pedersen's chatter in his ear.

At the University of Buffalo he made his way through small crowds of students, many of them girls, on his way to the library. He climbed a long, slow hill, watchful of the people about him—these young people who never seemed to notice him, or who glanced at him and then away, not recognizing him as a person nearly their own age. The girls seemed delicate and insubstantial, because he was accustomed to the heartier forms of his mother and sister. These girls, with their long, curled hair and their summer dresses, did not seem real to him. Such pretty faces!—but they were not quite real. Jesse sat reading in the library for hours. Electric fans cooled the building but did not reduce the humidity. Sometimes Jesse was distracted by a young woman sitting across from him, and his face grew warm, his forehead filmed over with perspiration, though he knew the girl would not look at him—he was not an attractive boy, he knew, with his serious heavy face and his suits and ties and perfect polished shoes. It would have been difficult for anyone to guess his age. Sixteen? Twenty-five? Thirty?

After hours of reading he had to rub his eyes to ease them. Was his vision failing? He would get glasses like Dr. Pedersen's, wide-rimmed, with wires that curved precisely behind the ears. And he would become a doctor, he would take on the appearance of a doctor. . . . Around him were young men who would probably be going into the army in a few months, whose conversation was often about the "war," when Jesse chanced to overhear it, but Jesse did not think about the war in Europe; it was not quite real to him. Dr. Pedersen had said that in twenty years there would be another war anyway. Always another war! *War is programmed in the genes of man*, Dr. Pedersen said. The thought seemed to please him and so it pleased Jesse as well. There would always be a war somewhere. Nothing came to an end; just like these streams of sweet-faced, birdlike young women who made their way along the university paths—there was no real ending to them, their legs carried them safely everywhere, pulsing like protoplasm in the warm rich sunlight. At times Jesse felt a sense of joy, knowing he was destined to serve such women. He would be a doctor. He would serve these people, save them from pain and terror, preserve the beauty of their bodies—the gross, sensual, gleaming beauty of female bodies, even these slender bodies! He sometimes paused, smiling, and stared at a girl—the look of her perfect body would inspire a peculiar, sharp hunger in him, in his mouth—pinpricks of desire in his mouth that caused his saliva to flow. When men came along his eye darted to them, jealously and then admiringly, for they were not really rivals of his . . . he was pleased at the way the young men strode by the women, men in a field of females, making their way firmly, unconsciously; he loved to see the men overtake the women, fall into step with them, talk to them, brush against them accidentally. . . . The females seemed to Jesse mere lovely animal life, surging and shimmering in the sun, and he, Jesse Pedersen, a point of scrutiny inside the field of their movement, an intelligence to give direction to their energy, sharing in the accidental touching of their flesh by the men. Their skin was so tender, so sweet, it might be stretched out seamlessly for hundreds of yards, lacking identity, belonging to any of them. . . . Occasionally he saw a younger boy, skinny and ill-clothed, maybe half his size, hiking up the hills in long awkward strides, looking too frail for the race, and he felt his heartbeat quicken as he thought of his own future, his own fate as Karl Pedersen's son, going out into the world to serve the sick, to carry on his father's dedication. . . .

But he wouldn't be going into such a future if his other father hadn't killed everyone in the family.

And then, in August, a few weeks before he was to leave for Ann Arbor, two strange things happened.

Mrs. Pedersen had been begging him to take her along to Buffalo so that she could shop. Finally he agreed reluctantly—so many miles of her chatter! She was complaining now of dizzy spells, of Frederich not brushing his teeth, of Hilda not bothering to change her underwear for days at a time—"By the time she puts it in the wash it's just filthy!"—and her whining was like a constant draft against the side of his head, maddening him. She complained of his plans to go to college. In a few weeks he would be gone, she said. He would be far away in Michigan and he wouldn't think of them at all.

"I'll write every week. I'll call you," Jesse promised.

"You'll be too busy. You and your books," she said.

Jesse left her off at Main Street and he went to the library; but when he returned, at the time they had planned to meet, she was not there. He stood at the corner and waited, looking up and down the streets, waiting for her to appear and call to him. After a while he began to worry. Had he forgotten the correct time? Was he in the wrong place? If she wasn't there soon they would be late returning to Lockport and Dr. Pedersen —who did not know about these trips of Mrs. Pedersen's—would be very angry.

He got so nervous that he stepped into a drugstore and bought several candy bars to eat while waiting for her.

And then . . . and then he caught sight of an extremely fat woman in the distance, nearly hidden by a late-afternoon crowd of shoppers . . . she moved with a strange bobbing motion, like a boat or a huge cork . . . her bright yellow dress was a terrible assault upon the eye. It was Mrs. Pedersen. Yes. People turned to look at her, some children circled her, giggling, and Jesse was embarrassed for her until he saw that she didn't notice—she was walking in a daze, her face moonstruck and stark, and she would have passed by within a few feet of him if he hadn't called out, "Mother!"

She gaped at him, frightened. Her eyes could not focus.

"What's wrong? What happened to you?" Jesse cried.

"A little . . . little dizzy," she said. She stood for several minutes without moving, while Jesse glanced miserably at the faces of passers-by. He wondered if the sun had made her dizzy, if she had walked too far, if someone had insulted her . . . ? But she did not explain.

". . . time is it?"

"Almost four-thirty."

"Dr. Pedersen will be home . . . he'll be home. . . ."

She looked around, confused.

"He won't be home until six," Jesse said.

He was able to help her back to the car and they got home in time, but Mrs. Pedersen sent word with Dora that she was "dizzy" and couldn't come down to dinner. She did not even appear the next morning at breakfast.

Then, one day when Jesse came home late in the afternoon himself, his briefcase heavy with books and his head girdled with a headache like a tight crown, he noticed something strange about the house: no piano notes. He set the briefcase down in the foyer, he listened with his head inclined to one side—but no, nothing, no music.

"Mother?" he called out.

He went back to the kitchen where something was baking—it smelled like apple pie—but there was no one around. He went back to the sun porch, but Hilda was not there. In the music room there was no Frederich, only the deep-cushioned chair at the piano and many piles of books and music, and, on the piano, a large sheet of paper covered with spidery notes and lines. A dish with the remains of a mincemeat pudding lay on top of the piano.

Jesse heard voices upstairs and he ran up—there were Hilda, Frederich, Dora, and Henry in the hallway. Hilda turned to him. "Thank God," she said. "You can get her out—"

"What's wrong?"

Henry was at the door to the hall bathroom, and Dora and Frederich stood a few feet away, watching. Henry was turning the doorknob and saying in a wheedling, coaxing voice, "Mrs. Pedersen? Mrs. Pedersen? How come you got this door locked?"

"What happened?" Jesse cried.

"She went in there and she won't come out. It's been hours now," Dora said.

"She was bothering me downstairs," Hilda said nervously, "and I told her to leave me alone . . . and so she went out, about one-thirty . . . and Dora hasn't seen her since then. . . ."

"Are you sure she's in there?" Jesse said.

"She must be. The door is locked," said Henry.

Jesse wanted to rap on the door but he hesitated. "Mother?" he said.

"She won't answer," said Henry. "I been calling to her and she won't answer."

Jesse rapped timidly on the door.

"If Father comes home and finds her—" Hilda said.

"Don't say that. She might be listening to us," Jesse whispered.

Frederich began to back away quietly.

"She's crazy. I don't love her, I don't want to see her again," Hilda said.

"Don't talk like that!" said Jesse.

"I hope Father does come home. I hope he finds her!"

"Why don't you go away," Jesse said nervously, "until she comes out... why don't you all go away and let Henry and me try to get the door down?" He rapped again on the door but there was no answer. "Mother? Are you sick? Can't you open the door? Then Henry and I can take it off the hinges, all right? Should we take the door down? Mother?"

Silence.

Henry went to get a screwdriver. Jesse, his warm face pressed against the door, tried to talk Mrs. Pedersen into coming out. "Mother, it's almost dinnertime. Why won't you talk to us? Hilda didn't mean what she said, she loves you very much.... Mother, nobody is here now but Henry and me. Just Henry and me. We have a screwdriver and we're going to take the door off the hinges. Is that all right? We've got to open the door before Father comes home... Father wouldn't understand, he might be angry.... We're going to take the door off now, Mother. Don't be afraid."

He and Henry did not look at each other as they worked.

At last the door was unhinged and with a grunt Jesse lifted it away from the frame. And then he saw in the bathroom, on the floor by the tub, the body of Mrs. Pedersen. Henry cried out but did not move. Jesse's eyesight went blank, black, and then came into focus again: yes, it was Mrs. Pedersen. She lay naked, on her back. Her skin was stretched and flabby, a terrible sight, her face simply a further expanse of flushed skin, the eyes half-open upon dull moonish eyeballs, the mouth open and gaping. She breathed hoarsely. Her body trembled and shuddered unevenly, in waves, and the perfumed water in the tub behind her shivered as if in sympathy; tiny, almost invisible ripples ran along the floor to the wall....

Henry muttered something and turned away.

What an enormous body! Jesse saw that her breasts were swollen, yellowish bulbs of flesh, the nipples raw, a deep red, circled with rows of tiny goose pimples as if she were very cold, though the upper part of her torso was flushed with a heat rash and her belly and thighs were also flushed. She breathed feverishly, rapidly. Lumps of flesh hung down from her belly onto the floor tile. She was like a ball of warm breathing protoplasm, an air of something fruity, yeasty, sour rising from her—then Jesse saw that she had vomited onto the floor just behind her head, and a narrow line of stale vomit led from her mouth down her neck and shoulder to the floor. He stared, speechless. He could not move but stood alone in the doorway, unable to enter or to retreat. That body! That blank, empty, dazed face! The head at the far end of the body seemed too small for it, as if it were an afterthought. So blank, so mottled and curdled a face, it could have been any face at all—it was the body that was important, exaggerated, swollen to the shape of a large oblong box, a rectangle like a barn. Brown frizzy patches of hair.... The body was so large that Jesse felt it pull at him, tug at him. Come forward. He must come forward. He could not run away. An odor of sweat about her, an odor of dirt—the earth—a closed-in smell of vomit and breath—as if she had been waiting here for years for him to discover her, in this private interior room with bathwater heavily scented and bluish.

"Mother—" Jesse cried.

His voice was choked.

She stirred. Lumps of flesh like tumors hung from her hips and thighs and just above her knees, the skin mottled orange-purple, bluish, yellow; her ankles and feet were not quite so swollen, only plump and sturdy, as if about to seize him in an embrace. Jesse stared, and though he wanted to jump backward, back out into the hall, he could not move. He must wake her. He must make everything right again, he must take her robe from where it had fallen and put it on her, he must wash her face of that vomit, he must get rid of the empty liquor bottle that had rolled into a corner of the bathroom—he must act, he must take charge before Dr. Pedersen came home, and yet for several minutes he could not move at all. Mrs. Pedersen was coming to life. Her breaths thickened to groans. Her body shuddered. The eyes, milky and blind, fluttered so that Jesse could not hide, he could not turn away—he wanted to bend down and quickly close those eyes to keep her from discovering him—

She groaned—her breathing quickened—her eyes opened suddenly and fastened themselves upon him. She looked up at him. Jesse felt as if a veil had been ripped away from her face and from his own, that they were staring at each other openly, confronting one of the terrible secrets of the world.

10

For several days after that Jesse moved in a private pressurized space: the very air seemed to exert a terrible pressure upon him. He could not locate it exactly on any part of his body. Sometimes he felt as if his heart might burst as he urged his body up a flight of stairs or out for a quick, desperate walk around the city—he found himself walking all the time, reluctant to come home—and sometimes his lungs ached, though he tried to breathe lightly and shallowly. At other times it was a dull ache that circled his head. He could not read now for more than half an hour at a time. He would go back to the university library in Buffalo and sit at a deserted table, a book in his hand... and yet he found after a few minutes that he was not reading at all, that his mind had gone dead.

He considered the big, ornate doors of the room he was in, an old-fashioned reading room. Invisibly he was unscrewing the screws, pulling out the hinges, taking note of the discolored indentations in the wood....

In a panic, he turned back to the book he was reading: a series of lectures, given in England, on the central nervous system. Already he had read most of the books he would study in his first years of premedical school, and now he was reading books at random, suggested to him by Dr. Pedersen, books that belonged to Jesse's remote future, an unimaginable future....

Nine days left before he would leave for Ann Arbor.

They were all going with him, except Frederich. Mrs. Pedersen talked about the trip all the time. Dr. Pedersen was going to take time off from his work. Hilda, stubborn and coy at first, had finally agreed to come along. They would drive him to his dormitory room, take hotel rooms nearby, get him settled, and only when he was certain that he could manage alone would they leave him. "We won't abandon you," Mrs. Pedersen kept assuring him. She spoke tartly and breathlessly; she was always in a rush now, buying Jesse clothes, sewing small tidy labels on his things, even on towels—his initials, *J. P.* "That way nobody can steal your things. You have to be very careful," she cautioned. At dinner she was eager to talk about how she spent her days: "Today I finally picked out a good trunk. I bought it at Williams Brothers on the condition that you approve of it, dear. Will you look at it after dinner?" Dr. Pedersen shared in her enthusiasm, though he hadn't as much time as Mrs. Pedersen to spend on Jesse. He entrusted her with all the preparations for Jesse's departure. She was brisk and efficient, always on the telephone, arranging to take a taxi downtown in order to pick out something for Jesse, even telephoning the dormitory residence in Ann Arbor to ask about the color scheme in the room Jesse would have. So much to do! She was in a flurry, and yet she was always back in time to prepare large pleasant dinners, slipping on an apron, humming happily out in the kitchen so that Jesse always heard her as soon as he stepped in the door, is if she were humming for his benefit. *I am out in the kitchen, I am normal. I am making a big normal meal.*

When she spoke to Dora, it was in the same high, efficient tone, though she seemed now to be giving Dora orders all the time. At the dinner table, her movements were sometimes abrupt; she upset her water glass two evenings in a row and Dr. Pedersen said, "Mary, whatever is wrong with you? Are you nervous about something?" She bit her lip and dabbed at herself with a napkin. "No, no, nothing at all," she said. "I hope you aren't working too hard these days, getting Jesse ready for college," Dr. Pedersen said.

Mrs. Pedersen continued dabbing at herself, not meeting anyone's eye. "No. I made up a list, dear. I just go down the list item by item. I'm not hurried at all. I can take care of it. I'm not nervous at all."

Jesse tried not to look at her.

In just a few days he would be leaving.

But how could he leave? He loved them. He loved all of them, even Frederich. Since the day Mrs. Pedersen had locked herself in the bathroom, there was a silent, abashed bond among Jesse and Frederich and Hilda that they never spoke of, never acknowledged in any way. It seemed impossible to Jesse that he would be leaving them. The air rang with panic. His head ached. Yet it was necessary to leave them in order to take his proper place someday in this family—Dr. Pedersen had explained everything to him countless times. He invited Jesse into his study after dinner and talked to him cheerfully, dreamily, recalling his own days at the University of Michigan and his days in medical school there, talking for an hour or an hour and a half at a time while Jesse found himself staring at the closed door of Dr. Pedersen's study, imagining how the screws could be taken out, carefully, deliberately, and how the door might be lifted off its hinges.... But when Dr. Pedersen asked him how his studies were going, Jesse was able to answer at once. Another voice seemed to answer for him. He could recite pages, chapters, he could outline entire books, speaking quickly and mechanically while Dr. Pedersen nodded. Sometimes it seemed to Jesse, joylessly, that he already knew everything. He spoke in so clear and unfaltering a voice that Dr. Pedersen could do no more than murmur enthusiastic agreement.

He no longer asked Hilda for help with calculus. He had stopped worrying about calculus. He did not want to think about it. And he felt his sister closed against him now, her fear softening her and yet deadening her to him, while her brittle mockery in the past had been a kind of camaraderie he had guessed at by instinct; now he did not dare to test her. He did not want to meet her gaze again and remember what she said about Mrs. Pedersen. It was too ugly. The secrets between them were too ugly. If he happened to glance at Frederich he sometimes saw Frederich watching him, but it meant nothing; the bond among them had to be silent because it was so ugly. Jesse wondered if Hilda and Frederich had known all along that their mother drank, hiding in corners, in the bathroom, even in the basement —Jesse remembered the several times he had seen her coming up from the basement empty-handed, a bright fresh color to her cheeks, greeting him eagerly: "I was just checking to see if the basement is leaking. . . . All that rain. . . ."

But he loved her. He would be leaving in a week.

And then, one day after lunch, before he could get out of the house with his books, he heard a knock on his door. He knew it was Mrs. Pedersen before he answered it.

"Where are you running off to today?" she asked.

Flat-footed, she stood in the doorway. Not yet invited in. She filled the doorway in a huge mint-green cotton house dress; on her feet were straw shoes with orange tassels and small brass mock bells on the toes. She had brushed her hair so that the frizz was tamed into waves, lifting from her forehead. He could see the beginning of her pale scalp, where there were tiny flakes of skin.

"Just out," Jesse said.

He had put on a white shirt and a tie.

"Are you going to Buffalo?"

"I don't know."

"Yes, you're going to Buffalo, you're all dressed up."

Jesse stared at the tassels on her shoes.

"I—I just wanted to ask you about your laundry—what you plan on doing with your laundry when you're at school—"

"I haven't thought about it," Jesse said. He felt her eyes on his face, his downcast face. Her fingers moved nervously about the embroidered pocket of her dress.

"I bought a laundry case so that you can mail your laundry home, Jesse. I thought it would be the best thing, for you to put your soiled laundry in it and mail it home. . . ."

"All right," Jesse said.

"It would be so much trouble for you to do it yourself in a laundromat," she went on quickly, "or to have it done somewhere. . . . They don't know how we want things done. They might put too much starch in your shirts. They wouldn't bother matching your socks together for you. . . ."

"All right," Jesse said

"Did you say you were going to Buffalo?"

Jesse looked up miserably. "I think I will."

"Good, I have some shopping that has to be done. I'll go with you."

"But I'm not going to stay long...."

"We don't have to stay long. I just have a few things to buy."

Jesse said nothing.

"But before we leave I have a few things to do," Mrs. Pedersen said. "I have to telephone my father and see how he is. Then I have a list, a list of things to do.... I'm going through the list one item at a time so that I don't get confused or nervous.... Can you wait for me? Can you wait? It will only take ten minutes for me to get ready."

"All right."

"Only ten minutes, I promise!"

"I'll wait in the car."

After she left he seemed to smell, dizzily, the scent of alcohol. Or was he imagining it?

He got his books and his suit coat and went out to the car. He sighed. A twenty-five mile drive ahead. The entire right side of his body sagged, it felt aged and alarmed. To sit beside Mrs. Pedersen in the car! That distance! To feel her stirring beside him, crowded in the front seat, feeling her fierce, helpless gaze upon the side of his face....

He waited. Five minutes passed. Ten minutes. He leafed through a notebook in which he was taking notes, and his handwriting looked odd to him, the handwriting of a stranger. Maybe he had picked up the wrong notebook by mistake...? But no, it was his notebook. He could not concentrate.... He could already smell Mrs. Pedersen's presence, beside him in the cramped front seat of his car....

Dora came out of the side door and said, "Jesse, Mrs. Pedersen asked me to say she's hurrying fast as she can. She'll be just another minute." He thanked Dora and put the key in the ignition. Maybe if he started the engine the car would somehow move forward, he would somehow escape.... Another ten minutes passed. Jesse sat staring out the windshield, his eyes glassy. He could not remember how long he had been waiting. At last Mrs. Pedersen appeared in a rush, carrying a large shopping bag and a straw purse and her coat over one arm. She must have dropped something because she exclaimed and stooped to pick it up. Jesse opened the door for her. He wondered what she was doing with all these things—in the shopping bag there were a jar of cold cream and a hairbrush and a small plastic box of hairpins on top; the bag itself was quite heavy.

Jesse drove out to the highway while Mrs. Pedersen apologized for being so slow.

She began to talk as if making a well-rehearsed speech. She sat with her hands clasped in her lap, each hand gripping the other. Jesse's head swam. He was certain he could smell whiskey.

"Jesse, I have not thanked you for what you did the other day. For helping me as you did. I am thanking you now." Both she and Jesse stared straight ahead. "I made a mistake. A bad mistake. If Dr. Pedersen had come home too early . . . Jesse, I made a mistake but I am not going to make it again. I've made many mistakes but I'm not going to make them again. I have come to a crossroads in my life. I have been thinking very seriously. I have been talking to my father and to Reverend Wieden. I have assessed my life, my past life, and I have come to a certain decision. But I want to thank you for helping me the other day. Hilda and Frederich would never have helped me. They don't love me. They're afraid of their father. They don't love me." She spoke in rapid, breathy snatches now. "We all live together in the same house, I prepare them three meals a day, I am their mother, I love them in spite of their attitude toward me but . . . but . . . I am ready to make a certain decision in my life because I know what my fate must be. . . ."

What was she talking about?

Jesse yearned for the coolness of the library. The quiet movements of bodies, girls' bodies, distant from him, the grave serious impersonal silence. He could sit there for hours, absolutely alone. He could read for hours. Alone. Absolutely alone. And he would be safe there as Jesse Pedersen, a boy with a home and a family to return to, a table to sit down at in the evening, when it was safely evening and Dr. Pedersen was home.

Mrs. Pedersen was speaking in a feverish voice: "Jesse, I have made my decision. I spoke to my father. He has known about my . . . my problem. . . . He has tried to counsel me. But now he has failed me. He doesn't understand, he is too old to understand . . . he keeps asking me what will happen to me, won't I be ashamed— how will I take care of myself— He doesn't understand."

Jesse did not dare to ask her what she meant.

"Jesse, I am not asking for your approval. I don't want to involve you, just as I do not want to involve my father. He has offered me money but I said no. That would involve him. That would make Dr. Pedersen very angry at him. . . . I have my own money, I have all the money I need. Here," she said, lifting her straw purse, "here is everything I need. . . . I took a taxi to the bank yesterday and got everything I need. I'm ready."

Jesse drove for another mile before he could speak. Then he said, not looking at her. "What do you mean . . . ?"

"I am leaving my husband."

"What?"

"I am leaving Dr. Pedersen. I am leaving."

Jesse's heart lurched. "You're leaving? Leaving them—?"

"I am leaving them to start my own life."

"But—"

"Yes, I am leaving today. I am going to a hotel in Buffalo. Everything is planned," she said hotly. "I can make plans. I can make a list and carry it out. I am not drunk, I am absolutely sober. Look." And she held her hands out before her. They trembled only a little.

"You're going to a hotel now? Today? To a hotel?"

"If you won't take me downtown, I'll take a taxi. I have money. I can take care of myself."

"But— What will he—"

"He will be very angry. I know. But for years I've known I would have to leave him. It's a question of survival. My sanity. I tried to explain this to my father and to Reverend Wieden but they didn't understand; men don't understand, they don't see that I am a human being of my own, I am . . . I am Mary Shirer. . . . I am still Mary Shirer." She began to cry. "I want to go back to being her, that girl. I want . . . I want to be myself again . . . I don't know how this happened, this fat, the time that went by. . . . So many years have gone by. . . . I'm afraid I might go crazy, I might die if I don't leave him. . . ."

"But what are you going to do?" Jesse said. "How will you live?"

"Alone. I'll live alone," she said, crying. "For years I've known it, I've been planning for it, and now the time is here; I will die if I don't escape from him, from that house; I am not a freak like the rest of them, I didn't used to be a freak and you were not a freak in the beginning either.... I loved you right away, Jesse, because you were like me, the way I used to be. I wanted to be loved too, like you. I wanted to be loved by Dr. Pedersen and no one else. I wanted to be owned by him.... But I wasn't a freak in the beginning. I was Mary Shirer. I don't know what happened, what he did to me, but I have to leave him now because ... because in another week you'll be gone, Jesse, and there will be no one to help me...."

Jesse stared at the highway ahead. It looked as if there were heat waves, teasing, in the distance. Could he smell the heat itself, or was that sharp sweet scent from Mrs. Pedersen?

"You'll help me, won't you, Jesse, you'll help me ... ?"

She touched his arm. He flinched.

"Otherwise I will go crazy. I will die. I will have to take my own life."

Her sobbing became wild. Jesse drove along in that same weightless, suspended daze, the same pressurized trance he had endured for the past several days. "Jesse, please. Please. Answer me, don't turn away from me now.... I will die if I don't escape.... It's for the salvation of my soul!" Jesse turned to stare at her, alarmed, and it seemed to him that he was staring directly into her soul—he had seen it the day of her collapse in the bathroom—and he could not turn away—

"Jesse ... ?"

"Yes. All right," he whispered.

She began to weep helplessly, noisily, like a child. Jesse drove all the way downtown, bypassing the university, his face grown violently hot. In the rearview mirror he saw a red, puffy face, *was that his face?*—the face of a fat boy of uncertain age, a stranger. *You were not a freak in the beginning....*

Downtown, Jesse circled the hotel Mrs. Pedersen had chosen while she dabbed at her wet face and tried to fix herself up. Her flesh-toned make-up had smeared badly. She wiped her face and throat and the back of her neck. "Jesse, what will I say to them? I don't know how to check into a hotel.... Somebody else always did it for me...."

Jesse's voice sounded hollow. "I don't know. Just say you would like a room."

"I would like a room."

"Maybe you should ask the price first—"

"No, I don't care about the price! I have plenty of money. My family has always had plenty of money. I have enough for the rest of my life. . . . *I would like a room. A single room.*" Jesse rounded the block a second time, then a third time, while Mrs. Pedersen stared out at the crowded street. Downtown Buffalo was airless and warm. She said uncertainly, "You're coming in with me, Jesse, aren't you?"

"All right."

"Please come in. Please. Just stand by the door and wait for me. You don't have to come to the desk."

"All right."

"It's so busy here . . . everything is so confusing. . . ."

Jesse managed to park the car, and he and Mrs. Pedersen walked back to the hotel, both ungainly in the heat. Mrs. Pedersen carried her big straw purse and Jesse carried her shopping bag and coat. The shopping bag was beginning to tear. The entire right half of Jesse's body, the half near Mrs. Pedersen, had begun to prickle violently. He had never felt anything like it before. Jesse gnawed at his lip and stared into the faces of people passing them: these people knew everything. They could recognize freaks when they saw them. Mrs. Pedersen was talking nervously, loudly. It was obvious that she had been drinking. These strangers on the Main Street of Buffalo could see that perfectly well—a huge drunken woman and a huge boy, waddling along in the sunlight, both of them panicked.

They went into the hotel and approached the desk. Mrs. Pedersen clutched at Jesse's arm. Finally he went up to the desk clerk and said, "My mother would like a single room, please."

The desk clerk smiled past Jesse at Mrs. Pedersen, who stood a few feet away. "Yes, for how many nights?"

"I don't know," Jesse said.

He turned miserably to Mrs. Pedersen.

"I don't know. . . ." she said.

Silence.

"An indefinite amount of time?" asked the clerk politely.

"Yes, I think so," said Jesse.

A bellhop took them up to the room, which looked out onto the street several floors below. It was not a very pleasant room.

Mrs. Pedersen looked too large in it; she bumped into a writing desk, she nearly knocked over a lamp. Her face was florid and astonished. As soon as the bellhop left she went to the window and ran her finger along the sill. She held her finger for Jesse to see—it was dirty!

"I just can't believe this, Jesse," she said.

She sat down on the bed and it sagged beneath her. Jesse stood, not knowing what to do. Should he leave? What was going to happen? Mrs. Pedersen began taking things out of the shopping bag one by one, setting them on the bedspread, moving dumbly and slowly. She licked her lips. "Oh, I forgot something . . . I forgot something. . . ." she said slowly. "I should have stuffed some clothes in here. . . ."

"You didn't bring any clothes?"

"I forgot. I forgot about clothes."

They stared at each other. Mrs. Pedersen's eyes were bloodshot.

"Oh, I forgot. How did I forget? You were in such a rush and I didn't want to keep you waiting . . . I was afraid you might drive away without me. . . . I . . ."

"Maybe you could buy some clothes here," Jesse said.

"No, I don't want to go out. It's so busy down there—all those people. No. I can't go into a store. I think I'm going crazy, Jesse, I've got to get hold of myself. . . . *What he did to me, Jesse, what he did* . . . ! I will never forget, my body and my soul have been sickened by it, by him, by the years as his wife. . . . I don't know what will happen to me. . . ."

Jesse stared at her ugly, streaked face. What was going to happen? And then, wearily, after several minutes, he said what he had known all along he must say: "I'll drive back to Lockport and get your clothes."

"Oh, Jesse, will you? Will you? It would mean so much to me, Jesse, I left so much behind, I got confused and left so much behind. . . . I can make out a list and give it to you. . . ."

She looked around vaguely. Jesse got her some stationery from the desk. He lent her his own pen. It took her nearly twenty minutes to make out the list, her face contorted as she tried to think. Jesse went to the window and looked down at the street four stories below. He could hear Mrs. Pedersen's heavy, strained breath. Occasionally she muttered something inaudible. Was this happening? Was this really happening? The windowpane was very grimy and it refracted the sun's rays into a faint rainbow a few inches before Jesse's eyes. Was any of this happening?

Behind the dirty glass, in the sky, there were great fluffy clouds. Puffs of clouds. The sky was a dead, flat blue, the clouds were perfectly white. Silence in the sky. One of the clouds compelled Jesse to look at it: it had the beginnings of a face, the features broad and shallow and mocking. But firm. There were eyes there, and a faint nose, and the indication of a mouth. Its expression distant but mocking.

Jesse blinked.

Mrs. Pedersen got to her feet with difficulty. "Here, Jesse. I think I have everything written down now."

"Will you be all right while I'm gone?"

"Oh yes. Yes. I will be all right. Everything is all right. I'm not at all dizzy now, I'm perfectly well. Don't I look perfectly well? I'm perfectly sober."

Jesse nodded sadly.

He drove back to Lockport. It was four o'clock when he turned in the Pedersen driveway between the two wrought-iron spikes. He gave the list to Dora and said, "Mrs. Pedersen would like you to put these things in a suitcase, please." Astonished, Dora took the piece of paper from him. His heart hammering, Jesse went out to wait in their driveway. He pressed his hand against the hot metal of his car. That was real, that heat. That metal. After a while Dora appeared at the screen door, opening it awkwardly. Jesse went to help her. He took a large tan suitcase from her. She said, "This ain't all. There's more." Another suitcase. She went back to get an armful of dresses. So many dresses! What did Mrs. Pedersen want with all these dresses? One of them had a sequined bodice.

"Thank you," Jesse said.

The car was packed. Dora stood watching him back away, her hand against her mouth as if she were staring at something terrible. As he drove back to Buffalo his head swam with the speed, the heat, the smell of Mrs. Pedersen's clothes.

He had to park some distance from the hotel. Carrying the two suitcases and the armload of dresses, he saw how openly people stared at him. Their expressions were guarded. Even in the hotel lobby people stared at him. He took the elevator to the fourth floor, and when he knocked on Mrs. Pedersen's door she did not answer for several minutes. What was wrong? Then, at last, he heard her heavy footsteps. She slid the bolt and opened the door slowly, fearfully.

"Oh, Jesse, thank God.... I thought it might be *him*.... I thought you might have told him about me, that you might have brought him back with you.... Oh, thank God, thank God...."

He helped her hang the dresses in the closet. Her mood changed and she chattered at him, excited, yet on the verge of tears still, occasionally lapsing into a shrill, surprising gaiety. Now he was certain she had been drinking. "Oh, wait until he finds out! Just wait! He doesn't dream of the plans I've made, he could never believe that his wife, his stupid wife, could break free of him and begin her own life just like anyone else.... Oh, he'll be so surprised...."

As she was unpacking one of the suitcases, the telephone rang.

"What? But nobody knows I'm here.... Nobody knows where I am...." Mrs. Pedersen cried.

The telephone rang again. Jesse went over to it and stood above it, his hands clasped together in front of his chest.

"Jesse, don't answer it! It's *him*!"

"But—but it can't be—"

"I know it's him. I know it"

"But how would he know you were here?"

"He knows. He knows everything."

"It can't be Dr. Pedersen," Jesse said.

Suddenly, grimly, he picked up the receiver.

The voice at the other end, crying "hello," was Dr. Pedersen's.

"Hello," Jesse said blankly.

"Who is this? Jesse? Where is your mother? Is she there? Put her on the telephone, please."

"She's—she's—"

Mrs. Pedersen had backed away, shaking her head.

"Jesse, put her on the telephone at once. I demand to speak to her!"

"She can't—"

Mrs. Pedersen was shaking her head wildly.

"Jesse, do you hear me? I know where you are. Dora called me at the Clinic and I know exactly where your mother went, it's exactly where she would go. I demand to speak to her. At once. I know she's there, I know exactly what is going on. I am not coming to get her. I refuse to drive up there. Put your mother on the telephone at once, Jesse."

"She doesn't want to talk to you," Jesse whispered.

"I told you to put her on the phone!"

"I can't—"

"Jesse, do you hear me? Do you hear me?"

In a panic, Jesse slammed down the receiver.

He and Mrs. Pedersen stared at each other.

Finally she said in a quivering voice, "Thank you.... Thank you for saving me...."

The telephone began ringing again.

"We'll get out of here. We've got to get out of this room," Mrs. Pedersen said. She hurried to the door. "Come on, Jesse. Please. We'll go downstairs and let him call me, let him call all he wants. I won't answer. He wants me to come back to him, to that awful life. He thinks he has power over me, but he hasn't. Oh, listen to that telephone! He wants to drive me crazy!"

They went downstairs to the coffee shop. Mrs. Pedersen ordered cheeseburgers and French fries for both of them. Eating quickly, as if she were very hungry, Mrs. Pedersen began to revive. "I'll tell you things about him nobody knows, Jesse. Secrets. Terrible secrets," she said in a low voice. "Oh yes, he's a genius. Yes, a wonderful man. All of Lockport is proud of him, yes. They write stories about him. Yes. But there are secrets nobody knows except me.... He takes morphine, Jesse. Yes, morphine! Not every night, but often he gives himself an injection of morphine the way other people take a drink—and then he looks down upon people who drink; he said some nasty, unforgivable things about my mother, just because she liked to drink now and then. The hypocrite!" As Jesse stared, she wiped her mouth hard, as if to emphasize the truth of the words she spoke. "Yes, he takes morphine, all in secret; I'm the only person on earth who knows about it.... And the things he's done to punish me! Once when we were married only a year he refused to speak to me for a month. To this day I don't know why. I offended him somehow. He's incredibly vain and proud. He won't let me buy anything unless he has seen it or gives his approval of it. Once he took all my clothes away and I had to stay in the bedroom naked for three days . . . he brought my food up on a tray and left it by the door, as if I were an animal. . . . I thought I'd go crazy in that room! He did it to drive me crazy, Jesse. He likes to make me cry. Yes, it's true, don't look so surprised! He made me shave all the hair off my body for a long time, for years, and if it wasn't shaved off well enough for him he took his razor and went over me. . . . He enjoys making me cry. Did you ever see that locked cabinet in his study? It's always kept locked because he has certain books in it, awful books, with photographs of awful things. I can't tell you what they are. There are photographs of men and women—you know—and other photographs of dismembered bodies, with captions beneath them like jokes. Books that make fun of everything. I almost fainted the first time he showed them to me. We were only married a few months . . . he made me read them and he stood behind me, watching. . . ."

"I don't believe it," Jesse whispered.

"Oh, you don't believe it!" Mrs. Pedersen said. "Well, you weren't married to him for nineteen years, like me. And why did he marry me? Because my father was a doctor, and my uncle, and because my family has money and land and he knew he could get it. All his life he's been talking about this clinic of his, the Pedersen Clinic. He thinks it's going to be famous all over the world. He's crazy. He wants to save everyone from dying. My father has given him thousands of dollars, has lent him thousands of dollars, because my father is foolish enough to believe him. He's crazy, my husband, he wants to save everyone from dying! He thinks he will eventually be famous in every country of the world! Then he talked Father into retiring. He has destroyed my father. He wanted Frederich to become a doctor so that he could inherit the Clinic, but Frederich was never well enough to go to school and so . . . and so . . . he adopted you . . . it's all part of his plan, the one I've been hearing about for nineteen years. . . . These are things that don't appear in the news stories about Dr. Pedersen," she said, smiling bitterly. The food had rejuvenated her. She talked almost merrily and seemed about to wink at Jesse, amused at his surprise. "Ask him to tell you about his secret philosophy. He talks all the time about his public philosophy, but what about the secret one? Once a patient has come to him, he believes the patient is *his*. The patient's life is *his*. He owns the patient, he owns the disease, he owns everything. Oh, he's crazy. Ask him about these things. Just ask him. Not all his patients survive, you know. Ask him about the ones who die. His diagnoses are not always right. The great Dr. Pedersen has made mistakes. But he talks his patients into believing him so that they would rather die than go to another doctor, they have such faith in him, they get sicker and sicker and die, actually die, rather than call in another doctor . . . and he watches them die and won't bring in anyone else . . . right until the end he thinks he is right, he's unable to believe that he might be wrong. . . . He is literally unable to believe that he might be mistaken. Now do you still love him more than you love me?"

Jesse stared at her face, her moving jaws.

Who was this? A woman, a heavy, perspiring, excited woman; a stranger, or his mother? or a great piece of flesh that, shaken hard enough, might reveal the small pretty face of an ordinary woman? Jesse was losing control of his own thoughts. She sucked them out of his brain; it had something to do with her chatter and the hungry grinding of her jaws and her small winking mischievous eyes. "When we were married, he examined me to make sure I was a virgin. Ask him about that. Ask him about the experiments he makes on his patients without telling them. His hypnotism. He can hypnotize a person at any time, did you know that? Ask him. These things are not in the *Book of Fates*, they're written in his secret ledgers, kept in a safe. I don't know how many ledgers he has now—he began keeping them when he was in his twenties. He might have five hundred ledgers by now. Five hundred secret ledgers. He's going to will them to some international science foundation after his death, he thinks they will revolutionize medicine. . . . Just ask him! Ask him about his idea for using germs in bombs—germs and bacteria—it's his latest invention, he wants to patent the idea and sell it to the United States government. He's really crazy. He wants to drive me crazy. Just ask him about these things, you admire him so much! You!"

"I don't want to hear this," Jesse said weakly.

His plate was clean. Only a smear of ketchup and a dill pickle. He picked the pickle up and slowly wiped the ketchup off his plate with it and ate it.

Mrs. Pedersen had finished her cheeseburger. She checked her lipstick, looking into a small gold compact. She was breathing quickly; a hectic flush had risen into her face, giving it a vigorous, flirtatious look. "What is that saying he's always repeating when he is hunting me down, trying to destroy me? *What is buried will surface.* Yes. I've been hearing that for years. He whispers it into my ear. I tell him the truth always—I don't know how to lie to him!—but he never believes me, he's always threatening me, he's always jealous. *What is buried will surface,* he says. He asks me about my dreams. All about my dreams. I have to confess every thought to him. He hypnotizes me, he gets into my head, he says I belong to him. He says that a husband owns his wife. Hilda and Frederich belong to him too, but he can't do much with them because they're too smart. I think he's a little afraid of them—once he tried to spank Frederich and Frederich bit his hand, sank his teeth right into Dr. Pedersen's hand like a dog and wouldn't let go! then he went into convulsions. He's afraid of Frederich and Hilda and so he goes after me. He thinks I have some secret plans against him. He's always asking me to confess. *What is buried will surface,* he says, waiting for me to confess. I can't go back to him. I would rather die."

She called the waitress over and ordered two more cheeseburgers and two more Cokes.

"But aren't you afraid of living alone?" Jesse said. "Alone . . . ? When everybody else in the world lives in a family?"

She snorted. "A family! What do I care about a family!"

"But . . ."

A sense of terror was spreading in Jesse. He tried to clear his mind. What was she saying, what was this woman saying to him? A *family*! For a moment he could not remember what a real family was. The terror grew, a terror at being excluded from the family of men, jostled about on the streets by people in a hurry, people in crowds, with their own families back home, private lives that excluded him permanently. . . .

"I'll come to Ann Arbor with you," Mrs. Pedersen said simply.

Just then a man appeared in the doorway of the coffee shop—

such broad, thick shoulders that Jesse thought at first it must be Dr. Pedersen—and then, behind him, out on the sidewalk, another large man appeared, but this was not Dr. Pedersen either.

The cheeseburgers were brought. Mrs. Pedersen began eating at once, quickly but daintily, as if she were conscious of Jesse's attention. "Yes, I'll move to Ann Arbor. We'll have a house there. I can buy a lovely house and I'll cook for you and do all your clothes and I won't bother you at all. That's what we'll do. It's all clear to me." Then she hesitated, staring. "Oh . . . shoes. Jesse, I forgot my shoes. I left home this morning and forgot my shoes . . . I forgot to write them down on the list. . . . I have only the pair I'm wearing."

Jesse was chewing his cheeseburger without tasting it.

"First I forgot my dresses and now I forgot my shoes," Mrs. Pedersen said. "How could I be so silly . . . ?"

After a while Jesse said, sighing, "I'll go back and get them for you."

11

When Jesse drove up to the Pedersen house this time, he saw Henry already in the driveway waiting for him. He had a large suitcase at his feet.

Henry said evasively, not wanting to meet Jesse's expression of surprise and dread: "Mrs. Pedersen's shoes are in here. Dr. Pedersen says for you to take the suitcase and good-by to you."

"Her shoes . . . ?"

"Mrs. Pedersen called up and said you were coming. She said to get the shoes all ready for you and you'd be here in half an hour."

Jesse kept staring at the Negro's face, as if he feared looking anywhere else. Hilda might be watching him from her bedroom window. Dr. Pedersen himself might be watching. The thought of Dr. Pedersen inside the house, calmly inside the house, made Jesse tremble. "You mean Mrs. Pedersen called home . . . ? She called home to say I was coming . . . ?"

"Talked to Dora. She talked to Dora and told her."

"Oh. Yes. That's good. That's good. . . ." Jesse said vaguely. He had picked up the suitcase, found it surprisingly heavy, but did not move away. Henry seemed anxious to leave. What had Henry just said? Jesse could not quite remember.

"Thank you for the shoes," said Jesse.

"Well. . . ."

Jesse wanted to ask Henry to repeat his message. He had told him something that Dr. Pedersen had said—what was it? Jesse couldn't remember. He felt his eyes pounding with the desire to look away from Henry's face, to the door of the house, to any of the windows where Dr. Pedersen might be standing, watching him. . . .

"Yes, thank you. . . . Mrs. Pedersen will be very happy. . . ." Jesse said.

Henry backed away. There was nothing for Jesse to do except put the suitcase in the car and drive back to Buffalo again.

This time he drove slowly. For some reason he felt exhausted; it was an effort to press down upon the gas pedal, to keep a consistent speed. His foot began to get numb. He was vaguely conscious of the highway—Transit Road—and other traffic and stretches of farmland, but from time to time he felt his mind slipping off, dozing off, and it was perplexing to him to remember where he was going. Back to Buffalo, yes. To that hotel. He had a suitcase in the back seat of his car, a car Dr. Pedersen had given him, and the suitcase was filled with Mrs. Pedersen's shoes, and she was waiting for him to bring the suitcase to her. . . .

His body had itched violently but he had been unable to scratch it then, because other people were around. Now the itching seemed to have gone away but his body, especially the right side, felt numbed, heavy, aged. Jesse knew that people sometimes fell asleep while driving. But he could not understand why he was so tired, so drugged, when he had so much to do—many more miles to drive!—and so much responsibility. He wasn't driving well. Sometimes he drove at fifty miles an hour, sometimes he noticed that he was driving only thirty miles an hour; his foot seemed to ease up automatically on the gas pedal; it would take him forever to get back to Buffalo. . . .

A high bridge ahead. He slowed, cautious of oncoming traffic on this narrow bridge. He drove over the bridge slowly: a creek below, mud-colored and shallow with the heat of early September. The creek was beginning to be familiar to him now. He had driven over this bridge many times. On the other side of the creek was a large building, an old mill of some kind; sloping down from this building to the creek bank was a hill of a peculiar, rich orange-brown color. A cider mill. Jesse's foot slipped from the gas pedal, numbed. He had to rest for a few minutes. He had to stop.

He turned his car up a lane by the mill. For a while he sat in the car, resting. He smiled at the odor of the apples . . . there had been a smaller cider mill outside Yewville on one of the creeks, and he had sometimes gone with other boys to dig for worms in the rich apple refuse behind it. It was the best place to dig for fishing worms. He stared at the mill, which was boarded up, and it seemed to him that the mill had meaning for him, that he had been meant to stop here. He got out of his car wearily and looked around. The mill was dilapidated. Two stories high, with an old stone cellar that protruded above the ground, and two rotted cellar doors, spread open permanently, showing the dark damp blackness of the cellar. An ornate cobweb was strung across the opening. The smell of damp moist earth and the smell of apples pleased him. Behind the hill, sloping down to the creek, was the rich dark orange soil that had formed from the apple waste; on the creek bank there were those Y-shaped sticks stuck into the caked earth that meant fishermen, maybe boys like himself, as he had been in Yewville. . . . The apple waste smelled rich and warm. It seemed to shimmer in the light of the sun's setting, nearly the same glowering color, illuminating a bank of clouds. The clouds were pocked as if with many shallow, shadowy eyes.

Jesse looked around the mill for a while, walking through the tall weeds, approaching the cellar. A whiff of dank air. It was dark down there, it looked forbidding. . . . Farther up the lane an old truck was parked on four greasy blocks in a cluster of blue-flowered weeds. In the distance was a scrubby field with deserted hulks of automobiles and trucks, and what appeared to be part of a snowplow. Abandoned in the weeds. The lane was very narrow and probably not often used: weeds grew in its center. Jesse noticed on his left an apple orchard. This belonged to a family who lived in a nearby farmhouse on the highway. He peered through the orchard and saw on its other side a large backyard. There was an old swing, made of wood and metal, painted green, that could seat four people. Was someone in the swing...? Jesse could make out two people, a woman and a child. Chickens were picking in the grass around them, oblivious to them. Jesse wondered what they were saying to each other. He wanted suddenly to hear them, to get closer.... The woman seemed to be scolding the child. Her voice rose in sweet, indecipherable notes, single notes, syllables of sound. Jesse could not hear. The woman, the mother, began to make the swing move, and the little girl jumped up on the seat opposite, exclaiming in delight. The little girl was about three or four years old. She had long dark hair. The woman had thick brown hair, very light, very curly, almost red-blond, like Jesse's hair. She wore a yellow dress. For some reason Jesse's eyes watered to see them, the two of them, and to know that he could not join them on the swing.... A mother and her little girl on a swing, in the country, on a warm late-summer evening... and he could not join them, it was impossible for him to join them. Now a man came out of the back door of the farmhouse. Chickens scattered before him. He was tall, husky, with his shirtsleeves rolled up past his elbows. His hair was black. He was saying something, but Jesse could not make out the words.

Then, suddenly, this man was looking over at Jesse. He stared. He must have said something, a murmur of surprise or irritation, because now the woman also turned to look. Jesse was on the other side of their orchard, far enough away to show he meant no harm. He was not trespassing. But the couple stared at him suspiciously. The little girl had not seen him. She was chanting something in a high melodic voice.

Jesse thought: *I will explain myself to them. I will show them I mean no harm.*

The black-haired man approached the orchard slowly. Jesse saw a cautious, springy threat to his step, in the very look of his arms.

He must leave.

He must get out of here.

Panting, he hurried back to his car. As he backed out of the lane he saw the black-haired man watching him. He had lit a cigarette. In such a way, Jesse thought, does a man protect himself and his family. In such a way does a man, a normal man, exclude the rest of the world.

When Jesse returned to the hotel, Mrs. Pedersen did not answer his knock. He rapped politely on the door. He waited. No answer. A man passed him in the corridor, glancing at him. Jesse saw the man approach out of the corner of his eye and for a moment his size was a puzzle—could this be Dr. Pedersen? But no, Dr. Pedersen was back home. Jesse was safe. He set the suitcase down by the door and knocked again.

She did not answer. His heart began to pound with panic. It was possible that something had happened to Mrs. Pedersen. She might have collapsed.... For a moment he could not remember how long he had been gone. Maybe he had been gone many hours. Time was confusing to him. He knew that the drive back from Lockport to Buffalo had taken much longer than it should have taken, as if he were in a dream, fighting through a dream to come to the surface of his own consciousness. Hours might have passed. Maybe a day had gone by.

He knocked again timidly. This time he heard someone's voice. Mrs. Pedersen was calling out a question but he could not make it out. He waited patiently until she came to open the door, opening it to the width of its safety chain. She peered out at him, her face florid and cautious in the crack of the door. Jesse could smell whiskey.

"You've been gone so long.... I thought something had happened.... I thought *he* had come here instead of you...."

She let him in. Her hair was wild and ravaged, a scarecrow's hair. The front of her dress was stained. "I was so afraid. So afraid," she said in a thick, childish voice. "Is that the shoes? That there, the suitcase? Thank God for you, Jesse. You're all I have now."

Jesse opened the suitcase and took out the shoes, which had been wrapped carefully in tissue paper. Mrs. Pedersen leaned near him, and her tears fell on some of the thin white paper.

"The telephone has been ringing. He has been calling me, tormenting me. But I won't answer. I will never answer that telephone," she said. "Oh, thank God for you. And Dora. Dora is wonderful. How did he know I came here? To this hotel? He knows everything. He can read minds. Did I tell you that he can read minds? He can read minds and hypnotize people without them knowing it—just sit down with him and he looks right into your brain—he knows everything—he knew I would come to this hotel before I knew it myself—"

Jesse wondered where she had hidden the bottle. He noticed a tray on the night table, with a few food-encrusted plates from room service.

"I'm not going to talk about him," Mrs. Pedersen said. She sat down on the bed and the springs creaked in surprise. "I don't care if he gets a proper dinner or not tonight. I don't care about Hilda either. She never loved me. She hates me. And Frederich—he hates me. They love their father better and they always did. You always loved him too. Everybody loves him, it's a mystery. I heard someone out in the hall while you were gone and I thought it was him, his voice, my heart rushed like mad.... I don't know if I still love him. I don't want to love him. I'm going to be free of him forever.... What did he say to you when you got the shoes?"

"Nothing. Henry was waiting outside with the suitcase."

"Just Henry?"

"Yes."

"Dr. Pedersen didn't talk to you?"

"No."

Mrs. Pedersen sat for a while without speaking. She did not seem to be aware of Jesse at all.

The telephone rang.

She jumped to her feet. "Tell him to leave me alone. Tell him to leave me alone," she cried.

Jesse went to answer the telephone, but standing above it, he felt his arm suddenly go numb. Was it paralyzed? The telephone rang again. Mrs. Pedersen had backed up against the far wall, her knuckles pressed against her mouth. "I'll kill myself. I'll go crazy. Tell him to leave us alone, to leave us alone forever...."

Jesse forced himself to pick up the receiver. His eyes shut, he yelled: "Leave us alone!"

He hung up.

Mrs. Pedersen and Jesse stared at each other. Mrs. Pedersen embraced herself, shivering. "Jesse, I feel so strange. I feel so hungry.... Was that him, was that Dr. Pedersen?"

"Yes. I don't know."

"I feel so hungry, I'm just shaking.... Could you go and get me something to eat? Jesse? From a good restaurant?"

"Why don't we leave this room? Then you wouldn't have to listen to the telephone ring."

"I don't want to leave, no, I look awful, I'm not well.... I can't go out on the street... it's getting dark.... I don't want people to see me...."

"But—"

"Go and get us something to eat. Get us some dinner, please."

"We could call room service."

"No, not room service, I don't want room service. I want something else. Food from a good restaurant... different food.... I feel faint, I feel shaky.... Jesse, go and get us something to eat, something solid, and we'll have dinner together up here, just the two of us, and we won't answer the telephone when it rings...."

She was about to cry, so Jesse gave in.

He went down to the street and looked for a restaurant. He walked several blocks. At last he came to a dingy Chinese restaurant that was nearly empty; he looked at a menu and ordered the first four dinners on it—pressed almond duck, beef with Chinese vegetables, shrimps in lobster sauce, chicken chow mein. He had to wait for the food to be prepared and his mouth began to water. So he bought a few candy bars at the cashier's stand and chewed on them nervously. He wondered how Mrs. Pedersen was. Maybe she was drinking. Maybe the telephone had begun to ring again and was frightening her....

This day had lasted half his lifetime.

When he brought the dinners back to Mrs. Pedersen she was waiting for him at the door and opened it immediately. Now she wore her pink flowered bathrobe and her hair stood up in jagged tufts, as if she had been pulling at it with her hands. "I was afraid you weren't coming back, Jesse, I'm just so shaky, my nerves are ragged.... What is this, Chinese food? But Chinese food is so insubstantial... it's delicious, but there's nothing to it.... I feel so faint, I'm dying of hunger...."

"Everything is all right now," Jesse said.

Mrs. Pedersen sat on the edge of her bed and began to eat. She panted. Tears of gratitude inched out of her eyes and down her belling cheeks. Jesse hardly tasted the food; he ate quickly, dipping his head to the plate. Hurry. Hurry. The telephone might ring at any moment. He, too, was starving and must eat, he must fill his stomach. An actual ache had begun in his stomach, demanding to be filled.

"This food is delicious but there's just nothing to it... only one bowl of rice for both of us...." Mrs. Pedersen said. When they had finished, she wiped her mouth and sighed shakily. "Jesse, could you go and get something else? This wasn't nearly enough for both of us. We missed our regular meals today. All the driving and the nervousness and the telephone ringing have made me so weak... I'm afraid to go without eating, I might faint, and we don't know any doctors up here.... Jesse, could you get us something else? Please?"

Jesse rose slowly.

"You are all I have, Jesse," Mrs. Pedersen whispered.

He went out again. This time he walked aimlessly, nearly got lost, then found himself across the street from the Chinese restaurant again. He went in and ordered the same four dinners. The cashier, a young Oriental woman with exaggerated eyes, stared at him. He bought a handful of Hershey bars and ate them while he waited.

Twenty minutes later, crossing the hotel lobby, he noticed that the desk clerk was watching him closely. The bellboys were watching him. But he took the elevator up to the fourth floor, carrying the warm cardboard box in his arms, his mouth watering violently from the aroma of the food.

"Mrs. Pedersen? Mother?"

He knocked but no one answered.

He pressed his mouth to the crack of the door and said, "Mother! It's Jesse!"

But no answer. He knocked again. His stomach was aching with hunger and he felt shaky. He imagined her sprawled on the bathroom floor, the tub filled with water, warm water, trembling in thin, nearly invisible ripples.... He stood for a while with the package of food in his arms. Then he set it carefully down on the floor and knocked again. No answer. Why was she hiding from him? He was weak with hunger and, while waiting for her to unlock the door, he squatted and opened the package. What food! It smelled delicious. With his fingers he picked something up—slivers of chicken, noodles, dark green leaves of a vegetable he couldn't recognize—and began to eat. He would eat only a little. Minutes passed and Mrs. Pedersen still did not come to the door. What was wrong? Jesse, ravenously hungry, picked up another handful of food, then another....

He squatted there awkwardly and ate. Might as well eat. His mouth prickled with each handful of food—his tongue seemed to come alive, suddenly muscular. Evidently he had been very hungry and had needed this food. There was something desperate in his throat that urged the food down and demanded more. What if he didn't get enough? His stomach was an enormous open hole, a raw hole, a wound. He had to fill it with food. He had to stuff it. But he could not eat fast enough, and the Chinese food was so delicate, so thin, there was no substance to it.... He should have bought some hamburgers, some good solid American cheeseburgers from the hotel's coffee shop.... This food would never be enough for him. He felt weak, baffled. His jaw muscles ached from eating, even his arm ached from lifting food to his mouth, yet he was still hungry. His insides buzzed with hunger. He could almost feel the soft, frail, pulsating lining of his stomach trembling with hunger, demanding to be fed. Finally he sat down on the carpet to ease his aching knees and to give his stomach more room.

Mrs. Pedersen did not come to the door. Jesse ate all four dinners and when he was finished he looked up groggily and saw that he was sitting in a corridor that was dimly lit and smelled of dust and food. He was alone. He felt slightly drunk. With an effort, panting, he got to his feet and knocked again on Mrs. Pedersen's door.

No answer. Nothing.

Finally he folded the packages carefully together and put them back in the box, along with the napkins he had used. He took the elevator down to the lobby. There was a feeling of urgency in him, concentrated in his stomach. It led him to the desk clerk, who seemed to have been watching for him. "My mother won't answer her door," Jesse said. "I knocked on it but she wouldn't answer...." The desk clerk's polite gaze dropped to Jesse's belly. Then it rose again. "I'm afraid something happened to her," Jesse said.

"Your mother has checked out."

"What?"

"Mrs. Pedersen has checked out of room 405. She is your mother? A gentleman came to get her... he said he was Dr. Pedersen... the two of them left about half an hour ago. I think you were out then...? Mrs. Pedersen seemed to be crying." The desk clerk was watching Jesse's face solemnly. "There must be some misunderstanding. You are Jesse Pedersen?"

"What did they... did they say what..."

"Dr. Pedersen left this letter for you."

Jesse took a letter from the desk clerk. In a daze, he turned and walked out to the street.

He could not remember where he had parked his car. He walked for a while, the letter in his hand. It seemed very large. It attracted people's attention. Then he discovered his car—it looked like his car—parked on a side street. Warm greasy air being expelled from a vent made him realize suddenly how hungry he was. There was a diner nearby. He needed good solid American food.... He clutched at his stomach, he was so hungry.

The diner was empty except for two sailors, lean as children, at the counter. Jesse settled himself carefully on one of the stools and ordered six hamburgers with chili sauce on them, three side dishes of French fries, and a Coke. He finished the Coke before the food was ready, so he ordered another. He was very thirsty—why was that? It panicked him to think that he might not get the second bottle of Coke quickly enough. But the waitress brought it right over. What was happening to him? His hand trembled as he reached for the first hamburger in its large toasted bun. The chili sauce smelled sharp, delicious.... His insides were buzzing with expectation. Jesse bit into the bun and he had the idea that the sailors and the waitress were observing him, but he didn't look over at them. He was so hungry; he felt sick with hunger. He would have liked to explain to them . . . explain to them that something strange had happened to him, that he didn't understand, didn't know what it was . . . he would have liked to explain to them that he had only wanted to do what was right . . . that there was a shrill hunger in him that rose like a scream. . . .

Eating. Pressing the food into his mouth. He had to hurry, he felt so shaky. Then, carefully, he opened the envelope from Dr. Pedersen and took out a piece of paper. Before he read it he finished the bottle of Coke. For strength, he took another large bite of hamburger. Some of the sauce ran down his arm, so he had to wipe it with a paper napkin before he could examine the piece of paper. Tears of hunger dimmed his vision.

It was a check, made out to Jesse Pedersen, for one thousand dollars. It was signed by "Karl Pedersen, M.D."

Jesse turned the check over. Nothing on the back. He sat for a while, eating, and then he picked up the envelope and looked inside. Another piece of paper, folded. He chewed desperately at a mouthful of French fries as if he feared it might get away from him, then he swallowed and felt the food streaming down the insides of his body; and already he was biting into the next hamburger, though his back teeth had begun to ache from the chewing and his eyes were hot and dazed. There were raw onions on the hamburgers and he did not like raw onions. He finished one hamburger and picked up another, and he was disappointed to notice that the bun was a little stale; saliva rushed into his mouth as if in refutation of his disappointment. He was still shaky, weak with hunger . . . he stuffed his mouth. Somehow the bun slipped out of his hand and fell onto the edge of the counter, and before he could catch it, it fell onto the floor. He stooped, grunting, and picked it up. He brushed it off with a napkin and bit into it. He ordered another Coke and then remembered that he should have milk; so he ordered a glass of milk. Then he changed his mind and ordered a chocolate milkshake. He noticed the sailors watching him from the other end of the counter—their boyish, intent faces—and the waitress, a pretty young woman, served him deftly and politely, with a small smile of her own, a creased little forehead. He was shaky, dizzy with hunger, and yet he noticed, as if from a distance of many years, the concern of other people. He wanted to explain to them that something had gone wrong, something had happened, he was not to blame, they should not blame him, they should not think ill of him. . . .

Finally, when he felt strong enough, he took out Dr. Pedersen's letter.

Jesse:
With this check and with this letter I pronounce you dead to me. You have no existence. You are nothing. You have betrayed the Pedersen family, which accepted and loved you as a son, and now you are eradicated by the family. Never try to contact us again. You are dead. You do not exist.

Karl Pedersen, M.D.

Book II

The Finite Passing of an Infinite Passion

1

A flash of lightning: the great heavy banks of air part, there is a vacuum, and then a terrific crashing-together, a cataclysmic noise. So time parts for certain events. A life seems to come apart, to be violently slashed apart. But then it comes together again and time resumes again; ordinary life resumes.

Jesse did not have much time to contemplate himself.

His years at the University of Michigan were to break into a few sharp images for him: the memory of certain buildings late in the afternoon; the canned goods—spaghetti, corned-beef hash, stew—he bought to eat alone; the residence halls he worked in; his job as an attendant at a public health center in Ann Arbor; the wet paths and hills of the arboretum where he walked sometimes by himself or, in the last year of his studies, with Anne-Marie, his fiancée. When he began to think of himself, to contemplate himself, his entire body reacted as if in sudden panic—there were things he must not think, must not contemplate, must not remember. Over the years he developed a studious, grave exterior, a kind of mask that covered not only his face but his entire body, his way of moving and breathing.

To stop from thinking of himself he thought of his work. He felt a feverish impatience with his work, the progress he was making—two years jammed into a year and a half did not please him, left him exhausted and grim. Five years jammed into four; eight years jammed into six and a half.... No, he was not pleased, he did not have time to be pleased. Alone in his room, he contemplated the books that were always before him, yet to be read. He ran his hand along the edge of the books, those hundreds of pages, mysterious from the outside, neutral. Most of the books were second-hand. He was $2500 in debt; he had to take a semester off to work, but the work was not enough to pay back much of his debt to the University—just work in a boys' residence hall, dirty, exhausting work in the kitchen unloading big containers of food, scraping piles of plates, leaning far into great greasy pots to scour them out while the very hairs on his head prickled with revulsion.... Time yawned. At the table in his room that he used as a desk he leaned forward and cradled his head in his arms, feeling how raw, how exposed his brain was, how in danger it was of disintegrating. But time resumed. Daylight resumed, after even the worst of his dim, baffling nightmares, and he awoke to normal life. He was in disguise as a normal young man.

Twenty years old: he lived in a basement room on Williams Street in Ann Arbor, Michigan. It was his first year of medical school and he had classes from eight in the morning until five in the afternoon; then he went back in the early evening to take part in experiments some of his professors were doing—insulin tests, dermatological tests, one of the worst of them a psychological test in which Jesse and other students lay in darkened rooms for forty hours, without any sounds to distract them, losing and regaining and losing their minds. In his gross anatomy laboratory, a pickled cadaver, much-handled. Death stank. He came back to his meager dripping room with the raw odor of chemical preservatives on his hands. Death was familiar in such shabby corpses, it had the air of a public place, a public rest room. It was not really important. What mattered were the structures of the body's systems, the utter undissolvable reality of their existence in any body, alive or dead.... He was twenty-one years old and still in that Williams Street room, walking several miles every day back and forth to the Medical Center, his mind sorting out problems, experiments, the case histories of patients in his clinical work he had to prepare. He studied pathology; he became fascinated with the microscopic. Sick for two weeks in the university infirmary with an influenza that was going around, he dreamed of the cells of tissues, the bizarre changes of fetal cells in animals exposed to radiation, and it seemed to him that death would not be so terrifying: only a completion. There were reversible and irreversible problems. The reversible ones panicked him because they must be handled, must be explained, life must be continued.... His hands were rough from steel wool and scouring pads and disinfectant and the splintery handles of mops, so he changed jobs—he was an attendant at a city welfare clinic for one winter, never quite well himself, his head filled with facts, formulae, the important faces of his professors, and the blurred, dying faces of the very poor, who were always trapping him into conversations: *You are so young*, the old people sighed, breaking his heart. *What is it like to be young?* They were baffled, not remembering their own youth. No, it was impossible to think of them as young. Jesse wanted to turn from them and cover his face, feeling his skin, his facial structure, as if it were a deceit, a mockery. He would have liked to scream at them that he was not young. He had never been young. No, never young!

He washed his hands often, after working at the clinic or after laboratory classes, or just because he had the opportunity, in any public men's room. He was very poor. He could not afford toothpaste. He never read newspapers or magazines, never saw any movies, never listened to the radio. Bleary-eyed from a night of work, he would show up at classes to overhear other students talking excitedly of names that meant little to him—names of European nations, names of American politicians. These young men spoke casually and intimately in a language Jesse could not quite understand. And while he was listening to it, trying to listen to it, part of him would withdraw coldly, sensing that there was nothing in such conversation for him, nothing of value. *Such things are not very real*, he thought. What was real were his laboratory reports, his examinations, his grades, the way his throat closed up at the smell of food. Food, what mountains of food!—metamorphosed into garbage, scraped from slimy, crusty plates into huge garbage bins, the stench overwhelming. In the hospitals, people lay flat on their backs and tried to eat, tried to swallow, in order to keep living. If weight loss was too rapid they would be fed in other ways and, with the body's wise instinct, they knew about these ways and so they ate, tried to eat perpetually until they died or recovered and were sent home.... Jesse had time to contemplate the noise made by mouths as food was eaten. Sometime during his second year of medical school, after he got sick, he became unable to eat in the presence of others and even their eating upset him, though he tried not to show it. He drank a lot of coffee. He ate at the table in his room irregularly, spooning food out of tin cans he heated in his sink by running hot water over them. By always focusing his eyes upon what he was reading, he was able to eat quickly and invisibly, not really conscious of eating at all.

Months of sharp, dreary weather: the ache of colds, the ache of hunger, the sleepiness in his classmates' faces, the dull anemic camaraderie of overworked students. Jesse's head often buzzed with fatigue. He saw himself again and again approaching a patient in a bare white room, the walls no more than concrete blocks, the lighting raw, fluorescent, vicious, he saw the patient transformed into a corpse, a thing to be fingered, wondered at, labeled, studied. Again and again he dreamed of approaching someone; he dreamed of the yellowed white sheet, the stillness, the toenails, the body hairs, the utterly simple dead face.... He told this dream to no one, and only once did he break down. He was a clerk in pediatrics, assigned to a children's psychiatric ward; his supervisor invited him into his office, offered him a cigarette, asked him how he was doing, and Jesse began to weep. "I'm very happy to be here. I don't know how I deserved this. I'm very happy," Jesse said hysterically.

Multitudes of faces converge into a single blur: a sea of crowding life into a geographical unit, a nation. Is there a common language? What do the imploring hands mean? Jesse saw them threaten him before he fell asleep, and part of his mind acted at once to block them out, to overcome them. No. No. He was good at saying no, at withdrawing. He resisted people. His classmates invited him out drinking with them, but he resisted. He was always in a hurry. He had a part-time job; he had two part-time jobs. He owed more money to the University. He caught mononucleosis and was sick for three long weeks, fearing sleep and desiring it, trying to hold himself back from the twilight of drugged sleep where dreams might operate freely. What a crowd of faces sought him out in his sleep! Impossible to interpret their messages in such a mob—better to insist upon darkness, the icy silence of the vacuum, the bursting of the atom out of the sky, the absolute zero of the polar regions! It was during this sickness that he met Anne-Marie.

He was twenty-one years old when he went to court to change his name: *Jesse Vogel.* He was twenty-four years old and now he lived on the third floor of a rooming house on South University; he still ate hurriedly at his desk, when he bothered to eat. Sometimes he glanced up from his work and knew there was something he must think of, someone he must recall . . . and he would think of Anne-Marie with a peculiar, flinching violence. She would be Anne-Marie Vogel in a few months. *Anne-Marie Vogel.* He loved her and he resented his need to think of her. He could not get her close enough to him, could not break through the boundaries of their flesh so that she would be near enough for him to forget. Therefore she drained him, drained his energies when he needed to work, to study, to memorize, to plan. There were other parts of his brain, dim and insoluble, unfathomable, where other Jesses existed, sinister and unkillable; and he accepted them, he could not rid himself of them. If he could have snipped certain neural pathways in his brain bloodlessly, he would have done it—with one of the neat curving little surgical instruments he had become accustomed to handling!—but it was impossible. He would always live inside himself. He would always live out those separate, frozen lives. But another part of him, the real Jesse, planned confidently for the future, thought confidently of this girl who would become his wife. After all, his life had become predictable. He was forcing his future into place.

He felt his body becoming mechanical, predictable, very sane. "Human beings fear mechanisms because they do not understand that they are mechanisms themselves. Perfect machines," one of his professors said. This professor lectured in neurochemistry; he was a guest in the department, from Boston. Jesse attended his lectures, auditing the course because he hadn't time in his official schedule to take it. He was fascinated with the man's slow, gentle, gentlemanly manner, his lapses into "unscientific" words like *destiny, beauty, creation*—such words evoked in

Jesse a sense of dreaminess, of memory, as if he had heard much of this before but could not quite recall it. "There is no machine as perfect as the human body, nothing like it in all creation," Dr. Cady stated, speaking to an amphitheater of sleepy students, Jesse among them, attentive and intrigued, though he often came to this early-morning class without having slept the night before. It was easier to stay up all night instead of sleeping a few hours. A kind of excited momentum carried him along. Then, the next night, he could sleep an ordinary five or six hours and wake refreshed, as if he hadn't missed any sleep at all. During such stretches of activity he hadn't any appetite either, and he felt surges of an unaccountable joy, as if he were pushing himself up out of the sluggish confines of his body, his spirit emerging muscular and powerful and very sane.

Yes, even his spirit had become automated, mechanized. It worked perfectly for him. He had only to direct it and it responded. It grew wise.

He got special permission to work late and sometimes, in the nearly deserted laboratory, he suddenly felt a sense of panic, as if a door might open at any moment and someone might walk in—a dream ballooning out of the empty corridor outside. If he could not control the panic with a cigarette or one of the little pills Anne-Marie had given him, he went outside, hurrying out into the street. His heart pumped, his eyes were wild. He walked around the block, around the large darkened buildings of the Medical Center, sensing himself absolutely alone, as if he had stepped out of the normal dimension of time and were already in his own future. *There* was sanctity, purity, *there* he could contemplate himself without panic. What was time? The element in which he lived, automatically. What was life? He knew that a living cell performs certain miraculous acts, that it contains a kind of electricity, and that a dead cell performs no acts, goes through no sequence of characteristic, identifying acts, and is nothing. The definition of life, then, was only one of behavior: the living cell behaved, the dead cell did nothing. The living cell was godly, the dead cell a zero. Between the two there was a universe of time.

This overwhelmed him. Fascinated him. He had no time to be fascinated because he had to work, yet his mind came back again and again to such facts. . . . *He had changed his name to Vogel in 1945. Jesse Vogel. The end of the war, the beginning of Jesse Vogel.* The facts he must be concerned with in his own private, interior life were simple and unmysterious and unfascinating: he would begin an internship in Chicago in July; he would marry Anne-Marie; he would establish a certain life, professional and private. Wasn't this enough to pit against the universe? . . . Sometimes, on a night when his nerves were jumpy from too much coffee, too many half-hallucinations of opening doors, cells shaking themselves to life when they were dead, precise and dead, he went out to a drugstore and telephoned Anne-Marie. She woke, answered at once, before the telephone could ring a second time, because she lived with her mother and did not belong wholly to Jesse. He could see her only a few times a week because he was so busy. Always, telephoning her late at night, his heart tripped absurdly as he listened to the distant, fragile ring that seemed already transformed by Anne-Marie's presence.

When she answered in her soft voice, "Jesse?" he closed his eyes in relief. She had answered his call. She was real.

"Hello," he would say. "It's just me. How are you? Did I wake you up? Did you have a hard day?" This surprised him, the choppiness of his questions, the abruptness of his voice. He had forgotten that he was so young and demanding. If she was tired herself, Anne-Marie never said so; she insisted that she had not really been asleep but only lying in bed, thinking of him. And Jesse would ask her about her work that day, about the other nurses, about her mother, and he would tell her about his own work, going back over the events of his crowded day, the conversations he had had with other people, the state of his landlady's domain—there were always minor domestic crises in the rooming house, with Jesse at the center, a kind of intermediary between the landlady and her other tenants. After a few minutes of this Jesse would begin to slow down, to relax. Anne-Marie would say sleepily, "I love you . . . you're so serious . . . you work so hard. . . ." There was a kind of lightness about her that she seemed to insist upon in spite of her nursing schedule and her troubles with her mother. She was always offering herself to him lightly, childishly; even her problems were twisted about to seem trivial. She slighted herself: the complaints she offered to Jesse were not serious. A sense of gratitude for her, for her kindness, was focused for Jesse in the clumsy hearts carved on the inside of the telephone booth by high school girls—so many hearts, all of them touchingly distorted, dancing before his eyes— "When can I see you? When tomorrow?" Jesse would always ask urgently. And, waiting anxiously for her reply, he closed his eyes and saw Anne-Marie, this long-haired, healthy, pretty girl, freed of the very restraints of gravity itself, released in her perfect white nurse's uniform from the old hospital in which she worked or from the aging house in which she lived, released to his arms.

Anne-Marie Vogel.

She loved him and it caused him to think, on the darkest of his dark cloudy nights, that he was really a normal young man. Not isolated. Not fated to confusion, chaos. He stood six feet two inches tall, strong in the shoulders and self-consciously erect, his hair brushed back from his forehead, thick and slightly darkening now, no longer so blond; his gaze was clear and cautious, a level stare that scanned everything before him, out to the limits of the spatial horizon, before settling on what must be seen. There was a slowness about him, a ponderousness, that seemed to collide with a certain impatience in his speech, as if he were often prodding himself awake out of a confusion of memory, the very brusqueness of his words meant to wake Jesse himself. Moods rose and fell in him, challenged him and were vanquished, moods of intense happiness—in his laboratory work and in his reading and in his love for Anne-Marie—and moods of sudden, almost abandoned depression, a gaiety of depressions, as if he knew everything was lost and could do nothing about it, nothing to save himself, why bother? Catching his own eye in a mirror he sometimes noticed a strange intense heat about his face, the very tone of his skin heated, pink-toned, very healthy on even his dreariest Ann Arbor days, as if the subdued and even shy manner that was his usual personality were underscored by this brazen, curious stare. He had avoided people for years now, perplexed by their response to him and not really wanting to do battle with it or comprehend it: it must have been that his face, in repose, had a skeptical or argumentative look, because he sensed a nervousness, a slight hostility in men his own age or older when they were in his company. "No, no, people like you, people are very fond of you," Anne-Marie insisted. But he did not believe her. With her he felt confidence—even normality—he felt oddly protected. As long as he was with her he did not even need to believe her.

And yet, when he was away from her, he sometimes could not recall her face. He felt her essence, her presence, but only as an abstraction—she might have been any American beauty on a billboard, advertising a brand of cigarettes or a soft drink.

One quiet night in April, 1951, he left the pathology laboratory late, around eleven, and as he passed a group of men on the sidewalk he noticed that one of the men glanced toward him, then turned to look at him. He did not return the look. The young men were mostly students and he did not want to be invited out with them, he had no time or interest... no time for drinking, no interest in talking, arguing. He was a little dizzy from not having anything to eat since noon. But when he was out on his feet like this, outside in public, the dizziness usually abated. He was too proud to walk weakly.

Anne-Marie was working at the hospital and so he couldn't see her; she would not go off duty until morning. So he walked quickly toward home, feeling the start of a familiar panic; he walked fast, as if he thought he might outwalk the panic, might get home before it struck. All day long he had been thinking about the utterly simple, grave pronouncements of the lecturer in neurochemistry, Dr. Cady: *The world is our construction, peopled by us; it is a mystery. All we know of the world, even our most precise laboratory findings, rests on the perception of the senses, but this very knowledge cannot reveal the relations of the senses to the outside world.* Jesse had been struck by this; he had wanted to laugh in astonishment. He wanted to seek out Cady and argue with him. Cady was a short, slight, rather delicate man; Jesse would have to stoop a little to talk to him, he would have to speak gently to him. But he wanted, he wanted... he wanted to argue.... Isn't the great lesson of science *control*? The lessons of homeostasis and cybernetics: *control*? What else mattered?

If he had control of himself, Jesse Vogel, then nothing else mattered in the universe.

He walked quickly—the panic was feeding energy into his legs. He could hear faint noises from the fraternity houses on the other side of the campus, up along Washtenaw, and he knew that what had seemed so deeply and ominously silent to him was not silence at all but was filled with the special small language of human beings. But he could not understand this language. Even Anne-Marie's words, her love, her perfumy essence—he could not understand it. So he walked fast, heading home, hurrying home on a pleasant cloudy night in April. What would await him at the rooming house? It was a kind of home for him; yes, he was fond of it, dependent upon it—the other tenants laughed at him because he was so easily victimized by the landlady, who was without a husband, perhaps divorced? widowed? abandoned? and who got Jesse to leave his books and run errands for her, beat carpets in the back yard as they hung, enormously heavy, from a straining clothesline, or watch over her eight-year-old daughter, a sorrowful child with glasses. But he liked living there. It was filled with the noise of other students, with their yelping laughter and radios and heavy footsteps, with the landlady's scolding of her daughter, but he liked it—it helped to dispel his own thoughts, his memories, the problems of his being. *Control.* That was all he wanted. The noises other people made helped to dispel Jesse's private burdens a little. He did not want to complain, even to himself, and so he blocked off the channels that led back to certain thoughts, just as he had recklessly and desperately sold that car of his, at a great loss, just to be rid of it, rid of it permanently, years ago here in Ann Arbor.... But at times, when his panic threatened, he had the idea that his private memories fed somehow into a vast universal memory, a sorrow not his own that he had not lived through and therefore could not erase, even by the most intense rituals of thought—this confused sorrow that populated the universe, that constructed the universe. It was not local. It was not even contained in the vast wastes of the war or in the jumble of history in this century. Time was mobbed with people. How could he establish himself, construct himself, in such a mob...? It was harmonious, unlocalized, spread out evenly everywhere. There was nothing human to it.

He wanted to argue with that professor. He wanted to insist that these things did not matter.... No, he wanted to embrace Anne-Marie violently, sweetly, he wanted to whisper these things to her, he wanted to frighten her with their terror and then calm her, soothe her, bring her back to the cheerful busyness of her usual life. But he knew that she would not understand. He had no right to force her to understand. If he loved her he would guard her from such thoughts; if he loved her he would not really bring her into himself, into his consciousness, but would allow her to remain herself.... He had learned from the few novels he had read in his lifetime that love demanded rescue. He must rescue his beloved from danger, even the danger of himself. The story demanded that a male rescue a female from danger and he would be punished if he failed....

Glancing back over his shoulder, Jesse saw someone following him half a block away. This person—a man—looked familiar, but Jesse did not have time to see who it was before he turned back again uneasily. This street led past residence halls and was therefore noisy. Jesse glanced at the rows of lighted dormitory windows and felt a pang of jealousy for the simplicity of these undergraduates' lives—when he had worked in dining halls he'd envied the boys' sloppiness, their loud herding instincts. He felt an impulse to go into one of the halls, just to avoid the man behind him. It was probably a classmate of his, wanting help. Wanting to borrow notes. At least everyone knew enough not to ask to borrow money from him. He owed the university more money than ever, almost three thousand dollars.... Jesse turned up one of the walks and went into a residence hall, walking quickly, as if he lived here, and once inside he paused to wait a few minutes. It was crowded here. Jesse had always felt oddly benevolent toward the undergraduates at the university, though they had money and he was poor; he thought of them as children, they were so boisterous and sure of themselves. They lived in rooms jammed with junk, dirty clothes and towels flung everywhere, sheets that went unchanged for weeks, they played poker and drank happily and stupidly; they were children and could be blamed for nothing. Those who did not live in the residence halls lived in palatial fraternity houses—enormous houses where music blared and curtains were blown outside windows. Jesse thought of these young people as jammed together warmly, perpetually. They came alive in crowds. Their faces brightened in herds. He envied them but felt, in a way, protective of them: when he was a doctor he would be serving them.

After a few minutes he took a side door out to the street again and hurried the few blocks to his rooming house. Now no one was following him.

He went up to his room on the third floor and saw that the door was ajar—he had evidently left it open in his hurry to leave that morning—and then, in the doorway, he was shocked to see that someone was in the room, sitting at his "desk," the cluttered table he worked at. It was Dr. Monk, "Monk," the man who assisted Dr. Cady in the neurochemistry course. Jesse realized now that Monk had been following him.

"Hello!" Monk said with a big smile.

He got to his feet and extended his hand. For a moment Jesse stood in the doorway, too stunned to react. Then, feebly, he shook hands with Monk. He could not help glancing around the room, as if checking it.

"I took the liberty of making myself at home. I didn't think you'd mind. You don't mind?" Monk said. He had caught Jesse's instinctive checking of the room and this seemed to amuse him. "I swear I haven't taken a thing! I haven't been tempted even by that stale sweet roll on the radiator, I swear.... Are you comfortable here? You're fairly isolated, at least, on the third floor."

"Yes...." Jesse said vaguely, not catching all this.

"You're wondering how I knew where you live?" Monk said.

Jesse was too confused to reply.

"I knew that you certainly didn't live in that residence hall," Monk said with a grin. "Well, why don't you come in? Sit down? You'll make me think I'm not welcome."

Jesse knew Monk slightly. He was an instructor in the medical school, having taken a degree somewhere else—Minnesota, Jesse believed. Monk had interned and taken a year's residency at Michigan. He was supposed to be brilliant. He attended all of Dr. Cady's lectures, sitting up at the front of the room in the left-hand corner, facing both Cady and the class, leaning forward attentively, earnestly; he corrected examinations for Cady and ran a laboratory section. Jesse had had a few hurried conversations with him about something Cady had touched upon, and once he had met Monk in a building late in the afternoon, in that dreary yellowish late afternoon of university buildings that is like a condition of the soul—but he had never had time to accept Monk's invitations to have coffee together or to go out drinking. Now he felt awkward, apologetic, as if this cramped room were Monk's and he himself an intruder.

"Yes, it isn't bad up here," Monk said. "I wondered where you lived. You look so incredibly serious all the time, it's difficult to think of you living anywhere, actually sleeping, becoming unconscious occasionally. . . . Are all these books yours? Jesus. Are those more books over there? You truly are a serious student, aren't you? My friend Bob Winslow lives on the first floor here. He says the landlady is a little crazy and that she takes advantage of you. Is that true?"

"No," Jesse said.

Monk laughed.

Jesse smiled a small, patient smile. What did this man want? Why didn't he leave? But Monk did not quite meet his gaze—he was a big man, looking a few years older than his age because of his slack, thinning blond hair, which was uncombed, and the pouches beneath his eyes. He was about thirty. He had an abrupt nervous laugh, a generous, good-natured manner, tufts of eyebrows that rose continually in mock surprise, a voice that was too loud for intimate conversation. He was too loud, too large. The few times Jesse had spoken with Monk he had felt uneasy, uncomfortable, as if he were holding a book up too close to his eyes. That way you couldn't read: the print was just a threat.

"I saw you leave the lab tonight and wanted to say hello. It's about time we got to know each other; you'll be leaving in a few months, won't you? Where are you going?"

"Chicago, I hope."

"Where, LaSalle?"

"Yes."

"How are things going with you?"

"All right," Jesse said.

Jesse sat on the edge of his bed. Monk was sitting in Jesse's chair. He crossed his legs uneasily, as if he sensed Jesse's irritation. Then he smiled, ready to begin a new topic, approaching Jesse from another angle. He spoke buoyantly of the work he was doing—neurophysiological experiments for Cady, on a big research grant—endless cuttings of cats. "To be factual and therefore more pedantic and confusing," he said, "we're working with a monosynaptic reflex pathway of the cat spinal cord, a fascinating mechanism!"

"What are you doing?" Jesse asked.

"Oh—" Monk said, waving the question away, "oh, I think it will turn out to be for Cady's private fortune; maybe he wants to perfect another barbiturate and patent it... you know he's already wealthy from a patent he has? No, didn't you know that? I thought everyone knew."

"I don't know much about Cady."

"You admire him, though. Enormously."

"I suppose so," Jesse said.

"It shows in your face, even at nine in the morning. Obvious adulation. It's good to see that kind of thing, even at nine in the morning."

Jesse was silent.

"Well, yes, Cady is an extraordinary man and there aren't many like him. I don't blame you for admiring him. We all do." Monk's enthusiasm did not seem sincere to Jesse. It was a way of talking, a method, while his eyes prowled restlessly around the room and back and forth over Jesse's face. His face seemed larger than an ordinary face, as if it had been stretched, kneaded out of shape, a clown's face, the features meant for a stage and its exaggerating lights. Jesse had always heard of his brilliance and of his "good-heartedness"—which meant he tutored students for nothing, he sometimes lent them money, he was generally available for help with people who were having trouble understanding Cady.

"Of course, none of us know Dr. Cady very well. I like his clothes myself. Excellent. He has a daughter, did you know?—a brilliant young woman in chemistry, biochemistry, something like that. At Harvard."

Jesse nodded vaguely. He wondered how long Monk would keep on talking.

"Look, Jesse, don't be offended. I only wanted to say hello to you. We had a fascinating conversation that day, do you remember? a few weeks ago? You said you had insomnia, just like me."

"Did I?" Jesse did not remember this.

"Yes, you mentioned it. I have insomnia too. But it gives us more hours of the day, it prolongs our conscious lives—right?

Of course, I have a photographic memory and am therefore something of a freak. You're not like that, are you? You don't have a genuine photographic memory?"

"Not the real thing, no," Jesse said coldly.

"You're not a freak, no, I didn't think so. There's a fourteen-year-old kid in physics here, do you know about him? Skinny, pop-eyed, a real genius. He knows everything. He's going right for the Ph.D., the hell with the B.A. He makes me feel very old suddenly. Did I tell you I'm contemplating another kind of life?"

"No."

"Not marriage, like you, but another kind of life altogether...."

In spite of himself, Jesse felt curious. "What would you do?" he asked.

Monk shrugged his shoulders. "Retreat. Retire. I think of Northern Minnesota, I think of lakes and pure water and silence ... I'd like to write poems, I'd like to wear this perpetual stink off my hands.... But they'd need a doctor up there; sure enough some female would start to give birth and they'd call me in, and I'd be Dr. Monk again, I couldn't escape.... I put in a year as a G.P., you know."

Jesse did not remember if he knew this or not—but why should he have known it? He was not a friend of Monk's.

"Everyone thinks of dropping out occasionally," Jesse said. It was the first thing he had really said to Monk; he felt Monk's satisfaction.

"Jesse, you should call me Trick. My friends call me Trick. My name is Talbot Waller Monk, an impossible name, obviously uttered by my mother as she came out of the anesthetic, and so everyone calls me Trick. Do you know why?"

His manner was open and childlike and yet not very sincere. "I don't know why," Jesse said. "Maybe you play tricks on people."

"No, tricks are vulgar ... mere tricks are vulgar," Monk laughed. "No. I simply push the logistics of a situation as far as it will go; I exploit the dimension of the possible rather than the probable. But I don't intrude upon anyone's destiny. It's all predictable, in a way."

Jesse had heard of his practical jokes at second and third hand, but he had never paid much attention to them.

"I did a fairly good impersonation of Rothman last fall, when he couldn't make a genetic talk at Michigan State. They thought I was the great Rothman himself," Monk laughed. "But really I was much better because I can at least speak the English language. It was very strange, there were people there who had known him . . . and yet they believed I was Rothman for some reason. . . ."

"You don't look anything like him."

"Of course not. He's a Jew from New York, slumming out here, and I'm an archetypal Midwestern personality. Actually, I'm very prejudiced. In the interests of science I hide my bias, but in my soul I'm really anti-Semitic. Come on, don't look so surprised, why can't we be honest with each other? You and I are Midwestern types. Look at us. We even look something alike, in spite of my ugly face. I'm really very narrow in spite of my girth." His face had flushed with a kind of fanciful shame. Jesse stared at him, uncomprehending.

"Well, it's late, I should be leaving," Monk said. But he did not move. Something caught his eye: a towel of Jesse's on a rack just inside his closet. "Who did you steal that from, someone with the initials JP?—that towel, I mean. But no, never mind, I'm too curious for my own good. I only wanted to say hello to you and to congratulate you."

"On what?"

"Oh, on your work, your good grades, your industry, all that. . . . Cady asks to see the good papers and he was impressed with yours. Especially when I told him you weren't really enrolled in the course. He's got this idea that people out here, non-Harvard people, are idiots, and when anyone does well it seems to astonish him. He asked me a few questions about you. I told him what I knew—nobody knows much about you, Jesse, except that you're bad competition—you've been around for a while but nobody knows much. I ran into my old friend Anne-Marie Seton the other day—"

"Anne-Marie? Do you know her?"

Monk seemed to be screwing up one side of his face, about to wink, but at the last moment—as if guessing that Jesse was on the verge of anger—his face relaxed. It took on an appearance of slack, respectful, moronic seriousness. Jesse's heart began to pound as if he were in the presence of something deadly.

"Yes, of course I know Anne-Marie. I knew her when she was

in nursing school. She lives in Ann Arbor with her mother . . . a pretty girl. . . ."

He spoke quickly and tonelessly, with a kind of apologetic smile.

"It just occurred to me," Monk said, "in talking with Cady, that I didn't know you either. I think I would like to know you. As a scientist I have a natural interest in superior personalities." Now his manner changed, the mock-apologetic look drained away; he became again lordly, decorous, very patient, as if he were much older than Jesse. Jesse felt a renewal of his initial assessment of this man, made years ago: he was a puzzle. But Jesse had no time for puzzles. "A superior personality reduces me to Jell-O. In the presence of the great Benjamin Cady I provide an ashtray for him with my hands, automatically, unconsciously, and he taps his ashes out in my hands just as automatically, accepting me as an ashtray without even thinking about it. I feel flattered. I run out to get him coffee, but it can't just be ordinary coffee; he's very fussy. I arranged for the apartment he has. His daughter is coming to join him. I arranged for that. We sit in his office practically knee to knee, talking, but then something happens and he doesn't seem to want to talk about his work, he wants to talk suddenly about custom-built automobiles or Mozart or an Italian cheese, and I feel my soul deflate, the air seep out of it tragically. . . . What good is it, really, a life of science? a life in science?"

"There isn't any other life," Jesse said.

"Oh, hell."

"There isn't any other life," Jesse repeated.

"Why not?"

When Jesse did not answer, Monk pressed his fist against his chest and held that position for several seconds, as if he were thinking very seriously. "No, you're wrong. We're devoting our lives to bodies, masses. We'd be better off perfecting explosives. Man is a mouth and an anus. Man isn't worth our devotion."

"Are you deliberately stupid?" Jesse asked.

This caught Monk by surprise: he stared at Jesse. Then he smiled coldly.

"Yes, deliberately. It's part of my style," he said. He got to his feet. He was wearing mismatched clothes—an old brown sweater and gray corduroy trousers shiny at the knees. It was rumored that he had money but that he never spent it on himself. "I'm sorry I offended you, Jesse. I know you're devoted to medicine. You've consecrated yourself. But I have a flabby soul; it's like air leaking out of a balloon.... You can hear it escaping if you listen. Yes, I'm leaving. I'll leave. You didn't go to see her tonight, eh?"

Jesse stood. "Why do you talk about her like that?"

"Like what?"

"In that way—that voice— What do you want?"

Monk spread his hands. "Absolutely nothing. I don't understand you. I came only to congratulate you on the success of your work—I'm very jealous of you, your youth and your energy. And your pretty little girl."

"We're going to be married," Jesse said.

"Oh?"

"Yes. Married."

They stared at each other. Monk lingered in the doorway, filling it with his slightly rounded shoulders. He smiled. "I don't think you're going to get married," he said finally.

"Get the hell out of here!"

Monk waved good-by and left.

Jesse stood in the doorway of his room. His face twitched, he felt like running after Monk and grabbing hold of him.... Instead, he went to the window and looked down to the street. A lonely street. A feeble light. In a minute or so Monk's figure appeared, large and grave, the shoulders bent forward a little. His walk was odd, as if premeditated, each step planned with care: *now I will cross the street, now I will step up onto the curb, now I will glance over my shoulder to see if Jesse is watching me....*

Jesse drew back from the window. His heart pounded with a dull, puzzled anger.

"Bastard," he said aloud.

He did not intend to sleep, so he lay down on top of his bedspread, pushing a few books aside. He thought about Monk. He thought about Anne-Marie. Something surged in his blood, a heady chemical released by such thoughts, an anger close to elation.... Then his mouth was dry. He must have slept and jerked awake suddenly. He sat up, checked the time—quarter after five. He went to his worktable and sat down. A pile of books. Papers, lab reports. It took him a while to remember that Dr. Monk, "Trick" Monk, had been sitting here talking to him hours before. *I came only to congratulate you,* Monk had said. Why was his mouth so dry now? He must have slept unexpectedly and breathed through his mouth. He had not intended to sleep. Everything was slowed down in him now, at five in the morning, and he could not quite remember what Monk had said that had angered him. Maybe he'd imagined it. Monk was always joking, he had the reputation of being a good person, generous and wise. . . .

Jesse worked until quarter to eight, when he ran downstairs and over to the hospital where Anne-Marie was on duty. He got to the hospital five minutes before the shift changed, so he went down to the Outpatients' Clinic, where a row of people were already sitting beneath a big clock. Anne-Marie would take this way out. The hospital smelled good to him. A yellowed old woman, sitting near the door to the Outpatients' Clinic, tugged at his arm. "You have to take a number and wait your turn," she said importantly. All the patients were holding large plastic cards with numbers on them, the kind used in meat markets.

"Thank you," Jesse said politely. "But I'm not waiting for the clinic."

The activity of the corridor distracted him. Nurses coming in, wearing light spring coats over their uniforms; nurses preparing to go off duty, yawning. Their movements—the rapid soft-soled motion of their feet—pleased Jesse. There were no men around, no men on duty. The doors to the x-ray rooms and the Pathology Lab were still locked. There were only the nurses, most of them firm-bodied young women, brisk in their white uniforms and pale transparent stockings.

The door to the stairway opened a short distance away and Anne-Marie suddenly came through. Jesse sucked in his breath at the sight of her.

A beautiful copper-haired girl. A stranger.

She saw him and faltered. One hand rose as if in defense. But then she smiled broadly and they hurried to meet each other. Jesse wondered if his face showed that strange, evil elation of the night before.

"Is anything wrong?" Anne-Marie whispered.

"No. Nothing. I just wanted to see you," Jesse said.

He had taken her hand. His eyes seemed to grab at her.

"Couldn't you sleep last night? You look so tired. . . ." she said nervously.

"I just wanted to see you."

They walked toward the exit. Jesse was aware of the outpatients watching them, sitting obediently along the wall with their plastic cards in hand. But he could not release Anne-Marie's hand and he could not stop staring at her. He felt the tension in his face, in the muscles of his jaws.

"It was a bad night, everyone waking up and wanting sleeping pills and running us to death. . . . Oh, I must look awful," Anne-Marie said.

"You look very beautiful," Jesse said.

She lifted her face to him as if offering herself. Her eyes were large with weariness—dark brown eyes, almost black, fascinating. Yes, now that he was with her he remembered her exactly.

"I was thinking about you all last night," Jesse said.

Anne-Marie smiled uneasily.

"You couldn't sleep again . . . ?"

"I slept for a while. I feel fine," Jesse said.

"You're sure that nothing is wrong?"

"I felt that I wanted to see you," he said quickly. "I was thinking about you . . . I was talking about you. . . ."

"Oh, with who? You were talking about me?"

"No one you know, a man named Monk. He's an instructor in neurochemistry."

Anne-Marie smiled faintly.

"You don't know him?" Jesse said.

"Who? What is his name?"

"Monk."

"That's a strange name."

"They call him Trick. I don't know his real name—Talbot, maybe—Talbot Monk. Do you know him?"

She shook her head. Jesse squeezed her hand, as if to reassure her that he believed her. He took her gently by the arm and walked her out to the parking lot. "He's about thirty, he has blond hair, he's big, tall, going to fat a little . . . there's something strange about him . . . everyone likes him, he's very friendly, very popular. . . . You don't remember him?"

"No. Why should I remember him? I don't know him."

"He seemed to know you."

Anne-Marie stared at him, smiling. Again she shook her head. She had lovely fair skin, a small strong nose, perfect teeth. Jesse's head pounded with blood. He loved her, he was weak with love for her. . . .

"It must have been a misunderstanding then," he said.

"But why are you so . . . strange?"

"Do I look strange?"

"Yes, you look as if you're angry with me."

"No, no. I'm not angry, no," Jesse said, confused. He realized that he had tightened his grip on her arm and that he was frightening her. He forced himself to relax. Relax. A few slow, deep breaths. He would be all right.

"Who is this man again?" Anne-Marie asked.

"No one, nothing. It must have been a misunderstanding."

"He isn't a friend of yours, is he?"

"I don't have any friends," Jesse said. "Except you."

"What did he want with you?"

She kept looking at him, forcing him to look at her. He was weak with desire for her . . . or maybe he was weak with hunger . . . everything was confused, jumbled in his head. *I came only to congratulate you*, Monk had said. Why didn't he believe that, why didn't he accept it? A kind of wild elated anger kept tensing up his face, making his eyes narrow. He was frightening this girl. Obviously she did not know Monk.

"I wanted to see you this morning. I had to see you," Jesse said. "You're so beautiful. . . . You do love me?"

"You looked so angry for a minute," Anne-Marie said.

"You love me . . . ?"

He stared into her face: he might have been staring over a precipice. There was that instant of danger, of terrible weightlessness.

"Of course I love you," she whispered.

It was so easily said that he did not believe her. How could she love him? Forgive him? . . . But then he relented and believed her. In a part of his mind she was already his wife.

2

A few days later Trick gave Jesse a book of essays on biochemistry—he explained that the publishers had sent him two copies and he had thought Jesse might like one. The book was selling for fifteen dollars. Jesse was tempted to refuse, but Trick was so sunny and unpushing that Jesse gave in; maybe he had been mistaken about Trick. Now it seemed he was seeing Trick everywhere, at a distance, in the corridor of one building or another, and that Trick was friendly but not eager—content to wave at Jesse as he hurried along, having other people to talk to. Jesse saw him sometimes with Dr. Cady on the sidewalks around the Medical Center.

Trick was often the center of a group, some boisterous gang a little loud from overwork, their laughter sounding hysterical; he was taller than most of his friends, his fair hair a neutral, pallid gleam, his laughter cutting through theirs with that sudden, violent, lordly corrosiveness, as if he were at once both a young king and a court jester, a clown with license to say anything. And he did say anything in the company of students. Jesse overheard him joking about members of the medical school staff, about tumors, guts, brains, his own ingrown toenails, even about the medical experiments performed by Nazi doctors on human victims, the subject of a recent story in *Life* Magazine: "What I wouldn't give for such an opportunity!" Trick would say, winking. "Imagine extra-large cats, cats with handles a man could actually grab hold of, not those cold furry little sons of bitches we have to work with in American labs! You must admit that Hitler had a certain style, a certain flair lacking in our bourgeois medical men."

And he would stretch his face, clowning and melancholy, daring them to take him seriously.

One day he caught up with Jesse on the street and, out of nowhere, patted his slack stomach, which had begun to protrude in a small, soft, wavelike roll. "This life is decadent, we aren't really worked hard enough," he sighed merrily. "I miss the drama of the war. I wish it would return. Those concluding days did something to me, gave me a permanent taste for cheap suspense —this peacetime living is decadent, fattening. Even you could be worked harder, Jesse." If he offended people, they gave no sign. Perhaps, like Jesse, they were puzzled by Trick and reluctant to judge him. When Trick was in the lecture hall or in the laboratory, he was usually serious; the rest of the time, rarely. Was everything a joke, to be joked about? Maybe. Trick's large, genial face, his yodel of welcome and his stiff, rather formal handshake, even the deadpan remarks he made when passing out examination booklets made him extremely popular; Jesse noticed other students imitating Trick.

He wondered why he had always disliked the man.

One morning Trick took over a lecture for Dr. Cady, who was out of town. He explained at great length the procedures and tentative results of the research project he was heading, under Cady's general supervision. He wore a suit and a tie, he spoke clearly, precisely, his forehead furrowed with the need to be absolutely correct. All around Jesse students sat hunched forward, taking rapid notes; their desks creaked under the strain. Trick did not drift off into quaint metaphysical speculation, as Cady sometimes did, so the students had no rest, but were forced to write continually. Jesse was fascinated with what Trick had to say. He could hardly recognize Trick in that dignified young man who stood at the lectern—how serious he was after all, how impressive a scientist! Yes, Jesse thought, he was a man of exceptional quality.

Half the amphitheater burst into spontaneous applause at the end of the lecture. Jesse and a few other students hurried down front to congratulate Trick.

Afterward, still nervous and a little formal, Trick said to Jesse: "I'm glad you could appreciate what I had to say. I think it went over most of their heads."

They went out for coffee to a restaurant on State Street, and there Trick talked more about his research and his plans. Jesse, who was interested in clinical medicine, began to wonder if maybe research might be more exciting. He asked Trick questions and Trick replied seriously, respectfully. Yes, he did seem like another person. The formal clothing restrained him. After a while he relaxed and began to speak of the years he had put in himself, as a student, then an intern, then a resident. "People in my family have no idea what I am now. They think maybe I've gone backwards. It seems to them I should have a practice of fifty thousand a year by now instead of grubbing along as I am." Of his family he said little: his father was an "ordinary businessman in St. Paul," his mother an "ordinary housewife in St. Paul." Where did his genius come from then? he asked ironically. Well, a distant cousin of his was also gifted with a photographic memory and total recall. The cousin was a boy seventeen years old, but not mature enough to be trusted at a university; Trick had the idea, though no one in the family exactly said this, that the boy was a little crazy.... Everyone else in his family seemed normal. His mother baked him brownies and mailed them every two or three weeks; they arrived stale and broken, sometimes no more than crumbs, but he wrote back dutifully to thank her. Certain myths cannot be broken. He loved his parents because they were so decent, so normal. "We are all very Midwestern in my family, which means that we are decent, silent people. For all my talk, Jesse, you must understand that I am essentially a silent person." But there was no danger of his perpetuating his family's ordinary genes, he said, because he would never marry. He did not believe in the divinity of Christ, but he believed in Christ's purity. He seemed to be serious. He affected a horror of the body that was lyric and heavy, whimsical and grave: "We in medicine should go after the ultimate cure—the separation of the spirit from the flesh. Everything else is unsanitary nonsense."

Jesse laughed at this, bewildered.

Yet at other times, when they talked of their work, Trick confessed to a sentimental weakness for fixing up things, making the parts work together perfectly, "especially in children—I could never work up a healthy hatred of any child. Which makes me think I'll subside into being a country G.P. someday."

"Someone has to do that kind of work," Jesse said. He was cautious with Trick because Trick so often joked; but he did not seem to be joking now. So Jesse said, warming to the subject, "I know what you mean. I want to fix things up too. I have this dream, this bad dream, of my crossing a room to a patient who turns out to be dead... and everything is awful, everything dissolves, because the patient is *dead* and beyond my ability to help him.... I wake up sweating. I wake up in a real terror. Because if they die, if they die... then they have escaped to someplace where you can't follow them; it's as if they've carried away with them to another dimension the secret of their disorder and can't be reached. Slicing the body open, pulling out the brains, won't really tell you why they died."

"No, that won't. That won't really tell you why they died," Trick said.

"I want to fix people up. Children and everyone. I'd like to run a clinic, you know, a kind of welfare clinic but with good equipment, not a slum.... I want to save them all."

Trick listened closely. In spite of his habitual scowl of derision, he was really sympathetic; Jesse sensed that.

"I suppose I want to perform miracles," Jesse said warmly, "but I want the miracles ordinary—I want to make miraculous things ordinary again. And I would like to do this impersonally. Out of sight. I don't especially want to be Dr. Vogel, *Dr. Vogel*, I don't want people grateful to me. I'd like to be a presence that is invisible, impersonal. I don't want any personality involved—where there's personality everything is confused—"

Trick stared at him, smiling oddly.

"I imagine myself this way," Jesse said. "There will be my own family, my wife and children—"

"Wife and children? How many children?"

"Four or five. This family and me—together. We will understand one another. But the work I do, the patients I see, will be impersonal and without private history, just this abstract love for them—they will be a kind of family to me also, but abstract and impersonal—" And he was giddy with a sudden knowledge that this would happen somehow. "I want—I want to do good—"

Trick was looking at him blankly.

"You don't think it's possible?" Jesse asked.

"My opinion will have nothing to do with your future," Trick said slowly.

"Well, I want to do good," Jesse said. "Otherwise it isn't worth it."

Trick colored slightly, as if these words were too intimate for him.

Jesse waited for Trick to ask about Anne-Marie, but he never mentioned her. He began to wonder if he had imagined Trick's remarks about her. There were weeks of Trick's joking, his silence, his melancholy, his gossip, his comic complaints—and still Jesse waited uneasily for him to mention Anne-Marie. Had Trick forgotten her? One day, out walking with her, he believed he saw Trick in a crowd in front of the diagonal before the main library, and he was about to point Trick out to her when he thought better of it.... He did not want them to meet.

Late one afternoon Jesse was working in a third-floor laboratory when Trick dropped by to see him. He must have climbed the stairs in a hurry, because he was struggling to get his breath. "Jesse, hello! I haven't seen you all week," he said.

His face was pale and strained from the stairs.

"I've been working hard," Jesse said. "How about you?"

"Oh, the same as always, the same." He belled out his cheeks as if to make fun of his own breathlessness. He was really out of breath; he was almost panting. "I'm in perfect condition, as you can see."

"Nobody should run up those stairs," Jesse said.

"I didn't run. I came up carefully, one step at a time," Trick laughed.

Jesse watched him, concerned. But Trick waved him aside. He had a habit of dismissing personal questions or comments as if to show that he was not at anyone's service, he was not available to anyone's curiosity or sympathy. "Let me look at your work," he said. He adjusted the eyepiece of the microscope. "Ah, very pretty! Lovely little cobwebs you've been growing. Don't tell me what they are, that would spoil it. I like to think that such lovely things are cancer, maybe... people are so cruel about cancer, they are so grimly determined to wipe it out...." He smiled at Jesse. "Cancerous cells have as much divinity in them as so-called normal cells. There's too much prejudice against them. Did I ever tell you, Jesse, about my secret hopes for a career? It's a little late now, but I'm thinking of switching to OB work; I'd like to be a great gynecologist; I'd like to take loving, gentle smears from the bodies of women, and examine them like this, in the solitude of a laboratory. I would be the most devoted and discreet of lovers and I would keep every secret."

Jesse recoiled from him a little. He forced himself to smile.

Trick must have misunderstood the smile, for he stretched his narrow, dry lips in an instantaneous grin, as if a certain shock of sympathy had run between them. "If I could, I would impregnate them all—with my fingertips—I would be very gentle, I would be invisible. A certain young student, on his way to a brilliant career, told me once that he would like to be invisible and I understood that desire at once; I too would like to be invisible in this race of men, an instrument, a metallic model of an organ—for the real thing, the real organ, is apt to be disappointing, eh? Disappointing to a woman? Women are very demanding and very easily disappointed."

A winning smile, a flash of hectic joy— Trick seemed about to wink.

Jesse's face froze.

"I could love them with my rubber-gloved fingers but with nothing else. Women are so impatient. Did I tell you I've begun to write poems? I'll write one for you and Anne-Marie on the occasion of your wedding."

Jesse forced himself to laugh. "What, you're writing poetry?"

"Talent is suffused in me, like mercury on a table top. Little beads and stems. Anyway, Jesse, one kind of elimination is as good as another. Don't be a snob because you're in love. Discharging in your beloved's body, discharging in her brain with a few delicate words—which is more rewarding, after all? I have a horror of germs." Trick seemed better now; he was breathing more normally. Boyish and cheerful, he tapped Jesse's shoulder as if in farewell. "I won't take up any more of your time. I know how hard you work. What I came up here to tell you is that my parents will be in town this Saturday and they want to take me out to dinner. They would like to meet you; I've mentioned you to them—they take all my friendships very seriously, they want to see what kind of people I know— Maybe they're afraid to be alone with me and want someone else to talk to—?"

"This Saturday? I can't make it," Jesse said quickly.

"Just for dinner and part of the evening—"

"I can't make it."

"Oh, yes. Anne-Marie," Trick said flatly.

"I said I'd take her somewhere . . . to see her family. . . ." Jesse said, lying without skill. "Her sister . . ."

"All right."

"I'm sorry," Jesse said. "I'd like to meet your parents."

"It's all right," Trick said. "I understand."

He turned to leave, then hesitated. His gaze scanned the laboratory tabletop thoughtfully. He was much heavier than Jesse, more than two hundred pounds, but they were nearly the same height. Unlike Trick, Jesse was muscular in the shoulders and arms; once he had lost the excess weight he had gained, his body had grown hard, the muscles of his chest and stomach were trim, tense, the calves of his legs poised as if to spring him forward. *He would grip Trick by the throat, squeeze that fat neck and its chattering bones between his fingers....* But he only said carefully, "Is there something you want to tell me?"

Trick shook his head. "Nothing."

"You said you had known Anne-Marie but she denies it. She's never heard of you."

They did not look at each other. At the far end of the lab a student was working, hunched over. He did not seem to be listening. His solitary, drab figure drew both Jesse's and Trick's attention.

"You said you had known her. How well?"

Trick drew in his breath slowly.

"Did you love her?" Jesse asked.

Trick said nothing.

"She said she doesn't know you. She has never even heard of your name. She says— But what was it? Did you love her?"

Trick made a motion to leave.

"No, wait. Damn you," Jesse said sharply.

"What do you want to hear?" Trick said, turning to face him. "You people in love!"

"Just answer my question. Please."

"You people in love always insist upon intrigue.... It makes me sick."

"Makes you sick, what do you mean?" Jesse took a step forward. At the other end of the room that face turned toward them, startled by something in Jesse's voice. Jesse felt his soul ache to flee into that other neutral, strange face, to be so distant and so uncomplicated.... "You were hinting something about her that night, something about Anne-Marie. I want to hear it, goddamn you, I want this straightened out. Were you in love with her? What happened between you?"

Trick smiled ironically. "You don't want to hear."

"Were you in love with her?"

Trick, at the door, screwed his face up and made a sudden, almost convulsive spitting gesture. "Love! What the hell is love?" he said.

Jesse stared.

"Good-by! Good night!" Trick cried. He waved good-by. Escaped.

For a few minutes Jesse stood without moving, staring at the doorway where Trick had stood—he could see again that screwing-up of the man's face, the puckering of the lips. His heart pounded viciously. He kept seeing that face, that ugly face; it was as if this spectacle had been predictable and yet he had insisted upon it, upon drawing it out—

What the hell is love?

That wrinkling of the face, the deepening lines about the mouth, the creases in the flesh.... Had he actually spat? Jesse stared at the floor and saw nothing. No spittle. Yet he seemed to remember Trick actually spitting; dizzily he seemed to remember saliva spraying thinly about his lips....

He cleaned up and went back to his rooming house.

Shameful, it was shameful to be so weak. So agitated. He hurried back to the rooming house as if to hide.

It was a three-story frame house, simply a rectangular box, with drab red-black siding that was supposed to look like brick. Jesse had lived there since September of 1949. He had had to move out of his basement room—which was so damp he was always catching colds anyway—because his landlady had decided to rent it to two students, in that way doubling the rent. Jesse had found this room after days of searching, had moved all his things over in an angry, desperate burst of energy, without any help, up to a cramped room on the top floor with a ceiling that peaked in the middle and sloped cruelly on the sides so that he could really stand up straight only in the middle of the room. But what did it matter, Jesse had thought, taking heart from the fact that he would now be on the top floor of a decent house and not in a damp basement.

In spite of the noisiness of the house, he had been very happy up in that room.

His landlady, Mrs. Spewak, was in her late thirties, querulous and attractive in a thin, restless way, her eyebrows plucked too severely, as if she had copied them on faith from a movie magazine. Her clothes were never quite right—she wore low-cut silky blouses with ordinary cotton skirts or slacks and very tight synthetic sweaters, sleeveless, tucked into the wide plastic belts that emphasized her narrow waist; her skirts were apt to be flowery and buoyant, with petticoats underneath them in the style of the day, or they were too tight, showing the ridges of her underwear and the ends of her tucked-in blouses strained against her flesh. She had a busy, gypsy-like manner that Jesse liked. He did like her, in spite of her chatter and complaints and the demands she placed upon him. She was always calling out his name as he hurried upstairs, or rapping on his door, wanting to enlist him on her side against the other tenants, who, Jesse had to admit, were pigs. Most of them were pigs. Mrs. Spewak and her daughter lived in the rear, lower part of the house. Jesse caught glimpses of their quarters sometimes from the kitchen. The living room was not really a personalized family room, but rather a dingy, sooty space, furnished with a single leather couch that showed hundreds of cracks and some chairs and tables that might have been bought at a rummage sale, all mismatched and ungainly. A single braided rug had been placed in the middle of the floor, but it was far too small for the size of the room. The other students joked about this place, especially about the new wallpaper Mrs. Spewak was so proud of—all towers and castles and spires of silver, outlined sharply in black like cartoon drawings, looking European and medieval. Jesse was depressed by this room, which should have been homely and domestic; he rarely entered it.

The second and third floors of the house had been divided into six rooms on the second floor and three on the third, and though Jesse lived so far up he was never confident that he would be left alone. The other students wandered around, lazily anxious for conversation, for distractions, hopeful of borrowing cigarettes or money, sometimes sitting on the edge of Jesse's bed though he had nothing to say to them and was clearly working.

They were all younger than he. They came in late, drunk, and made a lot of noise on the stairs and in the bathroom. Even the landlady's daughter wandered around during the day, though this part of the house was forbidden to her. She sometimes turned up in Jesse's room when he returned unexpected, snooping around.... Jesse suspected her mother of snooping too, though no one had actually caught her.

When he came home from the laboratory that day Mrs. Spewak was on the second-floor landing. Her face was bony and witchlike and appealing beneath a yellow kerchief. She carried a mop and pail and looked very pleased, Jesse thought, at being discovered so hard at work.

"Hey, you knocking off work early today?" she said.

"Something came up," Jesse muttered.

"If you'd come five minutes ago I could of showed you something. Real nice surprise in the john up on your floor. It's that Simon Brodsky, I bet—"

Jesse tried to brush by her politely.

"Eh, you wouldn't believe the pigs that live here. Did their mothers bring them up to be pigs?"

Jesse hurried up to his room, closed the door, stood for a few moments with his back against the door and his heart pounding. *Pigs....* Yes, they were pigs. His skin crawled with the realization of the foulness that was everywhere around him, the deceit, the shame, the hopeless wasting-away of flesh.... He wanted to be sick to his stomach. But there was no time for that now. No time. If he made retching noises in the bathroom Mrs. Spewak would come up, hearing everything, sniffing out everything, and she would rap on the door to ask what was wrong. *I am going to lose Anne-Marie,* Jesse thought in a panic. For an instant he seemed to confuse Mrs. Spewak and Anne-Marie. Both, women: a certain kind of woman. They knew all his needs simply by looking at him. Good at guessing, at hunches, kindly and secretive behind their pretty faces.... Jesse went to the bathroom after all and latched the door behind him. Today was cleaning day and the room smelled of harsh soap. A woman had been in here cleaning. Scouring. The mop, the red plastic pail of soapy, dirty water, the droplets of water—softened scum falling from the mop.... Jesse felt the vague desire to be sick. To be sick and get it over with. *Discharging*. . . . He stood shakily at the small sink, staring at his face. A face filled with color, as if the smaller veins and capillaries were throbbing with a knowledge that was not Jesse's own knowledge, but the knowledge of his flesh, his species. Why couldn't he trust it? *I am going to lose her and lose everything,* he thought. Weakly, he closed his eyes upon his own familiar face—which he always did his best to assess generously, because he had nothing else, no other face to rely upon—and he summoned up Anne-Marie's womanly, pretty face and the sweet warm mass of her body. Surges of power—the center of her being, a socket of pure power that would suck him into it and charge him with its strength—asking nothing of him but the surrender and collapse of all his bones, the blacking-out of his consciousness. Yes, he would come to her. He was wild with desire for her. He remembered how she had looked that morning in the hospital, coming through the swinging doors from the stairway, staring at him, surprised. . . .

He was not going to lose her.

A knock at the door. "Jesse?" It was Mrs. Spewak. He thought wildly of opening the door and telling her to leave him alone. *Leave me alone!* He would grab her arm and pull her into the bathroom, pull the scarf from her head so that he could finger the tight, ugly little pincurls, the hairpins and the small wire-like curls fastened flat to her head; he would pull her dress open, yank it down from her shoulders. . . . "Hey, Jesse, you all right?"

"I'm all right," he said, his eyes closed.

"You sure? Not sick, are you?"

"No."

She waited a few seconds, her hand still on the doorknob. Jesse was alarmed at the desire he felt, which was angry and abstract, ripe as something teased beyond its natural growth. He cleared his throat. "I'm all right, Mrs. Spewak. Everything is all right."

"You looked pretty pale just now. Hey, come on downstairs and I'll give you some stew. It'll fix you up fine."

Jesse opened the door. He brushed his hair back from his forehead with both hands in a flicking gesture, as if to suggest to her that he had only been combing his hair in here. . . . "Everything is fine," he said, brushing past her. If only she wouldn't touch him! But the hall was narrow and he could not avoid brushing against her. She followed after him. Talking about stew, beef stew, why didn't he come downstairs and let her heat it up for him? why didn't he relax? It was no wonder he'd caught cold that winter, the way he was always running up and down the stairs... not eating right....

Jesse escaped and telephoned Anne-Marie from the drugstore. The phone rang five, six, seven times; then her mother answered. Jesse hung up. He was going to see her at seven that evening but he could not wait. He felt wild, frantic, precarious. If someone bumped into him in this store, if a woman bumped into him, he felt that he would go crazy, he might do something crazy.... He wandered through the drugstore, not really looking at anything, and a few minutes later dialed Anne-Marie's number again. Again her mother answered, suspiciously, and again he hung up.

He knew she was not home and yet he thought frantically that somehow she might answer, she might answer the telephone....

He walked across town to her house. He must have looked anxious or in a hurry, because people glanced at him as he passed. He felt himself careening across the miles of pavement, a tall body, a young man with a precise destination, a precise fate, his eyes a little glassy with the certainty of this fate—where was she, Anne-Marie, that young woman he did not exactly trust? Where was she at this moment, why wasn't she available to him? He could not stand it, he simply could not stand it, his separation from her. She was looking at people who were strangers to him, at this moment. She was smiling. Speaking. She maneuvered herself quite intimately and ordinarily with people Jesse did not know. It was awful, it would drive him crazy.... He loved her and it seemed to him that his love, which was so miserable, should be repaid at once. Anne-Marie should be with him right now. After they were married she would always be with him, or available to him instantly; no separation; no mystery. He would know everything she did, everyone she spoke with; she would lie sweetly in his arms every night; and the two of them, husband and wife, would press their faces together, their mouths and cheeks, loving, sleepbound, their energies flowing freely like warm water back and forth as if through the same veins....

He was two hours early when he got to her house, and he did not want to talk to her mother. So he waited nervously down the street. He felt a little faint. He could not stand still, his body craved Anne-Marie so angrily; he began to walk, not paying much attention to what he was doing, into the gray warm sluttish air of the street. How to wait out those two hours! Now and then he felt a wave of faintness. Maybe he had forgotten to eat. Maybe he should eat. But his stomach cringed at the thought.... Look at that man on the sidewalk ahead, strained and heaving with fat! Jesse stared. Fat, fat, a fat man, a fat face and body, even the feet big, swollen, a human being bursting with fat creamy flesh. Jesse could barely keep the disgust from showing on his face. But this man was sick. Fat people were sick. When he was a doctor he would have to understand: the sick needed help in their sickness, not hatred and not affection. You didn't love them in their sickness, but you didn't hate them either. You were swift and clean and detached.... The fat man was gone and Jesse found himself thinking of Anne-Marie in the man's place: his own anger, worry, disapproval focused upon her. Sick in the hospital, Jesse had understood the isolation of the patients, their exclusion from the bustle and chatter and the nurses' perpetual giggling out in the corridors, especially late at night, the banging of mysterious metal things and the squeaking wheels of carts, and those girls, those girls with their whispers and muted laughter.... One of them had turned out to be Anne-Marie. A fresh, stunning face, hair in loose rich waves, girlish and breathless: Anne-Marie. He had fallen in love with her despite his general nervous irritation with nurses. Why were they always making so much noise? But he had fallen in love with her. She was melodic, her voice had a lilting musical insincerity about it that charmed him; yet she turned out to be very firm with him, almost sisterly.

Listening to him, her face would go soft, as if his words entered her hearing and transformed her, as if his nearness had the magical power of transforming her into the woman he wanted, a wife who would be a match for him. She nodded slowly. Slowly. She was always agreeing with him. But then she would reply with an odd question that showed she hadn't quite understood or hadn't been listening closely; or she would smile archly and switch to another subject, as she had after they had attended a symposium on community health in Detroit—having been subjected to three hours of speeches, harangues, statistics, graphs, charts, diagrams, blueprints, slides, all of them pointing to the impoverished condition of public health resources for the poor; having seen a film of crowded wards and aged, vacuous faces, the senile and the mad and the desperately sick; having heard the speakers' flat pessimistic predictions for the future—having sat next to Jesse through all that horror, Anne-Marie had been able to switch it out of her mind at once, whispering into his ear: "Are you hungry, Jesse? You must be starving after all this!"

But though he recalled this now, he felt all the more desperate to see her. So many little vexations. Little disappointments. He had to get hold of her, he had to make certain of her. He would frame her face in his hands, he would press his mouth against hers, he would embrace her wildly.... Up ahead he saw a couple approaching and for a moment, shocked, he thought the girl was Anne-Marie. But no, it was a stranger, a girl dressed in white —a white dress that was not a uniform. Shakily, Jesse went back to Anne-Marie's street and waited.

When she finally came, getting off a bus at the corner, he again saw the surprise and the faint fear in her when she noticed him. "Jesse...?" she said, wondering. He hurried to her and took her hand. He tried to smile. They greeted each other, smiling. Jesse saw that her face was not quite ready for him—there was a coarse, greasy cast to her forehead and her hair was wind-blown. But she was still very beautiful.

"Don't bother going in the house. Let's leave here. Let's go for a walk," Jesse said.

"I—I want to change my clothes—"

"No, don't bother, you look beautiful. You look lovely," Jesse said.

She seemed evasive beneath her smiling surprise. He could sense her thinking rapidly. Maybe she did not love him, he thought angrily, maybe she wanted to marry him only because he was going to be a doctor. All these nurses, these clever little girls, hoped to marry doctors.... But why was he thinking such things? He loved her. He loved her very much. He liked her being a nurse, he felt the rightness of their marriage. Everything was right. It would work out.

They walked out along Geddes Street, to the arboretum. It was one of their frequent walks. Jesse could not pay attention to Anne-Marie's chatter; he thought only of embracing her, of making love to her. When they were in the arboretum, on one of the deserted paths, he embraced her and she slid her arms about him tightly. She was so sweet, so light in his arms.... His desire for her was painful.

Then she squirmed away. She took his hand and walked beside him, and he could sense her separateness, her isolation from him. What was she thinking? Jesse led her down a slope, so steep that they had to dig their heels into the earth. They were alone now. Jesse put his arms around her again. He could not stop mauling her, pressing himself against her. Everything about her seemed to him vital and mysterious, filmy with the gauze-like confusion of his closed eyes, the rubbing of their faces together, the warm flesh of her back through the uniform she wore, the tight straps his hands brushed against, the sense of her tight, compressed little body.... He was whispering something to her. He loved her. Loved her. He needed her. An image flashed into his mind: that girl on the street in the white dress, whom he had mistaken for Anne-Marie. A girl he might make love to, like this. Another image: Mrs. Spewak on the other side of the bathroom door, calling him. Taunting him. She was an attractive woman; she threw herself around the house half-dressed sometimes; she knew exactly what she was doing...and why was she always brushing against him or tugging at his arm, teasing him? He remembered. Trick in the laboratory doorway. Trick backing away. That look on his face. The bitter drawing-up of his lips, the contemptuous scowl. *Love! What the hell is love?* And Mrs. Spewak had made a bitter face too, though her skin was exhilarated with the energy of her anger: *Pigs.*

Jesse felt like sobbing. He was mad with love for Anne-Marie. He could not control himself. She was whispering, "Jesse? Jesse?" They lay down. Anne-Marie said, "Jesse, I love you, I love you, but I can't get used to you...all this emotion.... You're happy with me and then, when we meet again, you're angry.... I don't understand you." He kissed her wildly, happily. "I'm not angry with you. I'm not angry," he said. She had such a pretty face—why couldn't he trust it? Maybe he did not trust prettiness. Her skin was fair and smooth, her hair gleaming, always clean, lovingly tended . . . she was always tending herself, checking herself in mirrors. . . . "I'm afraid of you," she whispered. "Jesse, please don't hurt me. . . ."

He could no longer remember where they were. Often they had lain in each other's arms out here, far from the wide paths and from other people, and Jesse had felt at those times a small prickling sensation of being spied upon, though no one ever watched anyone else out here . . . and now he experienced the same sensation but it seemed to provoke him further, to increase his desire . . . the certainty that someone must be watching, that Trick himself was somehow staring sardonically at the two of them, his lips prepared to utter a contemptuous word: *Pigs*. . . . It was possible that Trick had been Anne-Marie's lover, that he had known her when she was a nursing student years ago. It was possible that she had lied about that and about other things. He could not believe her. "Don't be afraid, I love you, I love you," Jesse said in anguish as the poison built up in him, a sharp rhythmic pain. They had made love only a few times before, gently and guiltily; but today Jesse pressed himself against her, into her, with a sudden violence that made her cry out. Jesse's mind seemed to bounce everywhere, from one part of the hill to another, stricken with the blind agitation of this moment—

She wept in surprise, clinging to him.

"I love you. . . ." he said, as if this explained everything. But now, with his face pressed against her hair, his eyeballs numb, as if scorched, he felt the beginning of a long wavering sigh of despair. And he knew that he did not love her, not any longer. He did not believe that Trick had been her lover, and yet it was as if it had happened—as if he had witnessed it. Trick, curious and cynical in this beautiful girl's arms, in the silence of this place, in the damp grass. Trick screwing up his face and spitting. Pronouncing judgment upon her. Trick's wise, monkish face. . . .

No, he could not love her after this, though he would still marry her. He would marry her. It was not possible for him to love her but he would marry her as he had promised.

3

One day in late May, Jesse was behind the wheel of his landlady's car, parked in front of a grocery store in which Mrs. Spewak was shopping. The car was an old Ford with a splotched windshield and soiled, frayed seat covers. A small St. Christopher medal, of a yellowish plastic meant to look like ivory, was attached by a suction cup to the dashboard; in the back seat, the eight-year-old Carla sat, jarring Jesse's seat with her knees, chattering at him in her high-pitched, exasperated voice. Something about her mother—her mother's injustice to her. Carla had the frank, wistful, tortured expression of a dwarfed adult but the relentlessness of a child, continually circling the same topic: "I hate her. I *hate* her."

"No, you don't hate her," Jesse said sternly.

But he had his eye on a couple approaching the car, walking along the sidewalk.

The man was familiar but somehow out of place here—unexpected here—that careful, fastidious walk, the way he moved his hands in slow, artificial, restrained gestures—as if explaining something that must be visualized precisely. Jesse recognized Professor Cady. It was Cady. And the woman was probably his wife: she wore a dark green suit, the jacket a little mannish, plain, loose as a maternity outfit, giving her a sturdy, shapeless appearance. Jesse saw that her legs were quite slender, though, and probably inside that unflattering suit she was slender, lithe, appealing. Cady had evidently married a woman many years younger than himself. Jesse did not know if he approved of this or not. He stared at them, hoping they would not notice him—Cady was no taller than the woman, his near-white hair clipped short and clean about his handsome skull, his coat a dark khaki, plain and correct as a uniform. He looked British. Jesse had always supposed that his clothes were expensive; they were so understated, muted. Only the man's voice, by a certain trick, called attention to itself—the lifting of words at the conclusion of a sentence, a subtle accenting of the next-to-last words, so that he seemed about to call his listeners to account. They were alerted, a little intimidated by him. His expression was usually neutral and undramatic. His eyes were shrewd but rather small and closely set. Were they gray, some near-neutral color? Jesse wondered if the man's small, excellent white teeth could really be his own.

Jesse drew in his breath as he watched Cady and the woman approach, the two of them so obviously together, united. They were talking earnestly about something that united them. Cady's graceful hands, describing odd little circles and boxes in the air, united them with their seriousness and their precision. What were they saying? Cady had married an attractive young woman. Jesse stared critically at her and saw that her face was serious and intelligent, the pale lips curved to a tentative smile as Cady explained something to her. She nodded uncertainly. He smiled. Jesse wondered what they were talking about. What did married people talk about? Suddenly he wondered what it might be like to be that man, that distinguished man—Cady had been a colleague of Walter Cannon's at Harvard, years ago, he had been awarded a Nobel Prize along with two other men and certainly at Michigan he was highly respected, almost idolized by certain students—Jesse's mind raced with the thought of meeting Cady now, face to face on the sidewalk. Why not?

There he is. There. Here you are, sitting here. Don't let him get away.

They had passed the car. Jesse's heart beat with a heavy, sullen envy of their intimacy, that gray-haired man and his young wife, the two of them perfect together... ennobled....

He mumbled something to Carla and got out of the car.

"Dr. Cady!" he called out. Cady and the woman turned. Jesse hurried up to them, blushing. His mind was in a whirl—what would he say?—but he was encouraged by Cady's polite, alert smile. It was the public smile of the lectures, generous and impersonal but unthreatening. "I just wanted to say hello, Dr. Cady. I wanted to tell you how much I've liked—I've learned—I took your neurochemistry course this year—"

Cady smiled at him.

"It's good of you to say so," he said, extending his hand. "What is your name?"

"Jesse Vogel...."

"Ah, Jesse Vogel, I think I remember that name...." This

was probably not true and he did not stress the point; he simply shook Jesse's hand firmly and released it. He was a fairly short man, about five feet six. "Mr. Vogel, this is my daughter Helene; she's been kind enough to stay with me for the past few weeks, taking care of me."

Jesse and the young woman nodded shyly. Jesse saw that she was very young—obviously she could not have been Cady's wife; obviously she was his daughter. The outfit she wore was not a maternity suit, just a suit that was a little too large for her. "Do you like Ann Arbor?" Jesse asked her. He looked her full in the face and gave no sign of his own nervousness. She replied, and Cady began to speak again, chatting about Ann Arbor, which was so much more leisurely than Cambridge, so much more pleasant in certain ways. He spoke of a chamber-music recital he and his daughter had heard the evening before, and though Jesse knew nothing about it he nodded briskly, as though he too had attended. His smile was strained but ambitious, big enough for both Cady and his daughter. How easy it had been to shake Cady's hand! Cady seemed to have no idea of his own importance. He spoke to Jesse as casually as if Jesse were a friend of his or an equal at the university. "Yes, we are both charmed by Ann Arbor, but I'm afraid we're impatient to be back home. . . . Helene doesn't know anyone here, of course." Cady had a small man's love of precision, his words were neat and clipped and self-conscious, as if to call attention to some subtlety in his meaning. Jesse felt a surge of emotion—affection—and recalled how readily, how cheerfully, Cady had shaken hands with him. *He had done it. He had done it.* Always, all year, he had admired this man, knowing enough to be able to assess Cady's knowledge and his undramatic recitation of dramatic material, his patience, his ability to anticipate questions in the sleepy, shadowy heads of his students in that big amphitheater. He had always had the sense, too, that Cady was somehow aware of him.

Standing in front of Cady and his daughter, Jesse felt that his height was a burden—he was so much taller than either of them. Did he appear overgrown and clumsy in their eyes? And he was wearing old clothes—it was a Saturday morning—a frayed shirt with its sleeves rolled up, the collar not very clean, soiled cotton trousers, shoes without socks. He had not even shaved that morning.

Time for them all to part. Jesse thanked Cady for the course and Cady accepted this graciously. "I'm sorry to bother you," Jesse apologized, backing off. It had all gone well. Cady was obviously flattered, and the girl was proud of her father, casting a cool, demure sideways glance at him, a wifely glance. Jesse said good-by and turned to leave.

His heart was pounding.

He returned to the car just as Mrs. Spewak was leaving the store. What good luck that she had not come out while he had been talking with the Cadys. . . . "God, Jesse, it cost me twenty-five dollars in there. The stuff is just inside the door there, can you get it? It's too heavy for me. God, I feel sick." She was wearing lime-green slacks and a nylon sweater of pale peach, too tight for her small, sharp breasts.

"Sure, I'll get it. I'll get it," Jesse said quickly.

He no longer saw Anne-Marie. They had argued over something—her accusation of his not loving her—and had decided to break their engagement. It had been unofficial anyway. Unofficial. It didn't count, Anne-Marie had said bitterly. With Anne-Marie out of his life, Jesse found himself with Mrs. Spewak more and more. It happened. Inertia, a vague desire to please, a vague sense of guilt: her sighs, her headaches, her backaches, her continual amazement at the troubles a woman had to face. And that daughter! Carla was not really a child of superior intelligence, Jesse thought, but she had a quick, crippling mind, a premature cynicism that sometimes passed for intelligence. She was very thin in the chest, her arms and legs were so small that Jesse could easily have circled them with his thumb and forefinger. She had strange, undiagnosed allergies that Mrs. Spewak seemed to think would make her more interesting to Jesse because he was going to be a doctor—she was allergic to dust and pollen and food and fur and certain mixtures of sunlight and humidity; she was feverish, restless, she rarely smiled, she did a lot of kicking and hanging onto her mother or Jesse, clamoring for attention. But when she received attention she became quickly embarrassed and bored. She hated to be looked at. She would put her fingers over her eyes as if to hide.... When Mrs. Spewak went out, which was often, Jesse took care of Carla.

"Where is my mother? Where did she go?" Carla would demand.

When Jesse told her, she wouldn't believe it.

Trick didn't believe it either. He was probably right: Jesse's landlady was just using him. Taking advantage of his kindness. She was an ignorant, lazy woman and there was something not quite clear about her life, but she had not exactly hurt Jesse, she had not really interfered with his studies very much. Jesse was inclined to defend her. She had evidently been married at one time but her husband had left her or she had kicked him out; maybe she was officially divorced, maybe not; she spoke of herself as Catholic, though she did not often go to Mass. When she asked favors of Jesse she spoke in a swift, apologetic voice, staring fixedly at him so that Jesse did not have the heart to turn her down.

"She wants to eat you up, kid," Trick laughed.

But the domestic squabbles, in which Jesse was forced to join, the routine of Saturday shopping and the putting away of groceries in the kitchen, his care of the garbage cans, his beating the rugs for her, quieted the racing of his brain that sometimes frightened him. He was so weak, really.... In spite of what people thought, he was so weak, he dared not be alone too much, dared not allow himself to think much, to remember much.... He was grateful for the duties of household life, even the dull, demanding voices of Mrs. Spewak and Carla.

"I don't mind helping her out," Jesse said to Trick.

"She just wants to use you."

"What do you mean, use me? I don't mind."

"Does she offer to pay you?"

"She doesn't have any money."

"She could take it off your rent. She could do something for you."

"She couldn't afford that."

"Jesse, Jesse!—you're so eager to give yourself away!"

They were friends now, Jesse and Trick. Somehow they had become friends. Jesse did not know whether to resent Trick's interest in him or to be grateful that someone seemed to care about him. He had the idea that other students envied him his friendship with Trick—Dr. Monk—and so he did not mind when Trick showed up half an hour early to have coffee with him, interrupting his work, or when he dropped in on Jesse at night, complaining that he was unable to sleep.

"We insomniacs share a certain mystique," Trick said.

They never spoke of Anne-Marie.

Jesse would have liked to explain to Trick that he had fallen out of love with her entirely. It was over. It was nearly forgotten. He did not hate Trick. Trick really had nothing to do with it—Jesse had just stopped loving her, that was all. And if he had hated Trick, even a little, it was forgotten along with his love for Anne-Marie.... Trick was like an older brother, a fretful older relative. He was critical about Jesse's habits: "It's a kind of mania, the way you force yourself to work. But as long as you function so well, that's the only test, the only test of health." He seemed to Jesse a superior man, an exceptional man. What had appeared to be dangerous in him was really only his frankness and his whimsy, which were foreign to Jesse.

Sometimes he goaded Jesse gently, with a curious bright look to his face. "How is your landlady this week? Is she still after you?"

"You exaggerate things," Jesse said.

"She has a lecherous eye, I'm sure of it. She has a certain moist, downy look, even for her age . . . and she isn't so old really. Are you sure you're not her lover and you don't want to tell me about it?"

"I'm not anyone's lover," Jesse said.

Trick smiled. "There was this friend of my grandfather's in Minneapolis, a wealthy old man, who had his own zoo built for him—no, not a zoo, an animal sanctuary, a private jungle—and he appropriated also a number of wives in succession, the wives getting younger as he got older. One of the wives looked like your Mrs. Spewak, though better-looking. I think he acquired her along with some lions. She was a lady lion-tamer, or that was part of the stunt in the carnival she traveled with. She wore a riding outfit around the place, and boots that came up to her thighs, and she carried a little whip with a velvet handle. Ah, it was magnificent to see her striding around! The old man had a huge ugly house, like a warehouse made of brick. There were rooms in his house he had never seen. And this woman, though she stood to lose a few million dollars and to be tossed back into the carnival again, she would drive out through the jungle and let herself out the gate and drive along the highways—because there were highways, normal highways, this was an ordinary part of the world—to gas stations and country stores and pick up kids there, I mean kids in their twenties; she was a kind of legend in the county.... She never bothered me, though. She never even glanced at me. Maybe that was because there is nothing lionlike about me."

"What happened to her?" Jesse asked, amazed.

"She ran away and he divorced her eventually. He married a twenty-year-old girl."

"Did he really have lions there—in the United States?"

"He had lions, eagles, monkeys—lots of monkeys and chimpanzees and even some apes—and parrots and large hogs from the Everglades—and all these women, these wives."

"You *have* known freakish people," Jesse said slowly.

Later, he wondered if Trick's stories were true: they always began innocently enough, always connected to Trick through a relative or friend, and then they branched out, blossomed out, to touch upon worlds Jesse did not understand. He wanted to believe in the ordinary, in the normal. His mind was slow to admit the bizarre.

"Yes, freakish people are drawn to me," Trick said with a grin.

Close up, his face was mottled and inconsistent, though he was not an ugly man. But he had this uneven, rather coarse and large-pored complexion that looked as if stage make-up had been applied to it in layers that had begun to smudge and run. Out of this mixture of tones—lardy flesh, rosy flesh, sallow flesh—his small eyes peered with a cheerfulness that was exaggerated at times, out of proportion to its object, as if Trick saw through the ordinary to another dimension invisible to his listeners. There was something oversized and godly about him, a debased godliness, though, as if he were the son of a god and were failing at his inheritance. "I get a kick out of strange people. I would like to be a collector. Maybe I'll become a county pathologist and do autopsies for some little town.... I would be more gentle with the dead than with the living because, of course, you don't get any hypocrisy from the dead...."

Jesse laughed uneasily. He wondered if he were one of the freaks who were drawn to Trick.

He was thinking now, almost constantly, about Dr. Cady and his daughter. But he said nothing to Trick about this. He felt a peculiar agitation, almost a sense of despair, to think that the year was coming to an end—his years as a medical student were coming to an end—and yet something was missing. Trick asked him what was wrong: why was he so quiet? But he said nothing; he could not have explained. He was graduating at the top of his class, and this was a completion of all his plans, his most feverish, improbable plans, and yet something was missing; something had been lost. It was not Anne-Marie. He had stopped loving her and now even the memory of his love, his anguish, was baffling to him. It did not seem believable that he had loved her so much. At times he could not even recall her face except to remember its bright, impersonal healthy beauty that might have belonged to any girl. His loss was centered somehow upon Cady. He sat in the front row of the amphitheater staring at the man's calm, intelligent face, wondering how it had been possible for a young man to grow into that particular man, to mature into Benjamin Cady. The school year was coming to an end, and its hectic melancholy was somehow focused upon Cady's face.

How to become that man without debasing himself?

One afternoon he took Carla to a movie while Mrs. Spewak went to the dentist, "to the dentist," she said, and Jesse chose to believe her, and during the movie Jesse was inspired by the energy of the screen—giant cowboys and cattle thundering back and forth—and decided he would not let the year end so weakly. He would not let the Cadys escape him. He looked for their name in the telephone book, couldn't find it, and telephoned the medical school office to ask for Cady's address. He was the son of a friend from Harvard, he said. Jesse, who never lied, lied now flamboyantly and happily, feeling himself safe in the telephone booth at the rear of the nearly deserted theater. There were operatic possibilities in life that came out of the darkness of a movie house—flashing out of the confused splotches of color and light that made up the screen's images, like the underside of a dream forcing its way to the surface of the mind.

After the movie was over he took Carla for a walk. She liked to walk through the university campus. Jesse took her out Washtenaw for several blocks to the apartment building where Cady lived. Carla was in a good mood; she had enjoyed the movie. She looked so small, so docile, that she could have been Jesse's own daughter. In spite of her thin, strained face he was proud of being with her: someone might mistake him for her father. A father of a child. A father.

Carla chattered about the movie, but Jesse remembered only looming men, expressionless men, vast colored skies and horizons, the promise of eternal desert, mountains that looked like perfunctory limitations of the earth, the earth as it is imagined, needing an end. He remembered the disturbing thud of horses' hoofs and the monumental thud of stampeding cattle. Forces pounding in one direction and then back in the other. Back and forth. A tornado of the mind. A spiral dipping out of the sky. It was the Old Testament, all that activity! And he was absurdly, abruptly grateful for the movies, which he saw so rarely, for their progress in patches and spurts, not as a coherent story but as the jagged bits of a story that never quite added itself up to anything believable. Years ago, his freshman English instructor at the university had told him there was something odd about his understanding of literature—he was unable to follow a plot. He was unable to see the careful evolution of a story. The necessary pattern, the rhythm that demanded completion, the internal heat, the gravity that forced everything to a suitable conclusion . . . what did all these things mean? He had not understood, though he had tried. But in the end he did not know what a "story" was. He had the idea that what people thought were stories were fragments from shattered wholes, the patterns, the brain waves, of a certain man at a certain time in his life, the record of his controlled and uncontrolled inner life: therefore all writing was autobiography, wasn't it? His instructor, an earnest young New Yorker, had tried to explain what was wrong with Jesse's ideas. Or his temperament, maybe; he didn't have a "literary temperament." But Jesse still believed that all writing was factual and true, as part of a shattered whole that could not be put back together again but must be experienced only in parts, and yet was not "believable" in the way his medical texts were believable. You lived it but you could not believe it.

He was struck by a sense of shyness as he entered the Cadys' apartment building. It was fairly small, four stories high, made of stone that was weathered and stained, covered partly with ivy, with the appearance of an old church. Shadows everywhere in the foyer—a still, moist air that had the quality of secrecy, sternness; an elevator with an elaborate iron grillwork that put Jesse dizzily in mind of a fortress. There was a stern, secretive spirit here and a variety of styles—the curlicues of the grillwork, brass knobs, small heraldic beasts at the molding, nearly lost in shadow and dust, an aged but very respectable wallpaper that showed silvery leaflike designs, absolutely flat, motionless, unlike the turbulent screen of the movie house Jesse had just been in. Carla tugged at his arm and whined about going home—wasn't it time to go home? What were they doing here?

The Cadys' apartment was on the first floor, so he did not have to take the elevator. Carla would probably have refused to get into it. He found the door without any trouble, bent to spruce up Carla, hid his own nervousness. He rang the doorbell and Cady's daughter answered the door almost immediately. It happened so quickly that Jesse was not prepared to speak.

"Is Dr. Cady—?"

"He isn't home right now."

"Oh . . . he isn't home?"

She did not reply, looking from him to Carla and back again.

"When do you think he'll be home?"

"I don't know."

Jesse smiled nervously. "I wanted to say good-by before he left. . . . I wanted . . . this is a little friend of mine, Carla Spewak. You probably don't remember me . . . my name is Jesse Vogel. . . ."

She nodded, but so quickly and vaguely that Jesse could not tell if she had remembered. His face went hot with disappointment.

"Yes, I'll tell Father you stopped by."

"I'm sorry to disturb you."

"It's all right."

"Was I disturbing you . . . ? Are you busy? I wonder if I could talk to you for a minute," Jesse said.

She hesitated.

Now Jesse knew why he had brought Carla along.

"I don't want to take up your time, but I'd like to talk to you for a minute," Jesse said.

Cady's daughter did not quite meet his eye. The skin of her forehead seemed to tighten, as if with dread or expectation; Jesse found himself staring at the dead-white part in the center of her head. Her black hair had been brushed back on either side of this part, starkly and smoothly, but in front of her ears there were filmy tendrils of hair, not thick enough to be curls. Her face was pale and clear—no make-up, no lipstick. A face denuded of guile, no tricks there, no bright false surges of enthusiasm of the kind he got from other girls and that had disturbed him so in Anne-Marie. He wanted only the truth from women. He wanted their true faces. He did not care about beauty, Jesse told himself as he stared at this young woman, who was not beautiful but who seemed to him stronger and more valuable because she was not beautiful and possessed instead that stern, doubtful face. . . .

She smiled suddenly. A courteous smile, exactly like her father's. "Yes, please come in. Father will probably be home soon." She led them inside and Jesse was pleased with the sparseness, cleanness—furniture that was well-worn, an oval table with a scalloped tablecloth draped over it, a gleaming white bowl that was empty of fruit or decoration, lamps that looked squat and old-fashioned and hunched, shades that were a little yellowed. His eye jumped at once to a photograph in a dark metal frame, set on a table—he saw Cady in a group of men, standing in what appeared to be a garden. He bent to look at it. *Stockholm, 1947.*

"Your father—Dr. Cady—that was when he won the Nobel Prize?" Jesse stammered.

He felt giddy with the fact of being here, standing here.

Helene Cady seemed about to say something, then hesitated. Perhaps she sensed Jesse's agitation. She met his gaze a little from the side, so that he saw her dark, still eyes across the slender side of her cheek, and something moved in him: he would love this woman.

Later, he would recall Carla Spewak as if she had been their first daughter. Their most basic and helpless child, a complaining, sickly, precociously troubled little girl, whose eyes had begun to water in the first five minutes of their visit—set off by a frayed black fur thrown across one of the sofas. So much would come of this visit that it was necessary to believe a great deal had gone into it—more than his straying desires, ripened by the late, warm spring, or his vexing recollection of Anne-Marie, Anne-Marie's body, or the odd half-recalled tale of Trick's about a woman in a riding outfit who carried a small velvet-handled whip, searching for lovers along a Minnesota highway. What could he bring to Helene, directly to her, unflinching and unashamed, except the keenness of his respect for her, his envy of her still, intelligent, listening body?

4

A clear, sun-splotched day. The mist of early morning had burned off, the sky was enormous, they were driving along a country road that dipped and seemed to bounce around curves, as if any surprise might be waiting for them. The road was empty all the way. Jesse sat between Trick and Helene, his hand clasped around Helene's, and beyond their casual conversation—Trick was talking about his plans for next year, his internship at Massachusetts General, where he would study with Francis Ehrlich in psychiatric medicine—Jesse felt the pull of the distance, the cultivated Michigan hills. Running right up to the road was a field of new corn, hardly a foot high. Air swam through it, silent ripples; it looked as if it were being stroked by an invisible hand. Jesse felt caressed by that same wind, able to pay only slight attention to Trick's voice.

His fingers moved restlessly over the ring on Helene's finger.

He had borrowed money from Trick in order to buy Helene an engagement ring—a ring with a small diamond, a plain band and setting. He was proud of it. He was proud of Helene's obvious happiness in wearing it. His eye involuntarily always sought out this ring on her finger, anxious to see if she was still promised to him, if he had not been mistaken. At times he lay awake, sleepless, and it seemed incredible to him that they would really be married—he would really marry Helene Cady? He would become a married man, she would become his wife? . . . In her shyness she was eager to please him, already wifely and observant. She had learned quickly from him the affectionate camaraderie of this kind of heady, intimate friendship; Jesse had found in himself an ability to guide both himself and her, refusing to be self-conscious or embarrassed, refusing to give in to his perpetual sense of unworthiness. He must hide that from her. He had never been friendly with Anne-Marie, not really. They had been lovers and nothing more. If they had seemed to talk of other things, it was really love they were talking about—Jesse eager, keyed up, jealous of her attention and her beauty, untrusting—though they had never been frank enough to use the vocabulary of love. With Helene, Jesse kept thinking of the rightness of their marriage. He kept thinking of Anne-Marie's limitations. She had been able to respond to him only as a pretty woman, always conscious of her prettiness, conscious of Jesse as a young man who desired her, the two of them walking parallel in these roles as if on railroad tracks that would never meet . . . and so he had never felt any friendship for her, he had never trusted her the way he trusted Helene. He had never been friendly with any girl before Helene. *Not even Hilda Pedersen.* His "sister." No, he had never been friendly with any girl, and he had to invent the casualness with which he greeted Helene each time they met, as if he felt no apprehension of losing her or of somehow violating the affection she felt for him. It was all so precarious, this business of trading in emotions—exactly what was love, what was it? Could it be depended upon?

He loved Helene.

He loved her, yes. He wanted to talk to her, to bring to her bizarre and random questions about life; he wanted to talk to her about oddities, promises, incidents, newspaper items, the gossip of his rooming house, the weather, anything. He wanted to confer with her about the handling of each day. This must have meant, Jesse believed, that he was now truly in love; he did not feel combative or anxious in her presence. He was not driven by a desperate lust to bury himself in her body.

They planned to marry when Jesse completed his intern year, the following July.

On this day Trick had invited them for a drive in the country. He was very surprised and pleased about the engagement, he told them repeatedly—he had never guessed the two of them were even seeing each other. How strange, how surprising.... Trick had looked stunned when Jesse told him, but in the next instant he had smiled a quick, courteous, rather paternal smile, congratulating Jesse. He had met Helene a few times. After Jesse told him about the engagement, as the weeks passed, Trick began to allude familiarly to it, smilingly, enthusiastically, as if he had really meant to bring the two of them together all along. "I had it in mind, I really did. She's a remarkable young woman—very intelligent—just right for you. A very intelligent woman," Trick told Jesse repeatedly. Jesse searched his face for a flash of cynicism, but Trick was sincere. He spoke rapidly, in a flat, earnest voice. *She is just right for you. Just right.*

In front of Helene, Trick praised Jesse in the same earnest voice. It ran on and on, flattened, a little dead, the voice of a clown who is forced to be serious. "Jesse works harder than anyone I know. He's totally dedicated. Almost possessed. It's a gift of his, being able to work so hard. Your father told me he thinks Jesse has a brilliant career ahead of him in anything, anything he wants to do... he has to be careful not to waste himself...." They were pushing him toward research, pure research. Jesse was uneasily flattered by Cady's suggestions: he could get a postdoctoral grant at Harvard and work with Cady himself. Or he could get a similar grant somewhere else and work with a friend of Cady's, another prominent man. Jesse tried to explain that he was interested in clinical work. He wanted to work with people. He talked over his plans with Trick, with Helene, and one long evening with Cady himself, when Helene had made dinner for the three of them. The food on Jesse's plate had cooled, turned unappetizing, as they talked. Jesse's forehead crinkled with the flood of advice, suggestions, his own need to decide while everyone told him kindly not to make any decision now, to take his time. Cady was generous. He said gently to Jesse, "I see in you a genuine liking for people, maybe even a need for people. You want to feel your way along by gauging other people's opinions of you, their satisfaction with you, and this seems easiest in terms of patients. The sick are always hopeful and always grateful. They are always immediate. They are very real. I can understand your interest in that kind of medicine.... But research is also a matter of other people. These people are not physically available to you but that doesn't mean they don't exist. They exist in great numbers, a multiplication of the people you would ever actually help in medical practice. After all, Jesse, a man doesn't exist simply in his skin, so that we must go around touching everyone!... And then you will have a certain relationship with your colleagues, even those who are in other parts of the world. You will be communicating with them constantly. And this is ultimately what is most satisfying about research. What you achieve—the progress you make—will enable thousands of other doctors to treat the sick, it will multiply you by thousands, you yourself multiplied by thousands, even millions.... You must think of that, Jesse; always keep that in mind!"

Multiplied by millions....

He came away from Cady burning with excitement, almost convinced. He felt so healthy now, so strong! He even ate regularly. He was careful to eat hot food, to sleep as long as he could. He had become very important suddenly. If only he could have taken Cady's advice and at the same time do what he really wanted to do, fulfill an ordinary internship and go into community health work, a general medical practice... he had been so moved by his work in the welfare wards that he could not imagine himself in any other setting.... *Dr. Vogel, Director of...*

Helene, respecting his privacy, did not try to argue with him.

Trick teased him a little about his liking for the bustle of hospital wards: *You want to raise up the halt and the crippled, you want to raise the dead—a small ambition!* But he did not put much pressure on Jesse. He liked most to talk about himself, and on this drive Jesse was relieved that Trick was not bothering him. He spoke lightly, good-natured and very attentive to Helene. "And from then on I will fly from one capital city of the world to another," he was saying, "treating only wealthy madmen and dining with kings and dictators. I will invent a new psychotheological movement and announce myself its Messiah and appear on the cover of *Time* Magazine. And I will write poems, beautiful poems, poems of love and tenderness, and I will turn up in the intimate journals of the most outlandish people. But

I will never be too busy to visit you and Jesse, my dear, any time you want me; I'll be a candidate for any position in your life—a godfather to your first-born, a resident psychiatrist, anything! You have only to command me to your side."

The car seemed to bounce with Trick's good wishes. It was one of his good days, a surprisingly good day. He had evidently made up his mind about going to Massachusetts. For a while he had talked vaguely of quitting medicine and retiring, at the age of thirty-one, to some farm, an uncle's farm in northern Minnesota, or of volunteering for a United Nations medical program, or of working somewhere with his hands. He had even sighed and hinted of marriage. "Should I marry? Should I take that risk?" But Jesse supposed this to be a joke, since he had never seen Trick with any woman. And Trick never spoke of any woman in particular. If he alluded to women, it was usually in the plural, a fuzzy cynical mob of Ann Arbor females who clamored for him because he was going to be a doctor, and everyone knew that women were mad for doctors and for their money, for their skilled, practiced hands. "Unfortunately, the only woman suitable for someone like you and me, Jesse, is a woman like Helene, because she's from a family of doctors and knows what to expect. She knows everything and yet she's brave enough to marry a doctor. But you got to her first."

He said now, leaning across Jesse to speak to Helene, "Will you command me? To come to your side, I mean. In the years ahead. Will I be Uncle Trick to your children? You won't forget me, will you?"

"Of course not," Helene said.

"Because, you know, though I joke around a lot, you two are the people I like best—I admire most—along with your father, Helene, and a few other people, a very few other people—Everyone else has let me down somehow. They've disappointed me. The years have gone by and you two are about all that's left to me—but I don't want to embarrass you—"

"You're not embarrassing us," Helene said uneasily.

Jesse was silent, disliking Trick's exaggeration. Why the hell did he always exaggerate?

"Jesse disapproves," Trick said slyly. "I can always sense when Jesse disapproves. He isn't sure he will invite me to be his child's godfather, or even trust me around his children. I can read his mind."

"Can you really read my mind, Trick?" Jesse said lightly.

"From the very first. Your mind is a complicated one but it repays study." Trick's voice sounded with delight. His good humor, his enthusiasm, made Jesse want to put his hand over Trick's mouth and shut him up before he said too much. His shamelessness brought out shame in others.

"I'm not thinking about the future or about anything," Jesse said. "I was just watching the countryside." He rubbed his fingers back and forth over Helene's hand nervously. It was a private gesture, and yet he had the idea that Trick was aware of it.

"Jesse, you're not being entirely truthful. It is impossible to think about nothing."

He was taking them to the pathology farm, about which Jesse had heard wild tales; Trick had spent a few weeks out there doing experiments on dogs for a professor named Ross, who was famous at the Medical Center for the federal grants he had brought them. The grants were confidential in their details—Jesse had heard extravagant rumors of million-dollar projects, research teams sworn to secrecy—all of it, he guessed, a jealous rerunning of the drama that had surrounded the nuclear chemists and physicists in the early forties. And how their secret work had become public, how it had flowered into a cataclysmic reality! No wonder other people were jealous. And now there was talk of biochemical research, counter-radiation work, the explorations of antidotes for germ-cloud formations. Medical students who announced themselves "politically honest" began to defend the money they would be making in a few years. It was a fact, they stated, that the "other side" would be doing this work whether they did it or not, so there was no moral problem involved—it was historical necessity that carried them on. Jesse kept quiet about this. It did not involve him personally. He did not believe he had to declare himself in any relationship to it. For as far back as he wanted to remember—that is, as far back as he had been Jesse Vogel—he had made his way through the tremulous packed streets of this life by fastening his gaze firmly before him, minding his own business, and if the pavement were to shrink suddenly to the width of a tightrope, he would have kept on in this steady, firm, unimaginative way; knowing that salvation is won only by hoarding the emotions.

"Gatti is in charge out at the farm, but he rarely drops in. He says he's allergic to the smell of manure. But really he's got a bleeding ulcer and is not a well man, I'm afraid," Trick was saying. He knew everything, everyone; no stray rumor or oddity escaped him. He seemed to forget nothing and sometimes entertained Jesse and Helene by repeating conversations he had had with other people. "Do you know Gatti, Helene? He looks like an Eskimo. There's something cold and savage about his face. A big mustache, a broad, flat face, a sloped forehead. You've probably met him. I can't imagine anyone more antithetical to your father, who is so aristocratic—I mean in his bearing, his brains; Gatti is crude and clumsy, he has a team of kids working for him out here who are like a circus act. I'll introduce you. If Gatti had more sense he would outlaw visits like mine, but there is speculation that he might want to bring the whole farm down into shambles in order to get back at Ross.... Or don't you know about that? Jesse knows about that, the feud between Ross and Gatti."

"No, I don't know about it. But never mind," Jesse said.

"It really goes back before your time in Ann Arbor. No need to dig it up. There's enough shit flying loose at the moment without loosening up more material," Trick said, and launched into a string of names and projects on the farm while Jesse tried to listen. He rubbed his thumb against the back of Helene's hand, across the fine small knucklebones. "Helene," Trick said, "you were wise to stick with chemistry. And you were wise to quit after getting your Master's degree. Once you fool around in biology, once you stick your fingers in blood, something is absorbed into your own system and contaminates you. Ask your husband-to-be. He nearly puked when he saw his first cadaver, but the second one was easier, and after that they're all alike. Isn't that so? Jesse aspires to a condition of personal bloodlessness—he told me that in an unguarded moment—but that necessitates the expulsion of a lot of fluid. In chemistry it isn't very clean either; in fact, it stinks a lot, but at least the stink is not anything personal. Out here... well, out here on the farm... there are some hilarious moments, if you don't have a weak stomach."

Helene stirred uneasily.

"That's the farm ahead. We've been passing their pastureland. See all the No Trespassing signs? A few farm kids from the area climbed over the fence one day and were exploring. They must have been surprised as hell to see our livestock exhibiting itself; they were sort of paralyzed and didn't even run away when the caretaker drove out in a jeep to yell at them.... See the gate ahead? When some really high-level work was being done out here everyone had to have an ID card with fingerprints and all. Then something happened, the project fell through, someone abandoned us for Berkeley, and things have loosened up a bit. How do you like the smell? Do you smell anything unusual yet?"

Jesse smelled something acrid, an odor of faint rot.

"I don't think so," Helene said uncertainly.

"Maybe I'm hypersensitive," Trick said. They stopped at the gate and Trick rang a bell. After a short wait a middle-aged man came hurrying out; he looked like an ordinary farmer in overalls, with a placid, bald head and a suntanned face. "This is the caretaker. It's a weird setup, he and his wife and six or seven kids living in there and the rest of us out doing experiments—Hello, Franklin. How are you today? How is everything out here?" The man flushed slightly at Trick's gay attention and swung open the gate so Trick could drive through.

The driveway was made of cinders. Behind the farmhouse was what must have been the farm's original barn, a large, humped building with a fresh coating of red paint and, in rows on either side of this barn, low, slant-roofed sheds made of metal and painted red also, with corrugated metal roofs. Jesse could see cattle moving about in the space between the buildings. A few cars were parked nearby, and a large, battered yellow truck marked *U-M Pathology Laboratory.* Two small boys, the farmer's children, were playing in the driveway and glanced up as Trick parked.

"Can you smell anything yet?" Trick said.

They got out of the car. A fly immediately blundered against Jesse's face and Jesse brushed it away. There was the sound of dogs barking, yipping. Someone was laughing. Trick led the way to the nearest shed, and Helene took Jesse's arm. The strangeness of this place, the acrid smell, and the laughter made them both feel formal. "Anybody home?" Trick shouted. The screen door of the shed opened and a young man poked his head out. Then a girl brushed past him, wearing shorts and a sweatshirt, and she cried out happily to Trick: "Dr. Monk, you fat thing! Why are *you* honoring us with a visit?" Then, catching sight of Jesse and Helene, she hesitated—self-conscious suddenly, she brushed something out of her hair and it fell to the ground. Behind her, in the doorway, two students were laughing about something. Jesse did not know them well. The girl's name was Peggy, but Jesse could not remember her last name. She was short and very perky, with a coy, monkeyish face. The thing she had brushed from her hair lay by her feet; it looked like a pink strip of something, maybe rubber. She reddened and shook Trick's hand. They appeared to be old friends. In turn, he introduced her to Jesse and Helene. Hearing that Helene was Benjamin Cady's daughter, she nodded gravely; to Jesse she said, "Oh, yes! Jesse Vogel! I think we know each other, don't we? I've heard good things about you." The students behind her stepped out into the sunlight, stretching their arms. One of them put on a pair of sunglasses. They were all wearing old clothes and sweat-shirts with smears of blood or grease on them.

"Hey, it's about lunchtime! What are you cooking in there?" Trick said, rubbing his hands.

"Oh—don't look! Don't look in there," Peggy said quickly. "It's sort of messy—these guys have been fooling around all day— You know what they're like, Trick."

She brushed at her hair again, as if she thought something might still be caught in it. Jesse saw that the thing at her feet was a small piece of intestine.

"What's your project, still cats? The same with me," Trick said, making a face. "Who's out here now? Whose cars are these?"

"The green one is Edna Bruner's. Her kids are fooling around with monkeys next door," the boy with the sunglasses said. "Jesus, you should hear those things scream! It's worse than when you were out here. The next prefab is vacant but Ray Easton is supposed to come in for the summer session. I hope to be working for him, if I can swing it. Then, down there, the big prefab, they're fooling around with sheep. You can see the sheep in the runway over there. Aren't they the damnedest looking things?"

In a pen behind the shed were a number of sheep of all sizes, even lambs. Most stood still. A few moved painfully around in the puddles of mud and manure. Flies buzzed everywhere. Jesse and Helene went over to look. The sheep had had their wool shaved off in large, ungainly patches, and numbers had been painted on their hides with bright red and yellow paint. A strange smell was loosed by their movement, not of the soil but of metal.

Jesse brushed flies away from himself and Helene. "Then the sheep still have lambs, even out here?"

"Oh, sure. That's part of it," the boy said.

"It certainly is part of it," Peggy laughed. Her face had gone scarlet, not from embarrassment but from excitement; she kept smiling at Jesse as if they were indeed old friends. Jesse thought her peculiar. "They're always herding the poor old ewes in with those damned rams. There are three rams out here. The females get the worst of it naturally, as in so-called human circles, and the rams just stuff themselves at the trough. Look at that poor ewe there! Do you see the one I mean? Barry Wilkinson had a bunch of first-year students, I swear they were freshmen, out here one day fooling around, I don't think he paid them more than fifty cents an hour, and they were trying to inject stuff into the sheep. That one started bleeding like hell and the kids ran over to us for help. What do I know about applying a tourniquet to a goddamn sheep?"

"But Peggy saved the thing's life. She was very noble!"

"I could hardly breathe, the thing stank so. Oh, those blue eyes! The sheep have such crazy blue eyes! I dream about those awful dumb blue eyes, like the eyes of crazy or dying people," Peggy said with a fake shudder. She was standing beside Jesse and she hugged herself as if cold, grinning up at him. "See that big barn? That's where they do the work. It's specially equipped for radiation work. Is it ever creepy in there—you see those crazy blue eyes staring at you from all over— A lot of sheep die in there and they've got a nerve to complain about *us*—because Wilkinson is trying all these new teaching methods, you know, bringing undergraduates out and letting them experiment. He says it's an elite community out here and that it should be democratized. The hell with the budget. They don't work with the radiation stuff itself, the kids, I think they just prep the sheep. But they can't do that right. They're so clumsy with a razor, I don't know how they manage to shave themselves in the morning."

A young man came out of the next prefab, letting the screen door slam behind him. Jesse recognized him as a faculty member. "Hello, Trick, what are you doing back here?" He grinned and waved at the others. "It's a bad day for a visit. The flies are biting." Everywhere there were large blue-black flies, drowsy with their weight or with the rich, slightly rotting odor of the place. They crawled on the sheep's splotched hides and passive, patient faces. A bedraggled sheep with the number 18 painted in red on her side approached the fence near Jesse, nudging it. Jesse and Helene glanced at each other. On the side of the sheep's neck were a number of pus-rimmed scabs. Flies crawled on them lazily.

"What are they doing with the sheep?" Jesse asked Peggy.

"Oh, it's a fertility experiment. I think they put some stuff in the jugular vein and see what happens—I mean, how the lambs turn out. How they're changed. I don't know what results they've gotten yet. They have an awful lot of money to fool around with though," she said, dropping her voice, "and Phil over there is jealous as hell about it. *His* project is going under, everybody says. Come look in the window at his stuff; he won't mind," she said. She took Jesse's arm. She was so short she had to stand on a concrete block to look in the window, but Jesse could look right in just by standing on his toes—he saw pens with dogs crowded into them, a number of single, small metal cages crammed with dogs. Most of the dogs were hunched over and motionless. A large collie with most of its fur shaved away and long purplish incisions on its body stared back at Jesse from a few feet away; it reminded Jesse of a patient he had seen the day before on his rounds at the hospital. A cocker spaniel lay beneath the collie, between its legs. The spaniel's fur was frayed and was coming off in unsightly strips. Flies crawled over a large open sore on its neck. "Maybe you shouldn't look," Jesse said to Helene, but she had already looked in. She turned away coolly, showing no distress.

"Why are the dogs so quiet?" Jesse asked.

"They've been fixed up," Peggy said, drawing a finger swiftly across her throat; "they had their barks removed. God, can you imagine what it would be like? That's what makes everyone mad about Bruner's monkeys. It's like a jungle out here sometimes, the way those things shriek! Luckily, old Edna is the only one out today and she must be writing up reports, so it's quiet. They're experimenting with burns, using flame throwers, and it's the goddamnedest smell you ever smelled. You can smell it right now, and they haven't been fooling around since last week. That singed smell—it smells like fur and meat—that's from the monkeys. Do you smell it?"

"I guess so," Jesse said.

"God, I hate monkeys," Peggy said. "They shoot some of the fire down the things' throats, so those monkeys don't make much noise. But it's like a slaughterhouse out here, the way it stinks sometimes. I've been asked to join a reform committee and I just might do it."

Jesse saw more sheep moving in a corral behind the barn. They moved slowly, stiffly. He had a sudden vision, an involuntary vision, of the countryside filling up with sheep, their battered, clumsy, dirty bodies moving slowly, sleepily, bumping into one another as their eyesight deteriorated, sinking to the ground as tumors rose in their bodies, the lambs nudging the ewes, all of them crowded sleepily together and too stupid to cry out in pain, crowding the landscape, easing outward so that they strained against the fences and broke them down....

If Helene was upset by this she did not show it; she stood a little apart from the others, watchful and poised.

Trick took them to another shed, where several people were sitting eating sandwiches. One of them, a man in his forties, was Gordon Howe, a professor in the biology department; the two younger men Jesse did not know by name; and the single girl, who had Asian features, was a stranger to him. They were sitting on the front steps of their prefab, waxed paper spread neatly on their knees. They offered everyone coffee but only Trick accepted. Peggy came hurrying after them and cried out that they should not miss the "egg room": "It's refrigerated—it's the only place out here that's bearable." The Oriental girl stood, as if made uneasy by the visitors or by Peggy's loud voice. She wrapped up what remained of her sandwich in a piece of waxed paper. The talk here was of hamsters, evidently an unexciting topic. Howe took them inside to look at the cages: row after row of nervous little animals with pink ratlike tails and curious twitching faces. The stench was sharp. "We're working with their tongues. Sensory paths," Howe said. As he walked between the rows of cages he tapped at them fondly. Trick seemed quite interested in the project. "We've got a new grant for next year," Howe said, and Trick congratulated him.

Nearby there was a shriek—a rising series of shrieks—then silence.

Howe showed them a graph with a complicated system of lines and bars of red and black. Jesse tried to interest himself in it but he kept glancing at Helene. She had worn a yellow dress that day, and though the color was attractive, it gave her complexion a yellowish cast; she looked a little sick. Her hair was parted neatly as always, drawn back behind her ears, and she wore small jade earrings. She seemed cautious, guarded. There was something of her father's cool haughtiness in her. The shriek came again from next door—Howe explained that it was a monkey—and Helene's mouth tightened. Jesse took her hand. It remained in his, inert and damp.

They went back outside. Someone had just driven up in a station wagon and several students were busy unloading boxes. Trick walked them down to the end of the row of prefabs where a radio was blaring and around to the sheep pen again. Jesse noticed how passively and fixedly Helene stared at the sheep. "This is a very important project they've got going," Trick said excitedly. "Putting radioactive stuff in the sheep to test for mutations— It should make big news. I wish them well. But I wonder what the hell they do with the dead sheep? I don't think you could dispose of a dead radioactive sheep in any ordinary way, do you?"

"No," said Jesse.

"I must ask about that," Trick said.

Peggy took them across a meadow strewn with concrete blocks and other junk, to the big barn. They could hear a humming noise. Another radio was playing inside, turned up high, and as they entered the barn Jesse smelled the sharp, half-pleasant stench of old blood. Yes, there were bloodstains on the floor, great dried pools everywhere. Only a few graduate assistants were around but they didn't look busy. On the counters there were rags and needles and bottles, tubes, rolls of tape, lunch bags, half-empty bottles of soda pop, tin cans, boxes. Against one wall were shelves of jars with embryos in them, one embryo to a jar, row upon row. The embryos were small, hunched-over, perfect little creatures.

"At least this place is air-conditioned," Peggy said. "Gatti himself designed the inside. He has a thing about stuff collected in bottles. He insists upon his people collecting a few hundred specimens, so in case of fire or breakage or anything he has a lot left over. He's very conservative. Isn't this place elegant? They give themselves airs over here. But I wouldn't want to work with all these dead things."

"Peggy likes live things. Sheep and goats and things like that," someone snickered.

"Oh, shut up! Just because I saved your sheep from bleeding to death. . . . Tell your kids not to bother me next time. I got blood all over my clothes, even down inside my shoes. How the hell do you think I looked going back to Ann Arbor?" she said angrily.

The boys laughed.

They went back out into the warm air. Jesse looked at Helene, but her expression was demure and opaque. She seemed slightly withdrawn from him, as if surrendering him to Peggy's boisterousness. Her passivity disturbed him. Trick kept turning to her, trying to include her in his noisy conversation with the others, but she did no more than smile tensely, slightly. Once he even reached out to touch her shoulder, an absentminded gesture, only part of his conversation. Helene's expression did not change but she stepped back. "As with the animals, so with us," Trick said. "They heal without as many complications, though, and don't know enough to sue us. I thought I was fed up with cats, but on second thought I prefer them to your sheep. They don't stink as much. The best material to work with would be human beings, of course, but that's not possible in this country. We are so civilized," he said, leering, scowling. He walked briskly ahead of the others as if leading them, the center of their attention. Jesse, walking with Helene, felt sodden, satiated with the sights of this place and with the odor of singed flesh and blood and rot. He was tired of Trick's voice. He would have liked to take

Helene aside and explain to her that he had not chosen this kind of life for himself, not this particular life: it was necessary to work through it, to push oneself through it, to come out at the other end as . . . as a man who might save the lives of other men. . . . What other way was there, except to pursue truth through the bodies of animals?

Trick was saying something about beer. Would they all like to drive out for some beer?

"It's getting late for us. We'd better go home," Jesse said.

"What? Why?"

"We have to get back."

"Oh, hell. Don't let him push you around, Helene," Trick said. "He always wants to bring the party to an end, he always wants to work! Let's all go out somewhere and have some beer."

"I'd rather go back to Ann Arbor," Jesse said. "I have some hospital reports to write up."

"God, my dear girl," Trick said, sliding his arm around Helene's shoulders, "you are obviously not going to remain faithful to Jesse for long. Work, all he knows is work! Not being a genius like me—how many of you are?—the poor guy has to frazzle his brain out. He'll disappoint you—and when he does, remember to give old Trick a call; command me and I am yours, I'll hurry to your side—"

Jesse flinched; Helene, unsmiling, moved away from Trick. The others laughed. Peggy poked Trick in the stomach. "You, what do you need beer for? You carry it all over with you like a camel!" she cried.

"Don't do that," said Trick. "I haven't had a bowel movement for fifteen days. I'm a walking disaster. It's all coiled up inside me and I need the extra space." They laughed. Jesse grinned in a sudden hot anger and walked Helene back to the car. The others laughed behind them. Trick called out: "Be right with you, kids! Be right with you!"

And he did hurry after them, puffing, panting, red in the face, and looked ashamed.

With a weary yodel he slid into the car beside Jesse. "Ah, I talk too much. I know it," he said.

Jesse and Helene were silent.

"I just thought it might be a nice idea to have a few beers,"

Trick said lamely. "But you probably have no appetite for it. You were right, Jesse, absolutely right. I don't like this crowd anyway. Except for Gordon Howe, they're bores." He chatted at them all the way back to Ann Arbor, his spirits rising slowly even though Jesse did not bother to reply. Helene stared out the window.

Trick seemed not to know the extent of their displeasure, or pretended not to know. When he let them out near campus he grinned happily at them. "Well, it was interesting, wasn't it? Great day for a drive in the country!"

When they were alone in the Cadys' apartment Helene sat down as if exhausted. She put her hands to her face, massaging her eyes. Jesse, standing above her, was fearful of touching her—she was so cool, so withdrawn, so independent of him.

"Did it upset you?" he asked.

She shook her head slightly, without looking at him. Outside the window an elm tree blocked out the sun; this room, a kind of sitting room, was shaded and cool. Jesse felt the presence of Dr. Cady here, though they were alone. On a nearby table stood the framed photograph—Cady and his two co-winners of the Nobel Prize, smiling gentlemen who seemed to be looking directly at Jesse, inviting him to join them. If he had to make his way to them through the stink of blood and intestines and burned flesh, taking wisdom where he found it, what did that matter? What did it matter?

Jesse kissed Helene's forehead and embraced her without force. She did not draw away. He wondered what she was thinking. Her scent was light, pale, blond-colored scent. She was a mystery, like the mysteries explored out there in the sheds, beneath the rusty corrugated roofs, in the din of portable radios and lunchtime joking. What was living performed the rites of living; when it no longer performed these rites it was not "living." Wasn't Jesse himself a kingdom of these living cells, all of them performing excellently? Wasn't Helene, so sternly attractive, so stubborn beneath her appearance of submission, herself a marvelous kingdom of cells, unfathomable cells that demanded awe? It was necessary that a man throw himself into the study of such mysteries, Jesse thought. All truth, any truth, justified itself. *That collie's large glassy eyes. The stink of putrid flesh, singed flesh, the shriek of a terrified animal, Peggy's shrill flirting with him.*

"Did all that upset you?" Jesse asked.

"No. But I'm thinking of what we have to go through."

"What? Who has to go through?"

"You and me. People. How we have to live and die. How our bodies will smell," she said faintly.

She looked up at him. Her eyes were darkened by threads of blood, as if by the seriousness of her thinking. Jesse was astonished. He had wanted to comfort her, but how could he comfort such words? It hurt him to think that she should contemplate suffering like that, moving restlessly and independently of him, of his love for her, as if he had not the power to protect her.... Did she really think they must suffer like those animals? Her flesh and his flesh, flesh no more divine than that of the animals, doomed to the same bawdy fates?

5

And your family is...

Scattered.

Your entire family is scattered...?

My parents are dead.

I'm very sorry to hear that.

An automobile accident. It happened a long time ago. Around Christmas... the roads were icy.

Silence, during which questions rose like bubbles in Cady's head: Jesse imagined he could see them. *What, what did you say exactly? Your family is scattered or dead? Your parents are dead? How exactly did they die?*

Jesse sat facing this man, an inheritor, a hopeful son-in-law, a kind of thief. He wanted to explain to Cady that those deaths were long ago, long ago. They did not matter now. How could they matter now? He wanted to erase all thought of those deaths from Cady's mind, he wanted to seize hold of the man by his frail noble shoulders and shake him.... *Dead? All dead? Where are they buried? Where do the dead go? Where are the dead at this moment, Jesse?*

After a few moments Cady began to speak gently. He told Jesse about his wife's death many years ago. Helene had been twelve at the time. Years, years had passed, and yet the death was somehow fresh, permanently fresh in their lives. Jesse stared at Cady's hands; at his small, perfect, oval fingernails, which were well-tended. Those hands had outlived his wife's hands. What did that mean? *Where are the dead at this moment?* Jesse began to feel lightheaded. Panicky. A copy of *Time* Magazine lay on a nearby table and Jesse could see the picture of Harry Truman on the cover. It lay at a slant toward him, the face distorted, shortened, the eyes hardly more than slits. A father's face. Alive or dead?

Jesse sat with his knees pressed together, suddenly afraid he might say something wrong. Make a mistake. He might ask Cady where the dead went, and where they were all these years—he could almost hear his voice breaking into Cady's voice, demanding to be told the truth—

An automobile accident. Christmastime. Long ago.

And you have no more relatives, Jesse?

No. Yes. They're scattered. I can't find them. Couldn't find them.

Have you tried to find them?

No.

Why not?

They're in the cemetery, waiting.

Do you go to visit them?

No, no!

Why not, Jesse?

"... so we were fortunate enough to have two sets of grandparents, very loving grandparents, for Helene. ..." Cady was saying.

Jesse nodded gravely, sympathetically. What was this man talking about? It was hard for Jesse to follow. When he sat in Cady's lecture he could follow everything the man said, no matter how complex it was; here, so close to him, as they talked of these soft-spoken matters, Jesse's mind seemed to jump all over.

"... you said you lived with your grandfather, Jesse?"

"Yes."

"How long was that?"

"A few years, until I went away to school ... a few years ... I don't remember exactly. ..."

My God, Jesse thought, how many questions can he ask! What

does he want from me?... Benjamin Cady had won the Nobel Prize for his work in cerebellar physiology and always, always he was asking questions, staring at faces. Jesse felt an awe that verged on dread in his presence. He was always thinking. Thinking. Jesse wished that Helene would join them—a third person would help, would tilt the conversation in another direction, would save him. *And is your grandfather dead too? What, they're all dead? Everybody is dead? Don't you think that's strange?*

"...and your grandfather...?"

"He died a few years ago"

Cady nodded. His face was grave as Jesse's, but still he fixed Jesse with a certain clear-eyed look, as if assessing him.

Where was Helene? She was chaste and comradely, his Helene. He loved her. *He loved her.* With her he forgot about the past; or, if he had to talk about it, he lied without fear. He always lied. He lied automatically, without fear, but when Cady questioned him like this he lied miserably—he could not keep his shame down. Helene was in the rear of the apartment and Jesse waited anxiously to hear her footstep—if he just heard her coming, or could pretend to hear her, he could get to his feet and bring this conversation to a halt.

He glanced up, imagining that he heard her. Cady noted his attentiveness and seemed pleased. "My daughter is a very serious, very steady young woman... a very special young woman, I think," Cady said. "You've made her very happy already. I am grateful to you for that. Yes, very grateful. I hope you will love Helene and respect her always, all your life," Cady said, his voice dimming suddenly as if he were about to weep.

"Yes, I will," Jesse said, startled and a little ashamed. "I will always love and respect your daughter, yes...."

He seemed to be making a vow.

He hurried up the steps of the apartment house with the piece of paper folded in his pocket, crumpled first in anger and then folded in two. She was waiting for him nervously, wearing the same yellow dress she had worn that day at the experimental farm. Was she wearing it on purpose? Her face was hectic and tender. Jesse wondered if Trick had already telephoned her. How much did she know? What was going on?

"You sounded so troubled over the phone. . . ." Jesse said.

He squinted at her bright, confused face. It was not like Helene to be so nervous.

"I don't think it's important, Jesse. It's just—something that came in the mail— I thought I should show it to you," she said.

Jesse took the paper from her, saw that it was the same dull, heavy white stationery that Trick had used for Jesse's letter. No surprise. Grimly, his face set for disapproval, Jesse read Trick's letter to Helene:

> Dearest Helene:
>
> I have always been of the conviction that love, because it is based upon the sexual drive, is an illusion, just as the sexual drive is to some extent an illusion, dependent solely upon ideal biological and environmental conditions. Sexual desire is a superficial "instinct" that vanishes at the first sign of danger, as you know, and therefore any emotion based upon it is fantastic and wasteful. But you know all this! What you also know, and what I have learned, is that love can exist truly, apart from accidents of the body and the environment. For some time now I have been in love. But I hesitated to tell you because of the embarrassment and awkwardness it might cause you. I know that you are going to marry Jesse and that there is no chance of my changing your mind. How could I change your mind? He is an exceptional young man, far superior to me. Everyone admires his ambition, even if they do not always appreciate Jesse himself. When I first became aware of him, I was struck by his seriousness, his dedication to his work, a strange inner *certainty* of his that the rest of us lack. At times he has such a strange look! Am I exaggerating if I say that he is a dangerous man?—or would be dangerous if he hadn't your love and his work to confine him?
>
> Yours always, sadly,
> Trick

Helene was watching Jesse's face. "Are you very angry with him?" she said.

Jesse shrugged his shoulders irritably.

"I . . . I was so surprised. . . . I never thought . . . Please don't be angry with him, Jesse."

"I'm not angry. I don't get angry," Jesse said. He had an impulse to crumple this piece of paper too. He was certain that Helene had enjoyed reading it and having him read it. She was very warm, agitated, excited. How womanly she was in her excitement! Turning from her, disturbed by her, Jesse read the letter through again, more slowly. He could recognize Trick's glinting smile behind it, that cautious skeptical leer of his. *A dangerous man. . . .*

"He didn't say I shouldn't show the letter to you," Helene said. "I feel very sorry for him . . . and we won't be seeing him again, Jesse, after next week. . . ."

"No, we won't be seeing him again."

He took his own letter out to show her. It was not typed, as Helene's was, but scrawled in Trick's slanting handwriting, falling ignobly and clownishly down the page.

"Here. Read this," Jesse said.

Dear Jesse:

She has received a letter from me today. Will she show it to you? Or will she keep it a secret? If she loves you she'll show it to you.

Will you forgive me, Jesse?

I mailed a declaration of love to her this morning. All day long I have been sick with shame, I want to die, believe me when I say that my life disgusts me, that I am disgusted with my work and my jokes, disgusted to the point of death. Jesse, there is such a gift in you! There is nothing in me. Your soul is as tough as the muscles of your body but my soul is flabby and drained and mealy from disuse. I am always examining myself in the mirror, hoping for a change. You don't know what my room is like because you've never come up here. You've never seen the mirror in my bathroom. You can't imagine how ugly a face looks in that mirror, especially my face. I am always staring at myself. I am always pulling my cheeks to show my eyes edged with red and crazy. I look like an ape. I joke with myself in the mirror. You are a man who does not even bother looking at himself in the mirror, because he knows just what he looks like. Always.

I was wrong to send her that letter. Forgive me. After next

week I will never see the two of you again. I will never bother you. Can I retreat from your lives with your good will, can I see you just once more? I will telephone Helene and ask if you will forgive me. I beg you to forgive me. May I take you out to dinner? And then I will vanish from your lives forever. I have been working on some poems. I think I will call them "Poems Without People." I am the speaker in all of them but I don't count myself as a human being, because I am drained out and soulless. Here is a poem I wrote this morning:

SONG OF MYSELF

I am a vile jelly
that grew wings
and a bumpy facial structure

beneath your bare feet
I would subside again
to jelly
to joy

Yours always,
Trick

Helene read the letter through twice, carefully. "I don't understand that poem," she said.

"The hell with it," Jesse said.

"What is he trying to say...?"

Jesse took the letter from her and crumpled it in his fist.

"Jesse, you shouldn't do that. Please, Jesse. It's like striking him... it's... He loves us both very much...."

"The hell with his love."

"But he is a good person. He is a good person," Helene said slowly.

"He's crazy."

He took Helene's letter and angrily crumpled it too.

"He asks us to forgive him...."

The telephone rang.

Helene hesitated. Jesse waved her away, his heart pounding. "All right, answer it. Go ahead. Let him take us out. And that's all, that's the end of it, we'll never see him again. Tell him that."

She went to answer the telephone, relieved. Yes, it was Trick. Jesse stood by the window and covertly watched her, jealous of the rosiness of her skin, the delicate energy of her face. She was a handsome young woman, yes, and this rivalry made her more attractive. He understood. He told himself that it was natural, he should not be so angry with her; he must control himself. Once they were married there would be no rival for her love. No Trick preening and weeping over himself . . . in fact, Jesse thought suddenly, she would not meet very many men at all, she would not meet his colleagues, she would be his wife and the mother of his children and she would belong to him entirely. She would belong to him. His heart pounded with the hot urgency of this fact, his need to make it come true, while Helene stood a few yards away, listening to Trick. Jesse could make out Trick's voice—how could he talk so much! How did he dare to call! Helene was saying softly, "No. . . . Oh, no. Not at all, Trick. No. He isn't angry, no. Please don't talk like that. . . . Yes. . . ." After a moment she put her hand over the receiver and said, "He wants to talk to you, Jesse. He wants to arrange a time to take us out to dinner."

"I don't want to talk to him."

"Jesse . . . ?"

"Make the plans yourself."

So she made the plans.

Trick was to pick them up on Sunday, at seven o'clock; but for some reason he arrived an hour early. Jesse was already there. He remembered the several times Trick had come early to have coffee with him, always insisting that he was on time and that Jesse was mistaken; now, rather gaily, he insisted that he was to arrive at six o'clock, that Helene must have made a mistake, he even accused her of being "charmingly feeble-minded. . . ." He had bought a new outfit for the occasion: a jacket of white and powder-blue stripes, a dark checked tie that did not quite match the jacket but looked very smart, and pale-blue trousers that were tight at the waist, so that Trick's stomach protruded painfully. His hair had been cut. Jesse saw, involuntarily, that Trick's skull looked pinkish and weak at its crown.

"Yes, we agreed on six o'clock—don't you remember?" Trick said to Helene.

"I must have forgotten," Helene said slowly.

"Six o'clock. Absolutely."

He drove them downtown to a large steak house. Trick and Helene did most of the talking. They were nimble and abstract with each other, their remarks scuttling across Jesse without quite touching upon him, as if they were both afraid of Jesse. Jesse himself felt unaccountably nervous. It was difficult for him to look Trick in the face. Trick chattered rapidly about any number of things, always circling back to the topic of the letters and the poem. "I shouldn't have burdened you with my troubles," he said. "Bad poetry should always be kept secret. It's as boring as dreams—as private and as boring as dreams—"

He ordered cocktails for them and made suggestions for dinner, reading off the menu to them. "I've been here several times. They serve excellent food here. It's very reliable. In fact, my parents wanted to take Jesse here the last time they were visiting me but Jesse was too busy that evening."

Jesse's head ached. All this troubled him, irritated him: Trick's talk and Helene's cautious quick agreement . . . the drone of other Sunday customers, travelers and parents visiting their children at the university. . . . So many people, so many crowded tables, so many confusing conversations! Jesse never ate in restaurants like this. It sickened him a little, the din of voices and silverware, the expense, the ceremony of food heaped upon plates, each table centered inward upon food and drink. Their drinks arrived and Trick proposed a toast to their wedding and their lifelong happiness. Jesse wondered if he was joking: but no, he looked serious.

"Yes, to your lifelong happiness—to your happiness!" Trick said.

Jesse fixed his gaze upon a complicated brass chandelier and tried not to pay much attention to what Trick was saying. He returned to the topic of the letters again, apologized again, and chided Helene gently once again about having forgotten about the correct time. Jesse's heart pounded with a sudden rage, because of course Helene had been right about the time and Trick wrong—and yet Trick kept insisting that he was right! Jesse did not dare to look at him. He was relieved when Helene murmured something placid, something agreeable—a vague apology for having forgotten the time—"I have so much to think of," she said.

"Ah yes, obviously you do!" Trick said at once. "In your life I am not a very crucial event. Obviously! In spite of my bulk, I am about the size of the jack of hearts seen sideways—or am I the joker maybe?" When Helene did not reply and Jesse sat silent, he went on to talk about the coming year and his expectations in Boston. He had many years of study ahead and he would have to undergo a formal psychoanalysis. He intended to be a psychoanalyst himself. "How ironic, you are thinking . . . ?" he joked, but it was no joke, and neither Helene nor Jesse responded. After a moment Helene spoke of their plans for the next week. They would drive down and move Jesse into the interns' residence hall. She planned to stay in Chicago for a while, perhaps she would get a job there, try to save a little money. . . . Trick laughed at this, as if to suggest that Helene did not need to have money with so wealthy a father; Jesse felt another pang of rage. He finished his drink.

Trick ordered another round immediately.

"But Trick, I haven't finished my drink . . . I really don't want another," Helene said.

Trick leaned against the table, big and anxious, his hair coming loose on one side of his head and falling lankly forward. Jesse narrowed his eyes and tried to look at Trick. He had been seeing that earnest, mottled skin for too many months. And that mouth. That moving mouth. And Trick's big feet under the table, crowding against Jesse's. Even when Jesse moved his legs to one side Trick bumped into them.

"A cigarette. Let's all have a cigarette," Trick said.

He offered cigarettes to Helene, who did not smoke, and to Jesse, who thought suddenly that he would like to smoke—but he hesitated, then refused. He would not take one of Trick's cigarettes.

Trick's hands were trembling. He sucked at the cigarette and then at his drink, holding one in each hand. There was a feverish cast to his eyes. "I don't think you forgive me," he said finally.

"Trick, please—" Helene said.

"It's Jesse. Jesse doesn't forgive me."

"Jesse does. He does."

"Why doesn't he look at me?"

With difficulty Jesse forced himself to look Trick in the eye. "I am looking at you. I forgive you," he said. His mouth smiled absurdly.

"As soon as I mailed the first letter I knew I had made a terrible mistake...."

"Please don't keep thinking about it," Helene said.

"But I'll keep thinking about it the rest of my life. It's one of the events of my life," Trick said.

"We can talk of other things tonight...."

"Yes, other things... we can talk of other things.... I should be able to express myself more coherently," Trick muttered. "I want only to please you. The two of you. I don't want you to leave Ann Arbor hating me. But what can a man say to two people in love, people who are going away together...? People in love don't need anyone else to complete them or to say good-by to them or to take them out to dinner. Obviously not. They only acquiesce to their friends out of charity."

"Oh, Jesus," Jesse said.

"Jesse is irritated with me. Yes. I knew it. I anticipated it. I stayed up all night last night and wrote some poems.... Would you like to see them?"

Trick seemed not to notice that the waitress was bringing their dinners to them, and as he reached awkwardly into his coat pocket he nearly jostled her. "Oh, excuse me!" he cried. "I didn't see you... are you back already?... Everything is going so fast...."

"We can read the poems later. It's too dark in here," Jesse said.

"You can hold them up to the light," Trick said.

He handed them across the table to Jesse and Helene while the waitress put down their plates. Jesse wanted to tear up the pieces of paper and toss them in Trick's face.

Helene held up the first piece of paper. "Why do you call them 'Poems Without People'? That's such a strange title...."

"Because, because I can't write about people. I don't know anything about people," Trick said eagerly. He hunched forward against the table, pushing himself onto the edge of his chair. His knee nudged Jesse's. "What do you think? Which one are you reading? I'm sorry I didn't have time to type them out... my handwriting looks like hell...."

Jesse looked on while Helene held the piece of paper up to the light.

THE MADNESS OF CROWDS

the pavement is cracking with the fever
of their feet
buildings shudder with their springy weight
newly built, still the buildings are obsolete:
their elevator cables sigh even at night

look, there are smoke-smudges blossoming
into souls!
beings the size of thumbprints bloom
bubbling up out of sewers
the tightest manhole covers cannot keep them down
they are falling lightly on bits of soot
angels the size of our smallest fingernails

sparkling protoplasm!
we are drowning
it is like carbonated water
it is like crystals baked into tons of ice
we are drowning
our fingers thresh the glittering air
we drown back into ourselves
into the shouting wave
we are helpless as the meeting of two blank
hot walls of air
or two lovers pressed together
in perpetual daylight

"What do you think? What do you think of it?" Trick said. He was talking very loudly.

Jesse, who made no sense of the poem and who felt a sudden violent exasperation with Trick, took the poems from Helene and folded them in two. "We can talk about this after dinner," he said.

"Oh... did you fold them?" Trick asked.

They turned to their dinner—Jesse picked up his fork angrily; Trick picked up his knife and fork as if he had no idea of what to do with them. He sawed at the meat on his plate. He cut his steak into several large pieces and raised one to his mouth. "I'm only guessing at life," he said humbly. "The only person I can write about is myself. That's why I call the sequence of poems 'Poems Without People.' Because the only person in them is myself and I don't count."

Trick glanced at the meat on his fork and lowered it to his plate, confused.

For some reason Jesse felt his mouth twisting into a smile—a grin. He laughed out loud. Trick glanced up at once, blinking. "Why are you laughing, Jesse? Are you laughing at me? In front of *her*?"

"I didn't mean anything by it," Jesse said.

But his face was still oddly, brightly amused—he could hardly keep from laughing again.

Trick cut the piece of meat into two smaller pieces. His movements were brisk and self-conscious. "I like to see Jesse laugh. I shouldn't complain. He doesn't laugh often enough for a young man his age. I like to see the two of you together, smiling together. Do you know I've followed you? Oh yes," he said gravely, nodding. He put down both his knife and fork and stared at the heaped food on his plate. Mashed potatoes, glazed carrots, a large greasy juicy steak.... He seemed unable to think of what to do with all this. He glanced up at Jesse, smiling. "Yes, I might as well admit it. I have no shame. I've often followed the two of you at a discreet distance, in disguise. Sometimes in disguise as a trash barrel, sometimes as a dancing bear.... But it's so cruel to be always kept at a distance, especially a discreet distance...."

"Trick, are you joking?" Helene asked nervously.

"Joking," Trick said flatly. He seemed to be testing, tasting the words. He shook his head no. *No.* Confused, he picked up a large roll and broke it into smaller pieces; he buttered one of the pieces crudely, but then put it down on the tablecloth near his plate. His eyes skimmed over Jesse's and Helene's plates.

"You aren't enjoying your dinner. You aren't eating anything."

Jesse and Helene had not touched their food.

"Why aren't you eating with me? Do I offend you?" Trick said.

"Trick, please.... You must be joking," Helene said.

"You accepted my offer to take you out and then you forgot about the time. Deliberately. You tried to imply that I had come an hour early in order to embarrass me. And now you've come out with me, as my guests, and you won't eat in order to embarrass me. You are demonstrating that in my presence you have no appetite!" Trick pushed his own plate away from him abruptly. The tablecloth was pulled up and Trick's water glass would have been upset if Jesse hadn't steadied it. "You are passing judgment on me and I can't stop you. You can see right through me into my brain. Shall I confess something...? I did a terrible thing a few days ago. I did it with *you* in mind, Helene. In a cadaver room... I had an idea suddenly... the idea came to me the way my poems come to me, in a fierce rush, like a dream... in a cadaver room I helped myself to a piece of a human being...."

He smiled slyly at them.

"Yes, a human being... I helped myself.... I know I shouldn't be telling you this. But I think I will. I want to confess everything. I cut out of a female about your age, Helene, a uterus that was not at all damaged, and I took it home with me in a brown paper bag and kept it in the refrigerator for a while... and then I did a very strange thing; I tried to broil it.... I wanted to broil it and eat it like chicken, which it resembles to some extent...."

Jesse and Helene stared.

"What...?" Jesse said.

"It broiled unevenly. Part of it got burned and part of it was raw. And it didn't taste like chicken," Trick said with a shiver, though he was still smiling.

"Are you joking again?" Jesse said in amazement.

Trick's face hardened. "Jokes. What are jokes? I don't know what a joke is," he said contemptuously. He glanced at Helene and his face screwed up as if he were about to spit. "You don't have any appetite, eh? You are rather bloodless, Helene. How will you be a match for this fiery young man?"

"Jesse, I think we should leave," Helene said faintly.

Jesse helped her up.

"We'll get a taxi back. Don't bother coming with us," Jesse said.

"Leaving, you're leaving already...? Why is everything going so fast?" Trick said vacantly. He stared at Jesse. "Oh, please...

don't leave so soon. . . . I've been waiting for this evening for so long, for so many hours. . . ."

"We're leaving," Jesse said angrily.

Trick followed them, protesting. He was carrying his napkin. "Oh, please don't leave?" he cried. People stared at him. "Don't abandon me! Why do people fear honesty, why do they betray their friends when their friends expose their hearts? You know I love you, both of you. But you're walking away. You're forcing me to chase after you."

"Stay the hell away from us," Jesse said. "Nobody's forcing you to do anything."

"He's sick," Helene whispered.

"Come on. Let's get a taxi," Jesse said.

They hurried to the corner but Trick followed after them, panting. When, in a rage, Jesse glanced around, he saw Trick's big flushed face and his hand, with the napkin in it, closed into a fist and pressed against his chest. Behind him, in the large, ornate doorway of the restaurant, someone was calling after them. Trick said loudly, "A poet can express himself obliquely, in poems, he can say things that his friend won't allow him to say in the daylight! I have another poem called 'Mouth' that is dedicated to Jesse. It's about my own mouth. You left it back in the restaurant but I can recite it—"

"Go to hell!"

Trick called after them in a shrill, oratorical voice. "My poem is called 'Mouth.' It goes like this—*That mouth. Enormous. / It is an opening like sand / falling beneath your feet— / a surprise of a hole, falling away / suddenly—*"

"Will you shut up! Go to hell" Jesse cried.

"*At the rim of the mouth / you surprise yourself / you are eager to be—*"

"Shut up!"

"You're confusing me, I can't remember the rest of it—Jesse, you're confusing me— *At the rim of the mouth—at the rim— You become this pulp / you surrender your name—* I can't remember the right order. You've confused me." People on the sidewalk had stopped to stare at Trick. He caught up to Jesse and Helene and took hold of Jesse's arm. "Jesse, you have no lyricism in your soul. Your soul is pure and abstract. He has plans for his future, Helene, that are pure and abstract and criminal! He told me himself. He wants to do only good and to save people, he doesn't want to stick his nose in anybody's mucus—but still he's planning a family, Helene, four or five children at least—he told me so himself! But the mother-to-be at that time was wider in the pelvis than you. Or does he want five children from you, too?"

Jesse shoved Trick away.

"Oh, you want to fight! You want to fight me!" Trick said.

"Will you get the hell away from us?"

"Fight me then. Come on."

"Get out of here!"

He rushed at Jesse. Jesse shoved him away again. Around them on the sidewalk people stood, gaping, and the manager of the restaurant had come out. Trick tried to grab Jesse, tried to embrace him, and this time Jesse shoved him away with his knee. His knee caught Trick in the belly. Trick grunted in surprise but came back at once—he threw himself at Jesse and the two of them stumbled and fell. Trick fell on top of Jesse. Jesse rolled away nimbly; he had not been hurt, he felt only an enormous exhilarating rage. What surprise, to feel this rage! To feel his blood coursing so strongly! He jumped up, strong in the legs, the very muscles of his legs long prepared for this, and the muscles of his torso and shoulders and arms long prepared, eager, to get hold of this man, to slam him in the face—Jesse's fists felt hard and distant as rocks. Painless. Helene was calling his name and trying to pull him away. But it was distant, painless. His panting breath was painless.

Trick, on his feet again, stood bent over in agony, swaying. He gripped his stomach. Blood was flowing from his nose down onto his shirt, dripping onto the sidewalk. He swayed and shuddered and yet seemed to be gathering strength for another lunge at Jesse.

"Don't do it! I'll kill you!" Jesse whispered.

But he ran at Jesse again, hardly able to straighten himself. This time he managed to get his big arms around Jesse in a tight strangling hold, but Jesse pushed himself free— Trick's strength suddenly gave out and he staggered backwards, his fist pressed against his chest. He cried out in pain.

His legs buckled. He fell heavily onto the sidewalk.

"I told you—I told you!" Jesse cried.

6

Waiting in the hospital, immense vapid hours: the smell of panic about Jesse's body, his cold body. His head felt hollow and cold. Jesse sitting in a cheap chair of metal tubing, with foam-rubber cushion, waiting. Helene with him, holding his hand, lowering her head wearily until she pressed her forehead against his knuckles; he gave a little jump when he saw her so docile, so close to him. In public. He was very sleepy....

The resident on the floor told Jesse to go home. But Jesse wanted to wait, he had to wait. *Was Trick going to live?*

"It wasn't your fault," Helene whispered.

It wasn't his fault, but Cady had called an attorney at once. The man was brisk and unconversational. This Sunday-evening emergency displeased him. He kept asking about the witnesses: yes, there were three witnesses apart from Helene, three men willing to testify. Good. *Jesse remembered that blow in the stomach—his knee rising hard right into Trick—* Did the young man, Dr. Monk, strike you first? *Yes.* Did he insist upon a fight? *Yes.* Had he been provoked in any way? *No.* Not in any way? *No.* Did you know about his heart condition? *No.* A rheumatic heart condition—he never mentioned it to you? Never? *No.*

Jesse jumping up, his blood coursing through him—rage bursting in him—

You repeatedly told Dr. Monk to leave you alone...?

Yes.

"He was the one who wanted to fight. He insisted upon fighting Jesse," Helene said. She was fired with a strange energy, leaning forward from the hips to look intently at the attorney, declaring herself. A certain ferocity, an air of ownership, gave her tired face a keen, girlish look.

To Jesse she said, "He wanted you to fight him so that you would kill him. I understand it now. He wanted you to kill him."

Jesse rubbed his eyes as if to get this clear. But he could not understand.

"Yes, it's true. I understand. I understand it now," Helene said.

She waited in the hospital with him, holding his hand. She would marry him at once; they would get married at once. Why should they wait until Jesse's intern year was over? Why? She knew what it would be like to be an intern's wife, it would be no surprise to her, the daughter and granddaughter of doctors— Yes, they must get married soon, in a week or two. She would never leave him. *Those first running steps of Trick's . . . the clumsy wrestling embrace . . . Jesse's knee brought up into his belly. . . .* She comforted him. He wanted to weep, she was so close to him and so public, so loving, so angry for him. She would never leave him.

"Why would he want to die?" Jesse asked her.

"He wanted you to kill him."

"But why? Why?"

He stared at Helene.

"Why would he want me to kill him?"

It was the same question the attorney had asked. *Why would this young man want you to hurt him? Why would he deliberately provoke you when he had a weak heart?*

Jesse's face was turning into a muscle that yearned to show pain, intense pain. He wanted to cry. But he did not allow himself to cry. *Trick was dying, who would cry for Trick?* Sparkling protoplasm: Trick. Drowning. We are drowning, Trick had said. Jesse had not understood the poem and now he could not remember it. The words were jumbled. *Protoplasm . . . lovers . . . lovers pressed together in daylight. . . .*

No, he did not understand.

7

A balloon, flimsy and transparent. There is something terrifying about it. It floats upon a background of darkness, a universe of darkness, pinpricked by tiny dots of light. They are like stars. They are hardly more than suggestions of light. The balloon does not move but looks as if it might move, suddenly—if you were to lean down and breathe upon it, surely it would float away?

No, it does not float away.

Pass your fingers near it lightly, not touching it. What are those grainy lines? They are like pencil lines. Like hairs. They seem about to lift themselves, to rise to the warmth of your fingers. But they do not move. The balloon itself is motionless, as if dormant for centuries. You can see through it, yet there is nothing behind it. Along its edges there are long thin lesions, as if someone had torn into the flesh of this thing with a knife. You can run your fingernail along the edge of the balloon and destroy it, and your fingernail springs into the microscope's lens like a planet. . . .

Helene was staring through Jesse's microscope. It was an enormous, costly instrument that her father had given him. She was alone in the apartment; it was five-thirty in the morning and Jesse was on duty at the hospital for the second night. Unable to sleep, uninterested in sleep, Helene had wandered through the apartment with her robe tied tightly around her.

She had turned on the light in Jesse's study and was leaning over the microscope, her arms folded. She did not adjust the lens because that would mean she had been looking through the microscope, that she had been in Jesse's study—a small back room hardly large enough for a child's room. She did not want him to know she'd been in here. He would come home exhausted, glance in at his things, and sense that she had been here. . . . She wanted to keep herself separate from him; she felt a strange, almost angry fascination with the need to be separate from her husband. She loved him and understood that he loved her, yet she must retain this separateness. . . .

How strange it was, this thing beneath the microscope's lens!—a filmy balloon, transparent cellulose, an enormous sun, an ocean of light, a face without features—

Helene looked through the stack of papers Jesse had left on his desk—notes on patients, magazines, journals, a glossy offprint of an article by her father, originally published in a neurological journal. Jesse's things were kept in careful piles, in order, papers clipped together and staggered along the edge of his desk so that he could see in an instant what was what. Helene felt a peculiar, heady excitement at the possibility of destroying this order—but she put everything back in place again.

It was early September. Jesse had been on the intern staff at LaSalle for two months now. His first assignment was in Medicine and he had one more month to go; he worked as Helene had known he would have to work, returning home stunned with fatigue, hollow-eyed, twitching and murmuring in his sleep. There he relived his first failures. Helene lay awake and tried to comfort him as he slept, knowing that her calm would have to serve for both of them. Loving him, pitying him, she stroked his damp forehead, brushing the hair back, studying him. His facial muscles gathered themselves up into an expression of anguish; it was so brutal and so useless, whatever frightened him. What good did it do? What was he reliving?

She imagined him hurrying through the corridors of the hospital, being paged as *Dr. Vogel, Dr. Vogel,* a man in a dream. She imagined that half second of utter blackness as he picked up a telephone receiver to answer the call: lifting the receiver like that was like stepping into space.

He brought home news of the bad cases, the nasty surprises. Other news—patients who did well, were released, vanished back into the city—had no interest for him. He kept talking to her of his mistakes, his near-mistakes, his failures. He had Emergency Room duties every two weeks, when he was on twenty-four-hour call and had to stay at the hospital. Anything could happen then. It must have been the gelatinous air of late summer in Chicago, the murky humid nights, the teasing air of the streets, the itching in brains that led to such bizarre accidents—mangled automobiles wrapped together, workmen falling through the air, skulls split by playful gestures. Jesse's hands could not work fast enough, his mind could not take in all these people. Once he came home and asked Helene to lie down with him, to hold him. He wept. He told her about a child brought into Emergency: a two-year-old with a wreck of a body, bruises and welts everywhere, one eye hammered shut and probably destroyed by tiny hemorrhages, ribs cracked, several fingers broken. Jesse shut his eyes tight and rubbed his face against Helene, weeping, surrendering his consciousness to hers, as if trying to impregnate her with his horror so that he could sleep.

She had tried to comfort him but had no words to use.

Now, in his place, she found it difficult to sleep. Jesse stayed at the hospital two nights every week, in a stifling room in the interns' quarters. At home, Helene thought of him constantly.

She tried to read; she glanced through the things on his desk as if to evoke another, more studious Jesse, a man not harassed and overcome with disaster; she stared out the window, she wandered listlessly about the empty apartment. She could sleep only a few hours every night. Jesse could sleep anywhere now. He could sleep in the hospital cafeteria, putting his head down on his arms for a five-minute nap. When he woke he would be as refreshed, he claimed, as if he'd slept an hour. He could doze leaning against a wall. He could sleep in a telephone booth while he was calling Helene, waiting for her to pick up the phone; dozing off suddenly, completely, so that when she answered the call, she was connected to nothing, latched onto nothing. "Is that you, Jesse?" she would cry, her voice rising in alarm.

But she never spoke of her loneliness or her bitterness. The other interns' wives complained constantly, angrily surprised by what they had contracted for, but Helene knew enough to remain silent. She never said aloud what seemed so clear: that it had been a mistake for them to marry so soon. Her father had tried to talk them out of it, and in private he had told Helene what she would have to endure. But she had insisted. *She had to marry him, must marry him.* Trick's collapse had terrified him. He had needed her, he had been mute with fear, needing her . . . she had had to marry him, to comfort him. . . . And Trick had not died. So in the end her father had agreed with her reluctantly, and then sternly, possessively, gave her money and commanded her to use it. *Never mind telling Jesse about it,* her father had said. *Jesse's life is too complicated at this time for him to be worried about money.* As an intern, Jesse received little salary. Helene worked part-time in the chemistry department at the University of Chicago, and she exaggerated the amount of her pay so that Jesse need not know about her father's checks. The checks came every two weeks. Sometimes there was a brief letter with them, hardly more than a commandment—*Telephone me collect on Sunday, please*—sometimes nothing.

She floated between them, her father and her husband. They seemed to have no real consciousness of her except as a point of contact, an object, a beloved object. She would telephone her father obediently and sense her soul straining out to him across the distance, as if she wanted nothing more than to leap back into his life... the study with the watermarked ceiling, the antiques, the heavy-framed paintings, the Victorian home in Cambridge where she had spent most of her life. But did she really want that? Her head swam. No, she wanted Jesse, her husband. She wanted him to lie in her arms and speak gently to her of love, she wanted to feel herself separate from him and yet linked to him by the careful articulation of his love, not his nullity of fear and passion.

He would make love to her in the dark, as if secretly, hastily, before falling asleep. It was one act among many he had to perform. He was responsible for so much, he had to act swiftly, skillfully, and then he had to fall heavily asleep so that he could wake up again strong enough to get through another day. It was heavy, the burden of his love! It was stifling, unnatural. Helene felt his anguish passing over into her, into the pit of her belly, where she was vulnerable to him, open and unresisting. There was always some spare horror he left her with: *In the baby's excrement there were all these worms....* So he slept while she lay awake, stunned. Her skin prickled with his sorrow. It was a presence in bed with them that she must keep at a distance, Helene alone, protecting Jesse while he slept.

...She checked the microscope again. That balloon. It was like a mouth, a mouth without a body. Pure mouth. Flimsy and transparent and eternally hungry. Was it dead or living? Were any of these cells really dead? She swayed above Jesse's desk, lightheaded at the thought of the crowd of cells that surrounded her and were inside her, which could never really die and which were invisible. Invisible energy. She herself, Helene herself, was made up of such cells and nothing else.... If she had the baby Jesse so strangely, desperately wanted, she would erupt into a cluster of new cells leaping out of hers, newer, richer, brighter energy pushing out of the nullity of her womb....

Her father had made the appointment for her, telephoning all the way from Cambridge. Today at eleven. To make sure she would go, he himself had called to make the appointment with a man he had known for many years, a Chicago obstetrician and gynecologist.

Today at eleven.

And now it was twenty-five minutes to six, a September morning. Already hot. Helene straightened Jesse's desk top so that it was in perfect order. She felt drugged, lightheaded, as if she had just had another of those quiet arguments with Jesse: *How can you want me to have a baby? At this time in our lives?* Or with her father: *Why do you keep telling me to make Jesse do this, do that?* Fiercely, she would defend her husband against her father. She would not talk Jesse into coming East. No. Though she wanted to return to Boston herself, she would not press Jesse. No application for a research position. No application for a grant. She did not really want Jesse to be a doctor, a practicing doctor; she hated the thought of his running a big clinic someday; but she would not try to argue with him. She told her father that he must not ask her to argue, he must leave her marriage alone. With Jesse, she defended her separateness, her crystalline, frightened body: why couldn't he understand how bad an idea it was to have a baby now? Why couldn't he understand her fear of the pain, the bitter, inevitable ripeness her body had to suffer? And then she would be a mother for life. *For life.* She did not want to be a mother. She was frightened. She did not want to enter that new state, to be delivered over into that new condition for a lifetime.... *Mrs. Vogel, a mother.*

Her father did not seem to listen to her and Jesse did not seem to listen to her. They talked at her. They talked at her and then went about the business of their lives, which had little to do with her.

She went out into the small kitchen and heated water for coffee. She lit a cigarette. Since coming to Chicago she had begun to smoke, though Jesse disapproved and she herself did not like the look of people smoking. Her forehead wrinkled sharply at the thought of women smoking, pregnant women smoking, pregnant bellies.... No, it was too ugly. It was impossible. She could not really be pregnant. Her body was too lean and somber, it had no glow to it, no resiliency. She had become acquainted with the young wife of one of Jesse's residents in Medicine. The residents, like the interns, received little pay. And yet this woman was pregnant and her face and body were hearty, almost arrogant with health, and she expressed only scorn for the reprimands given her by her family. Her name was Susan; her husband, Milton Kuzma, seemed to think highly of Jesse. Milton said of

Jesse: "They're not going to break *him*." And this was meant to be a compliment. They're not going to break *him*.

Helene stared out the kitchen window. She wondered if she would be broken. What did that mean, to be broken? She kept seeing Trick collapsing to the sidewalk, his legs giving out.... He was in a private hospital in Minnesota now. She kept seeing, half-seeing, the patients Jesse spoke of when he came home especially saddened, until the rooms of this small apartment were crowded with ghostly strangers, all pleading for attention. Helene stared out the window, feeling herself very much alone. Their apartment was on the fourth story of an aged brownstone not far from the hospital. The neighborhood was decaying: big, handsome, ruined buildings with tall windows and doors and columns, front stoops that flared outward to the street, everything dirty and weathered and very human, so that Helene wanted to stop on the street at times to stare, to memorize. The buildings had been handsome at one time. Ridged with scrollwork, with odd eroded animals and human heads, even their chimneys impressive. Their spirit stern, masculine. Now they were marked for extinction. Some were already razed, and you could see the marks of stairways on walls that still stood; the veinlike marks of pipes; the places where wires had been torn out or hung dangling like exposed nerves. Negro children played in the rubble. A few lots had already been cleared and bulldozers had covered the gutted valleys with fill of sand and clay and brick, preparing for new construction. Smaller buildings remained, like the one in which Jesse and Helene lived, and other brownstones that were two family houses. The air of the street was excited and dusty on any weekday—always a sense of wonderment, the surprise of walls about to collapse, bricks about to crumble, always the dull heavy half-pleasant rhythm of a weight striking something. The workmen would arrive at eight o'clock and begin work at once. Pounding, breaking, the high sharp angry buzz of machines, the churning of great wheels in soft earth.... The Kuzmas lived only a half a block away, on a side street. Their apartment was smaller than Helene and Jesse's, closer to the demolition work. Susan would sit and press her hands against her stomach, frowning, and complain about the noise. The vibrations. She hated the noise but Helene secretly liked it because it was not human. Jesse and Milton didn't notice it, they hadn't time for such things. But Helene liked it because it was not a human noise, not like the shrieks and footsteps in this old building that brought the faceless tenants too close to her, inflicted an intimacy on her that she did not want. When she was alone in the apartment, which was often, she tried to concentrate on the distant noise, the heavy reliable noise of machinery, in order to blot out from her consciousness this nearer, more disturbing noise. A father yelling at his son . . . a child's scream of frustration . . . women yelling perpetually at children, as if these children were still bound to their bodies by some frantic, agonizing strand of flesh.

It was not possible that she was pregnant. . . .

All her life she had felt wild rushes of expectation and fear. *To be a woman. A wife.* You needed a man to complete you; that was obvious. In order to be a woman, a wife. She had been afraid to think about love, about loving a man, because it had seemed to her impossible, ugly, brutish. She had resisted thinking about it the way she resisted thinking about death. It was too ugly. She had grown up with a dislike of being touched, even by her parents. Yet she knew she must be touched eventually. She must be touched, loved, completed by a man and made over into a woman. *A woman: a wife.*

She wanted to be loved but to be separate and suspended, inside the idea of love, so that the man might exist in a part of her mind, chastely. Always she had feared her body. Her mother had referred to certain things obliquely, with a curt clipped shame—her father had never referred to them at all—and Helene had grown up with a resistance to them, to the thought of them, and to her own body with its helpless flesh. What did that mean exactly, to have a body? To live in a body? Did she inhabit her body like a tenant? She imagined her body as a substance of a certain weight, pure and inviolable from the outside. And so it did not seem possible that a man, a man's body, might freely enter her own and do such damage to it. . . . Layer upon layer the years formed her: Helene was now a married woman, the same age as her husband, and yet she was also nineteen years old, she was twelve years old again, she was a child. All the layers were intense, quivering, conscious of existing. Conscious of being female, a little ashamed of being female.

Susan Kuzma showed no shame about anything. She talked about her bladder irritation in front of anyone, had made up a kind of joke about the humiliation of a gynecological examination at the hospital. Helene listened in amazement. It hardly seemed possible that another woman could speak of such things. She could never have spoken that way herself. Never. She was suspended in a fearful, cautious state, cautious especially of Jesse's love, as if surrendering to him would infect her with that coarse blatant bodiliness she hated so in other women.

She took a shower, dreading the ugly shower stall and its perpetual smell. But it was one of the things she must do every day. The drain was rusty and always clogged with hairs and soap, though she cleaned it often. Jesse showered at both the hospital and at home, and every time he showered he washed his hair. Soap came apart in his fingers, he must have used it so brutally. He brought home from the hospital the habit of scrubbing himself hard, for many minutes. The hospital was so contagious... and Jesse himself, his hands, was so contagious....

Yes, small bits of soap were caught in the drain this morning and Helene bent to pick them out one by one.

When she got dressed the workmen had begun their pounding. Great weights seemed to fall from the sky upon solid, resisting masses. It was eight o'clock, and by eleven she would be in the waiting room of her father's friend. He would decide her fate. It had nothing to do now with her or Jesse or even her father's wishes. *Jesse gathering her up in his arms, breathless, in that instant before his mind blacked out....* But now it had nothing to do with him. The doctor would examine her, he would test her, and then he would tell her what had happened to her. To her body.

Jesse knew nothing about this. Tonight he would spend the night here and she would have to tell him. He would bring home with him the faint sorrowful odor of sickness, a two days' duty on seven floors of a hospital; he would pass his hands over his eyes and whisper, "My God, there are some people I've gotten to hate...." and she would feel the tension in him, that he should admit to such an emotion: Jesse, who rarely hated. Then, with an effort, he would ask her about herself. How was her job? Exhausted, he would try to talk to her as if she were a special, challenging patient he must work up, her sickness a mystery. It would take probing, prying, to discover what was wrong with her. It would take all his youthful shrewdness. But a certain wavering of his gaze would tell Helene that he was about to collapse, and so she would lead him gently to bed, like a child, while he tried to talk with her, shaking his head to stay awake. It had happened so many times.... Sometimes Jesse went for thirty-six hours without sleeping when he was on duty. His eyes were ringed with exhaustion and he had lost weight. But he never complained except to tell Helene in amazement that he hated someone, or had lost track of a patient, or had been cut down by one of the staff, or had made a mistake. But these were not really complaints. Jesse seemed to contemplate himself, Dr. Vogel, as if this person were a stranger, without emotions. There was no time for emotions. Jesse, a husband, sometimes seemed to have emotions because he understood that people had them, that he owed it to his young wife to display them. But really there was no time. She would lead him to bed and lie beside him, holding him in her arms, and he would sink into a sudden stuporous sleep. Sometimes he ground his jaws. Sometimes he seemed to be arguing inaudibly. Helene would whisper, "Jesse, you're home. You're in bed." But still his muscles twitched, his eyeballs moved behind his closed eyes. What was he struggling with? Helene had a dim view of people running in the hospital's corridors—Jesse among them, running— Sometimes he said out loud, "The elevator is stuck," or "Where is the light?"

Helene wanted to sleep that night, so she went out to a drugstore to get some pills. Ordinary sleeping pills, the kind sold over the counter. She had never taken anything stronger because she had never wanted to ask her father for a prescription; she hadn't wanted him to know about any of her weaknesses. Her father had made a great deal of money on several types of barbiturates he had patented, so this seemed a further reason to resist taking them. In the drugstore she hesitated over several brands of pills. She imagined the pharmacist was watching her closely. Her fingers were trembling a little. Yes, they were trembling, and at the front counter, where she paid for the pills, a woman clerk seemed to feel sorry for her. There must have been some meager, helpless sorrow on her face.

She walked out with a jar of one hundred pink pills. The entire day belonged to her.

She could telephone Dr. Blazack and cancel the appointment. It would only take a minute. Then she could drive downtown and around the city aimlessly, or she could drive out along the lake, anywhere, in the car her father had given her and Jesse back in Ann Arbor.

Her wristwatch was small and delicate. It had been her mother's. The face was a tiny oval, its numbers dots of white gold. The strap was like a bracelet, a lacy interweaving of threads of white gold. *Only ten-thirty.* She had been up since five-thirty that morning, waiting for eleven o'clock to come, her face going hard and ironic at the knowledge that it would come so slowly. She held her watch up to her ear to see if it was ticking. The dots had the look of being blind. She wondered what time meant, why she was sitting here in this strange city, a city she didn't know or like, why she was beginning to fill with a cold sick panic, why she had married and had completed herself. She was a woman now, a wife. She was completed; if she was pregnant she would be completed. It would be a sign of how a man had completed her. She stared at her watch and saw that time moved very slowly. *That anonymous jellyfish, that balloon, its lesions and hairs and flimsy stubborn transparency. . . .*

She decided to drive downtown now. She had always wanted to explore Chicago on one of her days off from the university. She and Jesse had planned to explore it together, but Jesse had never had time. He said he liked to walk, but he never had time to walk. In Cambridge, Helene and her father had often gone for long walks on Sunday. They had also walked a great deal in Ann Arbor; in fact, it had been on one of their weekend walks that Helene had met Jesse. Someone had called "Dr. Cady!" and they had turned to see a tall young man, red-haired, very fair in the face and yet not pale with that sickly paleness of some red-haired people, dressed in old clothes, a certain quick urgency to his step that alarmed Helene—for it had seemed to her, in the first few seconds' confusion, that he had called out to warn her father of some danger. But it was only a student, a medical student. He was polite, frank, a little nervous. Helene, staring at him, had felt a familiar sense of helplessness rise in her, for this was the kind of man she had never been able to confront calmly—she had never felt herself equal to such a man; she had always turned away shyly, withdrawing. He had an excited, intelligent, attractive face. It was obvious that he was intimidated by her father, and yet he spoke clearly and frankly. There was something new about him, something very new, unique, that startled this young man himself as if with its audacity, as if he were creating himself as he talked, inventing himself. That day he had seemed to Helene too vigorous. A threat. She had turned away from him slightly, distrusting him.

She would go into the city alone, she would walk there alone. At the back of her mind she imagined herself walking all day, losing herself in the city. Jesse warned her about walking around by herself. Chicago was dangerous, he said. He told her of a woman brought into the emergency ward, raped and then slashed with a knife, her body still heaving with the effort of fighting off an assailant—how she had fought Jesse himself, believing him to be her assailant. *The enemy. Men are the enemy.* Even in this old dress of hers, with her flat-heeled shoes, Helene might attract the attention of men who yearned for women, for the blood of women; why not? It was possible. There were many such men in a city this large. In the world. Helene's legs looked bare because her stockings were so sheer. . . .

What, it was still ten-thirty?

Dr. Blazack's office was in a high, attractive building on the Drive. Helene was grateful for that. She wanted nothing to do with LaSalle or with its harassed interns and residents. Thank God her father had money! Dr. Blazack was one of the obstetrics men whom other doctors scorned and envied, a rich man, with a practice of rich women. She must go to him because her father had made an appointment for her: there was no way out of it.

Nothing to see in the direction of the lake—the air lifted neutrally from it, very humid.

Helene entered Dr. Blazack's suite of offices and her eye jumped nervously about the sofas and the tall "modern" lamps. A woman in a maternity dress looked up from a magazine at Helene, as if ready to recognize her, but Helene looked quickly away. She sat. A nurse came out to greet her as if she were an old friend. "Mrs. Vogel . . . ? Please come in here with me." She had a small, neat office of her own, where she asked Helene questions for the doctor's records. These questions already marked Helene as a patient of his. . . . Her heart began to accelerate, anticipating the examination. She hated to be examined. Hated to be touched.

"How long have you been married, Mrs. Vogel?"

"Since July."

"Oh, only since July?" the nurse said sweetly.

Helene was released and went back to the waiting room. Another nurse appeared and took away the woman in the maternity dress. Helene watched their legs as they walked away: the nurse's were muscular and gauzy in white stockings, the patient's legs were trim and fashionable. A young woman, as young as Helene. She glanced involuntarily at her own legs and saw that she was only a woman among women, after all. A woman's body among women's bodies.

Jesse had already helped deliver babies at the hospital.

She picked up a magazine but could not read. Could not concentrate on anything. She tried to make her mind go hard and precise; tried to think of the angles of this room, which were more real than the lamps and the sofas and the expensive carpeting. The room was a box that could not be disguised. A third nurse appeared—a girl of about twenty—and called her by name. "Mrs. Vogel?" Helene followed her into a back corridor, where fluorescent lights hummed dimly. An odor of plastic and tile. "Dr. Blazack will be with you in a minute," the nurse said in a whisper. Helene sat down again numbly. This was the doctor's own office—he had an extremely large oval desk; there were costly lithographs on two walls and one large window looked out onto the lake. Someone was washing his hands nearby. Water splashed. How many times a day did he have to wash his hands, this doctor? *Jesse lingered in the shower for ten, fifteen minutes, as if afraid he couldn't get clean. . . .* On a table near the big desk were piles of letters and magazines and advertisements. Helene could see the glossy cover of a popular science magazine, a photograph of a cell. A photograph blown up so that the cell was enormous, magnified more fiercely than the cell under Jesse's microscope.

Behind Helene, in the lavatory, faucets were being shut off briskly. The door opened and she looked around.

"Well, Mrs. Vogel! How are you this morning?"

Dr. Blazack was a fairly old man, she saw. Small, wiry, ambitious; when he smiled his teeth were a perfect off-white shade, exactly the color of real teeth. He smelled of soap. Helene recognized him not in himself but in the form of a certain kind of doctor, friends of her father's, who were successful and kindly and in perpetual joyful motion like her father. His hands were pinkened as if with a fresh surge of blood.

"No need to look so tense, my dear. It's a lovely day and no one is going to hurt you," he said gently. "First, I want to ask you about your father, if you don't mind. How is he? It's been ten years—at least ten years!—since I've seen Benjamin face to face—"

And so she spoke dutifully of her father. Dr. Blazack smiled brightly, nodded at her recitation, sighed as if in envy of Benjamin Cady's life; it was the courtesy of a wealthy obstetrician for a man of pure science. In his turn he talked of her father as if they had been very close friends. Helene doubted this. Her father had had no close friends. Helene pretended to agree but her mind wandered nervously. The magazine with its slick black-and-white cover seemed to shimmer. Protoplasm that was about to come to life—like jelly, like a balloon. Helene had examined thousands of cells under slides. Smears of cells. Jesse, in the pathology labs in which he'd worked, had gotten practice at examining cells of all kinds. The universe might open up into a snowstorm of cells.... Living units. Dead units. And yet the dead units were perhaps not really dead. Nothing dies. *Nothing dies permanently*—was that a law of physics? Life in each cell, like grit, like a grain of sand in the eye that can't be annihilated. The cell shrivels down to this pinprick of life... or perhaps it goes mad and starts dividing, multiplying, blowing itself up into a balloon-sized tumor....

"I think I'm pregnant," Helene said finally.

"Ah!"

Dr. Blazack smiled as if he had never heard such a statement before. Now he opened a folder, picked up a pen, prepared to take notes. The nurse had given him Helene's folder. Already she was a patient of his, in his records. "When was your period due, Helene?" he asked.

Helene was staring at his hands. Women fell in love with their obstetricians, she knew. Nine months of love. Their doctors became the true fathers of their babies. Their doctors became *their* true fathers, for nine months.

"I don't remember. . . ." she whispered.

"You don't remember?" he asked in surprise.

"I think . . . I think it was two weeks ago, two or three weeks ago. . . ."

She was silent.

He must have thought this was strange; he smiled sternly at her. Then, looking at a calendar on his desk, he said cheerfully, "Ah, yes, that would have been the fifteenth . . . ? If it was two weeks ago?"

"Yes, yes. . . ."

"Or was it three weeks ago?"

She stared in silence at his hands.

After an awkward pause Dr. Blazack said, "I'll examine you and then arrange for you to take the test. How does that sound?"

"All right."

"No need to look so nervous, Helene! You know better than that. There is never any point in worrying about anything, in assuming anything. . . . Wait until we see the results of the test."

"Yes, I know."

"Any hospital will run the test for you. Did you say your husband was at LaSalle?"

She had not told him this; he must have learned it from her father. But she nodded anyway.

"There's really no need to look so worried!"

Helene tried to smile.

One of the nurses rapped softly on the opened door. "Dr. Blazack, Dr. Brant is on the telephone. Can you talk to him?" Dr. Blazack made a gesture of helplessness, sighed, gave in and picked up the telephone. "Hello . . . ? I can't hear you. Oh, yes. When? Tomorrow? But I didn't think he would be willing to sell so soon . . . what about the highway commission? What happened? . . . Well, then tomorrow? At two?"

Tomorrow at two everything will be changed, Helene thought.

She could still leave. She could get out of here, run out onto the street, out loose in the streets of Chicago. She could lose herself in the crowds, walking freely in the crowds. No one would know her. Her heels hard on the pavement. Inside her, that warm little core would not be dislodged . . . she would walk fast and rap her heels on the sidewalks . . . she would feel the warmth spreading up through her, a radiance that could not be dislodged.

Dr. Blazack stood and closed the manila folder.

Now the examination.

The young nurse reappeared and escorted Helene into the examination room. Helene's heart was pounding. The room smelled of new fresh leather. At the sight of the table Helene felt something move inside her, in her loins. Was it the start of a flow? The beginning of blood? "I think . . . I think maybe. . . ." she stammered.

The nurse smiled at her. "Yes, Mrs. Vogel?"

But nothing. Of course not.

"Nothing."

The nurse's face was bright with efficiency. What was this room, Helene thought dizzily, why was she here? *A young man had called out her father's name. . . .* And here was the examination table with its stirrups. All women are equal on that table, their heels caught in those stirrups. All women are the same woman. The nurse was opening drawers deftly—she was arranging instruments on a tray. She drew a length of clean white paper up over the examination table.

"Would you like to get ready for the examination?" the nurse said.

Helene came numbly to life. She sensed the nurse's bewilderment. Why was she so stiff, so frightened? It was not normal. All of Dr. Blazack's patients were beaming with life, grateful to be pregnant and to be his patients. Normal women. And so Helene stepped forward, feeling a kind of power in herself. A bitter dark power. She would be examined on that table, she would feel pain, and this pain was necessary. She deserved it. Her body deserved it, after what Jesse had done to it. She had lain in that man's arms, obedient to his demands, though she had feared pregnancy and had feared Jesse himself. She had allowed him to make love to her. She had violated herself. Now she would lie down again, on her back, for another man.

Lie down. Lie down.

She was naked now, wearing only a coarse white smock that was too large for her. It tied loosely in back. She lay down on the cold leather table and the paper rattled beneath her like tin. The nurse, courteous and sweet as a sister, said, "Could you slide down farther, Mrs. Vogel?" Helene fixed her bare heels in the stirrups at the end of the table. She slid down awkwardly. "Just a little farther, please. A little farther."

The nurse spread her legs. One small palm on each of Helene's knees, spreading them. Now everything in her was open. The nurse drew a white cloth over her, up to her waist. She might have been covering a corpse.

"That's fine, Mrs. Vogel. The doctor will be right with you."

Women lay with their legs apart like this every day.

Helene looked at the window opposite her through her eyelashes. It was rimmed with eerie light—dark light—the sky outside had clouded over. In Chicago light changed rapidly. You could not trust the sun. It was hard for her to remember that she was in Chicago and not somewhere else. In Chicago. She was married now. Her father had arranged for this examination and so she was in good hands. *In good hands.* Time would stop now. The ticking of that relentless little watch would stop. And then, later, when the examination was over, the watch would begin again.... She would rush out of here when the examination was over and disappear into the city. Thousands of women disappeared into the city. She would go to Kresge's and buy a knitting needle—or did they come only in pairs? She would take a room in a hotel and use that metal knitting needle on herself, the way girls used knitting needles on themselves....

Dr. Blazack entered the room quietly. He was fatherly and holy. He said, "This won't hurt. It will only take a few minutes." That was evidently his style; he made his patients ashamed of feeling pain, so that they would bear pain in silence rather than disappoint him.

"Please relax, Mrs. Vogel."

And now a quick, peeling sound—flesh against something slippery—he must have been putting on his rubber gloves. The young nurse stood beside him, taller than he. Helene did not dare open her eyes to really look at them. If the pupils of her eyes flashed open she might scream. Between her legs, in that magic space, something flashed. The nurse was dabbing something on her. An odor of chemicals, disinfectant... she was being cleaned and made ready for him. The sound of instruments on a tray, rattling. Dr. Blazack said something she could not hear.

"This will only take a few minutes, Helene."

Then he inserted the instrument. It was very cold and sharp. Helene tried not to move, she willed herself to lie still. But something happened and she recoiled.

"I'm sorry," she said. She forced herself back to the edge of the table.

"It shouldn't hurt, Helene. You've been examined before, haven't you?"

"But I think I'm pregnant...."

That answer did not seem to mean anything.

"I think I'm pregnant," she said.

"If you could slide down again, please, Mrs. Vogel...." the nurse said.

"I think I'm pregnant, I..." Helene said wildly.

"Do you want the examination to continue?" Dr. Blazack said.

"Yes. Yes."

She prepared herself again. Clumsily, brutely, she slid back down and let her knees fall apart. Dr. Blazack took hold of her knees firmly and spread them farther. When the instrument was inserted in her this time she kept herself still.

Now he began to open it. Twisting it open.

She forced herself to lie still. Absolutely still. She could not remember this man's name. A man of late middle age, a stranger, with this thing stuck inside her body. It was metallic and sharp. Now he was opening it, spreading her body wider. It seemed to be turning. Slowly the instrument turned and expanded. It was like a circle of nothing, expanding, opening her and turning her inside out.

I didn't want... this is a mistake....

She began to breathe quickly. Someone might have been pressing a hand up and down on her chest, pumping her lungs. On the edge of the table her hands clenched and unclenched. The leather had become damp; it was slippery against her fingers. How could everything in her be so exposed now? The most secret veins of her body were open to the air of this impersonal room. Her head began to move, slowly at first, from side to side. She could not stop it. *No. No.* She did not want this thing inside her, she did not want a baby, she did not want a husband, she did not want to be completed. . . . "What does it mean?" she muttered, not knowing what she said. The clamp was cold and hard inside her, making a rim, a bracelet inside her, exposing her. Her body began to contract. She could not stop it. Her womb wanted to shrink back, hide itself. The secret parts of her body were drawing together in terror. Her knees came together hard—

"No, please, Mrs. Vogel," a man said in surprise.

He gripped her knees and spread them apart again.

She was trying to lie still but her heart had begun to pound wildly. Sweat on her face, under the heavy coils of her hair, which had come loose. A flash of heat shot upward from the cold dark between her legs, that open darkness, telling her she would die. She was going to die. It would come to her like this, the insertion of an instrument, opening her and turning her inside out, the dark heat rising to her heart with the ferocity of love—

She began to struggle.

"Mrs. Vogel—you'll hurt yourself—"

The nurse seized her hands.

But her body had begun to fight and it could not be stopped. The table rattled. Something came loose—one of the stirrups. Helene felt herself recoiling backward on the table, away from that instrument, but it came along with her, inside her, hurting her. . . . She saw a wild, black space, open to the light and its veins pounding, something not meant to be seen. The strange man could see it. Jesse could see it. The rim of that instrument was like intense searing light.

She heard herself screaming.

The doctor was saying something to her. He was giving instructions. Helene threw her head from side to side. She could hear nothing. Why was this man talking to her? There was something stuck up inside her body, a terrible bright pain, and this man was trying to talk to her! She could kill him!

"Mrs. Vogel—"

Her smock was bunched up beneath her body. The muscles in her legs fought. She screamed. Another jerk of her body—a small thin shot of pain—

Then it was over. The thing was out. Gone.

Still she threw herself from side to side. Her head struck the table; her cheeks hot against the leather, which felt like a cheek itself. Faces against faces. All of them sweaty and slippery. So Jesse, her husband, had slapped himself against her, his face grinding against hers in the dark, so he had entered her body with his own, his flesh into her flesh, marrying them.

No. . . .

And suddenly she saw a young woman lying on a table. Herself, contorted like that: a woman on a table, on her back, her face twisted and demented. She had fallen from a great height and her face was twisted permanently.

"Mrs. Vogel . . . ?"

What was that raw reddened gap between her legs? So vivid it sucked all the air into it—the entire white sky might be drawn into it and lost—a face more powerful than her own face, a raw demanding mouth.

"Mrs. Vogel, please—"

"—not my name!—"

She sat up, weeping. Alone with the nurse. Had she frightened the nurse? The doctor had left. Two women alone in this room, both frightened. Helene could not understand what had happened.

"You hurt yourself, it's bleeding. . . . Here, wait. . . ."

She fussed with something, not looking at Helene. Helene caught a glimpse of a wad of cotton with a smear of fresh blood on it.

"You could have hurt yourself badly," the nurse said.

Helene forced herself to stop crying. She took long, slow, deliberate breaths to calm herself

"I'm sorry," she said.

She tried to get up. Her legs were shaky.

"He didn't finish the examination?" she asked.

"I'm afraid not."

The nurse handed her a tissue and she wiped her wet face. "Are you feeling better now?"

"Yes. Yes. I'm sorry I lost control of myself."

She glanced covertly at the nurse's prim face. She had disappointed this girl.

Left alone, Helene dressed quickly. She threw the white gown onto a chair and saw with disgust that it was streaked with blood. There was nothing for her to think now; she stood in a kind of vacuum, dressed for the street, ready to escape. In one of her university courses she had studied physical defects that sometimes accompanied retardation—children without arms, without legs, some of them even without faces—and she had thought, staring in a chilled fascination at the photographs, *There is nothing to think about these children.* Thinking demanded a space that could be entered—you stepped forward into that space, pushing other things out of the way, claiming a victory, a territory. In a vacuum you could not move one way or another. Everything was transparent and eternal. There was nothing to think.

An eternity in the body of a woman: the explosion of small, soft, gentle cells, coils of absolute power. Nothing could stop that power. *It floats upon a background of darkness, pinpricked by tiny dots of light.*

Her flesh still tingled between her legs. It might have been glowing. A tiny burning clot of moisture seeped down . . . Helene took a tissue out of her purse and dabbed between her legs with it. *Let it be blood. The start of five days of blood.* But when she brought the crumpled tissue back out, careful not to touch her clothes with it, she saw that it was bright blood—too bright for menstrual blood. So she stood very still, waiting. The past three weeks had been a nightmare of waiting like this. She would feel something move in her loins, seeping down hotly . . . but it would turn out to be only a vapid colorless moisture, not blood. Mucus. A quarter's size of dark clotted blood would have redeemed her. But no. No blood. The cycle was not going to end this time.

She was already in her second month of pregnancy. She knew this. She wanted to shout at them in anger, at their satisfied faces: *Jesse, I'm pregnant, are you happy? Father, I'm pregnant!* It was a fact that had nothing to do with her personally. It could have been said of any woman, anyone at all. Something was floating lightly, invisibly, inside her. It swam in a cupful of liquid that was its universe, transparent and eternal. . . .

When she stepped out into the corridor she saw Dr. Blazack himself waiting for her. He was a small man, after all. "Mrs. Vogel, could you step in here for a minute . . . ?"

"I'm leaving. I'm going home," she said quickly.

"But Mrs. Vogel . . ."

She hurried out, looking at no one. She had failed. Dr. Blazack would telephone her father, and this evening the telephone would ring and she would have to answer it before Jesse did. *Her father.* She would have to talk to him. . . . What had happened to her fingernails? Two were broken. She must have broken them in her panic, during the examination. She was still tense and contorted. Her muscles cringed. She walked awkwardly, aware of the chafing of her thighs, where the insides of her thighs rubbed together. She was very conscious of them touching and wondered why she had never noticed this before.

Jesse was always telling her about the bad surprises at the hospital. Things broke, went wrong, collapsed, burst. There were hours of routine work, the filling out of reports, the blood samples, the spinal taps, transfusions, shots, intravenous feedings— and then suddenly there were the surprises, lungs filling suddenly with fluid, lips gone white, blood pressure falling, falling, as arteries somewhere collapsed— How did you make sense of such things? The body is a machine, but the machine sometimes breaks down.

It could happen to her: she could pick at the wall of the womb until it broke down into bleeding.

She drove along State Street in a haze of traffic. She was free for the day now. She would find a hotel, rent a room. She would run over to Kresge's. Then, in the hotel room, she would run hot water in the bathtub and undress and sit in the tub, her legs slowly spreading. She would ease the thing up into herself. Angrily and calmly. Its pressure would be very sharp and very thin, unlike the broad, coarse pressure Jesse brought to her.

Pressure. Then a sudden sighing release as the needle sank in. The water pinkening with blood.

What she must remember is *to leave the tub unplugged and the water on.* That way there would be a continual flow of fresh water, splashing and hot. The blood would drain out and new water would rush in and everything would be clean.

Noon: a clock advertising tires. Cars and trucks were moving through downtown Chicago steadily, in a constant noisy bustle. The sound of horns. More horns. One lane was blocked off ahead, in front of the Drake Hotel; there must have been an accident. She would have to get into the left lane. She hadn't been paying attention and now she was being drawn into the blocked-off lane, she couldn't get out of it... a police car was parked there and men stood around. She waited patiently. What she must remember: *to keep the hot water running into the tub.*

After a few minutes she eased into the left lane. Slowly, achingly, the line of traffic drew her onward. What she must remember— The traffic light ahead turned from green to red. What did that mean? She waited until it turned green again. Driving was a struggle: she sensed vehicles on all sides of her, about to lunge into her. But when she looked out she saw only cars and trucks with ordinary people in them, their hands gripped like hers on their steering wheels.

She braked to a stop suddenly. Then she drove forward again and everything was suspended. She could not remember exactly what she was doing. Where was she headed? She must not forget the bathtub, she would have to scour it first, make sure it was clean, then turn on the hot water... very hot water.... Behind her, around her, on all sides of her traffic moved onward. It pressed against her and would not let her free. She would scream at Jesse: *There are too many people! I can't have a baby in all these people!*

Steel knitting needles.

She would park the car and abandon it. Run, get into the crowd on the sidewalk, become anonymous. Become protoplasm. But she could not find a place to park. The balloon was inside her, fixed. She was passing drugstores, taverns, shoe stores, pawnshops, liquor stores, clothing stores. Movie houses. Old men loitered on the sidewalks here, looking around blankly, without judgment. Downtown at noon. These sights confused Helene. She might have intruded upon a sacred landscape, it was so certain, so definite. All the buildings were old, fixed, had the look of having been here for decades. The people all knew their way around perfectly. Everyone who was here belonged here. They had chosen to come here, walking in slow, measured strides or standing on the sidewalk, motionless, looking around. They had all been born at one time or another, at a precise moment. If their mothers had tried in desperation to scrape them out and lose them in bathwater they would have resisted—would have clutched the walls of flesh and refused to let go—why? Why should anyone give up life? Why not fight for it? There was an army in the womb and it would not die without a fight.

Helene's eye was drawn to three young women strolling on the sidewalk—flashily dressed, very cheap and pretty, their hair bleached and puffed out around their stark, glamorous, high-colored faces—how she hated them! feared them! *Must remember to buy Dutch Cleanser.* The tub would probably be dirty. She would scour it clean and get rid of all that impersonal dirt.... She followed the girls with her eye, repulsed by their cheerful sexual glow that was like a beacon shining out of their faces, so obvious, so disgusting, and she thought of the faint line of dirt that formed on the collars of her clothes and Jesse's shirts after a single wearing. Where did it come from, that dirt? Clean as she and Jesse were, they were not really clean. She must remember to buy cleanser. Otherwise she would not be able to force herself to sit in that tub.

Pedestrians passed close about her, crossing with the light. They walked with their collars turned up against their faces, like Arabs, trying to protect themselves from small whirling clouds of grit and papers. The wind was quite strong today. Their eyes were half-shut, as if with a strange contentment. *All of them swelling outward in sacs, their lips thirsty and pressed against the walls of sacs, sucking blood.* Nothing could dislodge them.

She could not find a place to park. She kept driving helplessly, heading north toward LaSalle Metropolitan Hospital. She felt herself drawn there, the car drawn there. There was something she must do but she could not quite remember it: the bathtub, the Dutch Cleanser, the hot water. Scalding water. People passed in front of her car when she stopped for a red light, walking tirelessly, fiercely. They had the look of city people who have spent all the days of their lives tramping the city streets, up and down, contented, knowing exactly where they were going. Helene feared their strength. She felt lightheaded suddenly, knowing that something was going to happen to her.

What she must remember. . . .

She wanted to stop this car, park it at a curb. Anywhere. She wanted to abandon it. She wanted to run to a telephone booth and call her father and scream at him. *I am Helene Cady! What has happened to me? I was supposed to grow up into a certain person, but where is that person? I've waited for years and nothing has happened, marriage hasn't made any difference . . . and now my life is over, I can't tell myself that it will happen in the future, I am through waiting for my life to happen. . . . I am everything now, at this moment, that I will ever be. It's over.*

She parked in the visitors' parking lot of the hospital. No moisture between her legs? No ache in the pit of her belly? The hospital was a large seven-story building with a broad, sand-blasted façade and scores of windows. It had an old, decrepit, stained look—tar seemed to have seeped down from its roofs; its chimneys were enormous and blackened, like the chimneys of factories. The big front lawn was a bright false green, dotted with refuse. A new wing was being added, but work had been temporarily halted and girders were exposed like raw, orange, comically exaggerated bones.

Helene entered the hospital through the big front door. A sound of wheezing as the door revolved. Inside, the familiar odor of a hospital. Helene went at once to the elevator and took it to the basement, conscious of people milling about her, the bustle of noontime. In the elevator with her were two young doctors, probably interns, Jesse's age, and a small flirtatious nurse, and a woman in expensive street clothes who glanced around hopefully. Helene hurried down to the staff cafeteria. She had met Jesse here a few times. But now she didn't see him, so she sat by herself at a corner table, exhausted, and stared straight ahead of her. Her mind shuddered and went blank. Doctors, young men, passed by her—someone was laughing loudly, with laughter as robust as Trick's had been; the men conferred together as if they sensed how everything was in their keeping, everything belonged to them. Their tired, laugh-lined faces, youthful and aged faces, possessed certainty, a power, a maleness that was unconscious in them. Helene stared at them leadenly.

Someone touched her.

She woke to herself, alarmed. Hours had passed.

"What are you doing here, Helene?"

It was Jesse, as alarmed as she.

A man of above-average height: thick red hair, eyes tired and dark in their sockets like her own eyes. Her twin. Her husband. He was a stranger to her, happening upon her like this, one of the many men dressed in white who passed so quickly and so unconsciously about her, hardly glancing at her; yet he was not a stranger at all but her husband. He had taken hold of her arm, as if in anger.

"Is anything wrong?" Jesse asked, frowning.

"No."

He sat down beside her, very close. He stared at her. "I'm just going to have my breakfast now, I've been running like hell all day.... Are you sure nothing is wrong?"

"I had a doctor's appointment this morning."

"What? Where?"

His face seemed enormous to her. She could see the freckles, the faint splotches of freckles across his forehead.

"What do you mean?" Jesse whispered.

His fingers tightened on her arm. It was nearly a convulsion, the way he clutched at her. *He knows.* It was unmistakable, the way he had come over to her and claimed her.

"Jesse, you look so tired," she said.

They stared at each other, their faces hard.

Around them, behind them, people milled and bumped against chairs. A man in white sat across from them with a cup of coffee, but Jesse did not look around. He stared at Helene and there was a power, a feverish urgency, in the very bones of his face.

She had not wanted it to happen this way.

But it had happened: she was here with him, this particular man. They were together. He knew. She leaned her forehead against the edge of his shoulder, the stiff white material of his outfit, and closed her eyes. Exhausted, she closed her eyes.

"Helene—" Jesse whispered.

She could not speak. She pressed her forehead against this man and everything stopped.

8

"What kind of bleeding?"

"Regular blood."

"But what kind? Do you pass blood?"

"Nosebleeds."

"Nosebleeds?"

"Yes. Nosebleeds."

Jesse stared at the man and had the idea that he was lying. But why lie? He wrote down this information.

"Bad dreams. I have bad dreams too."

Jesse nodded abstractedly.

"This old restaurant we used to live over . . . I keep seeing it . . . something about the stairway, my old man. . . . Real bad nightmares. I keep having the same one all the time. . . . They're all dead now."

He spoke with a dull anger. Propped up in bed, his big chest and stomach swelling against the hospital gown, he glared at Jesse as if Jesse were to blame for his trouble. A foxy, cagey look in spite of his weariness. His breath smelled. He had been hospitalized for uremia. Jesse was making out a report on him hurriedly, and he felt the tension rising between them, a senseless tension, as if this man blamed Jesse for the fact that he was there in bed, sick, while Jesse was making out a report on him. He was a fierce animal in an area marked off sharply by the bedclothes, the exact edges of the bed.

"Then since I come here, in the morning, I can't get my eyesight right. I will sue if you people are doping me up wrong. Flashes of light in my eyes, like going blind. I know a lawyer and I will sue for all you've got."

Already it was nine-thirty in the morning and Jesse was behind his schedule. He had to hurry. There was no time to investigate the intimate, cunning, frightened note in this man's voice; a curiosity, this notation on his record—he was a "professional wrestler," or had been; now he was fifty-five years old and going to fat. He wanted to talk to Jesse about his bad dreams, but Jesse was in a hurry and could only nod abruptly, vaguely, thinking of Helene back in the apartment—she had been sick again that morning, wretchedly sick, she was now in her seventh month of pregnancy and they were both afraid she might lose the baby, after so many months of misery—he had to telephone her as soon as he had a chance, he had run out of the apartment without saying good-by because Helene hadn't come out of the bathroom. She had stayed in there as if hiding from him. How could he make sense of this man's wheedling complaints? "I can smell myself. I stink. I can smell myself stinking," the man said angrily. "You are all waiting for me to die."

Jesse hurried to the next patient. An hour behind the schedule he had set for himself. At the back of his mind his wife's form wavered, more flimsy to him than the patient in this room—a woman of thirty-four with a very bright, intense, fixed stare. Months ago a stare like hers would have unnerved him; now it hardly bothered him because he knew he was only a shape in the air that drew out her bitterness, it had nothing to do with him personally. But he kept losing Helene, losing her into the weary drone of the hospital, the sound of the loudspeaker and the squeaking of wheels and the sound of his own voice, asking questions, questions. Nothing came to an end. Little stories began and then broke off abruptly. Nothing was completed, nothing was finished; he ran out of questions and had to hurry on to the next room.

A hard, gleaming skull to this woman; her hair was very thin. Forehead big, brutal, ominous. She had been hospitalized two days before but there was no diagnosis yet. She continued to stare at Jesse brightly, almost sociably, but she would not answer his questions. *Jesus Christ,* Jesse thought. A nurse came between them, moving across the woman's line of vision, but she did not seem to see the nurse. Jesse had to do a spinal tap. His hands went cold. She was going to fight him, going to tear him up—he imagined that square, hard mouth of hers opening and the teeth clenching down hard on his wrist. Jesse prepared the needle and observed his hands closely. Not trembling. Not yet. The woman began to whimper as he approached her. A single high shriek. But her body acquiesced, heavy and voluptuous in spite of the white gown she wore; when it was over she convulsed or pretended to convulse, so that Jesse had to soothe her. "It's all over.

No trouble. All over." She had been sent to LaSalle from a private mental hospital to be checked for a brain tumor.

It was Jesse's private opinion that she was just crazy, but he would probably never find out what happened to her.

Now an old man who had had a stroke. Jesse searched all over for a good vein. He began to sweat. Where the hell was a good vein, hadn't this old man anything left? His arms and legs were thin, ghastly. Jesse poked around for nearly ten minutes, using a tourniquet. A young doctor named Diebold, the chief resident on this service, came by to watch. Jesse got a vein located in the man's left foot and began the fluids. Diebold made a wry clever comment about something—Jesse tried to respond with a laugh—but he was aware, vaguely and nervously, of another consciousness in the room, the old man who breathed wheezingly, eyes closed, mouth slightly open. But there was really no time to think about him.

In the corridor Diebold said, "The old guy is dead, just between you and me. He's finished."

Jesse nodded and backed away.

He called the apartment but no one answered. On the sixth ring he heard himself being paged—"Dr. Vogel. Dr. Vogel." He was wanted in the emergency room, which he was covering for another intern who had come down with mononucleosis. The elevator was too slow for Jesse so he ran down the back stairs; outside the March air shimmered with sunlight and health that seemed very distant to him. He had no time for it. In the emergency room he had to clean up a young Negro, brought in by the police after a chase and an automobile accident; he mopped blood and fixed the boy up, while in his brain the ringing of that telephone sounded. Why hadn't she answered the telephone? Was she standing there, watching it, knowing it was Jesse?

They never argued. Her silence, her strange stubborn meekness, baffled him. The pregnancy had worn her down, her legs ached constantly, and yet she never complained—she hid her sickness as if it shamed her, just as being a woman seemed to shame her. But she never complained. And yet Jesse had come across a letter to her from Cady, in which Cady made references to something Helene must have written to him: *You are taking his desire to go into public health too seriously. Yes, I agree it is a delusion, but it will pass. Jesse exaggerates....* He had been stung at that letter. He had wanted to rip it up. Had Helene really said that he was deluded, had she actually used the word "delusion"?—she had accused him once, but very gently, of wanting to accomplish too much, wanting to move too quickly. But what did this mean, what did Cady mean, by saying that he "exaggerated"? The phrases kept coming back to him. *I agree it is a delusion, but it will pass. Jesse exaggerates....* It was Jesse's intention to take a residency in General Medicine here and to join a public health clinic in a year or two; this was really a modest goal. Cady would have wanted him to train for much more. Jesse did not understand how he exaggerated anything.

But she had become pregnant, for him. She would have his baby, the first of his babies.

The police took the young man away. By this time it was too late for lunch and anyway Jesse had no appetite, so he went right to the sixth floor to work up another new admission with Myron Diebold; a woman of sixty who had been brought in with heart failure. Her legs were grotesque, swollen to bursting. Diebold fired questions at her and Jesse took down the answers. He wrote quickly, in a large spacious hand he had invented for himself: *Dr. Vogel taking down information, Dr. Vogel inventing himself.* Evidently this woman had had rheumatic fever as a child; Jesse thought at once of Trick, who had passed into heart failure in Ann Arbor, but who had been brought out of it and had recovered, because the last Jesse had heard, Trick was living with his parents in Minnesota. Jesse was grateful that he had survived, and yet he was uneasy at the thought that he might run into Trick again someday.... Myron muttered to Jesse on the way out, "The old gal doesn't look good to me. Hope she doesn't die right away." He walked with Jesse down the corridor, walking fast. Myron was talking about something, complaining, making vague absent-minded swipes at his nose, and Jesse felt a surge of despair at the thought that nothing was ever finished, nothing was ever really clear to him. Since last July he had been running constantly. He had to cover too many patients, he worked with too many other interns and residents, overlapping their duties, he came to the end of nothing, he lost contact with patients who interested him, he had no time to look up records in this hospital and certainly not in other hospitals—in the beginning he had wanted zealously to trace the records of beaten-up children, knowing that their parents were bringing them from one hospital to another, but he had never had time, and anyway he was warned against this because he could get into trouble. He did not sleep enough and he did not eat enough, he had sudden rushes of panic, he had sudden impulses to laugh at the wrong time. Myron was chiding him for missing a luncheon meeting for the second time in a week. Jesse smiled dimly and said he had been busy. "Yes, you look worn out," Myron said perfunctorily, sighing; he looked worn out himself. Everyone looked worn out. But Jesse had really forgotten about the luncheon meeting. The word "luncheon" struck him as a strange word. He said it aloud, as if testing it: "Luncheon." He could not remember having used that word before in his life. "I forgot about luncheon," he said, while Myron looked at him oddly. "Lunch. Luncheon. Lunch. *Lunch.*"

He got away from Myron and went up to the interns' lounge, where he had to force himself to decide between going to the lavatory or lying down at once. Milton Kuzma was sleeping in a chair. His clothes were soiled with faint smears of blood and vomit. Jesse did not want to wake him—Milton was having trouble at the hospital and their two-month-old baby at home disturbed his nights. Jesse could not decide: should he go to the lavatory or lie down? He was very tired. But if he lay down he might have to get up again in a few minutes. He stood by a cot, thinking. Minutes passed. He pressed his forefinger against his teeth, rubbing at the fine, rather slimy coating on them—the leftover scum of a minute's panic, now forgotten. There was something else he was supposed to do. Telephone his wife. Yes, he should telephone his wife. But he could not decide about moving forward or backward or in any direction at all. His legs felt distant from him, not tired but impersonal, remote. That woman in heart failure: swollen legs. Fluid puffing up her flesh. Curious, Jesse bent to touch his own legs, to see what they felt like. Could not remember having done this before. He could sit on the edge of the cot and rest like that, or he could lie down and sleep, or go to the lavatory right now and get it over with; or he could telephone Helene.

Milton Kuzma woke with a groan.

"Jesse . . . ? What are you doing? What time is it?" Milton said vaguely. He passed his hands over his face. "Jesus, did I have a bad time. You heard about it, I suppose. That little girl . . . ?"

Jesse was startled at Milton's bleary eyes and dry, stained lips.

". . . they brought her in with meningitis . . . ? Jesus, was she going fast, and if you know what happened please don't tell me. . . . "

Then he was paged—*Dr. Vogel, Dr. Vogel*—in that efficient expressionless voice, and with relief he ran to the telephone. It was good to know what he must do! Only someone who had died, and would Dr. Vogel please come up to pronounce him dead? It was only one flight up. The patient, an old man, looked familiar to Jesse but Jesse could not remember him. He pronounced him dead. Yes, he was dead. A young blond nurse was saying shakily to Jesse, "This is the first time anybody died on me. . . ." but Jesse was already on his way. He had new admissions to check all afternoon, and since he had decided not to take a nap and not to have lunch, he might as well get started on them at once. Now that he was moving, his legs moving energetically again, he would take advantage of momentum. It was a kind of gravity, sideways gravity. Horizontal gravity. He was pleased with himself.

Sat on the edge of a windowsill and asked about complaints, symptoms, troubles, having to raise his voice so that the man in the bed could hear. Not very old, but he was nearly deaf; diabetes; trouble with gall bladder. And what about his past illnesses?—must ask about everything, every small bit of bad news. The man stared at him stupidly. *Past illnesses?* After a few awkward minutes Jesse got an answer, at least something to write down. Now, what about the illnesses of a man's parents, grandparents, brothers and sisters? A baffled stare. Could this old man have had parents? Grandparents? Jesse managed to get something out of him, something to write down. Yes, yes.

Now a blood sample. A simple operation. But the old man flinched, then recoiled. Then began to shout in Jesse's face. "No! Get away! You too young! Not you!" Jesse tried to soothe him. He took hold of the old man's arm and the old man snatched it away. Then, swinging it back, he struck Jesse on the side of the face. "No blood from me, not me! I'll kill you! Stick you with it instead!" Jesse was afraid the needle had been broken but it looked all right. He approached the old man again, explaining something he had explained a hundred times before. His face stung lightly. This time the old man's feet seemed to be coming to life, stirring beneath the bedclothes. He was cringing back against the stiff pillows, moaning, "No. No. No." Jesse eyed his foot under the covers and wondered if he was strong enough to swing it out and kick Jesse with it. Probably not.

White in the face, the man stared at him. Saliva glistening around his lips. Jesse talked gently to him. Gently. Someone leaned in the doorway and said, "You need any help in here?" and Jesse, not glancing around, said that everything was under control. The old man shuddered and extended his arm to Jesse. Ah, that was good. Good. . . . Next, on the fourth floor, a dwarfish banged-up child of fifteen; his mother pacing in the aisle between the beds, heavily perfumed and impatient as a dancer. The child was homely, bruised in the face and shoulders, scratched, dazed. His lip was swollen and discolored. He had fallen down a flight of stairs. Fallen or was pushed?—Jesse wondered as he took notes. The boy was very small for his age. Listless, his eyes open but unfocused. Was he feebleminded? Jesse was amazed at the number of feebleminded people he saw here. The mother stood close to Jesse and complained, "He fell. He's always falling. He can't walk right. Or maybe he can't see right. He even falls upstairs. The kids push him around, the bastards are always chasing him. He's been falling since he was a baby. Falls on his head. His nose bleeds for no reason—when he picks it, it bleeds twice as bad." Her breath was intimate and liquorish. Jesse tried not to look at her tight pullover sweater and her red slacks, very tight in the hips. Open-toed shoes. Something tinkled—jewelry, maybe her earrings—but he did not want to glance up. She kept touching Jesse, but very lightly, as if they were simply making conversation. "What do you think, Doctor? You are a doctor, aren't you? You look kind of young to me. But I bet you know what you're doing, huh? What do you think of him? They said probable concussion. What's that? When can I bring him home?" Jesse examined the boy and saw the old scars, the old sprawling yellowish bruises of a few weeks before, old bumps, the bad teeth, the curious drab eyes. No resistance. Jesse moved his hand in front of the boy's face and his eyes did not seem to notice anything. Blind?

The mother was complaining in a voice that rose and fell as she thought of the other patients in nearby beds and then forgot them in her anger, then recalled them again with a kind of demure shame. "I can't take much more of this. You hear? He's a bad boy. He's always getting knocked around. Won't listen. They kicked him out of school, he was so dumb. His goddamn father sucks ale and that's that. It's not my responsibility all by myself. Listen, you have to cuff him to make him even look at you. I'm not kidding. I had to take off work today just for this. . . ." After a few minutes Jesse located one of the young doctors on the staff and consulted with him. Then, the woman's voice still shrill and flirtatious in his head, he took the back stairs all the way down to the cafeteria. Must eat. It was important to eat.

He remembered the day Helene had been sitting here, just sitting here by herself. What a shock that had been, to approach her and to realize that she was noticing nothing! She had awakened only when he had touched her. . . . The odors of food discouraged Jesse but he pressed forward through a small crowd and picked up a tray. It was still wet. Jack Galt, another intern, turned to talk to him. He lived near Jesse and sometimes he dropped in to visit Jesse and Helene; a tall, thin, slightly stooped young man with glasses, very intelligent, very nervous. He was talking to Jesse excitedly. Something about an out-of-town physician who had had a coronary during a routine appendectomy that morning. Jack was on surgical service. Jesse could not pay much attention because he had to decide about what to eat—a tuna fish sandwich, which was on white bread and wrapped in cellophane, or should he take a chicken salad sandwich, which was on cracked wheat bread? He stared at the sandwiches while Jack talked. Jack poked his arm. "There's a line behind you," he said. Jesse hurried along and took only a cup of coffee. He was not really hungry after all. Jack sat across from him, sighing with exhaustion and a kind of counterfeit despair. "What a mess upstairs! The guy just fell over. We were all panicked!" Once when Jack had come to visit the Vogels he had complained to them in the same voice about a friend of his who had returned a Mahler symphony, a record, badly scratched; and now Jesse got this old news confused with the news about this coronary in the operating room. He felt lightheaded. Something nagged at him: should he go back and check on the uremia case? He had not worked up the man properly. And when the man had tried to talk about his bad dreams Jesse had not responded.... And the banged-up boy with the mother. Should check him out, see if he had a record of hospitalizations. Someone was beating him, obviously. Now Jack Galt was gossiping about Milton Kuzma, who had been given hell by Dr. Perrault just the day before. Had Jesse heard? Everyone agreed that it had not been Milton's fault, whatever happened. And something else had happened, not a patient of Perrault's but an out-of-town man's: an ulcer patient who had hemorrhaged about a quart of blood in the hall. Jack said sharply, "You're spilling your coffee, Jesse." For some reason this reminded Jesse of his need to telephone home.

He left his coffee and Jack Galt and went to look for a telephone. All in use. He could go back up to the lounge. Or wait. He decided to wait. Then he heard his name being paged, and was called back up to the fourth floor to look in on a patient with Myron Diebold and Dr. Costello, who was explaining the patient's trouble when Jesse entered the room. Dr. Costello had a pleasant high-pitched voice. Undiagnosed pain in the abdomen; not gall bladder; hernia, a stone somewhere? Costello was a very businesslike man in his forties, with neat, stern eyebrows and a manner of lecturing to his inferiors in all conversation. Jesse was always humble around him. Now he asked Jesse a question, and though Jesse could have made a reasonable guess, he thought it more prudent to say that he didn't know. Diebold attempted an answer and was interrupted triumphantly by Costello. "Hah! Where'd you dig that up?" Diebold flushed. After this, Jesse went up to the lounge and the lavatory, at last, and now another intern was sleeping in the chair Milton Kuzma had been in, his breath raspy and labored. Jesse washed his hands for quite a while, dreamily. Then he was called down to the emergency room again; a child no more than three or four years old, his face and head swollen, especially his eyelids and lips. He was unconscious. Jesse estimated a hundred bites—insect bites of some kind. Big red swellings, tiny angry blood-flecked dots, purplish areas of flesh... bright-colored, elaborate bumps that overlapped one another. The mother, who looked about sixteen years old, hovered nearby, weeping. "Jesus, isn't that a sight," one of the staff doctors said, whistling thinly. The child's eyelids were swollen shut, his lips enormous, as if blown up, the skin bright pink and tender, very thin from being stretched so hard. Jesse felt sick. A taste in his mouth suddenly of poison: the poison in that child's bloodstream.

When he was finished there, he telephoned Helene again. This time she did answer the phone. "Yes, hello, is this Jesse . . . ?" she asked faintly. He felt a rush of love for her that had something to do with the child he had just seen; it unnerved him, his love for her and for the baby she was carrying, his dependency upon her. He asked her how she felt. She answered briefly: a little nauseated yet, but nothing worse. Then they fell into silence. Characteristic silence. Jesse was suddenly eager to make her talk, he was desperate, guilty . . . he must get her through this pregnancy, he must prevent her escaping him. . . . He began to rub his eye in that silence, wondering what she was thinking. He feared her escaping to her father, back to Cambridge and the comfortable insular life she had led there. What had her father's letter meant, what had he meant by Jesse's "exaggeration"? But he did not dare ask. Instead, he asked, as if he had just thought of it, "Helene, what time is it?" "Ten o'clock." "Ten o'clock at night?" he said, surprised. He stopped rubbing his eye and looked around the lounge. Yes, it must be the end of a day, for newspapers lay around on the floor; cigarette butts in the ashtrays, some of which were on the floor too. A spent, stale smell. But where had the day gone . . . ? He felt that he might be losing his mind. "Are you sure it's ten o'clock at night?" he asked.

The windows of the lounge showed that it was dark out. He had not noticed that before.

Helene spoke softly to him, as if aware of his amazement. Yes, yes, keep talking. Love me, Jesse thought. He tried to imagine her, his wife—her fine skin fading with pregnancy, her hair listless and broken off at the ends, no longer so smoothly brushed back from her face. Enlarged veins in her legs. Slender legs, breaking veins. A body swollen out of proportion and difficult to balance. Her spine ached. Her spine was too delicate for her belly. It made no allowance for the baby, unwilling to give in, to be resilient. A stubborn spine. A spine so stubborn might snap.... Beneath her ordinary wifely words there was a silence, still, that reproached him for not knowing her. But did Jesse really know anyone; how close could he come to knowing anyone? What must he do to know her?

Once she had come to the hospital to pick him up, at eight in the morning. He had seen her walking through the parking lot, quickly and deftly making her way around the parked cars, and out of nowhere a man had appeared—this man seemed to be heading her off, and then he paused, stopped, lit a cigarette with his hands cupped about a match, turning slowly on his heels to watch her hurry by. Jesse had been angry at the arrogance of the man, but Helene had simply glanced at him coldly and contemptuously, without flinching, raising her face toward the man at just the right moment, saying nothing, dismissing him with her own arrogance. Whether the man had said anything to her or not Jesse didn't know and he would not have wanted to ask. In that instant he himself had felt somehow weakened and banished, as if he were a brother to that man who had been so coldly snubbed and not that woman's husband....

Her private smile, slow and girlish. Her ashen skin. The length of her ashen body, oddly slender except for that swollen belly. He thought of her constantly and it seemed to him that the secret of the world was somehow in her, in her body, casually possessed by her but hidden from him. What must he do to learn it, to learn her? His eye itched painfully and he rubbed it hard. He had known Anne-Marie better. He had been closer to Anne-Marie. "How often were you sick today?" he asked hesitantly, knowing that she hated to talk about this. She did not answer at once. Then she said, "I just didn't feel like answering the telephone when it rang. I didn't feel like it." "Yes, I know, but how were you? Are you better now?" Jesse asked. "Yes, I'm better now. I'm better," she said bitterly. A few more seconds of silence ...Jesse began to perspire, wondering what to do. Then Helene went on in the same voice, "I ate some dinner so that I'd have something to vomit up later this evening. I'm grateful for your concern. In the morning I'll vomit again—a pint or a quart—it's all predictable. Does that answer your question?" Jesse, shocked, stared out the window at the darkness, the parking-lot lights.

After a minute or so Helene said in a different voice, "When are you coming home, in the morning?" "Yes," said Jesse. "Do you want me to pick you up?" she asked.

Jesse did not seem to hear this question. He stood rubbing his eye slowly, ponderously. Helene said, "Jesse, if I have this baby you won't make me have another. Will you? Not another baby, Jesse. You won't make me have another baby, will you . . . ?" There was something in his eye, maybe an eyelash. The other day he had worked for a hard ten minutes getting an eyelash out of the reddened eye of a woman. Tears. A tiny stinging lash. "I'd better come home," Jesse said. Helene laughed and said lightly, "No. No. There's no reason. I don't mean anything of what I just said. I'm not sure I even said those things."

They said good-by and Jesse remained with the telephone receiver in his hand. A dead end. Not even a dial tone. Nothing.

Women showed up at the hospital, bleeding. All the time. Trying to dislodge the flesh inside their wombs, feverish with the need to scrape themselves out. What a mess they made for someone else to mop up . . . ! Fetuses big as a man's fist. Basins of blood. The doctors said they were crazy. Why so wild? So vicious? Savage as animals turning upon themselves, but also very sly and imaginative. The doctors said they were crazy but Jesse did not think it was that simple. A few weeks ago a night nurse had called Jesse down. There was a woman bleeding badly, looking surprised and distraught. In fact, she had just walked in off the street; she had asked where the ladies' room was. Wanted to fix herself up, she said. When Jesse got downstairs the blood was dripping freely on the floor, turning into a small stream. The woman, in her early twenties, was a large-boned healthy girl with a heavy chest and stomach. Wouldn't sit down. Kept staggering around, clutching at the backs of chairs, a table. Oddly dressed for this time of year—she wore only a sleeveless top of some silky, cheap beige material, tucked loosely into a tweed skirt that was too short for the fashions of the last several years. She was shivering convulsively. Her chest heaved. Still, with all that bleeding, she would not sit down. Jesse and Jack Galt, who were covering the emergency room together, had to calm her down. Blood ran down into her shoes. Onto the floor. Jack tried to urge her one way, but she would turn and brush against Jesse blindly, and then back toward Jack again, while one of the nurses tried to coax her into lying down. Finally they got her onto the table. She seized Jesse's arm and cried, "I don't know what it is, Doctor! It just happened. I don't know what it is—" There was blood everywhere and when Jesse tried to do a vaginal exam the woman began to fight him. It took several people to hold her down. "No, let me go! They don't know where I went—they're waiting for me back home—" The bleeding seemed to be getting worse. Jesse, now panicked, was covered with blood. She was going to bleed to death right in front of him. Bleed to death. He tried to examine her again. This time he came out with a handful of dark clotted blood and flesh and what looked like slivers of glass.... Could it be glass? The slivers were fairly large, curved pieces of ordinary glass, probably from a small fruit-juice glass; Jesse had stared at the red-and-yellow diamond design on the outside....

The woman's screams. Screams.

A fruit-juice glass jammed up toward the womb.

Myron Diebold came into the lounge. Jesse, startled, put the telephone receiver back. Myron held a sandwich out to Jesse. "Dr. Vogel, my friend, Jack Galt was telling us you didn't look well. Here. Maybe you're hungry." Jesse unwrapped the sandwich eagerly. It was a cheese and lettuce sandwich on white bread, not from the cafeteria but from the vending machine; but his mouth watered violently. He ate it in four or five bites. "Now, why don't you sleep?" Myron said. "I'm going to hang around for another hour and I can cover for you."

"All right," Jesse said.

"Did you hear about Milt Kuzma... ?"

"Yes," Jesse said, not wanting to hear anything more.

"Perrault really gave him hell. Steer clear of Perrault."

"Yes."

"Anything interesting come in today?"

"No."

"Myron left and Jesse sat down on the edge of one of the cots. He did not feel tired. Something was nagging him: that dwarfish boy. Those dull unfocused eyes. He certainly had not seen the boy before. But the boy looked familiar. He must check the boy again, must get back to the room when the mother wasn't around and question him. Must make a special note on the record—"injuries suspicious"— Restless, Jesse got up and, having nothing to do, went down to the fourth floor. At night, with things quieted down, the hospital did not seem so confusing; each floor had its own unmistakable appearance, its own shadowy lights cast by certain arrangements in the nurses' stations and from vending machines that sold coffee and cigarettes. Each floor seemed to have its own smell, its own taste. Jesse could not remember which room the boy was in. He was certain it was on this floor. He questioned one of the nurses, who smiled at him curiously. When he asked her about the boy with the head injuries, she didn't seem to know whom he was talking about. . . . They had coffee together and Jesse thought uneasily of Anne-Marie. Yes, he had been close to her, he had loved her. He remembered the violence of his passion for her. Then his mind skipped onto Trick, then onto Trick's collapse on the sidewalk. Caving in. His legs caving in. Jesse began to breathe quickly, as if he had escaped some awful danger.

After a few minutes he began to feel better. He would check on the boy again in a few days. He would check other hospitals, see if he could find the boy's records somewhere else. It seemed possible to him that he could do this. Now that things had quieted down. . . . There was the possibility of completion, of seeing someone through, and not these jagged snatches of people, their personalities reduced to a gall bladder, a lacerated scalp, a patch of burned skin. He loved them, how he wanted to help them . . . ! He did love them. He could crawl in bed with them, matching his length against theirs. Hook himself up to them: his blood and fluids flowing into them. His strong heartbeat would encourage theirs. . . . This little nurse told him her name was Rosemary. She was very interested in whatever he had to say. Exhausted, Jesse began to talk. He talked about the child with the insect bites, the old man who had hit him, the dwarfish wreck of a boy and how his parents should be treated, not just him, because of course they were sick, they were all crazy, the entire family would have to be brought in. "Not just a victim. The entire family," Jesse said. Rosemary thought that was a wonderful idea.

People shouldn't be allowed to die, Jesse said in a rush. Shouldn't be abandoned. Doctors should never give up, never, no matter how tired they are. . . .

Rosemary thought that was a wonderful idea.

Jesse's throat felt raw. He was talking too much. Reluctantly he said good-by, backing away, and the little nurse smiled reluctantly after him as if hating to give him up.

He went up to the interns' on-call room, where he lay down stiffly and considered sleeping. But if he fell asleep the telephone would probably ring. He waited for it to ring, jerking from time to time as if he were asleep, conscious of his muscles oddly jerking. He was not asleep, but he dreamed of that fistful of black clotty blood and bright red blood he had hauled out. A broken fruit-juice glass. What a surprise that young woman had given him! Women were always surprises, though; anything could come out of their bodies.... He sat up, frightened. He thought the telephone had rung but evidently it hadn't. So he lay back again and fell asleep. At once he returned to his dream of that woman's body, all the blood, the mess, the mutilated fetus. A woman's body and its dark surprises. Like a corridor: like the corridor outside the door of this room. The room was too hot. The corridor was drafty, especially near the back stairs. Heat and draft. Heat rising, cold air cutting through it, hot and cold, up and down. Corridors were adventures. Doors opened off to the right or to the left, doors that tempted you to enter. First you open the screen door, then the inside door. Turn the knob. Push in.

The telephone rang, jarring him awake. He jumped up in terror.

Only one o'clock.

He was called over to look at a postoperative gall-bladder case. The woman whimpered that she was afraid of dying. Jesse did not bother to get angry with the nurse, he simply brushed past her and went to check over the woman. She was crying and clutching at Jesse's arm. This was a semiprivate room, and the other patient, a sleeping woman, snored through the frantic consultation. A woman's face changes so rapidly, Jesse thought, it seems to change colors.... "But why cry now? You're fine," Jesse said gently.

Her face was enormous with fear, twitching, shivering, all its human womanly strength focused upon him, needing him. He could not leave. He stayed with her while she whimpered about dying, about the pain she felt, the snippy nurses, the taste in her mouth. . . . Jesse soothed her with words. Words. He was not sure if this was real or part of his dream. She mumbled something about his age: he was her son's age. Jesse blushed as if she had flattered him grossly. After about twenty minutes of this, with the night nurse hanging around silent and curious, Jesse was called over to the psychiatric ward, where a patient had started vomiting violently. The nurse on the telephone told Jesse that the man was trying to throw up his insides. Jesse hurried over there, wondering if the nurse was teasing him, if maybe there wasn't some conspiracy at night to keep him going, to keep him from sleeping, to flirt with him, to draw him out to the most trivial and unspectacular of troubles. . . . But he was slowed down at the sight of the patient. Yes, this did look serious. A huge fat man, not much older than Jesse; billows of flesh, flab, blubber, a bare wobbling chest smeared with vomit and blood—darting crazy eyes. Oh, those eyes! Jesse was becoming accustomed to them.

He hated fat people. Hated crazy people. Well, perhaps he did not really hate them, no, because hatred was out of place in his work; he was disturbed by them. They were sick in a way that did not interest him. With crazy people you could not stick a tube down them and drain out the poison or the excess fluid; you couldn't hook up some plasma and fluids and get them healthy again. Their sickness was a stubborn sickness, stubborn as a fist that could not be unclenched. . . . This patient was convulsing. Throwing himself around like a small elephant, a small whale. Jesse wondered if he had managed to poison himself somehow, his vomit stank so unnaturally. He put the man in restraints and said in a hypnotic, weary voice, "You're not going to die. Not going to die. Don't be afraid." The man's heart was going like mad, as if wanting to burst; but Jesse was not going to let it burst. Not tonight. Not while Jesse was on duty. The needle he tried to use on the man snapped in two so he gave him a rectal sedative instead, and by now the place reeked. Ugh, how he hated fat! And such layers of fat! No part of the body was ugly in itself, no face was truly ugly, but such quantities of flesh were hardly physical at all—they were a kind of spiritual obscenity.

Eyes rolling back in his head. The man lost consciousness in the beginning of a convulsion. "Ah, there," Jesse said softly. He sponged off the man's wet face. Then he sponged off his own face, breathing hard. He asked the nurses about the patient, curious as always, and yet cautiously, for he sometimes dreaded what he might be told. "In real life," a nurse said, frowning, "he was a high school teacher."

In real life!

Jesse stared at the fat man. Harsh labored breathing, minute twitches of his flesh, spasmodic twitches of his fingers.... Jesse felt his own skin tingle, as if about to twitch in sympathy with the man. Jesse hated death. He hated the way people tried for death, as if stretching to reach it, grunting with the effort. Why did so many of them want to die? It was terrible to see a human being convinced he must die.

The nurses, splattered with vomit, told Jesse about all the trouble this young man had been to them. As they spoke, sullen and faintly excited, Jesse stared at the unconscious man, this fat, sick creature who seemed to him to exist at the limits of human life, human reality, hardly in the family of mankind at all. It frightened him, the man's massive fleshly certainty, his absolute being, as if so much flesh were a mockery of Jesse's own spare flesh. The man's face twitched and seemed to be undergoing changes. Rapid flashes of dreams—nightmares—stretching his face out of shape, then relaxing it again. What was he dreaming? Jesse felt a sudden desire, an almost painful desire, to know what that man was dreaming. He would spend a lifetime in the service of sick people, he was prepared to give up much of his own life to them, and yet he would never know what went on in their heads....

He ran upstairs to take a shower, to get that filth off him. He couldn't stand it. The fat man's big straining face remained in his mind. It was almost a human face, yet not quite human. Jesse believed he had a secret face himself, a monstrous face that gave its special cast to his own normal features and that he had to fight, to hold back. He had never really seen this secret face of his. That monstrous fat man had shown his true face angrily, viciously, without shame. And his heart—Jesse had felt that heart, enormous and pounding. Such intimacy, Jesse feeling the heart of a stranger! How close they had been, like brothers, like twins!... Jesse puzzled over the outrageous stink of the vomit. Had it been poison of some kind?

Soaped and rinsed clean, rubbed dry with a towel. He sighed. He lay down and the back of his mind muddied at once. It was peaceful and good in this ugly little room, his private room for the night... yes, it was good to be on duty, to be responsible for so many people. It gave him happiness to be here and to know that he was needed. In another week he would go on the surgical service, which he feared a little because he feared Dr. Perrault, who was Chief of Surgery... and really he had no interest in surgery, he wanted to go into general medical practice. General medical practice: his life was leading him in that direction.

...Awakened suddenly by a telephone call: three o'clock. A nurse somewhere in the hospital wanted permission to give someone a sleeping pill half an hour before it was scheduled. Jesse lay down again and must have slept, because the telephone rang again, ringing loudly, and he jumped up with his heart pounding and could not think for an instant where he was. *Helene? Had something happened to Helene?* It was from the emergency room; a nurse who sounded hysterical. Jesse pulled on his trousers, stumbling. Five-fifteen. When Jesse got down there he saw why the nurse was hysterical—a man bleeding in a thick stream from what looked like the very pit of his belly, his groin, held down onto a table by two ambulance attendants and a nurse. Cries. Confusion. "My God," Jesse said when he saw what the wound was. For a moment he could not move, he was paralyzed, and then the horror of the sight made something click off in his brain—it was too much to assess, he must go through the steps one at a time. First, get the man down. Down flat. A young woman who must have ridden along in the ambulance was in Jesse's way and he pushed her impatiently aside and got to work. So much blood! Why was there so much blood? The man was in his late thirties; he had a face that must have been handsome but had now gone white and hard, smeared with his own blood. Blood in his hair. His lips were white and he was struggling to breathe, struggling with the nurse and Jesse. His pulse raced out of control; he had gone into shock. Jesse got the shock blocks into place and the table was tipped back, and still the man struggled, and Jesse had to fight down a gagging sensation. All this blood unnerved him, he was even slipping in it, and yet he knew that blood was not very important—the easiest thing to be equipped with—all he had to do was get a sample and prepare for a transfusion, yes, he had done this many times before, except now his own hands were so bloody and the nurses so frightened and the strange young woman—she was hardly more than a girl, maybe twenty years old—so terrified that his mind seemed in danger of breaking into splinters. *What if he found parts of a broken glass jammed up into the man's groin?* But the man had done it with a knife, according to the ambulance attendant, all by himself with a knife. A knife! Jesse listened and kept working, working so fast that he didn't have time to break. *The testicles slashed, hated so viciously and slashed so viciously....* But everything was under control. Jesse would not make a mistake. *No you don't,* he thought as the man tried to lunge backward, as if fleeing his own wound. *No you don't, no dying tonight, not on my hands!* A sharp odor of alcohol. An odor of panic.

The young woman, backing away, had bumped into another table. Her hands were out before her in a gesture of supplication. Blood-smeared hands. Fingernails that had been painted carefully, a very pale pink, and now the hands smeared with blood. Jesse glanced up at her face. She was staring at the bleeding man, staring fixedly at him, her face childish with alarm. The skin seemed to be of slightly differing colors, or shades of color, like petals overlaid upon petals. A very fine, healthy skin. The girl's eyes were dilated, dazed, as if she were staring toward Jesse through water, unable to get her vision into focus, into belief. Slender, blond. Strokes of blood on her face like faint water-color brush strokes. She wore something beige—also smeared with blood, soaked with blood in front— *All we need is for her to faint,* Jesse thought.

"Got a call that somebody tried to kill himself," the ambulance driver was telling Jesse excitedly, "but Jesus, what a surprise! I almost puked! Had to carry him right out through the lobby of the Palmer House, bleeding like a pig!"

Jesse blinked.

It crossed his mind that he had not paid for the cheese sandwich he had eaten that night.

In a few minutes the bleeding was under control, the man hooked up; his trousers in a bloody clump underfoot, as if they had been part of him, amputated and discarded. Jesse felt as if he were being blown along on a rich gust of wind, an element that was boisterous and good. Around him were shaky, exhausted people. They looked sick. Almost as pale as the man on the table. But Jesse was lightheaded and he could not help gloating: *Nobody is going to die tonight if I can help it.* Mopping himself off, he looked around the messy room, its glinting metallic surfaces, its splatterings of blood that were like exclamation marks, and everything seemed to him manageable now, in his power, a sacred area he had mastered. *Nobody is going to die....*

"Where did she go?" Jesse cried.

The young woman was gone.

They ran out into the corridor. She was gone. One of the nurses went down to a women's lavatory but it was empty.

"Where did she go? What happened?" Jesse asked.

He had to make out the report with the help of the ambulance attendant and the man's wallet, fished out of his bloody trousers. Jesse was writing up the report when Milton Kuzma came in.

"Jesse," he said. It was more than a greeting. Jesse glanced up, a little confused. Milton was wearing street clothes and for an instant Jesse did not recognize him. "Jesse.... Everyone's talking about what happened here; it's really a mess, it looks like a mess.... But look, Jesse, there's nothing to worry about," he said, laying his hand on Jesse's arm while Jesse tried to keep part of his attention on the report form, "the fact is I came over to get you because of Helene, but there's nothing to worry about, everything is normal and regular.... Jesse? Helene started having pains a few hours ago and she called us, and Susan drove her to Women's Hospital. She couldn't get hold of you. It's all right, Jesse, everything is under control, don't worry.... Blazack knows about it and he's on his way, at this time of the morning... I think that's pretty damn good of him.... Jesse, are you listening? The contractions are close together now—so, Jesse—look, Jesse, I'll cover for you now and you can go to the hospital. Women's Hospital, right? You know what to do? I told the taxi to wait out back and he's going to wait for you."

"What did you say?" Jesse said, looking up.

"Put that thing down, come upstairs with me and take a shower and change your clothes. You've got enough time," Milton said sternly. "Come on. There's nothing to worry about but you'd better get over there as soon as you can. She's a few weeks early. . . ."

Jesse could not understand what this man was talking about. It was strange to see him in this part of the hospital in ordinary street clothes; Milton looked diminished and trivial. He needed a shave.

"There was a girl here, a witness, who walked out," Jesse said, dazed. "She just walked out. She had blond hair and blood all over. . . ."

"Come on, Jesse, let's get you showered and fixed up. You're going to be a father."

"What?"

Jesse allowed himself to be led to the elevator. His eye was still sore. He began to rub it slowly. His hand was like a large clumsy paw now, just an ordinary hand, stained with drying blood.

"Susan is with her and Blazack must be there by now," Milton said. "There's a taxi waiting for you in back. I told him to be damned sure to wait. I've already paid him."

"I forgot to pay you for that sandwich," Jesse said suddenly.

"What sandwich?"

"It must have been a quarter," Jesse said. "It was cheese."

Jesse reached in his pocket to get some change, but Milt pushed his hand away.

"What, what? Jesse, you're out of your mind!"

"But I owe you a quarter—"

Milt gripped him by the shoulders and shook him.

"Will you wake up! Will you listen to me? You're going to be a father!"

Jesse stared at him raggedly. They were ascending in the elevator and everything was eerie and weightless. A father. A *father.* "Did you say a father? A father?" Jesse asked. A strange word. Strange sound. He could not remember having spoken it out loud before. *Father. Father. Father.*

". . . a *father?*" Jesse whispered.

9

One spring day in 1955, Jesse was taking his daughter Jeanne to a pediatrician on Adams Street when he saw someone he recognized. He thought he recognized her: a woman waiting to cross the street, her face in profile. He had seen her somewhere before. His heart tripped suddenly; there was an intimacy between him and that woman, something that had happened under stress, nagging and unforgettable . . . yet he could not quite remember.

He paused to stare at her. She wore a fawn-colored spring coat, tailored and simple, and the flesh of her legs seemed to ripple in the cool spring air of Chicago, muscular and smooth. Or did he imagine this? Her flesh seemed to shiver as if she were aware of him. She wore no gloves. No rings. She wore no hat either—her long, thick blond hair was ruffled by the wind, and as Jesse watched she reached up to press it down against the side of her throat in a gesture that seemed somehow familiar to Jesse.

Had she been a patient of his?

His daughter tugged at his hand. "Daddy . . . ?

Jesse was still watching the woman. He saw that his attention had begun to draw her attention, that she glanced nervously toward him. Yet their eyes did not meet. She glanced away, troubled. And yet her face seemed to be turned toward his, lifting itself toward his gaze like a flower drawn by the sun, the petals ripening.

A striking woman. A surprise: as if Jesse had known her when she hadn't been so beautiful.

Jeanne was nudging his legs

"Just a minute, honey," Jesse said.

She pressed against him and pulled at his hand. Ready to cry. All morning she had been crying off and on because she hated Dr. Leventhal. "It's all right, Jeanne," Jesse said gently, vaguely, while he tried to figure out where he had met that woman and whether she might remember him. He wondered if she might be the wife of a doctor. But no, he didn't think so. He didn't think she was anyone's wife.

It angered him that he could not remember her.

At the hospital he had the reputation of a man who remembered everything. He could remember patients' histories, medical records, charts, though he had seen them only once; he could keep miscellaneous items in his head for weeks. If a patient was readmitted after having been out of the hospital for several months, Jesse could recall at once the oddities of the case, the patient's name and family. . . . He was unable to explain this talent of his, which was nothing he had especially desired or had trained himself in, but he was certain of it; it was permanent. And yet this woman was a puzzle to him.

Now she glanced at him, as if accidentally. She saw Jeanne. A kind of smile appeared on her face—tentative and cautious—and as the light changed from red to green she made a movement to step off the curb.

"Wait," said Jesse suddenly, "wait—"

The woman stared at him. She hesitated. Jesse said hello, forcing himself to smile at her, to comfort her—what a beautiful face this young woman had! "Hello, I think we've met," he said. He was so accustomed to ugly people that this girl's beauty was a pleasure to him. He did not want to lose her so quickly.

She said nothing. She looked frankly and curiously at him.

"I'm Jesse Vogel. Don't you remember me?"

He put out his hand. The gesture was so direct that she almost returned it; she almost shook his hand. She stood very still, looking down at Jeanne, up at Jesse again, trying to figure out who this man and his daughter were, her expression still cautious. She had a very fair face, framed by heavy blond hair that was brushed back from her forehead and fell loosely onto her shoulders. It was a thick, exaggerated style. It had the effect of weighing her down. Her face was oval, the bones of her cheeks prominent and somewhat emphasized by the clear, whitish air. Her nose was long, pale, almost white at its tip. There was an impersonal, almost unhuman waxiness to her nose and chin. But her cheekbones were high and fair and of a good color, and her lips were darkened in the bright red style of the day, outlined and filled in with a shade the color of berries. She was a tall woman in her late twenties.

She laughed to disguise her confusion. "Should I know you?" she said.

An airy, girlish voice. Jesse did not recognize it.

"Yes, I'm Jesse Vogel. Dr. Vogel," he said, "and this is my little girl, Jeanne. But you've never met Jeannie.... You and I have met, don't you remember me?"

"Dr. Vogel...?"

She brushed hair out of her eyes. Sighing as if exasperated with herself, or with Jesse, she bent to shake hands with Jeannie, "Hello, Jeannie Vogel," she said in the same airy, insincere voice. "How are you on this windy morning?"

Jeannie pressed against her father's legs, shy.

"I'm afraid I don't remember your name," Jesse said.

"It's Reva."

"Reva...?"

She straightened, laughing. Her gaze moved away from Jesse and onto something behind him, as if she thought all this very crazy, very arrogant. It was clear that she was a woman not afraid of men, that she admired Jesse for his nerve. Jesse smiled deeply, grateful for her laughter and her good clean, even white teeth. Years of asking questions had given him the confident air of an authority who expects to be answered and who must be answered.

"Reva Denk. But I thought you knew me," she said.

"Everything but your name...." Jesse said.

Now they shook hands.

The girl drew her hand back nervously. People passed around them, strangers, nudging them closer together. Jesse felt as if he were close to an important revelation. But—but he could not quite understand what it might be— And now the girl was about to escape him, because there was no reason for her to hesitate any longer; the giddy momentum of their meeting had about run its course, and not even Jeanne's presence could keep her talking to him any longer....

"Well—good-by, Doctor," she said.

She narrowed her eyes mockingly to let him know that he had taken advantage of her. Again Jesse's heart tripped. But—but—

"It's so strange that we've forgotten each other," Jesse said seriously.

He did not smile.

The young woman backed away, no longer smiling, recoiling from his severity. She walked quickly away. Jesse watched her and saw her on the other side of the street, in a jumble of people, glance back at him once and then turn away.

She disappeared.

"Who was that? Why did we stop?" Jeanne whined.

Jesse stooped to pick her up in his arms, feeling he must comfort her. He was strangely excited. His mood was mixed up somehow with the whirling of the bright cool air and the hodgepodge of people around them, all of them strangers. No one knew. No one had seen.

He carried his daughter the half block to Leventhal's office, talking in their private "pet-talk" to her, which pleased her and put all fear out of her mind.

The next morning. Seven forty-five. He was going over an unpleasant case with Dr. Perrault in Perrault's office at the hospital.

At first Perrault sat facing the window, stubborn and squinting in the sunshine. He was a thin man with a cast of features that put Jesse in mind of a statue—a death mask, something from an earlier century, rigidly preserved. Very neat, thinning dark hair, combed back from his sizable forehead, always moist, as if he had just flicked a wet comb through it. There were pale but rather prominent veins on his temples, which jerked as he squinted into the sunlight. Finally he sneezed. Then he shoved his chair angrily over to the window and turned his back to the light. But now Jesse had to shade his eyes in order to look at Perrault.

"I am forcing you to go blind, eh?" Perrault said. He had a husky voice. "Excuse me. I sometimes forget that I'm not alone. It's just as my wife says—I forget that I'm not alone in the universe."

He moved his swivel chair impatiently over to the wall.

"Is that better?" he asked.

"Everything is fine," Jesse said.

"Oh—fine! Yes, everything is fine. Of course."

He let his hand fall heavily on the folder in his lap. A small bitter smile showed itself fleetingly. Perrault had handsome firm lips, the lower lip especially strong. His chin might have been the chin of a much larger man. There was a tightness about it, a severity, that made Jesse think Perrault was always holding himself back, holding his words back.

"Well," Jesse said hesitantly, "there has been some improvement. . . . He should be dead by now."

"Yes. Improvement. That is what we mean by improvement," Perrault said slowly.

He had a deep, throaty voice, almost a whisper. Out of that intimate voice his soul sometimes leaped: Jesse tried not to flinch.

"We knew . . . we knew before we operated. . . ." Jesse said. There were certain words that were always spoken. Saying them was a ritual, a way of growing older. A way of growing fatherly.

Roderick Perrault smiled ironically at Jesse, as if he guessed that Jesse's thoughts and this burden of knowledge, this burden of omniscience, were painful to him. He seemed always to know everything. The skin of his head had tightened with the irony of his total knowledge, emphasizing his small, shrewd, monkeyish skull.

"Yes, we knew before we operated," Perrault said softly. "But either a man dies or he does not die. Nature rebels against these twilight states; there is something obscene and confusing about them. They violate our definitions of reality. Improvement is not a definition. It is a joke, a gag-line. We have improved the man into a swine so that he might lay himself down among the other swine in contentment. Is that what we want, Jesse?"

Jesse stared. The sound of his name on this man's lips—the famous Dr. Perrault, who called no one by his first name—Jesse was Perrault's Chief Resident at LaSalle; he had been awarded this position over at least eight other third-year residents he knew about who had been anxious to assist Perrault, and certainly there had been other applicants he had known nothing about.

"Here. Read this again," Perrault said, handing him the folder.

Jesse had no need to read it, since he had written up most of it. But he opened the folder obediently and scanned the material.

Statsky William. 48. Subarachnoid hemorrhage . . . a right posterior communicating artery aneurysm . . . two days later a second hemorrhage. . . .

Perrault had performed a clean little miracle of a craniotomy; Jesse had assisted him, an eager pair of hands and an eager pair of eyes, precise as a machine. Another resident had stood by. Hours had passed timelessly, drained away like the bright blood,

Perrault's instruments flashing and darting in the intricate maze of a man's brains. Jesse had been hypnotized by the performance.

And now—

A mute patient. Leaden skin. Eyes that would not focus, would not see. *Akinetic with left hemiparesis. Intracranial occlusion....* Pages of melancholy news. Isotope cisternographies, looking like fingerprints blotted with too much ink. Jesse leafed through the report and felt a terrible weariness rise in him.

"And Mrs. Statsky...." Perrault muttered.

He took out a crumpled white handkerchief and blew his nose.

"People live. People die. But in between, in between these two states, they cry out against nature itself, they are obscene and most destructive to a happy interpretation of the universe. I do not wonder at Mrs. Statsky's hatred of me."

"She doesn't hate you," Jesse said at once.

Statsky was the owner of an aluminum company, called Standard Aluminum Products. Over the past several weeks Jesse had spent so much time in Statsky's room that he had begun to feel himself a member of Statsky's big, gregarious, wealthy family, the college kids showing up blunt and breezy in their camel's-hair coats, the sisters teary-eyed and vicious, the wife overcome by furs of cerulean mink, ermine, whatever exotic and foolish skins that were expensive enough for her. Jesse felt how they grabbed at him for his identity, his sympathy, his good will, as if he had some control over Statsky's bad luck, being so close to the great Roderick Perrault.

"Everyone understands that this is no one's fault," Jesse said wearily.

Perrault said nothing. He remained sitting in his swivel chair, hardly moving. Five minutes passed. Another five minutes passed. Jesse adjusted himself to the wait in silence and was prepared for a sudden angry movement on the part of the older man. But Perrault only took a cigarette out of a pack on his desk, moving numbly.

"You don't smoke?"—the eyebrows lifting in polite, distracted surprise.

"No."

"Ah, my good little doctor. My better self. My six-foot self," Perrault said.

He sat for another space of time, without lighting the cigarette. His face was drawn together into a rigid, masklike set of features, terribly lined. Jesse leafed through the folder again, wondering if he had overlooked anything. Here was a story, a short story not yet complete; when would it be complete? Death completed all these reports. A dismissal from the hospital was temporary and unsatisfying, really; only death put an end to questions of health and recovery. *There was once a man named Statsky.* Two years of high school, educated "on his own." Partnership in a meat-packing company. Partnership in a paint company. In asbestos siding. In aluminum siding. Married to a woman with a slurry, intimate voice, an ex-beauty, the daughter of a wealthy Chicago stock specialist. Worth ten, fifteen million.

It made no difference.

Perrault was stroking his forehead without affection. He treated himself rudely. After several minutes he glanced at Jesse, as if just remembering him. "Ah," he said, "you are waiting for our conference on Bruce Dahl."

Dahl was scheduled to be operated on that morning. He had been in the hospital before; in fact, Jesse had been allowed to do much of the work, the removal of a fast-growing tumor. But the tumor had been seeded out of cancer in the left lung and now it had reappeared in the brain. Perrault had become strangely irritated with Dahl.

"Him again! Him again!" Perrault had muttered.

A peculiar desperation to his voice, an almost flighty, flippant anger.

Jesse had wanted to tell Perrault that it was not Dahl's fault that the initial operation had been a failure. Enough that he had lost the whole upper lobe of his left lung. Enough that he had survived a vicious postoperative recovery period, dazed and wasted. He had stepped into Perrault's professional life as a sweet, friendly man, a builder of suburban shopping malls with plans to put great areas of the United States under pavement and temperature-control domes, and his friendliness had subsided in a matter of days to stark, staring, childish pleas to Perrault. *Help me. Save me. If it's a question of money...*

He suffered spectacular seizures, convulsions that involved

the entire body. First his thumb would begin to twitch, then all his fingers, then his entire hand, then his arm . . . and so on through the body . . . and he would have periods of confusion, near blackouts. Though Perrault was always reserved in the presence of his patients and their families, staring much of the time out the window or at the floor, he had been enthusiastic at first about the Dahl case. "I'm going in after it," he had said. "I'm going to send my boy in after it." His face had wrinkled up with a muscular, intense joy.

Then it had been discovered that Dahl had cancer in the lung, and Perrault had been crushed as a disappointed lover. He had been betrayed.

It was not likely that the cancer had seeded only a single cell to the brain, so it would be another dark plunge for Perrault, another probable disappointment. He would be left ironic and round-shouldered after hours of work. He had given most of the original job to Jesse and had assisted him, though brusquely, through the long operation. Jesse understood that he had done well, that he had held up well. It did not seem fair now that Dahl should be readmitted with the same problem. Another metastatic lesion in the brain! Another! And so quickly!

"I think I'm ready for it," Jesse said quietly.

"We will make a ritual of it. Mr. Dahl on the first of every month as long as his cash holds out," Perrault said.

His sarcasm was rude, blunt, painful. Yet Jesse smiled blindly into it, as if into a blazing light. He was Roderick Perrault's assistant! He told himself this fact a dozen times a day. He woke each morning very early, with a sense of wonderment, a sense of being blessed. All the years of his life had brought him to this, this almost unbelievable good fortune— He admired Perrault, worshipped Perrault. Let the old man say anything. His words did not matter.

Years ago he had hoped only to do a residency in General Medicine and to work in a clinic, probably in Chicago, dealing with multitudes of ordinary sick people. Bulletins from the Federal government and from the states argued monthly for the need of such doctors. What a shortage of doctors there was, and how much worse it would be in another decade! Jesse had believed he could manage a clinic. Then, as time passed, he had discovered in himself a growing need, a yearning, for what was most difficult, most challenging. Ordinary sicknesses were cured ordinarily. Ordinary chronic sicknesses continued month after month, year after year, ordinarily. When he put in his time as a surgical assistant he discovered that this kind of work, which had not appealed to him, which was so bloody and private and precise, was what gave him most satisfaction. He had come to the attention of Perrault himself. A few words of praise by one of the surgeons, someone's surprise at Jesse's thoroughness.... He had been drawn into Perrault's circle, unresisting.

The inviolable nature of the operating room fascinated him. The timelessness, the intimacy, the conversational bickering and joking that showed how trivial human language was, after all, compared to the work of a surgeon's hands... the way the self was concentrated, fiercely, in the fingertips.... When he operated under Perrault's guidance he felt his own fingers drawing out of himself his deepest, numbest, least personal self, and out of the older man, power that was pure control, unimagined until this time.

He was subordinated to it, to this power. He could have explained it to no one, not even his wife, not even his father-in-law—who was very pleased at his decision to stay on for additional years of residency in surgery. He could not have explained it even to Perrault, especially not to Perrault. He was subordinated to this sense of pure, impersonal, brute control, a control of the nerves and the finest muscles: he imagined the waves of his own brain subsiding to a greater pattern, that of Perrault's, adjusting themselves to his. He felt at times, in the privacy of Perrault's office, the approach of a dramatic, dangerous moment—a revelation of some kind; the possibility that Perrault might speak to him without irony, frankly, clearly, perhaps with love; the possibility that Perrault might suddenly reach out across his cluttered desk, his long nimble fingers stretched out to Jesse, to Jesse's own extended fingers—

What if their fingers touched, like that? Innocently and frankly, like that?

On his way to examine a patient he sometimes felt a sense of fear, of childish apprehension. Had he really dug into someone's brain, had Jesse Vogel really been picking around in a human being's brain? Small, violent shudders passed over him at the thought of his audacity. He had to tell himself again and again what Perrault seemed to know by instinct and would never have thought of explaining: that the human brain was not sacred. It was not sacred, it was touchable. It was matter. Like anything else: matter, mass, weight, substance, a weighable and measurable thing. Beneath the thumb it could be squeezed and prodded like anything else. Once dead, it was dead permanently: it was no miracle in creation. There was nothing to fear.

But he feared it. He feared himself, the possibility of making a mistake... it would be so easy to make a mistake.... Perrault, who never made mistakes, could not understand. It would have been pointless to talk to him. Since Jesse's first days at LaSalle he had been hearing of Perrault's indifference, his coolness, his impersonal precision. He lectured his residents in full hearing of his patients, working with a pin to demonstrate where feeling began in a patient's face or body. "And now here, you see, here it is dead," he would say in his low, confidential voice, jabbing someone's cheek. "See? Dead. Nothing. Inert. But here—here pain begins—here is life," he would say, as the patient flinched or cried out. "Life begins with pain," he would say. "Life is pain. Pain is life. Do you understand?"

When Jesse was named Chief Resident, one of the men he had beaten out was his friend Jack Galt; but Jack had said bitterly that he hadn't really wanted to work with Perrault anyway, he had not really wanted to become known as one of Roderick Perrault's men: "A copy of a copy of a human being." Jesse had flushed with anger. Helene, hearing this remark, had assured him that Jack had been speaking only out of jealousy and disappointment. Wasn't everyone jealous of Jesse now? And whose fault was that? *A copy of a copy of a human being.* Perhaps it was true. But Jesse had set out to copy the man, reproducing in his work as a surgeon Perrault's flawless technique, so that Perrault came to trust him and no one else. He even called him Jesse. He spoke ironically and fondly of him. In Jesse's hearing he said once that he trusted Dr. Vogel because "when Dr. Vogel operates it is myself operating, my six-foot self." Sometimes he joked with the nurses, sometimes he was silent and bullying with them, sometimes he teased the other assistants and the anesthetists;

but beneath his surface abrasiveness Jesse guessed at a deeper, droller, even lyric abrasiveness, seeded everywhere in Perrault's system.

"After my most miserable days I go home and play the harpsichord," Perrault was saying, lighting his cigarette in a series of quick, finicky motions. "I recommend it to you, Dr. Vogel."

Jesse smiled self-consciously.

"But of course you have a private life of your own, a domestic life. Your wife and daughter—or is it son?"

"Daughter."

"Ah, yes. Fine," Perrault said vaguely. When he tried to be courteous, his vision seemed to slip out of focus, his eyes' luster seemed to fade. Jesse did not know whether to be insulted or amused by this. "Yes, domestic life . . . real life. . . . We must all catch up on it whenever possible. So you are prepped up for our Mr. Dahl? And you are anxious to repeat your excellent performance?"

Jesse nodded. If Perrault meant this remark to be ironic, Jesse would not acknowledge it.

"I hope so," he said.

"And tomorrow at nine there is Mrs. Miller. You are going to save some of your inspiration for Mrs. Miller?"

"Yes."

Perrault rubbed his hands together enthusiastically. "I have a feeling about her, that left eye. We'll go in there and fix it, eh?" Mrs. Miller was a woman in her late thirties with headaches and partial blindness; she was an echo of a similar case Perrault had handled the year before, when Jesse had only watched, a case of deteriorating vision that had been fixed up in three long operations, Perrault at the top of his form, triumphant. The story had come to a temporary completion with the patient's return to normal, to normal vision: an unexpected bonus! Perrault had presented the case at an international conference not long ago. He felt great affection for that patient, though he could never remember the name correctly and would not have recognized the man if he had walked into his office and shook hands with him. But the affection was real enough.

Time to leave.

Perrault had fallen silent and Jesse understood that he wished to be alone. Jesse excused himself and went to the locker room to scrub for the Dahl case. He had never felt more excited, more sure of himself. It was a spring day: his future awaited him. Since the day Jeanne had been born life had begun to ascend, moving upward as though he were charting it himself, a boy with a pencil and a map. A map that showed the surface of the land, extending up into the atmosphere, into the mysterious clouds and the mysterious dimension above the clouds. . . . It was true that certain things had happened in the last three years that had made his life difficult, things that had troubled his marriage —Helene had had a miscarriage a year ago, and Jesse was in debt now to her father for $6000, and their tentative love-making sometimes faded into vague questioning murmurs and these murmurs into a baffled silence—but still Jesse understood that his life was in his control and that he was ascending. If he worked as hard as he had in the past, if he trusted to Perrault's guidance, he would be saved.

Nine-thirty. Perrault appeared gloved and gowned, soundless on his small feet, as deft as a moth or any colorless winged creature. He assisted Jesse. Jesse worked swiftly and mechanically. At one point the blood made a strange spluttering noise and Jesse found himself thinking of that woman he had met downtown the other day—that woman with the blond hair and the mocking, knowing smile— "Faster. Work faster," Perrault said. He was always a little nervous when he was not in control himself; Jesse expected this and did not allow it to upset him. "Why are you standing like that, in a crouch? Is that a crouch? You make my shoulders ache, watching you," Perrault said peevishly.

Jesse kept on, nodding silently.

It was Perrault's habit to bother Jesse for the first hour or so, because he was nervous or restless, or because he truly found fault with Jesse's methodical work; then it was his habit to suddenly lose interest, to grow visibly bored. Jesse understood this and waited. While Perrault picked at him he pretended to be unmoved, but really he was tense in every part of his body, filled with an excitement that could discharge itself only through his fingertips; he felt that if it did not discharge itself that way, perfectly, he would die.

"All right. That looks good. That will do," Perrault said casually.

The operation must have taken a long time. Jesse had become drenched with perspiration. Weak. Shaky. Out in the corridor Perrault shook his hand and said, "It was a good academic exercise, my friend," and smiled in a ghastly, confidential way, so that Jesse really understood for the first time that Dahl was going to die.

Jesse stared after him. The young resident who had assisted, who had been given nothing to do by Perrault and had only stood around for several hours, shifting his weight from foot to foot, now came up to Jesse to congratulate him. He was a dark, dour young man Jesse's age, ambitious and prying; his name was Lyle and Jesse understood that he was very jealous.

"The old man was edgy today," Lyle said.

"He was all right," Jesse said.

"Didn't want to touch Dahl himself, huh?"

"That's probably it."

In the locker room Jesse undressed and suddenly felt very sad, inert.

"I think you did a good job," Lyle said. "Even if he does die. . . ."

Jesse nodded.

"Maybe he'll die of pneumonia, huh, and that will sound better to his family. . . ."

Jesse showered. The hours were washed from him—close, tedious, painful work—the hours of intimacy with that open skull, the instruments, the presence of Perrault close by— He wanted to be back in the operating room. He wanted to relive the operation. Step by step, each movement of his, each teasing little remark of Perrault's. . . . But he must go home. Must hurry home. He had promised to take his daughter out to the park; Helene hadn't felt well enough to take her out for several days, and she loved the park. . . . But he yearned to be back in the operating room, to do over again the Dahl operation, or to begin at once on Mrs. Miller and her giant aneurysm, under Perrault's watchful eye. . . .

On his way out he caught sight of a telephone booth. He went into it and leafed through the directory. *Denk, Denk, Denk. . . .* He could not find her name. Was it Reva? Did he remember it correctly? *Reva Denk.* A puzzling name. He did not know if it was ugly or not. It was soft, soothing, and then hard as a clamp; it was girlish and then abruptly masculine, airy and then heavy as dirt. Airy. Heavy. The scattering of a shovelful of dirt in the air; then the plopping of this dirt on the ground. An opening and then a closing, as if jaws were clamped together. *Reva Denk.*

He couldn't find her name. It didn't exist. He was relieved and decided to forget her: he must go home and take his daughter out for a walk, and in the morning he must return to Perrault and to the operating room.

10

Jesse awoke that night out of a heavy, troubled sleep. He awoke to a certain thought; two years before, on a routine night duty, he had taken care of a man brought into Emergency with a bullet in his leg. It had been no more than a flesh wound but there had been a lot of blood and excitement and the police had been involved; once out of the hospital, the man had sent Jesse his business card with a hundred-dollar bill clipped to it. The card had said *A. A. Lowe, Private Investigator.*

Jesse had wanted to return the money, but finally kept it though he was to think, off and on, of his acceptance as something shameful. He had thrown away the card. But evidently he had remembered the name and in the morning he telephoned Lowe from the hospital.... Lowe remembered him at once and kept interrupting Jesse to thank him for having saved his life. "Any favor I can do for you would be great, just great," Lowe said loudly. "It isn't as if the class of people I get in my business is so hot; I mean, I could stand to mix with more cultured people like doctors...." Jesse asked him if he could locate a certain young woman for him. "Just tell me her name," Lowe said. "Anybody that saved my life is certainly worth a solid week of my time, I mean that, I don't say things I don't mean," he said, though Jesse tried to explain that his life had never been in danger, that his wound had been a superficial one. "Just tell me her name, Doctor. Maybe I got a file on her already. It's a small town, you'd be surprised, there's women that two, three, maybe four guys are sometimes hunting down at the same time—I could write a book on some of these cases! Look, there's nobody I admire in this world more than doctors. You got to hand it to all of them. I imagine your family is pretty proud of you, Doctor."

Jesse wondered if he should hang up.

"Well, Doctor, what is her name? The young lady's name?"

"Reva Denk," Jesse said.

"Give me twenty-four hours," said Lowe.

He telephoned Jesse back that very afternoon: he had Reva Denk's telephone number and her present address.

"Okay, you want to know about her private life?" Lowe said.

"No. No thank you," Jesse said quickly.

"Any names you want mentioned? You know—names of guys, and all that? Sometimes it helps, with a case like this, to sort of drop names around them, you know—let them know you're not so stupid, they're not pulling anything over on you. I could maybe just give you a couple of names for you to let fall accidentally—"

"No, that's all right. That isn't necessary," said Jesse.

"Her age, at least? You want to know that, don't you?"

Jesse hesitated. Then he said, "No, not even that."

As soon as he hung up, he dialed the number Lowe had given him. A woman answered sleepily.

"Is this Reva?" he said.

His heart leaped again as it had out on the street that day.

"Yes?"

"This is Jesse Vogel calling. You remember—?"

"Who?"

"Jesse Vogel."

A pause. Then she said slowly, "You mean Dr. Vogel? *You?*"

"Do you remember me?"

"Only from out on the street. Only that one meeting," she said faintly.

"Well."

She said nothing.

Jesse closed his eyes and a series of faces floated in his vision—his wife's surprised face, his daughter's face, the faces of Cady, of Perrault, shadowy faces that could not be identified but that belonged to Jesse, to his confused past. He tried to summon up this woman's face in order to blot out those other faces. But her sudden closeness, her breathy cautious voice, blocked him; he was so close to her that he could not see her. She seemed to be inside his head.

"I would like to see you sometime soon," Jesse said, his eyes still closed.

"I don't think so, no."

"But—why not?"

He remembered now her airiness, the thin curve of her eyebrow. A glow to her skin like the flesh of flowers, petals, which has no depth. He felt that he was breathing in her secrecy over the telephone.

"Why not, Reva? I want to talk to you. I only want to talk. . . ."

"I don't think so."

He wanted her, and a kind of peevish, childish rage rose in him that he would be denied her: he had wanted so few things in his life!

"I would like to talk to you," he said, his voice faltering so that he did not sound like Dr. Vogel at all. He sounded like one of Perrault's patients, appealing behind Perrault's back to him, Jesse, for help, advice, aid, sympathy, the real truth. But the real truth was always inaccessible. "It wouldn't involve much time—an hour or two—"

"Why are you calling me at this time? What time is it . . . ? I just woke up."

"It's after five o'clock."

"In the afternoon . . . ? But why are you calling now? Oh, I see what time it is, that's strange. . . . Who are you exactly?"

"I'm sorry if I woke you up, I'm sorry for bothering you. . . ."

"My life is too complicated right now," she said. He felt her straining to be polite; there was a kind of musical generosity in her voice. "This is a bad time to be calling me, even if I did know you. What exactly do you want? And how did you get this number?—it isn't my number and it isn't even listed! But I won't be angry with you. I just don't understand."

"There is a reason I want to see you," Jesse said.

She laughed nervously. "But please believe me, my life is too complicated right now. Don't come into it. Why do you . . . why do you want to come into it? No, it's impossible. I have to hang up now."

"No, wait—"

"But what do you want? What do you want?" He could imagine her face growing harder, sharper. That pallor beneath the powdery sheen of her young skin growing frightened. He did not want to frighten her, but it was at least a way of forcing her to listen to him.

"I only want to talk to you. I think there is something . . . there is something about you. . . . I can't explain," he said slowly, "I mean over the telephone like this, but I'm very serious, this isn't anything trivial or impulsive. . . ."

"Do you know me, have we met? But where have we met?"

"I can't remember."

"I can't remember either. I think you're lying."

Jesse was shocked. He thought her disappointing and vulgar. "But—why would I lie? I'm not lying," he said sharply, "I don't lie."

"I have to hang up now."

"When can I see you?"

"There isn't time for this. And you're married, you have a daughter. Don't forget I saw your daughter."

"Why isn't there time? I won't take up much time. I think that something might become clear if I could meet you again, if . . ."

"But, but, but—then you might want to see me again after that!"

"No, just this once. Tomorrow?"

"I don't know."

A sense of peace, of sudden stillness came over Jesse: she would see him. He knew it.

"At noon tomorrow?" Jesse said.

"But that's so soon . . . I don't know. . . . My life is very complicated and this just makes it worse. When anyone comes into my life someone else has to go out of it, someone has to be eliminated . . . I can't afford to bring you into my life or even to think about you right now. . . ."

She seemed so helpless, in spite of her cool, cautious tone; she seemed to be thinking as she spoke. He felt as if he were somehow inside her head, drifting with the impulsive currents of her thought.

"You don't have to think about me at all," Jesse said. "Just see me. That's all. I won't make any trouble for you."

"But out on the street you looked so serious, you were so . . . so assertive, so sure of yourself. I don't know. There isn't room in my life for you right now, it isn't anything personal, but this is a very bad time. . . ."

She laughed.

Jesse smiled.

"Let me come over tomorrow at noon," Jesse said.

"Over where? Here? But how do you know where I live?" she said.

"I could meet you somewhere else then."

"All right, for half an hour. All right."

"Thank you," Jesse said weakly.

They arranged a meeting, and after he hung up he grimaced at his reflection in the door of the telephone booth. A surreptitious, criminal face, Jesse's intangible face, as smeared as his soul. No clarity to this, to his pounding heart. No dignity to it. Adultery. *Adultery.* He wanted to remember this feeling of degradation, of shame; it would help him to dislike Reva.

He ran from the telephone booth to check on Bruce Dahl: no change. Tubes, wheezing breath, ashen skin. He talked to the nurse on duty, who told him that Mrs. Dahl was on her way —she'd gone home for a few hours—and Jesse thought that he must escape quickly or he would have to talk to her, no way to avoid a fifteen-minute session of hysteria. But as he thought this he deliberately stayed behind, talking to the nurse, giving her orders to call him at once if anything went wrong . . . he deliberately lingered until it was too late and Mrs. Dahl rushed into the room, her coat unbuttoned. Jesse was thankful for the long white clinical coat he wore. It seemed to protect him from the flurry of such women, such grieving wives. At once she asked him about Perrault. Where was he? Why wouldn't he talk to her? A serious case was being flown in for Perrault to work with early the next morning; a young girl from Mexico. Perrault was very busy. "I call his office but the nurse won't let me talk to him. I can't understand this," Mrs. Dahl said angrily. Jesse tried to explain that Perrault was very busy, very busy, and for a man his age . . . he wore himself out as it was, he exhausted himself, he did far too much. . . .

"How early should I get here? I'll stay here all night," Mrs. Dahl said. "Tell me. Just tell me. What about *that*—" she said, gesturing toward her husband, "what about *him*? You tell me. I'll get here at eight in the morning, no, at six. I'll stay here all night if that's what it takes to talk to him. . . ."

"I'm sure he'll talk to you tomorrow morning," Jesse said.

"I hope so. Yes, I hope so," Mrs. Dahl said.

She had the crow's-feet, the hacking shadowy cough of a widow; even her large body, gowned in black, looked ponderous and stilled as if at a graveside. Jesse wished that she would not keep glaring at her husband, who was unconscious, hooked up with i.v. fluids and wasted to about a hundred and ten pounds, a long flat lump in bed. It would have been simpler for Mrs. Dahl to go home and forget all this, Jesse thought miserably, but how could he tell her that?

After this he checked Perrault's other patients, then went home, where he had to begin working up a presentation Perrault had asked him to make the next morning at one of the hospital conferences; he was up most of the night going over his notes and rereading certain articles Perrault had given him. He woke Helene at five o'clock to read her part of what he had written—he was anxious to do well, he was a little worried about Perrault's opinion of him. "Why didn't he give you more time for this?" Helene asked bitterly. "I have enough time," Jesse said. "You always defend him. You defend him mechanically, without thinking," Helene said.

As Perrault's assistant at the hospital Jesse was responsible for the work of all the other residents in Surgery; he had to help Perrault with every case, following patients from admission to surgery to discharge, writing up histories, keeping their records up to date, writing orders for their tests and medications, checking on them twice a day, intervening between Perrault and Perrault's many enemies. . . . He was hounded by Perrault's small wizened shrewd face, by his raspy voice, by his nuances and frictions and imaginings. It was not enough that Jesse had to keep sick people alive. He had to intervene between Perrault and anxious, desperate, demanding families; he had to calm down women like Mrs. Dahl, he had to pick up the pieces after Perrault, always in a hurry, blurted out to a worried husband or wife that "the case is hopeless—you came to me too late—" and went on to the next patient. He had to be pawed by weeping men and women whom Perrault was always eluding. And he had to intervene between Perrault and other staff men with whom the old man was always quarreling; there were squabbles that went back for a decade, squabbles that made no sense to Jesse but that he had had to enter vaguely, reluctantly. Perrault had a habit of scrawling angry remarks on little yellow slips of paper and leaving them for other doctors and nurses. Jesse had to sort out all this trouble and make sense of it. He spent time running down to the x-ray suite because Perrault was especially insulting to the x-ray technicians. He spent time trying to straighten out misunderstandings with nurses, to whom Perrault spoke dryly and impatiently, without bothering to look at them. . . . Jesse spent time apologizing, trying to apologize, trying to explain, straightening up the disorder that Perrault caused in his demand for absolute order.

He had to represent Perrault in triumph at presentations like this: *Polymyoclonia with Opsoclonus.* That was the title of the case.

"He treats you like a servant," Helene said.

"No," said Jesse.

Never impatient. Never angry. And he did not expect, as other assistants of Perrault's had expected in the past, to be taken on as a junior partner in Perrault's practice. That was a traditional joke around the hospital—Perrault's assistants were always led to believe that he might take them on permanently, they sacrificed everything for him, and at the end of their residencies he simply said good-by to them.

Jesse got some sleep, dreamed of Reva, woke and showered and went to the hospital early. He had written a little case study called *Polymyoclonia with Opsoclonus.* The words continued to unfold in his head, confused with the vague dream of Reva Denk; words flowing backward and forward; Jesse in his hospital outfit thinking of *The Tragedy of Joseph Ross,* which should have been the real title of his paper but was not; the title was *Polymyoclonia with Opsoclonus.* No tragedy. Perrault did not believe in tragedy.

Jesse had a few minutes before the meeting began, so he looked in upon Mr. Dahl—still the same—maybe a little worse—*a good academic exercise.* Mrs. Dahl hovering nearby, waiting to trap Perrault. Jesse escaped her and went down to the conference room, where people were gathering; Perrault himself punctual and urbane, dressed in a dark blue pin-stripe suit that was several years out of fashion. Joseph Ross had been one of Perrault's satisfying cases; he had been a case that had made sense in Perrault's terms. No tragedy involved. The words Jesse had written the night before flowed backward and forward in his mind. He had been dreaming of them. He had been dreaming of Joseph Ross and of Reva. Was the dream completed? Perrault put his hand up on Jesse's shoulder and complained to him about something. Jesse ducked his head and listened. Nervous, proud to be seen by the rest of the staff like this, embarrassed, uncertain of how to respond.... *He treats you like a servant,* Helene was always saying. She did not understand. If she could have seen Perrault whispering into Jesse's ear now she would not understand. Jesse was a survivor. Jesse did not have a personality. He did not want a personality. His heartbeat told him always: *here you are, here is Jesse, a survivor.* One by one the men around Jesse, the men his own age, had disappeared. Their personalities had disappeared. Some had gone into private practice, some had gone to other hospitals because they had not been advanced at LaSalle. Jesse knew why they hadn't been asked to stay. Jack Galt had gone to Seattle, to continue his residency in surgery; Milt Kuzma had settled for private general practice somewhere in southern Illinois, where there wasn't much competition; Myron Diebold was an internist in Evanston, doing fairly well but frantic with the competition. Jesse alone had been asked to stay on for this fourth-year residency, Jesse alone had come to the attention of Roderick Perrault....

Unlike Joseph Ross, he was a survivor.

Time to begin. He started to talk about the case, conscious of Perrault's immediate restlessness; conscious of smoke in the air, of interns whispering somewhere in the back of the room, like schoolboys. Here is the story of Joseph Ross, seventeen-year-old Caucasian, referred to Dr. Perrault March 1, 1954, with complaints of vomiting, headache, difficulty in walking, jerking eye movements, decreased energy, depression.... A diary of Joseph Ross's miseries: April 4, April 11, April 14, April 17.... Jesse had spent many hours with Joseph Ross and with his parents. Many hours. *Eyes: horizontal conjugate oscillations.* He had come to like Joseph Ross. *Paroxysms. Laboratory tests normal; electroencephalogram normal.* Jesse felt Perrault's eye sharply upon him; he wondered if he was speaking too rapidly, too nervously. Not presenting the case clearly, not clearly... the staff could not see Joseph Ross's face, could not imagine him... someone was snuffing out a cigarette butt inside an empty paper coffee cup. *Therapy. Brief episodes of oscillopsia. Pneumoencephalogram: posterior fossa tumor. Craniotomy, therapy.* Joseph Ross, tube-fed and lying meekly beneath Perrault's contemplative gaze. His skin sore from the bedclothes. A victim. A victim hit and then cured. Operated upon, cured. *Postoperative period marked by surprising return of normal reflexes. Neurological examination normal except for mild unsteadiness in tandem walking.* Now Joseph Ross could walk normally across a room; if Jesse or any doctor were to hammer at his knee he would respond with the proper little kick. A good patient. Intelligent. Humble. Terrified.

The presentation came to an end; a few questions; Perrault frowned with a kind of reluctant pleasure; evidently the talk had gone well. Jesse was anxious to get out. One of Perrault's old enemies approached him afterward, coffee cup in hand. "Has Perrault been seeing the boy regularly since then?" he asked. "I don't think so," Jesse said.

Out of courtesy, the man asked nothing more.

Now his mind careened ahead to the meeting with Reva. She had told him to meet her at the corner of Adams and Michigan. Something came up at the last minute and Jesse was ten minutes late, vexed, worried that she would have come and gone. He waited on the corner. Stared over at the Art Institute—he had wanted to go there for years, since he'd first moved to Chicago, but for some reason he had never had time. His nervousness increased, almost to panic. He had wanted so few things in his life.... He had dreamed about Reva but he could not remember the dream. Maybe it wasn't over yet. He had lain beside his wife and dreamed of Reva and of Joseph Ross, *a skull opened to expose the brain,* and maybe tonight he would dream of Mrs. Miller, yesterday's case, and Mr. Dahl, *a skull opened to expose the brain,* any brain. When Jesse told his wife that he loved her, he was telling the truth. Those words were the truth. *I love you,* he told her. Mrs. Dahl had pawed at his arm again that morning. A face flabby with stale grief. Did Mrs. Dahl love Mr. Dahl now? Liver going, I.Q. gone, perception impulses shot. Married love. Mrs. Dahl loved the man in that room because he was her husband, assigned to her. A certain bulk of flesh assigned to her. Blind. Mute: no arguments. Jesse thought of Reva, and all these people, these faces, were swept out of his head.

At a quarter to one a limousine pulled over to the curb near Jesse. An absurd, giant car, manned by a chauffeur with a thatch of silver hair. This man got out as if to display himself on the sidewalk—the hair brilliantly silver but much too long, almost like a girl's. He wore no conventional uniform, only black trousers and a black pullover sweater with short sleeves, stretched tight across his fat chest and stomach and arms. This man approached Jesse. "Dr. Vogel?" he said politely. His accent was Southern. Jesse blinked away his surprise and stooped to see who was in the back seat of the car—was it Reva?—and saw a woman he supposed must be she, though he would not have recognized her because she looked so different.

The chauffeur opened the back door for him.

No, he wouldn't have recognized her. Her hair was up, coiled around her head; her white outfit blinded him. "Hello," Jesse said nervously. "Hello," she said.

Smiling. She was pleased with herself. Cunning and remote, safe from him in spite of their sudden, jarring closeness. He was sitting so very close to her. . . . "I thought we'd just drive around, because I have an appointment in a little while," she said.

"When?"

"In a little while."

Jesse stared at her, too confused to be disappointed.

"But how long will it be . . . ?"

Reva laughed. "You ask too many questions. Why are you so strange? If you knew all the trouble I went to just to see you today! I have a thousand things on my mind, I have to buy things, I have a long list of things to check off. I'm getting ready to go on a trip. See—" And she did an extraordinary thing, which Jesse was to remember often: she opened the white coat to expose her upper arm, where there was a small pink needle-prick. She opened her coat so quickly, intimately, as if Jesse were an old friend, and then she primly closed the coat again.

"It only hurts a little. Nothing much," she said.

Jesse stared. "But I thought we were going to have lunch.... I thought we'd be alone, we'd have time to talk...."

"*He* can't hear us, say anything you want. But I can't spend much time with you. I'm sorry. I'm leaving for Italy Saturday morning."

"Italy."

"Yes, Italy."

"By yourself?"

"No."

"But—when will you be back?"

"Then we're going to Majorca. I don't know when we'll be back, exactly. Maybe in the fall."

"You're going to be gone that long?"

"Yes," she said, smiling oddly. "Why do you look so disappointed? You and I aren't friends. We don't know each other. You don't have the right to look disappointed," she said, laughing. "Was that little girl really your own child?"

"Yes," Jesse said. "And we're expecting another baby in three months...."

Reva laughed, delighted. "And you tell me that so honestly!"

"Why shouldn't I tell you?"

"You talk like a doctor, you're so honest and sincere. Would you tell me if I had cancer?"

"Cancer... ?"

She was so guarded and beautiful that he could not really see her. He kept staring at her but somehow he did not see her. Her beauty was extraordinary. The white outfit, the hair wound up around her head in a long heavy braid, as if she were wearing a crown, hair brushed down thick on her forehead, so low that her eyebrows were nearly covered... a gold necklace, or necklaces, a confusion of golden chains dotted with small pearls.... She looked foreign. Barbaric. Her skin, which Jesse had remembered being pale, was now healthy, girlish. She moved her arm and something rattled—small gold bracelets. And her fingers, which she extended to him in a teasing little gesture, patting his arm in mock consolation, were covered with rings today—four rings—solid gold and silver bands studded with small pearls and diamonds. The back of Jesse's head crawled. He could only stare at her. While she chattered he could not even listen to her.... How to stop from dissolving in the back seat of this limousine? How to keep up the mask of his face?

"Don't stare at me. Please," Reva said.

"But...what is all this? This car? Who does it belong to?" Jesse asked weakly. "Who are you going to Italy with?"

"A friend of mine."

"Who?"

"I'm in love," Reva said shyly.

"In love...?"

Jesse forced himself to think clearly: she is not a possibility. She is already in love.

"Yes, in love, is that so strange? You're married, aren't you?"

Jesse nodded vaguely. So she was not free, she belonged to someone else. He wondered why he had arranged to meet her and why he was being driven around downtown in the back seat of this great ludicrous car, a hearse-like car, when he had so much to do at the hospital.

"What is your marriage like?" Reva asked.

"An ordinary marriage. A good marriage," Jesse said.

"Your wife is going to have another baby?"

"Yes, a baby, another baby, a second baby. Yes, in three months. I'm permanently married," he said slowly. He heard his voice but could not have predicted what it might say. "You don't think you'll be back until fall?"

"I don't know. Are you a doctor now or just in training?"

"I'm finishing my residency. In surgery."

"Surgery...?"

The heavy crown of hair seemed too much for her fragile head and neck. But her posture was perfect, even a little exaggerated, as if she, like Jesse, were very excited and self-conscious. She had begun to remind him of a typical woman patient, a young woman aware of him as a man, too aware, too intense.

"What I would like to have happen to me," Jesse said, talking freely and helplessly, "is to be invited to stay on with the man

I'm assisting... to join him in his private practice.... But I'm very much in debt, I owe my father-in-law a lot of money, I..."

Reva, stared at him in silence. He wondered what he had just said: something about money? Why had he mentioned that?

"You're going to be a surgeon?" Reva said.

"A neurosurgeon."

"Ah," she said, as if she had guessed this. She stared at him doubtfully.

"Of course," Jesse said quickly, "if I had enough money maybe I'd forget about all that and take you to Italy myself... I've never seen Italy... in fact, I've never seen anything, I don't know anything except medicine and surgery.... I don't know anything at all."

Reva shook her head. He wondered if she suddenly thought him a bad risk.

"The last man I was with," she said slowly, "was always going to the doctor, but it didn't help too much. He was always imagining he was sick. Then when he drove to Detroit to see his mother one day he had an accident, he collided with a trailer-truck and was killed...."

"Who? Who was this?" Jesse asked in distress.

"Oh, someone. A man." Reva frowned. "I want to tell you about myself so you'll know that I'm not interested in you. I'm being very honest. It isn't because I'm in love and my life is taken care of now, really there couldn't be anything between us because ... because what you do frightens me, the idea of surgery frightens me.... The way you look at me is frightening too. That man, the one who got killed in the accident, was just an ordinary man and didn't even have much of an education, but I loved him."

"He got killed?"

"Yes, I told you. On the way to Detroit. After that I spent a few months alone, not wanting to see anyone. I finally got over it. I managed to get over it, and now my life has changed again.... You know," she said suddenly, "I remember now where I met you."

"Where?"

"But you don't remember... ?"

"Where was it? When?"

She smiled slyly, broadly. Jesse was excited by that smile, which seemed to him both delicate and barbaric—the dazzling white teeth, the moistened lips, the flawless, elastic skin! Her beauty was preposterous. Like this big, silent, handsome automobile; like the silver-haired chauffeur behind the glass partition. Preposterous. Yet he wanted only to get closer to her, to feel her fingers again on his arm, so lightly and mockingly. He wanted to take hold of her shoulders and look her full in the face. His body prickled with an excitement that was generalized, many-branched, a push of great animal impatience behind his skin.

"Aren't you going to tell me?" Jesse said in anguish.

"You'll remember."

"Why won't you tell me?"

"You'll remember in a while. After you leave me."

"But how much time do I have? Are you in a hurry? I know you're in a hurry, yes, and I shouldn't be bothering you, but... When are you going away?"

"In a few days."

"I won't be able to see you again before you leave...?

"No."

"When exactly are you leaving?"

She made a short, negative gesture with her hand, putting him off. He had said too much. He was too eager. Her dismissal hurt him, but he only smiled and said at once, "The driver can leave me off anywhere he wants. This corner is fine."

"It's because my life is too crowded right now," Reva said vaguely.

Jesse shook his head as if to clear it. *If she only understood....* But she would have recoiled from him, from his desire. It was loaded with blood.

"Yes, he can let me off, anywhere is fine. Someone is dying back there. I shouldn't have left," Jesse said.

"Dying? Where?"

"At LaSalle."

She looked at him doubtfully. "Someone you operated on?"

"Yes. I'm afraid he won't make it. His wife is hysterical but I don't have time for it," Jesse said, "I don't have time for anyone's hysteria.... People have to die, it's like a door they must take, but they have so much trouble choosing the door and getting it open and walking through the doorway. Yes, you say my work frightens you, I know that, it frightens me too . . . I understand that. . . . And another thing, another patient, I'm thinking of another patient I had got to know. . . ."

"Who was that?"

"A boy, seventeen years old."

"Is he going to die too?"

He saw that she was suspended in a kind of breathlessness, a counterfeit fear. Or was it real? A woman's natural reaction to such words, as mechanical a reaction as Jesse's desire to seize her. She had been turning one of her thick rings around her finger and it almost came off—slid to the end of her finger—and Jesse reached out to catch it from falling, feeling her sudden alarm in all of his body. But the ring did not fall. She pushed it quickly back onto her finger and it was safe.

"He's only seventeen and he's sick . . . ?" she asked.

"No, he's well again. He had a hard time but he survived. A very strange disorder, complicated by a tumor . . . a benign tumor . . . but it did him in anyway. . . . I got to like him. I liked him."

"What happened?"

"He's become schizophrenic."

"Oh—what?"

"Schizophrenic. Insane."

"But that had nothing to do with you, did it . . . ?"

"No, nothing to do with me. Nothing to do with us," Jesse said. He sighed. "All the tests, the operation, lying in bed for so long . . . he gave up and we couldn't argue him out of it. . . . Still, the treatment was a success. We were all pleased with it."

She frowned, as if his mood displeased her. Jesse tried to smile, gallantly, mockingly, because he felt now that he had made this woman hate him and there was nothing for him to lose.

"Thank you for talking with me," he said.

"But was it worth it? Did you get out of this what you wanted?"

She seemed sincere. Her brown eyes were fixed upon him frankly. He wanted to take her head in his hands, cradle it in his hands.

"No," he said.

When he got back to the hospital it was after two. He arrived at Dahl's room just in time to pronounce him dead.

11

"But why do such a thing?"

"That's a strange question."

"To preserve life at such a cost.... And what kind of life would it be? Your services go to the highest bidder, don't they?"

"But the highest bidder would be the United States Government," Perrault said.

He looked around the table, elfin and cheerful. He hadn't eaten much, hadn't touched his wine. His gaze kept moving onto Jesse as if teasing him, taunting him, and Jesse himself had had no appetite.

What did Perrault want from him?

Cady said, "Absolutely true."

Jesse and Helene and Helene's father had been invited to the Perraults' home for the evening. So far as Jesse knew, no one from the hospital had ever been invited there before. No one had seen Perrault's wife for years. Jesse had happened to mention to Perrault that his father-in-law was going to be in Chicago, and Perrault's secretary had telephoned Helene the next day. It had been arranged in such a roundabout, formal way that the strange open casualness of the Perrault household was a surprise to Jesse.

"A great mind doesn't belong simply to the body it happens to have been born in," Perrault was saying argumentatively. Everyone listened uneasily. There was a peculiar edginess to the evening, a puritanical vigor to Perrault's raspy voice that forbade intimacy, though they were all crowded around this rather small table. Jesse did not dare to glance at Helene, fearful of seeing that sallow sickliness in her face—that stubborn, held-back disapproval. What was Perrault talking about? Why did he smile in that small, shrewd way?

This household was plain, homely, even slovenly. Obviously he was a wealthy man—Jesse knew how much he charged certain of his patients—and yet he lived in an ordinary brick home in Wilmette, surrounded by decent, ordinary homes, as if the old man's imagination had never turned itself upon the place in which he would live out his life. Mrs. Perrault was large, clumsy, good-natured, fussily maternal to Helene and concerned for her condition—Helene, pregnant, was reluctant to come here this evening but had been comforted a little by the untidiness of the Perrault living room, a kind of museum of odds and ends of travel, mostly from the Southwest and Mexico: shawls, blankets, woven items, icons of copper and brass. A strange place. Jesse could not detect Perrault's touch anywhere. Perrault's private office in downtown Chicago had been professionally decorated and was entirely in white—walls, ceiling, even the floor tile; he peered out of that sinister whiteness as if out of a cave flooded with light. Here at home he seemed content to sit like a cunning old man, a grandfather, at the head of this rickety dining room table or in a rocking chair with a footstool in front of it and a garish red rug beneath the stool, a hand-woven rug that matched another larger rug beneath the mahogany coffee table. On the walls were sunbursts of copper, and lithographs of many nervous lines and slashes, a mystery to Jesse; dried flowers and weeds had been stuffed into several oversized clay vases. The living room sofa was bright green, scratchy to the touch. Dr. Cady, entering this room, had glanced around in bewilderment, as if he had wandered into the wrong place.

"Come in, come in," Perrault had ordered.

He pressed drinks upon them, though he himself would not drink. Something might come up at the hospital, who could tell? His wife said with a laugh, "Do you hear that? His mind is always half there and half here. Half here, half there. Forty years of this...."

They were not certain of her attitude, so they smiled. Cady laughed. Helene, who had been ill earlier that day, looked better now and seemed to be taking a great interest in the Perraults' family photographs. She handled herself tenderly and self-consciously and a little bitterly, hugely pregnant again. She had had a miscarriage the year before and dreaded having another one. Jesse worried about her too, thinking of the violent irrevocable expulsion of blood and pulp.... He was careful of Helene, he never argued with her. Dr. Cady, whom he hadn't seen for some time, surprised him by looking so sleek and well. He must have gained twenty, twenty-five pounds in the past year. He had bought new glasses with thick black frames, knobby and fashionable. His suit was expensive, as always, but of a much more stylish cut than those Jesse remembered from Ann Arbor. By contrast, Perrault, who was about Cady's height, appeared thin and insubstantial and myopic this evening, as if all this preliminary visiting, this exchange of greetings and stray superficial commentary on his house and souvenirs bored him. *A genius,* Jesse thought, holding himself apart from Perrault and Perrault's busy bustling wife, *a genius who can't handle anything outside the field of his work. . . .*

Cady talked fluently and cheerfully, as if he and Perrault were old friends. They were no more than acquaintances and would not have recognized each other, and Jesse sensed a certain guardedness about them in the first several minutes. Cady had flown to Chicago only that morning, explaining that he was sentimental about his little granddaughter, whom he hadn't seen for some time, and worried about his daughter—not seriously worried, but concerned. He had sat on the bright green sofa and chatted with Perrault about men they knew, associates and acquaintances, successes and failures and mysteries who had disappeared into America. Jesse smiled uneasily, listening to this talk. He felt like a son-in-law with two fathers.

Mrs. Perrault was asking Helene about something, in a rough, hearty singsong voice. Jesse overheard her saying something about *forty years* again.

"Helene—your name is Helene—a very pretty name—Helene, you see what your life will be like, their minds are half with you and half *there,* and when they fall asleep at night—who can tell what they're doing? Better to let them do it in their sleep!"

This awkward period had lasted about half an hour.

Then Mrs. Perrault served dinner. She interrupted a conversation between her husband and Cady, telling them that the food was ready, it would be getting cold. They rose and went a few yards into the dining room, which opened onto the living room. The table was already set. "Anywhere, please sit anywhere," she said. Her pleasant, plain face gleamed with enthusiasm. Jesse ended up sitting next to her and was called upon to help her dish out food, plate after plate, loaded with beef and potatoes and string beans and creamed onions. He didn't know whether to be irritated by this or grateful for something to do. What about his wife? How was his wife? Sometimes the odor of food nauseated her. But she seemed all right. Dr. Cady ate everything that was given to him with a show of pleasure, though this food must have disappointed him. Dr. Perrault, at one end of the table, spent much of the meal staring down at his plate with a small, fuzzy smile, as if wondering why he had invited these people. Maybe he had had some reason and now he had forgotten it . . . ?

Jesse glanced at his watch.

Overhead, an old-fashioned chandelier burned too brightly. The light bulbs were imitation flames that stuck out of dusty cardboard cylinders meant to represent candles. Yes, the lights were far too bright. The ordeal reminded Jesse of an operation; but the room was too warm. . . . To get through it, he thought of Reva. Reva's face. That perfect, flawless face. . . . The mouth with its perfect smile. . . .

Though he had not seen her for many months, he had fallen in love with her. He could remember only fragments of their dissatisfying conversation. *Did you get out of this what you wanted?* she had asked.

What had he wanted?

He had wanted her, but then what? What would come next?

But his imagination went blank when he thought of what might have come next. It was not possible to think of anything coming next. Reva's face, Reva's body, and then. . . . Jesse picked at his food, lovesick for Reva. He felt at such times an almost physical distress, a cramping of the belly. But he had to eat because he was a guest at Dr. Perrault's home, an enviable guest. After a ten-day period of enduring more insults than usual from the old man he had been invited over for dinner, so he had to eat, had to keep passing dishes of food around the table in a cheerful never-ending circle. It was like belonging to a family . . . like belonging to a family . . . and yet he kept thinking of Reva, who was so solitary and inaccessible to him. He could not imagine her captured and subdued like Helene, weighed down by pregnancy, sitting beside her father and across the table from her husband.

Still, he loved Helene. He would have died for her.

Thick slabs of roast beef, oozing watery blood. They ate. Perrault would not touch his wine, though his wife teased him; he snapped at her, he smiled an angry apology, something about wanting to remain clear-headed in case anything happened at the hospital.... Mrs. Perrault glanced meaningfully over at Helene. *Forty years of this!* her mild self-pitying glance said.

Now the talk drifted onto Dr. Cady's experimentation at Harvard—work in the histochemistry of motor neurons and interneurons in cat spinal cords; just the sound of it made Mrs. Perrault shake her head. She abandoned them to their subject, going out to the kitchen for more food. Jesse could not decide if he liked the woman or if she made him uneasy. He felt relieved when she left his side. Through the archway of the old-fashioned dining room he could see a row of photographs arranged above Dr. Perrault's harpsichord, graduation pictures of two boys and a girl, the Perrault children. Jesse gathered that the boys had gone to Harvard Medical School like their father, and were now somewhere in the East. Maybe he spent his money on them, setting them up in practices...? Still, he would have a lot of money left over. Perrault's staff physicians liked to speculate about the old man's fortune. It was hard to think of him as a father who would lavish money upon his children, and Jesse felt a pang of envy for those young men....

Mrs. Perrault came back with some food. She walked firmly, like a peasant, coming straight to him. *Eat, Eat. Don't listen to them talking, just eat.* There was hardly room on the table for another bowl. A big red ceramic bowl of mashed potatoes. Jesse saw that Helene was smiling vaguely at Mrs. Perrault, and he wondered at her look of happiness. In their own apartment she was rarely happy. Her smiles were thin and forced. Even when she fussed over Jeanne, when she dressed Jeanne or played with her, Helene's smile was strained and unconvincing. Tonight, the deep pink material of her dress cast up a frail, rose light onto her face.

"You'll have some more, won't you, Helene? Just a little more?" Mrs. Perrault said. She was gently bullying.

Helene acquiesced. She glanced at Jesse, smiling. He tried to smile back. But he distrusted her, he was puzzled by her... what was there about this crowded table with its ornate, chipped china and its mismatched wine glasses and water goblets and its old-fashioned, heavy, slightly tarnished silverware that pleased her?

"Good. Good. You need to nourish yourself," Mrs. Perrault muttered.

Dr. Cady was talking about his work. "... yes, but it isn't satisfying, working with animals. Yes, it's pure and open-ended, but there are no personalities involved."

Helene turned to him, surprised. "Personalities ... ?"

"You would want personalities?" Perrault asked carefully.

"I think so, yes."

"No, really, that element is distressing," Perrault said. He crossed his knife and fork neatly on his plate to indicate that he was finished with this meal. He cleared his throat as if trying to clear his hoarseness. "Because the personality is not permanent. It's absolutely unstable. Therefore you find yourself working with—you might say experimenting with—a substance you naively believe to be stable, when in reality it is ephemeral. An animal has as much personality as a man."

Mrs. Perrault laughed quietly.

"Listen to that! I don't believe that," she said.

Perrault ignored her. He addressed the others as if they had questioned him. "What is a personality?" he said politely. "I will tell you, it is a conscious system of language. And when the language deteriorates, as it must, the personality vanishes and we have only the brute matter left—the brain and its electric impulses. Benjamin, do you agree?"

"But still there's an unconscious layer of personality. The mind is in the brain, though it's invisible," Cady said at once. "And up to a certain point it can communicate with you; it can tell you about the process of its own deterioration."

"It isn't reliable," Perrault said.

"But of course it's reliable, as reliable as anything else. When a person tells you that he has felt a small explosion in his head, and he dies an hour later, you can assume before an examination that he has suffered a hemorrhage, that something blew out—"

Perrault glanced at Jesse as if urging him to speak. Jesse said, wondering at this odd conversation, "They don't need to tell you that...."

Perrault interrupted impatiently. "No, of course, they don't need to tell us anything. We tell them. Or we don't bother telling them at all, we simply make a record of it for our own information. No, the personality is an illusion, and there is no one of us sitting around this table who truly possesses any personality, any permanent system of conscious or unconscious language. It is just a tradition. Personality is just a tradition that dies hard."

"A tradition . . . ?" Helene said. "I don't understand."

Dr. Perrault smiled his myopic, blurry smile, as if seeking out Helene in a dimension that was not real to him, a kind of dream. "I mean that belief in it is a tradition. It is a belief that dies hard."

A few moments of silence. Perrault continued to smile toward Helene. Jesse realized slowly that the old man did not believe in women, in their existence. They did not matter. They could not understand, it was hopeless to talk to them; and yet one had to talk to them out of politeness. That, too, was a tradition. And perhaps Jesse himself did not believe in women the way he believed in men. . . . Perrault was saying argumentatively, "What is the personality, then, that we encounter in those we think we love? I will tell you this also: It is a pattern of attitudes that are expressed in certain language patterns we recognize because we are accustomed to them, you might say *conditioned* to them, to be technical, the attitudes being a barrier to protect these people and ourselves against the infinite. The original chaos. Who can deny this? I am not contradicting you, Benjamin, but simply expanding upon what you obviously believe. There's no surprise in this. We each have a hidden obsession, I suppose, a kind of monster that has made our facial structures what they are on the surface, the facial mask that is our own, uniquely in the universe, and we try to keep this monster secret, except perhaps to ourselves. And some of us never see the monsters in ourselves. . . . This is the personality people defend. But it is only ephemeral. With a tiny pin in my fingers," he said, raising his hand and touching his forefinger to his thumb, "I can destroy any personality in about thirty seconds, sixty seconds at the most."

Helene was staring at him. Jesse felt a strange thrill of certainty in what Perrault had said.

"I don't understand that," Helene said. "Do you mean . . . what do you mean . . . ?"

"My daughter is very sentimental," Cady teased. He patted Helene's arm. But Jesse could see that he himself was doubtful.

"What you're saying is terrible," Helene said.

"The truth can't be terrible," said Jesse.

Perrault looked at him, pleased. Triumphant.

"Ah, Jesse! Yes, Jesse, absolutely yes, yes—the truth can't be terrible—that's the first law of science! What is terrible can be true or not true, but what is true cannot be terrible. You're reading my mind, Jesse."

Jesse felt his face grow warm.

Helene was watching him with a still, small smile. He felt the hysteria rising in her.

"What did you say, Jesse?" she asked.

Dr. Cady, trying to make a joke of this, turned to Helene. "I think my little girl is nervous tonight. She isn't herself tonight. Maybe you're worried about Jeannie . . . ?"

"Jeannie? No."

"Maybe you should call the baby-sitter and check with her . . . ?"

"Why? I'm not worried. Jesse is the one who worries about our daughter, not I," Helene said evenly. "I don't worry. No, I'm thinking about what Dr. Perrault said just now, about the pin . . . the pin and the personality that can be destroyed with the pin. . . ."

"Your wife is a very serious young woman," Perrault said to Jesse, with that special look he shot Jesse whenever one of the less able assistants blundered during an operation. "She should consider the fate of the personality when the brain is lifted out of its encasement and placed in another substance, when it is hooked up to another system. What then? Without its senses, is the brain any longer a personality?"

"Yes," said Helene.

"What do you mean, yes?"

"Yes. It is a personality."

Perrault laughed. He lifted his hands as if to show that he could not argue, he had no interest in arguing.

Cady said at once, "You mean the transplanting of brains. Yes, that's good. A good point. It seems to me that the brain would still be a personality because it would have a memory; a personality is largely memory, conscious or unconscious. An unfathomable number of memory units. So it would hold in these units its shattered 'personality,' unless that personality could be wiped out."

"Hooked up to another body, let's say," Perrault said, "and with the demands of the new body's senses, what then? The same personality, a new one belonging to the body, or a synthesis of the two?"

"It depends upon the memory. . . ."

"We will allow the memory."

Helene said sharply, "But this can't be done."

"Certainly it can be done, Helene," said Cady. "It will be done in the next decade."

"I don't believe it."

"Kidneys will be transplanted, hearts will be transplanted, everything," Cady said. "The body is a jumble of mechanical parts, some of which work well and some of which rattle. The parts can be detached and exchanged for new ones. Is this evil? Helene, you know all this, you're just pretending to be shocked. I think it's that baby you're going to have . . . you're rehearsing innocence for it, the innocence of a young mother. . . ."

"Don't upset the young lady. What good does it do to talk about these things? Just go and do them according to your plans, complete them and write your reports and collect your prizes," Mrs. Perrault said lightly. She might have been talking to children. She got to her feet and asked if anyone wanted coffee.

Perrault ignored her. He turned peevishly to Jesse. "I'll put it to Dr. Vogel. Are you going to be transplanting brains in your lifetime, Dr. Vogel?"

"I suppose so," Jesse said.

"Will it be so terrible?"

"No."

"Why not?"

Because nothing is terrible any longer. "Because . . . because it will have to be done . . . someone will have to do it," Jesse said.

"Yes, and if not Dr. Vogel, then who?" Perrault said triumphantly. "Who else? I admire your son-in-law, Benjamin, beyond any other man I know. This isn't flattery. It's a fact. He has part of my brain right now, memorized in his fingertips. That, too, is a tradition, the old tradition of training, of ritual. It will do for another generation or two. But then—the future—well, the future is going to be very interesting."

"The future. . . ." Cady said slowly.

"Yes, we're making the future very interesting," Perrault laughed.

Helene was staring across the table at Jesse.

"You . . . you plan on doing that kind of work?" she whispered.

Jesse shrugged his shoulders.

"The brain might be better off without a body," Perrault said. "It wouldn't be so distracted then by the senses. It would be pure. Whatever its function might be, it would respond more quickly."

Helene turned to him. "But why do such a thing?"

"That's a strange question."

Helene smiled thinly at him. Jesse could see the strain in her face. "To preserve life at such a cost. . . . And what kind of life would it be? Your services go to the highest bidder, don't they?"

"But the highest bidder would be the United States Government," Perrault said, again with that raising of his hands, as if this were all beyond his control. "A great mind doesn't belong simply to the body it happens to have been born in. It belongs to its culture, its physical and mental environment. Therefore we can say that no man owns himself, no personality owns the brain it inhabits, any more than we can own other people. It's taken us many centuries to understand that we can't own other people—I mean, in private life, in private relationships. We are all unique and free. Why, then, should we own ourselves? The government may have a perfect right to demand that certain brains be preserved."

"Preserved—why?" Helene asked.

"For the good of the nation."

"And the brains themselves would have no choice about it . . . ?"

"Now, when you talk about *brains,* and not about old-fashioned *personalities*, now you are speaking a language I can understand," Perrault said politely. "Of course the brains would not have any ultimate decision concerning their own disposal. When you consider the enormous value of the brain of, let's say, Benjamin Cady, who is worth more than all the computers that exist—his brain is absolutely priceless and could not be discarded because of any whim of his. But I would imagine brains will enthusiastically will themselves to science just as people today will their organs or their entire bodies. The brains will be honored, they will be truly resurrected, the first forms of life on this planet to be really resurrected! Maybe this is what was meant by Christ's promise to us, or by that teasing little statement: *The Kingdom of God is within you.*"

Helene brought her hand to her face. The lights of the chandelier were too bright, and her features looked stark, strained. Her distress communicated itself to Jesse, to his body. "But there isn't any choice. . . ." she said.

"There never was any choice about resurrection, was there?" Perrault said with a smile. "Men were judged whether they wanted to be judged or not. There was no possibility of escape. Why should we be any easier on men? Of course there can't be any choice. Men live in both health and disease—they die in disease, unless they die suddenly. We could not tolerate a prodigious brain losing its health because of a sentimental attachment to its body. We cling to our bodies even when they are diseased because they are all we have known. We are terrified at the thought of losing them. It's like the old terror of leaving one world and going to another, taking one's chances with the next world. But, unlike that old cosmology, the new world—the new body—would always be superior to the old. Guaranteed. So resurrection would be real; you would wake up in paradise. The old body, the old earth: cast away for a true heaven. But first we must educate people out of the vicious sentimentality of loving the body, loving the personality, the personal self, the *soul,* that old illusion. . . . What is the old self, after all? Only the promise of disease. And disease is antisocial, mortal, private, rebellious, eccentric, unpredictable, useless, unimaginative, unprogressive, uncomely!"

Self-conscious, he let his hands fall in his lap. Jesse had never heard Dr. Perrault speak at such length.

"Disease is private. . . ." Helene murmured.

"Yes, certainly. And to be utterly free is to be diseased. To go one's own private way, that is a disease," Perrault said. "Health is something else entirely—a relaxation of the ego, the self, the name on the card, the name on the birth certificate. Health is in the public domain, it always has been a matter of medical standards and regulations. It's in the public domain the way outer space is. Inner space and outer space can't belong to individuals. No brain owns itself; it resides in nature like the atmosphere, it rises out of nature and subsides back into it, and only a panel of scientists is equipped to decide when a superior brain must be taken from its old body. . . ."

"When it *must* be taken?" Cady said.

"Yes, when it must be taken, when there is no choice about waiting any longer," Perrault said.

"You're serious about this, aren't you?" Helene said. "It's the same as murder, what you've been saying. Yes, it's the same as murder." Mrs. Perrault had gone to Helene's place with a large silver coffee pot, but Helene did not seem to notice her. She was shaking her head, smiling. "You're sick, a sick man, you're crazy, you're a killer, and it's because you want to kill that you've thought all this out, you and men like you . . . you know that no one can stop you. . . ."

"Helene!" Cady cried.

She got to her feet, pushing back her chair. She pressed her hands against her face and pulled at the skin beneath her eyes, a curious, private gesture of utter weariness. Jesse hurried over to her. She turned from him as if she did not know who he was and walked away—toward the rear of the house, staggering. Jesse followed her. "Are you going to be sick?" he whispered. He put his arm around her shoulders and walked with her back to the Perraults' bathroom—a tiny room with peeling walls and a dull, scuffed linoleum floor. "It's all right, Helene. We can go home. As soon as you feel better we'll go home." His heart was pounding. Helene turned from him, gagging. She swayed. Her swollen stomach looked ripe and fragile to Jesse; he was afraid something terrible would happen to her. "Helene . . . ?" he said. She would not look at him. He wondered if he hated her for what she had said to Perrault and what she was doing to herself and to him—

"Leave me alone. Please," she said.

"But Helene—"

"Leave me alone!"

He left her. Back in the dining room everyone was standing—these old, aging people with their worried faces. Jesse stared angrily at them. Perrault's face was reddened. "I'm sorry—" he began.

Jesse nodded abruptly.

He went to the front closet to get Helene's coat. Perrault followed.

"You're upset," he said flatly.

"It doesn't matter."

"Yes, you're upset, your wife is very nervous. It's her condition, isn't it? This pregnancy?"

"I suppose so."

"Look at me, please. Look straight at me," Perrault said.

Jesse looked at him. He was such a short man, frail and meek in his body—Jesse could not think why he feared him so much.

"Do you agree with her?" Perrault said.

Jesse said nothing.

"Your wife's words, her accusation—do you agree?"

Jesse stared at him and did not reply.

"Then don't answer. All right. I had invited you tonight for a certain reason . . . for a private, personal reason," Perrault said quickly. His face was very red. "But now . . . now I . . . we . . . We can talk about it some other time. . . ."

Jesse nodded slowly. His mind was a blank, even his anger and alarm had run down: he felt the terrible, open purity of his brain, which belonged to no one at all.

12

A week before Jesse's thirty-first birthday, in October of 1956, his receptionist came back to his office and said, "There's a young woman who wants to see you. Her name is Rita Smith."

"Who?"

"Rita Smith. She says it's very important that she talk with you. She doesn't have an appointment."

"No referral?"

"No. She says it's very important. . . . I told her you were very busy, but she says she'll wait, she says you know her."

Jesse tried to think: did he know anyone named Rita Smith? The name meant nothing to him. Some nervousness, some very slight resentment in the receptionist's manner made Jesse wonder about this young woman. . . . Well, he couldn't resist. He would have to see her.

"Please show her in," he said politely.

The receptionist brought back Reva Denk.

She came right up to him, leaned over his desk, and shook hands happily. "Dr. Vogel! It's so nice of you to remember me!" she laughed. She laughed at his surprise, leaning across his large desk with a childlike pleasure at giving surprise. In the sharp sunlight of noon her beauty glared at him.

"You—you came back— You're here—" Jesse stammered.

"And you remember me," she said triumphantly.

She stood back as if to give him time to look at her, to assess her. Lowering her gaze, she seemed to be assessing herself. Shorter than he remembered her appearing. More contained, petite. She was wearing high-heeled shoes and a dress of smooth, silky wool, a very light blue. Her hair was tied back from her face in two thick, loose clumps, tied with ordinary yarn, and it was parted in the middle in a long wavering line. Her face was clean of make-up and looked very young, younger than Jesse recalled. Her skin was smooth and a little shiny, accentuated by the sunlight of noon.

That this woman should come to him at noon!

"But what—how— How did you find me?" Jesse asked.

"I looked you up in the directory. I've never forgotten you."

His heart had begun to pound heavily. He got to his feet, behind the desk—on which were arranged neat piles of letters, files, papers, an entire life, a maze of a life—as if fearful of coming out from behind it, of facing this woman directly. He stared at her face, her mouth. Her smiling mouth. It was artless, pleased, happy. The flash of her gums startled him; he might have glanced at something forbidden.

What was she saying?

Looking around his office. Smiling happily. "This is so high in the air, it's like being in a tower—up in a castle—up in the air," she said. "And what are all these things? Diplomas? Do they belong to you, all of them to one person? You? I can't read that—is that Latin? I don't know any foreign languages. Ah, what a wonderful place this is, so high up!—do you spend a lot of time standing at the window here, looking at the lake? I'd stand here all the time. I'd let my mind sail out the window and into the lake. . . ."

He could not follow her words. He was so struck by her—the

sudden intimacy of her presence, her being. That slender, lively body, those girlish legs, that head of blond hair now tied into two loose, swishing strands, the gleam of a gold bracelet on one arm, the constant movement of her eyes and lashes.... She was rhythmic, slowly moving, a slow delicate whirl of various shades and shallows of light, the gleam of her eyes, her moist lips, her very white teeth, the whorls of her ears, the pale, almost waxy whorls of her ears, the very tip of her fragile nose confused with the rhythmic whirl and dip of her words. Rises, hollows. The intense glare of the sunlight that seemed to make her skin opaque, poreless, smooth as flesh painted on a canvas. She was turning to him, teasing him, calling him to her. Didn't he hear her voice beneath that chattering voice calling *Jesse? Jesse?*

Or did he imagine her?

He had been imagining her for many months, he had been dreaming and exaggerating her. Along with Helene he had dreamed of Reva: he had made love to Reva in the form of a husband of Helene's. Two bodies had come together in love, a pantomime of love, and Jesse had manipulated them from a small sacred hollow somewhere in his own head, chaste and untouched, sending out the nerve impulses of love, wishing that love be made flesh. But the love was in honor of Reva and Jesse.

Now she was here, with him. Unexaggerated. She put out one exploratory hand, not toward Jesse but toward the window, as if drawn by it. Something about the sunlight, the height, the vaporous horizon of the lake and the sky seemed to draw her. She was wearing a gold bracelet that looked primitive, barbaric, a huntress's armband four or five inches wide. It must have been very heavy on her slight wrist. It was oddly out of proportion to her size.

"That's very beautiful," Jesse said quickly. He had to use the word *beautiful.* He had to utter it. "Are you—are you back in Chicago permanently? I tried to call you at that number several times but—"

"Oh, that's over, you mean that place on the North Side? That's over. I came back in the winter by myself and lived for a while in New York, and now I'm here for a while—in Chicago—and then I think I'll be going up to northern Wisconsin."

"Northern Wisconsin? When?"

"Oh, in a week," she said lightly.

Jesse stared at her. She was so bright a presence—the color of her dress so brilliant, so supernaturally intense—that he could not concentrate on what was being said. He did not know how important these words were. There were words he had rehearsed in silence: *I am in love with you.* But perhaps she already knew these words. *I want nothing from you.* But now that she was with him, in this room with him, the air between them was agitated and unserious, as if stirred by winds from outside the building, from the autumn sky, and he felt himself smiling slowly, unresisting, giving in, the way Reva was smiling at him.

The intimacy of that smile: they had known each other long ago, perhaps. They were lovers who did not have to hurry about touching each other. They were brother and sister.

"Take me out to lunch," Reva said suddenly. "Let's go for a walk."

Jesse had no time. He could not leave the office, really. But he said at once, "Yes, of course. . . ."

"I want to walk around and talk to you. I've thought of you so much," Reva said. "I feel like a sister to you. I feel that we're in a plot together, you know, a story, after that strange way you looked me up—did you hire a detective to check on me? Did you? Oh, don't look so worried! It doesn't matter now. It doesn't matter how we got to know each other; that belongs in the past. My life at that time belongs in the past, it's better forgotten—that big, crazy car I took you for a ride in, remember, as if we were in a movie together and had to ride together for five or ten minutes, on film, using up film!—oh, it's better forgotten, forget it all! I feel so warm toward you, Jesse, and I'm very happy about your success here—because I think you're doing well in your life, aren't you?"

"Yes, I'm doing well," Jesse said weakly.

He had approached her but he did not dare touch her. She didn't seem to have given him permission to touch her. And he wore white: he was in costume as Dr. Vogel. He did not dare touch her without her permission. She seemed so lithe, so clever, constantly in motion as if to elude him and confuse his vision—now examining the photographs of his family on the desk—wouldn't she slip out of his hands if he tried to embrace her?

"Is this woman your wife?" Reva asked. She gave no sign of noticing Jesse's agitation. "She looks very intelligent. Yes, very intelligent." She frowned at the picture of Helene. It was a strange picture of Helene, having caught only the surface of her being. The eye glanced at it and off it, lightly pleased, unworried. But when Jesse stared at it he could hear the murmur in that woman's brain, the constant stubborn flow of her consciousness, arguing silently with him. An argument he did not understand. "These are beautiful children," Reva said softly. "This is the little girl I saw that day—I can't remember her name—she didn't seem to like me, remember? And is this another girl? Or a boy?"

"A girl. Michele."

"Michele. That's a lovely name. Is the other girl named Jeanne? Yes, I thought so. I remembered that," Reva said, pleased with herself. She looked up at Jesse as if congratulating him for having fathered these children. The flow of her words, like her movements, was liquid and somehow elusive, hypnotic. "Are you happy with having a family, with being a father?" Reva asked.

"There's nothing that could mean more to me," Jesse said slowly.

"Yes, that's true. That's how it is with you," Reva agreed.

"But you . . . you look different. You're very beautiful," Jesse said, "but . . ."

She turned away from him, arranging the photographs back in their original order. A neat row of faces: Helene and the two girls. A mother and her two daughters.

"A mother and her two daughters," Reva whispered.

"Why did you come here, Reva?" Jesse asked.

Her gaze wandered onto the walls, the floor. Perrault's white, his taste for off-white, a sterility that did not quite blind the eye. Jesse wanted to explain to Reva that this was not his true setting, this office. Not this powerful white, this airiness, this extravagant tower overlooking the lake. She seemed suddenly nervous, evasive. He regretted having asked her that question.

"I only want to be friends with you," Reva said. "You met me at a time in my life when I was very happy, and I associate you with that time somehow, because between the two of us nothing has changed; we don't know each other and we never knew each other.... But the rest of my life has changed completely. And you're still here in Chicago, you still look the same, as if no time has gone by. But of course a great deal has happened in your life; you have another child, you're here in this office... who is that man, Perrault? Is he your partner?"

"I'm a junior partner," Jesse said.

"Is he an old man? Is he good?"

"What do you mean—good? He's an excellent surgeon," Jesse said. He was discovering how unaccustomed he was, as Helene's husband, to women who were not intelligent. "I've never known anyone like him; he's an extraordinary man...."

"Do you like working with him?"

"Well," Jesse said with a sudden laugh, "well, no...."

Reva smiled strangely at him.

"Yes, I like working with Dr. Perrault. He's a very difficult person but I like working with him. He keeps me going at a pace I couldn't maintain by myself... he forces me to be much better than I really am."

Reva nodded slowly. She stood with her hands clasped before her, in an attitude of attentive, meek, insincere submissiveness; if he didn't look at her he was able to speak quite easily.

"Dr. Perrault forces me to be a person I didn't know I was," Jesse said. "I'm learning constantly, I'm exhausted with all the things there are to learn in the world, because... because I thought I had come near to the end of them when I finished at the hospital. But... Dr. Perrault is writing a book and he has asked me to help him with it. He never rests, he never stops. He never stops thinking."

Jesse believed he could feel Dr. Perrault's presence in the suite of offices—he sensed Reva's awareness of Perrault also. She kept glancing at Jesse and behind him, over his shoulder at the closed door. Dr. Perrault was not in today, but Jesse felt him near just the same.

"You look a little tired," Reva said gently.

"Do I?"

"You look a little strained."

"I think it's because of you."

"Me, because of me?" she asked, as if genuinely surprised. And then, pleased, catlike, she stood gazing toward him, not quite at him, as if contemplating herself. He could sense her lowered gaze taking in her feet, her legs, her slender hips, her body, passing up to her face, assessing and calculating and dismissing lightly. "Shouldn't I have come to see you?"

"Yes. I didn't mean that. But you surprised me, I never expected . . ."

"Oh, Rita Smith? That was just a name I made up. I don't like my real name written down—you know—the nurse wanted my name, and I had to think quickly to make up a name, and—and really Reva Denk isn't my name either; it's a name I made up once when I had a while to think of a name. If I had fifteen minutes I could think of a better name than Rita Smith," she laughed. Jesse was smiling, grinning. His mouth seemed to be twisting out of his control, into the shape of a thin, strained quarter moon. Reva said, in the same light, evasive tone, "It was at a racetrack. I was with someone and then I met someone else—I belonged to someone, but when I met this other person I sensed that I would pass over to him, I—I sensed it, the way you sense that something is not quite even, a tilted platform or a porch or something—do you know what I mean?" She put out her hand, palm up, and turned it lazily, inquisitively, as if testing the balance of this room. She glanced at Jesse slyly. "So I had time to make up a name; but, you know, you never really make up a name, so that person explained to me later—a certain name comes to your lips and that's that, it fixes you. It tells you who you are much more than the name you were born with. . . . Oh, is this for headaches?" she said. She picked up a brochure from Jesse's desk, an advertisement for a new drug. "Migraine headaches? Sometimes I get headaches myself. I never take anything for them though. Somebody told my mother—it was a nurse—not to take anything if she could help it, not even aspirin. So I don't. I want to keep my system pure and natural. I want to be clean inside and out. The headaches don't really give me much pain. I never feel much pain. I'm very strong. Today I feel especially strong," she said with a smile at Jesse that made his blood grow suddenly heavy, and yet in the next instant her voice had become playful again. "Well, are you going to take me out? I want to show you something. There is something beautiful here in Chicago I want to show you. My mind fastened onto you

—Dr. Jesse Vogel—I'll tell you why later—and I looked you up at once and came here. Did I make a mistake?"

"No."

"Do you have time now?"

"I have time now, yes. Now. Later on this afternoon I have to go to the hospital, but now—I have time."

"That nurse out there didn't seem to like me. She said you were busy," Reva said.

Jesse wondered if his agitation showed. He was afraid she would decide suddenly to leave, to walk out. She kept moving about his office, playfully and yet with a kind of intention, unsettling everything, stirring heaving blocks of air between them. Jesse would have to change his clothes and he was afraid she would be gone when he returned.... "I like you in that white outfit. You look very handsome, very official," Reva said. "You look like a man who could have any name at all. I suppose a lot of women come to you, do they—and you examine them? That must be very strange. Do you like it?"

Jesse, rattled, could not think of any answer.

Reva's heavy bracelet gleamed. It was a gleaming like her sure, slow, healthy white smile. He had a sudden vision of a man tearing at her, tearing at her clothes, burying his face against her belly, her loins.... It made him dizzy to see himself doing that and yet to realize that another man was doing it, leaving Jesse innocent.

"I'll wait for you outside in the corridor. Not in your waiting room but in the corridor," Reva said.

He changed his clothes quickly. Fast-moving, cold, damp fingers. His flushed face. He was so impregnable here in this large suite of offices—it was a maze, a clean expensive maze, and patients were led to him and Dr. Perrault only after a complicated system of examinations and referrals. Reva had come to him directly. Yet Reva was not sick: she was very healthy, very strong. It was obvious at a glance that she was very strong.

On his way out, Jesse explained that he had to leave on a personal errand; he would be back as soon as possible; no, nothing serious, nothing to worry about. Perrault's nurses were not young women, but mature technicians, devoted to him as if they were blood relatives of his, absolutely uncritical. His bad manners and his impatience did not upset them, not permanently. They loved him. Jesse was a kind of younger relative, a son or a nephew of Perrault, promising, hard-working, a good young man but not one to be taken too seriously, not yet. Even when Perrault was nowhere around, Jesse did not occupy the center of the place: Perrault occupied it.

But Reva had come to him, and not to the old man!

Hurrying to Reva, Jesse felt something graze against his face in the empty air: her hair, the idea of her hair, its softness, its gentle odor. What if she had left? But she was there, waiting. Waiting by the elevators. She turned to him and her face was amazing, so clean and soft and yet very strong, uncanny. Jesse wanted to seize her head, to stroke the bones of her cheeks, to stroke her large, restless eyes....

"Now you look different. Now you look in disguise," Reva said. "You aren't that first man I met so long ago—but you don't remember, do you? Don't remember the time we first met?"

"No, not the first time. No, I don't remember," Jesse said. She smelled of something rich and burnished—perfume, sunlight? The odor of sunlight? Jesse let his hand fall upon her shoulder, as if by accident. He could not help himself.

Reva stepped away gracefully.

Embarrassed, nervously pleased, not looking at each other, they waited for the elevator to arrive. They watched the panel of numbers above the elevator. Jesse's face was flushed. A heartbeat seemed to begin in his forehead. *What to say to Reva, how to explain himself!* With Helene he often felt the same need to explain himself, to confess, to put himself into words. Somewhere there were words for him, for Jesse, the exact words that would explain his life. But he did not know them. He used words shyly, crudely. It remained for someone else—a woman, perhaps—to draw these sacred words out of him, to justify him, redeem him as Jesse—he could not create them himself. Not alone.

"No, I don't remember... I don't know what you mean...." Jesse murmured.

Beyond this Reva there was no one. No Reva. Nothing. An earlier, more mysterious Reva: he could not remember. If he tried to remember the first time he had actually seen her, his mind went blank. Blank as the chaste hard white walls of Perrault's office. He found himself thinking of silence, of years of silence, but that had nothing to do with Reva. He was a married man and he had married a kind of silence. With Helene at night, night after night, he experienced a panicked, almost sweetly panicked certainty: men married silence. In expectation of hearing those private, sacred words that would redeem them they married; but they married silence. He lay beside his wife and thought of the words that must be uttered, but the exact words did not come to him. They did not allow themselves to be shaped because he was alone, he was really sleeping alone. A dark, indistinct, confusing muddle of words, unvoiced words, and then the gradual fading into sleep, into night. Once he was asleep he was independent of Helene and of all women, even of himself. No one could follow him into sleep. He slept beside his sleeping wife, all the wild unpredictable hours of the night, the two of them wandering in their separate dreams, their heads ringing with words and forms and acts that would never be brought to daylight . . . in disguise, they lay sleeping as husband and wife, their bodies untouching or accidentally touching, it did not matter. If they woke, if Jesse made love to his wife, he had to imagine this love performed upon a woman who was Reva . . . and yet he did love Helene when he thought of her. He loved her. His dreams sometimes focused sharply upon her: anguish that he might impregnate her one more time and kill her.

After the birth of Michele, Helene had come home from the hospital with Dr. Blazack's command: *No more children.* She had wept. She had become hysterical, hating herself, accusing herself: *A failure as a woman. . . .*

"What's wrong?" Reva said. "You look worried about something."

"I was thinking . . . about pregnancy, about a woman having a baby. . . ."

Reva laughed, startled. "But how strange. . . . Why are you thinking of that?"

They were alone in the elevator. Jesse wanted to shake his head to clear it of the sorrow of his marriage. He wanted to get rid of all thoughts of his marriage. "I've missed you," he began nervously, "I've thought of you all the time, almost all the time.... I'm in love with you.... No, don't laugh, please, I'm very serious and...and I don't want you to laugh at me...."

"You don't love me. You don't know me," Reva said, embarrassed.

He was staring down at her lowered head, at the part wavering like a vein across the delicate curve of her skull.

"No, it isn't possible," she said.

When the elevator stopped at the ground floor she seemed to dance away from him. He followed her out to the street. Down here the sunlight was not so sharp. The noise of the traffic confused Jesse. He had the idea that he should take hold of Reva in order to make sure of her.

"I want to show you something," she said.

The noontime crowd surged upon them, around them. Reva looked so fragile—Jesse should take hold of her, protect her. But she kept moving away from him, leading him away. She seemed to have forgotten about lunch, and Jesse was grateful for this—how could he eat in Reva's presence? Instead, she walked him very fast somewhere—she took quick, vigorous strides—she chattered as they walked, fluttering, unobservant, trusting, while Jesse glanced nervously around, on the lookout for people who might recognize him.

Jesse and Reva, out together on the street.

She was walking so naturally beside him, unaware of her beauty, that he began to think they might already be lovers. They looked like lovers. If anyone from the hospital saw them—if old Perrault saw them—it would be a public fact, their love. Jesse was proud of being with her. He was proud of her birdlike little gestures, the habit she had of lifting one palm flat up, to emphasize a point that to her was absolutely clear; she was so trivial, so charming! Jesse kept touching her by accident. Gravitating toward her, toward her, and Reva kept stepping to the side, unaware, cautious, rather modest.... Jesse wondered why he had lived so much of his life without love. He had never loved anyone.... But, yes, he had loved Helene, he loved her even now, but he kept forgetting her. She was not the kind of woman to stay in the mind. No, not Helene. He loved her but he was not in love with her. He did not love her with this fierce, sickening certainty.... Why had he wasted so many years of his life? Years of his life? He needed only to take this woman in his arms and bury himself in her, to forget himself in her, in the pit of her belly, in the most secret part of her being, to blot out his consciousness and to rise again inside her, transformed by the moist shadowed labyrinthine secrecy of her brain, resurrected there....

"You shouldn't look at me like that out on the street," Reva whispered. She was very girlish, very tense. "I'll have to say good-by to you."

"I love you."

"You said you were married permanently. Don't do that, don't keep leaning against me... I don't like it...."

They had stopped, embarrassed. "I'm sorry," Jesse said.

"Last year you seemed to like me so much, without any reason, without any advantage," Reva said. "I didn't understand it. But it was... it was wonderful to me, it was so pure... I want to keep myself pure and healthy.... In the past year I loved a man very much, but then over the months I fell out of love with him; I couldn't help myself, and I had to leave him because it was all ugly and false, it was a lie. It made me old, to tell lies to him. It aged me," she said, and she had never looked younger, "and it aged him.... But I made the break and came home by myself. From time to time I thought of you, when I was alone or couldn't sleep or walking in a city I didn't know, wondering what the hell I was doing there. I had never met anyone like you. There's something about you that is mysterious and protective... and powerful.... I feel like a sister to you. You would have been a very wonderful, protective brother. You would have changed my life. I can't explain it. This is the most I've ever said to a man, I mean about my feelings toward him. It never pays to say much. Confessions are mistakes. Anyway, I don't understand my own feelings and I'm not very interested in them. I only know that I thought of you often. I wished you well. You had said that your wife was going to have another baby, and I wondered how that turned out. I've never had a baby myself. I'm not maternal. Do I look maternal?" she said with a peculiar, sharp laugh.

"What? Yes, I think you do," Jesse said. He was still hurt by her recoiling from him. He did not know what to say.

Reva frowned. "The gallery is just up the block," she said.

Jesse wished she would ask him again: *Did she look maternal? She could have his babies. His babies.*

She was leading him to a shop, an art gallery with storefront windows, crammed with paintings and sketches and pieces of modern sculpture. Jesse stared doubtfully. Inside, the place was cramped. The molding at the ceiling was filthy. Slowly, reluctantly, Jesse looked at the paintings on exhibit—a dozen large canvases, oil paintings in bright colors, green and yellow and orange. Zigzagging lines that made his eyes boggle. Reva seized his hand and led him somewhere. "This one. Look at this," she said quietly. The canvas was at least six by nine feet—enormous, bloated, a riot of lines and ugly shapes, vaguely human. Jesse stared coldly. This nightmare was not his and it did not interest him. He did not understand it.

"What do you think?" Reva asked excitedly.

Jesse shook his head.

"Does it frighten you? Does it make you think of anything?"

A short, bald man in youthful clothes approached and Reva greeted him with the same enthusiasm she had shown Jesse up in his office. Jesse smiled ironically at her, but she took no notice. She introduced him to this man—thank God she introduced him only as "Jesse Vogel"—and Jesse deliberately did not catch his name. A pert, busy little man. Jesse waited patiently, impatiently, while Reva talked with this man as if she had hours to spare.

"... it might work out with Annie again. I don't know," Reva was saying. "He doesn't have much hope himself. But he doesn't talk about it. I'm going up in another week, he wants me to, but I don't know what will happen ... I feel drained of everything.... I feel so sorry for *her*. He says he doesn't care what she has gone through," Reva said, tilting her head toward one of the big ugly canvases as she spoke; and Jesse understood at once that she was speaking of the painter of these things. The knowledge flashed through him. "She's such a slippery, snaky person, she's so ... so dwarfed ... but I feel very sorry for her...."

"Don't," the man said brightly.

Jesse hated him.

In a panic Jesse glanced at his watch: so much time had passed! She was going to leave him again. Going to walk away. Though she had taken his arm now as if they belonged together, though she led him up and down the aisles of this miserable little exhibit, Jesse knew that she was going to leave him again and that he would be unable to stop her. He was silent, sullen. Reva chattered. What the hell did she see in these paintings? All this mess was a mockery of life, of the natural forms of life. Deterioration of vision. Unbalance, collapse. Spasms. Brain damage. Cancer. A crowding of the natural forms of life, a crowding of the form of the canvases itself—the madness of colors and shapes without human sense.

Cancer.

Cancer.

Ah, now: they were looking at a man's picture. A face that filled the entire photograph, big, dark, wild eyebrows, stern features, creases on his forehead as if he were frowning painfully, angrily, bundles of hair, tufts of hair in his ears. A man in his forties. A grainy wood background that seemed more gentle than the man himself.

"That's Raeder," Reva said.

Jesse nodded.

"What do you think of him?" she asked eagerly.

"I don't think anything."

"But his face . . . ? His face?" Reva said, stroking her own face hesitantly.

The gallery owner approached them with a framed drawing. "Reva is much too shy to call your attention to this," he said flirtatiously. He held it up for Jesse to see, pressed against his own chest, and glanced down intimately at it himself. It was an utterly incomprehensible mess of lines—Jesse didn't know if they were ink, or what. He peered at the drawing and saw that its title was "Reva."

"Oh, don't show him that!" Reva laughed.

"Amazing, isn't it?" the little man said, smiling at Jesse. "So much energy! So much life!"

Jesse's mouth twisted angrily.

"All this is useless, this stuff," he said, indicating the other paintings, the whole shop. "It's ugly. There is no value to it. . . ."

Reva stared at him.

"No value to it . . . ?"

"Nothing. There's nothing to it," Jesse said angrily.

Reva turned and walked away slowly. He followed her. The little man was saying in a sprightly, ironic voice: "Come back again soon, soon! The two of you, please!"

Reva did not look back.

Outside, she turned to him but did not look at him. She said quickly, "I shouldn't have come to see you. It was a mistake."

"It wasn't a mistake."

"I have to leave you now."

"You're not leaving," Jesse said.

They began walking quickly. Jesse was careful not to brush against her.

It was a madness, his desire to hold her, to hurt her, to blot out that look of stubborn disapproval! What right did a woman have to disapprove of *him*? Of Jesse Vogel? He loved her and he wanted to grab her, to hurt her. He took hold of her wrist to slow her down. His fingers closed over the hard cool metal of her bracelet.

"Where are you going next week? Where in Wisconsin?"

"A little town. It doesn't matter to you."

"Where?"

"Oh—Hilsinger—"

She did not smile. Jesse felt the absence of her smile.

"Do you love him? That man in the photograph?—that face?"

Reva said nothing.

"Don't go back to him. Stay with me."

"I can't do that."

"Yes, you can. You can."

"You're permanently married," Reva said ironically. "Didn't you tell me that? Anyway, I don't love you."

"I won't ask anything of you. I won't involve you in my life."

"You're permanently married," Reva said.

Jesse hesitated.

"That might not be true," he said slowly.

Reva did not reply.

They were walking quickly, quickly. Jesse felt time running away. He felt an immense, dangerous pulsation—as if the hot, hollow, radiant core of his being, the elusive Jesse itself, were very close to his grasp. He still had hold of Reva's wrist. She was obedient, strangely passive, though she walked so swiftly, with her eyes fixed straight ahead. He felt that he could lead her anywhere, off the street, out of the city itself, he could lead her into the darkness with him, he could force her to lie down.... Once he made love to her the mystery of Reva would be ended: she would be his wife then.

"If I had money... if I had a little money.... If I weren't in debt...." Jesse stammered. He glanced sideways at Reva. She strode forward with the brisk, easy walk of a huntress, not drawing away from him and yet not really subdued, her arm passively against his, her eyes fixed straight ahead. She was hurrying. Hurrying out of his life. Jesse's mind raced in a series of twists and blots and zigzags of thought.... *What if...? What if...?*

"I might not be married permanently," he said.

"But I don't love you."

"Then why did you come to me?" Jesse said angrily.

"Because... because..."

"Why are you here, why are we walking here together? I could kill you," Jesse said.

Reva drew her arm away from his.

"I believe you," she said.

A crowd of noontime shoppers threatened to separate them. Jesse pushed her back against a building and they stood together, face to face, staring. There was a flushed, vigorous color to Reva's face. Her lips trembled; she stood with her arms tightly, primly folded over her stomach. It seemed to Jesse an odd stance.

"This is killing me," Jesse said in anguish. "*He's* killing me—the old man. I peel out the tumors, ripe as little plums, and there are always more—half a dozen more—thousands more waiting and getting ripe— I can't take it. I can't take you—what you're doing to me—"

"I'm sorry," Reva said. She brushed her forehead with one hand. "I didn't know what else to do."

Jesse stooped to hear her better.

"What?" he said.

"I didn't know what else to do," she whispered. "I need... I need help.... I remembered your name and that you were a doctor...."

Jesse stared at her. "What do you mean?"

She looked up toward him, not meeting his eye. He felt his scalp tightening, the hairs of his head rising. A dark red thatch of hair, a swirl of hair rising from his scalp. His forehead was tightening as if with the energy, the anguish of thought. His face, the muscles of his cheeks and neck, tightened. Jesse felt that his face must be like a shout to her.

"What, what do you mean?" he cried.

She did not answer. She only stared toward him, a frightened woman. He gripped her shoulders, the sharp bones of her shoulders, and had to restrain himself from shaking her violently. *I could kill you!*

"You—you can go to hell!" he said instead.

He walked away.

13

Several weeks later Jesse was glancing quickly through his mail at the hospital—most of it advertisements—when he came across an envelope postmarked Lockport, New York.

"My God. . . ."

He felt sick. He hid the envelope in the pile of mail. *Lockport.*

In a daze he waited for the elevator. Someone was speaking to him. He nodded and backed away, decided to take the stairs up to the fourth floor and so he ran up, his legs straining, his heart pounding lightly and rapidly, and when he got to the fourth floor, the elevator door opened and the doctor who had been talking to him downstairs got out.

"How is everything in your life, Jesse?" he said with an odd smile.

"Fine. Everything is fine," Jesse said. He had forgotten this doctor's name in his confusion. They walked together toward the operating suite. The doctor seemed curious about something—maybe about Perrault, there was a rumor about Perrault's health caving in, an untrue rumor—maybe about Jesse, who must have looked extremely nervous. He was scheduled for a simple operation at nine-thirty, one he had performed many times, but it seemed to him now an impossibility. He kept licking his lips and saying, "Good, fine, everything is fine . . . yes . . . everything is working out. . . ."

"When I want to know anything around here I ask the nurses," the doctor said. "That's how I find out who's on the way up and who's on the way down."

"Who's on the way down . . . ?" Jesse asked vaguely.

"How do you like your office with Perrault? It's in the Blake Building, isn't it?"

"Yes," Jesse said, edging away.

"How is the old man these days?"

"Oh, good, fine, everything is fine," Jesse said hurriedly.

"Some of us were wondering how he was," the doctor said, smiling at Jesse.

Jesse managed to get away from this conversation. He contemplated the handful of mail. If he opened the letter now, before the operation. . . . That might be bad luck. Might destroy him. He was already sickish, trembling, and in a few minutes he had to operate. . . . His mind went dark: how could he make the simplest incision, let alone saw away at the bone of the skull? What about the blood? How could he knowingly, willingly, start the flow of a stranger's blood? He kept seeing that envelope, that postmark. *Lockport, New York.* He kept seeing the flashing, balooning face of Dr. Pedersen, the upraised forefinger, he kept hearing that voice bouncing through the air. . . .

"Good morning, Doctor," someone was saying.

No, he would read the letter afterward. When the danger was past. It might bring news of Dr. Pedersen's death. In that case he would not be able to operate and would have to run out of the hospital; everyone would stare after him. Dr. Perrault would be notified. The patient—who was the patient? who was going to be operated on this morning? what was the trouble?—the patient would be under the anesthetic already and Jesse would run away from him, away from the sawing, the blood, the brain, the tumor, he would run out onto the street weeping, and so it would be better not to open the envelope now. After the operation, when everything was over, he would take it into the lavatory and read it there.

He left his mail in the surgeons' lounge.

He scrubbed and got dressed and felt reassured when he saw the patient actually up where he was supposed to be, at nine-thirty, with plenty of blood on hand and an anesthetist he respected, even a scrub nurse he liked, a middle-aged woman devoted to Perrault. Jesse had inherited all Perrault's likes and dislikes. He slipped into them as he slipped into his hospital clothes, into his gloves and mask, leaving the trembling Jesse outside in the corridor. Better not to think about that envelope and the letter inside. Better not to think about Jesse, waiting back in the corridor, nervously licking his lips and wondering what would become of him. Better to think only of the job ahead, a few hours' hard work. . . . Lyle Carter was his assistant for the operation. Jesse felt much older and luckier than Lyle, though they were about the same age. Now that Jesse was in private practice, safely taken care of, he did not feel uneasy in front of him; Lyle was not going to take his place with Perrault; no one would take Jesse's place with Perrault. He was safe, absolutely safe. That was why he spoke so quietly with Lyle, telling him what he intended to do. He was quiet, passionless, modest with everyone.

Because he was away from the hospital so much, Jesse had lost track of its hierarchy except at the very top. The small army of interns and residents were strangers to him. The interns looked boyish and undependable. He knew a few of the first- and second-year residents, but he hesitated to trust them with his own patients. He checked and double-checked his own patients, worried that other people would make mistakes with them and that they would die: he remembered his own confusion as an intern. Now he did not trust anyone. *Did not trust anyone.* Jesse stared down at the man he was going to operate upon and it occurred to him that the man might die, might die under the anesthetic, might bleed to death, might spurt blood up onto the lighting fixtures, might sit up with a laugh and knock the instrument out of Jesse's hand. . . . The nurse was looking at him. At Jesse. Lyle was standing near him, watching, ready to watch. Ready to learn what Jesse had to teach him. The body was waiting. The tumor was waiting.

Jesse began, moving jerkily. This was not his usual style. But he had to get started, he couldn't stand there all day while people stared at him. A body, a skull, the interesting profusion of nerves and tissue and bones knit together into a shield. Well, attack it and open it. No fooling around. No time to waste.

A simple removal of a tumor. Jesse had to slow himself down, he had to keep his hands going slowly, slowly. The tumor peeled out so nicely: it was surely benign. Simple and benign. Jesse was therefore bringing life, bringing a gift of life, to the body on the operating table. A droplet of sweat fell from Jesse's forehead onto his own arm. Like a tear. Jesse worked in silence, going slowly. Lyle hung over him. He wanted to know everything. Wanted to learn everything. Well, let him watch, let him learn, Jesse had no secrets. The intern assigned to the operation had nothing to do but watch. He was a nice-faced boy with a crew cut, very young. Jesse glanced at him from time to time. The boy looked very tired. Wanted to get out of here, wanted to run out into the street weeping, sick of the odor of anesthetic and blood.... Jesse thought of Perrault and of how swiftly the old man worked, especially when he was in a bad mood. And so he forced himself to slow down. He would be slow, methodical, passionless.

The patient? A man of about thirty-five. Referred to Perrault by a neurologist in Dayton: headaches, small spasms of the right arm, a stony, plain face, too rigid to show fear. A hulking body of the sort Jesse had seen often on the psychiatric ward; typical schizophrenic thickness, a premature stoop to the shoulders. He was the son of a wealthy Ohio industrialist. He was the "son" of someone with money, therefore he lay unconscious on this table while Jesse picked inside his skull and saved his life. Not a person for Jesse, not really. A body and a brain. A large container of blood—was the blood too dark? too light? Jesse always worried about blood—that had to be kept percolating or Perrault would be furious with him.

The pathologist's report came back in fifteen minutes: good news. The tumor was benign.

"Ah, thank God," Jesse said. He wanted to weep, this was such good news.

Now Jesse had Lyle work. He stared at Lyle's hands, at his mannerisms. Who was Lyle imitating? Jesse himself? Perrault? Jesse dreaded the operation coming to an end. Outside, the letter waited for him; but in here, in this confined, chilly room, he was safe. He knew what he was doing and what he had done. He trusted himself. He trusted Lyle. Nothing could go wrong now. Lyle's hand would not slip, it was impossible that he should make a mistake.... Once, as an intern, Jesse had assisted a surgeon who had opened a chest with one cutting of the knife, an extraordinary fifteen- or sixteen-inch incision to get at a hernia in the diaphragm, filling up with blood, bubbling with blood, and the instruments had been enormous, like mechanic's tools, crunching and spreading the ribs, making a huge hole in the chest. Minutes had expanded and contracted like the pulsations of the exposed heart and the lung, spongy and moving and slippery, an uncanny sight. Jesse had stared down into that hole, into someone's chest opened up... opened up like that for five and a half hours... and after that stint Jesse had great faith in the body's ability to withstand anything, any kind of battering and crunching and snipping.

It was not possible that this man would die. Jesse kept telling himself that, sweating, anxious to the point of pain. Other men died, other patients of his and Perrault's died, but not this man, not today, not when Jesse was so feeble and exposed....

Afterward, he withdrew shakily. It looked all right. He praised Lyle, backing away from him, anxious to get away and back to the lounge. Lyle remained to dictate the account of the operation. Jesse thanked the scrub nurse and the others and backed away, went out to the lounge again—there was his pile of mail, still—no one had walked off with it—

Jesse picked up the letter and closed his eyes.

What if Dr. Pedersen was dead?

He did not dare look at the return address on the envelope. Instead, he opened it hurriedly; roughly he drew out a piece of thick paper that rattled as he opened it; he read in a rush, in a panic, standing there in his green gown: "... estate of William H. Shirer... bequeathed to Jesse Vogel (Jesse Pedersen)... a sum of $600,000...." This made no sense. He forced himself to go back and read it over again. It appeared to be a formal statement from a Lockport attorney notifying him that he had been left certain assets and investments totaling $600,000 by his grandfather, William H. Shirer. The attorney had been searching for him as Jesse Pedersen and had been informed at the University of Michigan that Jesse Vogel was Jesse Pedersen, and now . . . and now he had been bequeathed $600,000 by the late William H. Shirer . . . who had died at the age of ninety-one in Lockport, New York. . . .

Someone was speaking to Jesse. Jesse nodded, edged away, and read the letter over again.

He looked at the back of the letter: nothing. His eye could not take even that in, not exactly. So he remained staring at it for several seconds. There were very small, very light, almost imperceptible dots on the back of the white paper, made by periods and semicolons on the other side that had pressed through with more force than the other typed letters. Jesse turned the letter back over and, when his vision cleared, read the first paragraph again. Each word seemed to make sense and flowed smoothly into the next; but the sentences themselves did not seem to go together. One sentence stood out: *Mr. Shirer expressed a wish to remember you for your kindness and sympathy concerning his daughter. He did not elaborate upon this point with me, but I assume you understand his meaning.*

Jesse saw a fat woman, massive and fluttery, and an enormous waddling fat boy, the two of them hurrying through a hotel lobby. The two of them cringing as a telephone rang. The two of them opening packages of Chinese food, their mouths watering fiercely, desperately. . . .

Jesse began to tremble.

"Is it bad news, Dr. Vogel?" someone asked.

The young intern. Jesse stared at him wildly.

"Is it . . . bad news?" the intern asked.

"No, good news. Good news," Jesse said blankly. *A fat woman and a fat boy on Ontario's fish-strewn shore, opening a picnic basket, their eyes narrowing sharply with hunger, with lust. . . .*

He would have to remember all of that life. He was doomed to relive it.

Little Jeanne was right outside the bedroom door, rapping on it. With her frantic small fists. She thumped against it, banging her shoulder against it so that one of them would have to call out, "Jeanne! Don't hurt yourself!"

Helene sprang to her feet, then hesitated. She stared toward the door as if she did not know what to do. Jesse called out, "Jeanne, don't hurt yourself—stop that—"

Silence. Jeanne's giggling.

Jesse stared at his wife. Her face was turned from him, in profile—stunned, joyless.

"I'd better let her in," Jesse said.

Helene did not reply.

"I didn't mean to . . . didn't mean to upset you so. . . . This won't change our lives," Jesse said.

Jeanne began rapping on the door again. Maybe she thought this was a game: her mother and father hiding on her.

"You never told me that you had a grandfather who had so much money," Helene said slowly.

"I didn't know it myself. I mean, that he had so much," Jesse said evasively.

The letter lay on the bed where Helene had let it drop. She turned to look at him; her gaze was level, suspicious, frightened.

"Helene, why are you so unhappy?" Jesse said.

Her face seemed to collapse.

"This won't change our lives. . . ."

"Won't it?" Helene said.

Jeanne was calling to them. Her small, petulant, frightened voice: *Mommy, Daddy.* Jesse went to the door. He picked up his daughter in his arms and hid his face against her, so that she giggled in surprise, squirming.

"Daddy, let me down! Let me down!"

But when he tried to put her down she hung onto his neck, still giggling. Jesse bounced her in his arms; he did not dare turn back to Helene for several seconds.

"Won't it change our lives?" Helene said.

"What do you mean?" Jesse asked.

"Won't you want to leave now? Pay off your debts here and leave?"

"My debts?"

"To my father. To me. Pay us off and leave. . . ."

"I don't know what you're talking about," Jesse said.

Helene picked up the letter again and tried to read it. Then she let it fall back onto the bedspread; Jesse saw that her eyes were bright and bitter with tears.

"You're in love with someone. I know it," Helene said.

"Don't talk like that," Jesse said angrily, "not in front of—"

"Go to hell," Helene said.

Jesse carried his daughter back out into the living room and sat down with her in the large armchair near the window, "his" chair, and forced himself numbly to listen to her chatter—shrill, hurried chatter, because Jeanne sensed his love for the new baby, her parents' preference for that newer, smaller baby. He forced himself to listen. He kept seeing Helene's tight, anxious face, the absolutely straight part in her black hair, and beyond her familiar face, as if transforming it, the warmer, younger face of Reva, Reva's eyes and their restlessness, Reva's mouth....

When Helene came out she had washed her face. She brought the baby with her, trying to smile, as if nothing had passed between them in the other room. Michele. Jesse stared at the baby. *Michele and Jeanne. His daughters.* He had wanted other children, sons, but he would not have them; Helene could not have any more children.

Staring at the baby, Jesse said, "I could never leave...."

Helene smiled stiffly at him.

He could not eat dinner, couldn't bring himself to sit down. Nervously, apologetically, he backed away and thought wildly of something to tell this woman, this wife of his, some excuse to offer to her—he had to go back to the office, he had forgotten to bring home a chapter of that book Perrault was working on. "I'm supposed to go over it for him. I forgot to bring it home," Jesse said.

"All right," said Helene.

"It won't take me long...."

He drove out and parked somewhere and sat for a while in his car. Then he went to a telephone booth, though he knew Reva's name would not be in the directory. He leafed through the big Chicago directory, listlessly, in a kind of daze, thinking of *that enormous woman and that enormous son of hers, the son taking the hinges off the bathroom door, the hinges off the door, off the door.* No Reva Denk in the directory. No Reva Denk. She did not exist: not as Reva Denk. Standing on the street corner, in public, with her arms folded primly, protectively over that belly of hers. Still flat, he had thought. Girlish and flat. Mrs. Pedersen had been swollen as if with a pregnancy that had bloated her entire body, her entire being, making her cheeks bell out with a flirtatious alarm. Ah, pregnant women. . . . Jesse could not remember whom he himself had impregnated. Did it matter? What did it matter? His sperm or another man's sperm, all of it clotted and anonymous, what did it matter?

It was possible that Reva had not yet had an abortion.

He would drive up to Hilsinger and get her. Save her. No, he would not perform any abortion on her; he would marry her; he would be the father of that baby. *I didn't know what else to do,* Reva had said, frightened. He would be the father of that unborn baby, that mysterious baby, perhaps the one baby he was meant to father out of the entire universe of confused, blundering human beings. . . . Excited, he leafed through the directory again, glancing at the names, the columns of names . . . and none of them meant anything to him, he didn't give a damn for any of them, not one. . . . If Reva Denk's name was not in this book, the book had no value.

He shoved the directory back onto its metallic shelf and went out to his car. He started driving north, north toward Milwaukee; at a gas station thirty miles away he stopped to get gas and a road map, and he thought that maybe he should call his wife, maybe it was now time. . . . But to tell her what? That she was right, he wanted to pay off his debts and be free, he would never see her again? Never see the girls again?

He drove on.

He could not call her. He did not dare call her. He imagined his saying, *Helene, I have to leave you,* and he imagined her perfectly cool voice in reply: *But I will have another baby for you. Another baby for you. Isn't that what you want, another baby?*

And then he would never be able to leave her.

14

Dawn. Jesse woke in the front seat of his car, his mouth pounding with dry heat, his eyes sore, raw. He knew at once where he was and something moved in his stomach, low in his belly, a sense of disaster.

He was somewhere outside Hilsinger, Wisconsin. His car on the shoulder of a narrow highway. Nearby, a ditch choked with weeds—pastureland—a stunted, sparse clump of trees. He rubbed his eyes and the landscape took on no more significance. His mouth was dry, the back of his tongue raw with heat as if he had a fever there, concentrated there. Had he spent the night arguing? He remembered arguing in his sleep. Arguing with Helene, with Mrs. Pedersen, with Reva . . . there were too many women in his life and he needed to clear himself of them permanently.

He sat up stiffly. Moved himself with care. Got behind the steering wheel again, peered at his face in the mirror—that thatch of red-blond hair, wild from a night of misery, of argument, lifting from his forehead with its usual despairing energy. *I am going to marry you. No abortion.*

Why?

He did not believe in abortion, in death. He believed only in life.

Yes, but why?

In life. In life.

But why in life?

He got the car going again, backed around on the highway, and passed at once the "tourist court" that had been closed the night before—the proprietor, a middle-aged man, had refused to give him a cabin last night and had told him to come back in the morning. Well, it was morning now but he was damned if he was going there. He drove angrily past—just a row of ugly little cabins, no more than shacks with screens that belled out loosely and a garbage dump only a few hundred yards away.

Hilsinger: a name on Reva's lips, melodic and inviting. He had been thinking of that name for some weeks. But Hilsinger itself, the real place, the town itself, was not melodic and inviting at all; it was a dull, dismal, ordinary town of about three thousand people, built along the banks of a narrow river, with a few mills and warehouses and some new gas stations and hamburger stands out along the highway. In the distance were hills, a hazy blend of earth and sky no one but Jesse would bother to look at. The air was chilly and assaulting. He needed to wake up. He needed to get that taste of death out of his mouth.

He turned into the parking lot of a diner. Several large trucks were already parked there. Inside, he ordered a cup of coffee. The woman behind the counter gave him an appraising look. How was he dressed? How had he left home? He couldn't quite remember but he suspected he had a hunted, perplexed look. He rubbed his sore eyes and finished his coffee and asked for a glass of water. His stomach was heavy, pulling him down. He felt sick. Noticing the waitress staring at him, he felt how easily he had become another person—someone to be stared at, someone to rub his eyes slowly and miserably, in bewilderment, in a sleazy diner in Hilsinger, Wisconsin. It did not seem probable that he was Jesse Vogel, M.D., an associate of Roderick Perrault. It did not seem probable that he was a married man, the father of two children, or that he had inherited $600,000, or that he could perform delicate, patient little operations upon the human brain, yes, the human brain, though right at the moment his eyes and mouth felt encrusted with a kind of dull, pulsating, feverish scum.

"Could you give me some information?" Jesse said.

The waitress, startled, seemed to leap forward. She picked up a filthy yellow sponge and began fingering it, picking at it.

"I'm looking for an art school that's supposed to be up here. An art colony . . . ?"

"Art colony?"

"I'm from Chicago and I'm looking for an artist named Raeder. I understand he has a kind of art school up here," Jesse said.

The waitress began wiping the counter in front of him slowly, thoughtfully, with the yellow sponge. "Well, there's some painters outside town," she said, "they rented the old Case farm. . . ."

"Where is that?"

"Oh, just up the highway, outside town, maybe a mile away. . . ." She looked at him and Jesse saw a very ordinary, friendly, cautious woman of about thirty-five, he felt a sudden surge of pity for her and for her life. But the look she gave him was pitying. "On the mailbox it probably says Case, they probably didn't bother to change it. A big old place with some barns. . . . Are you a painter too? They had some painters up from the city to take courses or something. I don't know what happened. There was some fracas, something went on, a fight or something . . . it didn't get in the newspaper . . . that was maybe five months ago. . . ."

"I'm not a painter. I'm just up for a visit," Jesse said.

Jesse found the farm without any trouble. Over the name CASE on the mailbox there had been painted the name MAX RAEDER in big white bloated balloon letters, the kind of expansive letters used in cartoons to indicate mirth. Self-parodying mirth. Jesse turned up the bumpy drive and at once a large dirty collie ran out after him, barking. Some chickens ran loose. The farmhouse was in poor condition, and behind it were other, more dilapidated buildings—a barn, a kind of coop that had been painted half-way around in a bright unbelievable red color, a few shanties. Two mud-splattered cars and a pickup truck were parked in the driveway.

Jesse got out of the car in spite of the angry dog. "Go away. Get. Go to hell," he muttered. A man peered out of the house, opening the door cautiously, Jesse saw that it was not Raeder. "Hello," he called, "hello—can I talk to you? Is Max Raeder there?"

The man came out onto the porch, shivering. He wore only an undershirt and jeans. "Max is in bed," he said. "Are you a friend of his or what?"

"I'm a friend of Reva's."

"Oh, Reva. Reva. Well yes, Reva. . . ." the man said slowly. He was not quite a man, really a boy of about nineteen—sandy-haired, smiling, bearded. His skin was rough and some of the pimples had run together into patches of red that looked painful, like burns. "Did you say Reva? Are you a friend of hers?"

"Yes, I think she's expecting me."

"Well, yes. . . . Reva's in bed too."

Jesse's pulse leaped.

Now a woman came out of the house, wearing a raincoat and slippers. Her bare legs were very pale in the morning light.

The boy said to her politely, "Annie, this is a friend of Reva's. Is she maybe up yet?"

"You know nobody's up yet," the woman said irritably. She called the dog back. Jesse, trying to smile at her, afraid of the dog and afraid of what was waiting for him inside the house, felt with a peculiar, lightheaded, almost sweetish panic the sickness of his bowels, his head, the back of his mouth. It was at the back of his mouth that his soul began, and there the sickness began. The woman looked at him, sharp-eyed. Her hair was stringy and long. "How come you're up here so early, mister? It's pretty early to be causing so much trouble."

Jesse imagined Reva in bed with that man—the man of the photograph—the two of them clutching each other in a musty, ill-smelling bed, on a dirty mattress, beneath dirty quilts. Reva entangled in a stranger's arms and perfectly happy.

"I can wait until they wake up," Jesse said.

He was very excited.

The boy came forward to shake Jesse's hand. "I'm Allen, I'm from Kentucky originally. I call this my home now. Where are you from?"

"Chicago."

"Oh, hell, Chicago is an evil city," the boy said seriously. "Forget it. Up here is the end of the world. Your mind doesn't have to race to keep up with itself here because it's the end of the world already—everything is at peace. Isn't it, Annie?"

The woman made a brief scoffing sound.

"You want to see some of our work?" the boy asked. "A lot of us were here all summer. Then it began to break up, people can't keep themselves pure, they bring evil and discord everywhere.... We slept outside in the barn then, when it wasn't so cold. You should have come up this summer."

"You want me to wake them up?" the woman interrupted angrily.

"Well—I don't know—" Jesse said.

"This goddamn dog will get him out of bed on the run. Mad as hell first thing in the morning," the woman said. She wore a man's raincoat that was spotted with paint. Her legs were bluish. "Look, what is your name and what do you want? He'll want to know."

"I'm a friend of Reva's."

The woman smiled brutally. "What's your name?"

"Jesse."

"Is she expecting you?" the woman said with a bright, brutal smile. "Or is it a surprise? Her birthday, maybe? Or your birthday? You her brother or something? An old husband or something?"

"Just a friend," Jesse said.

He spoke calmly but he was very excited, very agitated.

"Okay, fine. You wait out here and I'll see what's what," the woman said.

The boy who was trying to drag the collie back from Jesse, smiled in embarrassment. "Annie isn't like that really. She's a good woman," he said unconvincingly. "You paint, or what?"

"No."

"No? Nothing?"

"Nothing."

The boy stood stooped over, with his arms around the collie's neck. He smiled up at Jesse. "I work in oils exclusively. I'm so goddamn slow you wouldn't believe it! Only five or six canvases to show for the whole summer, but Max says they're worth it.... You know Max's work, huh? You saw his show in Chicago?"

"Yes, I did."

"All that big stuff, huh? Yeah, he's good, he's a genius. No doubt. A bunch of us followed him up here from Ithaca. There were—I would estimate—about forty people in the beginning, off and on, and then this summer about twelve, but that was because Max was in the hospital for a while. Oh, yes, and he was in New York for a while too. He didn't know what his plans were, couldn't make up his mind. He only charges us for board up here. He's a wonderful teacher—I had him at Cornell. He was a great teacher. Did you ever work with him?"

"No."

"You're just a friend of—of—"

"Of Reva's," Jesse said quickly.

Jesse let his eyes move about the place: the old house, the piles of rotting lumber, an old haystack, aged barns. What was this? Why was he here? A scrawny boy with a very badly blemished face was smiling at him, staring at him curiously. If Reva was actually here, inside this house, if she was actually about to appear to him... why, then, Reva would be degraded by this setting, she would be as ugly as the place itself. Jesse thrilled suddenly at that thought: Reva become degraded, ugly....

"She's such a . . . pretty woman. . . ." the boy said shyly.

Jesse flinched.

"There's one other guy up here right now," the boy said, lowering his voice, "but he's not much good. He sleeps in the front room. He's sort of an old guy. He works all the time though, you got to admire his energy. Forty canvases since July, Jesus! They're in the barn mostly. In fact most of them are pictures of barns, different angles and lighting. You know—Monet—'The Haystacks'—that kind of thing."

"What?"

"Monet."

Jesse smiled in confusion. Money?

"Like 'The Haystacks' and 'Water Lilies,' playing around with different light and stuff. He wants to treat the barn very subtly, but it doesn't come out quite like Monet's work. Ha! He tries to be utterly faithful to reality," the boy said confidentially, "in spite of what Raeder tells him, and as a matter of fact we all tell him. Like painting the barn the way it actually is, halfway done in red—and it only turns out looking crazy. Because the real barn, the barn *right there,* looks kind of crazy halfway painted, so why should a painting of that barn look any better? I don't believe you should be faithful to reality when reality doesn't warrant it, do you? Reality isn't everything!"

Jesse could not pay attention to all this. His heart was pounding mightily, nervously, he kept staring at the house and waiting for Reva to appear.

"Look, tell me your opinion precisely. Do you think that reality warrants our absolute fidelity?"

"No—I don't know—" Jesse said vaguely.

"What is reality, that it should so enchant us? Entice us? Wear our fingers down to the bone with love for it?" the boy said. He had begun to sound a little vexed, even angry. "Reva is like that, she's so demanding and heavy . . . I mean heavy in her expectations. . . ."

"What?"

"When she models for us. Her expectations of what we paint."

Jesse stared at the boy. "She modeled for you?"

"Sure, lots of times."

"Reva modeled for you?"

"She isn't very good, really. She isn't professional. She just sits there. Max fixes her up, twists her arms around and all that. He made her sit with her neck stretched back, her head way back like she was looking up at the sky. She could hold that pose for fifteen minutes maybe, which is fairly good, but she isn't a professional because she is too self-conscious. You always know it's Reva, it's *Reva,* and you get sort of... sort of excited...."

Jesse smiled tensely.

"We all model for one another," the boy said. "The kids are pretty good, for kids—Max's kids—but kids don't make good subjects, there is something very banal and sentimental and boring about the very shape of a child, you know. Unless you want to emaciate them or stretch them out or something, you know, something fanciful. But a kid is just death to draw."

Jesse could hear someone arguing inside the house.

"Dr. Vogel?"

Reva had poked her head out the back door. Her blond hair was wild. It fell loose about her face and onto her shoulders, uncombed. She was blinking out into the morning light, a face glazed over with sleep, filmy and beautiful. Jesse stared at her and felt his own helplessness like a wave passing through him.

"My God, Dr. Vogel—Jesse— Is that really you?" Reva cried.

"Don't be angry," Jesse said quickly. "I had to see you—"

Reva stepped out onto the porch. She was wearing a bathrobe that was too large for her, wrapped around her, of some dim, soiled material; it had come open in front as if to show that she was wearing nothing beneath it. Her legs were bare and her small pinkened feet were bare, the toes curling on the doorstep. "Is it really you?" Reva cried.

"Can I talk to you?"

"But— Allen, take the dog away, please, that barking is awful— But, Jesse, what do you want with me? I mean, what do you want?" Reva held the bathrobe tightly closed about her, both hands at her throat. She was smiling sleepily, apologetically. The boy led the collie toward the house, dragging it away from Jesse; he saluted Jesse briskly, backing away. "Oh, that dog is awful, that dog is demented. It isn't friendly," Reva laughed.

She smiled from Jesse to Allen and back to Jesse again, as if this were a joke and nothing serious, as if Jesse were not staring at her.

"I only want to talk with you. Can you come with me for a few minutes?" Jesse said.

"I'm not dressed."

"Get dressed and come out."

"Yes, but—but—"

"I only want to talk to you, I have to talk to you," Jesse said miserably. "Why are you barefoot? You're going to cut your feet, Reva. Why did you come out here barefoot?"

"I didn't know who was out here."

"What kind of answer is that?" Jesse asked in anguish.

"The last time you saw me, you told me to go to hell," Reva said seriously. But he could see that she meant no harm to him; already she had begun to smile again. It was so strange, so effortless, that smile of Reva's! Jesse stared at her. She looked so complete, so unsurprised, so warmly confident. Her skin seemed to glow with health. Was it the pregnancy? Jesse wanted to open the oversized robe she had on and look at her. It was a dazzling, bitter revelation to him, Reva's beauty; the power that women have over men, to make them acknowledge their beauty.... A kind of mist passed over Jesse's brain. He thought of dragging this woman to his car, driving out of here, driving down a lane, back into some scrawny melancholy cornfield....

"You're very beautiful...." Jesse whispered.

Reva smiled dreamily at him. There was no part in her hair for him to stare at. Her hair was very thick, full, flowing up from her forehead down past her shoulders like a mane, burnished and blond, her neck rising from her shoulders gracefully, fluidly, everything about her fluid and alive. He could not truly remember having seen her before, not this particular Reva, this particular woman. There was something massively surprising about her, jarring. Jesse stared at her bare legs—tanned and slender—and at her very slender ankles, which were not too clean, dotted with small red marks that were probably insect bites. Insect bites! Her toes were grimy. He loved her. He wanted to urge her over to his car, get her inside his car and slam the door and drive her out of here—

"Are you in love with that man, that man in there?" Jesse whispered.

"Yes," Reva said.

"And you're living with him? In the same house with his wife?"

"Oh, and other people too," Reva said, surprised at Jesse's tone, "it isn't the way it sounds.... Annie and Max have been together a long time, seventeen years, and Max has not always lived with her, but a few years ago they decided to have these babies... they have two boys, four and five years old, and the boys turned out to be disappointing, I mean they were supposed to bring Annie and Max together again and to be sort of childlike and beautiful, but instead they're hard to manage, they aren't very interesting... and Annie doesn't want to take care of them by herself. I don't blame her. And one of the boys is a little crazy, people think... so Max came back to see how things were.... I met Max in New York. He's a genius, of course, and very talented, but he has had bad luck most of his life and he drinks too much, and... and I'm afraid to talk to him about leaving because he gets so angry...."

"You think he'll hurt you? Is that it?"

"Yes, maybe," Reva said slowly. "Or maybe Annie or one of the boys.... He gets very angry. I don't want to cause more trouble in his life. He was in the hospital while I was gone—Annie says his liver is weak. That's very serious, isn't it? Max is forty-three years old and a very talented man; his students keep following him all around the country, but I'm afraid of the future with him.... I just can't leave him, I can't walk out. I love him."

"What about the baby?"

"Oh, the baby," Reva said, reddening, "well, I guess Max doesn't want me to have it. I guess I'll have to..."

"Come for a drive with me, please. Come with me. I have to talk to you," Jesse begged.

"I'm not dressed—"

"Reva, for God's sake! I want you so badly, I love you, I would do anything for you— Why are you just standing there staring at me?"

"Jesse," she said, pronouncing his name carefully, as if it were not a name she knew well, "Jesse, I don't think I could love you. I don't know you very well. Max is the one who needs me...."

"He doesn't need you!"

"Why are you so angry? Has something happened in your life, that you've driven all the way up here? After that day in Chicago I thought you wouldn't want to see me again. You were so angry with me, so disgusted... your face showed such disgust.... But now you seem to love me again. Why is that?"

Jesse took hold of her wrists, her hands.

"Reva, please. There's a place down the highway—a tourist court—some cabins—I could get us one of them—please, I want to talk to you—"

"I can't leave like this," Reva laughed. But her expression was becoming guarded, cautious. She glanced back at the house, and Jesse was maddened for an instant, wondering if her lover were watching. He would kill that man! "The truth is, Jesse, that Annie and I have been having a very serious discussion for the last several days. We've talked everything through and I probably will be leaving him in a while, but..."

"All right!" Jesse said. "All right, fine! I'll take you back today."

"But not so abruptly," Reva whispered. She pulled away from him. "Do you want to kill him? He's not well, and you're so strong—you look so angry, so healthy! I think you want to drive me crazy. What would it be like to live with you? To marry you? You would push me around, you'd suffocate me—"

"No—"

"You'd suffocate me with your love. I know what you want," Reva said, narrowing her eyes. She was so sweet, so cunning, that Jesse could not tell whether she was serious or teasing. "Yes, I know you... I know men like you.... When I was a girl I knew men just like you, oh, exactly like you... your eyes are getting red at the rims just from looking at me... what you'd really like is to drag me out of here and back in some old barn or some old cornfield, I know you, I know what you want.... A big country boy! You look so healthy and so angry...."

Reva took Jesse's hand. She was smiling tauntingly. Closing her eyes, she pressed Jesse's palm against the side of her face—he felt the slight chill of her cheek in amazement—

Jesse thought he might faint.

"Well, if you become my lover, you must promise this: never make me remember that day I looked you up to ask for an abortion. Never bring up the past to me," Reva said in a swift, rather perfunctory voice. "It will begin all over again, for us. It will begin today. Everything new. A new start. No Max for me and no wife for you. Is that a promise? Is it?"

"Yes—yes—"

"And do you still want me to be Reva to you?"

"Yes—"

"You have no objection to that name?"

"I love that name—"

"And you won't force me to love you? Not right away? Because I don't love you right now, but I will try to love you. I will be faithful to you and try to love you, and eventually I will love you, I can guarantee that. Yes, I can guarantee that. But don't bully me, don't suffocate me. . . ."

"I won't bully you. Never," Jesse whispered.

"And you'll marry me?"

"Yes."

"And the baby—?"

"I want you to have the baby."

Reva smiled at this. "So you'll be the father of this baby, good! That baby will be very proud of his father! And so you'll marry me, you'll let me have the baby," she said lightly, as if running through a list of items, "you'll never bring up the past to me, and never bully me, never? And you'll never see your children again, never, and never your wife? Never your wife? Will I be your wife? Will I be your only wife?"

"Yes," Jesse said.

He tried to embrace her but she stepped away. "No, Max might be watching, we're out in the open," she said. Her face was feverish, beautiful. It seemed to glare at him. "Can you give me an hour, Jesse? An hour? Jesse, can you go away and wait an hour? I will explain this to him, that I'm leaving, I will get free of him, I'll get ready for you—I want to take a bath—I need to take a bath—"

Suddenly she and Jesse both laughed. There was a shrill, terrible, glaring sound to their laughter.

"Will you go away, Jesse, and give me an hour, just an hour?" she said.

"Yes."

"And you, you should fix yourself too. For me. You should get ready for me. Your eyes are bloodshot and you haven't shaved—your clothes are all wrinkled and musty—"

She was speaking in an intimate, hypnotic voice, almost a singsong voice, maddening Jesse. He could not speak.

"Go away, please, and give me an hour. I want to take a bath."

Jesse backed to his car.

"An hour. Just an hour," she said.

He backed away, stumbling. Took hold of the door handle of his car. The fever in his mouth and throat had begun to glow like a flame. Reva was backing away from him at the same time, waving.

"One hour!" Reva cried.

One hour.

"My God. . . ." Jesse said aloud.

He backed his car out of the driveway. He was so excited he could hardly manage to drive, his limbs moved of their own accord, in spasmodic jerks. Where was he? Hilsinger, Wisconsin. Where was that? He got the car turned around somehow and drove back along the highway, past the diner, back to the tourist court. This time the proprietor was willing to give him a room. "It's three dollars a day," he said. "How many days do you want it for?"

"Just a few hours," Jesse said. "I want to get washed up. Shaved."

The man led him through a patch of weeds to the first cabin, which had been whitewashed not long ago; the grass around it was flecked with whitewash. "Well," he said, grunting, "you can get washed up just fine—here's some water—see?" He turned on a faucet and rusty water splashed out. Jesse's face broke into a radiant grin.

He paid in advance for the cabin: three dollars.

Left alone, he hurried to the sink. Panting. He stared at his face in the mirror and, yes, it was really his face, *Jesse,* the face of a thirty-one-year-old man, skin fair and firm, mouth strong, temples strong, a hectic glare to the eye and to the broad ridge of his cheekbones. What had Reva said? So angry and so healthy! So angry and so healthy. But now he must shave. He must shave. He ran his hands hurriedly over his face, his rough cheeks and jaw.

He had no razor. Nothing.

Stunned, Jesse opened the door of the old medicine cabinet above the sink. Three shelves, covered with filthy strips of paper. Paper towels. Nothing. No, wait, he saw on the top shelf a single razor blade—yes, a razor blade!—slightly rusty along its edges but shining in the center.

He tested it against his thumb: sharp enough.

But he needed a safety razor to put it in. Otherwise how could he shave? Trembling, he looked around . . . around at the little room. . . . A lumpy bed, bare walls, wan, listless curtains made of plastic. Screens that were loose. Dead flies on the windowsill, a dead bumblebee, how could he shave without a razor to put the razor blade in? He stared out the window. His own car was parked nearby.

Only a razor blade.

He was crazy with love for her. He would bring her back here, right here, to this rented cabin, and on top of that narrow lumpy sordid little bed he would make love to her. He would marry her in that way. The fetus she was carrying would become his. His baby. Magic. His power as a male. But first he had to wash, he had to shave. . . . He unbuttoned his shirt and tore it off. He sniffed at himself under his arms. A stale odor. Panic. Alarm. Had Reva smelled this? He turned on the faucet and the rusty water spurted out, tepid to the touch; he waited but it got no hotter. Now for some soap. A bar of soap. He looked around and found only a thin, shell-like piece of pink soap . . . but it was enough, it would do! He began lathering the soap, then realized that he should take all his clothes off, should wash his entire body. Reva herself was taking a bath. *Give me an hour,* she had said. He undid his trousers and stumbled out of them, thinking of Reva bathing herself for him; he undid his shorts and stood now in his socks, trembling. The water had begun to splash out onto the floor. He worked the soap into a frantic lather again and stroked it up onto his face, up from his neck and onto his chin and cheeks, the strokes swift and hard and upward . . . and then he tried to wash his chest, impatient with the ticklish curly red hair, matting it down, and then his stomach, his belly, his genitals. . . . *Give me an hour,* Reva had said, backing away from him, and he had felt his soul being tugged out of him by her smile, her lazy dreamy melodic smile, the promise of her body, her name. . . .

In the mirror Jesse's living body faced him, the living surface of his soul: an opaque feverish form standing at its limits, hovering in the yellowish mirror of this room. The skin clammy, as if with terror. Whitish, clammy, unreal. Was this Jesse? His skin, which looked good enough at a distance of inches, was really a fanciful conglomeration of colors, the pigment mottled, like a quilt, all bumps and tiny hills and goose-pimples and hair and moles and formations that were exotic and unintelligible, like something shaped by the warm caressing currents of the sea, or of the wind. His hands raced over his body, soaping it. Must get clean. Must get that odor of panic clean. His face, seen at a respectful distance, was a good face. But, seen up close, it was a curious terrain of slopes and ridges, skin and cartilage and freckles and small veins and hairs, brute dark hairs, pits, bumps, hollows. Reva would see him like this, she would see him up close. Pressed close. He had good, muscular shoulders, biceps that were small but hard, a good chest, a trunk he need not be ashamed of, but Reva would lie close in his arms, delirious in his arms, and he must get clean for her, absolutely clean, he must wash the shadowy pits beneath his arms, and the bluish, frail stomach and abdomen, and the monstrous part of him he half-admired, half-loathed, it was so public, so shameless, so arrogant. *On that bed there, on that very bed. . . .*

His body swayed with a joyful certainty, a lust that radiated out from his loins to make everything glow, the most distant muscle, the bony structures behind his ears, the smallest toes—everything, a festival of parts!—glowing with certainty, with lust, with love for that woman. As he would penetrate her he seemed to penetrate himself, all the parts of himself, well-oiled and warm with a honeyish certainty, the cavities of his body aching to be filled as her body ached for him, his muscles straining to please, his organs swelling and pumping blood in harmony, in love.

He stared at himself. His lips were loose, a loose terrified grin.

Soap on his face. The lather was fading, dissolving. The water wasn't warm enough, but no matter, no matter, he had to get clean and shaved and ready for that woman. He held the razor blade awkwardly in his right hand. How to work this? He had never tried to shave like this before. He wasn't sure if it could be done. Stooping, squinting, he peered at himself in the dingy mirror and tried to see where he should begin. The razor blade was slippery. His fingers were slippery. What if he cut himself . . . ? But he had to shave, he had no choice. He tried to maneuver the slippery little blade against his jaw but he was so timid that nothing happened, the blade just grazed his beard. . . .

Try again.

He got a firmer hold this time. But at the very last instant he was afraid of nicking himself and he dropped the blade into the sink.

He picked it up again carefully, as if it were a delicate surgical instrument. Must take care. Take care. He was panting. The entire area of his mouth and upper throat ached with fever like a flame. He held the razor in place against his left cheek, and felt up and down the length of his body a sharp thrill of lust, so keen that he nearly doubled over . . . but he did not drop the razor blade again; instead he held it firmly and stretched the skin of his left cheek downward with one hand. . . . And then lightly, timidly, he scraped the blade against his skin and blood spurted out at once.

He stared at his own blood.

Then again, as if hypnotized, he drew the blade against the other side of his face.

More blood.

He was fascinated by the sudden streaming of blood. It ran thinly, brightly, through the lather. Nothing could stop it. He brought the blade down against the top of his chest and drew it against his skin—such soft skin, shivering beneath his touch—another immediate flash of blood!—and then against the very top of his stomach, the firm muscular skin. More blood. A sluggish flow. He made the cut deeper and the blood jumped out at once, as if springing forward.

And now . . . ? He touched his left shoulder. Another scratch. He bent and touched the top of his left thigh, frowning. And then, hesitantly, reverently, he drew the blade through the tangle of pubic hair, feeling only a light, acrid stinging, but seeing no blood . . . then digging the blade in a little deeper. . . .

Ah, blood!

He stood there, bleeding from a dozen places, unconnected places, streaming blood so lightly, experimentally, giddily....

He waited but the bleeding did not stop. He tried to blot it with the old paper towels, but it did not stop. The scratches stung. In the end, impatiently, he decided to put his clothes back on over the bleeding. He drove back to Chicago that way.

Book III

Dreaming America

1

July 1970

Dear Father,

The voice must say *I love you.* If it does not say *I love you* it is not an authentic voice.

Today we hitched a ride with two old people in a camper. Retired, from Minneapolis. Gray-faced. Chatting, chatting. You should hear Noel chat with strangers! Sometimes he isn't Noel but gives out other names—sometimes I am his sister—sometimes his little bride—sometimes he is from Canada, or Maine, or California, or Florida—his voice mimics all voices, changes itself to suit all ears, coddles and caresses and hypnotizes—*Father, I want to come home*—no, that isn't my voice and it isn't Noel's, don't listen to that voice—

Hitched a ride to Homestead, Florida. Don't look it up on the map. As soon as you put your finger on it, your clean pared fingernail, I will no longer be there. In fact I am already gone. Worked out in the fields for a day, I forget how long, *U-Pick Tomatoes* 10¢ lb.—Noel says work is good for us, you eat as you work, lots of pulpy seedy messy tomatoes squashed under our bare feet—oh, my shoulders and arms and neck are pink, red, they ache—the voice is always changing itself like the runny fluid of tomatoes, the seedy insides of tomatoes—the voice is always mimicking other voices—it is not Noel's voice but my own, it is always saying *I love you I want to come back.*

U-Pick Pole Beans. U-Pick Avocados. Ten for a dollar here. The fields glimmer with heat, with heat waves, there are old battered buses parked in ditches, Negroes with grimy straw hats and no smiles, glancing at Noel and me without interest. Noel is so bright, so blond! But you have never seen Noel. You have never seen him even in your imagination, though you have wanted him dead and have had to imagine him to want him dead. Father, are you listening? Or are you on the telephone? The police can't find me, I am too far away; if they tried to head me off in one of these fields they would see me melt into the waves of heat, Noel and I both melting together, dissolving—

Can you hear the voice? Does the voice say *I love you?*

I am writing this on the Gulf of Mexico, on the edge of the Gulf. Noel has been gone for two hours. When he comes back he'll have a surprise for us—always a surprise—sometimes money, sometimes other people; once he lugged a color television unplugged from some motel room, he's so clever, and if anybody approaches him he melts right into the air, nobody could catch him! You couldn't catch him. Couldn't put him under an anesthetic and pare out his soul. Couldn't strap him down on an operating table the way you did the rest of us.

The outside of my hand is getting red, but the inside, the palm, is still pale. Clammy. It's dirty but clammy and pale. My fingernails are all broken and black. Mother should see them! I think I will rip one off and enclose it with this letter, so you can show it to Mother and to the police for identification. Then they can match it up with me when they find me.... My hands are dirty but that's not all. You are such a clean man. I tried to explain that to Noel but he couldn't understand. He thinks that clean means clean hands, soap, he doesn't know it is a jug of distilled water, a jug made of that very clean, light, unbreakable plastic, not dangerous like glass but unbreakable. There is no taste to distilled water. There is no taste because it is not contaminated.

Did you get my letter from Savannah? That was me. I sent that for a joke. Did you know it was me? Or did you think it was really from one of your dead patients? If they could write from the dead, think from the dead, dream back on you from the dead?

Noel is very late coming back to me. The sun is very bright, I can feel how much closer it is to the earth here than in Chicago, I am lying on the edge of the land waiting for him and dreaming of you, dreaming of him and you, melting you together. Little shells all around me. Millions of shells. I try not to think about them—how small they are—the shells of little animals but the animal meat has melted out of them—their bodies are beneath me—all we have to give are our outside bodies, our shells, trying to make something beautiful of them and then draining out of them, great piles, mountains of shells that are bodies for giants to lie upon. Noel has instructed me to rid myself of you. "You must dream back right over him," Noel whispers in my ear. *Dream back.* "Dream his face and his voice. Erase as you dream," Noel says, stroking my backbone up and down—because it was sore—and it is the center of the body, everything radiates out from it—my backbone is so sore and limp—what good did it do, Mother's nagging about my posture? Don't forget to show Mother my fingernail! Oh my black ragged fingernail!

I don't love her. The voice has nothing to say about her.

Noel rubs his forehead hard against mine sometimes, to make me think his thoughts. They rise up in him and in me like surprised, dangerous waves. Giant birds are diving into the water here. I think they are pelicans, with terrible beaks. They rear into the air and then dive down again, suddenly, three or four of them together; my heart jumps when they crash like that, flat into the water.... Noel's ideas are like that. Once he said to me when we were on the back of a truck, a farmer's pickup truck, my head ached from being so tired and he said *Give me a shove* and stared at me, to see if I could do it. *Give me a shove off onto the road, honey.* But it was a joke. I think it was a joke. To see if I could kill him when he instructed me, but I couldn't move, that is the way his ideas flash into my head sometimes like the birds diving or the biggest waves, that throw the shells around and drag them back again, up and back again, again and again as I lie here, trying to wash me away and erase what is in my head, Father, all the thoughts you put in my head. "Systematically

—because I believe in order—you dream back and erase yourself," Noel told me, "step by step, year by year, erasing the monsters so that you can be free. Then you will be mine, Shell," Noel promised. And he never lies.

The voice must say I love you or else it is not an authentic voice. I don't love her. I dream about you—so tall, your head filled with thoughts like the shadows of birds' wings, the skin around your eyes darkening with all the deaths you had to perform, death on your fingers and in your lungs. Carrying me. I remember you carrying me in your arms. I remember Jeanne frowning up at us, ready to cry, so jealous of us—Jeanne sputtering with her asthma—I can hear you talking to me in babytalk and I can hear your voice switching to another voice for Mother, the drone of your talk with Mother, necessary talk about how to get from A to B, one year to another year, I can feel myself carried high in your arms with the ceiling and the walls reeling around my head, and Jeanne so far below and Mother in another room, trying to talk to you.

I am an unadopted baby.

I don't like to think about being born. If you had adopted me I wouldn't have had to be born like that. You and Mother were going to adopt a baby for so many years—a little brother for Jeanne and me—"baby brother"—I was ready for a baby brother but he didn't come. Jeanne was ready for a nightmare but it didn't come. Jeanne's face all mottled but no baby brother came.

"Imitate his voice in your head," Noel told me. He weighs me down and keeps me from slipping off into the sky. His soul weighs mine down, otherwise it would trail up into smoke and be gone. Noel. My lover. "Imitate his voice in your head. And then you will be free," Noel said. But I can't do it. Can't make your voice come out of me. Or hers. It is only my voice saying *I love you I want to come home* and I have to press my hands against my mouth so that Noel can't hear that, otherwise he would grind my face into the sand here until I suffocated. "Imitate his handshake," Noel said. I have seen you shake the hands of many men, Father, stooping eagerly to them because you are taller than most men, frowning a little, your face going cloudy and baffled as if you felt yourself colliding with other people as if with mysteries, was that it . . . ? Dense cloudy faces, souls. Try to figure them out. People stick in me the way they stick in you. Can't slide off them, even my slippery body can't slide away. Your smile had to be coaxed. You stared at me without seeing me and then a form appeared that was your daughter and you saw her and then you smiled. But not before. What did you see before you saw me, when you were staring at me?

If I could get behind your face, Father. Manipulate your handshake. If I could make your voice sound in me, in my head. Your tufted eyebrows, you red hair lighter than mine—your strange light green eyes, like mine—why can't I see out of them? Then I could see myself. The daughter. Then I could erase myself and be free.

Noel says: You came out of a cell expelled by your father, and you must go back into that cell.

A cell is like an eye, with a dot in it. Is that the soul?

Mother had nothing to do with it. I don't dream about her. I see her in flashes the way you see old stray memories of strangers, people you didn't know you were seeing at the time. Somehow they get inside your brain. I see her at the front window of our big house, staring down the big front lawn, staring at the street. . . . I see her nervously pulling a bedsheet up to cover something, so that I wouldn't see . . . blood on Jeanne's bed, was that it? Blood in the shape of a star.

Close your eyes, Shell. Place your finger upon a certain day, the beginning of what you remember. That was what Noel told me before he went away. *Write your father a letter. . . . Your father is a famous man, with such grave pouched eyes and a noble forehead, he deserves a letter of love! In your own voice, Shell, and not in mine. You have to do this yourself.*

Noel came running to me, Father, a pounding noisy weight on the stairs, his face bright and panting, his hair flying, his voice already threading into my head, my precious brain, and the buttons on my dress squirmed at the sight of his hands. My heart was already fattening up at the sight of him. Something unbearable about him, his purse of a mouth. A ringing sound set off by him next to me, oh I could not help myself—little Shelley thinking in terror *I could not help myself.* He wasn't the first anyway. Not the first. Not the second or the third either but after that my mind fades away. Don't ask questions.... Father, you don't want to know! Don't want to know how I could not help myself!

Of your two daughters it is Michele who cannot help herself. Jeanne does very well.

My father is a famous surgeon, little Shelley giggles. Makes herself dizzy. Your eyes look light and transparent but mine look opaque —an imbecile is growing out of me—sometimes I can't read, Father, it frightens me when I can't read the billboards along the highway, the letters don't add up to words and I think I am in another place like on another planet where the language has changed—but Noel tells me I will be all right, Noel sings in my ear and puts me to sleep—

Once I was terrified and couldn't stop screaming but Noel brought me out of it. Made me laugh instead. Oh I laughed and laughed! The muscles of my sore face jumped around like crazy, careened off the walls, jumped back into me. I was terrified because a book was going to fall off your shelf and onto my head, the book was by a man named Lord Brain. I had to explain this to Noel but I couldn't stop screaming. The book was about brains. I used to look through it in your study. It was by a man named Lord Brain and it was about brains. I saw the diagrams, I read the words.

Think of November 22, 1963.

Can you remember? Remember for me. Help me. Noel says I must remember and I must begin at the beginning. *Father, I love you, don't call the police but help me, listen to me....*

Noel wasn't the first anyway.

November 22, 1963. We were in New York City. I was eight years old. Mother and Jeanne and I were at the back of a large room, sitting on folding chairs. You were standing at a podium. Talking. Your clear steady voice saying something about memory. *Memory.* The audience was nearly all men. Heavy heads, serious heads, heads stuffed with brains. Like yours. Eyes behind eyeglasses, aging men with fragile heads, men like bulls, so shaggy you can't believe they are doctors.... They are all listening to you, to Dr. Vogel, on memory.

It is New York City. A hotel "ballroom." Chandeliers of blinding crystal, turned on because the inside of this old hotel is dark. The walls decorated with velvet in strange designs, bright green like the green of pool-table tops. . . . You are talking about memory and what it is. The men are listening to you. *Dr. Vogel is my father.* Mother is listening quietly, her hands folded on top of her purse on top of her knees. Jeanne sits on her other side, her thumb pressed against the bottom row of her teeth, exerting great pressure there while she listens and listens. Jeanne, my ugly pathetic sister. She is trying to push her teeth back all the time because she thinks they stick out too far. She is a head taller than I am, always nudging me away, poking me with her elbows. Hating me.

Jeanne is clean outside and in. Distilled water. A clean light unbreakable jug of distilled water. No man has stuck a finger into it to contaminate it, you can bet on that.

Your voice penetrates all the corners of the room. Even and unhurried. *Dr. Vogel. Jesse Vogel. The Vogel Clinic.* Listening to you, Mother opens her purse quietly and takes out a tissue to dab at her nose, then at her forehead. Mother is always doing that. You can't ask your mother why she is always dabbing at her face. She is afraid of grease oozing out of her pores, maybe. But her skin has no pores. *Mother dreaming out the window, kept perfectly clean by the maid. Waiting for you to come home? Waiting as the sun went down?* Don't think evil of me, Father, but I don't love her. I could never think of anything to buy her for her birthday or for Christmas. Once when I bought her that little village, the "New England Village" made of cardboard and sparkling with fake snow, with Santa Claus and his reindeer flying over the church steeple, she couldn't even pretend that she liked it—her face careful, unresponsive, as she bent to arrange it under the Christmas tree—I kept looking at her, looking, waiting for her to say that she liked it, but she was careful only to say *thank you, Shelley.*

You came to the end of the paper you were reading. A period of questions. Glinting of eyeglasses, assessing frowns. I watched as men priced you, Father. Added up your parts. They asked you complicated questions and you answered them slowly, carefully, Dr. Vogel cautious as always: such an expensive man! I wanted to put my hands over my ears, afraid I would hear you make a mistake. Afraid someone would attack you. I looked around and saw them all pricing you, adding you up. Back home everyone knew what you were worth. Jesus, everyone knew. The kids at school knew, they knew everything, there was no place for me to hide. Even in the girls' lavatory I couldn't hide except in the toilet stalls. That's the last place in the world. When you are alone there with the door latched, just standing there, you have come to the last place in the world and you can't go any farther. That's where you might go crazy if your head is uncertain. That's why doors should not have latches. Or there should be a back way out of toilets. In the overnight jail the lavatories are all lit up all night long, and the doors don't have latches, you can bet on that.

November 22, 1963.

I am eight years old.

It is a short while after the reading of your paper, but you are not with us. Mother and another woman have taken Jeanne and me out somewhere, to an ice cream parlor—it has a name out of a fairy tale—it smells of chocolate syrup and the warm perfumed whisperings of mothers and daughters—I remember the stuffed animals, the giant pink and white pandas and the rag dolls with their benign sunflower faces, all eyes and grins. Mother seems happy, as happy as I've seen her. But I don't dare look too closely at her for fear I will see something about her face I will regret. (I told Noel my nightmare about Mother: her face smooth and hollowed out as if with a surgical instrument, nothing but slopes in the skin for eyes and nose and mouth, indentations that are thoughtful and shadowed, valleys in a pale bloodless face. But it's not Mother I am dreaming about.) The woman with us . . . yes, of course, it is Mrs. Myer, Lauren Myer, Dr. Myer's cheerful wife . . . Dr. Myer is coming to Chicago to join you in your Clinic. You will become close acquaintances. You don't make any friends, Father, but Dr. Myer will become a valuable acquaintance. Mother doesn't make any friends, but Lauren Myer will become a name on her lips, a name Jeanne and I will hear often. I remember Mrs. Myer's lime-green coat, her puff of hair, the watch with a thick wristband of platinum, with emeralds on either side of the face . . . I couldn't have known they were emeralds at the time, someone must have told me later. Yet, I remember her and her watch, I remember it precisely and as I remember it I am erasing it.

I am erasing her. And Mother. I am erasing their talk. I am erasing that day.

"You must be very proud of your husband—" Mrs. Myer is saying.

An ice cream parlor decked out in expensive deep pinks and velvet-whites: wrought-iron chairs and tables, the smell of glop, vanilla, fudge, giant lollipops, giant teddy bears with their shining wise eyes, perched up on shelves. Their paws have been cut off and stitched over. Harmless blunt rounded paws. There are clowns with bellies of yellow and black stripes, their grins a little too wide. Boxes of candy that are as living as the clowns and the stuffed animals, wide crinkling bows, wrapping paper smooth and gleaming as satin. Mrs. Myer fusses over Jeanne and me, *you must be very proud,* she seems a little perplexed at Jeanne's moodiness, *isn't this a lovely place?* She has a face like one of those boxes of candy—heart-shaped, too brightly made up, a satiny sheen to her lips. Her eyes are slightly recessed, smaller than Mother's. She is coming with her husband to Chicago to fall in love with you, but you won't be bothered by this fact; probably you never knew it.

Sucking a thick syrupy concoction up a straw: my heart pounds with the pressure to get all this eaten, out of the way. The excitement of the trip has made me a little nauseated. It is some rich strawberry drink, a soda or a milk shake in an enormous frosted glass, too big for me, sickening, and around me everyone is chatting, laughing, *what are they saying?* Mother is looking around suddenly. Mrs. Myer stops talking. The place goes silent—up at the front, at the cashier's counter, someone is talking loudly. Our waitress—a girl with hair curled like tiny sausages—walks toward our table without seeing us, staring at the front of the shop, blundering into a chair— *What, what are they saying?*

Mother gets to her feet.

"What happened to him? Is he shot? Where is he shot?" Mother cries.

But the waitress does not answer her, and now other customers are standing, bewildered, frightened, someone puts his napkin down slowly and is very white, very distracting . . . an old woman wanders out into the center of the restaurant, staring. . . .

Mother and Mrs. Myer hurry us out. Now there is a hurry to

get out of here, everyone hurries, at the door people glance at one another, their eyes snatch at one another's faces . . . Jeanne is whining at Mother, wanting to know what is wrong, I am excited and frightened and relieved not to have to finish all that ice cream. . . . A radio has been turned up high. A man is speaking as if he has just rushed in with a terrible sight in his head. He is almost shouting. Behind the counter the cashier has begun to cry, a middle-aged woman with layers of make-up on her face, crying, I am frightened to see how her make-up stays on the top of her face while the face itself contracts and changes—

"Is the President killed?" Jeanne whines. "Is he here in New York? Where is Daddy?"

Out on the street we are being hurried along. Mother and Mrs. Myer hurry us, their heels clattering on the sidewalk, must hurry, hurry, and everything has a different look—people are hurrying like us, or else they are standing oddly still, with nowhere to go. Looking around. Waiting to hear news. Waiting. "What if there's an uprising? A revolution?" Mrs. Myer says.

Mother drags us along. At a newsstand she pauses to glance at the newspapers, but their headlines tell her nothing. We cross over to the hotel, its enormous entrance, enormous sprawling steps, and everywhere people are strange, they stare at us and at one another—I hear someone say, "Is he dead yet? Is he dead yet?" There are whistles around us, sirens, horns of automobiles, someone crying, or is that Shelley crying? like a baby, crying? so that Jeanne gives me a push. We hurry through the revolving door and other people are hurrying out. Eager. Pushing hard. Inside the big hotel lobby there is a rush of people. I am panicked, I pull at Mother's gloved hand.

The ornate lighting of the lobby makes faces look like masks. Unused to this condition, this noise. The women's clothes seem put on crooked. *Is he dead? Is he dead?* A young man with an overcoat flapping around him rushes through the crowd, knocking people aside. Men stare sternly from face to face as if searching for someone responsible—I know that look—I am fearful of it in your face—*Father, I love you I want to come back to you*—the elevator doors open and a stream of men jostle by, men's legs and arms brushing close to me, I start to scream, Mother's hand slips from mine and I am pushed to one side, I see you across the lobby, Father, and I start over to you—I am pushed against a chair, a leather chair, and I slip under it and get free of the crowd—and a man in uniform is opening a plate-glass door to let someone hurry through, wild-eyed himself but very stiff, straight—I run in a panic, not seeing you but running toward you, toward where you were, people brush against me without seeing me and take no notice of my screams—

Yet I am screaming.

Noel says, waking me out of bad dreams: *You're only imagining pain, Shell. Pain is a fiction.*

Yet I am screaming.

I overheard you telling someone about a patient of yours who began to scream when the tubes were put in him. A man who weighed only eighty pounds but fought everyone off and crawled under the bedcovers to the foot of his bed to hide, to hide from you.

We are all screaming.

Here in the lobby it makes no difference if you scream out loud or inside. Nobody can hear. The screams rise in a pyramid but still they are silent, caught inside the faces. A current is dragging us all. There is a wind inside this building that lifts us, pushes us hard, cuts off our screams, suffocates us, we stampede back and forth, trapped, and yet we are all free here, nobody knows us, we are all children running loose without adults to hold us back, we see people who look familiar to us like people in a dream, but they turn out to be strangers—

And then you have hold of me. You are crying, "Shelley! Stop that!"

You catch me in your arms.

I stare up at you and see the fear in your face, even in your face.

"Shelley, stop that! Shelley!"

I am trying to get away from you, throwing myself backward, striking something hard, being kicked by someone—and you try to pick me up, you are struggling with me—I can't stop screaming—you shout at me to stop but I can't stop, I can't stop—

I am still screaming.

2

In the early morning of November 23, 1963, Dr. Vogel lay awake in his room in the Plaza Hotel beside his sleeping wife, and he thought of things failing, crumpling, the bone of the skull collapsing, and his body was rigid with terror.

He would have liked to turn to his wife, but he respected her sleep. He feared her a little. If he had turned to her she would have guessed that he sought only her flesh, the certainty of her flesh, something he could embrace.

He thought of the President: dying, and dead. He thought of his daughter: her hysterical little body, her drained face. All that crying, struggling. As if she hadn't known him. Staring up into his face as if, so close to him, she hadn't recognized him. *Someone was dying, no, dead. . . .* For hours someone had been dying but had really been dead. Now he was dead. The world was filled with people who were dying, and dead. The dead have been dead a long time. Jesse lay flat on his back, a chill of terror passing through him as he thought of the dead and their claim upon the earth—how many more dead there were than living, how deeply the earth was filled with the fine siftings of their bones!

Tomorrow we'll be home, Jesse thought. Tomorrow this will be history.

The conference had ended abruptly. Confusion and grief. Jesse thought of his paper on memory, of how well it had been received, of his own cautious satisfaction—and now all that had fled from him, rapidly, into the past, the inconsequential past of the day before. There was only one truth about that day: someone had been killed.

Dr. Vogel and his wife had spent the evening with a small group of doctors and their wives, people who hadn't been able to get out of New York that evening. They had watched television—the film clips, the endless reports—and after a while they had milled around loosely, nervously, beginning to joke, drinking too much. Jesse had stayed by the television set, watching. There was something he must learn. Must understand. He could not quite believe that the President was dead. What did that mean? Dead? A bullet in the head—the brain—yes, the brain—and so someone was dying, someone was dead? The President was permanently dead?

He kept thinking of how Shelley had seemed to run to him, and then to run away from him—her terror, her screams. She was a high-strung, very pretty little girl; he was fascinated by her, and yet, when she had struggled with him in that crowd, he had felt rage like a flicker of heat passing over his brain, maddening him. Why had she fought him?

Shelley, stop that! he had shouted.

He had not told his wife about Shelley.

Now he lay awake and did not dare to move. The bedclothes beneath him were damp with his sweat. All his nerves were keen, as if pinched hotly; he was exhausted; his mind raced back and forth over the day he had just lived through. All day long someone had been dying, and had died. Finally died. He had been dead all along and Dr. Vogel had known it, but when he had finally died Dr. Vogel had been unable to comprehend it.

He wanted to get out of bed, throw on his clothes, run down into the street—

The Vogel Clinic, Chicago, Illinois.

He would be The Vogel Clinic. Himself.

Dr. Perrault had not bothered to come to this conference of neurologists and neurosurgeons. He kept saying to Dr. Vogel: "Yes, yes, you are ahead of me when I was your age, is that what you want to know? You are ahead of yourself. The world is ahead of itself."

Dr. Vogel, with his own plans for the future, awaiting quietly the future when Dr. Perrault would be retired, respected the old man's bitterness and said nothing. He knew how to be silent. Never argue. Never. His face stiffened at such times, but he said nothing.

"Why are you looking at me like that?" Dr. Perrault sometimes asked. "Do you think I am something to stare at? Eh?"

Jesse defended him at the hospital. The old man's insults were getting worse—he was getting crude, offensive. Jesse defended him to the families of patients. *Why, why was he so unfeeling?—*

didn't he respect death? It was Dr. Vogel's belief that Dr. Perrault did not respect death, no. That was the old man's secret. But he would have never said this out loud, not to anyone. It was a secret of Dr. Perrault's that Perrault himself did not understand.

At the conference he had skillfully avoided saying much about Perrault to men who asked about him. Working hard as ever, Jesse told them. Working on his book. As he talked with these ex-students and associates of Perrault, some of them fairly old themselves, he had felt an eerie tugging at the back of his mind, as if Dr. Perrault were present, listening, spying on him, taking in all this with his sardonic birdlike expression.... Dr. Perrault hated Dr. Vogel, obviously. Staring at Dr. Vogel, he would appear fascinated, utterly enraptured, as if something about Dr. Vogel's face gave him no peace. He could sit for fifteen, twenty minutes without moving, in a kind of catatonic calm, staring and thinking. What was he thinking about? Dr. Vogel felt the old man always thinking, always contemplating him, even when he was nowhere near. He felt the old man opposing him. He shivered, thinking of that persistent, eternal opposition, not understanding it. "Your hair is an extraordinary color," Perrault sometimes said, smiling.

"My hair?" Jesse said, alarmed.

"Yes, your hair. An extraordinary unhuman color."

Perrault wanted to drag him down. But he would not drag him down, not Dr. Vogel.

In a few more months Jesse would be free of him. And he was really free of him now. Always, he was subservient to Perrault, he accepted Perrault's most biased criticism, he did what Perrault wanted, and yet he was free, freeing himself. It had to be done cautiously. *Someone was dying, was dead.* Jesse had gone to talk with Grandfather Shirer's attorney in Lockport and he had settled out of court—Dr. Pedersen had intended to contest the will—for half of what he had been left, so he had money, he had a great deal of money to finance a small hospital of his own; in a sense he was already free but he had to move cautiously. Dr. Perrault could still ruin Jesse if he wanted. He could shake himself out of his dark inertia and ruin Jesse.... It took him so long to withdraw, to sink; as he drifted farther from life Jesse moved to take his place, taking on more and more of Perrault's responsibilities, being exposed himself. At times he felt the raw panic of exposure. Working himself free of the old man, so caught up with the old man, he yet realized that Perrault protected him from the world even now. He knew that. He could not erase in himself a sense of absolute, utter, sweetish dependency, a helplessness in the presence of the old man that grew out of love. It was permanent in him. But at the same time he thought eagerly, guiltily, of the years when he would be free . . . a better surgeon than Perrault himself . . . with a clinic of his own, a private clinic that would be the center in the Midwest for certain types of work. . . . And then all that would remain of Dr. Perrault would be Dr. Vogel's carefully cherished memory of him.

Someone was dying, was dead.

Helene stirred. Jesse, wanting suddenly to embrace her, to talk with her, leaned up on one elbow. "Are you awake?" he whispered.

She did not reply.

"Helene?"

She had had too much to drink last evening. Her father had been in and out of New York, too busy, too mysteriously busy, to take part in the conference. He had stayed around for a while that evening, dashing and yet pert, delivering his opinions on the assassination—the "assassination plot"—in the crowded hotel room, fixing himself and his daughter drinks, standing for a while behind Jesse to watch the television coverage, but gradually drifting away to join a circle of other people. Jesse was relieved that Dr. Cady hadn't bothered much with him. He was relieved to have been spared Cady's perpetual questions about his work and about Perrault and about his family life. . . . Cady was aging, but not shabbily. Not like Perrault at all. He seemed to be getting nervier, sharper. Neither Perrault nor Cady had finished his book, but Perrault kept on with his or gave the appearance of keeping on—Jesse did much of the research for him, the compiling of figures, he had a large file of correspondence with other doctors, in fact he was almost writing the book himself—while Cady only joked about his book. His work was a semiclassified project that had been funded over the past fifteen years by government agencies. "With all they've poured into me they could have financed a small war," Cady joked. "They could certainly have financed an assassination done with more finesse, with more style."

He had shocked a few people by saying that. Jesse, annoyed, had pretended not to hear. "Now Robert Kennedy will be next, that is a prudent assumption," Cady said. Helene had smiled a small, strained smile at this. But most of Cady's conversation had been about a car he was having built for him. Jesse had tried not to listen to this, wanting to put his hands over his ears, staring at the television screen—but there was his father-in-law, the renowned Benjamin Cady, talking loudly about an automobile someone was building for him. On this day the President of the United States had been killed, but Dr. Cady insisted upon talking about an automobile.

"It's absolutely a custom job; there will be only one of its kind in the world," Cady had explained. "The chassis, engine, and automatic transmission are being built by General Motors, then modified by hand by the Richler engineers. The final assembly, coachwork, instrumentation, and finishing will be done in Germany, of course. The leather interior will be done by Connolly Brothers—they supply Rolls, you know—it should be done shortly after the first of the year—"

Jesse had not dared look at his wife's face.

Now they lay side by side in this hotel bed, the two of them in the darkness of a strange room. They seemed to be floating upon the darkness, separate. Whatever sorrow Helene felt about her father, Jesse did not know about it; whatever sorrow Jesse felt about Perrault, Helene did not know about it and would not have wanted to know. Other women had wept at the President's death, but Helene had not wept. Jesse had felt tears of anger and frustration burn in his eyes, but Helene had remained calm because she hadn't wanted to frighten the girls. "Jeanne is already too morbid. Shelley is feverish," Helene had said. She was always assessing the girls, speaking of Jeanne and then of Shelley as if reporting on them to Jesse or to herself, making sure of them. "Too much is going to be made of this," she had said of the assassination, "the country always makes too much of everything.... It will turn out vulgarized and clownish. I don't want the girls to wallow in it."

The President had been killed. Now there was a new President. Before two o'clock it had all happened and had become history: the motorcade in Dallas fired at, the President struck in the head, the President pronounced dead. Jesse felt again and again the impact of those bullets in his own body; the head, the vulnerable head, the precious brain.... Why was it always this way, men dying, men dead? Why the exploded skull, the burst brain, why so many men in a procession that led to death? Dr. Vogel, sweating, could not understand it.

He would think of Reva instead.

No, not Reva. Not tonight.

His senses stirred suddenly, painfully. Always Reva. Reva. But he would not think of her tonight. He would remain faithful to Helene.

When he could not sleep he often thought of Reva, and a kind of storm would grow in him. But he must not think of her tonight, not when someone had just died. His mind raced, looking for something to attach itself to. Not Reva. Not the demands of his body. He often lay awake for hours at night, unable to sleep, and in his head there were people, patients, deaths, diagnoses, problems, recoveries, improvements, surprises. Dr. Perrault had just filed a suit against someone, and Jesse would be dragged into it. No way out. He must acquire an attorney of his own. Must protect himself. His mind filled up with Perrault's words, Perrault's grimaces, Perrault's soul. He lay awake in a perpetual consciousness, a perpetual flow of words. He could never catch up with his own consciousness.

What was consciousness, what was life? What was death?

He thought he heard a sound in the adjoining room, where the girls were sleeping. One of the girls moaning in her sleep?

He wondered if he should get up to check. But Helene was sleeping purely, flawlessly, and he did not want to disturb her. He listened and heard nothing more. Shelley had been so frightened, so wild.... He had not been able to say the right words to Shelley. He had not been able to console her. Holding her, embracing her, trying to comfort her, he had felt with a terrible certainty the failure of his words, his touch, even the fact of his fatherhood...what could he bring to this terrified eight-year-old, this pretty, feverish child? It was terrible, that he should love his daughter so much and yet be unable to help her.

He listened but heard nothing. No sound from the other room. Only sounds from the street eight stories below, ordinary city noises, impersonal and out of his control. Helene slept beside him, turned from him. Jesse wondered bitterly if she was human, that woman. She was so virginal and impersonal in her half of the bed, the kind of woman who sometimes came to his office—refined, tense, very intelligent—carrying her flesh lightly, as if it belonged to someone else. He did not understand these women. Shelley was not going to be like that. These were women inhabiting bodies that did not belong to them and did not interest them. *A man could not connect himself to a woman without a body.* Just before flying to New York, Jesse had talked with a young female patient and had explained that her condition had been diagnosed as myasthenia; and before he could go on to assure her that this was treatable, she had interrupted and asked coolly, indifferently, "How long do I have to live, Doctor?"

He had the idea that his diagnosis had disappointed her.

The thought of Reva was still with him, not the thought of her exactly, but the sensation of her. He touched Helene's shoulder, which was uncovered. Cool, smooth flesh. It was subordinate to him and yet separate from him. He wanted to make love to it—to his wife—but the strain would be too great, the need for conversation, the conflict between them that was never verbal, never exposed, her pretense at sleepiness and her reluctance and her final acquiescence. She would become affectionate when it was almost too late—when it was almost too late.

He would never sleep if he thought about love.

He would never sleep if he thought about the dead President, about the death of the President, the fact of death.

Jesse lay unable to sleep. Occasionally, out in the hotel corridor, a voice lifted with faint perplexity or impatience, as if this long troubled day had kept people up too late, pushing them to the limits of their strength, their capacity for grief. Eventually you ran out of grief. He himself was only thirty-eight years old, he was only beginning his life, and yet he was unaccountably tired, his soul was tired, as if he had lived through several lifetimes already . . . as if, somehow, Dr. Perrault's aging were his own, something he had already experienced and was experiencing now, through Perrault, and must someday experience once again in Jesse Vogel. . . .

Jesse Vogel: who was that?

He heard a sound from the girls' room. He sat up, startled.

He got up, put on his bathrobe, and crossed over into the other room. His eyes darted at once to the twin beds, the covers that looked light, almost glowing, in the shadowy room, the girls' slight bodies beneath the covers—his daughters. His. Both seemed to be asleep. He closed the door behind him and stood there, staring at them, his heart still pounding as if he had thought them in danger. He wanted them only to sleep like this —to be at peace, unharmed, unconscious.

Yes, they were both asleep. No danger.

When Jeanne had been born, Jesse had loved her so that it had frightened him. Fascinated by her smallness, her perfection, the fact of her existence. . . . And then Shelley had been born, Michele, an even lovelier child, and Jesse had felt, helplessly, the deepest current of his love flowing out to her, a truly hot, glowing, illuminating passion that was like an intense beam of light, out of his control. It was terrible, his love for her: he had felt her hysteria in that crowd as if it were an opening in the earth, and impossibility suddenly pushed upon him.

He was going to lose her.

He approached her bed: a child hunched beneath the covers, asleep. Mouth open. The sound of her breath. Jesse bent and pulled the covers up higher about her. She did not stir. In the other bed, Jeanne slept with the back of her head flat on the pillow. It startled Jesse to look from Shelley to Jeanne, unprepared for Jeanne's being so much older. She was eleven years old now. Her dark hair had been cut short and it was curly, wavy, disordered. She seemed to push herself out tight against her skin, so that her forehead looked tense even in sleep. Shelley was softer, more vulnerable. She lay with her face turned to one side on the pillow, her full, rather plump cheeks absolutely still, her eyes lightly closed, as if she were not truly asleep but watching Jesse secretly. Her lips were parted; Jesse saw a gleam of moisture on her chin. He stared at her.

He sat quietly in a chair near Shelley's bed. A blower somewhere in the room circulated air, making a hollow, gusty, remote sound. *Why are you crying? Stop crying!* He felt a dull anger toward his daughter, mixed with confused emotions of fear, pity, love—had she struggled with him, trying to break free of him? She had stared up at him as if not recognizing him.

She had a small, perfect face. Heartbreaking skin. It was uncanny, that child's beauty—she was only a child, with a child's face, and yet there was a womanish pertness to her features, an accidental and startling perfection about her small nose and mouth and her large, thickly-lashed eyes that seemed even now to be peering at him. He half-expected her to sit up in bed and laugh. It stung him to see Shelley's soft, unconscious beauty; it was almost a painful, stinging sensation, to sit there by her bed—feeling himself better off here than in that other bed, lying sleepless in a half of a marriage.

And suddenly a sense of panic overcame him.

The President was dead: that was the beginning.

It was the beginning of something.

Jesse sat in that chair the rest of the night, thinking of the young, dead President, who was already a historical fact, a dead fact, and thinking of his own daughters, who slept so deeply and unconsciously. Tears gathered in his eyes and ran down onto his cheeks. His mind was clear, but he could not help those tears; something panicked and bitter drove them out, seemed to be pinching his nerves to the point of pain. He felt that he was sitting up like this, mourning the President, and yet mourning something else—but he did not know what.

He marveled at his daughters' sleep. They were so delicate and precarious, his daughters, they could be destroyed so easily, so easily smashed, it was a wonder they had lived to be as old as they were. It was a wonder. A marvel. He wanted only to protect their lives, to protect all that existed in his life, precisely as it existed at this moment.

When he got back to Chicago he bought a gun, a pistol to be carried in his coat pocket; he got a permit to carry a concealed weapon. This was in 1963. He carried a pistol with him for the next seven and a half years.

3

October 1970

Dear Father,

Today we got a ride with four boys from New York in a broken-down car—wild kids! Hair long as Noel's. He conned them about himself and me being from Alaska. Spoke of me as "the Fetish." Drank beer and threw the cans out the window. Cans bouncing on the road behind us—bouncing in my head—gave me a headache.

I am "the Fetish."

Noel dressed me up the other night for the beach. Painted red stripes and circles on me. All he had was red paint but he was very ornate. His touch is ornate, just to feel him touch you. Painted me up and down, curls and tendrils and complex interweaving lines. Decked me out with beads, five or six strands of beads, one made of sharks' teeth, wound more beads around my thighs, my ankles, linked me to him with a long strand of glass beads, led me around the beach naked.

Those old bastards from Iowa, from Michigan, the retired folks from Indiana couldn't believe their eyes, kept staring at me. Couldn't believe it! Noel, very politely, introduced me as "the Fetish." He had painted big red eyes on my eyelids so when I closed my eyes other eyes appeared. I wish I could have seen that. But I couldn't. Wound rows of beads tight around my forehead that left a mark afterward.

Up where the cars were parked, some guy with a huge stomach approached Noel. Guess what he wanted. His eyes all bloodshot from the sun and the birds crashing down all the time and his belly heaving; Jesus, I wished that Noel had spat in his face instead of just answering politely that I belonged to him.

Somebody called the police but we got out before they arrived.

December 1970

Dear Father,

I am thinking of Christmas 1967, which is three years ago now but very close to me. I am thinking of the night you walked out on us.

Noel teases it out of me, my dreams. I owe everything to him. You owe my letters to him, you should be grateful to him—or else I would have melted away by now, just thin wispy smoke going up into the sky!

We are in a hot, hot sun here. In Chicago it is freezing but here the sun bakes us. I am very brown, dried out and brown. Noel is very brown but his hair is bleaching out. Saintly and blond, Noel. My red hair is shining from the sun. Noel washes it for me whenever we have soap. The salt water is sticky and the sand sticks like mud, very fine mud, like salt itself, everything very fine and invisible.

Noel loves me and teases you out of me. He says he can feel the shape of you in my head. He never heard of you, never heard of the Vogel Clinic, never heard of Benjamin Cady or Roderick Perrault, but I told him that Dr. Perrault looked like one of the pelicans we see here, the same mean clever beak and squat body, the way they fly and suddenly dive down into the water for their prey. The pelicans are dying. Becoming extinct. Someone got excited about this in a bar somewhere but Noel argued that it didn't matter. *We are all becoming extinct,* Noel explained.

Noel is my lover, my lover, my lover. I know the shape of him in me when he is far from me, even when I don't know where he is or when he is coming back or even if he will come back. But I know him. I feel him. *I feel you.* He teases me until I cry out to him, I scream out to him—not words but only sounds, noises—there is the mark of my fingernails on him and on my body the marks of his nails, the bruises, the crown wrapped tight around my forehead that stung and made little indentations like teeth.

I am thinking of the marks you made around my head, neat little scars from incisions.

Inventory for 1967: Winnetka, where you brought us. Near the lake. Formless little lanes that are not streets or roads, enormous elms and oaks and evergreens, and spiky thin evergreens arranged around houses to keep them from floating away. You brought us to an expensive house of old, age-softened brick, three stories high, with a garage that was a house of its own, turreted and neat as a gingerbread house. A big dipping lawn. Elms, oaks, evergreens, etc. You soared with us to this house and dipped us down to it, landing us on the bright green lawn one spring day. You said, "Do you like it? It belongs to you."

When I was nine years old Grandfather Cady gave me a large illustrated copy of *Alice in Wonderland* and *Alice's Adventures Through the Looking-Glass.* I sat with it up on the table before me, a big heavy book, reading the paragraphs one by one and trying not to fall into them and lose myself, trying not to feel terror, *it's only a book*; staring at the drawings of this girl with the long, long neck and the straggly hair and the wild, enlarged eyes, the girl reduced to the size of a mouse, sailing through the air dragged by the Red Queen's hand, sitting at the end of a banquet table while legs of mutton waddled down toward her to eat her. I would close my eyes in a panic and feel you dragging me through the air, feel my head coming loose with the exertions of the wind and all the noise of Winnetka that was not said out loud, screaming at the back of your head, the side of your face, *that noble face.* Noel asked me what my worst terror was and I told him, "A book falls down from a library shelf and comes open. It is a very large book with a heavy binding. It falls onto me, knocking me down, and then everything is very still—no one knows about it, the book is not alive and has no will, it means no evil against me—and I am lying there, paralyzed, I can't make out what the book is about, only a few letters or parts of words close to my eyes—"

I told Noel I was going crazy with the need to figure you out.

Noel said there was no need on earth to figure anyone out.

I said you were a book I had to read but I couldn't read because my mind was going. The alphabet was all broken up. Letters could be put together in any way, to say anything, and then scrambled again to say anything else, but they all said the same thing, pressed too close to my face for me to read.

Noel said that human beings had no need to learn how to read. Reading was dead. The alphabet was dead.

I said how would you know history then, if you couldn't read?

Noel said history was dead.

I said how would you know the shape of your own body then, if you couldn't read about other bodies?

Noel said it wasn't only history that was dead but anatomy too.

I covered my face with my hands because I couldn't understand him and he scared me.

Noel said, "History is dead and anatomy is dead. Passion is the only destiny."

Noel is not from Alaska but when I first saw him he was so pale, his eyes so big and dark and burning in his pale, curdled skin, his beard grown out so ragged and crazy, that I knew he was from a place where the language is different and you can't understand what people mean.

Noel made me love his body, all the parts of his body, with my fingers and my mouth and my eyes, so that I would never hold myself apart from him. "The Fetish must be humiliated," Noel told me.

I told Noel I wanted to crawl out from under that book and see what it said. Noel told me it was a book I wrote myself. He told me I could forget you by dreaming back over you and writing it down for you to read, up there in Chicago in the Vogel Clinic; books are dead, says Noel, the hell with books and reading, the hell with your father, the hell with language, the hell with America, the hell with the Fetish, all that must be humiliated and forgotten. "Drive your cart over the bones of the dead," Noel says with a wink.

I told him about the Vogel Clinic. The plate glass, the aluminum, the marble; the beds of evergreen and white, bulky stone. *Oh I loved you there.* Where you were Dr. Vogel and invisible. Where you were Dr. Vogel, my father. I told Noel about counting the windows in our house—forty-eight windows, some of them very high and narrow and complicated. I think Mother counted them too, one by one, each window a place to stare out. I told Noel about our slate roof, rising in graduated ranks, heavy as a cloud, thunderous and beautiful. I told Noel about your insomnia, how we would hear you walking through the house, the rooms of the mansion you bought for us, maybe thinking about the tons of slate over your head and wondering if they would collapse on you.

A perfect tomb.

Kennilworth Drive: the concluding lane of a maze of lanes. No stranger could find us.

Close your eyes, Shell, says Noel, *and wander barefoot through that house. Do you see anyone there? Your father or your mother? Maybe little Shelley herself . . . ?* Yes, I see her. A honey-faced girl with long curly red hair. Soft cheeks always a little flushed, as if from exercise or embarrassment or excitement. Sitting at the table on the sun porch, making a mess with water colors, drawing flowers and cats on their hind legs stalking one another with furry smiling faces and curly whiskers, women flying through the air with their legs dwindling off into tangled skirts, like smoke, everyone smiling and mysterious. I couldn't draw men. No men in my pictures.

At school the art teacher hung my paintings all around the room. It was meant to be a story, a little book. A cat that turns into a girl, lots of bright yellow and orange and green, my favorite colors, and then turns back into a cat again. Happier being a cat. Mother didn't know what to make of this and you didn't either. You stared at the paintings. I felt you staring at them and at me. In your sight it was like a hive of bees, trying to breathe in the hive, your mind buzzed about us and would not leave us alone.

I see Jeanne's face stung by you, your love for me. For me. I see Jeanne hating me. I see her narrow eyes edging onto me, onto pretty little Shelley, hating hating little Shelley, I see you staring at me late one summer afternoon when I rode my bicycle up the drive, I hear your strange, anxious questions: *Where were you? Who were you with? Your face is flushed, you must have been riding that bicycle too fast....* You were never home, but when you came home you wanted us there. Before you. Humbled before you. I did not dare stand straight, did not dare let you see how my body was growing. I did not dare risk your eyes on me. Your nervousness. Love lapping onto me like waves, like the warm waves of the pool you built for me. Then, after the pool was built, Mother said, "Your father wants you to use it every day, he doesn't want you wandering around. Don't make him angry." You were never home but when you came home you would sit at the edge of the pool and watch me swim—*oh I burned in the sunshine in the glare of your watching me; walking naked in front of any men now is no task, no risk for me, not after you—* If you came home and I wasn't there, if I was late coming back from school, I could never think of the right words to explain, I had to explain but I couldn't, I saw the anger and the fear and the worry in your face, I cringed at your voice: *What? What are you saying? Don't speak that way, Shelley. Speak only in complete sentences. Give us your complete thoughts.*

What is a complete thought?

I am not a complete thought. Not in my head or anyone else's. Passing close to men, to tease them, I feel the brush of their thought but it is never complete. It is never complete because it is about the Fetish and not me.

Why did you walk out on us that night?

To be a complete thought you have to come to the end of yourself, you have to see your own birth and your own death, summed up. Maybe into a book. Beginnings and endings. I didn't want to know about death but you kept bringing it home to us—the smell of it on your clothes, on your hands, no matter how often you washed them. Certain smells can't be washed away. They are embedded in those serious, fine, almost-invisible lines on your face, the lines that are beginning to ruin your handsome face. *Your father could operate on me any day,* one of my girl friends joked.

Father, here is Noel sleeping. The length of him heavy on the sand, his face turned to the sun, blind and complete. You can never sleep through a night, but Noel sleeps deeply, soundly, like a child. He can fall asleep anywhere. His sleep is like an angel's sleep. He is tall—over six feet tall—not as tall as you—but very thin, his waist and hips are thin—his cheeks are narrow and hollow. Sleeping. I lie here beside him, fearful of his melting into the sunshine and my melting with him.... Noel says I am vain. Because of my face, my body. He says that beautiful girls are damned unless they humiliate their beauty. Father, I am drowning in the heat here, in the sunlight that is so steady and relentless. I am used to the sooty sky of Chicago and this world is too silent and clear. Lying here, I can stare up into the sky and I might fall into it forever, forever.... I must be humiliated, my face must be ground into the earth or I will be damned....

I think I am going to have a baby.

Mother always wanted another baby—a baby boy—why didn't she have one? For you. I would have had another baby. I would have. We needed boys in our family—you needed sons—so that Jeanne and I could be left alone.

Too late now.

It is nearing Christmas and the decorations are ugly, bright fizzy red and green cellophane, tinsel, red-cheeked Santa Claus faces made out of cardboard—and the world is summer, the palm trees are summer, a perpetual, hot glittering summer. I don't want to think about Christmas. I don't want to remember.

Christmas, 1967.

On that day a story was published about you and the Clinic in the Chicago *Sun-Times*. Then you were photographed in your white clinic coat, your face serious and saintly, there you were described in print, in public, so that I knew you must be real. I bought six copies of the paper. Waiting for you to come home, I read the story out loud to Mother. Waiting for you to come home. I read out loud those words that were about you, my father, and each of the words was a puzzle to me: *His colleagues speak of him as elusive, ambitious, hard-working, brilliant. . . .* I read over and over the description of the Clinic, which was like a kingdom I couldn't enter *with its own laboratory, its own X-ray and diagnostic facilities, departments of radiology, pathology, anesthesia. . . .* There was some secret here that I couldn't understand.

When you finally came home, you said nothing to us. Went to your study, your face closed from us, turned away; you tried to shut the door but I called out to you. . . . You looked at me. Not seeing me. Your eyes hard and bright with that fear in them, that fear. . . .

You shut the door.

I cried out to Mother, "Why is he hiding from us?"

Mother said, "Don't bother him. Leave him alone."

She was sitting alone in the big living room, which no one ever used. She had decorated it in grays and golds and whites, but no one ever used it or looked at it. Now there was a small fir tree in one corner, decorated with gold ornaments. Mother sat with her perfect stillness in that room, her eyes like wounds. *Why did you hide from us?* Small strain marks at the corners of her mouth. She sat there until it got dark and I turned on the lights.

"Why is he hiding? What's wrong?" I asked her angrily.

No answer.

"Why are you sitting in here?"

You held down your silences, you and she. In different parts of the house.

I didn't love her and so I could look directly at her. Her cool, tired, perfect face, the eyes finely lashed, tender, with that softness that belongs to someone who can no longer be hurt. Hair dark, combed back flat on her head, not flattering, a few tendrils at her temples and before her ears. Almost a beautiful woman, except for the strain of her tight skin. I think she became a beautiful woman as she grew free of you.

"Is it because of the newspaper story? What's wrong?" I asked.

"Leave him alone," Mother said.

I started to cry. I started to cry and I remembered what you used to tell me when I cried, when I was still a child—*Living begins when crying leaves off*—and I could hear your voice saying these words—

"Does he hate us? All of us?" I asked Mother.

Close your eyes, Noel instructs me, *and let your fingers run over his face. Caress him back into nothing.*

Finally you came out of that room. Your face haggard. Closed-in, strange. You stared at me as if you didn't recognize me. I saw again that fear, that fear, as if you didn't recognize me, didn't know where you were. "Are you mad about the newspaper story?" I asked, afraid of you. "Are you mad at me?" You stared at me. Your forehead looked pinched. Your hair straggly, damp with perspiration, uncombed. Not like you, to look like this, a man walking in a dream, stiff-legged, dangerous. Mother came to the doorway of the living room, as if to greet you. But the two of you were silent. Jeanne, who had come downstairs, stood pressing her thumb anxiously against her front teeth, silent. Only I kept whimpering, asking what was wrong, what was wrong . . . ?

I could smell the fear in you.

You walked past me to the front door. You got your coat and opened the door and went outside.

"I hate him," I whispered.

Mother turned to me. "Don't say that," she said.

"I hate him, I hate him!" I shouted.

And now my hatred floats up in me like a bubble: how to prick it, that poisonous little bubble? Too many bubbles float along the passages to the heart and wear it out. I want to prick that bubble. I want darkness, the flow of blood without bubbles of oxygen or memory, I want to be free of you, I want to be free.

You walked out on us that night, Christmas night. You were gone all night. I don't want to think about where you walked, or why you left us like that, or why I sat at the top of the stairs waiting for you to come back, in secret, in the dark, afraid to go to bed.

I want to be free.

Love,
Shelley

4

Early morning.

May 1968

The bed in which she lay was long and warm, unhealthily warm. It felt to her like a boat: a slight rocking, rocking to it, the ebbing of invisible tides in this room. The pulsation of blood.

Open your eyes: there the familiar windows, the four high narrow windows, the sky not yet ready to be seen. Like the underside of an eye.

Helene's senses, waking, seemed to flow downward, suddenly downward to the pit of her stomach, her loins. She lay for a moment, baffled. Then she realized that Jesse was not in bed. He must not have come to bed at all.

It was five o'clock in the morning, she was alone in bed on a cold May morning, baffled, her body pulsing with a strange heavy despair. From all the parts of her body, all its remote sterile surface parts, this flowing moved to the center of her, turgid and bulging; she could almost feel the veins bulging with the increased flow of blood.

Jesse. . . .

She sat up. At the back of her skull a darkness like the darkness of the room had shaped itself. She pressed her hand against the back of her head. He had been up all night again, working all night again, or sitting down there in his study staring at the window, at his own reflection in the window. Or he had been walking quietly through the rooms downstairs, quietly, thinking.

What did he think about?

She got out of bed. The dim, chilly room was very empty. She turned on the light and saw with a bitter approval the handsome, formal room she had created—the bed overlarge, as in a photograph, with linen sheets and a light blue blanket and a bedspread neatly pulled back and flowing to the floor, a very light yellow, silky and elegant, looking new, though she had bought it years ago. A deep buff carpet, wallpaper of dark gold streaked with lighter gold, like sunlight. A long, low bureau with a large mirror in which her face was reflected, itself oddly formal. The room looked unlived in, as if planned for a marriage yet to be consummated.

She put on a robe, trying not to look at herself in the mirror. Moving deftly, hastily. She did not need a mirror to pose before; she hated mirrors. She hated that moment just before the mirror self is recognized and acknowledged. All her life she had been posing, moving, speaking in front of other people who watched her closely, and so she did not need mirrors. Other people were always present, watching and assessing. These people crowded the bedroom now, invisible. Helene pressed her hand against the back of her head again, as if the crowd of people were somehow inside her head.

Her body ached.

She thought of her husband in another part of the house: his mind turned brightly, feverishly onto his work, like a beacon turned out into the dark, intense and narrow. Her body ached for him or for a man who might come to her in the form of her husband.

When Jesse did come to bed it was always after she had lain there for a while, waiting—he was like a sleepwalker returning to bed, stumbling upon the bed as if by accident, exhausted, seeing nothing, noticing nothing. And, once he lay stiffly beside her, she could feel the urgency of his hope for sleep. He was superstitious about sleep. Sometimes he slept for a while, off and on, but often he had no luck; he was edgy and excited, ready to begin the next day's work.

Her sleep, beside him, was thin and puzzling. She thought of their marriage. Their love. What was love: Was it the contact between people? The touching of people? She did not understand. Why this pushing, this plunging, this falling into an abyss, a sacred abyss? She could not push herself into it, she had always drawn back weakly, fearfully. She feared Jesse. But at the same time she loved him, she wanted him. . . . He had abandoned her years ago, before their first child was born, really. Sixteen years before. She knew this. She knew it with an angry, wise ripeness, though she could not have explained it to herself. She had loved him and had opened herself to him, had allowed him to plunge into her, drown into her, reshaping himself inside her. Then he had withdrawn; the fleshly part of him withdrew from her, used up, sweetly spent, indifferent. She had given him two daughters. *But what is love,* she wanted to demand of someone, *that it must be the contact between two people?*

Her body ached for Jesse. It ached for a man who might come to her in the form of Jesse. Yet she understood that he would not come to her; it would always return to this, back to this, her basic loneliness and resentment. Her eyes seemed to fall downward, in their stark, heavy, sleep-befuddled gaze, toward the center of herself: Helene, a woman in despair. *You are a beautiful woman,* a man had said quietly to her not long ago—an associate of Jesse's at the Clinic, a small, ugly, pinch-faced doctor, himself unloved and untouched. She had turned away from him, disturbed. Yet her senses had been stirred by him, by the warmth of his words, which seemed to have been uttered against his will.

Isn't my wife a beautiful woman? her father had asked, bringing them his new bride proudly, jauntily.

A beautiful woman. A woman.

Her father's new wife was nearly as young as Helene herself. She did not want to think about her.

Downstairs, Jesse sat at his cluttered desk. His face a sleeper's face, perplexed and drained. He was losing the robust high color of his youth, Helene thought. He turned to her, startled, and Helene saw that his beard had grown out to a light red-blond stubble: some of the tiny hairs were gray.

"Have I . . . have I been up all night?" Jesse asked.

"It's five o'clock."

Jesse rubbed his hands over his face. "Five o'clock. I might as well change my clothes and go down to the Clinic. . . ."

Helene stared at the papers on his desk. It had been years since she had understood Jesse's work. He was too far ahead of her, why bother to try? Somewhere a pile of magazines lay, marked for her to read, and though she had requested these assignments she had never really tried to read them. She could not understand the neurological terms.

"What have you been doing?" she asked gently.

"The preface for Perrault's book," Jesse said.

Again he rubbed his hands over his face. Perrault had died earlier this year and Jesse, his "literary executor," was preparing his book for publication. For years he had been helping Perrault with it, and now he would be completing it, alone.

"God, I'm tired of this . . . all of this. . . ." Jesse said.

"Why don't you come to bed and try to sleep?"

"No. I can't."

He had spoken impatiently. She wanted to touch him, to soothe him, but she was afraid he might recoil from her. He seemed to be living tight against his skin these days, pushing himself, urging himself forward, the muscles of his shoulders always tensing, his fingers always moving restlessly, restlessly. As his public life had become more successful, his private, inner, secret life had become more unfathomable to her. He was a dark puzzle. She remembered him as a young man, calling out her father's name so eagerly—she remembered that face, that man—and she felt a heavy, erotic dizziness rise in her, the excitement a woman can feel only for a stranger.

"I keep thinking of the old man. How he died," Jesse said.

"What do you mean?"

"Losing his temper over something an intern did, dying so fast, right in the intern's arms. . . . I keep thinking of it. Imagining it. Nobody ever could figure out what Perrault was doing at the hospital so late at night, why he was wandering around . . . evidently he got mixed up and thought someone had changed the orders on a patient of his. He was actually going to yank the tube out of someone's nostril when the intern stopped him. I keep imagining myself in the intern's place, wrestling with Perrault, holding him at the instant he died. . . ."

"Why do you keep thinking about it?"

"I don't know."

"You bring it up so often. . . ."

"I can understand death scientifically," Jesse said slowly. "It's no longer mysterious or frightening to me. It's these deaths . . .

certain deaths. . . . The deaths of certain people. These deaths fascinate me."

He was blank to her, like a wall or the side of a rocky hill. Everything was tense at the surface of his body, his skin impenetrable and luminous with a fine gleaming white, like ivory. Yes, he was mineral, elemental in his opposition to her: but it was an opposition that had no awareness of itself.

He was not a man; he was Dr. Vogel. He was no longer Jesse. He was not available to her. Nightly he held himself from her without any awareness of what he did. Every night. His mind raced feverishly and would not let him sleep, racing with the image of *Dr. Vogel, Dr. Vogel.* He was no longer Jesse, the young man who had called out her father's name and stridden into her life. He only appeared to be in this room with her, speaking to her as a husband to his wife; really he was elsewhere. His presence here was a lie. If his mind cast itself about in this house, exploring his possessions, it would only assure itself of their existing, bluntly and coarsely, without spirit: a wife, a daughter, another daughter.

"I wish you would try to sleep," Helene said helplessly.

Jesse stood. His height always surprised her. She was the daughter of a short man—a man her own height—and Jesse's size seemed a kind of threat.

"I'm not tired now," he said.

"Don't think about Dr. Perrault, please. . . ."

Jesse stared at her. "But why shouldn't I think about him? I can't turn my mind off after thirteen years. Who else will remember him? Even his wife doesn't remember him correctly. . . . She's always calling me at the Clinic, you know. Wants to have us over for dinner, even the little girls, as she calls them. . . . But she can't really remember him, she didn't understand his work; he was a great man and he needs someone who can appreciate him. . . . Do you see what I mean?"

Helene said faintly, "Dr. Perrault is dead."

"What? Dead . . . ? Yes, he's dead, I know that, I knew that," Jesse said. "But I keep seeing him in my imagination. I keep having conversations with him. After thirteen years I can't forget. People work themselves into the lives of others, into their brains. He exists in me, in my brain. In certain cells in my brain. Helene," he said suddenly, "where do they go when they die? These people? They seem to be backing off from me, leaving me, I can't keep hold of them . . . there is always something unfinished about them, about them and me. . . . I want to ask Dr. Perrault certain questions, I want that man to answer me truthfully, for once, not to be sly and sardonic but to tell me truthfully the secret of his life and of his death. It's as if he still exists somewhere, but he's mocking me, he won't come back to me. . . . I need these people. I love them and I need them. . . . I keep imagining myself there at his death, instead of that intern. I see myself boring little holes into his skull and opening it up and draining the blood out, fixing him up somehow, saving him. . . ." Jesse said, holding out his hands for Helene to see. His fingers twitched as if with a desire to act, to grab hold of something.

Helene could not speak. She was afraid of him.

"I'm very tired. But I can't sleep. Forget what I've just said."

He went upstairs and Helene remained behind, watching his back, her husband's back, wondering at him. She did not know if she loved him for his strangeness, if she desired him as always, or if she feared him. . . . She remembered the way he had walked out of the house on Christmas evening, the way he had frightened the girls. But he had not frightened her: his walking out like that, so quickly and so strangely, had been a kind of relief to her.

He was taking a shower upstairs. She lingered in his study, looking through the things on his desk. Typewritten pages, notes, offprints of articles. . . . Everything was scattered, and it was hopeless, the attempt to put the parts together. They would not add up to Jesse Vogel. She had married him but she did not know him. She had thought that marriage would be the beginning of her life; she had had a long life as a daughter, a famous man's daughter, and she had been eager to begin her real life. She would be a woman, womanly and fulfilled. A wife. But this had not come about. . . . And then, puzzled, she had believed that the birth of her first child would fulfill her. So much apprehension and pain and joy. . . . But the birth had left her exhausted and at a distance from herself, from her own body. Her baby had overwhelmed her. She was ashamed of herself and it occurred to her that she must have another baby, another baby to make her normal, a real woman. But after the second baby nothing was different. She felt a final, terrible certainty about her strangeness: she would never become a real woman.

She was being destroyed by her husband, she thought, annihilated by him. He could not imagine her, had not the time to imagine her existence, and so he was destroying her.

She picked up a sheet of paper. It seemed to be what Jesse had been working on when she had interrupted him. The paper was covered with his large, fine handwriting, looping letters and strong slashes that crossed *t's* as if with impatience, dots over *i's* that were like small pricks in the paper itself.

> Dr. Roderick Perrault was working on this book at the time of his death in February, 1968. For several years I had been assisting him in the preparation of certain chapters, and he had indicated his wish for me to complete the book in the event of his death. There has been little need for extensive editing, except in the case of the chapter on otoneurology, which I have brought up to date in collaboration with Dr. Ronald Myer. Dr. Perrault's contribution to his field has, of course, been enormous—not simply in the quality of his written work, but in the quality of his personal work, his dedication and example to those of us fortunate enough to have studied with him. He was a model of scientific excellence. All of us who knew Dr. Perrault have been shaped by him and will never outlive him. We will never outlive outlive outlive his death death death

The last sentence trailed away.

Helene read the paragraph again.

She put the paper down where she had found it. She folded her arms quickly, bringing her hands firmly against her ribs, tucked under her arms as if she were cold. After a moment she picked up a copy of a magazine that lay on top of some books—*Studies in Neuropsychiatry*—and saw from the table of contents that Jesse had an article in it. "Oddities of Retrograde Amnesia." Helene skimmed the case histories of Jesse's patients—a fifty-year-old man who believed himself ten years old, who kept asking the same question about the weather again and again, unable to remember any answer given him; another man who listened to the same record again and again, unable to remember having heard it before; a woman who remembered details of her childhood forty years before but who had forgotten everything that belonged to her adult life. She read:

> After certain types of traumatic injuries there seems to be a block between sensory reception and the process of retention. RA that is extended indicates severe damage that blocks out current and recent memory, so that the patient can recall distant memories clearly and believe he is much younger than he is. It seems that events of the distant past are more firmly established in the memory, with no regard to their relative (conscious) significance or insignificance to the individual; current and recent events are precarious and may be extinguished completely by traumatic injury. Why should not distant memories be most easily extinguished? And yet in fact they are most firmly retained. We might hypothesize the following: that memory is not a patterned or predictable process. Brain damage may result in the extinction of all memory, of course, but it seems that the mere organic existence of the brain assures a constantly strengthening foundation of distant memories. Is it the function of the normal brain to hold the present cheaply and to honor only the distant past?

She closed the magazine and put it back on top of the stack of books. The voice of Dr. Vogel, his presence, his hard, radiant, luminous mind.... She opened a drawer: notecards held together loosely by rubber bands. Notes taken in red, green, and blue ink. She opened another drawer: newsclippings. Strange. She picked up one of them—it was a brief article about a suspected murderer who remembered his victim's name but not his own name, knew everything about his victim's life but nothing about his own life. He had evidently murdered a young woman in Tampa, Florida, had stolen a small powerboat, and gone out into the Gulf of Mexico, where he had been picked up by the Coast Guard. Another news item was about a derelict who was hospitalized in Bellevue and who began gradually to recall that he was a doctor himself, or had been a doctor; the story had a happy ending, with the derelict restored to his family in Yonkers, New York, whom he had left eight years before. Another clipping told of a coal miner of twenty-nine in Hazard, Kentucky, who had shot to death his wife, his infant son, and his own mother, evidently on Christmas Day, leaving them dead in the living room of his home and going out to the barn to shoot himself.

How do these things come together? Helene wondered.

Jesse was out of the house by six-thirty. The girls were up by eight and Helen made breakfast for them. She was still nervous from the encounter with Jesse. There was some tension between the girls, some irritation, but she did not want to inquire about it.

Jeanne and Shelley were totally different—no possibility of their being friends, only sisters. Jeanne was fairly tall, about five feet eight, much too thin, too serious. She was always staring critically, contemplating. She was sixteen years old and, like Jesse, paid scrupulous, courteous attention to all the details of her work—she was going to study biology when she entered college, hopefully at Radcliffe. But ordinary life seemed to baffle her.

Shelley, with her sloppy posture, her noisy eating habits—she ate her toast quickly, dropping the crusts on her plate—was inattentive, dreamy, very pretty. She appeared older than her thirteen years. Her red-blond hair was brushed down to her shoulders; her cheeks were pink, even ruddy. She was a few pounds overweight and very healthy. Jeanne was always catching colds, always complaining of headaches, but Shelley ran out in the rain and returned in the cold from swimming practice with her hair wet and never got sick. Her only troubles were nicks and scratches and bruises. She was always slouching as if embarrassed by her figure; she twisted strands of hair around her fingers and sucked at them, she was surging, pushing forward, yet oddly lazy, exasperating, nervy. This morning she was sitting with her eyes downcast, that pure, pale, light green of her gaze turned down to her plate and the crusts of toast, as if she were afraid to look up.

"Look at the mess of crumbs you made," Jeanne said suddenly.

Shelley said nothing, blushing. It was strange that she did not reply to her sister.

"Why can't she learn to eat decently?" Jeanne asked.

Something was wrong between them. Wearily Helene felt the jabs and thrusts between them, like the pokings of an elbow.

"Don't bother Shelley so early in the morning," Helene said.

"Bother her? Who's bothering who? She bothers me," Jeanne said. She was staring contemptuously at her sister. "She doesn't have any manners, at her age."

Suddenly Shelley pushed her plate away. She looked up at Jeanne.

"You can go to hell," she whispered.

Helene looked with irritated amusement from one girl to the other. What was this? What did it have to do with her?

"Shelley, you can leave the room," she said.

Shelley jumped up. Clumsily, she backed into the opened silverware drawer, made a sobbing, choking noise— "She promised she wouldn't bring it up and now she's going to!" she cried.

"Bring what up? Who's bringing what up?" Jeanne said.

"You are! You promised you wouldn't tell and now you're going to!"

Jeanne smiled in amazement. "Nobody's bringing anything up," she said.

"I don't want to listen to this. Any of this," Helene said.

"There—you see! There!" Shelley cried.

Jeanne shrugged her shoulders. Her face was sickly in its antagonism.

"I mean it," Helene said.

Shelley put her dishes in the sink, ran the water noisily onto them, and left the kitchen. They could hear her heavy footsteps all the way out to the front door.

"Shelley—" Jeanne began.

"I said I don't want to hear about it," Helene said flatly.

"But—"

"No. I don't want to hear about it."

"But Shelley—"

"I said no."

Jeanne stared at her, startled.

No, Helene could not listen to this, no more news of Shelley, no more bad news. Not this morning.

"All right," Jeanne said, her voice trembling, "if you don't want to hear about it, you won't. . . ."

"I don't want to hear about it."

Two weeks ago Jeanne had come in breathless from school to tell Helene that her sister was being talked about even in the high school, that the name "Shelley Vogel" was being passed around and joked about—that she had done something crazy—Helene, frightened at Jeanne's ferocity, her anger, had wanted to shake her into silence. But Jeanne rushed on to tell her that Shelley had allowed herself to be picked up by a bunch of high school boys and to be used for target practice by them.

"For what?" Helene had cried.

"Target practice. With rifles. Real rifles," Jeanne said.

"But I don't understand—"

"Some boys picked her up and got her to hold out matches for them to shoot at. She's crazy! I'm so ashamed! They had .22 rifles and instead of using paper targets the way they usually do, they got that stupid fool to hold out matches for them to shoot. And then—this is when the mother of one of the boys looked out the window—then they got her to stand with a cigarette in her mouth, and they were shooting it out of her mouth! Out of her mouth!"

"I don't believe it," Helene said.

Jeanne began to cry angrily. "I'm so ashamed. How could she be so stupid, to let them use her like that . . . to laugh at her like that. . . ."

"She could have been killed," Helene said.

She felt faint. She had to sit down.

"I'm so ashamed, everybody is talking about her. . . . She's so stupid, so stupid!" Jeanne said. Her tears were hot and spiteful.

Helene's mind had whirled: how could this be true? She thought of her pretty daughter, with that face she herself envied a little, she thought of that face exposed to bullets. . . .

When she confronted Shelley with this news, Shelley said nervously, "Oh, they were just fooling around . . . they're nice kids . . . it was only a BB gun and I shot it myself a few times. . . . Nothing happened."

"How could you let anyone do such a thing to you!" Helene had asked.

"They didn't do anything!" Shelley protested, not meeting her mother's eye. "Oh, Jeanne is always exaggerating things, she hates me, she's always after me— They didn't do anything, they're nice kids and they're my friends, they just like to fool around— Nothing happened."

Helene stared at her.

"No, nothing happened," Shelley said hotly.

Helene had not dared to tell Jesse about this.

Now, this morning, she said slowly to Jeanne: "I don't want to hear about it. Please."

Alone. It was a relief to be alone.

She drove out into noontime traffic. At a new shopping center —Wonderland East—she hurried through a few stores on errands. She hated to shop and moved quickly, nervously through the crowds of other women.

Crossing a concrete square—cheaply decorated with "modern" multicolored cubes and benches of garish carnival colors—she heard the start of music, greatly amplified—then it stopped abruptly. The other shoppers, most of them women and many of them middle-aged, glanced around at the noise, bewildered. Then it began again: a crashing of guitars, drums, indecipherable instruments.

Helene wanted to press her hands against her ears. The racket was almost unbearable.

She tried to hurry to her car, but she had to cross these small artificial "courtyards"—square after square of cubes and benches and potted plants, female shoppers, small children, teenagers in slovenly dress, with the screeching, harshly rhythmic music piped at her from speakers set high on posts. It was windy and she had to close her eyes against the flying grit. So much noise, the pounding of drums and voices, the ache in her legs to hurry, hurry, to get her out of this—

It was mocking her, mocking the misery in her body.

You are too old, too old. Give up. Forget. You are far too old.

She was to meet Mannie Breck for lunch. For days she had wondered if she would really meet him, but now she was obviously on her way. The restaurant was located a few miles from Wonderland East, an older place set back from the white tile and strident signs of newer restaurants and shops, near a park. When Helene drove by the park she noticed a small crowd there, a kind of demonstration, young people with signs, a single policeman on horseback.

Too old, too old. Forget. Forget everything.

At twelve-thirty she walked into the dim foyer of the restaurant, carrying the sound of the rock music in her head, a little dazed, irritated, frightened. A single unwanted glimpse of her strained face in a mirror—and then Mannie sprang forward to greet her.

"I wasn't sure— I thought you might not come—" Mannie said.

He was eager, formal, very nervous.

They shook hands like people newly introduced to each other. "I'm so happy to see you," Mannie said.

He was wearing a light suit and a shirt of some dark, coarse material that threw a shadow up onto the lower part of his face. He was a specialist at the Vogel Clinic in diseases of the spinal cord, especially those in children, in "floppy infants"; there seemed to be something miniaturized about him, his voice, his features, his manner. He was no taller than Helene herself, of a slight frame, his complexion olivish, dark, with a certain dusky, unhealthy pallor. His features were pinched and strained, as if he were constantly fighting a headache. Above his small, wise face his hair rose in stiff bunches, beginning to gray. He had given up a good private practice in New York to join Jesse here.

Helene smiled at him nervously.

As they talked, she found herself recalling the shopping plaza and the windy squares and the blare of music, the music of young people. She recalled the hurrying women, the shoppers with their purchases in colored paper bags and their hair blown in the wind that was not friendly to them. The rhythmic thumping of the guitar, the drums. What had it to do with these women shoppers, with their forlorn faces and mottled legs? She kept seeing herself hurrying away from the music but not escaping it. *Too old. All of you are too old.*

She and Mannie were shy together. He talked about the clinic. Of course. About Jesse. Of course. Asked her about the girls, about her own life. Pausing politely to listen to her account of her own life. Asked about her father. Helene stiffened but managed to say, "He's living in Palm Beach now. You probably heard that he married again. . . ." Mannie nodded eagerly. He asked her again about "things at home," with the attentive, self-deprecating manner of someone who has no home himself and to whom "home" is sacred.

Mannie chattered about his work, his problems, his gains, the words a kind of musical interlude meant to put them both at ease. Helene warmed a little. Listening to Mannie, watching him she wondered why he was attracted to her and what would come of them. The two of them: a couple in this restaurant of strangers, a couple sitting alone together. She felt herself sinking into a warm, puzzled, erotic daze, so that the music she had heard at the shopping plaza flowed, subdued and lyric and sweetened, in and out of her consciousness. Mannie seemed inspired by her, leaning forward, talking so eagerly that she could see small flecks of saliva on his lips.

"You're not unhappy about anything . . . ?" Mannie asked.

"No," said Helene.

"People who live alone are often unhappy because they think too much. They have nothing to do at home but think," Mannie said with a smile. "That's my trouble. I was very attached to my family, my parents, and now . . . now things are all changed. . . ." Ugly little man, with that monkeyish face! He was weak, charming, harmless. A brother. A child in the form of a small man, masquerading as a man. *I want Jesse,* Helene thought in a sudden misery. "It's wonderful that your father has remarried, at his age. I imagine you're happy about it . . . ?"

Helene hesitated. Her father, at the age of sixty-seven, had married a woman of no more than forty-five, a "speech therapist" in Boston with dyed blond hair, a regal, swaying, hard-corseted body, supposedly a widow. They had driven out to Chicago to visit, in an enormous black automobile. Cady had talked incessantly about the car and a boat he was buying and the home he had bought for his bride, with a quarter-mile frontage on the ocean. His face was tanned from Palm Beach, his clothes youthful and nautical in style, with brass buttons. He had retired from his work entirely.

"Yes, I'm happy about it," Helene said tonelessly.

Mannie sensed her mood and fell silent, embarrassed. Then he changed the subject: "Did you see the antiwar demonstration across the street? The kids?"

"Is it an antiwar demonstration?"

"I don't think they have a permit. There's some complication."

Mannie talked about the war for a while, shaking his head sadly. Helene did not pay attention to him, wanting to ask about Jesse, her husband—what was he like?—what was he really like? Another man might know him. As they ate lunch self-consciously, Mannie went on to talk about the effect of the war on America and what it had done to people he knew. His small, dark face would be matched by a small, dark body; there would probably be dark curly hair on his chest, swirls of hair on his stomach. Short, pale legs, knobby feet. He would be a gentle lover, fearful of failing her.... Jesse was not afraid of failing her. He did not think of her at all.

"Even in my own family something happened that would not have happened a few years ago," Mannie said. "My sister's girl, who is only twenty, dropped out of Smith to get married. She and the boy bummed around Europe and when they came back they had an infant with them, which they plan on giving away for adoption—in fact, I think they already have given it away. My sister is heartbroken. This is her only grandchild. She didn't even know her daughter had had a baby, and now the girl is giving it away, coldly and deliberately... she won't even let my sister bring the child up, she wants it given to strangers...."

"Why does she want to do that?" Helene asked, genuinely surprised.

"We don't know. It's killing my sister. The baby is only a few months old, a boy...."

"Women shouldn't be allowed to do things like that," Helene said slowly.

"Exactly, she shouldn't be allowed, because in a few years she will regret it. When she grows up. She will regret it the rest of her life. Nobody can talk sense to her."

"But what about her husband?"

"He wants to get rid of the baby too. Neither one of them wants to be held down. My niece says she isn't interested in being a mother. She isn't interested!"

Helene felt her face warming with anger. An abstract, mysterious ferocity. Ah, how she hated—

But she did not know exactly what she hated.

"Did I upset you with that news? I shouldn't talk about such ugly things," Mannie said uncertainly.

"We always wanted to adopt another child, a boy. Two more children. Jesse wanted two more children," Helene said vaguely. "I wanted to have another baby but . . . but there was some risk. . . . I shouldn't have listened to my doctor. I don't think he was right. And so we were going to adopt another baby. . . ."

Mannie nodded sympathetically. "Yes?"

"But it was never the right time, I don't know why . . . Jesse was always so busy with the clinic, and for a while Jeanne's health was bad . . . she had pleurisy one winter. . . . I don't know what happened. But we never adopted a child."

They had finished their lunch. Helene had hardly eaten hers.

"We wanted to give love to a baby, a strange baby," Helene went on, a little giddy with the intensity of Mannie's interest, "but we could never decide which baby it should be, we could never decide upon the right time, Jesse and I. . . . Jesse always wanted a son. He used to talk about having a son. I think he loved me best when I was pregnant. He loves the girls very much, especially Shelley . . . he was meant to be a father. . . . He could be a father to a whole crowd of children. A hospital of children. Did you know that when he was an intern he had intended to work in public health?"

"It's necessary work, but ordinary men can do it," Mannie said.

"Yes, that's right," Helene said quickly. "Jesse is not an ordinary man. He is . . ."

"Yes?"

Mannie's face crinkled, as if resisting the strong glare of Jesse Vogel; but he smiled shyly, encouragingly.

"He is a jumble of men. . . . There are many people in him," Helene said. She felt a little drunk. The rhythm of that music sounded in her, deep in her loins. "And he wants more. He wants his daughters, and he wants me . . . I mean he wants us in him. . . . He wants to be us. I can't explain. He wants to own us, to be us. . . . Are there types of neurological disorders in which people are multiple . . . ? Their personalities are multiple . . . ?"

"They're considered psychological disorders," Mannie said.

"No, I don't mean that. I don't mean people who think they are more than one person, but people who really are multiple. Real units of personality, tissue or atoms or nerve cells," she said vaguely, wildly, "bits of flesh that are real and not imaginary, not insane...."

Mannie smiled at her, sympathetically and baffled.

"I don't believe in delusions of the spirit," Helene said, trying to speak more calmly. "I believe in real events, statistical events, things that can be measured. The blood count is real, the secretions of the glands are real, the chemical composition of our bodies is real; the ideas we have are not real and are sometimes dangerous... I think we have an instinct for dangerous ideas, for errors...."

They sat in embarrassed silence. Helene was agitated and yet she felt the need to keep on, to keep this man's bewildered attention, not to surrender him. "Years ago I found some scribblings of Jesse's," she said, "just pieces of scrap paper with strange designs all over, resembling human faces, and the word *homeostasis* written over and over again, maybe a hundred times.... *Homeostasis. Homeostasis.* Is that an idea, or is that real?"

"I don't know," Mannie said. His tone was cautious, as if he feared being hurt by her.

They left the restaurant. Helene felt that she had prevented him from loving her, as if she had pressed a brisk, unwomanly hand flat against his chest. Yet she was excited, agitated, she had to continue.

"*Homeostasis.* It's just an idea, the idea of a man," she said.

"I suppose so...."

"Inside the body—equilibrium. Outside the body—equilibrium. Either equilibrium or death, isn't that it?"

"Yes," said Mannie. "Equilibrium or death."

He looked at her sadly.

"I don't suppose... I don't suppose we could talk a little more, we could go for a ride...?" he said.

She smiled suddenly, surprised at him. They had come out into the sunshine now and Helene shaded her eyes.

Across the street there was a commotion—a small crowd of people, some of them dressed bizarrely, carrying picket signs, others dressed in ordinary clothes. Several policemen on foot, one on horseback. A squad car was parked nearby.

"What are they shouting about?" Helene said.

"It looks like trouble. We'd better leave," Mannie said.

"But . . . what are those people shouting at them?"

Helene started across the street and Mannie followed reluctantly. On the outside of the small group of young people, in a loose, unruly ring, were men in ordinary working clothes and a few men in suits, even a few women in housedresses and slacks. A number of people were shouting. Helene saw a picket sign tilted at an angle—something about "war"—the young man who carried it wore an Indian headband. He was arguing with one of the policemen.

"Who says so? Who says so?" someone was yelling.

Helene approached the crowd, fascinated. She was struck by the strange silence that fell between isolated shouts. She had never heard that silence before. Mannie was saying something to her but she paid no attention—she was staring at the girls here, their hair long and uncombed and ratty, skinny girls of no definite age. Sixteen, twenty, twenty-five? They glanced at her in their confusion. Their faces were pale and frightened and angry. Their mouths twisted with hate.

Helene could smell it in the air.

Hate. We hate you. We hate you.

Another squad car pulled up to the curb. A few people cheered. Helene noticed a girl with long shining black hair, black as an Indian's, who stood with a cigarette in her mouth, angrily jerking a picket sign up and down. The sign showed a crudely painted skull and crossbones, with the initials LBJ beneath it. She was shouting something, shouting around the stub of a cigarette; she wore a sacklike outfit of some very fine, almost gauzy material, exposing much of her bony chest. She happened to notice Helene and stared hatefully at her. Helene, catching the strange hot weight of this stare, felt them all look at her as she approached.

"Helene—" Mannie said.

One of the policemen seemed to be saying something to her too. But she paid no attention; she went right into the center of the crowd, fascinated by their faces, their droopy soiled clothes, their blank faces. They were young and they hated her.

"Take your fucking war and shove it!" the girl shouted.

Was she shouting at Helene?

Helene took several steps toward her. The girl with the picket sign did not back up. She hated Helene; here was hatred; here Helene had finally found it! *It is over for you,* they all seemed to be saying, ready to shout murderously at her, *it is over, over, over for you! For you!*

Helene whipped her hand around and knocked the cigarette out of the girl's mouth.

The girl cried out in surprise and amazement. The cigarette flipped up high into the air.

Someone cheered, and someone else pulled Helene back—it must have been Mannie—and one of the boys grabbed hold of the girl, who had started to rush forward. She was screaming at Helene. Screaming. "Let me go, let me go!" But Helene turned and began walking away quickly. People parted for her. Back on the sidewalk, where the crowd of shoppers and men in shirt-sleeves stood, she waited for Mannie to catch up with her.

She had finished everything for herself, she thought. Good! It was good! Her heart was pounding fiercely. The erotic glow in her loins, so teasing and warm, had spread lightly through her body now, light as May air, harmless. She was fulfilled. She was free of the man who hurried beside her, who could not love her now, and she was free of her husband, her daughters, the people in the park, her own youth. It was over: the tyranny of her body, the yearning for other bodies, for talking and touching and dreaming and loving. She had freed herself. It was over for her.

5

January 1971

Noel? Are you awake?

There are no lights here and the daylight fades and opens again and opens us to each other. The day is stretched out of shape because it begins so early—before dawn—and ends so early, always confusing me. But there are no real days, Father.

Days are an invention of the newspaper, which has to have a date at the top of each page.

Noel?

Yes?

Do I exist, Noel?

No, Shell.

Is there anyone here?

No.

Then why do I dream, why is my head all filled with dreams?

Because people are walking through your head, Shell.

How can I stop them?

Dream back over them and murder them, Shell.

Father you have got to let me go. You have got to stop thinking about me and let me go.

You hypnotized me. I am like a deer standing in the road, hypnotized by the headlights of a car. Noel shakes me to get me loose of you, he slaps my face—one side, then the other—he would like to enter my head and fight you there, but his own head is filled with people walking in it too, his own people.

Since we left the South, Noel carries a little kit of surgical equipment everywhere with him. He sleeps with it under his pillow, which is a rolled-up towel we got from somewhere. Not just the needle and the spoon, but the other spoon—a sharp filed spoon he uses to open locks—and a file that is really a knife, and a leather belt with a big buckle. He walks like anyone in New York now. You would never guess he is a stranger here.

I told him that my father carried a gun with him everywhere.

I knew about that gun for years. It was no secret.

A man named Jethro was traveling with us but he got picked up by the police; Noel and I turned a corner just in time. Noel grabbed my arm up near the shoulder and we ran, we ran.... Tears flew sideways out of my eyes; it was so cold on the street here, the tears were like little slivers flying out. *I love you I am coming home.* Jethro stuttered and when he stuttered he got angry. I was afraid Noel would kill him with his file, which is really a knife, but now he is in jail somewhere and we won't see him again.

I am not going to jail again.

I am thinking tonight of that day in 1969 when you came to Toledo to get me. Did you love me then? Why did you cry? I am thinking of that rainy September day that went on for so long. I am thinking of Shelley in her bleached-out blue jeans, her hair ratty from no sleep and no hairbrush, her face puffed up with crying, everything babyish about her except the dark rings under her eyes. I am thinking of that jail, which I remember so clearly—the Clinton Street Jail—the county jail and its rich, ripe, dark odors, where the lights never really went off but were only dimmed, but never really came on again either, so that we could sleep all the time and stir in our sleep, whimpering and sniffing. We all had colds. We could bang around in our sleep. We could seize the bars and bang our heads against them. *Wake up! Wake up!* But you can't wake up no matter how fast your heart goes, because it is all a dream, the other girls prowling for loose change and complaining and blowing their noses and whispering and screaming at one another in a dream, begging to make telephone calls or to be released ahead of time, begging in babyish, awful voices, over and over: "Miss Goldie, I got to get hold of a certain party. I got to make contact. Miss Goldie, this is a matter of life and death, you got to take me seriously."

The matron, Miss Goldie, was tall and wise and her hair was snipped short; her head was too small for her body. That way she could move her head around fast, without any fuss. Whip her head around to see what was going on behind her. When I turned my head, all my hair had to come with it, a mane of hair, it got me down. Miss Goldie smoothed down my hair and tried to make me smile. My teeth chattered. Miss Goldie said, "Well, if you won't tell us your name, we'll have to make one up for you. How about Honey? A honey of a name for a honey of a girl."

I couldn't smile. My teeth chattered.

Honey! Honey!

Some of the girls snickered, some of them liked the name. A black girl my age, in pajamas with a tiger-skin design, took up the cry, teasing me, "Ain't *you* a honey, though!"

I sit shivering, afraid of the other girls. They are so bouncy and loud. Miss Goldie smiles at me, but she smells like the jail itself, the musty cot, the dirty mattress— on her stocky legs she seems about to fall on me. She will crush me. The black girl is very thin, nervous. She is always singing under her breath and cracking her knuckles; her name is Toddie. Her pajamas are brand-new, a present from her grandmother, so she says, in honor of her return to Clinton Street. She sees how cold I am and takes my hands and tries to rub them warm again, muttering under her breath, "Honey, ain't you a honey, though! Huh! You from out of town, huh? Don't tell *me.* You don't look like nobody I ever saw in this city before."

I draw away from her and sit in the corner of Cell 5.

My thighs are plump and juicy, making the legs of these old jeans swell. I am wearing a yellow cashmere sweater stained with vomit. Father, I am not thinking of you. No. I am not thinking of you at home, the telephone calls you are making, the way you must look, the way your face must look.... I would rather think of Jeanne, who is your only daughter now. Jeanne, the only Vogel girl left at home, the only girl, the victor. Jeanne plodding back and forth inside your love, taking classes at Northwestern so that she can live at home. Forever. I would rather think of Mother, who hates me. Mother, who knows why I had to leave home, who could have stopped me if she had wanted to, I passed by her and she could have touched me and stopped me....

My eyelids are heavy, sluggish. I am afraid to go to sleep. I don't trust the girls here and I am afraid to sleep. They are so noisy and gossipy, padding around in their bare feet or in bedroom slippers, girls my own age, white and black and mulatto, all at home here like daughters with a staff of mothers (there are three matrons) and no fathers at all, no fathers. Everyone is a sister to everyone else. The jail is called "the house."

Who's new in the house today?

What's all this noise in the house?

Why's the house so gloomy—this ain't no tomb!

Sometimes a giggling yell goes up—*Man in the house! Man in the house!*—when the doctor breezes in for a few fast examinations.

He is a doctor without a name. No time for a name. Miss Goldie herds me into the room and right away his stethoscope is pressed over my heart, his hard quick fingers tilt my head to the fluorescent light, he stares right into my eyes and into my brain. "Won't tell us where you're from, eh?" he says kindly, without interest. He picks my arm for a vein, he asks me to make a fist but my hand is too weak, so he ties a rubber tube around my arm and makes a vein swell. He draws the blood sample up into the needle and I watch the blood rise. Afterward there are drops of dark blood on the table.

He does not see Shelley. Not your Shelley.

"This isn't going to hurt," he says, warning me, but I can't lie still. Miss Goldie holds me down on the table. I am screaming. But he doesn't stop: the thing in his hand keeps going in, going in.

Led back to Cell 5, I am giggled and gaped at. They all know what went on. Toddie winks at me and cracks her knuckles. She is singing a popular song under her breath, the same words over and over. Across the way a girl with the heavy brows of a boy, her face gleaming, glowing, yodels over at me, "Hiya, Honey! How was it, Honey!" She wears a pair of jeans and a boy's shirt. She is in Clinton Street for beating up another girl and "resisting arrest," this girl of fourteen, and Toddie has told me she gave a cop a broken nose before he knocked her hard on her ass—"That Jackie is one tough babe, I kid you not," Toddie tells me.

Crooning. Mocking. All the girls sing out loud, their voices crisscrossing and interrupting one another. I sit in the corner of Cell 5 with my eyelids burning. They don't close. I can't sleep. I won't lie on that filthy cot, no. Won't sleep. I have been awake since Tuesday morning, when I walked out of the house. Wednesday on the Greyhound bus. Wednesday night: walking around crying. Big stupid baby, crying. The bus station. Those kids following me. Thursday morning in Toledo, sick to my stomach out on the street. People gaping at me. A mailman in his little truck watching me. Where is Toledo? All day Thursday, a long day, walking fast around the city to keep people from following me, and Thursday night picked up by a squad car . . . and now it's Friday night and I can't sleep . . . I haven't slept since Tuesday morning and I will never sleep again. . . .

"Honey," says Toddie, "you better lay down and sleep before they lay you down personally."

"What are you, stubborn child?" someone calls over to me. "Runaway or what? Not A & S, are you?" she giggles.

"She's vagrancy," Toddie says importantly.

There is a girl whose name I don't know, with a long face and kinky blond hair, a smirking smile, lines on her forehead. She paces back and forth in her cell, light on her feet, grabbing hold of the bars and trying to shake them. "Hey," she whispers over to Toddie and me, "hey, hey you two! Hey, what'cha doing there, you two? What'cha doing in there, black-and-white, huh?"

She is alone in her cell, pacing like an animal. They won't put anyone else in with her.

"Go to hell," Toddie cries. "Whatd'ya know about anything?"

"Black and white speckles, you two! Hey! I got something to tell you. Come closer. Come over by the bars," the girl says, pressing herself against the bars of her cell, sliding her long thin arms through, stretching out her fingers. "Come closer! Here! C'mon!"

"Go to hell! Go to sleep!" Toddie shouts.

Other girls begin shouting: "Lay down and go to sleep! Shut up!"

The girl says mockingly: "I ain't going to sleep at any nine-thirty at *night*, not me. . . ."

Toddie sits on the edge of her cot, furious or pretending to be furious.

"Don't you listen to big mouth," she says.

Eyeing my puffy face, my fear. With a raspy little laugh she chatters at me but I sit with my teeth gripped hard, trying not to shiver. She tells me about how she got in this place. "We was hauling stuff out of that store all night long before anybody got wise," she says excitedly. "Got big boxes of Kleenex enough to blow your nose in the rest of your livelong days! All kinds of stuff—for our mothers, like Band-Aids and toothpaste—filled up a box with lipsticks, we figured we could sell them—dumped a whole lot of pill bottles and stuff in a box, vitamins and cough drops, you know— My sister tells me one of my girl friends turned me in. I'm going to burn her ass when I get out of here. I got thirty days in this dump, what about you? They do a V.D. on you?"

Shelley shivers, remembering that cold piercing instrument. She shivers in spite of the heated-up look of her skin.

Toddie lies down to sleep. Shelley sits up all night, her head aching. She knows that she will remember Clinton Street all her life—the murmur of the girls' sleep, their waking arguments and laughter, the boyish, flirtatious, sensuous noise of their personalities mixed together in the old jail. She has only to think of it to hear it again: like picking up a telephone receiver to hear the dial tone. Always there. Always there. *The past is always there, in your head.*

Near morning there is yelling from another part of the jail—the addicts' wing—and Toddie jumps up, inclining her head that way, like an animal. "Jesus God!" she says with a sigh. "Listen to them poor dumb bitches over there, you think *we* got it bad!"

Then it is morning.

Everyone has survived the night and looks from face to face, alert and ready for news. Good news? Bad news? Only the heavy-browed girl stays in her cell, doesn't want to move. The matron shakes her. To the washroom, a bunch of us, I walk along in a daze, slowed-down with exhaustion while the other girls are ready to run, hopped up with a strange energy, grinning and teasing one another so that their teeth flash happily in the spotted mirrors. "Who you think you are, fat-mouthin' me?" one of the girls laughs. Someone shoves someone else, playfully. The stinking hygienic white of the washroom doesn't depress them. Two short stocky girls, like twins, are washing fast and dripping all over. One of them is telling the other a story in a guttural, rising and falling, lyric voice: "He told me he had all these other women, a lot older than me, he said, and he didn't need me; he kept pushing me, you know, and I told him the hell, I wasn't scared, it was just if it was a Saturday night, you know, when it can get rough. I was out there standing and some guys drove by and tried to get me in the car, and him and his friends was in a bar, and they came out, and all hell broke loose . . . and the cruiser came by without no siren or warning or anything and that one cop, he had my number, he was always giving me the eye, and so we all got out of there and ran like hell, but they picked me up later at home . . . because that cop had my number and wanted to get rough with me. My mother yelled at him not to lay no hands on me, but a hell of a lot of good that did. . . ."

Breakfast. Long dark nicked tables, tin trays with breakfast food in their hollows, Shelley sickened by the odor of the food and the other girls growling and laughing over their food. I want to shrink away from them, their strange happiness in this place. I want to shrink inside myself. At the farther tables are older girls, women, their voices hoarse and jocular. Some of them look crazy. Slack-faced, smiling too much. Maybe they are retarded. Sick. Right beside me a girl with hair the same color as mine, but fuzzy and ugly, and a huge belly, sits eating and staring down at her food. Her eyebrows move up and down as if in a silent, pleasant conversation with her plate, which she wipes with a piece of bread. "How soon are you?" someone asks the girl, but she doesn't glance up, though her face shows comprehension and a kind of conversational pleasure. She is about fifteen. The bread on her plate makes a faint squeaking sound.

Father, I want to fall asleep in your arms.

"Hey, why'd you leave home?" a girl is asking me.

She is looking right at me.

"Which one of them was it?" she says.

I shake my head—I don't understand.

"Which one of them—mother or father?"

I can't answer. I stare at her, feeling the tears in my eyes.

The girl doesn't want to release me. She says with a laugh, "With me it was my mother—*she* turned me in, how d'ya like that! What about you?"

But I can't answer.

"Leave her alone," says Toddie.

"She think she's too good to talk to me?" cries the girl.

Afterward they all go to the laundry room to work. *You are waiting for me.* The matron gets me ready, scolds me for being so slow and clumsy, she isn't nice like Miss Goldie because she says: "You're a lucky little girl to have your father come pick you up. Some of these sad little mutts, their fathers don't give a damn about them."

I don't want to leave Cell 5. But I am dressed in my jeans and my filthy cashmere sweater, trembling, shuddering, all ready to be presented to my father. I don't want to leave. I start to cry. The matron makes a disgusted noise.

What must I do to stay here?

But it is too late. I am expertly handled: walked briskly along the corridor. I am being steered by a two-hundred-pound woman who knows how to handle little girls.

There you are, waiting for me—

There you are, with your face that glares at me, your tired eyes, your staring, staring eyes—

So you brought me back home again, home from Toledo one rainy September noon.

6

That fall and winter he lay sick and unable to sleep. He began to wander through the house—staying away from his study, his desk, because he couldn't have been able to concentrate anyway—and he walked with his head slightly lowered, as if in a baffled blind rage, like an animal, narrowing his eyes so that he might smell his prey better. He seemed not to want to see, not clearly. And his hearing was too sensitive, it pained him to hear clearly, to be forced to hear everything.

Why did you do it? Run away? he had asked her.

I don't know.

Her face pale with fatigue, her eyes pocketed with shadows like bruises, Shelley sitting beside him in the car, pushed over against the door.... He had driven from Toledo to Chicago with her sitting like that, her breathing raspy as a child's, almost panting, as if she were terrified. He remembered a dog of his: that dog, the black dog. Yes. The black dog. What was its name...? Duke. That dog had panted too, in terror. A deep panting, deep into the chest, the lungs, the sound of terror.

Why did you do it?

Shelley's frightened silence.

He was sick with anguish for her. He thought about her constantly. At the clinic, there was the image of Dr. Vogel moving restlessly about, like a shadow jerking across the wall of his office or along the corridor or even in the operating room, the panicked Dr. Vogel who could think of only one thing: his daughter. The other Dr. Vogel did his work slowly and methodically; he found it difficult to concentrate but he did his work, he got it done always, but he was aware of the shadow-self, pacing restlessly about, trying to disrupt his life. That other Dr. Vogel, who worried so much about his daughter, wanted to draw him into a deeper anguish and destroy him.

This other self had sprung out of him on that ride home from Toledo. It had taken hold of Shelley and shaken her violently, knocking her head from side to side. *Why did you leave home! Why! Tell me why!* But Jesse himself kept on driving, forced himself to concentrate on his driving and to show no agitation. He did not want to frighten her any more. He did not want to punish her. Enough that she was breathing so hoarsely, that she had spent the night in a county jail, brought to him by a big, tough-looking matron with a man's nose and jaw—

But why did you run away from me? he wanted to ask.

Back in Winnetka, he checked her into a hospital where an acquaintance of his could examine her. She had not protested. She seemed to fling her body along as they walked up the sidewalk, throwing herself forward. She had taken off the old clothes she'd been wearing for days and wore now a dress, stockings, shoes with small wooden heels. Jesse had stared at these shoes, charmed by them. He had forgotten momentarily where he and Shelley were, what they were doing—he thought his daughter's shoes were very attractive and wondered why he had never noticed them before—

"Your shoes are very pretty," he had said.

"Thank you," Shelley had said, startled.

When he lay in bed beside Helene he felt the agitation of that other Dr. Vogel who prowled the house in the dark. He had to get up to join him. The other self, the ghost self, tugged at him and insisted that he get out of bed and come downstairs, where he could sit in the dark of the large, long living room, thinking of the night and of his daughter, sleeping upstairs, in a room almost directly above him.

His hearing was too sensitive, especially at night. He could hear everything. Tires screeching on a street far away... the ticking of the clocks of the house, of his own wrist watch... the whipping fall of sleet in late November... the first sounds of morning, Helene's footsteps overhead. Helene would try to comfort him. She was always saying of Shelley: "She's much better now. She's changed. She's much more mature." When Jesse called his wife from the clinic, urged by that other Dr. Vogel to telephone—something might have happened in his absence—Helene told him gently, surely, "Nothing is wrong, Jesse. Nothing. Shelley came directly home from school. She's in her room right now. She's much better, she's changed a great deal... she and Jeanne never fight anymore.... She doesn't mind going to bed early. And she really goes to bed; I've checked. And her grades will improve, I'm sure. Why do you worry so much?"

He could not believe that his daughter had run away from home. *Runaway,* the police had termed her. *Runaway.* The police were efficient and indifferent and courteous. Jesse's shame could have been any father's shame, not Dr. Vogel's. They did not know him. They did not know Shelley. The police matron who had dragged Shelley into the reception room had not known her.

He could not sleep. His brain ached. He wandered through the strange rooms of this big house. Where was he? In a large brick home that was evidently his own home now. Why was he pacing like this, pressing himself on from room to room? Because he had to hunt out something. Had to find out some truth. Why was his head lowered, his hair shaggy with the night? Because he had to figure something out, had to make sense out of something....

In late 1969 he opened the front door one night and watched the snow fall for some time. It was nearing Christmas. The street lights of Kennilworth Drive were faint, distant from one another and from his front door. Everything was silent. He felt a sudden urge, an almost violent urge, to go outside, to get out of this house... to get into the falling snow and walk fast, fast, before it was too late, before he exploded.... So he walked down the front walk to the street, already breathing hard, his head lowered with the beginning of a headache, the vapor shaping and dissolving about his mouth like angry unspoken words, shouts. *Why did you leave me...?* He walked down the middle of the winding street. If he glanced over his shoulder he saw only his own footsteps in the snow, the fine falling of snow, snow beginning to drift. His footsteps covered over gently. Scuffed, scanty footsteps, becoming invisible. No one could follow him. He walked faster, wanting to run. His heart urged him to run. That other Dr. Vogel, anxious to get into the fresh, freezing air, tried to climb out of him and run....

The panic lessened. He was very cold, exhausted. Panic faded as his strength faded. He found that he had circled around his house, a circle that must have taken him five miles, the house remaining in its center, in the very center of his consciousness, his wife and daughters sleeping in the center, while snow fell in their sleep and all about him. . . . He approached his house, aware of the sharp, intense odor of winter, the dampness of the air, his senses sharpened and brutal and somehow detached from him, as if belonging to an animal, a hunting animal, a creature run like a machine, without personality. He could smell everything, he thought. Could see too well—the flickering Christmas lights of the few houses that were decorated, flickering and nervous through the falling snow, yet still vivid to him, disturbing. Could hear too well. It was a curse, he thought. He was cursed with such sharpened senses, how could he ever sleep?

The next morning he would have to operate: a patient at nine-thirty, another at twelve. A third in the afternoon. He would have to operate on them no matter how exhausted he was. And yet, exhausted, almost stunned with cold, he felt a certainty that he would perform well; he would not fail. He would never fail.

Excitement stirred in him at the thought of operating. He would peel out those poisonous little beads one by one. . . .

He slept.

. . . Shelley's great anxious eyes. Her nervousness at the dinner table. Stared at, observed, even when no one was looking at her. Jesse thought, seeing her through a film of pity and apprehension, a kind of film over his vision, that she was taking on the manner of an animal that knows it cannot avoid its fate. Furtive and gracious, as if squirming under the pressure of her father's concentration, even when Jesse did not dare look at her; a boyish, neutral inclination to her head, with that heavy rope of hair that she wore now braided and straight down her back. She seemed much younger than she had before running away. She had lost ten or fifteen pounds.

In Toledo she had been given a V.D. test. It was negative. *A V.D. test.*

His mind turned upon that fact giddily and would not release it, as it turned upon this house he had bought for his family, his wife and two daughters, Shelley static in the center of it.

He telephoned the principal of her high school himself, not wanting his receptionist to make the appointment. His voice sounded uncertain, timid. But it was not the principal he would see; instead he must make an appointment with the "guidance counsellor." Someone named Miss Kesey. So he made the appointment and learned with surprise that his wife had been in to see this woman a few months before. . . .

Miss Kesey turned out to be very young, a disappointment to Jesse. Too young. She was staccato-voiced, with an arm-load of tests and transcripts and notations pulled out of a file. "*Michele Ellen Vogel,*" the young woman said, frowning, wetting her lips as she leafed through these records, "in ninth grade she scored exceptionally high, with an I.Q. rating of 144 (verbal 141, performance 132) . . . but her grades were never quite up to her ability. . . . In her sophomore year she slipped a little . . . yes . . . the I.Q. rating is 140, but there is a notation from her examiner that she was extremely nervous during the testing session. Her performance in mathematics was not very good, and this was the semester she failed mathematics . . . failed plane geometry. . . . She shows an excellent sense of the manipulation of words. The Madden Language Skills score is very high. . . ."

Jesse squirmed in his chair. "May I look at the records myself?" he asked.

"I'm sorry, Dr. Vogel, but that isn't allowed."

"I would like very much to examine them myself," Jesse said tensely.

"That's out of the question, I'm sorry, I'm very sorry but there are rules. . . ."

Jesse tried to smile.

"There are rules," the young woman said, frowning, "we must have rules. . . . Parents are always coming in here, they're upset and angry and . . . And we have to follow certain rules. . . ."

"I understand," Jesse said.

He got to his feet. The young woman was saying something further, her voice gone helpful and bright again, as if eager to please him, but Jesse paid no attention to her. He walked out into the corridor. A bell had just rung and students were changing classes. Warm-faced, a little out of breath, Jesse was conscious of dozens of girls who might be his daughter. They glanced at him, frankly and with curiosity, their eyes strangely keen, sharp —these were exaggerated eyes, outlined carefully in black. Like eyes drawn onto eyes. All the girls wore long, straight hair. They were thin, in sweaters dragged down over their hips, wearing stockings of all colors—bright red, bright yellow, green, black. They dawdled in the corridor between classes, carrying books and purses up against their small chests. The high school boys, looking much younger than the girls, ducked in and out of their birdlike clusters.

He was forty-four years old now.

He lingered in the hall as if waiting to see her, his daughter, to catch her by surprise in this strange context. Where was she? Had she already sighted him? These girls were tall, so agile. They moved with a peculiar internal cunning; their voices and their laughter were light, mocking. When they happened to notice Jesse their eyes went opaque, as if sighting an enemy. He was forty-four years old now. Some of the girls were sloppily, slovenly dressed, their shoes scuffed the floor, they let their hair swing loosely and messily forward across their faces. Staring at Jesse, sizing him up. There were hundreds of students in this school, Shelley was hiding somewhere among them... all the legs, the flashing colors, sword-like legs of girls, the laziness of their bodies, their smiles, their lips outlined in preposterous glowing pale colors, almost white, like the lips of corpses... shoulders slightly rounded, chests small, flat, concave with coyness, that strange internal cunning that governed their bodies... little stomachs hollow, the bones of the pelvis showing as if to emphasize the boyish fragility of their bodies....

This was a very new school, very expensive. The halls were enormously wide. The walls appeared to be made of ceramic tile —multicolored and striking—and the floor was carpeted. A dark blue carpet. There were open spaces, lounges, with furniture of transparent plastic, faintly fluorescent orange and green "chairs" in which students sat, very much at home. Windows of Thermoplex glass reached nearly to the ceiling, looking out upon the vast snow-stubbled front lawn of the school and the enormous black-topped parking lot, where the students' cars were parked in long rows, with a regularity that seemed remarkably adult. Jesse's heart yearned suddenly....

He walked along through the thinning crowd of students. Passed beneath the portraits of Lincoln and Kennedy in their modern sleek pale-blond wooden frames. Sick with yearning, he was heartsick, lovesick. . . .

Jesse loves . . .

There were no little messages of love scribbled on the ceramic walls. No messages at all, unless they were wiped off by a janitor every night. Everything was polished and clean, all surface. You couldn't carve anything into the walls. *Jesse loves . . . loved. . . .*

He had never seen Reva again, after that morning in Wisconsin.

Shelley?

Yes, Father?

How do you feel today? Are you getting over that cold?

Yes. I stayed out from swimming class today. I'm much better.

He talked with her after dinner, even when he had work to do. A calm level unangry unfrightened conversation like a period of prayer. His eyes suddenly filled with love for her: he could not help himself. *The V.D. test was negative. Runaway.* She had not given her name in Toledo. Had not answered to Shelley Vogel.

Every afternoon Jesse called his wife around four-thirty to see if Shelley had come home yet. She always came home, yes. Yes, Helene reported, yes. Shelley was home. Up in her room. If Jesse did not call he could not concentrate on his work—if he was talking to someone he could not follow the conversation. The other Dr. Vogel leaped up from his desk, paced the room anxiously, demanded that he pick up that telephone and dial home.

Shelley?

Yes, Father?

I was very pleased with your grades . . . your grade in Art. . . .

Thank you.

He tried to imagine her in her room—a room with pink-and-white wallpaper, a girl's room, sweet and fresh and pleasing to him when he looked in it during her absence; he imagined her sitting on the edge of her bed in the short nightgown she wore, a white gown dotted with pink rosebuds that had faded from many washings, Shelley brushing her hair, one, two, three, a hundred strokes, two hundred strokes, safe in her room at ten o'clock every night, unangry, his daughter brushing her hair before bed. *The V.D. test was negative.*

Shelley?

Yes, Father?

Who are your girl friends now? Why don't you ask them over to the house? Don't you see that tall girl with the freckles any longer... ?

Who? Sandy? Oh, yes....

Who were you talking on the telephone with just now?

Oh, nobody, just Babs Baird....

Who?

Babs Baird....

He had the idea she was lying to him.

At the clinic he worked quickly, excitedly. He could not fail. His poor-risk patients did not always die, not even from the anesthetic; urged on by that other Dr. Vogel, who was always eager to operate, Jesse dissected aneurysms and ran the risk of hemorrhages; he never hesitated, he worked as if still under the cautious, shrewd eyes of Dr. Perrault himself, daring Perrault to find fault with anything he did. The brain damage was never so bad as it might have been. His patients were never so bad as they might have been. At staff conferences, Jesse's associates worried and argued and hinted at squabbles Jesse did not know about, glancing at Jesse's thinning, perplexed face and seeing in it a centrality of all their wonder, a sense of growing neutral amazement over the problems of diagnosis, the frequent hopeless cuttings, even the habits of the cleaning women—Mannie Breck was always bringing this odd point up—who left scouring stains in the sinks.

Breck and Ronald Myer could never agree on what they called a matter of ethics. When should nerves be snipped to put a cancer patient out of pain?

Though Jesse was paying attention, he was also aware of small, striking details that somehow confused him. Mannie's frizzy hair and wise, worried face. Ronald Myer's hefty, high-colored face. The window behind them, darkly glaring with winter sunshine—a tinted window. Traffic moving out on the street. He recalled a hypodermic needle someone had stolen at LaSalle, years ago; he had always suspected a certain young nurse.

Silence in the room told him that he was expected to say something.

At other times he heard everything, heard too much; words stayed in his head but floated without connections, without the syntax of ordinary language to tie them together. That was why he was anxious to work, to work with his hands. His hands forgot nothing. He could do five, six difficult operations in a couple of days—operations that lasted for hours; one of them ran from nine in the morning until eleven-thirty at night and released him buoyed and excited by success, ready for the next day, the next problem.

He found himself wasting many minutes with letters that came to him at the clinic. After an article appeared in a local paper there were always stray letters that Jesse opened personally, fascinated, knowing this was a waste of his time; and yet he had the feeling that someone might be trying to reach him, with a message meant only for him.

Dear Dr. Vogel:

Can you tell me the explanation of this: my fingers get numb like ice and it spreads up my arms to my elbows, but my face is very hot. I hear roaring in the ears. When I was sixteen I had a burst appendix. Is the poison still in me? Sometimes I taste a substance that is green, like poison, and gritty. What I want to know is: do other people taste this poison, or only me? Is it something in the air.

Dear Dr. Vogel:

My telephone number is below. Please call me any night after seven. I have long times of blindness and have to stay in bed. I am not a drinker. I have a good appetite and since a child I have always concentrated on good green vegetables and very little red meat. My spells of blindness will interfere with my job. I am waiting for your call.

Dear Dr. Vogel:

I am sixty-two years old and recently my periods began again, a heavy period of blood that lasted five days. I stayed in bed all that time. Is my body going backwards to where I could have a baby again. I am afraid to go to a doctor to talk about this. Please answer on this postcard which I have stamped.

And there were the notes from Mrs. Perrault. She telephoned and left messages for Jesse to call her; one week Jesse counted eleven messages. He dreaded calling her, but one day, at noon, already feverish from a morning of work that was not going well, he picked up the phone and dialed her number. When she answered, her voice sounded stale and sleepy. "Oh, Jesse, thank you for calling, I have to talk to someone and you're the only one who would understand," she said. "It's about my son Bruce and his wife. . . . I don't like to complain, Jesse, but I'm alone now and I don't have anyone who understands me. . . . I remember how courteous you always were, Jesse, to Dr. Perrault, and how he loved you . . . yes, we both loved you, and . . . and . . . For Christmas they gave me a bowl of cut glass, you know, for flowers and things . . . they're living in Sacramento, you know, and she hates to fly so they never come visit . . . I never see the grandchildren . . . and . . . and, Jesse, they sent me this cut-glass bowl from a department store, it was packaged and wrapped and mailed from the store, for Christmas," Mrs. Perrault said, beginning to cry in hoarse ugly gulps, "and it shows they gave no thought to me at all, just ordered something from a store, maybe Bruce wasn't even along but *she* picked it out and it was the only present they sent me for Christmas, it was the only chance they had to send me something for Christmas and I might not be around next Christmas . . . it was just that one chance, when I opened the present, and it turned out to be that. . . . Dr. Perrault is dead now, Jesse, he's dead," Mrs. Perrault said, sobbing, "do you know what that means? He's dead, do you know what that means?"

For half an hour Jesse listened in misery, to this, unable to hang up.

Once, in March, he telephoned home to check on Shelley, and Helene explained to him that she had given Shelley permission to stay after school for a meeting of some club—the journalism club, she thought, or the drama club. Jesse hid his irritation. He called back in an hour and this time Shelley was home. He asked his wife to put her on the telephone. "How are you, Shelley?" he asked. For a few seconds she was silent. He had the idea that she was about to scream at him. Then she said in her light, rapid voice, the voice of any high school girl, "I'm just fine, Father. When will you be home tonight?"

He put the receiver back slowly, knowing that he was going to lose her.

But he had to be certain of her. He had to prevent her from being misused by strangers, by men. The world could get at his daughter through the orifices of her body, pushing into the willing elastic streams of her blood, and she would smile dumbly, enticingly. Yet at the same time he had to think about the clinic. It could not handle all the patients who were referred for tests and treatment. It must be expanded. More money. A new wing, a new group of doctors. A further extension of Jesse's brain, his energy. And his own field was expanding all the time; he could hardly keep up with the journals and papers that came to him. He spent an extra night trying to make sense of a long monograph on isotope encephalography, "brain-scanning," by means of a radioactive isotope injected into the blood, but he could not concentrate because he kept thinking of Shelley upstairs, sleeping; or, rather, not thinking of her but envisioning her. Yet he did not really envision her, not the girl Shelley, but rather the ghostly "scan" of his own brain, Dr. Vogel's brain, a photograph of a grainy oblong in which a certain area was heavily shaded by the radioactive isotope in the form of his daughter's face, like a tumor . . . located in the frontal region of his brain. A posterior frontal tumor in Dr. Vogel's brain.

He forced himself to read: *Abnormal tissues show abnormal scans.*

The first Saturday in April, Shelley was allowed to spend an afternoon at a girl friend's house about a mile away. She left the address and the telephone number. Jesse went down to the clinic to check on some patients of his; then, on an impulse, he called the number. A girl answered. He asked to speak to Shelley and, with a breathless little laugh, the girl said that she was Shelley: didn't he recognize her voice?

Jesse hesitated. Yes, it was her voice. Of course. His daughter. He felt as if his head were slowly being squeezed out of shape.

He stayed at the clinic for another hour, but the other Dr. Vogel was eager, anxious to get going, to do something, to get out from behind that desk. No operations scheduled for the next day. Nothing until Monday at nine-thirty. Nervously, he opened two or three letters and glanced at their contents, let them fall back onto his desk. . . . Finally he could stand it no longer. He drove back to Winnetka, to the address Shelley had given him. The house was handsome, large, a fake English Tudor with a garage big enough for four cars. The lawn was oddly raw, torn up, as if repair work had been done on it last fall and had never been completed. There was a large shallow pit near the front steps where a pipe lay exposed, partly covered with leaves and debris and dirty patches of snow. When Jesse rang the bell he heard nothing inside—the bell must be out of order.

Fighting his panic, he waited quietly. The material of the front porch had begun to crumble. The mailbox was an ordinary dime-store mailbox, rusty and bent, and in it were stuck shopping circulars, their colors run together.

Finally he knocked on the door.

And now . . . now . . . someone was coming. He heard a voice.

But the door was not opened. Jesse rapped again, gently. He did not want to frighten this person away. He heard someone speaking, asking a question. But he could not hear what it was. *My God,* Jesse thought in misery, wanting to bring his head forward and smash it against the door.

He knocked again. Gently. Courteous. And, after another long wait, he heard the lock being undone.

A woman his own age stood there, staring at him. She wore a bathrobe of some violet quilted material.

"Yes? Who is it? What do you want?" she said.

Her face was pale, her eyebrows and eyelashes pale, undefined. Messy hair. A smell of disuse about her.

"Mrs. Baird?"

"My name is Nancy."

"I'm Jesse Vogel. . . ."

She stared boldly at him and said nothing.

"I think my daughter is visiting your daughter . . . ?"

"Oh. Your daughter. Somebody with Babs. Oh, wait. Do you want to step inside?"

The entryway was dim. A flagstone floor, a low-hanging chandelier of wrought iron. The woman was saying, "Somebody is with Babs, yes. I heard them come in. Now, let's see. Let's see," she said, confused. She stumbled back against something—a piece of heavy ornate furniture, a Spanish chest that was very dusty. "I was taking a nap. I have my room now in the study, right up close to the front door. So I can answer the doorbell. Otherwise I wouldn't hear it. I can't get anyone to come fix the doorbell. Repairmen just laugh at me, they never pay any attention to a woman by herself.... Which one is your daughter, is she the blond? They have a place in the Bahamas?"

"Shelley has red hair."

"*Shelley.* Oh, yes. Shelley. She's very sweet. She's Babs's best friend. They went to St. Ursula's together before Babs transferred...?"

"You must be thinking of someone else," Jesse said nervously.

The woman was leading him into a long, dark living room, where the furniture was not quite in place, the sofas and chairs moved about into odd arrangements. A table was overturned in front of the fireplace. Most of the shades were drawn, but not evenly. "This room is a dungeon. I hate it. I want to do it all over in off-white, you know, oyster. But I can't get started. This place has a curse on it," the woman said rapidly. "First of all, I hate this style of house. It wasn't my choice of a house.... Oh, I know where they are. They're swimming," she said, shaking her head as if to clear it.

She led him through the living room into a corridor, where the carpet was coming loose. It looked as if children had been running and skidding on it. "There's a curse on this house, believe me," the woman said peevishly. She led Jesse into a huge room of domed glass. The pool was empty, drained out, the air was very chilly. "Oh, they're not here after all. Where are they? I thought they went swimming... I thought I heard them in here...."

Jesse walked to the edge of the pool and stared down. At this end it was cluttered with cans and bottles, debris from ashtrays, old newspapers, waxed milk cartons, bright yellow cereal boxes.

Jesse could not speak.

"Well, maybe they went out. To the roller rink maybe. They all wear these cute little skirts and colored panties and high-topped white roller skates. Aren't they cute, those outfits? That's where they are, probably."

"She isn't here?"

"Why don't you relax? Are you new in the neighborhood or something? You look like you're new. Why don't you sit down somewhere, I'll make us a drink...."

"They're not here? My daughter isn't here . . . ?"

"Why don't you relax, please. I'll make us both a drink and we can talk this over. . . ."

Jesse stared at her. His head pounded with revulsion. That pale, out-of-focus face, her squinting eyes, her odor— It was so hard to keep a family, Jesse thought suddenly, that maybe it was better to give up. Better to give up, erase them all, destroy them, obliterate them and the memory of them, wipe everything out. A father could wipe out everything he had ever done and be free. A clean, pure, empty being, a void. . . .

"You sure you're not new in the neighborhood?" the woman asked, following him to the front door.

Jesse went home. Seeing his face, Helene asked what had happened. He said nothing. "You didn't check on Shelley, did you? You didn't go to the house and embarrass her in front of her friends?" Helene asked anxiously.

"No," Jesse said.

When Shelley came home, it was nearly dark. She let herself in the back door and he heard her speaking to Helene—the two of them speaking ordinarily, lightly, loud enough for Jesse to hear if he wished, so that he could know there were no secrets in this house.

She appeared in the doorway. Jesse was sitting in the living room without the lights on.

She stared at him. "Are you . . . is it . . . am I late?" Shelley asked.

"No."

She was unbuttoning her jacket. It was made of some coarse beige material, lined with fake fur, an imitation of a farmer's or a laborer's jacket. She wore jeans and boots. Her face itself looked a little coarse, as if from hurrying, breathing hard.

"What's wrong . . . ?" she whispered.

"Is anything wrong?" Jesse asked ironically.

They stared at each other. It was nearly dark. Light from the hallway fell past Shelley and into the living room, all the way to Jesse's legs. He stood. He was not going to do anything.

"Did you go there?" Shelley said faintly.

"Go where?"

"To the Bairds'."

Jesse said nothing.

"You . . . you want to kill me. . . ." Shelley whispered.

She turned and ran upstairs.

That was on Saturday. The next morning she did not get out of bed; she complained of a cold, a sore throat. She looked feverish. Jesse went up to her room and she was sitting propped up in bed, the Sunday papers scattered about her, a few pages fallen onto the floor. She wiped her nose with a tissue that was already crumpled and damp.

"How do you feel?" he asked carefully.

"It's just a cold. I'm all right."

Her hair bad been brushed away from her face; near the hairline there was a row of small dull pimples.

The next morning she did not go to school. At the clinic, preparing for an operation, Jesse thought of her red-rimmed eyes and he froze, he could not move. He had been washing, scrubbing for the operating room. A minute before he had been eager to get in there, to peel out some poisonous little beads of flesh he knew he would find . . . in just a short while he would find them, he'd peel them out and destroy them . . . but now he froze, he heard someone talking to him but he could not bring himself to make the effort to listen—

He couldn't do it. Couldn't take the risk. Someone else would have to do the operation.

That afternoon at two the telephone rang and he knew it would be his wife. He listened to her careful, calm voice like a man in a dream, his eyes closed. "I only went out for half an hour. She was gone when I came back. There's no note, nothing. Nothing. It's just like the last time. . . ."

7

Jesse drove down into Chicago, on the lookout for girls of a certain age, a certain height. He seemed to see them all over. He saw them walking along the street or waiting for buses or lingering in doorways. His eye jumped onto them. Occasionally they noticed him, his cruising automobile, and stepped out to see him better, to give him a better look at them—some of the girls even younger than Shelley, some of them black, with that same hip-rocking sardonic flirtatiousness he had noticed in the high school girls. It meant nothing, he thought. Nothing. Or it meant everything.

He stopped from time to time to telephone his wife, but there was no news at home, no good news. The police hadn't found her. The police were sympathetic but busy; they were on the trails of a thousand girls like Shelley, so they said.

At her high school he tried to talk to her teachers, her friends, tried to learn something about her. Her teachers didn't seem to know her well. Yes, a pretty girl, a redheaded girl, not very responsive . . . daydreaming. . . . Their pity for Jesse embarrassed him. Shelley's "friends" were no more helpful. They were embarrassed and a little sullen. Babs Baird said coolly, "Shell had a mind of her own, she didn't really run with us. She did what she wanted to do. Nobody could boss her around."

"Who wanted to boss her around?" Jesse asked.

"Oh, you know. Guys."

"Who?"

"People. Just people. They always want to boss you around," Babs said.

She was a lean, round-shouldered girl, insolent in an impersonal, weary way. Jesse would have liked to shake her by the shoulders, but he spoke to her politely. *Where did she think Shelley had gone?*

"Look, I didn't know her that well. She sort of used me, you know? She used my name. She had more on me than I had on her. She'll probably be back."

"Why do you say that? When will she be back?"

"Who knows?" she said, shrugging her shoulders.

Jesse drove around other high schools in the city, cruising slowly. His eyes had begun to ache. He saw crowds of high school students, boys and girls, a tide of them, the sexes confused, mixed together, surging across school lawns and intersections. He saw a hundred girls who might have been his daughter. He strolled along the sidewalk, letting the girls overtake him, pass him, his heart lurching at their shadows, which skidded past and touched him deftly, boldly. . . . Snatches of their conversations:

"Oh, Louise told me that already. What else? Who's kidding who?" A mysterious, fluid jumble of words that seemed sacred to him. If he turned to glance at these girls he saw how vacuous they were, how easy with one another, not guessing at the sacred quality of their words, their faces. . . . Girls with colored stockings, ornamental stockings stitched into diamond shapes, even into shapes of tiny hearts, some legs so tight with flesh that the black stitching was uneven in places, starting to unravel. Their voices were occasionally flat and harsh, even the voices of the prettiest girls. But Jesse had faith in their inner music, which paused and stalled and rushed onward, mocking and derisive, while their long hair flicked with the wind, their heads snapping like horses' heads to get the hair out of their eyes. Any one of them could have been his daughter.

He kept calling the police station. Yes, they were looking for her. So they said. They had a thousand girls to catch up with, so they said.

On April 15, Jesse drove downtown again to watch the crowds gathering for an antiwar demonstration. He got there early in the afternoon so that he would miss nothing. It was a fairly cold spring day, but the crowd grew rapidly. Thousands of people. Most of them were young, kids in their twenties, teenagers in groups, the girls with their usual long straight listless hair, the boys with greasy hair in shoulder-length strands, their faces pasty and wild and set for excitement. A slow surging march along the street. Policemen lined the sidewalks to hold back the spectators.

Jesse's eyes jumped everywhere, looking for Shelley.

The stamp of marching feet. Chanting. Random shouts. Bright splashes of sound—pure voices, without words. Jesse's heart ached to hear those voices, the girls' voices, so pure and bodiless and angry. He was elbowed, shoved, pushed by people on the sidewalks, spectators who were getting impatient. A gang of Negro boys ran through the crowd, ducking and giggling. A girl with a picket sign was knocked down. She shrieked. A policeman on horseback started through the marchers, the horse's tail swishing, aristocratic and unhurried; people strained to get out of the way, a few of the younger girls cried out in alarm. . . . Someone was being pressed up against a building. *Help! Stop!* The policeman continued without looking down. Jesse had been pushed along himself and could not see what had happened to the girls.

A surging, milling crowd, the stamping of feet, picket signs waving in the light—END THE WAR IN VIETNAM! END THE KILLING! Jesse stared at the faces, knowing how necessary it was to see each face. His own face must have been brilliant with desire, like a beacon, because people occasionally glanced at him, struck by something they saw in him. He sensed in the young people who were marching a curious impersonal contempt for him, perhaps because of his clothes. Or his age. It was not personal, it was not bodily or physical or sensual, this contempt. It was an abstract, spiritual hatred of him, a dismissal that was frightening. A man like Dr. Vogel might die and it would not matter.

He felt their hatred, it made him lightheaded, fearful. He did not understand it. He thought of cancerous protoplasm: that fatal spreading essence. He had seen it many times through a microscope. Eating away its own boundaries, no limits to it, an inflammation seeding everywhere—to the spinal fluid, to the brain. How they surged in the chill open air of Chicago, roused as if by godly chimes—the bells of sunken churches, pealing and pulsating in a rhythm that people like Jesse could feel only remotely, being too old. It was a rhythm that beat in the loins of the young and showed in their faces. Their eyes were glazed, filmed over by the cold wind—in a hurry, they were in a hurry! they were shouting with the need to hurry! They were so young, they could push everyone else off the edge of the continent, being in such a hurry!

Girls younger than his daughter were tramping around downtown in this mob, being pushed and shoved and pressed against, all elbows themselves, ducking under arms and squirming away, running, chanting, taunting the police and their own hecklers, their faces wind-blown and arrogant. Jesse was out of breath and could not keep up with them. He was behind the police line, safe with people his own age and older, not in the surging crowd that had taken over the street. He watched. No good to shout at them to wait. No good to shout at all. They would not hear, waving their signs in a communion of noise. They were children's faces in the street, rising and blossoming and on the verge of detonation. Their faces strained to explode. Mouths and eyes out of shape, distorted, a lovely sleeping yearning to them as they pressed forward into the backs of other kids....

Jesse hated this formlessness. He was seized with a sudden hatred for it, almost a nausea. He hated it, hated them. Hated the crowd and its joy in being trampled. Hated the noise. The communion. The sensuous rising heat of the faces, the shapes of the mouths...hated that merging, that mobbing.... Better to destroy them all, Jesse thought. Better to die than to descend into this frenzy, to be lost in this anonymous garbage. This strange mass consciousness revolted him. He hated it, hated all these people, even those watching from the sidewalks. So much garbage in the world! And most of it human! Heaving, pulsing, sighing, surging with blood, their common breaths congealing in the used-up air, forming a sooty, smoggy, warm breath that was human and guttery, the comfortable odor of sewage.... Jesse could not help but think that this crowd was about to part and reveal something, a single figure, a truth. Wasn't there a truth, a single truth, a single human being at the center of this mob? A single eye that would see everyone, everything, and pronounce judgment upon it?

But nothing. Only noise. Only bodies.

Jesse fought his way out of it. Back to where his car was parked, a mile away. Panting. Breathless. Stunned by the smell of them, this human flow, this avalanche, his head rocky with their chants, their feet. Yet his eyes still darted about hotly. He had to find her. He would find her. He had been tempted to lose himself in that crowd, yes, to pass into its frenzy as if his brain had burst, but he would not give into it: he would return to the world in which he was a single human being, a single consciousness with a destiny he must fulfill.

The next week, a postcard came to him at the clinic postmarked Savannah, Georgia. Very faint scrawling, in pencil, which he could hardly read. It said something about a head, a "fast-moving head," something about an operation, about brains. He turned the postcard over in his fingers: an ordinary street scene, a boulevard with palm trees, in Savannah. So she had gotten that far. Georgia.

He knew he would never find her.

8

In July he received a letter from Florida, a long letter on tablet paper, covered with Shelley's slanted handwriting. And, in the envelope, part of a broken fingernail.

He read the letter several times. *The voice must say I love you. If it does not say I love you it is not an authentic voice.* Trembling, unable to control his trembling, he read about Noel, read about someone named Noel, his daughter's lover.

He read the letter and yet he had the idea that she was dead: that the police were hiding information from him. Somewhere they had discovered her decomposing body, in a ditch somewhere, strangled and left by a man, a man named Noel.

He called the police. Went to the station and showed them the letter but would not surrender it to them, wouldn't let them read it all the way through. "She's with a man. Someone named Noel. Named Noel," Jesse said.

"If she writes you letters she'll be coming back. Don't worry," he was told.

And Helene told him: "If she writes you that means she'll come back. I know it. I'm certain of it."

He tortured himself with certain passages from this letter: *Noel says, Noel rubs his forehead against mine, Noel weighs me down. . . .* He waited for another letter but nothing came until October: again postmarked Florida, a small city on the western side of the state. *I am "the Fetish." Noel dressed me up . . . led me around the beach naked. . . .* Jesse read this letter and a flame passed over his brain, paralyzing him. She was teasing, taunting him. This couldn't be true. He told Helene about the letter but would not let her read it. She did not insist. She kept saying gently, unconvincingly: "If she writes you, Jesse, she'll come back. Why else would she write?"

The next month another long letter came, an almost unintelligible letter, and Jesse read it with a stiff angry smile, sitting at his desk at the clinic, where he spent most of his time though he no longer operated. He went to the clinic mainly on the chance that a letter from his daughter might arrive—she never sent any of the letters home. Ronald Myer had taken over much of his work. Jesse's "work." Jesse's "patients." He waited for the mail each morning and afternoon, waiting for Shelley to write, but when her letter did come he thought at first it must be a trick: he was sure that she was dead. Her murderer was writing these letters to drive him mad.

Then, in January of 1971, he got a letter from New York City, and he wondered if she might be on her way home. Coming north, coming back to him. He no longer bothered to call the police. No use to show them the letter. He kept it at the clinic, in the center drawer of his desk, where he could read it slowly through again and again. *You hypnotized me,* Shelley said. Or someone said, in Shelley's voice and in her childish handwriting.

She was teasing him, taunting him. Like the girls in the street that day last April: their faces savage with the delight of teasing, taunting.

The next letter came only a few days later, also postmarked New York City.

Dr. Vogel: never committed murder.
T. W. Monk: never got killed.
Not for Mother's eyes. T. W. Monk read his poems last night at St. Marks. Do you remember him? Remember the man you almost killed?
He told me all about you.
So you tried to kill somebody once! Oh I love you.
Thought I saw you the other day in the square. Man with red hair, walking fast. Oh it wasn't you. Oh there are thousands of men not you.
I am going to have a baby.

Love love love,
Shelley

9

"And that was your daughter? That girl your daughter, really?"

Monk was staring at Jesse and smiling vacuously.

"You mean you have a daughter, that was really your daughter? I thought it was a joke or something . . . I was a little mixed-up that night. . . . That little girl was really the daughter of Jesse Vogel?"

Jesse nodded stiffly.

"Well, Dr. Vogel, my friend, I would recognize you, yes, but it's quite a surprise for me and an honor, truly an honor," Monk was saying rapidly, "to open the door and see you standing there. . . . I'm a little confused, but eventually I make perfect sense. There is a code to my confusion. And so you're looking for her, that little girl who was evidently your daughter, no joke about it . . . ?"

"Yes. I thought you could help me."

"Oh yes. Yes. I can help you. Indeed, yes," Monk said with a smile.

Monk's room was above a bar in the East Village. Jesse sat rigidly, in a kind of chair, while Monk sat on a ruined sofa with piles of candy wrappers on the cushions around him. The room stank.

"You must have been surprised to discover that I am famous, after all that nonsense at Ann Arbor," Monk said. He was thick and clammy, stripped to the waist, perspiring in spite of the chilly room. His chest was mottled, many colors, even bruised in great yellow and orangish and violet welts, and his chest hair was stubbly—it had evidently been shaved off some time ago and allowed to grow back in. His head was completely bald. The gleaming scalp was rotund and boastful. Even when Monk was not speaking, his mouth moved in silent, moist, circular movements, as if he were chewing gum though he did not seem to be chewing gum.

"Yes, I was surprised to hear about you. I was surprised," Jesse admitted.

"Well, this is a time of magic. Anything can happen today," Monk said. "My first book was published under the name T. W. Monk, not Trick Monk. I rejected Trick because it was undignified. Did you read my book?"

"I'm afraid not," Jesse said.

"I knew you wouldn't, and I don't hold it against you," Monk said with a swift, sweet smile, moving his mouth. "The title was *Poems Without People.* Do you remember that title?"

Jesse frowned. No, he did not remember.

"Ah, you don't remember.... Poems are written to people like you, who don't remember any of them," Monk said wistfully. He had a garish, lined face; he appeared middle-aged. His face sagged. The skin of his scalp differed noticeably from the skin on his face, which was ruddy and pale in spots, caked over with something bright and muddy—it must have been make-up—that caught the light cruelly in this room.

"Anyway, it's good to meet an old friend after so many years," Monk said, reaching out to shake Jesse's hand again. It was the third time he had shaken Jesse's hand. "I feel that I am about to synthesize great areas of American thought, I feel that I am on the brink of revelation—and then you appear! Jesse Vogel appears knocking at my door! Did you happen to read that review of my second book last year in—what was it—the *Saturday Review?* The reviewer took on twenty-five books of poetry, an avalanche, but such an avalanche is correct in our time because it reflects the avalanche that is to come. I don't mind being considered in a mountain of other human beings. I feel, Dr. Vogel," he said with a snicker, "that in a mountain of bodies my own will fare well enough—eh? An arm sticking out here, a leg there, a vital organ exhibited to public view, eh? There is a cult down here, you know, strongly behind President Nixon. I had a vision of him descending to us from the sky. I think he is the Second Coming in person. It was that conviction I tried to express in my book... it was not an easy vision to express...." Monk got to his feet with a grunt. He began to pace back and forth in the cramped space in front of Jesse. "The reviewer for the *Saturday Review* misunderstood my poem, but with charity. There is no evil, Dr. Vogel, my dear Jesse, my friend Jesse...." He turned to Jesse with a sudden warm, loose smile. Jesse tried not to draw back. "Oh, how I loved you! Seeing you at those morning lectures of Cady's, sitting in the front row, sleepy and angelic and so attentive, so very attentive, as if your soul's salvation depended upon your hearing everything, learning everything! Your strength and your brains, your lovely brains— There is no love without the struggle of the brains, sexual chess, no, nothing at all—but you had a kind of Protestant soul then, an unimaginative dreary Protestant soul, and there was no chance of your being converted . . . and . . . and so decades have passed. . . . Now, now what was I saying . . . ?"

"You were going to tell me about my daughter," Jesse said nervously.

"Your daughter. Yes. It's strange, that you are a father." Monk went to sit on the edge of a tub. Evidently, the tub was not used for baths but was piled with books and magazines and papers and clothes. Behind Monk's head a banging had begun on the other side of the wall, but he did not seem to notice it. "Did you follow her footsteps to me, or what? I mean, is it still snowing?"

"What?"

Monk got up with another grunt and went to peer out of the window.

"They must have shoveled it up. Who sent you here?"

"Someone clerking in a bookstore. I asked about you and he told me where you live."

"But, look . . . the girl never came up here, did she?" Monk said, frowning. "She never came up to this room. I'm sure of that. So how did you follow her here?"

Jesse stared at Monk and could think of no reply.

Monk said vaguely, as he looked out the window, "I met her or someone like her at the Tupperware Corner, where I give poetry readings. I read them my Nixon sonnet a dozen times. They always ask for it, it's an audience-pleaser. I am working on another poem about the President. But I have trouble keeping track of my notebook. People are anxious to see what I'm doing, so they borrow it. They don't steal, they don't mean harm. But the notebook is not here now, I notice. Are you sitting on it? I have a problem with the central image. I want the scene to be the Washington Easter-egg roll, and I want a giant egg that will crack open so that the President can step out of it, but at the same time ... I have this disturbing, maddening image of a baked potato ... yes ... a very American baked potato that is cut open, and it too will reveal the President.... Art is hallucinatory, it comes up out of the depths and cannot be explained. It is instinctive. I must follow my instincts and I can't decide between these two images."

"You gave a poetry reading," Jesse said. "That was last week, wasn't it? And my daughter somehow met you, talked with you at that time ... ?"

"The Tupperware Corner, a coffeehouse. I'm their star. They have my picture on the wall next to Mae West and Calvin Coolidge. It was the picture that ran in the *New York Times* two years ago, did you happen to see it? A professor at Columbia put together an anthology of antiwar poems and he asked me for a poem. Well, I didn't have anything about Vietnam or any other war, but everyone really wanted me in this anthology because of my reputation in the Village here, they wanted to spread me across the nation ... they are so kind ... well, I had a poem on the central nervous system, four pages long, so I retitled it "Vietnam" and somehow it became the star of the anthology ... the *New York Times* singled it out to discuss.... Here, I have the picture handy. Don't think I'm aggressive about this, really I am only part of a national movement and in advancing myself I am advancing all my brothers and sisters. See, here...." He searched through the pockets of his tight-fitting trousers. Jesse watched him with apprehension. But Monk did have a wallet, made of imitation reptile skin, and he took from it a news clipping that had been covered carefully with transparent adhesive tape. Just the look of this—the care that had gone into its preservation—made Jesse realize suddenly that there might be some truth to what Monk was saying.

Monk handed him the clipping and stood at the window self-consciously. He began to hum and clap his hands lightly together.

The clipping was several inches long. A photograph of Monk, just as bald as he was today, with a shy beatific grin and pouched eyes; the caption read "T. W. Monk." Jesse skimmed the review:

> ... the increasing irony of the distance between the object as *perceived* and the object as *conceived* in American society has

given rise to a new school of tragic-minded poets . . . for whom the tactile is the only measure of historical value. . . . One of the poets in this shocking little anthology declares that "Paisley print is a Braille of love/but our fingers must be sanctified"—and the reader comes away immensely shaken, immensely changed. The most original poet of all, T. W. Monk, seems to sum up an entire decade—perhaps an entire era—of our apocalyptic American experience, in his cool, brilliant denunciation of the Vietnam tragedy. His poems, which I wish I could quote in full, contain these lines: "fed fed fed by small arteries/an epilepsy unpetals/it is electric in the discs/the brain heaving like a penis/oh unleash us! unteach us! carcinoma of/the brain hail/full/of grace/now and at the hour of our birth/Amen."

This made little sense to Jesse, who was extremely nervous anyway, so he handed it back to Monk. Monk said quickly, "I despise exhibitionists and I only offered this to you as a gesture, so that we might meet as equals. I want to spare you the embarrassment of not knowing that I . . . I am . . . well, I am . . . a kind of equivalent of yours, Dr. Vogel, though not," he said hastily, "not in the world of reality, only in the world of poetry. This reviewer was perceptive and kind, don't you think? The other review . . . which I seem to have misplaced, unless someone borrowed it . . . is kind also, but seems to have misunderstood my stand on President Nixon. The reviewer seems to think that I am attacking our President. But really he is a kind of hero to me . . . he is a cult down here actually, America's attempt to create the *Ubermensch*. . . . When I shoot myself up I ask only to be transformed into him, for that lovely split second of radiance, you know . . . or don't you know? At any rate I would never attack our President."

"And your life is . . . it consists of writing and reading poetry now?" Jesse said, baffled. "Can you make a living that way?"

"I have consecrated myself to purity of all kinds," Monk said. "My only grossness is a craving for Milky Way candy bars. Do you like them? Excuse all these wrappers," he said, embarrassed, as the papers crackled beneath his feet like leaves. "I have come a long way, Jesse, since the last time we saw each other. Utterly transformed. I can't remember much except a series of hospitals after Ann Arbor... and then my freedom, my apotheosis. You see before you not a man but an abstraction, an essence. My only grossness is chocolate candy. I have to take care of my head, you know, and the only way is by tending the stalk that leads up. I am very speedy even without shooting. There's a joke in the Village, that T. W. Monk should be put in the nearest refrigerator when he is high, but I cherish my metabolism because it is the metabolism of a poet. No artist wishes to be cured."

"You're taking drugs?—speed?"

"I handle one-third of a gram nicely," Monk said with a large smile. "I'm the original T. W. Monk. You should see me in my own environment. Give me another chance, you might become affectionate after all," he said wistfully. "But... but... I have consecrated myself to purity... I can't let my audience down.... What did you want to see me about? I know you're a doctor now, are you doing a routine examination?"

At this moment the banging on the other side of the wall began.

"What is that?" Jesse said, alarmed.

The door opened, kicked inward. It slammed back against the wall. Monk crouched and put his arms over his head.

A boy in his early twenties stood in the doorway, staring at Jesse.

"Just checking!" he cried.

He turned and ran away. Monk shut the door.

"What was... what was that?" Jesse asked faintly.

"Conrad. He must have seen you come up. I don't blame him, you look so prepared and so dangerous," Monk whispered. "When you walk through us, the crowd shivers and ripples. Dr. Vogel, my dear Jesse, you don't understand. You want to kill us. Don't kill us. Don't look at us like that," Monk said. He had begun to cry. "I can feel it in you, the desire to do something—to dissect us, or operate on us—to snip our nerves—to clean us out with a scouring pad— Oh yes! We sense it! Conrad is like my own son. He gets off and everywhere he goes I accompany him, in my soul. Don't hurt us, don't kill us...."

"But why are you crying?" Jesse asked, amazed. "I'm not going to hurt you. I explained my reason for looking you up...."

Monk shook his head sorrowfully, as if he could not believe this.

"You want to walk through us and part us, like parting the sea. Your shoes hurt us. Look at my poor chest . . . my arms, the inside of my arms. . . ." He held out his arms for Jesse to inspect: a mess of scarry tissue, bruises and welts, veins that must have been like leather. "You want to dissect us with your special instruments, but to us they feel like ice picks. Believe me. I know you are a surgeon. But have mercy. More patients die under anesthetic than under the tracks of a steamroller. . . ."

"My daughter," Jesse said. "The girl you were talking to. Try to remember her, please."

"Your daughter. . . ."

"A very pretty girl. You should have noticed her, anyone would notice her. She has red hair, she's about five foot four, she wrote me a letter and said she had met you. She's been missing from home for several months. Evidently, the two of you talked about me. Did that happen? Or didn't it?" Jesse said wildly. He was beginning to doubt everything. "Please, Trick, please help me . . . I have to find her. . . . I love her and I have to bring her back home; please, you could help me if you'd just remember, remember. . . ."

"A girl. Last name Vogel. Yes," Monk muttered. "I have all that straight. A long time ago. Vogel. Vogel. Jesse. You wouldn't accept my poems, you tried to murder me. A boy of passion who tried to murder me," Monk said, beginning to weep again so that tears gathered in creases in his face. "A girl. But I need money. My head is clean today and I can plan for the future, except for my notebook, but they'll tell me where it is if I can get out on the street. I feel very clean today. I need money."

"Money . . . ?"

"Yes, money. Money."

Jesse took out his wallet. He fumbled, opening it, and took out a hundred-dollar bill.

"Thank you," Monk whispered.

He sighed. His head was smoothly shining, his eyes sunken but oddly sweet, even innocent, frank as a child's. "I don't see very well. But I thank you for whatever you've given me. I know you're generous."

"It's a hundred dollars. . . ." Jesse said uncertainly.

"I don't see too well, there's no point to it," Monk said. He folded the bill carefully and put it in his pocket and sat down on the floor. He sighed heavily. He no longer seemed to be aware of Jesse.

"But . . . but what about Shelley?" Jesse said after a few seconds.

Monk leaned his head back against the wall. His pouchy eyes went slowly out of focus.

"Trick? Trick? Aren't you well?" Jesse cried. "Wait, don't fall asleep, I need your help. Please. I need your help. . . ."

Trick waved him away. "A baked potato . . . would destroy life inside it . . . cracked and puffed open. . . . An Easter egg is our approximation of the divinity. Out of the egg comes new life. Out of the potato . . . sprouts. . . ." He shook his head as if besieged by fears, doubts, complexities. "No. No. Don't keep after me."

Jesse got to his feet. "I didn't try to murder you—I don't remember it that way—I was only trying to defend myself, I tried to push you away from me—that was all—I didn't—"

He watched as Monk fell asleep, or fell into a state of semi-consciousness. Then it seemed to him that he was alone in the room. He was alone. Monk sat with his stomach grotesquely squeezed together, in long lardy ridges, his head back against the wall, his eyes partly closed. Jesse understood that he was alone.

After three or four days in New York City, looking for Shelley, he gave up and went back home.

10

Dear Dr. Vogel:

Ancient here & ruined. The sun has done its work, you can see that. The land is all one giant body. We were in San Angelo for a few days, they wanted us to leave. The sun is still cold. It gets on the inside of your head and worries you. Went to places I wrote down to save for you— Best, the Glass Mountains, the Christmas Mountains. They wouldn't let us over the Rio Grande. Are you surprised I came so far? Found a name on a map I wanted to get to—the Caverns of Sonora. But we never got there. Noel wants to get to California to meet up with someone. Best, Texas. That is a town. We went in and out again. Luth who is our friend and giving us a ride all across the country took me off to the side & told me to go back home. Said he would give me money for a bus ticket himself. He got sunburned in the desert even though it isn't warm yet. It's still winter.

Noel went under the name Judge Roy Bean for a while in Texas. I'm afraid of the sun. It makes my eyes water. I'm afraid I will crawl out into the desert sometime and die there. Something drains out of me—like pus. It is clear and smells fresh. Should I rub some on a piece of paper and mail it to you, Father, for a test? Either I should have a baby or I should start to bleed again, I don't know which, the insides of me should swell up with a baby or they should thin out and bleed again, but they don't. Noel says not to worry about it. He is the superior mind. Luth doesn't understand us.

I dream about you flying in the air around my head, a beak & claws & wings beating. If you would just forget me I could be free.

Love,
Shelley

Dear Dr. Vogel:

Venice Beach was rough. Hard to find a place to sleep. Noel was away for a week & I stayed with some wonderful people. He says for you to burn all snapshots of me & certificates; he says this is a time of bad magic.

Lost oh maybe a cup of blood altogether—ran out of me one day, then nothing more. Adri, a girl out here, says I should do something for myself, I told her my father was a famous doctor & all I had to do was write home for a free diagnosis. Pus gets on my clothes.

Don't come to Venice Beach because I am gone from there & still moving. Has it been a year I've been gone? Out here you can't tell the seasons. I never know the day of the week or the month. I think it is March already.

Did you burn things like I told you?

My head hurts from the sun all these months & seeing men like you, like I saw this morning out on the street. It wasn't you. Or was it you. Noel goes away because I am dragging him down but I can't help it. He says he loves me but I drag him down. He loves my hair & washes it for me, rubs it with a towel. I saw someone walking in the street, thought it was you. You. Not you. I don't know. Wanted to run after him and yell at him to leave me alone. They all ask me what you did to make me hate you and I tried to tell them how I was the evil one of the family, the bad magic is in me, not you or Mother. I am the evil one with the people walking through my head. I can't stop thinking. I was high for eight days & couldn't come down, then crashed down flat.

My belly is hollow, where the baby should be. How exactly is there room, Father, for a baby to grow in there. Noel lies with his head against my stomach listening but he doesn't hear anything. I am not the Fetish now. He says all that is drained out of me.

Don't come after me because Noel will kill you.

Love,
Shelley

Dear Dr. Vogel:

Did you wonder where I was for so long? Dead?

The White Angel of Death.

Guess how we got here to Yonge Street, guess how we got across the border! ! !

In Toronto people seem multiplied because it is a strange country, or I am very tired now. It is April and getting warm. I see people here I knew back home, I think, only they are different people, but they look the same. Why is that? Are there only a certain number of faces to go around in the world, and they get used again and again? Father, you should see Noel's face when he is angry. He has everything in him. His head dominates us like the sun. He told me not to write to you any longer, that's why I didn't write for so long, he thinks you are gaining strength from us because we are sick. Noel has been gone for three days, I don't know where. I don't care how long he stays away. When he is gone I don't get hungry & don't think about anything. No problem about me when he is gone because I can only remember myself when he is with me. By myself I just stare at the wall & want for nothing.

You wouldn't know me if you came here now. My face is not the same now. I am free of you. I don't remember you except in flashes, when things go bad in my head.

I am the Angel of Death here—fell off a ledge but didn't get hurt. No blood. There is no blood in me now. I saw the street coming & gave in to it, I let myself go, there is no resistance between matter and spirit if you can dominate. Noel taught me that.

They cried over me, even Noel. The White Angel of Death. But I didn't die. Woke up again. I thought you would come to me & bring me home, I tried to get away, on the street, but Noel told me *no, no,* to lie down & rest. *You are my angel,* says Noel, *don't be so afraid.* He rubs his forehead against mine & our tears come together. We were born with the same fear in us, that you would eat us up.

Noel won't talk about his father but I see him: see the shadow of him, the shape of him, in the back of Noel's head.

I am the White Angel of Death and I cannot be killed now, even by you.

Someone in our family here was killed. Randall, "the Dimpled Soldier." Did I tell you about him. Deserted from Iowa but the draft dodgers up here snubbed him. They are so loud, always so angry. Anger is no good. Randall kicked all over & his hand knocked a window out by mistake, & the surprise of it killed him. Nobody's fault. There is a broom on the landing somebody left. Roaches behind it. The glass flew all over. I started crying, to have to lie down in the glass, but Noel gripped me by the back of the neck & said *Pray for us! Help us!* Randall was high so long his heart gave out. You could see the edges of his mouth, bright red blood, & blood coming out of his nose & ears. St. John who moved in with us started to cry. We all got down on our knees. Out on the landing is the broom somebody left but I couldn't get it to sweep the glass up. Too tired. Noel has been gone three days but St. John is here. Out on the street you are multiplied, Father, a thousand times. I can't go out there because of you. They dragged Randall downstairs saying he was still alive, but I knew better, to take him over to the hospital, but in the street some police were coming so they left him. In the Hacienda doorway, but it was nobody's fault that he died. Noel is mad at somebody at the Hacienda. It was nobody's fault that Randall died. I swear that.

love,
Shelley

11

What are you going to do to her?

Bring her home.

How?

Bring her home.

Yes, but how? How will you bring her home?

He drove from Chicago to Detroit, thinking of his last conversation with his wife—her expression of caution, disbelief, fear—the way she kept staring at him. *Yes, but how?*

He would do it. He would bring Shelley home.

Though for the last several months he had been strangely lethargic, almost exhausted, though he had withdrawn to administrative work in the running of the hospital, feeling too shaky and too tired to work with patients, he now felt energetic, even youthful. He felt that nothing could stop him. He would drive to Toronto and find his daughter and bring her back home.

She wants me to find her, he told his wife.

Helene had pressed her hands against her face. What was she thinking? Seeing? *Better to think of her as dead,* Helene had said wearily.

But Jesse drove from Chicago to Detroit, rested half an hour in Detroit, and then, inspired by an energy he had not felt in years, drove through the tunnel that connected the United States and Canada. He was stopped at Customs. *Citizen of what country? What are you taking into Canada?* He had only one small leather suitcase and his leather bag; a letter from a professor at the McGill Medical School; and the pistol he had bought years ago, which he wore in his coat pocket, inside, so that he could feel it against the side of his chest. The Canadian customs official leaned in the window of his car, which was a black Cadillac with tinted windows, and glanced respectfully into the back seat.

"You have nothing to declare?" he asked.

Jesse felt no apprehension at all. "No," he said.

The official waved him on through.

So he crossed the border into Canada without any trouble. That was good luck. He had always had good luck.

He got to Toronto in the early evening, his eyes a little seared by all the driving and by the acrid air, which had a faint yellowish cast to it; but he was calm, calmed by the very weight of his expensive, respectable car. Shelley's half-dozen letters now lay opened on the seat beside him and when he had to stop for a street light he glanced at them, his eyes skimming the familiar lines. He could hear her voice inside those letters, calling him. She was certainly calling him. *Guess how we got here to Yonge Street. . . .* That letter had come only the day before; she was certainly calling him to her.

It was an evening in early April. Jesse could smell the coolness of the wind that blew from the lake, and he imagined that this city was more northerly, more pure, than the cities he had known in the United States. But it looked like an American city: the crowded streets, the neon lights, the blocked-off right-hand lanes, the trucks, buses, people crossing against traffic lights, and, when he finally got to Yonge Street itself, the confusion of colors and costumes—young people wearing blankets draped around them, fringed gowns, girls who might have been his daughter sitting with their backs against buildings, staring out into the street, their faces blank and pale and used up, yet expectant, as if waiting for Jesse himself. Waiting for something.

All these crowds perplexed him. Had he come so far only to lose her again in another crowd? His energy subsided a little. What good did it do, he wondered sadly, a life dedicated to explaining, to making an order of confusion—to testing, analyzing, diagnosing, correcting, curing?—what good did it do out on the street like this, bucking the crowds and the traffic, anxious only for fresh air? His life, his very self: it would mean nothing to these people. They were wandering, yearning. Like a tribe of baffled, nomadic strangers, a human avalanche flowing opaquely through the downtown streets, as if searching for some larger crowd, a vast sweet crowd, a gigantic consciousness that would take them in....

He decided against checking into a hotel. No time. It seemed important to find her before another night passed. *Anything could happen at night.* He parked his car in a lot and went to Yonge Street and stared at the crowds. So this was Yonge Street? The center of the city? The center of the world for him, for Shelley? The world had subsided to this street. He would walk in one direction, that was how he would begin.... He walked along quickly, a tall man, dressed in a dark coat of very light material, noticing that his reflection in the jumble of store windows moved along much too fast, almost darted along. He was one of the few people on the street who hurried. Someone approached him: a boy with long curly hair, on crutches, who whined something about needing a dollar. The boy smelled of stale, unwashed flesh. Jesse shook his head sternly, no, get away, leave me alone, and walked past the boy. But he realized that he must look like a stranger, a foreigner, dressed in these clothes. It was obvious that he did not belong in this part of the city.

As he walked he took off his tie and stuffed it in his pocket. And now the coat, which was too warm anyway; he carried it over his arm. Did he look less suspicious? In the bleary, glazed eyes of the young people who passed him he guessed he must still not look right. He was too old.

So this was Yonge Street!

He walked headlong into odors of food, fumes, currents that were stale and intimate and welcoming. An open-air fruit market: a whiff of the tropics. A meat market with objects dangling inside, plucked and withered, headless. Scrawny little wings. The odor of blood and sawdust. And all the restaurants—the pizza diners, the coffee shops, the hamburger joints that were no more than single counters. Jesse peered into these places, hesitating. The street was noisy with music from competing record stores. Blaring loudspeakers. Jesse had the idea, from all the noise, that no one could truly hear anyone else or even see anyone else, that the din and the jostling crowds would have confused even a spectator who was looking out of the windows of one of the high buildings, waiting for Jesse.

Crossing the street toward him when the light changed, a group of people broke into individuals: but they seemed harder that way, more abrasive, threatening. At a distance the crowds were fluid and gentle, despite their noise. He felt his energy returning, the sensation of certainty—he alone of all these people knew exactly what he wanted, *exactly what he wanted.* The others milled about helplessly. The motion of the crowds was somehow rhythmic, breathing with the music from the loudspeakers. Anxious to miss nothing, Jesse stared into the faces that passed near him; he felt a sudden perplexed pain between his eyes. *Will you know her after so long?* his wife had wept. But he kept walking. He stared into the crowds of people and was unable to find any center, any single place to look. That was the problem: maybe the young people themselves felt it, these baffling sexless creatures with their long trousered legs and frizzy hair and laconic, pleasant faces passing him effortlessly, as if in a dream, having no center to them, no core, no place to get to. Jesse felt that if he put his hand out to touch one of these people he would touch nothing, his hand would grope hopelessly in the air....

This was Toronto: a city in a foreign country. But it seemed like any other city. From time to time he caught sight of men like himself—men with suits and ties, yes, conventional costumes; there were couples, prosperous tourists with cameras, even a young sailor who reminded him suddenly, painfully, of his cousin Fritz...though he had not seen or thought of Fritz for decades.... It did look like an American city after all. The faces of Chicago and of New York. The same surging flow of fragments, the same conversations half-overheard; maybe even another Jesse here somewhere, hidden by the crowd, on the other side of the street, hunting... a perspiring, overweight Jesse, hurrying to keep up with this lean, anxious Jesse?... a scrawny, frightened young Jesse, hurrying along in this confusing tide?

Jesse tried to make out the horizon, but it was obscured by tall buildings that were in turn obscured by a haze of unwholesome, golden light. Was there, in that shadow-ridden heaven, another form of Jesse too, watching him, yearning to draw up to him Jesse's hollow, radiant, yearning self? Yearning to purify himself at last, after so many years?

He collided with a fat boy coming out of a coffee shop. No, a fat girl—monstrous, in bell-bottomed white trousers. She grinned at him and he muttered an apology, feeling his face go red. Had bumped into her, a stranger. Had touched her flesh. After another block of this he felt he must sit down; he went into a bar and sat at an empty table. His chair had one uneven leg. Around him people were already gathered, though it was early evening, girls and boys, their legs moving constantly, their voices lifting like shrieks of music. . . . He ordered a glass of beer. A young girl with an icy, brilliant face passed near him and stooped, as if to peer into his face. She stared rudely. She was wearing a costume that looked like a curtain, many layers of white lace wound around her, a kind of shroud. *The White Angel of Death.* Jesse smiled coolly at her and turned away. Alcohol might ease that growing pressure at the top of his skull. He did not want to be hurried, too anxious. It was unwise to be too anxious about anything. That was how fatal mistakes were made.

The girl wandered over to another table and stared into another man's face.

Jesse finished his beer and went back to the washroom. Washed his face, his wrists. He had to lay his coat over a wastepaper receptacle that was filthy. On the lavatory walls were the usual words, drawings—an odd picture of a woman's cadaver, the heart and the lungs exposed, the stomach sac, coils of intestines, the womb carefully drawn. Jesse found himself examining the drawing, surprised that it was so good. The organs were in their proper proportions. At the very center of the little womb was an eye, elaborately inked in.

Jesse transferred the pistol from his coat pocket to his trouser pocket. It was bulky but it rested closer to him now, compact and reassuring.

He had another glass of beer and when he returned to the street he felt stronger. The cold water and the beer had restored him. This part of the street looked better: expensive shops and galleries were interspersed with sleazy shops, the camping-outfit and gun stores, the blaring record stores, the immense stores that sold stereo and high-fidelity equipment that must have been costly, though it was crowded together in the display windows. Near him a few boys were begging. They begged shamelessly but without urgency, reaching out as if to touch the elbows of passers-by, but not quite touching them. An emaciated boy with a knapsack on his back stood wordlessly by the curb, his hand extended. No one bothered with him. Flat-chested, flat-bellied, a barefoot girl strolled by with the stony eyes of a statue: impossible to impregnate such a female, Jesse's instincts told him. She glanced at Jesse but did not seem to see him. No female left in her, no sense of his maleness. *I do not see you,* she seemed to say. Jesse realized how futile it would be to talk to any of these young people, even to approach them.... As he walked he noticed newer buildings: steel and glass and concrete, murals, mosaics, reflecting the jumble of neon lights, and even on the steps of these excellent new buildings people were sitting, with that exhausted unquestioning look Jesse saw in the faces of his terminally ill patients.

A long-haired boy was hawking newspapers. He held them up for people to see, but few passers-by bothered with him. His face was savage and weary; his hair bounced out angrily and comically. He showed no surprise when Jesse stopped to buy a paper for a quarter.

The little paper had red, white, and blue stripes across its front. It was called THE HOLE WITH A VOICE. The biggest headline was in black: NIXON PLANS MASS CONCENTRATION CAMPS. Other stories dealt with FBI agents' activities, the "Most Wanted" list back in the United States, a communal picnic of draft dodgers and "freaks" that had evidently been broken up a few days before, and Prime Minister Trudeau, "Canadian puppet of imperialistic war-mongering nations." Inside, a smudgy cartoon showed a middle-aged flabby man holding a gun to the head of a long-haired child, presumably his son. *We all die for our country,* the caption said.

Jesse glanced through the rest of the paper and tossed it into a trash can. He felt a quickening of his senses, a greedy, restless anticipation. He was going to find her and bring her home. He would not fail. That other Jesse urged him on, seemed to be straining his legs forward, forward. He was wasting time like this.

Why had he bothered with that little newspaper? Wasting time, wasting time! He passed decorators' shops where antique chairs were draped with costly silk or brocade material; galleries with enormous, awkward paintings that were mostly slashes of color; sleazy paperback stores; health-food stores; a cheap clothing store.... Jesse went into the store on an impulse. He bought a dark, pullover shirt of a cheap jersey material and asked the clerk to take out the tags and the pins. Then, while the clerk was ringing up his purchase, he thought of something else—new trousers. He picked out a pair of khaki pants on sale for $3.98, with standard cuffs. In a crowded little dressing room, with boxes and tissue paper scattered everywhere, he decided that the length was all right—a little short, but all right. So he transferred everything from his trouser pockets into these pockets, including the gun, and he pulled on the shirt, and had the clerk put his own clothes in a paper bag. Out on the street he threw the bag into a trash barrel. He was relieved to get rid of it so easily. But there was something more... something he should get rid of.... He took out his wallet, extracted his money, and placed the wallet inside the bag. This way he would have no identification in case anything happened. He could not be identified. Then, if all went well, he thought vaguely, he might stroll back this way and pick these things out of the trash barrel again... he must remember where the barrel was....

Now he felt light on his feet and very energetic. He could not fail. In a telephone booth he leafed through the directory, looking for the listing of the "Hacienda Restaurant." Under "Restaurants" he located something called the "Yonge Hacienda." Good. That would be it. It was only a few blocks away. As he approached it, on the far side of the street, he saw that there was a tall tenement building in that block; that would be it, the place where Shelley was living. Up there, behind one of those grimy windows, his daughter was waiting. Watching? The building was five stories high, decrepit and Victorian and still handsome in a terse, uniform way. But its ground floor, at least along the street, had been improved with a new façade. There was a drugstore with a front of white tile, and an open-air pizza place, all garish red wood. A clothing store with a black-and-white façade and a sign of a boy/girl dangling over its doorway, clinking little bells on a rope around the figure's neck. The "Hacienda" was an ordinary restaurant with a bright orange sombrero for a sign.

Jesse crossed the street. A few young people were sitting on the steps to a door that was ajar, so that Jesse could dimly see part of a stairway. One boy held out a plate with a few coins on it. Jesse approached the young people, sensing his height in their eyes. Though it was rather chilly, one of the boys was bare-chested, and his hair was twisted into a single thick strand that rose from the very top of his head, fixed with rubber bands. Everything in his face rose, straining upward. His eyebrows looked permanently arched. He was no more than twenty, but his eyes had that pouchy, blurred, childish look that Monk's had had. He held the plate up to Jesse.

These dying people!

Beside the boy, slouched as if exhausted, sat a girl of about eighteen, in a faded green outfit, a sari perhaps, pulled up carelessly above her knees. Her dirty feet were held out straight, small and blunt and charming in sandals decorated with beads. Jesse was struck by the sleepy tinted cast of her face, her eyelids smeared with a greasy blue ointment. In the center of her forehead there was a blue spot. Her brown hair fell to her waist.

The boy begged for something; Jesse could only catch the word "nutrition." He took a bill out of his pocket and put it on the plate. He smiled formally at them. "I'm looking for someone you might know," he said. They stared expressionlessly at him. He felt his heart enlarge with hope, with cunning. "A young man named Noel. I'm not bringing him bad news. Nothing bad."

The girl stared up at him without blinking.

"Do you know anyone named Noel?" Jesse asked. "Does he live here?"

Nervously they shook their heads, no, they didn't know, didn't know anything. Jesse had the idea that they were afraid of him. He wanted to comfort them; he stood staring down at them, puzzled, thoughtful, while another part of him urged him into motion.

"Excuse me, will you let me by?" Jesse asked.

They moved at once for him. The girl scrambled to her feet and the boy with the plate inched over to one side, on his haunches. Another boy—Jesse thought it was a boy—slid off the steps and squatted on the sidewalk, watching Jesse closely. There was no real alarm in their faces, only a momentary unsettling. They had the appearance of victims of war, photographed to illustrate the anonymity of war.

Jesse entered the dark foyer. He was intensely, lightly happy. It was as if he were coming home. The steep dark stairs in front of him might have been trick stairs, a fake cardboard obstacle that would collapse beneath his powerful weight. But he would get to where he wanted to go. It was dark: good. He needed darkness in which to breathe deeply, privately. From the street behind him lights flickered, showing a large feeble shadow of Jesse on the stairs. The shadow moved quickly, rippled quickly upward.

The tenement building was old, shabby, smelly. Unsurprising. Debris lay on the floor, a pile of garbage and papers. No light on the landing. The building was open, welcoming. Anyone could walk in. Anyone could run lightly up these stairs. It might have been the end of the world, with everything so open and dream-like and obliging! Jesse's blood pounded with certainty. He was so powerful, his back so suddenly strong, certain.... He did not pause until he reached the third floor. There he went to a door that was partly opened; he heard a radio playing inside. Jesse rapped politely on the door. A girl in a short dress, or perhaps in a man's shirt worn as a dress, poked her head out.

"I'm looking for a young man named Noel. He has blond hair...."

"Oh, them. They're upstairs," the girl said brightly.

Jesse thanked her.

On the next floor he came up to a door that had been crudely painted—a kind of rainbow—while the rest of the hall was a drab, dull green. The painting on the door was of a peacock's tail. Had Shelley painted it? He was about to open the door without knocking, when something made him hesitate. Sweat had broken out on his body. It was no good to be too anxious, too nervous; in that way fatal mistakes might be made.... And there was something profound about this door. Once opened, it might never be closed. Once he opened it, he would have to go in.

A light bulb burned in the hallway. No one was around. No one was watching.

He turned the knob.

Unlocked. He opened the door gently, stealthily. The room inside had been a kitchen, but for some reason the stove had been taken out. There were holes in the plaster where it had been detached. But the refrigerator remained, scuffed and dirty, its door decorated with a smaller version of the peacock's tail. A childish blurred spectrum of bright colors. Jesse frowned at the stench of the room. He saw the roaches crawling freely in the sink and along the floorboards.

"Is anyone here?" Jesse said.

Someone jumped up and ran toward him from another room—appeared in the doorway gaping at Jesse. He was about Jesse's height. His curly hair hung in damp ringlets about his face; it was silver-blond.

"Who are you? What do you want?" the man asked.

Jesse guessed he was about thirty. He was very thin. Emaciated chest, shoulder bones that seemed to lurch nervously forward, the bones of his face severe and ascetic.

"I'm a friend. . . ." Jesse said, his face frozen into a small stiff smile. He held out his hands as if to show that he was carrying nothing, no weapons.

"Are you from the peace clinic?" the man asked doubtfully.

"Yes," said Jesse.

"Is this Friday night, then?" the man asked, staring in bewilderment at Jesse. "No, this isn't Friday night. This isn't Friday night."

His eye fell to Jesse's trousers, and Jesse pulled his shirt down lower, still smiling. "How many of you live here?" he asked. He looked over the man's shoulder. The next room was not much larger than the kitchen. Someone was sitting by a window, looking toward him. Someone else—two figures—were lying on a mattress on the floor. The room was crowded with boxes and junk, piles of clothing, towels. Jesse saw the entire room in that first instant, but then his vision seemed to shift out of focus and he stood there, staring helplessly.

"What do you want?" the man with the silver-blond hair asked sternly.

"Is your name Noel?"

The man did not back away. Though his face was thin it was blunt and hard; he had a jaw like a man's fist.

"What...? Who...? My name is St. John," he said with an ironic bow.

"You are not St. John!" the person by the window cried, jumping up. "I am St. John!"

"Noel is gone. Took off. Vanished. Noel is not in Toronto tonight," the blond-haired man said, staring at Jesse. His thin, insolent lips shaped themselves into a nervous smile.

The boy by the window ran over and tried to seize Jesse's hand. "He isn't St. John, I'm St. John. He's been after me ever since I came here. He wants to take me over. I am St. John and no one else can claim to be St. John...." This boy was younger than the other, but not very young; he was not really a boy at all; his pock-marked face gleamed with anguish. Jesse paid no attention to him and looked again at the couple on the mattress—two boys—a boy with a dark untidy mustache and ragged hair, who was sitting up, and another, lying flat and senseless on his back, his arms folded across his stomach as if they had been laid there reverently.

Jesse's heart pounded. That he had come so far, only to fail....

"You're not St. John!" the boy cried. "Why do you persecute me, Noel? Isn't your own soul enough for you? Why do you want to possess us?"

He clutched at Jesse's arm and began to weep. "Noel wants to take me over. He wants to claim the authorship of the *Revelations*—my lifework—he wants to claim them for himself—"

"Noel is not in town tonight," the blond man said. "You won't find him. He's in Montreal on business."

"When do you expect him back?" Jesse asked.

"Noel is evil. Noel does not exist. Noel has no soul of his own," the boy cried angrily.

"Did you want to leave a message for Noel? Or did you bring him something?" the blond man asked.

Jesse was trembling. Did they notice? But the boy was so upset, whimpering, he kept dancing around and trying to tug at Jesse's arm...and the man with the silver-blond hair, his hands on his hips, appearing so stern, really had a raw, edgy, wild look to his eyes, as if he too were hiding his terror.

"No, no message. Nothing," said Jesse.

"Then why are you here?"

"You didn't bring us anything?" the boy sitting up on the mattress cried. Though his voice showed disappointment, he got to his feet with a bouncy spring and came over to shake hands. "My name is Wolcott. I'm from Peoria. I know you're an American, I know your accent—Chicago? I want some news from home, authentic news, not what you read in the newspaper. I want some citrus fruit. What I need is nutrition, good sound nutrition, and I need somebody to take me seriously," he said, rubbing at his mustache, "not like this clown Noel, Noel is just a joke... oh, Noel is evil, but evil can be laughed at too... I laugh at evil... I laugh at death itself. Mister, what are you running up here? What are you peddling?"

"Does anyone else live here with you?" Jesse asked.

"Oh, nobody, nobody! People come and go and we can't account for them. That's my little brother over there. We're all tented up here, we help one another, it's like the Boy Scouts back home.... There are deaths in the Boy Scouts too, but they are kept secret. Tents collapse, boys die in campfires and drown on canoe trips. Those deaths are kept secret, but ours are shouted from steeples...."

"Shut your mouth," the blond man said.

Wolcott darted away behind Jesse, giggling.

"You're Noel, then?" Jesse asked the blond man.

The man shrugged his shoulders.

The boy on the mattress stirred as if this noise annoyed him. He drew the back of his hand across his forehead the way Jesse often did. That weariness, that reluctance.... Jesse could see, in spite of the dim light in the room, that the boy's skin was yellow.

"Is he sick?" Jesse said.

"No. Oh, maybe the flu. Nothing much," Noel muttered.

"What flu?" said Jesse.

"The flu. Any flu. He's okay."

"Angel will be all right as soon as the nutrition man arrives," Wolcott said cheerfully. "That will clean out our systems nicely. Noel can't do it anymore. Noel is wearing out, eh, Noel? Lost his contacts. In fact, he's hiding. He'd like to be in Montreal, eh, but how can he get there without appearing on the street...?"

Jesse went over to the boy on the mattress. He stared down—

his heart pounding in that slow, heavy, clutching way—and saw that this was not a boy at all, but a girl—her hair cut off close to the skull, jaggedly, her face wasted, yellow, the lips caked with a stale dried substance.

"Shelley—?" he said.

"She needs something to clean out her system," Wolcott said anxiously.

She stared up at Jesse. Slowly, laboriously, she sat up and stared.

"Who are you?" she asked blankly.

Was this Shelley?

She muttered something and crawled away, across the mattress. She was wearing jeans and a boy's undershirt that hung loose on her. It was incredible how thin her body was—she looked like a child of nine or ten.

Jesse reached for her. "Shelley—"

"No! No!" she cried.

She scrambled to her feet and ran to the window. "Don't you come near me or I'll jump out! I know who you are! I heard your voice! I know who you are, you want to kill me—"

She shook her head slowly, to clear it. Her voice was thick and hoarse, each word she spoke seemed deliberately chosen. Jesse looked around, dazed. This man with the silvery-blond hair—Noel—the Noel of all the letters, now wild-eyed and anxious himself—he stood ready to run, the ringlets of his hair damp and frizzy. The stubble on his face was like part of a mask.

"So you're—you're the father, huh?" Noel said. "Dr. Vogel, huh?" But then, as if recovering himself, he laughed and waved Jesse away. "Oh hell, you don't expect us to believe that! That's a hot one! You just come in here off the street and . . . and you expect us to believe you, like God himself has to be believed—Our little Angel has nothing to do with you, she is our girl, our baby. We take care of her. She is our little sister and our wife and our little madonna, just wait a few days and we'll sweat the yellow out of her. She'll be magnificent again. And who are you, mister, *you*," he said wildly, his teeth chattering, "to barge in here and try to wreck our family? You came under false pretenses! I thought you had something to deal me! All this talk about

Noel, how do you dare mention his name, Noel is beyond all your C.I.A. plots and spying and betrayals. . . ."

"Noel don't—don't let him come near me—" Shelley whispered. She was staring at Jesse through her fingers. Her lips moved thickly. "If he comes to touch me I will have to die—"

"She already jumped out a window once," Noel said to Jesse angrily, as if this were Jesse's fault, "and this time it's the third floor! You better leave us all in peace, get the hell out of here and leave us all in peace!"

"Shelley, please," Jesse said. He could not believe this: her wasted body, her thin, puckered, pinched little face. . . . He took a few steps forward and she pressed herself against the window, her arms outspread. Someone had snipped her hair close against the skull; it was growing in unevenly, in patches of dark, greasy red. Was this Shelley? Was that her face? He would not have recognized her on the street. She had a boy's face now, a sexless face, the cheeks thin and the eyes sunk back into her head, darkly shadowed as if bruised. Her skin was a sharp sickly hue of yellow.

"I don't know who you are. I didn't mean for you to come here. I didn't know what it meant," Shelley babbled. "I live here and this is my family here. Everything comes from them. Noel is my husband here—not you—never you—when I have a baby it will be for all of them here, and not you— Why did you come after me? I can't go back. I'm all dried out. I'm dried out. Look—" And she lifted the undershirt to show her chest—her shriveled little breasts, her ribs, the shock of her yellow skin. "I'm all shut off, there is a curse on me to shut me off, my body, I don't know what happened—there is no blood and no baby either—the police have a radar machine that dries us all up—"

"You're making her very excited," Noel said. "You'd better leave."

"Get away from me," Jesse said.

He approached his daughter. She flattened herself back against the window and gaped at him. Jesse calculated the distance between them—he would be able to grab her if she tried to throw herself out the window—

"I am not here. There's nobody here," Shelley whispered.

"Shelley, please—" Jesse said.

"No. Nobody is here. You can't get me. I don't exist and you can't get me."

"Shelley, you're not well. You know that. You've got to let me help you," Jesse said carefully.

"I'm dried out and nothing works," Shelley said, staring at him. "I don't hate you for that. I don't hate Noel. Inside me everything is dried up. You were looking for Shelley, with that face Shelley had back home; well, Shelley is dead and there isn't anybody in her place. I don't have a passport. We wanted to go to Cuba for the sugar harvest. Noel was going to take us all. I don't have a birth certificate either. I wrote to you from California to destroy all the evidence. You can have another baby to take my place—you can adopt a baby—"

Only Noel and Jesse remained now; the other boys had fled. Noel drew his forefinger across his nose, sniffing in a kind of panic. He was barefoot, his toes long, angular, very dirty. He wore ordinary work trousers and a soiled white undershirt. "Hey look," he said gently to Jesse, "she started crashing last night. She was high for seven, eight days. Now you got her scared to death. You smell it? How afraid she is? She thinks you're going to kill her."

"I'm not going to leave her here."

"She isn't well," Noel said angrily, miserably, "she needs her head cleaned out! She doesn't need you!"

"Noel can take care of me," Shelley insisted. "I don't need anybody else. I'm sorry I wrote to you. Noel made me pure, like a madonna, like an angel.... He brought so many men to me to make me pure again, to make me into nothing. He made me free, you don't understand, he made my body float free of everything.... But you, *you,*" she said, confused, "you're standing right there so that I have to look at you, and you know my name and... you understand that I am the wife of all of them here and not of you...."

"Leave her alone," Noel said.

"Shelley, you're not well. Let me take you home," Jesse said.

"She isn't sick, it's just the flu...."

"She's very sick."

"The flu! Everybody up here has the flu, it's nothing serious!" Noel muttered.

"She's got jaundice. She might have hepatitis. She's going to die, she's going to die of liver failure. . . ." Jesse said in a slow, dream-like voice. He kept staring at her—was this Shelley, this child? This emaciated child?

He blundered into something on the floor, stumbled. Shelley cried out. Jesse said in that same thick, slow, dream-like voice, as if each word of his were rising with difficulty through a thick element, an air made gaseous and vile, "You want to come with me, Shelley. This is all over. You know you want to come with me. Come home."

Shelley pressed her hands against her ears. "Don't let him talk to me, Noel—he'll get inside my head again—"

Noel was breathing heavily. He inched alongside Jesse, his hands moving nervously, wildly, as if he wanted to take hold of Jesse but did not dare touch him. "You can't just break us up like this!" he cried. "That girl is my property, she willed herself to me—we have been married in a solemn ceremony—she told me how you tried to kill her all her life! Enough is enough! Last night she started crashing and it took two of us to hold her down, and tonight you show up in our kitchen, it's too goddam much for my head, doctor, you want me to crack up? I can't take all these agitations! I don't trust you, you could be with the C.I.A., you could be evil! Evil!" And Noel, so grim and rational at first, began to shriek wildly. He tried to wrestle Jesse backwards, toward the door. Jesse broke loose. Jesse shoved Noel aside and was surprised at how weak Noel was. Nothing to him after all! The Noel of all the letters!

"Shelley," Noel cried, "he's the devil himself, the devil! Jump out the window and save yourself!"

Jesse ran and grabbed her before she could move. Her arm was like a matchstick. "Don't hurt me, don't kill me. . . ." she whispered.

"He himself is the devil," Noel said from across the room. He was flailing his arms around. He seemed to be addressing other people in the room, an audience of sympathetic observers. "He's here to take her back into bondage. She was free here, the Angel, I made her nothing at all, I ground her down to nothing and freed her! She didn't even know her name, when I was through! I set her free and now he's got her again, she's giving in to him like a bitch of a woman, she's ready to lie down and open her knees for him, little bitch—pus-stinking whore—after I freed her and made her my own wife—"

Jesse felt a surge of joy. He had won.

"—all you need is a bath in Laverne's tub, I suppose! Get yourself ready for it, I suppose!" Noel said mockingly.

Jesse held Shelley with one hand and with the other reached for the pistol. He was utterly calm, triumphant. He had won. Hatred rose warmly in him and swelled the cords of his neck, all the vessels of his proud manly body—just to pull the trigger, to shoot that man in the face! What joy, to shoot him in the face! But Shelley leaned against him so passively, like the child she had been years ago, and Noel himself now looked so defeated, his lips damp with saliva, that Jesse paused out of pity.... If he shot this man, this stranger, what then? A corpse. What then? A pool of blood draining out from the smashed face. What then? What then?

Noel was staring at him.

"You're going to kill us both," he said.

Jesse held his daughter tight. No getting away from him, no leaping out the window to escape.... He put his hand into his pocket, he felt the pistol. And, in that instant, he seemed to see Noel's mocking, terrified face blasted: the life blasted out of it, the defeat and the terror themselves blasted, gone.

But he did not move.

Noel's head began to nod in a series of slow, terrified movements. "You're going to... going to... You have a gun, don't you? You came here to kill us...? You...."

For a long moment they stared at each other.

Then Jesse said, "Get out."

Noel was still nodding. And he began to back to the door carefully, carefully.

"You... you won't.... You won't...." Noel said.

"Get out."

At the door he hesitated. He licked his lips. "If I open the door... you're not going to... Do you have a gun with you? Do you... you... you're not...?"

Jesse saw again, as if in a flash of memory, Noel's face pouring blood. And his own blood warmed, leaped at the thought. But he did not move.

"No. Please. Get out," he said.

Nobody is going to die tonight. No dying tonight.

Not on my hands.

Noel made a sudden leap to the door, jerked it open, and in that instant Jesse gripped the pistol.

But he did not pull it out of his pocket.

"Nobody is going to die tonight," he said aloud. He listened to Noel outside, Noel running away, escaping. . . . The blood still surged in him, powerfully, frustrated. When Shelley pushed against him he shook her still and felt the enormous power of his muscles, his blood, his brain, the power to hold her here and to keep her from dying.

"Did he leave . . . ? Where is he, Noel, did he leave . . . ?" Shelley cried.

Jesse waited for his heart to calm again. He waited for the beating to subside, for his brain to come back into control of itself: how he loved this control, this certainty!

"He's gone and the hell with him," Jesse said shakily.

"No. I don't believe he—he—"

He began to walk her to the door.

She balked, she pushed against him. Wildly she looked around and Jesse was surprised at the strength in her body—it was a kind of fury, almost, a frenzy set against him.

"Noel is— Wait— Noel is still with me, he—"

"No."

"Noel is—"

"Noel is gone and the hell with Noel," Jesse said.

Shelley looked around the room, her head turning slowly from side to side. She was like a child, and yet her body had that curious, stubborn, almost demonic strength.

"He's gone," Jesse said.

After a moment she gave in: he felt the tension ebb.

"Nobody is going to die tonight," he said again.

She walked with him to the door. To the corridor, the landing. When she paused, swaying, he supported her and whispered angrily: "No, nobody is going to die. Not Noel. Not you."

"But you are still the devil," Shelley said faintly. She pressed her hands against her face. "He said . . . he said you were the devil and I believe him . . . I . . ."

"No, you don't believe him."

"I believe him . . . I . . . I love him and I believe him. . . ."

"No."

". . . he said you were the devil and I . . . I think you are the devil . . . come to get me to bring me home. . . ."

"Am I?" Jesse said.

AFTERWORD

Wonderland Revisited

> *So much of a novelist's writing takes place in the unconscious; in those depths the last word is written before the first word appears on paper. We remember the details of our story, we do not invent them.*
>
> —Graham Greene

We are led to value highest that which has cost us the most. Of my early novels, *Wonderland*, the fifth to be published, obviously the most bizarre and obsessive, stands out in my memory as having been the most painful to write. The most painful in conception and in execution. The most painful even in retrospect. For it was evidently so mesmerizing, so haunting, so exhausting an effort, I must have willed it to be completed before, in that regulatory limbo of the unconscious to which we have no direct access, it was ready to be completed. As Graham Greene so eloquently says, we remember the details of our story, we do not invent them. When I reread *Wonderland* after its hardcover publication I knew that the ending I'd written was not the true ending; in the months between finishing the manuscript, and seeing it published, I had continued to be haunted by it, "dreaming" its truer trajectory. I knew then that I had to recast the ending, at least for the paperback edition and subsequent reprints. The original ending, and a brief hallucinatory prologue that framed the thirty years of the novel, were jettisoned, and the "true" ending supplied. *Wonderland* could not end with a small boat drifting out helplessly to sea (specifically, Lake Ontario); it had to end with a gesture of demonic-paternal control. This was the tragedy of America in the 1960s, the story of a man who becomes the very figure he has been fleeing since boyhood: a son of the devouring Cronus who, unknowingly, becomes Cronus himself.

My practice as a novelist up to and including the composition of the similarly obsessive *Son of the Morning*, published in 1978, was to write a complete first draft in one long head-on plunge; by which, though this was perhaps not my conscious choice, I would be nearly as immersed in my characters' experiences as they themselves were. The first draft completed, I would be exhausted; often, overcome by a sense of psychic derailment; my graphic vision of the runaway Shelley, wasted and ungendered and sickly-yellow with jaundice at *Wonderland*'s end, is an exaggerated self-portrait, meant perhaps to exert authorial control over the torrential experience of novel-writing—which is the formal, daylight discipline of which novel-imagining is the passion. Once the first draft was completed, I would put it away for some weeks or months, and, after an interregnum during which I took on more finite projects, including, for who knows what restoration of the soul, the intensive reading and writing of poetry, I would systematically rewrite the entire manuscript, first word to last. And this was the triumph of art, it seemed to me: the re-writing, the re-casting, the re-imagining of what had been a sustained ecstatic plunge. A novel is prose artfully structured, structure imposed upon prose. Control imposed upon passion. *Wonderland*'s theme of a protagonist who seems without identity ("You do not exist," Dr. Pedersen tells Jesse) unless deeply involved in meaningful experience (who is more qualified than a neurologist to determine where brain and spirit fuse?) is an oblique portrait of the novelist as well.

This book is for all of us who pursue the phantasmagoria of personality —how boldly, how trustingly, *Wonderland*'s dedication exposes its secret heart! In the broadest terms, literature is of two distinct types: that which offers us a distillation of experience, and that which offers us experience itself. My method of composition in those years was ideally suited for my goal—that of offering, so far as literature may be said to offer anything palpable, tangible, "real," at all, not a cool, intellectualized distillation of fictitious characters' experiences, but experience itself, mediated by language and form. Instead of exploring the "phantasmagoria of personality" (the mystery of our *selfness* within our *species-hood*) obliquely, which is the more navigable way, *Wonderland*, from its first sentence to its last, plunges us into the vortex of being: we begin with a terrified fourteen-year-old boy who "knows" something terrible is going to happen to him, or has indeed already happened and is awaiting him at home; and we continue with him, adding on, as if in psychic replication, his wife and younger daughter, all of them caught up in this vortex of being as it confronts non-being—for that is the secret horror inside the costly microscope Dr. Cady has given his son-in-law Jesse. *Do we exist? What is "personality"? Is it permanent, is it ephemeral?*—can it be destroyed as easily as Dr. Perrault boasts, "with a tiny pin in my fingers"?

Because such questions are the novel's heart, its deep verticality and inwardness is driven by convulsive narrative leaps: months and even years pass, but only those actions possessing psychic significance are dramatized. Opening with an act of despair that seems to us so tragically American—the slaughter of a family by its "head," who then kills himself—*Wonderland* moves from the Depression through World War II through the Korean War and the "Cold War" and the Vietnam War and the turbulent years of that decade (approximately 1963–1973: from the assassination of President John F. Kennedy to the end of the Vietnam War) known as The Sixties. Background is foreground, in a sense, only in terms of the Depression, which has devastated Jesse Harte's father; the assassination of Kennedy, which is experienced by the Vogel family at a crucial time in their lives; and the grimly self-destructive yet intermittently radiant visions of The Sixties, to which both Jesse's mock-brother Trick Monk and his daughter Shelley fall victim. Like virtually all of my novels, *Wonderland* is political in genesis, however individualized its characters and settings. It could not have been conceived, still less written, at any other time than in post-1967 America, when divisive hatreds between the generations, over the war in Vietnam, and what was called, perhaps optimistically, the "counterculture," raged daily. (So too *them*, the novel immediately preceding *Wonderland*, could not have been written before the "long, hot summer" of urban race riots of 1967.) How specifically rooted in time and place *Wonderland* is, from the meticulously observed view of the Erie Canal, its cascading waterfalls and locks seen by Jesse from the perspective of a certain bridge in Lockport, to the demoralized street scene in Toronto, thirty years later, where the drug-addicted young, moribund, unsexed, affectless, begging from strangers, have "the appearance of victims of war, photographed to illustrate the anonymity of war." (Yes, that was Yonge Street, Toronto, in those days. A "street of the young" in any large North American city, in those days.)

For *Wonderland*, as a title, refers to both America, as a region of wonders, and the human brain, as a region of wonders. And "wonders" can be both dream and nightmare.

After rewriting the ending of *Wonderland* for its paperback reprinting in 1972, I ceased thinking about it; I did not want to think about it; of my early novels, it was the one of which readers sometimes spoke in odd, rapturous-accusatory terms—"I was eighteen years old, my roommate at college gave it to me to read, I was up all night, I couldn't put it down. *Why don't you write novels like that any longer?*" I did not want to write novels quite like that any longer, nor even to reread this specific one, the very thought of which made me feel faint, as if in recollection of some close call, some old, survived danger. (Perhaps I should mention parenthetically that my interest in neurology, so evident in *Wonderland*'s long speculative middle section, was the consequence of an apparent medical condition, which necessitated one or more tips to a neurologist in Windsor, Ontario, where my husband and I lived at the time: but the "condition" turned out to be, not physical, or in any case not seriously physical, but a temporary confluence of symptoms caused by what is today called, so commonly, "stress.") Approaching the novel now, a cavernous twenty-two years after its composition, I am probably most struck by what might be called its kinetic exuberance. I mean it as a purely neutral expression—neither laudatory nor condemnatory—to say that, both in its epic conception and its execution, *Wonderland* leaves me a bit breathless: as the narrative itself seems breathless, caught up in that vortex of being that is our human predicament.

Indeed, so fuelled by energy was *Wonderland*, it spilled over into a play, *Ontological Proof of My Existence*, a dramatization and expansion of Jesse's visit to Toronto, to win, or buy, his daughter back from her drug-dispenser lover; and into such short stories of that time as "How I Contemplated the World from the Detroit House of Correction, and Began My Life Over Again," an analogue of Shelley's experience as a runaway to Toledo. (In retrospect, it seems that Shelley Vogel was crying out for a novel of her own, a story that was not a mere appendage of her father's; but this was a novel that I could not, or would not write. The material was simply too devastating.)

Much in *Wonderland* has to do with memory. The escape from memory, the surrender to memory. Theories of memory. The "invention" of memory. Of all art-forms, the novel is the most indigenously equipped to take its populace through a delimited space of time, shoring up memory in both characters and readers; at a certain point, as if by magic, the memory of the novel is shared by both characters and readers. So, in *Wonderland*, when the adult Jesse remembers, or fails to remember, the attentive reader is a part of his consciousness; we sense the onset of his breakdown when isolated figures and memory-shards out of his deeply suppressed past begin to intrude into his rigidly controlled present. No other art-form so builds upon memory so *necessarily*, as the novel: in this it mimics, as Dr. Cady suggests, personality itself. (For there can be no *person* without memory.) And no other art-form is so dependent upon and so infatuated with memory, as the novel: the novelist might be defined as one who, in the guise of fiction, is involved in a ceaseless memorialization of the past. (*Wonderland* includes a postmodernist snapshot of a kind, when, in the concluding pages of the first section, the beleaguered Jesse, pausing in his desperate drive from Lockport to Buffalo, spies upon a young family in a green swing behind a farmhouse—Carolina and Frederic Oates and their three-year-old daughter Joyce.) The uses we make of our homesickness!

For the melancholy we feel when completing a novel is akin to the melancholy we feel when, by the inexorable process of time, we are expelled forever from home.

Joyce Carol Oates
January, 1992

ABOUT THE AUTHOR

JOYCE CAROL OATES is the author of a number of novels and many volumes of short stories, poems, essays, and plays. She is the recipient of numerous awards, including the National Book Award for her novel *them*. She lives in Princeton, New Jersey, where she is the Roger S. Berlind Distinguished Professor in the Humanities at Princeton University.